BLADES OF HAVOC

THE COMPLETE SERIES

EVA CHANCE
& HARLOW KING

Blades of Havoc: The Complete Series

First Digital Edition, 2023

Cover design: The Pretty Little Design Co.

Ebook ISBN: 978-1-998752-75-1

Hardcover ISBN: 978-1-998752-76-8

SHOTGUN SPIN

BLADES OF HAVOC #1

ONE

Luciana

MOST OF MY mother's gangster minions had obviously never considered that a skate could be a lethal weapon. Even with two of them dangling over my shoulders as I headed out of the house, the lackeys standing guard in the front rooms had to make their teasing remarks.

"There goes the Ice Princess, off to her frozen castle," one of the guys said from the living room doorway, with a salute that could have passed for respectful if he hadn't been smirking at the same time.

"When are you going to start ruling around here, chica?" another called out from across the foyer.

I paused to shoot a glower at the second guy. No doubt they'd have said a lot worse if I *hadn't* been the daughter of their boss, the Deadly Rose, one of the most powerful crime bosses in the world.

But Mom had taught me plenty of lessons as her heir apparent, including that I should never let anyone intimidate me or get the upper hand, not even for a moment.

"Si yo te gobernara, te estarías comiendo tus bolas," I replied. *If I ruled you, you'd be eating your balls.* After I sliced them off with the blade on one of these skates, maybe.

I kept my tone firm but even. Maintain control, show only confidence.

The criminal underworld wasn't an easy place to survive for anyone, but it was twice as hard when you didn't have balls at all. At least not the literal kind.

Mom liked to say we Cordova women had to make up for it by making our metaphorical bolas twice as big. She'd also insisted on me learning Spanish, though I'd never even gotten to meet my great-grandparents who'd emigrated from Mexico.

Every piece of knowledge you collect and every skill you cultivate gives you that much more of an advantage, she'd said. Funny how she didn't apply that philosophy to my figure skating.

At five foot one, I was nearly a foot shorter than the dude who'd shot his mouth off, but he knew his place well enough to shrink at my retort, ducking his head while the others chuckled. Rafael emerged from the shadows of the hallway to flank me, and suddenly all of the house guards had much more important things to focus their attention on than the nineteen-year-old mafia princess in their midst.

"Ready to go, Lou?" my bodyguard asked in his typical low, subdued voice.

Rafael could have won awards for his poker face. Even the short coils of his wiry black hair stayed perfectly still with the turn of his head.

I'd never seen him show any emotion except the few times some prick had hassled me enough that he'd felt the need to turn on some real rage.

It was a little annoying how quickly the asshole underlings got their act together when they had to face a man instead of just me, even though I had a gazillion times more authority than he did. But I was used to it.

"I think so." I cast a quick glance around before I strode on toward the front door, half expecting a random flunky to come running with a message that the Deadly Rose needed me for some important task right this minute.

Mom had never been particularly enthusiastic about my dedication to my skating, but in the last few months it'd felt like she was outright interrupting my training sessions more and more.

No one charged over this time, though, so I made it out the door unhindered.

The dry summer air hit me with a smack of heat even this early in the morning. I wasn't going to need the sweatshirt packed in my duffel bag until I reached the chilled air of the indoor arena.

I walked around the white-washed walls of our sprawling mansion, enjoying the brief glimpse of the Colorado River I got before I reached the garage.

Rafael didn't make any comment when I headed for the driver's side door of my Mini Coop. As soon as I'd gotten my license, we'd had the argument about who got to be behind the wheel, and he hadn't been able to deny that he'd have a much easier time protecting me in an emergency if he wasn't having to steer at the same time.

I slipped my small frame into the driver's seat easily. Rafael had to fold his tall, brawny form in beside me a little awkwardly even with the passenger seat pushed all the way back.

But he fit just fine once he was inside. And, I mean, he was *fine* in general. I couldn't help admiring his burnished brown skin and broad, muscled shoulders for a second before he flicked his intense burgundy gaze toward me and I jerked my eyes away.

There wasn't any point in looking for more than a bit of eye candy anyway. I'd already tried to hit that once when I was sixteen—and really should have known better, considering that Rafael's stoic discipline was one of the qualities I admired about him beyond his looks—and again once I was eighteen and totally legal.

He'd still turned me down the second time, with his usual calm reserve, and no amount of flirting had changed his mind, despite the hint of a smolder I thought I caught in his gaze now and then. I'd decided it was better to stop before I crossed the line between persistent and pathetic.

I was reaching to start the engine when my phone chimed with a text alert.

Oh, God, it'd better not be Mom calling me away for a mission after all.

I pulled the phone out of my pants pocket and flicked it on. One glance at the words that popped up on the screen had me frowning.

The message wasn't from Mom but from Coach Balakin, the man I'd been about to drive to meet at the arena.

I'm sorry to end things like this, but I can't watch you cling to this unfortunate dream any longer. You haven't progressed to the level you'd need to truly compete, and I don't think there's any point in continuing to coach you. Let's end this here, and you can move on to other dreams.

I stared at the sentences until they blurred together.

Rafael leaned toward me. "What's the matter?"

"I—I don't know. This doesn't make sense."

The bottom of my stomach had dropped out as I'd read Balakin's dismissal, a burn of shame and frustration forming in the back of my throat.

He'd been my coach since I'd first started training seriously when I was five, and in some ways the message shouldn't have been a surprise. He'd always said I wasn't quite there yet, not quite skilled enough that there was any point in entering competitions.

At nineteen, my time to reach that point was running out.

But getting this message right now felt wrong. Just a couple of days ago, Balakin had pulled me aside and told me, in a weirdly urgent voice, that he thought *he* was holding *me* back from what I could really achieve. That maybe I should find a new coach who could let me really take flight.

He'd seemed so twitchy when he'd said it that I'd asked him if everything was okay, and he'd covered it up with a nervous-sounding chuckle. I'd had no idea how to take that statement.

It was the total opposite of what he was saying in this text, though.

I swallowed the lump of emotion that'd constricted my throat. "Something strange is going on. I need to talk to him properly."

I tapped out a quick message telling Balakin to wait for me at the arena so I could hear him out and then shoved the phone back in my pocket.

The rest of Rafael's expression stayed typically reserved, but something flashed in his eyes. "If he said something that upset you—"

"I'm sure he didn't mean it like that," I insisted. "That's why I'm going to find out exactly what he did mean. I don't need you to protect me from my coach."

Rafael's jaw flexed, but he didn't push. If I *had* needed protection from the man I'd spent more time with than my own family for the past fourteen years, I had no doubt that my bodyguard would have leapt to my defense without a second's hesitation.

I drove along the outskirts of Austin to the small arena where I'd done most of my training for years. It was safer going someplace that wasn't very busy—easier for Rafael to keep an eye out for threats, less chance of anyone who might have a beef with my family even knowing I was there.

My body moved through the motions automatically. My heart was thumping heavily in my chest with a mix of apprehension and swelling grief.

What if the message was real? What if Balakin had just wanted to get out of coaching me without hurting my feelings the other day, and he'd been nervous because of how sick he was of trying to bring me up to par?

I gritted my teeth and focused on the road ahead. It didn't help anything thinking like that.

All that mattered was what Balakin would say when I could look him in the eyes. If he really felt that way, then I'd accept it.

The parking lot outside the dingy arena building was empty other than Balakin's blue Honda. At least he was here.

I hustled into the building, heading straight down the hall to the rink, where we usually met up. "Coach? I'm here. I don't want to argue with you—I just—"

I stalled in my tracks a few feet from the scuffed boards that surrounded the ice. A stark red smear had just come into view, standing out against the pale surface beyond.

My pulse hiccupped. I threw myself the rest of the way to the boards.

My hands hit the plexiglass, and a cry burst from my throat.

Coach Balakin lay sprawled on the ice at the base of the boards, his head lolled to the side. His pale eyes stared blankly.

His sweater was drenched with blood from multiple stab marks that'd broken through the fabric. The crimson fluid splattered his hair—once blond and now pure silver—and the waxy-looking skin of his face.

Above his head, someone had streaked more blood across the ice to form the words *Death to the Rose.*

"No," I mumbled, as if I could argue my coach back to life. "No, no, no. Why would anyone—how could they—?"

I'd seen dead bodies before. I'd killed more than one man myself. But that'd been in the other part of my life. The most violence I'd encountered while skating was a bruise from a badly landed jump.

Balakin had nothing to do with my family's criminal operations. He'd been patient and kind—he had a wife and two grown kids and a new granddaughter he'd been so pleased about last year…

Rafael grasped me by the arms and tugged me away, turning me in the same motion so the corpse was no longer in my view. "Come away from there, Lou."

He sounded strangely gentle.

I bit my lip, willing back the tears that burned at the back of my eyes, and clutched on to the anger that was rising up alongside my sense of loss.

"We have to find whoever did this. We have to find them and make them *pay.*"

"We'll do that," Rafael said in the same steady tone, but I could tell from the slight roughness that'd crept into his voice that he was pissed off too. "We'll take care of this. I need to make a couple of calls. But you shouldn't have to keep looking at him in that condition."

Maybe I should. It was my fault, wasn't it?

Death to the Rose.

This had something to do with my family's connections. Balakin had put so much time into training me when I'd never even been all that impressive, when I'd had to badger my own mother into letting me—

A chill swept through me that had nothing to do with the artificially cooled air. My heart skipped a beat.

I didn't want to even consider the possibility, but now that it was in my head…

I pushed away from Rafael. "I need to get back to the house. I need to talk to my mother."

It was evening before Mom answered my request to speak to her and summoned me to her home office. Apparently she'd been out of the house all day, although it was hard to tell for sure.

The Deadly Rose came and went at her pleasure, answering to no one.

The first confirmation that something was off was the fact that when I came into the grand room with its antique desk and bookcases, Mom sprang up from her chair and stalked over to wrap me in her wiry arms. She was tall enough that her chin rested against my forehead with the embrace.

The hug only lasted for a couple of seconds, but Mom rarely touched me at all. When she did, it was usually a poke or a smack to correct my position or to chide me for a mistake.

"I just heard," she said in her crisply smooth voice. She stepped back, giving my cheek a slightly patronizing pat that felt more in character. "I'm so sorry, Luciana. I know he was important to you."

I gazed back into her eyes, which were the same dark brown shade as mine. Her face had turned gaunt with middle-age, but she still looked elegant as ever with her bold but classically styled make-up and her black waves that she carefully dyed the gray out of.

We shouldn't have *to worry about being judged by how attractive we are, but we will be. So we do our best to turn that prejudice toward serving our purposes.*

Everything Mom did was part of a strategy. What was the purpose of the mask of mild sympathy she was showing me now?

"I don't understand why someone would have killed him," I said. "He never messed with anything criminal."

Mom tsked her tongue. "Plenty of our enemies might not have realized that. Most likely, though, they went after him because of his connection to you. They were looking to strike a blow at us. Maybe they hoped they'd get information out of him and killed him when he'd given everything he knew."

"He didn't know *anything* except how well I can move on the ice," I protested.

"Yes. It is unfortunate." Mom folded her arms over her chest. "I suppose we should take this as a sign that it's time you took on more responsibilities within our actual business. You can help me with keeping the lowlifes who'd attack us like this in line."

There it was. My heart sank.

She didn't even sound upset, just briskly business as usual. Because the horrific murder played right into her plans.

Wasn't that convenient?

I studied her expression as I prepared my next words. "What if I want to keep skating?"

Mom waved her hand dismissively. "I'm sure you'll find time to get out on the ice here and there. But the schedule you've been keeping—there've already been conflicts. And wasn't Balakin saying that you'd reached your limits anyway?"

I hadn't been totally sure before that moment. I hadn't *wanted* to be sure.

But I hadn't said anything about the text Balakin had sent me to anyone. How could Mom say that with so much confidence if she didn't know about it for other reasons?

Like, because she'd ordered whoever had actually written that text to send it on Balakin's phone after they'd slaughtered the poor man.

That would be a perfect strategic move, wouldn't it?

Mom didn't have to be the bad guy, ordering me to give up my aspirations. It was the coach telling me I'd reached the end of the road, a coach who was now gone so his supposed last words to me would stand unchallenged.

It was awful, but also completely on brand for the woman in front of me.

My stomach lurched queasily. I held on to my composure with the iron fist she'd beaten into me.

Part of me wanted to throw her deception in her face. But what purpose would *that* act serve?

If she realized I was on to her, she'd only up her game.

"I guess he was," I said, playing along with the rouse. "Are we going to find the people who murdered him?"

Mom's reaction was only further confirmation. If she hadn't intended this outcome, she'd have been furious about the violation, the direct threat aimed at her in the bloody message on the ice.

Instead, she simply said curtly, "They'll be tracked down and dealt with. We have men on it already."

"Good," I said, letting just a hint of my own anger color my voice, even if I couldn't fully direct it at its real target.

Then I exhaled as if in exhaustion. "It was so sudden—I know I shouldn't be shocked by something like this, but I'm still a little shaken up. I think I'm going to turn in early."

Mom nodded, not bothering to express disapproval of my admission of this small weakness when she thought she'd gotten what she wanted. "Nothing wrong with taking a little time to gather yourself while you have the chance."

I couldn't get out of her presence fast enough, but I forced my steps to stay measured until I'd shut the door of her office and was heading down the hall. Then I hustled the rest of the way to my bedroom at the back of the house.

The funny thing—in a sick way—was that I'd already been prepared for this moment. I just hadn't expected it to play out quite like this.

For the past several years, I'd been siphoning as much money from the family accounts as I could get away with into a hidden stash of cash as well as a secret bank account under a pseudonym Mom didn't know. I had a getaway bag packed and stashed in the attic, easy to grab from the trap door in my walk-in closet.

I'd been planning to leave this house and Mom's expectations behind eventually. I might have done it already if I hadn't kept convincing myself that I should hang in there a little longer, build up my nest egg a little more…

And I hadn't decided how I'd handle the issue of Balakin and my training, since obviously Mom could find me through him.

Little did she know that with her vicious gambit, she'd swept the main factor keeping me with her into oblivion. There was nothing left in this city that I really cared about—nothing I couldn't just as easily find someplace else.

Mom had taught me how to survive in a man's world, how to stand up for myself and take control of my life. And for the first time, I was actually going to enjoy putting those lessons to use.

I stuffed my skates into my training duffel along with a few other items I couldn't bear to leave behind that weren't in the emergency bag. Then I swapped my black-and-white striped leggings and hot pink muscle tee for an all-black ensemble.

For a second, I imagined how Balakin would have clapped to see me wearing more typical workout gear rather than sticking to my preferred style at the rink, and a fresh pang of grief rippled through me.

He would have wanted this escape for me too. He'd been trying to tell me that when we'd talked two days ago, hadn't he?

Had Mom been putting pressure on him to cut me off, and he'd defied her? That would explain his nervousness.

But God, how he'd paid for it.

I blinked hard and sank onto my bed, pulling my knees up to my chest.

I couldn't leave just yet anyway. There was too much activity in the house; the sun hadn't even finished setting.

I waited until midnight. Then I grabbed all my things, popped out the screen in my window, and shimmied down to the roof on the back porch.

From there it was an easy drop to the backyard. My sneakers only made a soft thump in the grass.

A couple of men patrolled the expansive yard, but I'd timed my departure well. I slipped through the night toward the hedge between our grounds and the neighbor's.

I already knew I could squeeze between the tall, conical bushes and—

I'd almost reached them when a brawny shape stepped out from behind one of the trees. I jerked to a halt, clutching my bags, narrowing my eyes at Rafael.

"Where the hell are you going?" he demanded under his breath, his gaze flicking to the house behind me.

If he raised the alarm, I'd simply have to run.

I stared back at him fiercely. "She killed him. She killed Balakin. I can't live under her roof for one more day. I'm leaving, and you'd better not try to stop me."

I couldn't tell whether my accusation startled him. Rafael gazed back at me for a beat, and then he said, "I'll come with you."

I blinked. "What?"

His voice left no room for argument. "You should have someone with you who's got your back."

Rafael had watched over me for almost a decade, since Mom had given him the assignment. I still wouldn't have expected him to throw in his lot with me that far.

If she found out—*when* she found out that he'd betrayed her…

But I could tell from the tension in his face that he knew the consequences of his decision at least as well as I did. The longer we stood here, the more likely it was that we'd get caught right now.

And the thought of having a little company while I threw everything else in my life away did give me a tiny rush of relief.

"Okay," I said, pushing past him. "Just make sure you keep up."

TWO

Luciana

THE ENGINE of the faded blue Mercury Grand Marquis grumbled more than it rumbled, but that fact didn't shake my sense of satisfaction as I leaned back in the creased leather seat behind the wheel.

The car was mine—all mine, in a way I couldn't say my old ride really had been. And thanks to the cash I'd been secreting away for the past two years, Mom could never trace the purchase.

Rafael and I were traveling completely incognito, which was a necessity, honestly. I could only imagine the rage that'd flared behind Mom's eyes when she'd realized I'd flown the coop.

In the passenger seat next to me, Rafael stretched out his legs and frowned at the glove compartment. Or maybe at the base of the windshield. It was a little hard to tell.

My bodyguard had frowned at the car a lot when I'd picked it out from a buy-and-sell website. But after peeking at the engine and taking a test drive around the block, he'd stepped back while I handed over the wad of hundred-dollar bills.

We'd put a lot of miles on it in the past couple of days, and it hadn't failed us yet. So I figured I'd earned my satisfaction.

Rafael rolled his shoulders. "We should make a pit stop soon. Get the joints moving before they totally stiffen up."

I made a face, but I had to admit my back was pretty achy. "I guess sleeping in a car for two nights will do that to you."

We hadn't wanted to risk getting rooms in motels along our way, even paying cash. And it hadn't seemed safe to stop driving for very long, period. During the nights, we'd taken turns napping in the back seat while the other drove.

But the bright sunlight streaming over the lush forest on either side of the narrow country road lifted my spirits all the same. "We're almost there, though. Why stop now?"

Rafael took out his phone and squinted at the GPS as if verifying my statement. His frown deepened. "Are you sure a place like this is going to be safe enough? It's not really your typical scene."

I snorted. No, Hobb Creek—a tiny town that was barely a speck on the map of Ontario, Canada—was the exact opposite of the chaotic city where I'd grown up. But that was what made it perfect.

"There's no chance Mom will bother looking there," I said. "There are only three thousand people—pretty much impossible any of them will know about the Cordovas and recognize me. Especially when it's over a thousand miles from home and across a national border on top of that."

"We're going to stick out."

"Not if we pretend like we're normal people. I think I can manage that. Can't you?"

Rafael glowered at me, which didn't have the effect he was probably going for. Instead of feeling chagrined, my body temperature rose by about five degrees.

The man was smoking-hot, what can I tell you?

"You'll be bored out of your mind," he said. "What are you going to do with yourself for days on end?"

"I don't know, I think I could use a little peace for once. And there's the skating rink."

Rafael let out a snort. "I doubt that's anything like you're used to either."

I resisted the urge to punch him. "I *shouldn't* be skating anywhere like I used to. Mom will have her people monitoring all the nice rinks in the major cities—that's the first place she'll look. And I picked Hobb Creek specifically because for such a small town, it's got a pretty nice arena. It's not hyped up in a way Mom would notice, but I found a few people talking about how good it is on more obscure sites online."

Rafael simply sighed. "And this house you're thinking we'll rent. It just happened to be available immediately?"

"It looked like the owner has been trying to rent it for a while." I shot my bodyguard a pointed look. "Which is another good thing, because it shows that this town isn't a happening spot in high demand. It won't be on anyone's radar, especially the Deadly Rose's."

At least, I sure as hell hoped it wasn't.

"We'll see what condition it's in." Rafael shifted his stance again, but rather than continuing his skeptical comments, he fell into silence.

His large frame looked a little squished even in the Grand Marquis' spacious seat. Although in comparison to my Mini Coop, I'd bet he considered it a step up.

He'd appreciate it more when he wasn't using it as a hotel room as well as a vehicle.

Maybe I did owe him a quick stretch break, though. My joints were starting to tingle with the need for a good stretch too.

I peered through the windshield at the tree-lined fields we were passing now, crops I couldn't identify swaying in the gentle late-summer breeze. Where would be a good spot to pull over for a couple of minutes?

What I caught sight of first made my heart leap in my chest.

I jerked straighter in my seat. "Hey! Look, there's the sign. We're here!"

Rafael's dark eyebrows rose, a gleam of relief in his burgundy eyes. "Hobb Creek, Ontario," he read. "I guess this is our new 'home, sweet home.'" His soft-yet-steady baritone held the hint of a smile tucked away in it, though it didn't show on his lips.

Typical Rafael. You could tell him he won the lottery, and I'd bet he wouldn't crack a grin.

I had to admit, it was calming having him by my side. I'd never expected him to go on the run with me.

He was still the stone-faced man I'd known since I was ten years old, but if there was one reminder of my old life that I didn't mind having with me, it was him. Nothing shook him. There was no one I'd ever been able to count on more.

He pushed himself up taller in the seat, and I let myself quietly appreciate the swell of muscles in his biceps while ignoring the itch in my fingers to touch them.

Maybe now that we'd be living together, he'd rethink his resistance to getting close in other ways.

I cruised past the sign, easing off the gas so we could get a good look at the town rather than speeding through it. "The house is on River Street. Watch for that."

Pointed rooftops came into view up ahead. We drove past a smattering of houses and then along what was clearly the main street.

Several pedestrians strolled along the sidewalks. The storefronts on either side looked quaint, but the people themselves could have fit in back in Austin just fine. They hefted grocery bags, pushed strollers, or scrolled through their cellphones.

It reminded me a little of Sixth Street, only, y'know, a trillion times more rural. A pang of homesickness rang through my chest, but it was softened by a swell of hope.

I could be happy in a place like this, couldn't I?

We drove by a coffee shop and a school where a gaggle of teens were busy in the courtyard in a very intense game of three-on-three. The next several blocks were stuffed full of small restaurants and stores, a bank, a doctor's office, and a tiny fitness center.

A large grocery store loomed on the left. We puttered past it, saw a couple more streets of houses, and then suddenly there were only a couple of warehouses on either side of us followed by a stretch of fields.

I pulled over onto the gravel curb and squinted into the distance. I couldn't see anything beyond the fields except some more forest.

"Was that it?" I said in disbelief. "The whole town? It's only, like, fifteen blocks long!" That was barely even a neighborhood back in Austin.

Rafael cocked his head. "You wanted small, you got small. I can see why you didn't have any trouble getting us that house."

"It shouldn't be too hard to find. Did you see River Street?"

He shook his head and motioned to his phone. "It looks like it's down Maple Avenue, which is about three blocks back the way we came. Take a right."

I yanked the wheel to take the car in a U-turn, still chewing over the situation. Somehow I hadn't imagined the town being quite *this* tiny.

What if Rafael was right and I'd be going stir-crazy in a few days?

But what were my other options? The bigger the town or city, the more likely Mom would have connections there. She wasn't going to let me go easily.

The image of Coach Balakin's bloody body flashed through my mind, and my hands tightened around the wheel.

I'd have to make Hobb Creek work. The only thing to do now was to keep my head down and make sure I didn't attract too much attention.

I followed Rafael's directions and aimed the car down a residential street lined with bungalows and two-story houses with large lawns. In less than a minute, I spotted the sign for River Street.

I turned the corner, and there we were.

The bungalow looked just like it had in the pictures in the online listing, all maroon clapboard and slate-gray shingles on the roof, with a mailbox at the foot of the driveway. But the photographs hadn't captured the flecks where the paint was peeling, or the dent in the side of the mailbox, or the weeds that were warring with the grass for dominance in the lawn.

That was all cosmetics, though. I couldn't see anything actually *wrong* with the building.

A smile started to tickle across my lips as I pulled up the driveway. This was the perfect home for lying low.

The bungalow's front door banged open as we stepped out onto the grass, and a portly man with tufts of gray hair poking up from his broad head made his way towards the car. His ruddy face shone with a broad grin.

"Miss Lou? You've made it!"

He extended his hand prematurely, before he was anywhere near close enough for me to reach it. When he was finally an arm's length away, I grasped it and shook it. He pumped his arm up and down enthusiastically.

"It's a pleasure to meet you," he said. "You remember me from the phone call, yes? Dimitris Papadakis?"

I did. The man's Greek accent had reminded me of Coach Balakin's eastern European articulation. It had immediately endeared him to me. Now that I'd experienced his warm jubilance in person, I liked him even more.

"Of course," I replied. "Thank you for giving us the chance to rent the house on such short notice. We're very grateful, aren't we, Rafael?"

My bodyguard only nodded in response. His eyes were trained on the bungalow. He was already assessing the area, his gaze honing in on the door and windows like laser-sights, evaluating every route in and out of the building.

Dimitris chuckled. "I'm grateful too. But come, come. Let me show you around."

The heavy-set man ushered the two of us up the front steps. They creaked so loudly under our combined weight that I had to suppress a flinch.

Dimitris simply beamed at me. "They like to welcome you home."

"Such an enthusiastic welcome too," Rafael said under his breath.

The landlord chuckled again. "Your husband has a good sense of humor. I like that. But I've done some renovations inside for more comfort. I promise you'll love living here."

Rafael cleared his throat. "I'm not her husband. Just a friend."

He said it calmly enough, but the admission had me wincing

inwardly in a different way. I searched Dimitris's face for any sign of disapproval, but he just shrugged his hulking shoulders.

"Ah, well," he said. "Whatever makes you happy. You see the living room—I should mention the air conditioning unit. Still very warm here in early September, so you'll be using her for a bit longer. Sometimes she gives a little leak now and then. Like a dog, not totally trained yet. But everything else is working perfectly fine!"

I eyed the gray unit protruding from one of the living room windows, which didn't appear to have piddled recently. I could handle mopping up an occasional puddle. No big deal.

At least it would only be water.

The space we'd come into was a tad dingy: the cushions on the narrow sofa worn in patches, scuff marks along the edge of the plain pine table. But at least it *had* furnishings.

Fresh country air flowed through the space. I sucked in a deep breath of it, and all I could think was that no one would come marching in to order me to do *anything* as long as I was living here.

Yeah, I could get used to that. Who needed a mansion when you could have freedom instead?

Dimitris showed us the main bedroom on the ground level, the bathroom with its slightly yellowed but ample bathtub, and the concrete steps that led to a second bedroom in the basement.

Overall, it was a pretty small home, but bigger than the one room I'd had to myself back under Mom's roof. And now I'd have a roof all my own.

"One tenant maybe ten years ago, he was writing a movie," Dimitris told us as we climbed back up the stairs to the first floor. "He said he never got as good inspiration as when he was living here."

"How did the film do?" I asked with honest curiosity.

Dimitris burst out into a guffaw, his great gut shaking. "Oh, it was a total flop. But I'm sure it wasn't because of the script. Now, let's get this unpleasant paperwork out of our hair, yes?"

I'd already reviewed the lease when he'd emailed me a copy. I scanned the printed version quickly to confirm the contract looked the same as the one I'd already considered, with its month-to-month agreement and other basic stipulations, and then signed it with a flourish.

As I handed over the cash for the deposit and the first month's rent, something I could only call joy sparked in my chest.

I'd done it. I'd finally broken from my chains and staked a claim on a life that was truly my own.

Dimitris thanked us with another emphatic shake of my hand, and then he waddled off with shouts over his shoulder about how we should contact him if we had any trouble. I waved him off and then hustled to the car to grab my things.

When I lugged my bags into the house, I found Rafael studying the lock on the door. I arched an eyebrow at him. "Does it meet your approval?"

"It's not awful," he said, which from him was high praise.

"You know, I hear that in small towns like this, most people don't even bother locking their doors."

Rafael's head snapped around just like I'd known it would. "We're keeping the door locked, Lou."

With a roll of my eyes, I held up my hands. "No kidding. I was just saying."

Sometimes it was way too easy to push his buttons.

He moved to the windows, inspecting the latches on them too. "I'll take the basement bedroom."

I paused. "Are you sure?" It was colder and darker, and the windows were tiny. I didn't really *want* to sleep down there, but on the other hand I could see turning it into a cool little cave.

Rafael had given up his whole life to follow me here. This wasn't *his* dream. I didn't want to make him any more uncomfortable than he already was.

But he simply shrugged. "I'd rather you were close to the exit if you need to get out in a hurry."

Well, when he put it in practical terms like that, it was hard to argue.

I hefted my bags onward to the main-floor bedroom, which had a picture window that was actually rather pretty and a double bed with a brass frame. The bedspread was a little frilly for my tastes, but I could always replace it if we stayed here long enough.

I could decide everything about how this house was decorated—with some input from Rafael, of course. The contract I'd just signed said it was all *mine*.

But the house wasn't the only reason I'd come here. As I unpacked my clothes from my emergency bag, taking a weird pleasure from adding them to the hangers in the closet, my gaze kept snagging on my training duffel.

When the urge became too much, I left the rest of my clothes and knelt by the equipment bag. I stuffed a few small items in my purse and then simply grabbed my skates.

I wasn't going to do anything hardcore on my first day here. Just… take a quick spin on the local rink. Break in the ice.

I slung the skates over my shoulder by the laces and walked to the doorway. "I'm going to check out the skating rink."

Rafael appeared at the top of the stairs. "Of course you are. Where exactly is it?"

I could picture the layout of the town in my head now. "It's at the opposite end from here, east side, right on the outskirts. But that means it's barely any distance at all."

"Doesn't matter. I'm coming with you."

I hadn't expected anything less—and though I wouldn't have admitted it, part of me was relieved to have the company. Not that it was likely anything around Hobb Creek would offer a significant threat.

"You can check all the locks on the arena too," I teased.

I opted to take the car so that I wasn't flashing my skates all over town on my first day. Even with the slow speed limit and one wrong turn, we reached the squat gray building that held the rink in less than ten minutes.

The parking lot was empty. I guessed early afternoon in the middle of the week wasn't a very happening time for rink rentals. Or maybe people just walked over.

In a quiet town like this, I'd probably have the whole arena to myself most of the time.

A giddy shiver passed through me. I walked up to the front doors and tugged on the handle.

The door jarred against its partner—locked. I knit my brow, peering through the smudged windows, but I couldn't see any sign stating the opening hours.

Rafael peered over my shoulder. "We could always come back tomorrow morning."

"Who knows if they'll be open then either?"

Impatience was prickling through my limbs. I'd come all the way over here—I'd come almost two thousand miles to make Hobb Creek my home. I was going to see the goddamn rink.

It shouldn't be that hard. What I'd said to Rafael about small-town security was generally true, wasn't it? The lock on the door looked awfully simple.

I glanced around and confirmed there was no one within sight. Thankfully the arena was set at the back of its parking lot on the outskirts of town, so there wasn't a whole lot of traffic.

Bending down, I reached into my sock and fished out the set of bobby pins I always kept there, just in case.

"Is this really how you want to spend your first day?" Rafael asked. "Breaking and entering?"

"Oh, stop. This place doesn't have cameras, and there are no cars in the parking lot. No one will ever know. If anyone *does* catch me inside, I can just claim I found it unlocked."

He sighed but didn't argue further.

I had the door open within the next three breaths. Tucking the bobby pins back into my sock, I smiled triumphantly.

We stepped into a dim entrance way with a front office that showed no signs of life. A hallway branched off to the side where presumably the changerooms lay, but my attention zoomed in on the swinging doors straight ahead that would give admission to the rink itself.

I pushed past them and stopped at the top of the steps to flick a light switch. A thrill tingled through me.

The stands were empty. The rink shone glossy under the overhead lights that'd just flooded it.

The ice was calling to me.

Rafael drifted to the side, melding into the shadows along the top of the stands as he preferred to. I hurried down the aisle to the benches that ringed the rink.

Perched on one, I tore off my sneakers and slid my feet into the familiar encasing of my skates. My fingers moved to lace them automatically.

I pulled my phone out of my purse along with my Bluetooth speaker and found my playlist that included my warm-up music and the songs for a few of my favorite routines. With it playing, I set the phone and speaker on the top of the boards around the ice and then pushed off.

My blades glided over the slick surface. The breeze I generated with the swift movement swept around me. I closed my eyes just for a second.

This—this was where my new life, my real life, truly began.

THREE

Jasper

I WAS JUST TYING up my sneakers when an energetic knock sounded on the apartment door.

"Time to get going, lazy bones!" my self-proclaimed coach called through the wooden slab in his typical playful tone. "The day's not going to wait forever."

"I'm coming, I'm coming," I grumbled half-heartedly. "A guy's got to put his shoes on, you know. Especially when his coach insists that he needs to walk to the rink."

"All part of your training. You can never have too much endurance work."

It was hard to feel truly annoyed listening to Niko Okabe's cheery, lightly accented voice. Even harder when I reminded myself that he'd flown halfway across the world from Japan just to haul me out of my slump.

But that didn't mean I was going to somehow transform into Mr. Sunshine myself.

"As you always say," I retorted dryly, and glanced at the hallway mirror. A few rakes of my fingers through my auburn hair was enough to tame it into shape.

I fumbled around for the keys of my garage-top apartment as I swung my equipment bag over one shoulder. When I shoved the door open, Niko grinned at me from the landing on the side of the garage, just as chipper as he'd been when he'd arrived at my grandparents' door in Ottawa a couple of months ago.

He was already in his workout attire of black athletic pants and brightly colored tee, his black hair spiked in his usual style. The hot pink streak he'd dyed through it caught a flash of sunlight, nearly blinding the shit out of me.

I locked the door behind me and shoved the keys into my pocket. Niko was renting a bachelor apartment over a store in the middle of town, closer to the arena than my place was, but he insisted on joining me for the walk over every day.

Maybe to make sure I did actually walk. But he said it was so we could warm up our minds too, talking over goals for this practice session.

He strode down the stairs ahead of me, a thermos dangling from one slender hand. "It's a beautiful day."

"As I'm sure we'll appreciate so much while we're hanging out in a windowless room."

"It sets the mood." Niko wagged a finger at me. "You know that attitude is at least fifty percent of the performance."

I couldn't stop one corner of my mouth from ticking upward in the start of a smile. "Then I guess I'll be skating clear and sunny today."

Niko simply chuckled, that light but warm laugh that gave the impression you genuinely *had* brightened his day. The sound sent a weird twinge through my stomach that I didn't want to look at too closely.

It really was a gorgeous day if you were into that sort of thing, the sun beaming down over Hobb Creek like it was setting it up for a picturesque Hollywood film set. Summer was still hanging on enough that the breeze that brushed over my bare arms was enjoyable rather than chilly.

As usual, Niko started chattering away about his opinions on the progress I'd made.

"Your Lutzes have been looking much better in the last few weeks. Good height, and you've barely popped out of any of them."

"Hurray!" I said in a sarcastic cheer.

"We need to celebrate our victories," Niko insisted. "That's attitude too. Be happy with where you're at, and the audience will be happy watching you."

"When I have an audience again."

"We're getting there."

There wasn't a particle of doubt in Niko's voice. He unscrewed the cap on his thermos, took a swig, and grimaced. He managed to swallow with a bob of his Adam's apple, but he poured the rest of the white liquid contents out into one of the decorative flower beds next to the sidewalk.

"Another failed experiment?" I couldn't help teasing. "When are you going to learn that carbonation and milk just don't go together?"

"They do!" he protested. "If you'd ever had proper Calpis… It's a crime that you can't buy it here. But if they can make it, there's got to be a way."

"Or you could just get your sister to send you some straight from Japan."

He snorted. "Then I'll never hear the end of it from Emi. I can be persistent. Better to teach a man to fish or something like that, isn't that what they say?"

"That's about right."

Niko had mentioned that he'd lived in the US for a few years as a kid while his father was stationed there for a job. He'd spent first through fifth grade in an American school, which explained why his accent was mild and his grasp of English idioms not bad. There were still a few concepts he didn't totally have down, though.

Like that everyone on this side of the ocean thought making pop out of milk was deeply bizarre.

He shook his empty thermos at me, grinning. "When I get it right, you'll see. You'll be guzzling it like you do that maple syrup you pour on everything."

"Sure, and then I'll land a quadruple Axel," I said, but my mouth had stretched into a full smile despite my skeptical tone.

Over the past several weeks, Niko and I had settled into something like a comfortable routine. He badgered me onto the ice in his upbeat way and delivered his coaching instructions with boundless enthusiasm. When my muscles were aching, we trekked back through town to grab a bite to eat, quickly hash out how the practice had gone, and go our separate ways. Then the next day we started over again.

But tramping along beside him, uncertainty still niggled at me.

If I was going to compete again, there was no one better to coach me back into the circuit than Niko Okabe. The guy was like music on the ice; he had a way with both the artistic and technical aspects of skating that I'd always admired.

I'd watched him compete for Japan and had been blown away by his ability to paint a picture through motion. I wanted to do the same more than anything in the world.

There was a reason he'd made it to two Olympic Games, earning silver at the last one.

He'd never coached before, though, as far as I knew—at least not professionally. He hadn't really explained why he'd tracked me down and insisted that he was going to whip me back into shape, only saying that he'd noticed my absence during the last sequence of competitions and decided he would see what he could do about it. That he'd been wanting a challenge.

Was that all he saw when he looked at me—a problem to solve? A difficult puzzle to work through to stretch his skills?

If it meant anything more than that, he certainly hadn't given any indication. He was cheerful and friendly, sure, but always with a professional air.

The thought made me feel prickly again, but really, did it matter?

I wanted to be out there performing in front of the crowds again. If Niko was willing to help me get back into the headspace where I could, who was I to look a gift horse in the mouth?

This once, there was a car parked outside the arena—a light blue sedan I didn't recognize. Most of the time the staff never showed up while we were practicing. Hopefully they weren't messing with the ice.

Niko must have observed it too. Rather than fishing the spare key the owners had given him out of his pocket, he tried the door. It opened easily.

"Looks like I might not be the only one who gets to appreciate your talents today," he said, tugging it wide.

"Unless they screwed up our scheduling and we're about to walk into some six-year-old's birthday party," I muttered, but headed on inside behind him.

We found the reception area eerily vacant, just as it always was. I craned my neck down the short hallway, but the manager's office was shut up tight too. No lights shone through the tiny window.

No party, then. Maybe a janitor was making the rounds?

As we approached the doors to the rink, a lilting melody filtered past them to my ears. My heart skipped a beat.

Someone was playing music in there. And not any kids, unless Chopin was the new standard for birthday parties.

I opened my mouth to call out and ask who was there. We'd booked this time, after all.

But Niko had already reached the doors and nudged them open. His hand jerked up to silence me as he stared through the gap.

Then he was off again, pushing right into the stands. I hustled after him, even more confused than before.

The second I burst into the rink area, my steps slowed.

The music was emanating from a small speaker perched on the boards around the rink, slightly tinny but the notes pealing clearly enough. And moving with the melody, a woman glided across the ice.

In an instant, I noted that she had a typical figure skater build: petite but muscular through her thighs and calves. Her dark ponytail streamed out behind her like a battle flag.

And man, could she *move*.

She held her hands high above her head, then leaned back as she trailed them down across the swell of her chest and out again. They curved with the rest of her body when her feet spun up in a beautiful triple Salchow.

She whirled through the air as though that wasn't one of the more difficult moves a skater could accomplish and landed it with a graceful sweep of her leg.

My mouth fell open. Her expression shifted in time with the music, the crescendo trilling higher until an entire storyline was playing through my head. The nocturne conveyed a sense of danger and romance intertwined, something so beautiful and touching that I couldn't tear my eyes away.

A pang reverberated through my chest. This was it. This was how I wanted to skate. The power and artistry I craved every time I set my blades on the ice.

The vision that never looked quite right even after all these weeks of Niko's guidance, no matter how much he praised my progress in the video recordings he took to show me after.

As I drifted down the steps to the boards, I searched my memory, trying to recall if I'd ever seen this woman before. But no: nothing from the town, nothing from any of my past competitions.

She'd definitely have stuck in my mind if I'd seen her before. So who the hell was she, and where had she come from?

I was about to ask Niko those questions as I came up beside him at the foot of the stands, but then I caught a glimpse of his face.

Of the awe etched in his avid expression.

His bright brown eyes followed along with every leap of her powerful legs and every subtle curl of her fingers. His lips had parted as if the imagery she was creating had struck him speechless.

Had he ever looked at *my* skating like that?

Jealousy coupled with a hefty heaping of insecurity spiked between my ribs. If we compared who a panel of judges would be most impressed by, she would probably blow me out of the water, and Niko clearly knew that too.

"Wow," he breathed, rubbing salt into the wound. "She's really something."

Yeah, she was—in more ways than one. She eased to a stop at the far end of the rink, and for the first time I could see her face clearly, if only in profile.

The exertion of the routine had brought a ruddy flush into the smooth brown skin of her cheeks. The perfectly chiseled bow of her lips curled up in a tiny smile. The graceful arc of her eyebrows matched the elegant slope of her nose.

She was fucking gorgeous.

My cock twitched involuntarily, and I set my duffel bag on the bench in front of me just in case I needed it to hide my reaction. At the same time, my jaw tightened.

A woman like that would be used to everyone falling all over her. The last thing I wanted was to come across like another lovestruck schoolboy tripping over himself to join her fan club.

Shoving down the flare of heat that'd stirred inside me, I raised my hands in a slow, pointed clap.

Yes, we see you. Yes, you're oh so wonderful.

Now get over here and explain what the fuck you're doing crashing my training time.

FOUR

Luciana

I SOARED THROUGH THE AIR, as smooth and elegant as a swan on the water. The very soul of grace itself.

I was made for this.

Or at least, that's what I told myself.

The words had become a mantra, a prayer on repeat, bouncing around inside my brain while I tried to summon all the dignified calm and effortless confidence of a professional figure skater. When nerves nibbled at the edges of my mind, I reminded myself why I'd risked sneaking into the rink in the first place.

There was no one here watching, no one judging. Only Rafael's eyes would be on me right now, and he barely counted after all these years.

I could glide around for as long as I cared to, really get acclimated to the feeling of this new rink beneath my skates.

After all, this strange, tiny town was home now. This little arena would be the backdrop for my skating from now on.

The familiar sound of my blades hissing over the ice filled my ears, chasing away all doubts. I shifted directions, pumping my legs with long, swift movements as my skates propelled me backwards.

My hands spread wide, my slender fingers reaching out towards the empty stands. A well of power had begun to course through me, surging in my veins and pulsing in my limbs.

Deep breath in, and out again.

This headspace was familiar. This was comfortable. Again, that mantra sailed through my thoughts, but this time, I knew the words were true.

I was made for this.

Sweeping one leg out behind me, I pushed up with the opposite foot and swung my arms around my slim form. I ascended like a bird in flight, the thrilling rush racing through my gut.

Pure, unfiltered bliss pumped throughout my body, pounding in my chest and bursting in my vision. I couldn't have stopped the smile from curving my lips even if I'd wanted to.

I knew in my heart that this was where I belonged. No matter what anyone said.

Landing felt more like floating. My skates met the ice again with a soft *shrrrk* before I pushed off again with one foot.

Another triple Salchow, this one even easier than the first. I might have tried for a triple Lutz if it hadn't been a few days since my last practice.

I closed my eyes when I landed this time, tilting the point of my toes and sweeping off once more. The moves felt natural, just as they always had before I'd left the only home I'd ever known.

I breezed across the ice in arcs and leaps, the blades connecting with the frozen surface almost magnetically. One, two, three, four, five…

By the time I reached the end of the routine's final sequence, my legs were screaming for a break, but giddy exhilaration still flowed through the rest of my body. I raised my hands in a graceful ending pose, fingertips reaching towards the arched ceiling.

My mind conjured the sound of applause, the adoring crowd roaring behind me. I almost let out a laugh.

Like that would ever happen.

A satisfied breath puffed through my lips. I was just about to turn towards the stands to tell Rafael that we should call it a day when a very real noise reached my ears.

Not a flurry of applause, but a single set of hands clapping in a slow rhythm that somehow didn't feel entirely complimentary.

As I spun toward the sound, another pair of hands joined the first, faster and more emphatic. I found myself staring at two men who'd come down to the boards at the other side of the rink.

Oh, shit.

How long had they been there? I hadn't noticed them as I'd been skating, but then again, how could I have? I'd drifted into that trance-like state of joy that had always come with being on the ice.

I grimaced. Maybe this plan wasn't so well thought out after all. I'd been in town for a whole hour and the first thing I did was get busted for trespassing. I could just imagine my mother shaking her head at me with disdain in her dark eyes.

At least neither of the guys appeared to be law enforcement or security. They weren't dressed in employee uniforms either, but regular T-shirts.

T-shirts that showed off a whole lot of impressive musculature on both of them, now that I was paying attention.

The bigger guy, who had to be as tall as Rafael and nearly as brawny, was the one clapping more slowly. Auburn waves tumbled across his face over full lips slanted at a skeptical angle. That didn't stop him from also being awfully delicious-looking.

The man next to him stood half a foot shorter, leaner but still plenty toned. A broad grin split his equally gorgeous face, sending a twinkle into his bright eyes that I could make out even across the distance.

A twinge of recognition shot through me, though I couldn't place it. Why did they look familiar? Had I seen them without really registering them when we drove through town?

Rafael hadn't emerged from his shadowy alcove to interrupt them, so he mustn't consider them much of a threat.

The slimmer man waved me over with obvious enthusiasm, still grinning away. He didn't look like he was about to accuse me of breaking and entering, but I wasn't so sure about his companion.

But I couldn't exactly pretend I wasn't here.

I skated over to the boards about ten feet down from where they stood and grabbed my phone to shut off the next song on the playlist.

"Great form," the enthusiastic man said before I could decide how to explain myself, his voice as cheerful as his expression. "Really excellent. Those two triple Salchows back to back, and then that ending sequence—you've obviously been training for a while. How have I not seen you on the competitive circuit before?"

I blinked at him, my brain not quite processing the compliment. Did he even know what he was talking about? He'd recognized the jump, so he obviously knew something about figure skating.

But Coach Balakin had always complained that I didn't achieve quite enough height, the angle of my arms looked clumsy. It wasn't likely all that had gotten fixed during the two-day drive to Canada.

"Thanks," I said warily, pushing a little closer across the ice. I couldn't shake the niggling sense that I should know who these two were…

Then the enthusiastic guy swept his lithe fingers through his smooth black hair, and a neon pink streak flashed beneath the rink lights.

I couldn't stop my mouth from dropping open. I hadn't fully recognized them at first because no part of my mind had been able to conceive of these two men actually being here.

But there was no mistaking them now that my brain had caught up.

"Oh my God," I blurted out. "You're Niko Okabe! And—" My gaze jerked to the grouchier, bigger guy next to him. "Jasper St. Pierre. Wow."

I snapped my mouth shut before I could babble any further, my cheeks flushing hot. I must have sounded like the ditsiest fangirl.

But I was a fan of both of them—I'd admired their routines from various championships more than once, glued to my TV screen.

Niko Okabe was known for his boldness both on and off the ice. He skated to music the judges raised eyebrows at, incorporated moves from other disciplines that raised those eyebrows even higher, and pulled it all off so well they couldn't help giving him top marks anyway.

In interviews, he never shied away from acknowledging his culturally controversial interest in both men and women. He refused to let anyone put him in a box.

How could I *not* admire that?

And Jasper St. Pierre… Despite his bulky build, he was pure artistry in motion. No one could paint a picture like he did when he whirled across a rink.

Of course, he wasn't making the prettiest picture right now with that stunning face of his getting increasingly grim.

He narrowed his stormy gray-green eyes at me. "Good job. You aren't blind."

Niko rolled his eyes at the taller guy and dipped into a jaunty bow. "A pleasure to meet you."

"What are you doing here?" I couldn't help asking.

Jasper folded his arms over his broad chest. "We should be asking you that. This is our ice time."

My cheeks flared hotter. Somehow two of the world's top skaters were training at this nice but admittedly rinky-dink arena in Nowhere, Ontario, and I'd gone and stolen their practice time.

I groped for the excuse I'd had ready, drawing myself a little straighter—though I couldn't come close to matching even Niko's height, skates or no. "I'm sorry. I found the door unlocked, and there was no one up front… I didn't think it'd be any problem for me to skate."

Niko waved off my concern and nudged Jasper with his elbow in what I took as a chiding way. "It's perfectly fine. I appreciated the chance to watch that amazing display of skill."

Right. He'd been saying something before about how great my routine had been. How well I'd performed it.

Hold up. Niko Okabe thought *I* was amazing?

No. That possibility did not compute. He must simply be acting friendly, overdoing it a little to make up for Jasper the Grouch.

"I had to take a little break from practice, but I'm glad to get back on the ice," I said, not knowing how else to respond, and then added quickly. "But I'll get off now so you can have it."

Jasper grunted as if my offer didn't come close to making up for the offense I'd committed. As I glided over to the opening in the boards, he dropped onto one of the benches and pulled his skates out of a duffel bag.

Niko was still studying me avidly. "You still haven't told us who you are. And why have you been keeping such a low profile? If you'd even entered the US national competitions, I'd have seen you."

He really was being awfully nice to someone who'd snuck in during their ice time. I obviously wasn't going to give him my full name, but I had to answer him somehow.

"My name's Luciana," I said. "But I prefer Lou. Competing, well, I just always seem to get little injuries at the worst times."

Timing that would have prevented me from competing for years on end would have been incredibly bad luck, but Niko didn't question it. He probably didn't really think I was good enough to make it even to Regionals anyway.

My gaze slid from him to Jasper—who was studiously ignoring me while he laced up his skates—and back again. "Why are you two training here?"

I mean, the rink had been highly praised by the few people who knew about it online, but it was hardly world-championship-skater prominent. And Jasper had always competed for the US, as far as I knew, while Niko was obviously Team Japan.

I half-expected to get another brush-off, but Niko leaned his tan arms against the top of the boards with no sign of concern about my nosiness.

He tipped his head toward Jasper with another flash of his impressive grin. "It's all this guy's fault, really. If he hadn't gone and tried to disappear, neither one of us would be here bothering you right now."

"Bothering *her*?" Jasper muttered without looking up.

Niko ignored him. "If you recognize him, you obviously know how fantastic *his* skills are. I expected to see him sweep through the last circuit, but he never showed. So I decided to make it my mission to drag him back into the spotlight. I tracked him down to his grandparents' place in Ottawa—"

Jasper interrupted with a cough. "*Stalked* me." But he didn't sound quite as irritated about it as he did when he was talking about me.

"—and found him lazing around in a slump. Since that was obviously not okay, I offered to give coaching him a try."

"More like he demanded I let him have a go at it and refused to leave until I said yes," Jasper put in, and met my gaze for the first time since I'd come closer. "But I didn't want it to be a big deal, so I asked around to find a place that would be very low key but still a good rink."

Huh. Their reasoning had been awfully similar to my own. I guessed that meant I'd made a good choice.

Jasper shot me a more pointed look and added, "So I'd better not see our faces plastered all over your Instagram or whatever."

I held up my hands in a gesture of innocence. Now that the initial shock of meeting two of my idols in the flesh was starting to wear off, my own prickliness was rearing its head in reaction to his.

"I came here to skate, not to take selfies. Or anyone else-ies."

He only scowled back at me. "And you just happened to turn up here?"

"I picked Hobb Creek for the same reason you did—seemed like a low-key place with a good arena," I said. "I needed a change of pace from the big city." That was a reasonable if vague explanation for my popping up out of nowhere, right? "Believe me, it would never have occurred to me that I'd run into you two here. I definitely won't spread the news."

"Good." Jasper turned to Niko. "Well, let's get on with it."

"Such a positive attitude, hmm?" Niko shot me a wry glance. I couldn't stop my lips from twitching with amusement, which from the glower Jasper shot me, hadn't gone unnoticed.

I snatched up my skate guards to pull them on and slipped past the boards to my own bag, even though a longing tugged at my gut to stay and watch. "I'll get out of your hair. Sorry again. If you let me know what slots you have booked, I'll make sure to work around them."

Niko's face brightened. "You shouldn't have to worry about that. There's lots of room on the rink, and we are here an awful lot. You should come train at the same time."

Jasper let out a sound that might have been a growl, but the offer made me too delirious with excitement for me to care.

"Are you serious? I really don't want to interrupt—"

"It's no trouble at all," Niko insisted. "I'd love to see what else you can do."

His gaze skimmed over my body, and warmth licked over my skin in its wake. Nothing he'd said had been overtly flirty, but all at once I had the impression that the appreciation in his gaze wasn't just for my skating.

Holy hell. Was *the* Niko Okabe attracted to me? I mean, I couldn't say the feeling wouldn't be mutual.

If he was… could anything actually happen between us? Had I fallen asleep on the ice and this was a crazy dream?

Just to make sure, I pinched myself where the men couldn't see. Nope, definitely awake.

Regardless of any other considerations, how could I possibly pass up the chance to train alongside two of the great skaters whose careers I'd been following?

A bright smile stretched across my face. "I'd love that. Thank you so much. I promise I won't get in the way."

"I'm sure you won't," Niko said over Jasper's skeptical grunt. "We're here every afternoon except Sundays from one until six."

"Then I'm sure I'll be seeing a lot of you."

Taking on training partners hadn't been part of my plan. Making friends—and maybe more?—with two very prominent skaters *definitely* hadn't been on my mind.

But they were laying low too. Practicing with them wouldn't cause any actual problems, right?

One thing was for sure: my new life had just gotten a whole lot more complicated.

FIVE

Luciana

"EVERYTHING OKAY, HUN?" my waitress asked, stopping by my little table outside the town's main café with a swish of her white apron.

I smiled up at her, taking a moment to peek at her nametag. I had learned a few useful things from my mother, one of which was that people appreciated it if you made the effort to address them personally.

"It's all been great, Beth," I said, poking my fork into one of my few remaining pierogies. The creamy goodness of the cheesy filling lingered in my mouth from those I'd already devoured. "Thank you."

Honestly, it was hard to imagine everything being *more* okay than it currently was. Over the last couple of days, I'd joined two of the skaters I'd admired most to practice, and tomorrow I would again. I was spending my Sunday off eating a delicious rendition of my favorite comfort food, not quite as good as my old nanny's cooking but close.

The weather was warm but not sweltering. Birds fluttered from one awning to the next along Hobb Creek's main street. Only a handful of cars had puttered up and down the road while I'd been having my lunch.

I couldn't remember ever enjoying this much *peace* in my entire life.

Maybe I was a small-town girl at heart after all.

A middle-aged couple strolled by, the woman shooting a glance at me that she quickly jerked away when she realized I'd caught her. I chewed on my pierogi without taking offense.

Rafael and I *did* kind of stick out here with our darker complexions. Small-town Ontario wasn't exactly a hub of multiculturalism. And on top of that, I was a newcomer.

No one had been outright unfriendly. I could handle a little wariness.

Really, I'd spent most of my life feeling like an outsider even back in Austin. It wasn't as if I could have gotten really chummy with any of the other kids at my schools. And I hadn't wanted to immerse myself in the family business and the people involved in that.

The only place I'd really felt at home was on the ice, and I'd never gotten to enjoy an actual community there, only Coach Balakin's company.

I was glad no one was badgering me about what I was doing in Hobb Creek, sticking to just observing. No doubt more pointed questions would come once the locals realized I was sticking around, not just visiting as a tourist.

Good thing I had my cover story all set for that moment. I smiled to myself before popping the last delicious morsel into my mouth.

As I drained the last of my cappuccino, a woman who didn't look all that different from me—other than being at least thirty years older—ambled up to the café door. Her wavy black hair was strung with silver strands, and her tan skin looked about as weathered as my mom's on the rare occasions I saw her without makeup. But there was a roundness and warmth to her face that I'd never have associated with Mom.

With the chime as she opened the café door, the voice of one of the waitresses rang out. "Oh, Dr. Ribeiro, you made it! Will you have your regular?"

The door closed before I could hear the doctor's answer. I couldn't help peering through the window and caught the waitress's sunny smile as she ushered the woman to a prime spot by the window.

She wasn't seen as an outsider, obviously. Maybe there was hope that I'd be offered similar enthusiasm someday.

I tried to imagine myself still living here in thirty years, and my mind balked at the idea. Mostly because I couldn't picture myself still skating as a forty-nine-year-old.

Well, I wouldn't be pulling off triples anymore, but if I kept myself limber, I didn't have to give it up completely.

My last gulp of the bittersweet coffee was spoiled by a puff of exhaust from a grumbling pickup truck that veered a little too close to the patio for comfort. I narrowed my eyes at it as it roared out of view—and noticed a guy sauntering in my direction on the opposite side of the street.

He didn't fit the typical small-town vibe at all: mid-twenties, sporting a couple of tattoos that poked from beneath his muscle tee, head tipped at a brash angle. About half a block away from where I sat, he turned toward a store and rapped his knuckles against the window.

I knit my brow. The place was a toy shop with the name *Harry's Treasures* painted across the glass in perfect cursive. Above and below the words were illustrations of a teddy bear, a bouncing ball, a jump rope, each rendered with careful precision.

What the hell did this cocky guy want there? And if he *did* want something in there, why had he simply propped himself against the doorframe with his sinewy arms folded over his chest like he was waiting for something?

This guy wasn't a regular customer. What was his deal?

As I watched, my nerves prickling with uneasiness, an elderly man appeared in the doorway. The younger guy pushed himself fully upright, flexing his shoulders in a posture that exuded menace. His laugh carried down the street, but there wasn't much warmth in it.

He jabbed his thumb toward the doorway. The old man raised his hands as if in protest, his own stance humble, but the guy shook his head. Drooping further, the old man—who I was pretty sure owned the toy shop—ducked back inside.

He returned less than a minute later with a letter-sized envelope he handed over with obvious reluctance. The cocky guy checked inside, clapped his target on the shoulder, and started ambling away.

"Sorry, Miss, are you ready for your bill?" a voice said, startling me out of my daze. I realized I'd gone rigid in my chair, and my waitress—Beth—was peering down at me with obvious concern.

"Oh, um, yes, please," I said hastily. My heart kept thudding as I dug my wallet out of my purse to pay for my meal.

I knew what a criminal transaction looked like when I saw it. No way were the contents of that envelope something legit. What the hell was going on in Hobb Creek?

The cocky guy was still in view a couple of blocks down the street. Not walking too fast but like he owned the place.

My teeth gritted. I tossed down a few bills that included a substantial tip and set off after him.

I stayed on the opposite side of the street and at least a block behind him, with regular glances at the store windows I passed as if I were simply taking a stroll. As I trailed the guy off the main street and through a residential section of town, it occurred to me that this might not be the smartest move I could make.

I should be staying as far away as possible from anything criminal. Anything that might tie back to my mother, no matter how tenuous the connections.

But I couldn't shake the memory of the hopelessness I'd seen in the old man's stance. My sense of peace had been fractured.

I needed to at least know what was going on. That was a reasonable strategy, wasn't it? Even if I decided to avoid getting involved, it'd be easier if I knew exactly *what* to avoid.

Yeah, even I wasn't totally buying that story. But it kept me meandering past the rows of houses to the edge of town. My hands rose, my fingers trailing over the subtly sharp edges on the set of rings I liked to wear when I wasn't skating.

They looked pretty, and they could cut a guy with a swipe of my fist. Both features I appreciated.

When the commercial buildings I'd noticed before on the outskirts came into view, I slowed my pace even more. The cocky guy strode right on across the sprawling parking lot to where the pickup truck I'd seen before, a van, and a sports car were parked close to a boxy white storage building.

I stopped in the shade of a tree at the edge of someone's lawn and pulled out my phone so I could pretend to be focused on it rather than the activity across the lot. If I got any closer, it'd be obvious what I was after.

A couple of other men came out of the storage building. I couldn't make out what they said, but the macho posturing came across just fine. They shouldered each other and barked laughs with an attitude that reminded me way too much of the lower lackeys who hung around Mom's mansion back home.

Even more apprehension gripped me. So when a low, deep voice spoke up from right behind me, I nearly jumped out of my skin.

"What do you think you're doing?"

My hand had already shot to the knife in my pocket before I recognized Rafael's voice. I spun around and elbowed him as discreetly as humanly possible.

"Are you trying to give me a heart attack?" I hissed under my breath.

I wasn't exactly surprised he was nearby—it was becoming clear that his bodyguard habits weren't dying just because we'd left the dangers of my old life behind. He'd probably been shadowing me from a discreet distance from the moment I'd left the bungalow.

But he didn't normally emerge from those shadows to hassle me with questions.

"I'm trying to figure out why you wandered all the way out here," Rafael said, still keeping his voice quiet.

I motioned vaguely behind me, toward the storage building. "There's something sketchy going on here—I'm sure of it. I saw one of those guys take an envelope from a store owner who really didn't look happy about it, and… just look at them!"

Rafael didn't miss a beat. "I already have."

I stared at him. "What?"

He gazed back at me steadily. "It's not exactly a big town. It didn't take me long to get a full lay of the land. Seems like a bunch of minor thugs decided to form a small-time gang out of that building."

"Here?" I said, still finding it hard to wrap my head around this development even after what I'd seen. "How much criminal business can they even get up to?"

Rafael shrugged. "They hit up Hobb Creek and a few other small towns in the area—collecting protection money, dealing drugs, stashing stuff in that storage building that's probably stolen or illegal. People who want to profit by breaking the law can always find some way of doing it."

I scowled. "And what the hell are the local police doing? Just sitting on their asses?"

"I don't know if they've even noticed what's going on. The regular locals are too intimidated to speak up. From what I've seen, the law enforcement presence in this area is stretched thin and not very competent anyway."

I turned my scowl directly on him. "And you found out all this stuff and didn't tell me?"

Rafael lifted his eyebrows just slightly. "Why would I have? What does it even matter?"

"Well, I—they're making trouble for the town! *My* town."

"Lou, you're supposed to be staying *out* of anything that looks like trouble, remember? Lay low and skate. Wasn't that the plan?"

"It was," I grumbled. "It is. But that doesn't mean I have to like it."

The townspeople I'd met so far didn't deserve this shit. They should get to enjoy their peaceful surroundings without some assholes ruining it.

And *I* didn't deserve this shit. I'd driven across an entire country to escape the criminal side of my life, and somehow I'd driven right into more of that garbage.

What if this gang did make a connection with the wrong person, and someone recognized me? As unlikely as it was, their very existence was a threat to my freedom.

I set off back toward town, shoving my hands in the pockets of my jeans, but my thoughts kept roiling in my head. No, I didn't like this at all.

But what exactly could I do about it that wouldn't make the threat even worse?

SIX

Luciana

MY LEGS PUMPED as I built up my speed, my dark hair trailing behind me in its ponytail. Bending my knees into a squatting position, I positioned my ankles back until they were beneath my thighs.

An ache spread through my muscles—this was one of the first moves I'd ever learned, but holding it always strained my endurance. I adjusted my weight until I was sure I was steady and then lifted my right foot while sinking even further down, clasping my gloved fingers around the toe of my skates.

One Mississippi. Two Mississippi.

God, this move was torture. I dropped my leg after several more seconds and stood only to speed up again.

All my senses were wired with the awareness of my two fellow skaters at the other end of the rink. This was my third time training alongside Niko Okabe and Jasper St. Pierre, but every time I glanced their way, butterflies fluttered in my stomach.

I still couldn't quite believe I was actually training on the same ice as them.

Not only that, but Niko had even given me a few tips here and there when Jasper was taking a breather or doing something simple like stretching. And always with plenty of praise, as if he really did believe I was somewhere close to the same caliber as the two of them.

That idea felt even more impossible. Could he really just be that nice?

But if he honestly thought I had that level of skill… then had all Coach Balakin's criticisms and discouragements been lies? Or had being in the presence of two greats somehow elevated me too?

I couldn't wrap my head around it, but one thing I knew for sure was that I intended to give a performance worthy of Niko's praise. If I was going to level up to the standards I'd been aspiring to so long, I couldn't settle for anything short of perfection.

Again, I lowered myself back into the move. This time, my bravado carried me through the ache in my legs for little more than thirty seconds.

But I would be damned if I let my weakness faze me. I tried over and over, until I thought my muscles would snap like rubber bands.

Finally breaking out of my position, I lowered my right leg and stood, albeit a little wobbly. I'd held the pose for as long as I could that time, but the pressure on my ankles and thighs was murder.

Leaning against the side of the rink, I stretched one leg and then the other, trying to keep my expression natural. The last thing I wanted was Niko or Jasper noticing my sweaty face and heaving chest.

"Great legwork with that shoot-the-duck," Niko called. "You were really cruising! Nudge that foot just half an inch higher, and it'll be even easier."

"Thanks!" I called back as evenly as I could. "I'll try that next time."

Which wouldn't be until tomorrow—or next week, if my legs got any say in it.

I would have glowed with the praise, but as my gaze slid from Niko to Jasper next to him, I caught the bigger man scowling at me.

The second our eyes met, Jasper jerked his head away, his mouth pressing flat. But I knew what I'd seen. Especially since I'd seen it more than once over our training sessions.

Anytime Niko paid much attention to me, Jasper started looking even grouchier than usual, which was a massive feat. The coolly handsome face he put on during his professional performances had to be as much of a costume as the intricate outfits he wore, because I'd only caught rare glimpses of it as he ran through his routines here.

I'd have thought he was simply annoyed that I was stealing some of his coach's attention… but he didn't seem all that happy when Niko was focused on *him* either.

Like right now, as Niko turned to him and murmured something I couldn't hear. Jasper shook his head sharply, a storminess coming back into his eyes that I could see even from halfway across the rink.

Sometimes they'd joke together, and I'd see a looser side of the hotshot skater. But just as often, an odd tension would come over his brawny frame for reasons I didn't understand.

What was buzzing around in that gorgeous head of his under those tussled auburn waves?

Niko had obviously noticed it too. As Jasper pushed off into a circuit of the rink, building up to a jump, the slimmer man's constant smile briefly faded.

For just a second, he looked almost… *sad.*

It wasn't the first time I'd seen Niko look at Jasper like that, either. I couldn't shake the impression that there was more to his insistence on crossing the ocean to train Jasper than either of them were letting on.

But it wasn't my business. If I got too nosy, I could kiss this once-in-a-lifetime chance good-bye.

Jasper launched himself into a breath-taking double Axel. As he swerved around past me, I offered a thumbs up. "Nice one!"

I'd been trying to make friendly, but Jasper just grimaced. "I was aiming for a triple," he muttered.

I would have said something about how it was impressive to be able to switch intentions and pull off a double so smoothly when you realized you weren't going to land the harder move, but I suspected he wouldn't appreciate my insight.

Gulping a little more water, I rolled my shoulders. My skin was starting to feel muggy under my long-sleeved thermal.

And I couldn't say it was totally due to my work on the ice and not the company I was keeping.

I tugged off the thermal and tossed it onto my bag in the stands. My faded Metallica tee hung to my hips, matching my plaid leggings better than the plain blue shirt had anyway.

Who said you couldn't bring a little style even to practice?

"What's that on your back?"

I glanced over to see Jasper tipping his head toward me, his expression still grim but a hint of curiosity in his voice. My hand moved to the rough-edged neckline of the shirt that dipped to reveal the tops of my shoulder blades.

Oh, he meant my tattoo.

I patted it and offered a tentative smile. "Got this a few years ago."

With a tug downward, I revealed enough of my back that they'd be able to decipher the dark lines as angel wings, swooping from my spine to the tops of my shoulders.

"It's kind of in honor of the skating," I added. "I love feeling like I'm flying."

The second the words came out, my face flushed. I'd never told anyone that before.

Jasper didn't say anything particularly caustic, though. He just grunted, his gaze skimming down over my clothes. "So you're a real punk, then."

As I rolled my eyes at him, Niko shot me one of his brilliant grins. "The tattoo is beautiful. And earned. You move like an angel when you're skating."

My cheeks were outright burning now. I didn't know what to say to that other than a mumbled, "Thanks," that felt totally inadequate.

"Well, come on," Jasper grumbled at the other man, and Niko swerved around with a flash of what might have been guilt crossing his face.

No, I really didn't understand their dynamic at all.

While I worked on a few of my spins in one corner of the rink, Jasper soared past me in another attempt at his triple Axel, and then another. The first time, he stumbled and swayed when he landed a smidge too soon in his rotation.

The second time, he pitched forward right onto his knees.

As he shoved himself upright, cursing under his breath, Niko skated over. He grasped Jasper's arm to help steady him.

"You're in your head too much. You know you can do this—I've seen you make it. But you need to relax and let yourself get into the flow."

"I need to get out of this fucking slump," Jasper growled. He pulled his arm away from Niko and frowned at the other man. "Are you here to be my coach or my therapist? Because I didn't ask for the former and I'm *definitely* not looking for the latter."

Niko held up his hands, too easygoing to take offense even as I bristled on his behalf. "Frustration will trip you up more than anything—speaking as a coach. Why don't you take ten, grab a drink, and cool off?"

Jasper ducked his head. "Sorry. I—" His jaw tightened, and he skated off to where he'd left his bag in the stands.

Niko turned to me, his smile returning if not quite as sunny as before. "That means *you've* got to deal with me now, Angel. I saw you struggling with that Biellmann spin."

I couldn't hold back a wince. I'd been doing so well for a moment, but then a wobble had crept through my legs.

Niko chuckled. "Oh, don't look like that. You almost had it! Here, let me show you —"

He moved to my side and ushered me towards the center of the ice. I glanced toward Jasper, wondering if this would piss him off even more, but he had his back to us as if he didn't care.

"Like this," Niko said. "Do you mind if I…?"

He gestured a few inches from my body, asking if he could touch me. I nodded, a sharp dip of my chin.

His slender fingers dropped down to my waist, holding me steady, while his other hand rested on the outside of my left leg. Warmth rushed over my skin.

Dear lord, I hoped he couldn't feel that his touch was turning me on.

He patted my leg lightly, which only sent more sparks up it. This close up, his gleaming eyes and warm smile were nothing less than magnetic.

"You'll want to keep this leg as straight as possible. And you might try catching your foot at your side rather than behind you to keep your center of gravity."

How was I supposed to process his advice when my brain was short-circuiting at his touch? Coach Balakin had definitely never had this effect on me.

Focus, Lou. You're supposed to be a professional here.

But as I inhaled Niko's light, oceanic scent, I couldn't help noticing that his gaze veered to the rise and fall of my breasts, just for an instant before he jerked his attention to my face. The gleam in his eyes now might have been a little heated too.

He kept his tone as breezy as before. "Does that make sense?"

"Yeah," I said, willing my voice to stay steady. "I just always seem to lose my balance a little just before I'm fully in position."

His hand dropped to the small of my back, and my pussy clenched. I leaned into him just slightly and *knew* I wasn't imagining the flash of interest in his expression.

He wet his lips, and then it was gone again, hidden behind his cheerfully casual demeanor. "If you lean back just a bit when you feel the wobble coming on, that might get you right again before it shows. If you're still having trouble, it always helps to practice standing by the boards, getting a solid feel for the position."

Would he ever let me get past the professional front and discover the passion I knew was simmering underneath? Or maybe he wouldn't think it was worth altering whatever odd relationship we had now.

Either way, I didn't think I'd be able to resist taking my shot with him if I got the chance.

Just not on the ice. And definitely not in front of Jasper. Who knew how the grouch would react if I started outright flirting with his coach?

Niko stepped away and set his hands on his hips. "Now let's see another Biellman spin in that signature Lou style. Don't look nervous! You've got this."

At his comments, a different sort of longing welled on—one that'd gripped me since I was five years old. One that Coach Balakin had never satisfied.

I let myself voice it before I could second-guess the impulse. "Do you *really* think I'm good enough to compete? Like, the real competitions, sectionals and all that?"

Niko's eyes widened. "Are you joking? You should have been out there already. I don't want any injuries this year, because it's a crime that the world hasn't already seen what you can do."

His voice was so emphatic that I felt both immensely relieved and ridiculous for having asked. "Okay. Good. I just—I wanted to be sure."

Something in Niko's expression softened. He squeezed my shoulder, sending another spike of warmth through my chest. "I wouldn't lie about something like that. It'd be cruel to send someone out with expectations they can't meet. But you've got it, Lou. I could see you not just competing but blowing everyone else out of the water."

Jasper's skates clicked against the ice where he was just stepping back onto the rink. He gave me a wary glance. "Whoever was coaching you before must have been an idiot if they never bothered to tell you you're good."

Bitterness tainted his voice, but I could tell he meant it. And if he meant it enough that he'd bothered to say it no matter how much my presence annoyed him…

I guessed I had to believe it too.

Niko glanced between the two of us, and a glint of mischief lit in his eyes. "You know what, I have a better idea than more spins. Lou, come over here."

He motioned me over to stand just a couple of feet from Jasper. The guy dwarfed me, standing a full foot taller and broader through his whole frame as well.

We both watched Niko, Jasper looking as puzzled as I felt.

"What are you doing?" he grumbled. "Sizing us up for a photoshoot?"

Niko squinted at both of us and rubbed his hands together with one of those eager smiles. "I'm thinking a little more ambitious than that. Let's mix things up a bit and do some basic exercises in synchronization. Jasper, take Lou's hand."

"What?" Jasper protested.

Niko raised his eyebrows. "Maybe you'll have an easier time getting out of your head if you have someone other than yourself to focus on."

Jasper stared at him for a few seconds. My gut knotted.

He really disliked me that much that he wouldn't even give it a try. Not that I was so keen on running through the basics hand-in-hand with the grouch beside me, but I'd still be willing to—

"Fine," Jasper bit out, and snatched my hand without any further warning.

His solid fingers engulfed my much slimmer ones. Something about the feel of them, despite how reluctant he was acting, sent a jolt of electricity up my arm.

Niko waved toward the other end of the rink. "All right, you two. Skate forward, but keep your arms up. Hands together. I want you to match the strokes of your skates. And… go!"

Niko sounded more like a coach than ever before. There was also a thrum of excitement in his smooth voice that was new.

As Jasper and I pushed off, I stole a glance over my shoulder. Niko looked like he was trying hard not to bounce off the walls with excitement. Something about that expression made my pulse stutter, like I was about to go over the big drop in a roller coaster.

"Hey, eyes forward." Jasper tapped the back of my hand with his thumb. "Whatever he wants us to do, I want to do it right."

Of course he did. If there was anything I knew about this man's career, it was that he was a perfectionist.

It sounded simple enough—just skate to the end of the rink. But Jasper's height meant we had to position ourselves carefully to keep our clasped hands raised without straining my shoulder, and keeping pace between my shorter legs and his longer ones required careful precision.

It took several strokes wildly off and then several more slightly out of sync, but I felt us catching on to each other's rhythm. By the time we reached the far boards, our feet were gliding forward in unison.

It was kind of thrilling, seeing it happen. Was this what Niko had been picturing?

"Spin in sync, a full 360 and then back to face me, and skate on over here a little faster," Niko called.

I glanced at Jasper, as intent on impressing Niko now as he was. We eased into the start of our spin, judging each other's speeds, and managed to curve around to face each other and then Niko at almost the same moment.

It would be easier with a plan and music to time our movements to, but we were doing pretty damn fantastic anyway.

We'd glided halfway back to Niko when he barked out another instruction. "Swivel and make the rest of the trip backwards!"

I whipped to the side automatically—unfortunately at a clashing angle to what Jasper's instinct had been. Our shoulders collided, and I skidded on the ice.

Jasper's arm shot out. He grasped my bare elbow to steady me, and I had to brace my other hand against his chest just for a second before I had my balance.

It was an incredibly nice chest, all packed with muscle. And when my gaze flicked upward as I drew my hand away, Jasper's gaze caught mine.

I could have caught fire from the heat that had flickered in those gray-green eyes. A giddy quiver rippled through my body.

The glint of hunger disappeared as quickly as it'd arrived. Jasper's face turned stormy again.

"Come on, let's get this done."

Well, it wasn't as if I didn't have plenty of other much more welcoming eye-candy to appreciate on this rink.

We pushed backward and made it to Niko with only a few slips out of sync. He was grinning even wider now, a feat I hadn't known was possible.

"I have a brilliant idea," he announced.

"More brilliant than this one?" Jasper asked in a dry tone.

"You could say it's more of the same idea." Niko cocked his head, his hair swishing across his forehead with a flash of the neon pink streak. "How would you two feel about trying pairs skating?"

"What?" I burst out at the same time as Jasper sputtered, "Are you kidding me?"

Niko wagged a finger at us. "Don't discount it out of hand. It would give you both a fresh perspective. By collaborating, Jasper will have different skills to focus on, and Lou won't have to face her first competitions alone. If you decide to keep at it that long. We'd just be seeing how it goes."

He turned to Jasper. "You should find it pretty easy to do lifts with Lou given your size difference. And the two of you got in sync so easily just now. It's meant to be."

My mind blanked with shock. Of all the things I might have expected him to suggest, this would never have occurred to me. I'd never skated with a partner in my life.

But we had gotten into the groove awfully quickly. It'd been *fun*, as jerky as Jasper could be.

I'd really get to stretch my skills, and embracing the challenge would mean skating literally alongside one of the greats. What did I have to lose?

Other than whatever speck of good will Jasper might have still felt toward me.

His hands had balled at his sides. He looked from Niko to me and back again.

I couldn't tell what he was thinking, but he was giving off the vibe of a volcano on the verge of eruption.

His jaw worked. Then his fingers uncurled from his palms with what looked like Herculean effort.

"Pairs?" he said. "Are you sure?"

Might as well jump in the deep end while I had the chance. "I'm in. If Niko thinks it's a good idea—it couldn't hurt to see how we handle it, right?"

Jasper aimed a brief glower at me before turning back to his coach. "I was never planning on working with a partner."

Niko laughed. "You never planned on having me coach you either, but look at how well that's working out. Give it a shot, St. Pierre. What's the worst that could happen?"

I guessed he had a point—enough of one that Jasper sighed.

"Okay. Sure. Why not?" He glanced at me again. "But the minute I sense that you're slacking off, Punk, I'm out."

I crossed my arms over my chest. "You won't have to worry about that."

And just like that, I'd somehow partnered with the grumpiest guy in Ontario.

SEVEN

Luciana

I TOOK a deep breath and leaned back on my hands. I'd say one thing for Ontario—it sure had beautiful lakes.

The scents of pine and cedar wafted from the trees standing along the hill I was sitting near the base of. A whiff of roasting meat carried from the barbeque pits farther along the shoreline. The water lapped gently at the rocks that gave way to a narrow stretch of sandy beach.

I wasn't the only one from Hobb Creek who'd come out to this spot just north of town on this fine afternoon. The warm early September day had brought some of the local kids right into the water, jumping and splashing.

Their parents watched from the towels they'd spread out on the sand. A little ways further, a group of teens had stretched out to sunbathe.

It all felt so perfectly, blissfully normal.

I'd always found that immersing myself in nature eased my nerves—and oh, did I have a lot of nerves skittering away right now.

Niko had ended today's training session early… because tomorrow, Jasper and I had our first pairs practice.

Tomorrow, we'd find out whether I could match him or end up looking like a total dunce despite Niko's faith in me.

It shouldn't have mattered. A week ago, I'd had no skating prospects at all. So what if I ended up back in the same place?

But I wanted to be the great skater Niko said I was.

And a larger part of me than I wanted to admit wanted to see admiration spark in Jasper's striking eyes too.

I grimaced at myself. Getting the hots for *both* of my new skating companions didn't seem like the best idea. Especially when the second one spent about ninety-nine percent of the time being a total grouch.

But telling that to the butterflies that'd taken permanent residence in my lungs hadn't worked out so far.

I inhaled another gulp of forest air and brushed the dry needles off my plaid leggings. A few of the older beachgoers had glanced my way with looks that weren't completely approving. Maybe they saw me as a "punk" too.

My fashion sense wasn't that out there, but it was definitely different from most of what I saw in Hobb Creek.

Oh well. They'd just have to get used to me as I was, because I was done squeezing myself into a box for anyone.

But I had picked a perch away from the main beach area where I wouldn't make the locals feel intruded on. That way I didn't have to worry about getting questioned either.

I glanced at my phone. Five-thirty. Rafael and I had made a habit of eating dinner together at seven every night, so I still had plenty of time to exhale my nerves.

God, it was perfect here.

Except maybe it wasn't exactly perfect. A voice reached my ears, faint and carrying from somewhere behind me.

I couldn't make out the words, but the tone was distinctly distressed.

I was way more familiar with that sound than I wanted to be.

With my senses on high alert, I got to my feet and ventured

through the trees up the hill. It only stood about twenty feet over the lake with an easy slope my toned legs had no trouble scaling.

As I reached the top, the voices became a little clearer. A cry rang out, still faint but with obvious pain.

My stomach knotted. I crept down the other side of the hill, peering between the tree trunks.

What the hell was going on?

When I got close enough to make out movement up ahead, I froze, keeping behind a broad oak tree for shelter. As I watched, I gradually picked out the figures in this drama.

A couple of guys who looked to be in their twenties were pacing in and out of view in a small clearing beyond the base of the hill. One of them was the cocky guy I'd seen badgering the toy store owner.

They were from that small-time gang Rafael had identified.

That would have been enough to raise my hackles on its own, but a third figure knelt on the ground between them. A teenaged boy, I saw—he couldn't have been more than sixteen from the peek I got at his smooth face, still a tad soft around the edges.

One of the goons lunged at him and smacked him across the head. The kid cowered and gasped in pain.

My body went rigid. This was so many levels of not okay that I wanted to scream.

"So what I'm hearing is that you don't have the money," one of the goons said. "Is that what I'm getting from you?"

The boy cringed. He let out another yelp when the prick behind him cuffed him in the head.

"I—I have some of it," he stammered. "The guys at school, they just wanted to try the stuff! T—they didn't have a lot of money, so —"

"So you let 'em have our product for free?" the first man asked. He tutted to himself. "I'm afraid that's not how we work around here. Tell him how we work around here, Barry."

Barry, the bigger goon by a good twenty or thirty pounds, pulled back his fist and slammed it into the kid's ribs. The highschooler slumped onto his side with a choked noise.

They'd tried to bring the kid on—to peddle drugs for them, probably, based on their conversation and the business endeavors

Rafael had mentioned. Stupid to turn to an inexperienced teen for that anyway.

It was their idiotic mistake, and they were making him pay for it.

My gut churned. I hated this, *hated* it.

It was far too easy to picture the faces of my mother's lackeys in these assholes' overconfident and cocky grins. It was like I'd run all the way across the continent for nothing. Nothing at all.

"I have some of the money." The high schooler coughed, choking out a string of phlegm that he hastily wiped away. "I can get the rest, I swear! J—just please give me a little time. Just a few more days!"

I peered from Barry to his fellow thug. They looked momentarily pensive, as though they were considering the kid's offer.

What should I be hoping for? The only thing I could ask from the universe was for two asteroids to come down and squash these two assholes, but of course, I couldn't count on killer space rocks.

I was here… but I really shouldn't draw attention to myself. If I burst into the clearing and gave the two goons a much-deserved ass-kicking, the very next thing I'd have to do was leave town.

The gang would still be here, just even more pissed off than before. And if Mom ever got wind of a petite young Latina woman who'd started handing wannabe gangsters their asses, she'd tear Hobb Creek apart looking for me even if I'd already left.

If I was going to do anything about these pricks, I had to plan it carefully. I had to make sure they were completely done and that they never realized who'd hit them.

"I don't know, Barry," the mouthy guy said. "Do you think we can trust this kid? I mean, he's already screwed us over once before…"

The high school kid's eyes zipped left and right as the thugs stalked around him. I braced my hand against the rough bark of the tree trunk, and conviction hardened in my chest.

I wasn't going to watch these goons kill this kid in front of me. Low profile or no, there were some places I drew the line.

If Rafael was shadowing me from afar like usual, he'd just have to bite his tongue and deal with my decision.

I had my trusty knife in my purse, but it wasn't going to do me any good at a distance. My gaze swept over the ground for something, anything, I could use.

There. I leapt forward a couple of steps and snatched a rock the size of my palm off the ground. Then another, and another, and another.

Tucking the extras under my arm, I eased closer through the trees. The goons were looming over the kid again.

One of them had gotten out a switchblade. Oh, hell no, there was no way I was letting this continue.

Before either of them could make any further threats or use that knife, I hurled the first rock from my hand.

It collided with Barry's flabby cheek, striking him directly below the eye.

"Hey!" The asshole spun away from the kid. "What the fuck was that?"

"What?" the skinny guy asked. "The hell are you going on about, dipweed?"

Barry squinted into the sunlight, staring toward my patch of forest. He was looking about forty degrees in the wrong direction, although even if he had looked my way, I doubted he'd have made me out in the shadows.

I bit down a laugh. If I thought he looked stupid before, the flabby douchebag looked even more like a buffoon now.

"I don't know," Barry sputtered. "Something *hit* me." He touched his cheek.

And it's Lou Cordova with the pitch. She lines up her shot… and there it is! Strike!

I nailed the skinny bastard with the second rock, right in the temple. His hands flew up to his face.

I whipped the last two rocks in quick succession, braining Barry in the side of the head and scraping the skinny guy's chin. With a yelp and an angry shout, they barged toward the trees.

I ducked behind the nearest trunk, but not before I spotted the kid sprinting to safety while they were distracted. Mission accomplished.

"Who the fuck is throwing shit at us?" Barry bellowed.

I didn't stick around to answer him. Hightailing it through the trees, I'd vanished over the top of the hill before I even heard their footsteps crunch into the layer of pine needles on the forest floor.

Emerging on the beach side, I slowed to a casual stroll and made my way to my car in the small parking lot. When I reached it, I glanced over my shoulder.

The two would-be gangsters were just marching out of the trees, scowling but with no real target to direct their anger at.

I hid a smirk as I slid into the driver's seat of my car. They'd never know who'd interrupted their beatdown.

But as I started the ignition, my good humor faded.

I'd interrupted them for now. Soon enough they'd be hassling that kid—and who knew how many other people in town—all over again.

But my next steps no longer felt like a question. Something was stirring within me, something righteous and full of fury.

I had to get these guys out of here. They were a threat to me and to everyone in this town, and I'd be damned if I was going to stand back and watch them take over the place while I was the only one around remotely prepared to do battle.

I'd made my decision: I was going to *fuck* with them. These guys were clearly brainless, leaderless idiots, nobodies who were just making a buck off the innocent locals.

It hadn't been hard to screw with the two goons here. There shouldn't be any need to resort to much violence. My mind would be enough to do this gang in.

I rolled my shoulders and thought of the tattoo stretched across my back.

Maybe Niko was right—maybe I was *exactly* what he had called me.

An angel. An avenging one.

EIGHT

Niko

MAGIC.

That's what I was watching. There was no other word for it.

My two trainees could create something miraculous on the ice, even if they weren't aware of it yet. My job was to make them see it themselves.

I followed them with my eyes, taking in every dip of their shoulders and every subtle movement of their limbs. They'd only gone through two practices with a focus on pairs, but their synchronization was already impressive.

I wasn't a total stranger to pairs skating. I'd done some as a teen before it'd become clear I was better off carving a path on my own, and after I'd made the suggestion, I'd gotten in touch with an old friend back in Japan who was more experienced in that area and had offered some tips. So I thought I'd been guiding them reasonably well as they spun and swayed across the rink.

But a lot of it they'd picked up without much help at all. Lou had risen to the challenge with the same fierceness I'd seen her approach every part of her skating, and the occasional snarky remarks she exchanged with Jasper only seemed to add more vigor to her powerfully graceful moves.

As for Jasper… He'd been tense to start, but he was pretty much always at least a little stiff during practice. I'd watched him loosen up more than ever before while he had to concentrate on Lou's timing as well as his own.

He wasn't worrying about how fast or how high he could go on his own, only about matching another skater with at least as much talent as him. He tried to act as if he was still skeptical, but I'd even caught a few brief smiles when they'd nailed a spin.

Which meant it was time to try something a little more complicated.

I leaned over the boards to call out to them. "I think that's enough work on the ice. We're going to move on to lifts next."

Lou skated over to me, looking unusually uncertain. "Lifts? Already?"

Jasper mirrored her expression; his silence was somehow louder than his usual sarcasm.

"You've got it." I waved them back towards the stands. "You can take your skates off over there. You won't need them for this."

The two of them shared a look.

"Come on," I stepped between them to lay my hands on each of their shoulders. "Don't doubt me. Look at how far you've come already. Here, follow me. Let's get our lift on!"

Jasper snorted. "Niko, no one says that."

"I say that. Now come on, let's —"

"Get our lift on," Lou finished for me. I could hear the smile hiding underneath her words. "Yeah, yeah."

They followed me back to one of the storerooms where I'd set up a little surprise for them earlier that day. Neither one spoke as they passed by the piles of equipment that I'd dragged out to make room for the —

"Foam pads?" Lou said once I'd pushed the door open.

A sea of thick blocks of foam layered the floor from wall to wall. We had to nudge some aside while walking inside, treading on others.

"Foam pads!" I said, grinning back at her. "So you don't bust your head open or break your neck if you fall. You're welcome."

She stared at me a moment before nudging me in the shoulder playfully. "Okay, okay. Thank you. This is… I feel *way* better about this now."

"Of course," Jasper said. "This is how serious figure skaters always practice lifts. Don't tell me you didn't know off-ice practice is a thing."

Oh, Jasper.

I knew he was touchy lately, but every now and again, he'd gone out of his way to prod her. Lou usually shot back in kind or annoyed him even further by giving him some silly, singsong retort, but this time, she just stared down at her sneakers.

"No, I didn't." She twirled a strand of dark hair around her pinkie. "I've never skated with anyone else before. When I trained, it was just me and my coach. That's all."

"There weren't any other skaters around trying things like this?" I asked.

Lou shook her head. "Nope, I've never seen lifts done except on TV and the live performances I've made it to." She shot a cheeky grin at Jasper that didn't totally reach her eyes. "So, if I suck at first, it's not totally my fault."

Jasper reached up to scratch behind the back of his head. I could see the discomfort scrawled across his face, but I wasn't about to step in and help him out here.

He was the one who'd stuck his foot in his mouth and provoked that slump in Lou's spirits when rarely anything seemed to faze her. Whatever was going on under his prickly exterior, I couldn't sort it out for him.

As much as I wished I could.

"I've never practiced them either," he admitted, staring pointedly at the foam pads I'd laid out on the floor. "So we can both suck together, Punk."

The first hour was full of a lot of awkward positioning and sudden tumbles. But though Lou's hesitation got the better of her at first, she gained confidence as quickly as she always seemed to. There was no denying her enthusiasm for giving the attempts her all.

Still, once she was up in the air, there were times when she would glance down at the ground and wobble in the palms of Jasper's hands. Something about the way she was holding her body didn't seem exactly right, but I couldn't tell what it was.

As Jasper lowered her back down after at least a few dozen trials, annoyance fluttered across her soft features.

She set her hands on her hips, frustration knitting her brow. Her hair had dampened along her forehead with sweat. "What am I doing wrong?"

I cocked my head. "There's definitely something a bit off, but it's hard for me to tell just watching. Here, let's try it you and me so I can feel exactly how you're shifting your weight in the air."

She moved to meet me without hesitation. Jasper stepped back, watching the two of us with hooded but curious eyes.

"Alright, whenever you're ready." I bent my knees, trying to picture us out there on the ice.

Lou didn't waste any time waiting around. She nodded once and squared her shoulders, stepping towards me. "Ready."

My left hand clasped her right one as I used my other palm to push upward on the junction between her hip and leg. With one shift of my shoulders, she was up in the air, her legs at a perfect ninety-degree angle.

Every brain cell in my head was trying to focus on the way Lou felt in my hands as a skater, but the awareness of her as a woman—a very attractive woman—filtered through despite my best efforts. Her limbs weren't just strong but also sleek, and a hint of a tart but warm scent that was all her filled my nose.

A small part of my mind started imagining how it'd feel to run my hands farther over her trim curves. A totally unacceptable thought from a coach.

I'd never been very good at suppressing my natural desires. But I could make sure they didn't affect the work we were doing together.

I raised her to the full height of the lift, noting the shifts in her body and tuning out the rest. Before I could dwell more on how wonderful she felt in my hold, I set her down on the foam pads again.

"What, too heavy for you?" Lou's eyes shined playfully.

"Oh, please." I tsked at her. "I could lift both you and our favorite raincloud here with one arm if I wanted to."

Jasper shot me a baleful look from the sidelines.

"I think I see where your trouble is," I went on. "You're tensing up your core. It needs to be steady but not rigid."

Lou laughed. "So tighten my abs, but also stay relaxed. Why didn't I think of that?"

From the humor in her tone, I could tell she wasn't actually dismissing my advice. I nudged her shoulder with my knuckles teasingly. "You know what I mean. It's all about balance—both in the air and within yourself."

"Hmm, are you sure you're not actually a yoga guru?"

Even as the joke spilled from her lips, her gaze turned more thoughtful. She looked down at herself, setting her palms against her stomach as if she were feeling out the differences in how she could flex the muscles there.

That dedication was what made this woman so compelling, wasn't it? She kept her spirits high through criticism, not letting any of it hit her hard but paying close attention all the same.

I wasn't sure I'd met another skater so determined to improve but also so able to roll with the punches.

Okay, that wasn't the only thing I admired about her. There was the energy she brought to every attempt, bold but not foolhardy beyond her capabilities. Her easygoing confidence that never drifted into arrogance.

She would have been justified in a little arrogance, really, but instead her lapses were in the other direction, into insecurity. Somehow she had no idea how skilled she already was.

She was an undiscovered star, a diamond hidden away here in Hobb Creek. I had made up my mind to change that.

After she and Jasper rose to their highest potential, everyone would know her name — and remember why they knew his. The whole world would be able to appreciate the stunning imagery that they were able to create.

She was the catalyst that would push Jasper out of his rut. I just knew it.

But when she momentarily swept her hair out of its ponytail to run her fingers through it, waking up the urge in me to touch those silky waves myself, I pulled myself backward, away from her. The attraction I felt could never be acted on, or I could ruin everything.

I motioned toward the doorway where the locker rooms awaited. "I think I've tormented you two enough for one day. You've come amazingly far already. Better to let today's lessons sink in so you can meet tomorrow's practice with a positive attitude."

Jasper narrowed his eyes at me. "You're quitting now?"

The edge in his voice sent an uneasy prickle over my skin. "I wouldn't call it quitting. There is such a thing as too much practice."

"I've never noticed that there was with you before," he muttered, and stalked out of the room before I could say anything else.

My stomach knotted. We'd managed not to talk about anything that'd happened before I'd shown up at his grandparents' house other than past skating performances. He grumbled a lot, but mildly enough that I didn't take it personally.

I thought I'd heard a little anger in his tone just now, though. Was he still angry at me underneath?

I'd tried to touch on that very sensitive subject a couple of times, but Jasper had deflected me before I'd gotten anywhere close. So I'd settled for making up for my screw-up last year as well as I could without bringing it up directly. It obviously hadn't been enough yet.

Lou gave me a little wave and vanished into the hall after Jasper. I stayed in the converted storage room for a few minutes, breathing deeply and clearing my head.

The training. I just had to focus on the training. Everything good I could do for either of my current charges would grow from there.

In my mind, I replayed the key moments from today's training. Lou's joke about me being a yoga guru came back to me with a spark of inspiration.

I had actually practiced yoga on and off at a studio back home. The main teacher had shown me a position that'd flipped a switch in my head when it came to maintaining balance. It might help Lou as well.

With a burst of hopeful enthusiasm, I hurried down the hall to the women's change room. If I caught her before she left, she could give it a shot tonight and it might have leveled up her abilities by tomorrow's session.

I knocked on the locker room door but didn't hear an answer. Had she already left?

Worried that I'd missed her, I pushed inside. "Lou?"

I'd only made it a few steps before I processed the hiss of running water. And the image that went with that sound.

Lou was in the shower area in the corner of the change room, behind the curtain that hung across one of the three stalls. It hid any details, but the silhouette of her lithely curved form showed vaguely against the translucent material.

My dick jumped to attention. The rest of me backpedaled as fast as humanly possible.

But she'd already heard my call. Before I made it to the door, Lou poked her face around the edge of the curtain, her dark hair plastered to her head. "Niko?"

Heat burned my cheeks as I averted my eyes. "I'm sorry. I didn't realize—I was in a hurry to tell you something—it can wait."

"No, no, it's fine. I was almost finished. Just give me a second."

I didn't know whether it would be more rude to stay on her request or insist on leaving anyway. I settled for turning so my back was to her.

But I heard every motion. The click of the water turning off. The rustle as she reached for the towel she'd left on a nearby bench. The soft whispers of it rubbing over her light brown skin.

Stop imagining what that looks like, I ordered my brain.

My brain did not cooperate.

"Are you going to tell me what's up or are you just going to leave me staring at your back?" Lou asked in an amused tone.

I dared to turn around, assuming she'd gotten dressed faster than

I'd expected. But she was standing by the bench with only her towel wrapped around her body.

Well, a little of her body. The thin terrycloth fabric covered the swell of her breasts while leaving plenty of smooth skin and a tempting dip of cleavage on display. It only hung to mid-thigh.

When she shifted her weight from one foot to the other, the ends of the towel slipped a little apart, opening a gap almost to her right hip. I jerked my gaze away, but not before noting the few droplets of water that still clung to her upper legs. My pants had gotten uncomfortably tight.

Could she tell? Oh, kuso!

Lou flipped her damp hair back over her bare shoulder and gave me a look that felt both curious and assessing. If my face had been hot before, now it was totally burning.

And it wasn't the only part of me on fire.

"Don't leave me hanging," she said. Did her voice usually sound that sultry?

Was I just imagining it because of how turned on I was right now?

"Well, I just—" I fumbled with my words and closed my eyes for a second to gather myself. "The training, the lift today. Balance. You mentioned yoga. I had a teacher who showed us a pose that was good for enhancing your sense of equilibrium."

Lou let out a low laugh that was undeniably sexy. "So you really are going yoga guru on us."

"Maybe a little bit."

She sauntered closer with a sway to her hips that brought my gaze sliding down her body before I caught it and yanked it upward again. A sly smile was playing with her lips.

Lou was always pretty, and I loved seeing her face set in its frequent determined expression. But this new seductive persona made her a whole different kind of gorgeous.

I couldn't say I liked it better, but certain parts of me were responding—a lot.

"What's the matter?" Lou said, close enough now to tap me right in the middle of my chest. That smile turned even slyer. "I'm not going to believe you've never seen this much of a woman before. I'm not sure

I've ever read an article about you that didn't make a point of mentioning how you swing both ways."

Somehow my cheeks seared even hotter. "I—well—that is true—I just wouldn't normally—"

She eased even closer, the warmth of her presence tingling over my skin, and trailed the finger she'd tapped me with down my sternum all the way to my belly. An ache formed in my stiffening cock.

Lou gazed up at me. "Is there a problem?" She didn't let her fingers slide any farther, which part of me was desperately grateful for and the other part deeply regretting. "I've gotten the impression that there's a spark between us. But if you're already dating someone or I've made a mistake, I won't be offended."

I swallowed hard.

"It's not that," I made myself say. The truth was I hadn't pursued anyone in months—and there were very few people, men or women, who'd ever affected me as much as she did.

"Then it's something else?"

It was, wasn't it? When had she become the flirty one and me the awkward dolt?

The answer came to me like a bolt out of the sky. "I'm your coach. It wouldn't be appropriate—"

Before I could continue, Lou snorted. "Is that what's bothering you? I don't see why it should matter."

I found my composure enough to put a little sternness in my expression, trying to ignore the feel of her fingers against my stomach. "Relationships between someone in an authority position and a student can easily become exploitive."

Lou arched her eyebrows at me. "I promise you I'm not the slightest bit concerned that you might 'exploit' me. Actually, I'd really like you to." Her smile stretched into a grin.

I could practically come in my boxers when she looked at me like that.

"I *am* still your coach," I had to say.

"Are you, though? I mean, it's a totally unofficial position. I'm not paying you. Neither of us has any power over the other. We're both consenting adults, no real authority either way."

I couldn't help acknowledging that she had a point. But was I only thinking that way because I wanted her more with every passing second?

At my continued hesitation, Lou's teasing demeanor faded. She moved her hand over to curl it around my own. My fingers squeezed hers of their own accord.

"Just to be clear," she said, her gaze searching mine, "this isn't just about scratching an itch or something. You know, you're the first person who's ever made me feel like me skating is something *good.* Like I could be bringing something great into the world by doing it. You have no idea how special that is to me. I can't stop myself from wondering if the spark between us means our connection could be incredible in other ways too."

The honesty in her voice sent a pang through me that was more than just desire.

She sounded like a woman who knew what she wanted—and who really did want *me*. Would I really be protecting her by denying her and myself?

Or maybe this was a chance to create a different kind of magic.

A few doubts still niggled at the back of my head, but they'd been quieted enough that the hunger in me overwhelmed them. I tugged her even closer, and my head bowed as if by a magnetic force.

Lou bobbed up to meet my lips halfway. The second her mouth melded with mine, whatever sparks had been forming between us flared into a total bonfire.

She tasted like cinnamon sugar with a hint of bitter coffee, sweet and invigorating in one petite package. With a swift movement of her soft lips, our mouths were parting and her tongue slipping over mine.

My free hand came to rest on her side and froze at the feel of the towel. I'd almost forgotten how little she was wearing.

But Lou leaned into my touch encouragingly, looping her own arm around the back of my neck. Her whole body pressed flush against mine.

I suppressed a groan and kissed her more deeply. My thumb stroked up and down her side.

My fingers tingled with anticipation, and I couldn't resist stroking them upward. My palm came to rest against the curve of her breast.

If I'd had any doubt about her enthusiasm for this encounter, the encouraging murmur that escaped her lips erased it in a flash. When I swiveled the heel of my hand over the pebbled peak beneath the fabric, I received a needy whimper.

Lou arched her back at the contact and kissed me as if she needed my touch like she needed air.

I *had* hooked up with plenty of partners in the past, but somehow this fiery woman had me as giddy as a teenager making his first confession.

Her hand trailed down my back. She tucked her fingers under the hem of my shirt and brushed her thumb across my bare skin.

I shifted my hips against her, desperate to feel those bare thighs against my own skin. More of the slope of her breasts spilled out from the towel beneath my fingers, the hem dipping almost to her nipples.

A little gasp of pleasure burst from her lips. That sound was heaven.

My dick throbbed as my thoughts ran wild. I envisioned the towel slipping lower, revealing all of the perfect mounds.

Lou's hand stroked higher, her mouth claiming mine in a wilder kiss—

And a buzzing sound emanated from the bench behind us.

Lou pulled away with a muttered curse. She glanced back at her phone, which buzzed again with another alert.

"Crap," she said. "I really have to get going. I hadn't planned for a detour."

Of course she couldn't have planned for me to barge into the change room while she was showering. My face heated all over again, but before I could do anything like apologize, Lou turned back to me and touched my cheek.

The eagerness in her eyes melted me. "I *do* want to plan for it to happen again. To be continued?"

Relief and joy shot through me in tandem despite the ache in my groin. "*Definitely* to be continued."

Lou flashed a smile that promised so much more to come. "Great. Can't wait for the sequel."

I stepped out of the change room to let her get dressed, adjusting my pants as I went and willing my erection to calm down. Once it was no longer obscene, I headed out through the streets to my apartment.

Halfway there, it occurred to me that I had never gotten around to telling Lou the details of that yoga pose. Well, I guessed it wasn't totally my fault that I'd gotten distracted.

I found a video of the pose online and texted her with it. Just as I was about to slide my phone back into my pocket, it chimed with an incoming email.

I glanced at the subject line and paused.

"Ninth Annual Dellville Figure Skating Competition," I read in a murmur. "What do we have here?"

NINE

Luciana

HOBB CREEK LOOKED like a totally different town in the dead of night. I could hardly believe that it was the same little hamlet that had captured my heart.

The continuing trickle of passersby from the early evening had headed home or onward in their tourist journey. Only a couple of lights still shone in windows.

Not a single soul roamed the streets. The only movement that caught my eye was a stray cat jumping from rooftop to rooftop and a brief streak of a shooting star.

I stopped for a second to take that sight in. When was the last time I'd been in a position to simply stop and stargaze?

Beside me, Rafael let out a soft grunt, reminding me that I wasn't exactly in that position *now*. We had a mission to carry out, one that'd been my idea.

"Everything looks kind of eerie at night, doesn't it?" I murmured, hefting the two large water jugs I had tucked under my arms, which were burning with a familiar ache from today's training session. The straps of a backpack that held a few more jugs dug into my shoulders. "Even in a peaceful town like this. Maybe more here."

Rafael let out the mildest of sighs as we tramped on down the street, dodging the dim pools of lamplight, toward the edge of town. "Well, it is three in the morning."

"Always the voice of reason," I teased, grinning over at him. My legs were sore too, but the thought of the mischief I'd planned kept me light on my feet. "Had to make sure our targets would be asleep."

My bodyguard adjusted the jugs cradled against his bulging arms and shot me a skeptical look. "Are you really sure this is necessary? You're sticking your nose into places it doesn't need to be."

I grimaced at him. "It's my town now. It's totally my business. It helps me and everyone else here—except the jerks who deserve a little hurt."

"If they realize you vandalized their property…"

"They're not going to find out. I know what I'm doing. And it probably isn't *their* property anyway. I bet they stole most of the vehicles they're driving."

"That doesn't make them worth bothering with."

I stopped and spun toward him. "If you don't like the plan, you can go home, and I'll do it all myself."

Rafael's mouth set in a tight line. "Let's go," he said gruffly, like I'd figured he would.

He might argue sometimes, but he never backed down from what he considered his duty. Although I didn't totally understand why he'd decided it was still his duty to protect me when no one was paying him to do that job anymore.

Not that I was complaining.

Sometimes he made good points. But tonight we were doing things my way.

Those goons were going to get a taste of their own medicine, and I was the wicked doctor doling out doses.

As we came up on the last few houses before the final road that separated the town proper from the nearby sprawl of storage buildings and warehouses, Rafael gave it one more try. "I thought you wanted to get away from the criminal side of your old life."

"I will when I have the option," I said. "I can't just ignore these goons. But that doesn't mean I have to use the kind of tactics Mom would either. This is all Lou, all the way."

Mom would have sent her men in with guns blazing and mowed the two-bit gang down. I was simply going to show them that sticking around this town was more hassle than it was worth.

No bloodshed, no scarring the good people of Hobb Creek. Just a little old-fashioned vehicular sabotage.

Even if I wanted to protect my new neighbors, that didn't mean I had to deal out the kind of carnage the Deadly Rose was known for. I wasn't her heir anymore.

I peered across the road and the wide parking lot. A few security lamps cast a yellow light around the front and sides of the big white building the gang operated out of. In the shadows that blanketed the rest of the lot, I made out the shapes of several cars, a couple of pickup trucks, a van, and a jeep.

As I scanned the scene, the front door to the storage building swung open. A couple of men sauntered out, swaying a little, and got into the nearest car. The thumps of the car doors shutting rang through the night.

After they drove off, the whole area was totally silent.

"No guards," I whispered to Rafael. "Could they be more amateur?"

When he looked at me, I thought I saw a hint of a smile curling his lips despite his previous protests. "They've never had to deal with anyone like you around here before."

I smirked back at him. "And it's about time they did. Masks on."

I figured we could sneak onto and off the lot without getting caught, but it was always wise to cover one's ass just in case. Rafael and I set down our jugs and dug our ski masks—black to coordinate with our long-sleeved tees and sweats—out of our pockets.

The cloth felt uncomfortably warm against my forehead and

cheeks, but it was a small price to pay to ensure no one who caught sight of us could ID us.

Jugs held tight, we glanced up and down the road and then loped across. I motioned for Rafael to start on the cars to the left of the lot while I swerved right.

At the closest car, I knelt by the fuel door and took out the flathead screwdriver I'd brought for this job. I fit the head into the gap between the door and the rest of the car.

All it took was a little pushing and wiggling, and the fuel door popped open. "Bingo," I said under my breath, and quickly unscrewed the fuel cap underneath.

Then I lifted one of the water jugs, held the narrow mouth to the opening, and poured the entire two gallons into the tank.

The sickly smell of the gasoline the water was sloshing around with prickled into my nostrils. Wrinkling my nose, I closed everything up and hurried on to the next vehicle.

The van's fuel door snapped open even more easily than the previous car. Another two gallons of water gurgled into its tank, then I was moving on to a junky-looking sports car, and finally one of the pickup trucks.

Every last one of their vehicles was going to be fucked. If they figured out what the problem was early on, they might be able to avoid most of the damage, but I was betting the bozos weren't quite smart enough for that.

I was just emptying the last dribbles of water into the truck's gas tank when the hinges squeaked on the storage building door—now less than twenty feet away from where I was crouched.

With a hitch of my pulse, I ducked down even farther. A voice called out as if to someone still in the building.

"Yeah, I'll be back in the morning. Can't leave her hanging too long, if you know what I mean."

The leering bravado in the asshole's voice set my teeth on edge. But what if he headed this way?

As quickly as I could, I twisted the fuel cap back on and eased the fuel door shut over it. Footsteps rasped across the asphalt.

They were heading in my direction. Shit.

I curled my fingers around the handles of the now light-as-air jugs and backed away from the truck toward the sports car, staying low to the ground. The last few steps, I dashed.

Dropping down behind the trunk of the sports car, I sucked in a breath and peeked the way I'd come. The man who'd come out of the storage building looked like he was heading around the hood of the truck rather than stopping to take it.

Fucking hell. I glanced around, judging the distance to the van and then to the road beyond.

The prick started whistling, and I took that as my cue to keep moving.

Setting my sneakers quietly on the pavement, I fled for the shelter of the van. I'd just flung myself around its rear end when the whistling stopped.

"Hey, is someone out here?"

I clamped my lips tight—and nearly choked when a large form emerged from the shadows next to me.

It was only Rafael, frowning with concern. He beckoned to me, and we both took off for the streets of the town now within reach.

We stayed low and kept the van between us and the goon. I didn't look back until we'd hurtled several steps down one of the town's streets past a couple of quaint houses.

I probably should have hustled on back all the way home. But I couldn't resist peeking back to watch the first results of our handiwork.

It didn't look like the wannabe gangster had worried too much about whatever he'd thought he'd seen or heard. He was whistling again, the sound cut off a second later by the thud of a car door closing.

As he revved the ignition, I braced myself. The engine rumbled.

Then came a sputter. A hacking like the engine was coughing its lungs up.

The guy shut it off and twisted the key again, and you'd have thought that poor car had come down with tuberculosis.

Delight dancing in my chest, I turned to Rafael and nodded that we should go. A grin plastered itself to my face the whole way back to the bungalow.

I'd wreaked my little bit of havoc. Let's see how tough these douchebags would actually be when push came to shove.

TEN

Luciana

"IF YOU COULD AVOID KNEEING me in the nose, that would be appreciated."

I glanced at Jasper as he lowered me, trying to judge the ratio of grumbling to dry humor in his voice. I was pretty sure this time he was leaning more toward the latter.

"As long as you don't gouge my thigh with that deadly thumb of yours," I retorted cheekily.

His mouth gave a twitch that I was pretty sure by now indicated a suppressed smile, because my new partner never seemed to worry much about showing his frowns and grimaces.

Of course, it was hard to tell with him, even with a few practices as a pair under our belts. I couldn't say he'd ever been actually *friendly* with me.

Did he really have a problem with skating with me, or did he simply feel like he had to maintain his reputation as a grump?

Niko clapped his hands together. "You're getting closer every time! Let's see that once more."

I shook the tension out of my limbs and glided around the rink to get back into the starting position for the simple star lift we'd been working on. Jasper synchronized his movements with mine without complaint.

From the corner of my eye, I tracked the rhythm of his blade strokes and the power that emanated from his brawny body. There was no denying that he could make a spectacle on the ice—one it was impossible not to appreciate.

We reversed course and glided backward, me veering in front of him. As I turned toward him, Jasper grasped my hip and one of my hands to sweep me into the air as if I weighed nothing at all.

I caught the start of a wobble with my hand against his broad shoulder. Extending one leg toward the ceiling, I stretched the other straight behind me.

Jasper whirled around and around, and my ponytail streamed out from my head. The exhilaration took my breath away.

Then he eased me down and set me on the ice at just the right pace for me to pull away from him.

No matter how much he grumbled, nothing mattered more to him than creating a beautiful image on the ice. If I hadn't been able to tell that from watching his performances on TV, working with him would have proven it.

I could respect the desire even if I wouldn't mind him getting an attitude readjustment. He had to realize how committed I was and warm up to me eventually, right?

As we skated toward Niko again, our self-appointed coach stretched his arms with a languid grace that reminded me of a cat in the sun. "I think that's enough for one day. Great job, you two. You're really killing it out there."

Jasper snorted and stomped toward the benches to grab his bag. "I guess we look a *little* less like idiots now."

I tried to restrain my wince at the sting of his words. Ouch.

I knew I was learning a hell of a lot from working with him, but maybe I was holding him back. Diverting him from the training that would put him back in the spotlight as a star.

That's what Coach Balakin would have told me, wasn't it?

I moved to retrieve my own duffel bag with my chin high, doing my best not to let my dampened spirits show in my posture. Apparently I didn't do a good enough job at hiding it.

"Hey." Niko planted himself next to me as I hefted my bag over my shoulders. He caught my gaze with a typical twinkle in his bright brown eyes. "Don't mind him. He just doesn't like being outside his comfort zone. The two of you really are making fantastic progress."

I couldn't exactly accuse him of lying. "It feels good," I admitted. "Working with someone, building a routine together instead of being limited to what I can do on my own."

Niko grinned. "Then my plan is succeeding. I can tell Jasper appreciates it too, even if he has a funny way of showing it."

"'Funny' is not the word I'd use," I muttered.

Niko muffled a snicker with his hand. "That's fair."

His gaze slid over me, stirring a sudden heat beneath my skin with the memory of our interlude in the change room a few days ago. "We're finishing a little earlier than usual. Do you feel up to adding a little endurance work to today's practice."

Curiosity sparked in my chest. "Sure. What did you have in mind?"

He motioned to my bag. "Get changed and toss that in your car, and we'll go for a hike."

That actually sounded like exactly what I needed right now to clear the cobwebs of doubt from my brain. I shot him a smile that I hoped didn't look too fawning. "Perfect. I'll meet you out front in ten."

When I found Niko in the parking lot, he didn't actually look like he'd changed much other than pulling off the fleece pullover he'd been wearing against the arena's chill. The black fitted tee showed off his lean muscles to delicious effect.

I was definitely not drooling. Okay, maybe a little.

I tossed my bag in the trunk of the car and glanced down at my cargo pants and sleeveless top with its glittery skull print. Maybe not typical hiking gear, but it'd do.

As I turned toward Niko, I made a subtle gesture with one hand beyond his view. *Stand down*, it said.

Rafael would be watching, as he always was. But I didn't want him following us on this expedition *too* closely, not when I had high hopes about all the sorts of endurance we might explore.

He'd trail behind where he could hear a gunshot or a yell for help, but he'd give me my space. Or at least, if he didn't, he'd have only himself to blame.

Niko motioned for me to follow him. "There's a good trail that starts just a few blocks from the arena."

I raised my eyebrows at him as we set off together. "I wouldn't have taken you for a hiker."

He beamed at me. "There's something about being surrounded by natural beauty… It soothes the soul. I think that's the right way to say it. You Americans don't have the same respect, but you can always start cultivating it now."

"Hey, I have plenty of respect for trees and lakes," I informed him.

He chuckled. "That's why I'll show you my favorite spot around here."

We set off through the streets and then veered into a patch of forest at the edge of town, not far from the road to the beach. When the ground slanted upward, I started to feel the burn in my legs with the exertion, but Niko chattered on about the various routes he'd discovered around town without any sign of flagging.

"First thing I do when I'm settling into a new place," he said. "Find all the best hiking paths and views. That's what helps me feel at home."

"It is beautiful out here," I said, dragging in a breath full of the fresh scent of fir needles.

"Wait until you see where you're going. That's the best part."

The path turned rockier and steeper, and I scrambled up a few stretches accepting Niko's hand for balance. The last time, he kept his fingers curled around mine and tugged me forward with him.

I wiped my brow, glanced up, and stalled in mid-step.

We'd come out to the crest of a hill overlooking a placid lake. I couldn't tell if it was the same one with the town's beach—no sand or people were visible from our vantage point.

The sunlight sparkled across the water as if it were a multi-faceted jewel. The leaves on the trees around the bank rippled with a light breeze, flashing hints of yellow and orange amid the green where the autumn colors were just starting to creep in.

"Wow," I said. "It looks like something out of a fairy tale."

"I told you." Niko shot me one of his grins and sat down cross legged on the wide slab of stone along the edge of the peak.

I sank down next to him, keeping a few inches of distance between us, not sure how bold I should be. The mood didn't feel right for suddenly jumping his bones.

"Are there places like this back in Japan?" I asked him.

"Oh, much prettier than this. But Canada can offer an acceptable temporary substitute." He winked at me. "As long as I find one peaceful spot, I'm good."

Somehow after all the articles and TV spots I'd perused about Niko Okabe, I'd never known he was a nature-lover. I guessed that didn't fit the rebel narrative the reporters liked to play up.

The words tumbled out before I could think better of them. "It must be nice to get away from the whole media circus. All those people constantly judging you."

Niko's eyes widened, and my gut plummeted. If I'd accidentally put my foot in my mouth—

Then he shook his head with a light laugh, clearly undisturbed. "People can have their opinions. It doesn't affect who I am. I always tell myself that if anyone shows a prejudice, it says more about them than me."

Relief washed over me that I hadn't offended him. "Good. That sounds like a really healthy way to look at it. I should probably work on that kind of mindset too."

Niko's voice took on a lightly teasing tone. "And what sort of pressures have you been dealing with, Angel?"

We were not getting into any details there.

"Nothing like what you've faced," I said. "I can't imagine having reporters shoving microphones in your face and asking such personal questions—like it's their business who you're dating or anything like that."

Niko shrugged, his gaze returning to the lake. His handsome face looked nothing but serene.

"It hasn't always been easy. There are some issues where my home country isn't as… progressive as yours. But that's exactly why it's important to me to always be upfront about it. I've made a reputation where being different from what's considered normal is part of my character. It's my—what's the word for it…?—trademark. So it's expected rather than shocking now. For the most part."

"It mustn't have been fun getting to that point."

"We all have our struggles." He nudged me with his elbow. "Focusing on other people's opinions doesn't do anything but hold you back."

I wished I believed that as fully as he clearly did. How did this man manage to keep such an upbeat attitude regardless of the pressures heaped on him about everything from his sexual orientation to his fashion choices?

The media portrayed him as a playboy and a daredevil, but I saw nothing but an incredibly resilient man who was playing the best game he could with the hand he'd been dealt. The best game he could while still being *himself* rather than conforming to anyone else's expectations.

Wasn't that why I'd come all this way too? I wished I could soak up his confidence until it became my own.

Maybe I couldn't absorb all of his self-assurance, but I could certainly get closer to him than I was right now.

I peered at him sideways, evaluating my next move. My pulse thumped faster, but I'd never been the type to take the coy route.

How much longer would I even get to revel in his company? The future felt so uncertain.

The one thing I knew for sure was that I wanted to enjoy his presence in every possible way while I could.

The swell of emotion in my chest was something I'd never really felt before. My hookups back home had been totally casual, burning off pent-up energy, never putting my heart on the line.

But Niko was different. Niko wasn't looking for anything from me or trying to prove a point. He *saw* me like no one else ever had—not even Rafael, as loyal as my bodyguard was.

How could I not want even more?

I scooted closer to him and slipped my hand back around his. "In the interests of not holding back… what do you think about picking up that 'to be continued' now?"

Niko met my gaze, both mischief and hunger flaring in his. "I think that's the best idea I've heard all day."

I pushed onto my knees and around to meet him as he dipped his head. Our lips collided with a giddy rush that swept through me from head to toe—and had my panties dampening in an instant.

His tongue twined around mine, his lips soft but steady. I groaned, wanting him more with each passing second.

My fingers found their way into his hair, tracing those black and pink strands as if I could permanently commit the feeling to memory. Niko let out a faint groan and wrapped his arm around me to pull me even tighter against his toned frame.

I couldn't resist sliding my hands down his body to the hem of his shirt. The dip of his abs was screaming to be touched, and there was nothing I could do but oblige it.

I knew I was right when he arched beneath me, a perfect cue to keep going. My fingertips trailed upward over his chest.

At the thudding of his pulse against my palm, a spike of excitement surged through me. I raked my nails softly against his shoulders and the slender curve of his neck.

He didn't protest when I tugged the tee right off him. I tossed it into a crumpled ball on the forest floor and took in his exquisitely sculpted torso with a sharper pang between my legs.

I only had a few seconds to appreciate the new view before Niko drew me into another kiss. He slipped his hand beneath my shirt and locked the peak of my breast between two of his lithe fingers.

I gasped at the jolt of pleasure, and he smiled against my mouth. Then his tongue swept between my lips again, stoking the flames already blazing inside me even higher.

Niko cupped my breasts, thumbing over my peaks. He teased me gently, bringing me to the brink of pleasure with only his deft hands.

It wasn't enough. I wanted more.

Taking the initiative, I tossed my shirt and sports bra after Niko's tee.

Niko murmured something in Japanese that sounded awed before switching back to English. "You're stunning." He dropped a kiss to my shoulder and then the crook of my neck before his fingers traced the top of my feathery tattoo. "An angel in every way."

I snorted. "Maybe not *every* way."

A grin that was downright devilish crossed Niko's face. "I happen to think angels should be allowed to have a good time too."

He nibbled the sensitive spot just below my earlobe, and a breath stuttered out of me.

"Hallelujah," I mumbled, and he chuckled with a wash of warm breath down my skin.

He massaged my breasts with little tweaks of my nipples until I was whimpering, then eased one hand down to trace along the waistline of my cargo pants. If my panties had been damp before, his touch so close to the place where I was aching most had me soaking them.

But he didn't delve farther, only stroked my belly and my breast while his lips worked their sweet magic on my neck. I squirmed, shifting my hips in a plea for his touch, and he simply nipped my jaw.

I gasped and decided that enough was enough. *I* wasn't going to be shy about what I wanted.

I slid my hand down his chest and pressed it against the bulge at the crotch of his sweatpants. The already rigid erection there twitched against my touch, and Niko groaned.

"A very impatient angel," Niko murmured. "I can take care of you."

In an instant, his deft fingers had the fly of my cargos open. He curled his hand right over my panties, his breath stuttering as he encountered the proof of my incredible arousal.

A burst of bliss radiated from my core at the contact. Niko's fingertips worked my pussy in gentle, slow circles through the thin layer of fabric. My head swayed back, my eyes closing.

I wanted to block out everything except Niko, close myself off to any sensation that wasn't purely him. I was barely aware of the soft coos of need that were making their way between my lips, joining the birdsong in the forest's quiet chorus.

The way he was able to read my body was unreal. He flicked his thumb over my clit and set a pulsing pace with his fingers until I thought I'd explode just like that.

But he kept my climax just out of reach. Every time my pleasure raced higher, he'd slow down his ministrations, until I was moaning in desperation.

Just when I thought Niko would tease me forever, he tipped me back on the rough stone. With a careful yank, he peeled my cargo pants off me.

The next thing I knew, he was pulling my panties to the side and opening his lips against my pussy.

At the first lap of his tongue, I cried out. My fingers clutched at his smooth hair, the only thing I could hold on to through the rush of startled ecstasy.

Sighing, I spread my hips slightly to allow him further access. At his groan of approval, the vibration of his voice sent a shiver up my spine.

His tongue was like magic against my clit. I shuddered at every deft touch, every slick swipe between my legs.

He shifted lower still, traveling further down towards my slit. When his tongue delved right inside of me, my vision hazed.

I had to have him right fucking now.

I got enough of a handle on myself to tilt his chin up with one finger. His eyes flicked to mine, amusement dancing in his bright brown irises.

His lips gleamed with my arousal. My pussy throbbed at the sight.

"Condom?" I rasped.

His smile turned wicked. He fished a foil packet from his pocket.

The next few moments were a blur. My hands were on Niko, peeling away the few remaining layers of clothing that he had left. He was gloriously hard, his dick searing against my palm.

I took a second to appreciate the straining length of him before my hands went to work, stroking and pumping him, toying with him in the same way as he'd done to me minutes before. I only released him so that he could handle the condom situation, and even that took too long for me.

He rolled it over his shaft, his eyes meeting mine. The glow of desire I caught in those two dark orbs left me breathless.

With no patience left at all, I pushed him down on the ground and straddled him. As I rocked against his rigid cock, he gripped my ass cheeks and squeezed.

"Fuck," I muttered, and lined myself up.

The tip of his cock pressed against my entrance. I sank down, biting my lip at the sensation of him filling me. When he pushed upward, my world transformed into blissful static.

I blipped back to reality in time to savor his first few thrusts. Even as he bucked his hips upward, he still managed to keep one hand massaging my breast to send extra quivers of delight through my body.

I set my hands on his shoulders and found my own rhythm soon enough. Locking eyes with Niko, I matched the motion of his hips.

His mouth dropped open as he expelled a soft groan. I ground my body against his, desperate to be closer to him even now.

I raked my nails lightly down his chest, urging him on, and he sped up his pace. The smacking of our bodies together tossed me upward—I felt like I was soaring above the tree line, my head high up in the clouds.

The only thing I could hear was our soft cries echoing through the forest and the sounds of our merging flesh.

"You're so hot," he managed to say. "So wet. So *perfect.*"

"Jesus, Niko." I arched my back as he thrust deeper. "Keep going, just like that."

My nails dug in further, my heart fluttering as he whispered an endless slew of praises. His name floated from my lips in a breathy sigh.

Niko pumped harder, his strong arms wrapping around my waist. I could tell that his climax was nearing, threatening to spill over at any moment.

I wasn't far behind him, if I was behind him at all. My mind reeled with every stroke of his shaft inside me.

His breaths transformed into heavy panting that twined with my heightened cries like a symphony. If I opened my eyes and looked at him, I would come immediately and I knew it.

"Lou…" His hand rose to my cheek, calling my gaze to him. It was almost as if he could read my mind, knowing exactly what I needed.

I couldn't hold back any longer. I gazed down at him, taking in the flush of his cheeks and the fervor shining in his eyes.

My thoughts went completely blank. The only thing I could focus on was the pulsing waves of pleasure that swept through me with each passing second.

My breathing became harsher, my pitch higher.

Heaven. Euphoria.

Pure fucking bliss.

"Niko, I'm—"

My moan of completion cut off my words. I shuddered against him with the power of my orgasm.

He cut me off with his own cry. I felt his grip tighten, and his cock twitched madly inside of me.

He gasped out my name, stiffening against me as he surrendered to the same rapture that I was spiraling through. We rocked to a halt against each other.

My head dropped down. Our lips touched again in a kiss that was strangely innocent, as light as a butterfly's landing.

For a moment, the only thing that either of us could do was catch our breath in each other's arms.

Niko gathered me against his chest and kissed my forehead. "That was incredible. You can be my hiking partner any day."

A giggle tumbled out of me. I snuggled against him, soaking up his warmth as the breeze brushed over my skin. "Worthy of a few encores?"

His tone turned sly. "I'd definitely enjoy collaborating with you like that again."

We couldn't cuddle there forever, though, as much as I longed to extend the moment. Evening was falling, and Rafael would be getting restless.

The last thing I needed was him barging in and making a mess of this. There'd be no encores then.

I peeled myself off Niko, and we reassembled our clothes. The walk back toward town passed in companionable silence, hand-in-hand.

Niko veered in a slightly different route than the one we'd taken to get on the path. I only realized when I saw the gang's storage building coming into view up ahead.

My stomach clenched.

An SUV had parked on the shoulder a couple of blocks closer to us. A frazzled looking woman got out, retrieved a toddler from the backseat, and lay her down beneath the open hatch.

Emergency diaper change, I guessed.

Rafael and I clearly hadn't outright destroyed the gang's entire fleet of vehicles, because at the same moment, a red truck peeled out of the lot, its tires screeching against the asphalt. As it sped toward the SUV, a guy leaned out the passenger side window.

"Stupid whore!" he shouted at the woman. "Get the hell outta here before we *make* you."

The young woman, clearly shaken, snatched up her son as the truck roared by. She clutched him against her and then hustled to return him to his seat as if terrified.

My chest had totally constricted, all the joy I'd been holding on to vanished. When I glanced at Niko, a cloud of worry had settled over his face.

My first effort hadn't been enough. The goons were still racing around being menaces, and they were threatening Niko's sense of peace as well as everything else.

I couldn't let them ruin even more.

ELEVEN

Rafael

POUR a dollop of olive oil in the pan.

Toss in the pepper, onion, and garlic.

Follow with the tomato puree and wine.

And let it simmer.

I inhaled, breathing in one of my favorite childhood scents, my mouth watering at my own handiwork.

This was it, the dish that was going to blow Lou out of the water. If I couldn't fix her broken taste buds with enchilada de camarones, then I didn't know what would do it.

"That actually smells really awesome, Rafael," she called from the living room.

"What do you mean, 'actually'?" I asked, stirring the marinated shrimps in. "Por supuesto! As a Latina woman, you should be drowning in drool already just from the aroma alone."

"Drowning in drool?" She flashed me a teasing smirk from over the back of the sofa where she was sitting flipping through TV channels. "Well, you'll have to excuse me if I don't need the water wings yet. It does smell awesome, but what matters is how it tastes."

"It tastes amazing. If you weren't so busy shoving pierogies and cabbage rolls in your mouth, you'd have discovered that by now."

She leaned her arm over the sofa back to better face me with a flash of her silver rings, the cheeky grin that I'd come to adore years ago lighting up her dark brown eyes as well. "Hey, now. You're *really* missing out by passing on the golumpki. My nanny could make some that would knock your socks off."

I shook my head, breathing out a heavy, mock sigh.

It was hard to get all that invested in the argument when we'd been having variations on it ever since I'd found out she preferred Polish food over anything close to the cuisine of her heritage. So what if she was three generations removed from the ancestors who'd arrived from Mexico? She had no idea what she was missing out on.

But on the other hand, I couldn't really blame her if she associated comfort more with the Polish nanny who'd raised her through most of her early childhood rather than that mother of hers. The Deadly Rose was about as maternal as a machine gun.

I'd resigned myself to her odd food preferences, and these days our well-rehearsed banter wasn't much more than an inside joke. But that didn't mean I was going to stop demonstrating the fantastic flavors she'd been missing out on. The Cuban recipes I'd grown up with might not be the exact same as what her great grandparents might have made, but they were a hell of a lot closer than her usual comfort food.

I glanced at the shrimps. Perfect.

"Well, hold on to your socks." I grabbed the ladle. "Because I'm about to rock your world."

Lou stuck both bare feet up in the air and wiggled her toes at me. The nails were painted in an alternating pattern of neon green and black. "Already one step ahead of you."

She broke into peals of laughter, her smile lighting up the room so brightly that it could have been sunrise instead of eight o'clock at night. Something tightened in the pits of my stomach even as my heart jumped up into my throat at the sight.

How had the scrawny, scrappy ten-year-old I'd been assigned to nine years ago grown into a woman this beautiful? How in all the levels of Hell was that acceptable?

I *had* known her since she was ten. The year she'd officially become an adult, I'd had my thirtieth fucking birthday.

I should not have been entertaining thoughts that would have gotten me consigned to Hell just for having them pass through my head.

Swallowing hard, I jerked my gaze toward the TV instead. A man in a suit stood in front of a bunch of colorful boxes while a nervous contestant sweated it out beside him.

I'd never liked game shows, but pretending to be interested in it was better than letting the slightest hint show of the heat that'd flared under my skin. I'd stare straight at the sun if it somehow drowned out the attraction that sparked when I least wanted it to.

Which was basically always.

Of course, it got even harder to ignore Lou when she peeled herself off the sofa and sauntered over to where I was doling out our dinner. She'd developed a slight sway to her hips that I wasn't sure was even purposeful.

And when she leaned her elbows onto the counter, the neckline of her tee dipping to reveal a deeper shadow of cleavage between her breasts…

"Here, eat up." I shoved the plate toward her a little harder than I'd meant to. "I don't see how you're eating enough after spending so much time skating. You're going to end up working your muscles to death if you keep this up."

"What are you, my nutritionist?" she asked, already popping a forkful into her mouth.

Her eyelids dropped in a swoon that both gratified the cook in me —and made my traitor cock twitch. "Mmm, this really is good. I'm not usually that into the peppers. Obviously Mom should have hired you as chef instead of that fancy pants we had at home."

I raised my eyebrows at her as we moved to the table. "But then who would have made sure your rebellious ass didn't get hung out to dry?"

It was the wrong comment, because it encouraged Lou to shake that undeniably pert ass before she settled it into her seat. Cue another cock twitch.

"I'm sure I'd have survived somehow," she said breezily.

I sank down across from her, grateful that the lower half of my body was now out of view. "Well, I'm glad you like it. It's one of my favorites. My abuela's old recipe that she brought with her from Cuba."

Lou shoved another forkful into her mouth. "I wonder if my great-grandparents didn't care about recipes or if Mom chucked all those out before I came into the picture."

She chewed thoughtfully for a moment and then waved her fork at me. "I was thinking. I saw a truckful of those douchebags outside their hideout yesterday. They're still going around being massive assholes. Obviously I didn't hit them hard enough for them to decide to get out of town."

"I'm not surprised," I said, watching her warily. "Idiots have a tendency to also be stubborn."

"Too bad for them that I am too. There are plenty of other ways we can pick away at them until they realize they're better off finding a new stomping ground."

I suppressed a groan. "I assume you're going to tell me about these other ways."

"Of course!" She shot me a mischievous grin that tugged at both my heart and my groin. "I thought about mocking them with graffiti, but I don't think that'd have enough impact. I've got to make things difficult for them, not just annoy them."

"Naturally," I said dryly, putting on an impassive expression to hide the worry spinning up through my stomach.

"I could smash some windows—on their cars or the building itself—but after just one, the noise would probably be enough to bring them running outside. A single window wouldn't really be big enough."

"You settled on something difficult and big, then. I'm thrilled."

Lou laughed at my deadpan remark. "Oh, don't worry, it's nothing *risky*. I came up with the perfect strategy: tire spikes. All you need is some scrap metal to play with. Set them down at night near the cars, the pricks drive over them the next day, and poof! No one's roaring through town terrorizing people."

She dug into her meal, radiating confidence in her plan. And I couldn't even fault her that assurance, as nerve-wracking as I found it.

How had the gang princess adapted to small-town life so quickly —while also championing the town in her own way? Lou had always been a bold spirit, but now that she'd had a taste of freedom, she was like a wild bird finally released from its cage.

I just had to make sure she didn't fly too far too fast.

"Remember, we're supposed to be keeping our heads down. If you're caught messing with these guys—"

Lou let out a dismissive huff of breath. "I won't be caught. Laying down a few strips of tire spikes will be a hell of a lot faster than pouring all that water into the tanks. It's not like I want those goons taking up more of my time than they have to when I have so many more interesting things to devote it to."

Something about the sly shift in her tone had me bracing myself. "You mean your skating," I said casually, knowing it was something more than that.

"I mean, there's always *that*." She tugged a strand of her dark hair free from its habitual ponytail and curled it around her finger. "But now I'm also hooking up with my sort-of coach, which makes the whole thing even more fun."

Even though I'd had some suspicious thoughts when she'd signaled for me to hang back the other afternoon, jealousy roared to the surface beneath my well-practiced cool. I tucked my hands under the table as they clenched, my jaw echoing the motion for a split-second before I caught my reaction.

Lou could sleep with whoever the fuck she wanted. I'd made it awfully clear that *I* wasn't game, hadn't I?

I could hardly expect her to become a nun.

But I couldn't stop the images from playing out in the back of my mind, sending an infuriated ruddy haze over my vision. That guy's slim hands running over her body, his lips pressed against hers…

Did he have any idea how to treat her the way she deserved? What kind of asshole got it on with a girl he was supposed to be coaching anyway?

"That seems a little hasty," I said, straining to keep my voice steady. "You haven't known him very long. Are you sure you can trust him?"

Lou snorted. "Trust him for what—not to be an undercover spy for my mother? Or a gang lackey? I think a couple of weeks of skating with him for hours nearly every day is plenty of time to be totally sure of that. Oh, and the *years* before that when I followed his competitions on TV."

"There are other ways he could hurt you."

She rolled her eyes. "I was the one who seduced *him*, FYI. You should be rejoicing. He's a huge step up from the kinds of guys I was stuck hanging around with back home."

Okay, she might have had a slight point there. But the guys in the gangs I understood. I knew how to read them.

I knew fuck-all about how some figure skating star operated.

"Just doing my job," I said with forced calm. "That's why I'm here."

Lou leaned back in her chair, narrowing her eyes at me. "Then I'll remind you that it was your idea to come along. You know, my skating partner is all kinds of hot too, even if he's a jerk half the time. Maybe I'll see if I can get him to loosen up in all the right ways too."

I obviously hadn't hidden my disapproving reaction quite well enough, and now she was pissed off at me—and trying to rile me up on purpose. At least, I sure as hell hoped that comment about the other rink-jock was throwaway provocation, not her real feelings.

I opened my mouth and ended up shoving the last few bites of my dinner into it rather than saying anything. The heat of the meal churned in my gut alongside the flares of temper I rarely struggled this hard to contain.

She wasn't a child anymore. I knew that. She was a grown woman, and it wasn't my place to boss her around, especially now.

But when she made jabs like that, fuck, did I want to bend her over the table and—

No, that was definitely not the direction my mind should be going in right now.

I pushed my chair back from the table, tossed my plate in the sink, and strode down to my room in the basement without another word.

Never had I been more grateful for the punching bag I'd been able to pick up at a sporting goods store in the larger town several miles outside of Hobb Creek. I went right at it, slamming one fist and then the other into the thick material.

The bag's chain squeaked. It swung away from me and back into another vicious punch.

I poured my tension out into the blows, letting the padded instrument absorb all of it. I hadn't bothered to wrap my hands, and in a matter of minutes, my knuckles were raw. But I kept going, letting the sting ground me.

I'd followed Lou all the way up here to keep her safe. She might be grown up and a woman who knew what she wanted, but anyone, no matter how tough, was vulnerable on their own.

Especially anyone with a mom like Mireya Cordova, who wasn't likely to take her heir's disappearance sitting down.

So I was going to do my fucking best to protect Lou from the things she actually needed protection from—and that included shielding her from all those urges I never should have felt to begin with.

TWELVE

Luciana

JASPER and I finished the final rotation and glided to a stop as our extended legs lowered to the ice in tandem. Our blades hit the ice perfectly in sync, and I couldn't restrain a broad grin.

Niko let out a whistle from where he was watching by the boards and gave an enthusiastic round of applause before skating over to join us. "You two are really killing it. That last spin was breathtaking. You've come a long way, you know—both of you."

The warmth of his smile sparked with my own joy, sending a deeper flood of triumph through my chest. But when I glanced at Jasper, he simply shrugged, his mouth slanted in a direction that had more in common with a frown.

Geez, was there *anything* that would perk this guy up?

Or was he still peeved that he had to put up with my constant presence?

The thorn of insecurity didn't have time to dig deep before Niko's eyes lit with a sly glint I was coming to recognize.

"Considering how much you two have evolved since we first gave pairs a try, I think it's time you got the chance to show off for a wider audience."

My gaze shot to the stands. "You want to invite people from town to watch us practice?"

Jasper sighed. "He's talking about some kind of competition. He wants us to perform someplace else—right, Niko?" He didn't sound happy about it.

The shorter man chuckled without any sign of noticing Jasper's lack of enthusiasm. "That's exactly what I'm getting at. Now before you say anything, it's just a small local competition. An event in Dellville—a city a couple of hours from here. No official criteria for competing, so it's fine that Lou is a newcomer and not registered anywhere yet. It'd give you the chance to get used to having more spectators and to get some objective feedback from judges without too much pressure."

"Judges," I murmured. The memory of Coach Balakin's disappointed tone when he pointed out my flaws echoed up from my memory.

I squared my shoulders against the recollection. The guy coaching me *now*, who absolutely knew what good skating looked like, thought I could handle this.

Luciana Cordova didn't let anyone else decide what chances she took a shot at.

Niko nodded, studying my reaction with a slight softening of his expression. "I can tell you how good you are all day long, but I know Jasper here will never believe me. This will give you objective proof of how far you've come."

He nudged Jasper teasingly with his elbow, but his gaze stayed on me. He could probably tell my confidence wasn't on the most stable ground either.

"I've never competed before," I said. "So starting with something small sounds just right to me. What's the point of doing any of this if I'm not going to put myself out there properly?"

I paused, taking in Jasper's uncertain expression. "Unless you think it's too small to be worth bothering with for *you*." Which was a stance

I could totally understand after he'd made it as far as the Olympics in the past.

Before Jasper could reply, another thought struck me with a jolt of panic. I turned back to Niko.

"How much publicity would a little local competition like this even get? It's not, like, broadcast outside the city or anything?"

Jasper snorted. "If you're looking to get on TV, I don't think a backwoods competition like that's going to do it for you."

I exhaled silently, not wanting him to realize I was incredibly relieved rather than disheartened by the fact. Thank the Lord.

I was supposed to be in hiding. I couldn't risk blowing my cover with any competition where someone who recognized me might spot me. But if it was only a small one in a city I'd never even heard of before—so no doubt Mom hadn't either—that should be safe.

A giddy shiver passed through me. I could finally get out there and make a spectacle on the ice like I'd always dreamed.

But Jasper still didn't look convinced.

"We just show up and skate?" he asked Niko.

"There's a qualifying round," Niko said. "But I have no doubt you'll be in the top ten pairs who're approved for the official competition day. I wouldn't be surprised if they don't even have more than ten pairs and it's just a formality."

Jasper rolled his eyes. "Such a vote of confidence."

Why did he always have to have such a stick up his ass? Couldn't he give this a chance?

I might have voiced those snarky questions, but Niko stepped in with a much more diplomatic attitude than came naturally to me. "I'm only putting the idea out there. You don't have to answer now. Just think about it."

Jasper hummed to himself noncommittally, his gaze veering back to the ice. I waited for the word *no* to roll off his tongue, but instead, he tilted his chin back upward, a steely expression on his face.

"I'll think about it—alone."

With one graceful push of his powerful legs, he was gone, soaring all the way to the other side of the rink. I eyed him, watching him mentally prepare himself before flying off into a series of jumps.

His form was impressive, stunning even. I didn't understand how Jasper could have any doubts about his abilities.

What was it in that handsome head of his that tripped him up when push came to shove?

Was he afraid that even the minor pressure of this "backwoods" competition would throw him off his game and he'd embarrass himself?

Before my eyes, he kicked off into a flawless triple Axel. My jaw dropped so fast it nearly hit the ice.

Here was a glimpse of the skater I'd seen on television, the man whose career I'd followed. Even with no music, Jasper swept across the ice as if he were moving along to a symphony, one only he could hear.

With his broad shoulders and brawny chest, he looked regal, princely even. I couldn't help but stare.

And possibly my fingers were tingling with the impulse to find out what those shoulders and that chest would feel like if I got to handle them for more than just fleeting lifts.

Niko's hand came to rest on the small of my back as he joined me in watching the other man. A headier tingle rushed through me at the ease of that casual intimacy—along with a little pang of guilt.

I probably shouldn't be checking out another guy while the one I'd been hooking up with was right next to me, should I?

Niko dipped his head so his warm breath ruffled my hair as he spoke. "He's pretty amazing, isn't he?"

"I can see why you'd cross an ocean for the chance to coach him."

"Mmhm. And is his skating the only thing you're admiring?"

A blush flared in my cheeks. Was I really that obvious?

I groped for an appropriate answer. "I—I mean, he is something to look at. Objectively speaking. If you can get past the infuriating personality."

Niko laughed. "That wasn't an accusation. I'm not going to be offended if you're interested in him too."

I guessed I might as well admit it now. "I might have a bit of a thing for hot, grouchy men, it turns out. But I also like the cheerful, sexy ones." I prodded Niko in the chest with my thumb. "So you don't need to worry."

Niko's smile didn't waver. "Not worried at all. If you can crack that man's shell, I'd be *happy* to see you do it. I didn't get the impression that you're the kind of woman who's looking to be tied down, Lou. I don't mind you playing the field as long as you stay honest with me."

I swallowed the rock that had somehow found its way into my throat and found it dissolved on its way into my stomach. He sounded like he was honestly okay with the idea of me pursuing Jasper too.

Not that I had any illusions about *Jasper* being okay with it. I wasn't sure it'd be worth the hassle of taking a hammer to that guy's shell in the first place.

I shot a glance over my shoulder, an unexpected wobble passing through my stomach. "Does that mean you're playing the field too?"

Niko gave my temple a quick peck. "Between training the two of you and enjoying your company in other ways, my days are pretty full as it is. I didn't expect even you to sweep me off my feet."

He said the last bit with a teasing note that I couldn't help giggling at. "So I'm your Prince Charming now?"

Niko flashed one of his brilliant grins. "Princess Charming-ko."

We both dissolved into laugher. When I got control of myself, I noticed Jasper had glided over to the boards where he'd left his water bottle.

He jerked his gaze away just as I looked at him. He was probably wondering what the hell was wrong with the two of us.

Niko's approval gave me a little boost of courage. I pushed off and skated over to join my partner.

Oh, fuck me. Did he have to toss his head back like that while he swallowed, his Adam's apple bobbing on full display?

Did some part of me have to want to lick the sweat right off it?

His dark blue tee clung to his well-muscled form. I yanked my attention back to his face.

I was coming over here to talk, not to ogle him.

Okay, maybe a little bit to ogle.

I tried to plan something clever and suave to say, but the words just tumbled out as I stopped next to him. "You looked amazing out there."

Jasper raised a skeptical eyebrow at me. "It was just a random string of moves."

"What, and I'm not allowed to appreciate the skill it took to pull them off?" I resisted the urge to stick my tongue out at him, which would make him *so* much more impressed with my maturity. "If you're fishing for compliments, sure, you're even more amazing when you're performing one of your routines. I always loved seeing you in the televised competitions—you manage to make even the most athletic moves flow together into such a gorgeous picture."

Jasper lowered the water bottle. He stared at me with such a startled expression that I had to fight the urge to look down at myself and make sure my faded concert tee hadn't caught fire.

"Really?" he said without a hint of his usual snark. Something in his gray-green eyes had shifted; the storm looked a little less tumultuous.

Did he really have to ask that?

I set my hands on my hips. "Yes, really. I wouldn't go around giving you compliments I don't mean just to thank you for being such a kind and considerate guy. Because you're not particularly kind and considerate so far."

Jasper let out a sudden sputtering sound as if he'd managed to choke on the air. "Got it. No false compliments around here."

I couldn't resist punching him—fairly lightly—in the shoulder. Or as close to his shoulder as I could easily reach when standing more than a foot shorter than him.

"The point is, I meant it. I always knew I'd get lost in the world you'd create on the ice. Never saw anyone else who could put on a show the same way."

Jasper scratched the back of his head, appearing lost for words. His awkwardness melted a little of my irritation with him.

As unbelievable as it seemed that a guy who'd once been seen as such a prodigy that his avid fans had dubbed him "Saint Jasper" might lack in confidence, he was clearly affected by my words.

"Well… thank you," he said finally, peering at the ice for a beat before meeting my eyes again. He hesitated and then offered a wary but genuine-looking smile. "That's always been my goal. Bringing the vision in my head to life so I can take the audience there with me. I'm glad to know it's worked."

"Of course it's worked. I bet it'd still work just fine if you let go of whatever's eating at you like Niko keeps saying."

I leaned back against the boards, thinking back over the routines of his I'd watched. A sigh twinged with longing slipped over my lips. "Like that Chopin piece you performed for your short program the first year you were at Nationals. I watched that so many times…"

Maybe I shouldn't have said that. Jasper's eyes narrowed—but then a flicker of wonder passed through it.

"That's the music you were skating to when we caught you in here during our practice time that first day."

I gave him a crooked smile. "Because I've been trying to recreate the same vibes." A longing wiggled up inside me, and I decided to risk the question. "I'd love to see your routine live. If you wanted to get in a little more solo practice today."

Jasper's lips parted, his stance tensing. For a second, I was sure that he was going to say no, to tell me to piss off.

He closed his mouth again, and his jaw worked. "It wouldn't be the same without the costume."

His voice was softer than I'd ever heard it before. It woke up a hunger in me to see him even more unguarded.

"I can imagine that part," I said coaxingly. "I've seen it enough times. But to have you right in front of me…"

He wet his lips, and I realized his face had flushed just a little. Had my interest affected him that much?

"All right," he said abruptly. "Why not? It'd be good to run through that program again anyway."

I managed not to clap my hands in joy like a total fangirl. "I'll cue up the music for you!"

He looked a little tense as he swept off toward the center of the rink. How long had it been since he'd performed this routine from years back?

Well, he'd agreed. He could always change his mind if he was that worried about it.

But when the first strains of the song reached him in his opening position, all the tension fell away from his posture. I hooked my arms over the top of the boards and leaned back to enjoy the moment to its fullest.

Symphony and skater became one. The music built to its familiar crescendo, one that I'd committed completely to memory.

Jasper's powerful body breezed across the ice, never missing a form, never skidding, never faltering. All the confidence I'd seen in past performances rose to the surface as if it'd never left.

He landed every jump with total grace. Whirled through his spins like the music had him in its grasp. Tears pricked my lashes, my emotions surging in time with the melody and the beautiful image that Jasper had created for me and me alone.

By the time he'd finished the routine, he'd totally stolen my breath away. My hands burned with the force of my clapping.

Jasper skated back to me, his chest heaving with the exertion and an odd mix of pride and puzzlement etched on his face. "I made it through the whole thing with no errors."

"It's not the first time."

"Well, no, I just—" He looked back toward the rink and then shook his head.

"Whatever you're thinking, stop," I had to order him. "You looked absolutely spectacular out there. Like, it's a miracle that I haven't dissolved into a puddle of awe just from seeing it firsthand."

I pressed my hands to my face in giddy embarrassment. "Holy crap."

Jasper blinked at me, but his face had brightened. "What?"

My voice came out in a whisper. "It just hit me again. Somehow I'm skating pairs with Jasper St. Pierre. How the fuck did that happen?"

I pinched myself just to make sure it really *was* happening. Jasper watched and then broke into the first real laugh I could remember hearing from him.

I started giggling too. "I'm sorry. You have no idea how crazy this seems to me. A month ago, I didn't think anyone was ever going to see me skate other than my long-suffering coach, and now somehow this is my life."

The memory of the very real suffering Coach Balakin must have gone through in the end cut through my good mood, but I kept the pang of loss off my face.

"And here I thought you were trying to avoid feeding my ego," Jasper said in an unusually relaxed tone. He paused. "I like watching you skate too, you know. You get across some pretty impressive visuals yourself. It's not like it's a hardship skating with you."

I caught my jaw before it dropped right out of my head. "Sometimes you sure make it sound like it is."

Jasper ducked his head. "That's not—that's not really about you. And I wasn't sure at first. But you've definitely got some moves, Punk."

The compliment set me aglow. "You don't know how much it means to me to hear you say that. Telling some kind of story on the ice with the picture I'm creating—that's what I'm always striving for. It might sound cheesy, but there's so much awfulness in the world. I want to be someone who's bringing more joy and beauty to people."

"Yeah," Jasper said, his attention completely focused on me again. He cocked his head. "Can I ask you a question?"

"Can I stop you?" I retorted with a smile to show I was teasing.

Jasper drummed his fingers on the boards. "Did you really not know you were good enough to compete—to tell those stories on the ice—any of it? How could you *not* know?"

How could I not have?

The question expanded in my mind, repeating over and over. Ever since Niko's first assurances of my skill, I'd asked myself that same thing until I could barely think about it anymore.

I could say it was Coach Balakin's fault—that he'd claimed I was falling short of even the most basic professional standards. But was it really?

He'd been an experienced figure skater. He'd competed for Ukraine decades ago.

Could he really have gotten it so wrong? Or had there been another hand at work, directing his coaching just as it'd orchestrated his murder?

Had he truly seen me as a failure… or had Mom paid him off to lie to me in the hopes of killing the dream she'd always seen as pointless?

I couldn't explain even a fraction of those possibilities in detail, so I settled for a vague approximation.

"I think it's mostly about my mother. She didn't really support my interest in skating—talked like it was a waste of time, like I wasn't good enough to bother. It's hard to have a clear idea of what you're capable of when you've got a voice from someone that close to you in your head all the time."

For the second time in this conversation, Jasper stared at me, momentarily speechless. He swiped his hand across his mouth.

His voice came out a bit hoarse. "Yeah, I can see how that could happen, especially if you never got the chance to get much outside feedback. My dad actually wasn't at all supportive either. If he'd had his way, I'd have quit before I was even competing in Juniors."

"What?" I burst out, shocked and horrified by the thought of a world without Jasper St. Pierre ever showing off his talent. "That's ridiculous."

The news stories about him had never even hinted at any conflict in his family. But then, the figure skating world usually shied away from drama when it could. The community preferred to give the impression of being as elegant in their lives as they were on the ice.

Jasper shrugged. "I'd say it's just as ridiculous that your mom tore you down. I hate to think how much we've missed seeing because you stayed out of the competitive circuit so long."

An unexpected sense of closeness settled over me. I reached out and rested my hand against his bare forearm.

A jolt of electricity shot through my nerves. Jasper's gaze darted to meet mine, and I thought I caught a flicker of answering heat there.

"I think things have worked out pretty well in the end," I said quietly. "Here I am, training with you—and Niko. I can't imagine what I'd trade to have instead of this."

A little of the flush I'd seen before colored Jasper's cheeks again. "I think it's pretty fantastic that you're finally out here pursuing your dream. And even if I act like an ass about it sometimes, I'm glad I can be a part of that."

I couldn't resist leaning a little closer and arching my eyebrows at him. My pulse thumped double-time, but even though an ache was forming between my legs, I had other things on my mind than getting busy.

At least, not that kind of busy.

"Does that mean you'll give this Dellville competition thing a try?"

Jasper's gaze slid down my body, trailing heat in its wake. I was going to melt into a very different sort of puddle if he kept looking at me like that.

He swallowed audibly but managed to stay on topic. "You really want to, huh?"

"I'd like to find out what I can do when I've got more than a couple of people watching."

His expression set into a more familiar expression of determination. He squeezed my hand—just for a second, but emphatically enough to spark another wave of heat through my body—and then pushed off toward Niko.

"Hey, Okabe! Sign us up. Those other Dellville skaters aren't going to know what hit them."

THIRTEEN

Jasper

GETTING HUNG up on some woman I hardly knew wasn't a good idea. I was supposed to be focusing on my art, not dreaming up erotic scenarios.

But as many times as I told myself that, as many pops of excitement as I squashed in my chest before heading into practice, here I was at nine o'clock at night sitting in my Mustang outside the bungalow Lou was renting, my heart thumping around like I was a preteen about to call his crush on the phone for the first time.

It was ridiculous. I was here to drop off the weights I'd said I'd lend her, nothing else.

I spent hours nearly every day around this woman. It wasn't as if seeing her for a few minutes right now was ever so thrilling.

Sure, so maybe I was a little curious to see our unexpected punk prodigy in her home environment, but it wasn't *that* big a deal.

Apparently I'd sat around too long convincing myself of that. As I pushed open the car door, Lou came bounding out of the bungalow.

"Hey! Thanks for bringing them by. Let me help you carry them in."

The next thing I knew, she'd loped across the weedy lawn in her bare feet, her slim curves teasingly visible through her rough-hemmed tee and distressed jean shorts. She leaned through the passenger side window I'd left open to let in the cooling evening air and snatched the set of ankle weights off the seat.

I grumbled something not particularly articulate about personal space and grabbed the two pairs of dumbbells, but the truth was her audacity left me more giddy than irritated.

She always kept me on my toes, wondering what she'd do next. I should have hated it.

Instead, way too often, I found myself waiting in awed anticipation. I hated *that.*

"It's no problem," I made myself say as I hefted the jumble of weights over to her house. "I didn't realize you had so little equipment with you for training off the rink. These are extras I had lying around."

"Still, I appreciate it. Come in, come in. The place isn't much, but it's home for now."

I hadn't meant to come inside, but here I was, stepping into the warm glow from a bowl-like light fixture that looked like it'd probably been installed in the seventies.

The furniture was kind of shabby compared to my apartment, but there was something appealing about the lived-in feel to it. I'd been inhabiting my Ikea-furnished space for three months, and it still barely looked like I'd moved in.

A hint of spice hung in the air, something rich and savory. Had she been cooking?

Was there anything she *couldn't* do?

I held up the weights awkwardly. "Where do you want these?"

"Um… I guess over in the corner next to the TV is fine. I like to get caught up on my talk shows while I'm working out."

I shot Lou a look, trying to judge if she was joking, but her hint of a smile gave nothing away.

I set the pairs of dumbbells down next to the maple TV stand and glanced around. A couple of doors stood at the far end of the living space beyond the kitchen area, presumably a bedroom and bathroom. Just past them, a shadowed flight of stairs let down to a basement.

Not a bad setup, really. It was bigger than my apartment, and a hell of a lot more private, with her own big yard and everything.

I rubbed the back of my neck, feeling twice as awkward now that I had nothing to hold on to. "Nice place you've got here."

"Oh, whatever." Her hands rested squarely upon those grabbable hips. "Leave my poor house alone. It's the best place I could find on short notice."

Did she really think I was being sarcastic?

I'd have protested, but I wasn't sure I wanted to encourage a friendlier vibe… and her last couple of words had caught my attention more.

"Short notice? You just out of the blue decided to crash into Hobb Creek?"

Something flickered in Lou's gaze, the trace of a smile vanishing before she plastered one that looked a little stiffer on her face. "That's about the size of it. Obviously I made the right choice, huh?"

"Seems like it," I had to admit. "You really came all the way up from the States just because you saw a few positive comments about the rink?"

She shrugged. "It just sounded like a nice place. And I wanted somewhere as different as possible from big city life."

There had to be more to it than that for her to have rushed here with so little preparation. Her answers were awfully vague.

I caught another question before the itch of curiosity propelled it from my throat. I wasn't here to badger her for her life story. Even if I *was* awfully curious now.

I couldn't really blame her for being hesitant to open up to me, could I? I'd spent more time grumbling at her than having a real conversation.

Could anyone blame me for having my doubts? She *had* crashed into town—and into my life. How the hell was I supposed to just accept that?

But the last couple of practices, it was like we'd found a common wavelength. I'd found myself not just fending off sparks of excitement when I reached the rink each day, but craving her company after she left at the end.

It felt… dangerous, how much I was starting to enjoy our partnership. I'd never imagined skating pairs before.

How could it work this well?

"Well," I started, figuring she probably wanted me out of her hair, but Lou chucked the ankle weights next to the dumbbells and made a beeline for the kitchen.

"You want something to drink? I shouldn't make you come all the way out here and forget how to be a good hostess."

My lips twitched into a crooked grin. "It was only a three-minute drive."

She shook her head. "I always forget how small this place is. But hey, the offer still stands. I think we deserve at least a beer after all the work we've been putting in."

Obviously she'd spent all of her time in the bigger city she'd mentioned. Where exactly had she come from?

I swallowed that question too and shrugged. "Yeah, okay. A beer would be great."

It'd have been pretty rude for me to totally shut down her offer, right? Accepting had nothing to do with not actually wanting to leave her presence.

I sank down onto the sofa, stretching my legs out on a diagonal so I could get more comfortable on the narrow cushions.

Lou appeared at the other end a moment later, clutching a bottle in each hand. "I changed my mind. Or, well, I forgot I don't have any beer. How's hard cider instead?"

How was she so charming even looking embarrassed over the slip?

I reached out. "Cider's even better."

She passed mine over and plopped down on the other end of the sofa without any hint of self-consciousness. From what I'd gathered, she'd only been living here for a few weeks, but she'd gotten comfortable fast.

A set of silver rings, a little thicker than I saw most women wearing, decorated the fingers of her right hand. I nodded to them. "Gotta ramp up the punk style when you're off the rink?"

Lou wiggled her slim fingers. "I don't think you'd appreciate it if I had these on while we *are* on the rink. I just like them. They make me feel tough."

She let out a laugh and fit her lips around the neck of the cider to throw back a gulp with an enthusiasm that made my dick twitch. I jerked my gaze away and took a sip of my own cider.

She had good taste. It was tart and crisp but still with a faint sweetness.

"Where'd you get these?" I asked.

Lou waved toward the front door. "Oh, there's a local brewery about a half hour outside of town that I stumbled on when I was cruising around on one of our days off. Couldn't help going in for a little taste test."

I raised my eyebrows. "Going totally local, huh?"

She laughed. "Might as well while I'm here. Especially when the locals have good stuff."

"Yeah. It's not a bad town at all, tiny as it is. I guess wherever you're from had a pretty different vibe."

I was kind of fishing for more information about her past, but Lou didn't take the bait. She leaned back against the sofa, a soft smile playing with her lips that made her look even prettier than usual, which was saying something.

"It really is a great town. A lot of people have been welcoming, and the people who aren't have kept it to themselves. Well—no, that doesn't count."

I studied her. "What doesn't?"

She waggled her bottle at me. "Nothing important. I thought I might get bored someplace this small, but I haven't really at all."

"Same," I admitted. "But then, Niko keeps us so busy there isn't a whole lot of time to get bored."

Another laugh tumbled from Lou's mouth. "That's the truth. So he was just as much of a slave-driver before I showed up?"

"Oh, yeah." I paused, feeling I owed the guy who'd flown halfway around the world to drag me out of my slump better than that. "A very nice slave-driver, though."

"The most cheerful slave-driver ever."

I couldn't restrain a chuckle. "Yep, that's him."

"He does know what he's talking about," Lou said. "I never would have thought of trying pairs if he hadn't brought it up."

"He's really very good at the whole coaching thing. I can't believe he's never done it professionally before." I paused, abruptly embarrassed both to have said that out loud and that I'd never given Niko the compliment to his face.

"He obviously thought you were pretty special, coming all the way over here to train you."

"Yeah."

The chaotic emotions her comment stirred up might have shown on my face. As I took another swig of my cider, Lou clapped her hands together and changed the subject.

"So, we're going to be competing. When do we get to pick out costumes?"

Her enthusiasm brought back my smile. "Normally I don't think about costumes until at least the basics of the routine are sorted out. So I can make sure it all fits together. But, ah, I wouldn't generally be picking them out."

The second the words had left my mouth, I kicked myself. I never talked about this part of my approach.

But Lou was eyeing me with nothing but eager curiosity. "What do you mean?"

I'd put it out there now. She was going to find out soon enough anyway, wasn't she?

I drained the last of the cider and set the bottle on the coffee table, nearly falling off the narrow cushion as I did. This sofa was not made for someone my size.

"I sew them myself. The costumes. I could never find anything that fit my vision perfectly off the rack, so I just… taught myself."

Lou's eyes widened. "Holy shit. No kidding? That's amazing. I never would have guessed—you obviously taught yourself well."

"I'm glad you think so."

"Why don't the reporters ever talk about that? It's such a cool part of your story."

I ducked my head. "I don't usually bring it up. Always assumed people would think it was more weird than cool, I guess. It's just something that kind of happened."

Lou snorted. "I could almost say that about skating in general for me. Went to see one of those stars on ice shows when I was five years old, begged my mom for a pair of skates and lessons, and the dream just kept getting bigger all on its own."

A momentary melancholy crossed her face, and my stomach clenched at the memory of her comments about her unsupportive mom. Not all of her associations with her skating career were happy ones.

"You want to talk about uncool," she added, springing up. "You should see—"

She darted over to where her equipment bag was resting by the wall and dug into one of the side pockets. Then she sank down onto the sofa—closer this time, just a few inches away from where I was leaning my arm across the back.

My awareness of her nearness tingled over my skin, but I pulled my attention to the scrap of fabric clutched in her hands.

"One of the laces from my very first pair of skates," she said, stroking her thumb over the fraying strip of woven material. "I like to have it with me to remind me of how far I've come, even when it didn't seem like I'd come anywhere near far enough. My good luck charm."

She grinned at me, but I hadn't missed the dash of pain in her statement. As hard as it was for me to wrap my head around it, this woman hadn't believed she was good enough for an awfully long time.

My voice dropped lower of its own accord. Somehow my hand ended up coming to rest on her shoulder with a tentative graze of my fingertips.

"Having seen you skate, I find it hard to imagine there's any limit on how far you'll take it."

Lou met my gaze, her dark eyes shimmering with enough emotion to flood me with heat. "And here I thought that to you I was just a punk who barged in on your practice time."

The heat rose to my face at that remark. God, I really had been a prick to her, hadn't I?

"That's just… me," I muttered. "I don't do people very well."

The light dancing in Lou's eyes turned sly. She teased her fingers over my own shoulder, watching my reaction. "Hmm. I'd like to believe you just haven't had enough experience with the right people. But we can keep working on that."

My throat had gotten abruptly rough. "On the ice?"

"Or maybe…"

She set the old lace down on the coffee table and rose up onto her knees on the sofa. Just the right height to touch my cheek and lower her mouth to mine.

The press of her lips sent a shock of total bliss straight through my body. I'd wanted this so much, but I'd tried to ignore that desire so determinedly that having it made real left my mind reeling.

My hands rose of their own accord, delving into her silky waves. Lou tussled my hair in turn, drawing sparks over my scalp with her fingertips.

She deepened the kiss with a flick of her tongue across my lips, and I parted them to welcome her in. My tongue swept over hers, tangling them together in a very different sort of partnership than we'd attempted before.

One kiss flowed into another. My cock rose behind my jeans, which were becoming uncomfortably tight as it hardened.

Our breaths mingled, and I claimed her mouth even more avidly than before. What was it about this woman that I wanted to meld her right into me?

One of my hands slid down her side to her hip. Lou took that as a cue to scoot closer, her knees coming to rest against my thigh.

My cock stiffened even more, and my fingers curled against the frayed fabric of her jeans. I adjusted them as if to tug her right onto my lap, but something about the impulse made me hesitate.

Desire clanged through me. My pulse was racing, my skin burning up. She was driving me crazy, and we hadn't done anything more than kiss yet.

This was dangerous.

Before I could catch my reaction, I jerked away from her. My hip banged into the arm of the sofa.

Lou stared at me, her own face flushed, her lips deliciously swollen. Fucking hell, how could I be throwing away this moment?

The same question seemed to be running through her mind. "Is something wrong?"

I fumbled for an answer. "I—I'm just not sure this is a good idea."

She cocked her head, knitting her brow. When she sucked her lower lip under her teeth to worry on it, I just about short-circuited and yanked her back into my arms after all.

"Do you think getting together like this would be bad for our skating partnership?" she ventured.

There—that was an excuse that made sense. A hell of a lot more sense than *I like you too fucking much*.

But I found I couldn't outright lie. My mouth opened and closed and opened again.

"I guess having that kind of physical connection might actually help us work better together. But the emotions that could come with it—that can get messy."

The glint of mischief came back into Lou's eyes. "Oh, then there's an easy solution to that. We'll just have to avoid falling in love, and it'll be no big deal."

"Right," I said, my throat suddenly hoarse. "I should have thought of that. No big deal."

Other than the fact that I had the sneaking suspicion I was already falling for her, hard.

Lou stroked her fingers along my jaw with a heady shiver of sensation that made it really difficult for me to care about my reservations.

I could keep myself detached, right? I'd managed to navigate training with Niko all this time.

And God, did I want this woman.

But Lou hesitated, gazing at me. All at once, she looked oddly shy.

"I should probably tell you before anything else happens between us—Niko and I have been getting pretty close too. He knows I wasn't planning on being exclusive. I don't want you to get the wrong idea about what I *can* offer."

Even as a jolt of jealousy hit me, I found I wasn't actually surprised. Not after seeing the two of them interacting at the rink.

All the shared laughter and the little touches came back to me. My gut twisted.

He'd gone after her—or she'd turned to him first—

What was I even bothered about? It wasn't as if I'd even been making overtures of friendship with either of them.

And I didn't really want to look too closely at the convoluted threads that jealousy split into.

Being with Lou like this felt good. Better than I'd felt off the ice in ages.

Why shouldn't I enjoy it while it lasted? For once in my life, surely I deserved a moment when I wasn't taking everything so damned seriously?

"That's totally fine," I said, with only a tiny strain I smoothed out of my voice. "No commitments. Just having fun."

Lou beamed at me. "I can do that."

I shifted forward, setting my hand on her waist. I'd been the one to pull away, so I'd better make it one hundred percent clear how much I wanted her after all.

"What are we waiting for, then?"

I tugged her onto my lap, and she straddled me as if there was no place she'd rather be. As my hands dove back into her hair, her mouth slammed down on mine.

My eyes closed. I wanted to relish this moment as much as I could, soak up as much as she allowed me. A shudder ran down the length of my spine, jolting me forward into her embrace.

Her hands splayed across my chest, running over my pecs and then down to my abs. Heat flared everywhere they touched.

I kissed her harder, and her teeth grazed my lower lip to electrifying effect. She slid her fingers right down to the hem of my shirt and then up underneath, tracing the planes of my muscles over my bare skin now.

Fuck, she was sex incarnate. I tore one hand out of her hair to match her explorations, dying to feel all of her beneath my fingers.

When I cupped her breast through her shirt, an encouraging gasp passed from her mouth into mine. It egged me on.

I stroked my palm back and forth over that delectable mound, and the gasp transformed into a series of short whimpers.

Lou started to rock on my lap. At the brush of her groin against mine, it was a wonder my erection didn't explode right out of my jeans.

I grabbed her hip and yanked her flush against me. A groan reverberated from my chest at the torturous contact.

While she ground against me as fervently as her mouth seared into mine, I tucked my hand under her shirt and traced the soft skin of her torso up to her bra. With a tug, I dislodged the cup from the swell of her breast, giving me full access.

Lou let loose a breathy moan as I tweaked her pert nipple. She leaned in, her position urging me to twist sideways on the sofa. My head bumped against the hard arm, but I didn't give a fuck about the minor pain when I had this woman writhing on top of me.

Our mouths crashed together again and again. I hiked her shirt higher and massaged both her breasts at the same time.

Lou rode me with little bucks of her hips, turning my cock hard as steel. I needed to feel *all* of her. I needed her riding me for real.

I drew my hand down to the fly of her shorts, adjusting my position to get the right angle—and realized a second too late that I'd misjudged the narrow sofa. My broad shoulder veered right over the edge of the cushion, and gravity took over.

The next thing I knew, we were tumbling onto the floor with a bone-jarring thud. We'd rolled as we fell, and I caught myself before I crushed Lou under my full weight.

Lou blinked up at me now braced over her, and her mouth twitched with the start of a giggle. We'd both have burst out laughing a moment later if footsteps hadn't thundered up from the basement at the same moment.

A huge man burst into the living room, his dark face hardened with rage. "Get the fuck off her, *now*!"

FOURTEEN

Luciana

THIS WAS a complete and total nightmare.

As Rafael charged at Jasper, looking like he planned to hurl him off me and straight through a wall, Jasper scrambled to the side. I leapt up, my body still flushed from the *very* enjoyable interlude my bodyguard had just interrupted.

Rafael raised his fist as if to slam it straight into my skating partner's gorgeous face, and I jumped between them with my arms spread wide.

"Stop it!"

Thank all that was holy for Rafael's swift protective reflexes. He didn't want to pummel *me*.

He jerked himself backward, dropping his fist. But his temper hadn't totally flamed out.

"That fucking asshole tried to—"

"It's fine," I broke in with the mafia princess tone I only brought out for special occasions. "We were messing around on the sofa, and we slipped off by accident. I'm totally okay. I *told* you I was having Jasper come over."

The furor in Rafael's dark eyes simmered down. He looked from me to Jasper, who was standing there tensed like he wasn't sure if he should be running for his life, and back again.

"I didn't know I'd find him tackling you to the floor," he growled.

I set my hands on my hips. "It. Was. An. Accident." One we could have recovered from to go on to much more fun if Mr. Overprotective here hadn't stormed into the room like a maniac. "And it was at least as much my fault as Jasper's. So calm the fuck down and go back to whatever you were doing before you started your volcano impression."

Rafael took a step to the side, not exactly retreating. His eyes narrowed as he studied Jasper, and the bulging muscles along his shoulders flexed with subtle menace.

Oh, for fuck's sake.

I spun toward Jasper, groping for a way to salvage this mess. "I'm sorry. Just a misunderstanding. Rafael's a friend of the family—he came along to watch out for me—he's just doing it *very badly* at the moment."

Rafael let out a grunt just shy of a growl.

Jasper's stance went even more rigid. He was nearly as tall as the other man, and brawny enough to have made me drool on more than one occasion I'd never admit to, but even to him, Rafael's massive frame and obvious hostility would have been intimidating. It wasn't as if the figure skater would ever have found himself in a gang brawl.

I turned back to my bodyguard. "Would you go back downstairs? We're both okay, and we were kind of in the middle of something."

I made those words as pointed as I could, and Rafael finally eased backward. But it was too little, too late.

Jasper was backing up too, edging toward the door. His wary gaze darted between me and Rafael. "Obviously you have a lot going on. I'd better head home. Gotta rest up before practice and all."

I wasn't going to argue with him to stay. Things had gotten way too awkward already.

"I'm really sorry," I said. "Stupid sofa."

I gave it a playful kick for good measure, trying to lighten the moment, but it didn't work. Maybe because Rafael hadn't quite reined in his glower.

Jasper rubbed his neck like he often seemed to do when he was uneasy and bobbed his head in acknowledgment. "No big deal. I'll see you at the arena tomorrow."

Then he was ducking out the doorway like he couldn't get to his car fast enough.

The door thudded shut in his wake. Rafael paused by the top of the basement stairs like he was waiting to make sure the guy wasn't going to sneak back in the second he lowered his guard.

Like there was any chance of Jasper *wanting* to return after the scare he'd just had.

Ugh. Was there any chance he'd forget all this in a day or two, and we could pick up where we'd left off without it being an issue?

Somehow I found that hard to believe.

The car's engine rumbled and faded as Jasper drove away. Rafael's shoulders came the rest of the way down, and he moved to head back downstairs like he hadn't just completely ruined my night.

A fresh wave of frustration crackled through me. "Where do you think you're going?"

He glanced back at me without a trace of remorse in his expression. His tone was back to its usual even deadpan.

"You told me to go downstairs. Just following orders."

Oh, he was going to play it that way, was he? I marched a couple of steps closer, glaring at him.

"I asked you to get going *before* the guy I was hoping to hook up with took off. You terrorized him. What the hell were you thinking?"

Rafael's mouth tightened into a frown. "I was thinking that I heard a bang and rushed upstairs to find you pinned to the floor under some guy twice your size who I'd never seen before. How could I have known he wasn't attacking you?"

I rolled my eyes. "I wasn't *pinned*, and you could have waited two seconds to see if I was actually in any danger. I have a mouth—I'd have yelled for help if I needed it. Hell, I'd have been kneeing him in the balls if I'd objected to what was going on."

"Two seconds could make the difference between life and death. That's not a chance I'm willing to take."

"Maybe with a fucking assassin. He's a figure skater, not a professional criminal. Christ, Rafael."

Rafael's frown deepened. "You trust these guys too much. Just because they're skaters and you watched them on TV or whatever doesn't mean they couldn't have bad intentions."

I threw my hands in the air. "You sound more like a mom than my actual mom ever did. I'm a big girl. Fully grown, officially an adult. And I've been training with them for weeks now, so yeah, I do know them enough to trust them not to rape me. But even if I didn't, *you* know I can look after myself better than any woman these guys have ever been with. You expect me to believe you honestly couldn't tell I wasn't fighting for my life?"

"I didn't have a whole lot of time to analyze the situation."

"Don't give me that bullshit," I snapped. "Even after I told you it was fine, you kept staring him down like you were trying to punch him with your goddamn eyes."

A flicker of discomfort crossed Rafael's face. He knew I was right —he knew he'd gone too far.

Seeing it only fueled my anger. "You got all grouchy when I told you he was coming by, just like you did when I mentioned I slept with Niko. You never wanted him here to begin with."

"I'm trying to protect you—"

"You're trying to stop me from having any kind of private life at all!"

Rafael shut his mouth and turned that glower of his on me. It wasn't fair that it could heat me up inside all over again even while I was so pissed off at him.

But that had always been the problem. He could get me hot and bothered, but he'd never let me act on the desire.

The words kept tumbling out, propelled by not just tonight's annoyance but years of pent-up frustration.

"You've decided you don't want me even though I pulled out all the stops to show you I was interested, and that's fine. I backed off. I'm not standing around mooning over you. But you don't get to turn me down and then block me from having fun with every other guy in the world too. You made it clear that it's none of your fucking business."

Rafael blinked at me, his stance stiffening. His frown had twisted into something vaguely sickly looking.

"Lou—"

I flicked my hand toward him. "I don't want to hear it. You won tonight—I didn't get to fuck a very hot guy who's actually interested in me. But if you're going to have a problem with me hooking up with whoever I damn well want, you can go back to Austin."

"Don't be ridiculous. You can't—"

"I can get by on my own just fine. *You* insisted on coming with me—I didn't ask you to. I left home so that I didn't have to live my life under someone else's thumb, and I'm not going to let you bully me into doing things your way now."

Rafael winced. He lowered his head, his expression still grim.

"I'm sorry," he said. "I shouldn't have interfered. I'd never try to take away your freedom. Of course you know what you're doing. I won't barge in like that again unless I'm sure you need me."

They were all the right words, but I couldn't hear much actual remorse in his voice. He sounded like he was speaking by rote, going through the motions of an apology when he didn't actually regret what he'd done one bit.

I gritted my teeth, because there wasn't anything specific I could call him on—and then he'd already spun on his heel and started trudging down to his basement room, ending the conversation completely.

For a minute or two, I stood there, my breath rushing in and out of me as I gathered my composure. When my nerves felt a little steadier, I sat down on the sofa hard, trying not to think about the delight Jasper had sparked in my body there less than half an hour ago.

Thoughts of the man downstairs loomed too much at the forefront of my mind.

Rafael and I had argued before, of course. I couldn't count how many spats we'd had when I'd chafed against his protective nature through my teens.

But since I'd passed my eighteenth birthday, he'd eased off on the domineering attitude, and we hadn't *really* clashed that whole time.

Until now. And this felt different from any argument we'd ever had before.

It didn't matter that he didn't want to jump in the sack with me. Rafael was the one constant presence in my life, the one person I'd always been able to count on. When he'd thrown in his lot with me over my mom, I'd thought that meant the trust between us ran as deep as could be.

But after the way he'd acted tonight, the way he'd defied me for no reason other than whatever petty grievances had provoked his hostility… I wasn't so sure after all.

Was he my rock, or a stone I'd have to stumble over on my way to claiming my freedom?

I didn't want to ask those questions. I wanted to believe this was just a temporary tiff.

But as I flicked on the TV to try to distract myself, I couldn't shake the sinking sensation creeping through my gut.

FIFTEEN

Luciana

SOMETIME BETWEEN LAST night's encounter and this afternoon's practice, Jasper had reverted back to the same prickly grouch that I'd started to know so well.

"Let's try that new lift again," Niko called from the sidelines. "I think you almost had it this time!"

Jasper grumbled something about not having it the last thousand times but got back into position anyway. My heart raced as his hand settled on my hip, the other grasping my hand. Then I was soaring up into the air.

For a moment, we were perfectly balanced.

But only for a moment.

As we whirled around, Jasper's arms wobbled. And over his head, so did I.

"Shit," I said, trying my best to right myself, and added an extra *Shitshitshit!* in my head for good measure.

His arms had shifted, throwing off my fragile balance. There wasn't much I could do from above.

He let out a few curses of his own as he attempted to adjust himself, but it was too late. The damage was done. I was teetering over.

I braced myself to fall in the least painful way, instincts honed by years of collisions with the ice, but Jasper managed to catch me against his chest before I hit the ground. He quickly set me on my feet, his face flushed and his eyes dark with frustration.

"That was my fault," he admitted with a grimace. "I fucked up. I'm sorry."

"It's okay. These things happen." I straightened up and smoothed my tee shirt. "You made sure I didn't eat ice too badly. No harm done."

The truth was that we both knew what was eating *him*. Obviously his visit to my house last night had thrown our dynamic out of kilter —whether because we'd made out or because of Rafael barging in or both, I couldn't tell.

I'd tried to bring it up at the start of practice and again during our snack break, but he'd brushed off my attempts both times. The second occasion, he'd taken off to the other end of the rink rather than talk to me.

So yeah. Things were definitely *not* okay, but I had no idea how to fix them.

When we skated back around toward Niko, he was watching us with a thoughtful expression. Had he guessed that something had gone down between us outside of practice?

Lord help me, had Jasper told him about it?

No, I was pretty sure I was safe from that embarrassment. When Jasper clammed up, you'd need a jackhammer to force him open.

But our coach had clearly caught on that something wasn't quite clicking between us. He motioned toward the stands.

"It's time to wrap it up for the day. You guys have been really putting your all in. Don't skimp on your cool-down stretches now!"

Jasper didn't argue that we should keep at it a little longer, but then, maybe he was just grateful not to have to be around me much longer today.

My heart sank. Was he really that pissed off with me for whatever reason, or was something else behind his renewed shitty mood?

We skated off in separate directions to loosen our muscles. I could feel Niko's gaze from the center of the rink, shifting between Jasper and me.

Maybe we needed some more time off the ice and away from each other. If Jasper and I were going to get the hang of the short routine Niko was choreographing for us even well enough to pass the qualifying round, then we had to get our heads straight.

And it seemed like being around me was having the opposite effect on my partner.

I stretched out my aching muscles, doing my best not to steal peeks at Jasper's muscles rippling beneath his own tee. Getting caught ogling him would only make this whole situation twice as embarrassing.

As I cooled down with slow glides across the rink, the chill of the arena's air seeped into my skin. Rubbing my arms, I cruised over to my bag in the stands to grab my hoodie.

I was just stepping off the ice, my gaze meandering across the stands, when a splotch of blood red caught my attention up near the top of the rows of seats.

My heart lurched, a colder sweat breaking over my skin. An image of Coach Balakin's bloody body flashed behind my eyes.

I grasped the boards, drawing in a shaky breath against the rush of horror.

It was fine. Just something red attached to the door—hanging there by the handle.

I had to get a grip on myself before I started freaking out all over the place every time I saw a freaking *color* at a rink.

Still, I couldn't help approaching the door cautiously, swaying a little on the skates I'd hastily hooked the guards onto. I didn't remember seeing anything dangling off the door before.

When I got close enough to squint through the shadows, I stopped in my tracks, my pulse hiccupping all over again.

Okay, I definitely would have remembered seeing that.

A gauzy red scarf was tied around the door handle—that was what had caught my attention. But one end of it wrapped around the neck of a fashion doll who hung there as if from a noose.

The doll's dark brown hair was wrapped in a ponytail. She'd been decked out in black leggings and a muscle tee—workout clothes.

Was that… supposed to represent *me*?

My stomach plummeted to the floor.

I yanked the scarf off the handle and examined the doll from front to back. Her perfect plastic smile glimmered, but her eyes had been Xed out.

As if to indicate she was dead.

Goosebumps quivered up and down my arms. I spun around, scanning the stands.

Who the hell had left this here? I hadn't noticed anyone coming in or out.

They must have slipped it on so stealthily even Rafael hadn't caught on, wherever he was lurking in the dark alcoves, because there was no way my bodyguard would have left this sick display for me to find on my own.

Niko had gone over to talk to Jasper in a low voice I couldn't make out. Neither of them was paying any attention to me.

My hand tightened around the doll. This incident had happened because of me—I didn't want to drag them into the mess if I didn't have to.

Balling the plastic figure in the fabric of the scarf, I shoved open the door and marched out into the hall. The space was empty, only a single voice carrying from the reception area up front.

"Yeah, we'll have that all set up for you on the sixteenth."

I hustled over in the hopes that I might catch the culprit, but all I found was the arena manager, Olive, leaning over the reception desk with her back to the entryway. She was scrawling something on a scrap of paper in the jumble of objects there that she'd somehow pull into a cohesive schedule.

"Perfect," she said, in that same saccharine sweet customer service voice. "We'll see you then. Uh-huh. Okay, g'bye."

She set the reception phone down, tapping her pen with her veiny hand, and startled a bit when she glanced up and noticed me.

"Oh, Lou," she said, relaxing immediately. Her gaze skimmed over me, taking in the skates I was still wearing and my lack of equipment bag. "Can I do anything for you?"

I didn't really want to wave the doll in front of her either. What would some small-town local make of ominous threats?

She'd either freak out or think I was crazy. Or maybe both.

"Oh, I just wondered if you've seen anyone come in while we were training. I thought I spotted someone by the door a little while ago, but I was so focused on the routine I couldn't pay attention, and then they were gone."

Olive frowned. "I'm sorry, dear. I only got in about fifteen minutes ago. I haven't seen anyone since then, but maybe they were already gone. Did they disturb you?"

Yeah, disturbing was definitely the word for it. But I plastered a smile on my face, since there was nothing the manager could do for me anyway.

"Oh, no, I was just curious. Thanks all the same!"

I hustled back to the rink and hurried down the stairs, watching Niko and Jasper from the corner of my vision. If I didn't want any strange looks and uneasy questions, I had to get my finding out of sight before the men came this way.

My heart didn't stop thudding double-speed until I'd tucked the bundle of gauzy fabric into the bottom of my equipment bag. My nerves were still twitching with apprehension as I leaned over to finish my cool down with a few sitting stretches.

Niko joined me a minute later, his head cocked. "You went out for a minute. What's up?"

I shrugged like it was no big deal, willing away the sour taste in my mouth. "Nothing, just thought I saw someone I knew by the door. My mistake."

His face relaxed, so I must have lied well enough. "If Jasper's attitude today has been getting to you—I know he can be kind of—"

"It's fine," I broke in. "Really. I know what he's like, and we all have off days." I stretched my arms over my head and forced another smile. "I for one am looking forward to chilling out and a big dinner."

Niko chuckled and went to grab his own bag. My gut twisted with the lies.

What could I tell them? That I might have brought down the wrath of a bunch of criminals not just on me but on my skating colleagues too?

Who else could have left this childish threat, after all? It would be just like those asshole wannabe gangsters.

I had no idea how they might have figured out that I was the one who'd messed with their cars on two occasions now. No one had spotted me so far, and I'd been wearing my ski mask both times.

Maybe they had no idea I was connected to their vehicular troubles. Maybe they'd just noticed there was a new chica in town and decided to haze me in their own sick way.

Jasper and Niko weren't equipped to deal with that kind of problem. But me—I could take them all down without breaking a sweat if I let myself go full Deadly Rose.

Rage replaced the queasy feeling in my stomach.

If these asshats thought they could scare me out of this town — *my new home* — then they had another thing coming. They were small fry, barely even a legitimate gang.

I'd ordered around squads larger than them as a fucking teenager. Mom's empire stretched around the globe.

They had no fucking idea who they'd just pissed off.

Niko headed up the stairs with a cheery wave. Jasper trudged by with significantly less enthusiasm. I chucked off my skates and gave the blades a brisk wipe before shoving my feet into my sneakers, hopped up on a combination of nervous and furious adrenaline.

My equipment bag weighed heavy on my shoulders, but I'd gotten used to making the walk to the bungalow rather than driving. All part of my endurance training.

And today it gave me a chance to burn off a little of my jangling unease while my gaze roved over the streets and my mind spun through the possibilities.

Buoyant music drifted through the door to the hair salon. The staff at my favorite café were busy stringing the patio railing with a garland of autumn leaves that the local trees were only just starting to match.

It wasn't right that a place this peaceful and happy had such a dark cloud looming over it.

And now that cloud was coming for me.

I picked up my pace as I headed into the quieter residential streets. The back of my neck prickled as the memory of finding the doll floated up through my mind.

But no one said a word to me until Rafael's brisk footsteps caught up with me just as the bungalow came into sight up ahead. Like usual, he preferred not to show himself until it was inevitable.

"Everything okay?" he asked in his usual low, even tone. "You seem a little more tense than usual."

He really hadn't noticed the gross gift that'd been left for me, then—or enough about my discovery of it to realize what had happened. Wherever he'd been watching from, it mustn't have given him a view of the door. His main priority was keeping an eye on me and the area around the ice, after all.

I opened my mouth automatically, ready to tell him the whole story… and then closed it again.

Did I really want to admit that my crusade against the shithead gangsters might have come back to haunt me? That one way or another, they'd managed to get under my skin, however slightly?

After the way he'd reacted to Jasper last night, I suddenly wasn't convinced I could expect him to handle this new threat with a cool head.

What if he demanded that we leave town immediately? What if he decided this whole running away thing had been a stupid idea and dragged me home?

I knew how to fight, but I wasn't kidding myself to think that I could overpower Rafael if he got it in his head that he knew what was best for me.

"We're having a little trouble with the routine Niko's choreographing for us," I said instead. "I don't like that we're struggling."

If Rafael made any connection between our possible difficulties and his intrusion last night, he didn't show it. He just nodded.

"Go easy on yourself for once. You work your ass off constantly."

He pushed a little ahead of me to open the bungalow door and hold it open, like I really was some kind of princess.

I strode inside, resolve hardening in my chest. Whatever was going on with those dipshits, I was going to handle it. My way, on my terms.

They wanted to play games? They'd poked the wrong tiger.

And now they were about to see just how vindictive this little ice princess could get.

SIXTEEN

Luciana

THE MOMENT that my phone alarm started quietly vibrating next to my ear, my eyes snapped open and I got to work.

Earlier in the day, I'd shoved some goodies I'd bought into a black backpack. Now, I slung it over my shoulder and took one look at myself in the mirror.

With my long-sleeved black shirt and matching pants, I looked like I was about to go burglarize half the neighborhood. Not quite what I had in mind tonight, but the less I was noticed, the better.

I patted the bag, making sure that everything was there.

One, two, three bottles of engine oil.

One bag of steel wool.

One pack of 9-volt batteries.

One extra-long screwdriver.

One black ski mask.

That was all I needed to fuck up a few cars in a particularly terrifying way.

Before I'd only been trying to make the wannabe gangsters annoyed. Now I wanted them to know that if I wanted to, I could blow them to bits.

They'd threatened me. Turnabout was fair play.

That thought didn't loosen the knot in my stomach as I slunk out of the house. I shut the door with the faintest click and paused with my ears pricked.

No sound from inside. Rafael was still fast asleep.

Good.

I darted across the lawn and into the streets of Hobb Creek. Years of training let my feet fall softly on the concrete sidewalks.

But it wasn't getting caught that I was most twisted up about. It was the mission *I* was planning on carrying out.

I'd told myself I was done with the mafia princess life. I wasn't going to let myself become what Mom had tried to mold me into.

What was I going to do if this threat wasn't enough to run these assholes out of town? If they were too stubborn or too stupid to realize they were outclassed?

I didn't want to *kill* anyone. That much I was sure of. Lou, semi-professional figure skater, was not a fucking murderer. At least, not when I had a choice in the matter.

Lord, how would Niko or Jasper look at me if they had any idea what I'd already had to do under my mother's orders?

That wasn't me. I hadn't wanted to do any of it then, and I wasn't going to sink to the same depths now.

There had to be a way to get the pricks out of here without resorting to full out war, and I was smart enough to figure it out.

If I was lucky, my current gambit might even do the trick all on its own.

The whole town was silent and dark except for the pools of light cast by the periodic streetlamps. I avoided those, making a quick dash whenever I had to cross a street.

The last thing I needed was for any of the locals to notice me skulking around and think I was the real problem here. Not that it seemed like them calling the police about a suspicious character would accomplish anything, good or bad, regardless.

When I came up on the end of the last street before the sprawl of the warehouses and their parking lots, I pulled out my ski mask and tugged it over my head. Thankfully it was cool enough at night these days that the layer of cloth actually brought a welcome warmth.

I scanned the parking lot outside the gang's storage building in the hazy glow of the security lamps. The windows on the hideout were dark, but a couple of figures were standing near the main entrance, passing a cigarette or a joint back and forth while they played a grating rock song from a Bluetooth speaker propped on a window ledge.

The idiots had finally figured out a little security was in order. Well, I'd expected as much.

It made my job harder, but not impossible. Too bad for them the bozos hadn't also figured out that blasting music to keep themselves entertained also meant it'd be that much harder to hear an intruder.

I glanced up and down the cross-street to make sure no headlights were anywhere inside and then hunkered down into an army crawl position. Gritting my teeth at the discomfort of the awkward stance, I slithered across the road and over to the nearest ideal target.

A pickup truck, its hood facing away from the would-be guards. Perfect.

I fished out my screwdriver and wiggled it along the edge of the hood, feeling for the latch. The screeching music drowned out the faint scraping sounds of the tool.

There it was. Slide, click, and nudge that sucker up.

Just a few inches, since I didn't want my project to be noticeable if the guards happened to glance this way. Now, the motor oil.

I unscrewed the cap and extended my arm under the hood to slosh the viscous liquid all across the engine area.

Next I balanced one of the batteries in the perfect nook and tucked a thin but wide swath of steel wool right under it. Then I yanked the bottle of oil back and eased the hood into place.

My heart was thumping hard, but a grin stretched across my face. Perfect.

I'd learned this trick from one of the guys who worked under my mom. He'd been incredibly proud of the revenge trick he'd played on a guy who'd hit on his girlfriend, and he'd shown me all the steps, "Just in case you ever need to teach a guy a lesson yourself, little Rose."

The moment one of these goons turned the ignition, the vibration would send the battery tumbling into the steel wool for an instant spark, and the front of the car would go up in the prettiest bonfire in all of Ontario. The engine wouldn't outright explode, because this wasn't a movie, but I'd bet the dipshits would throw themselves across the parking lot in terror, afraid that it would.

And they'd be left wondering just how much worse it could get if they insisted on continuing to do "business" around here.

A few more cars were parked close enough together that I could scurry from one to another without coming into the guards' line of sight. I set up my trap another three times and then paused to scan my surroundings, the cloying smell of the motor oil itching in my nose.

My gaze snagged on a massive white shape near the far end of the lot, close to the building's loading area. My pulse skipped a beat.

A delivery truck. That would be the perfect finishing touch for my don't-fuck-with-me demonstration. I wouldn't just be freaking them out but screwing up their plans for whatever they'd meant to transport in it.

But there were a few open stretches between my current position, the two cars at that end of the parking lot, and my ultimate goal. I worried at my lower lip, debating the risk.

If the guards spotted me, I could just run for it, but they might check the vehicles and find my traps before they could go off properly.

On the other hand, I *really* wanted to go for maximum impact here. The sooner the jerks decided it wasn't worth sticking around Hobb Creek, the better.

As I considered the odds, the guards pretty much made my decision for me. One of them started tapping at his phone, trying to find whatever song he wanted to bring up next and swearing at the device, and the other guy lowered his head to peer at the screen too.

They were both distracted. How could I not take this chance?

Sucking in a breath, I dashed for the first of the two cars, keeping low to the ground and softening my footsteps as much as I could. I froze there, listening.

The idiot was still muttering curse words while the current song blared on. I'd made it.

The distance to the second car was a little longer. I didn't let myself second-guess my choices but just ran for it.

I dropped down behind the car just as the song changed.

"There!" the guy said with a sharp laugh. "Fucking piece of junk."

They fell back into their mumbled conversation. I peeked around the car and saw them vaguely eyeing the lot around them again.

Shit.

Well, I'd come this far. It was only maybe ten feet to the truck now, and this side of the lot was particularly dark.

I waited several thumps of my heart until the guards' attention appeared to be pointed away from my area, and then I threw myself into one last sprint.

As I hurtled around the side of the truck, the toe of my sneaker caught in a dip I hadn't seen in the asphalt. With a lurch of my gut, I careened forward.

Wincing preemptively, I twisted into a roll rather than catching myself on my hands and knees like I wanted to. The pavement jarred my shoulder and ribs, but continuing the momentum of the fall dulled the sound of the impact.

I pushed myself out of the roll into a crouch, every muscle tensed.

"Did you hear something rustling around?" one guard asked the other, and my body went even more rigid.

The second guy let out a huff. "Probably another fucking raccoon. Gimme the light."

The beam of a flashlight streaked across the parking lot, rippling over the truck I was hiding behind without revealing me. The guards didn't bother leaving their post.

"No one there. Like anyone would try to mess with us when we're right here."

They guffawed, and my grin came back. That's what they thought.

I went through the steps of my trick one last time, moving even more carefully than before. This time, I sprinkled the entire last bottle of motor oil across the truck's innards before setting up the steel wool and the battery.

No one was going to drive this baby very far for a good long time. Ha.

I slunk away from the truck into the scruffy stretch of woodland between this parking lot and the warehouse farther north. When I'd put enough distance between me and the guards that my nerves started to settle and the trees completely hid me from view, I headed back into town the long way around.

As I loped through the streets, my good mood faded. My first two tricks hadn't scared the assholes off. What were the chances this one would, even if I had upped the ante?

It doesn't matter, I told myself. *As long as I keep at it, eventually I'll make their lives here so miserable they'll leave.*

As long as I did it *my* way, not my mom's, I could see this through.

When the bungalow came into view up ahead, I slowed my pace, watching for any sign that Rafael was up and patrolling after noticing my disappearance. The house looked perfectly still.

I circled around back and stashed my bag with the empty motor oil bottles in the dusty tool shed it looked like no one had used in years. Then I squirmed in my shirt to turn it right-side out again, so the faded neon graphic on the chest showed.

Just a perfectly normal set of lounge clothes. Definitely not stealth gear.

I edged open the door inch by inch and crept inside. No Rafael waited for me in the living room.

I exhaled with a rush of relief. Maybe I was going to pull this whole thing off without him having the slightest clue.

Then, as I turned toward my bedroom, the same traitorous toe that'd tripped me in the parking lot bumped into a beer bottle Rafael must have set down near the door to go out for recycling.

It tipped over and hit the floor with a thunk. And there was no blaring music in the house to cover the sound.

Hell, Rafael would probably have woken up even through a blast of alternative rock.

I'd swear it took all of two seconds for his door to creak open. Knowing there was no way I could scramble into my room without him realizing I'd been up to something, I instead spun toward the kitchen, only a few steps away.

When he reached the top of the stairs, I was standing by the fridge with my hand on the door. I glanced over my shoulder at him.

"Oh, hey," I mumbled as if half asleep. "Sorry I woke you up. You've got to stick those bottles someplace else."

My bodyguard squinted through the darkness, looking like he was suppressing a yawn. "Lou? Is something wrong?"

I cocked my head in what I thought was a pretty amazing performance considering my heart was jackhammering at my ribs. "What? No, I was just grabbing a midnight snack."

He frowned. "You got hungry at two in the morning?"

I raised my hands in the air. "It's hard to get back to sleep when your stomach is grumbling away, you know. It's got to be all those calories I'm burning in practice."

Rafael studied me for a moment longer. My skin prickled under his gaze.

I was pretty sure he was suspicious, but my explanation didn't offer any holes for him to poke at. He sighed and turned back toward the stairs.

"Better eat up then. Try to do it more quietly."

"Yeah, yeah," I shot back in typical snarky fashion, and managed not to topple over in relief when he tramped down the stairs.

To completely sell the story, in case he was listening from below, I opened the fridge and grabbed the tin with the last slice of the cherry pie we'd gotten for dessert a couple of days ago. I carried it to my bedroom and set it on the dresser.

I wasn't actually hungry. My stomach had clenched tight.

Well, I could have it for breakfast without Rafael knowing the difference.

As I climbed into my bed, the clenching sensation spread through my entire abdomen.

I didn't like lying to Rafael. He'd been my partner in crime—often literally—for so long.

But he'd proven that I couldn't trust him. What he didn't know wasn't going to hurt him.

And when I got rid of that bungling gang for good, I wouldn't have to sneak around anymore anyway.

SEVENTEEN

Luciana

THE NEXT DAY, the reality of the previous night sat heavy on my shoulders. I couldn't seem to get my bearings in training.

Jasper had been short with me before we began and barely deigned to look me in the eye after my first slip-up. When I fumbled the landing of one of my double jumps, which normally would have been child's play, I thought he'd *really* freak out.

Instead, he remained silent, his eyes trained on the stands over my shoulder, deliberately not looking at me. We were back to square one, all our progress and connection dashed against the ice.

Explaining why my head was in the clouds was out of the question, so I just kept quiet and hoped I was keeping in sync. My mind kept racing back to the stunt I'd pulled at the gang hangout last night, replaying every detail.

I'd felt good about what I'd accomplished right before I fell asleep, but the second I'd woken up, the full anxiety had hit me like a freight train. Here I was, back in the place where one of those assholes had threatened me with that stupid doll.

What if they came back? What if they did something worse next time as payback?

What if one of them somehow realized who I actually was or brought in allies who would? It seemed impossible that these bozos could have any connection to my mom all the way back in Austin, but the Deadly Rose had people all over the place.

And even that tiny chance niggled at me, eating away at my focus.

Had I terrorized the gang enough for them to decide it was better just to leave town? If they didn't, how in the hell could I come down on them harder without stooping to my mother's level of violence?

Even if I was prepared to slaughter the bunch of them, it'd be quite the challenge to take them all down with only Rafael for backup. Not to mention I'd totally traumatize the entire normal population of Hobb Creek in the process.

I'd end up tainting this peaceful place even more than the wannabe gangsters already had.

I tapped my hand against my thigh, my gaze fixed on the wall without really seeing it. If I could just —

"You in there, Lou?" Niko asked, his tone gentle. "You seem a little distracted today."

I waited for Jasper to chime in with his usual sarcasm. Somehow, his silence was louder than his snarky words could have been.

"Yeah," I replied. "Yeah, I'm paying attention. Sorry, I just didn't sleep so well."

"Okay," Niko said. "Not a problem. If you need a break or anything else, you just let me know, all right?"

God, I did need a break—from the problems that'd somehow chased me all the way up here to what was meant to be my escape.

But Niko couldn't give me that. I wished I could spill at least a little of the worries dogging me with him and soak up the reassurance and affection I knew he'd offer in return, but I had the feeling that if I got at all affectionate with *him* in front of Jasper, that might sour things with the other man I'd started falling for even more than I already had.

"Definitely." I reached up to scratch between the wings tattooed on my shoulder blades. "I'm doing my best to work through it. I'll be fine."

"Maybe we should avoid any lifts practice for the time being," Jasper muttered. "It's no good for either of us if your head isn't in the game."

Even though the words weren't outright hostile—and he had a point, especially when I was the one who'd be hurt worse if I took a bad tumble—I winced inwardly.

How was he going to take me seriously ever again when I kept screwing up practice, I had a strange man living with me who acted like he was going to pummel him, and I—?

I hesitated over that thought. Maybe there was one thing I could get out in the open with both of my fellow skaters, to clear the air and lift a little of the weight off me.

Jasper hadn't wanted to talk about the altercation with Rafael, but I could force the issue. Make him see that I hadn't been betraying anyone or shacking up with a total maniac who had no reason to act protective.

"Actually," I said, pitching my voice to carry, "before we keep going, I think there's someone I should introduce the two of you to. Since he's going to be around a lot, and I don't want you to be startled if you notice him, as good as he is at keeping a low profile."

Niko gave me a quizzical look, and Jasper tensed. I glided in a semi-circle to face the stands, scanning the shadowy alcoves that I knew my bodyguard would have favored.

I'd made my first comment loud enough that I was sure Rafael would have heard it, so he'd be ready, but now I lifted my voice even more. "Hey, Rafael! Could you come out so the guys can meet you properly?"

For a second, I thought Rafael might refuse, pretend to not even be there. *Not* actually being there at all simply wasn't a possibility.

Then he peeled himself out of one patch of shadows and moved toward the aisle with his typical brawny athleticism. He strode about halfway down the stands toward us, his expression impassive as he assessed the situation.

He didn't say anything, waiting for me to take the lead. Which made sense. He didn't know where I was going with this.

As pissed off as I'd been with him, I couldn't help being a little grateful that he was playing along this far.

I swung back toward my partner and my coach. "Jasper, you two met under not the best circumstances the other night. And I figure Niko should probably hear this story too. Guys, this is Rafael. He's… basically my bodyguard."

That was straightforward enough. Why lie about the parts I didn't have to?

Jasper's gaze jerked to me. "Why would you need a bodyguard?"

He sounded wary but not incredulous. I guessed that was a decent start.

I took a deep breath. "I mean, not officially. I haven't hired him or anything." It was Mom who'd done that, and he was off her payroll now. "You've probably wondered at least a little about exactly what I'm doing all the way out in Hobb Creek."

Niko cocked his head, glancing from Rafael to me. "That question had crossed my mind," he said with a reassuring smile. So certain this couldn't be anything too crazy.

Hopefully he'd never have to find out just how messed up my circumstances were.

I lowered my gaze, scraping the blade of one of my skates against the ice. "The thing is, my home life was… not great. My family was pretty messed up—I couldn't count on any of them—and it got to the point where I didn't even feel safe staying in the house. So I took off. Rafael's been a friend of the family for years. He's looked out for me since I was a kid. He realized what I was planning and insisted on helping me get out."

To my relief, understanding dawned on Jasper's face as he studied the larger man staring down at us. I could practically see him reevaluating their previous altercation in light of this new information.

"He's been kind of watching over me while I get settled into my new life," I added. "So he'll be around a lot of the time. But he knows that he doesn't have to worry about you two."

I said the last bit with particular emphasis for Rafael's benefit.

Jasper's eyebrows arched. "You left behind *your* life just to chase this punk across the continent and keep her out of trouble?" he asked Rafael with a small but audible teasing note in his voice.

Rafael's mouth curved into an equally small smile. His deep baritone echoed across the rink. "Since she is quite the punk, she needed it. I wasn't happy with my situation back in the city either. It was a good excuse to set down roots somewhere else."

Niko beamed at him, taking all the new information in stride—and trusting that I was telling him the truth. "That makes sense. I'm just glad that Lou has had someone looking out for her. Anyone she considers a friend is good with me."

His gaze slid to me again. "Are you okay now—with the home situation, and everything?"

I nodded, my stomach tightening. Technically, that was the biggest lie I'd just told, without speaking a single word.

Jasper rubbed the back of his neck like he often did when he was feeling awkward. "I guess I can see why you came on so strong the other night, considering how it must have looked when you came into the room."

Rafael tipped his head to the other guy in a mildly friendly gesture. "I'm sorry for the misunderstanding. I'm used to people playing not so nice back where we're from. Instincts honed by years of experience. But I was out of line."

Jasper's eyes widened. "Hey, don't worry about it now. No harm done in the end."

To my surprise, my normally taciturn bodyguard kept going. "Really, I don't see any reason for concern. You two have been good to Lou since we got here. I don't think I've ever seen her as happy as she is when she's skating with you. Thank you for that."

Niko chuckled. "She makes us pretty happy too, so it works out well for all of us. Right, Jasper?"

My skating partner cleared his throat. "Right."

A funny wobble passed through my stomach as I smiled up at Rafael. The fondness in his voice had been unmistakable.

It'd sounded like… like it really mattered to him that I *was* happy.

I guessed that shouldn't have been a surprise, but somehow, even now, it was hard to tell how much he actually cared and how much he was just fulfilling a duty he believed was owed.

Niko rubbed his hands together and motioned to Rafael with a playful gesture. "I don't suppose you're planning on getting into skating too? Do we have another prodigy on our hands?"

Rafael let out a snort. "No, my only interest in skating is seeing that Lou gets to keep doing it. It's not like there are a whole lot of guys who look like me getting out on the ice anyway."

I bit back a grimace. There weren't a whole lot of women figure skaters who shared my looks either.

My coach's expression turned more serious. "I suppose that's true. The average complexion does tend to be pretty… pale." He glanced at Jasper. "There is that medalist from Germany who was competing until a couple of years back… Colin! And I've crossed paths with a couple of others."

His attention slid back to Rafael, his tone lightening again. "I'm sure we could make room for you if you ever discovered a secret love for the ice."

A little amusement colored my bodyguard's voice. "I don't think there's much chance of that. I'll stick to watching the three of you defy gravity."

He gave me a short nod and loped back up to the alcove, where he melded back into the shadows. I turned to the rink, my spirits a little more at ease with that one secret off my chest.

Even though my biggest problem was still hanging over me, with my renewed sense of purpose, I managed to ignore worries about the gang well enough to get through the rest of practice without a hitch. Jasper and I flowed through the moves in sync and even landed all three of the lifts in the routine Niko had choreographed with only a little wobble on one.

When it was finally time to head out, I felt much better than I had coming in. I said my goodbyes to the guys, had a quick shower and change, and set off through the late afternoon sunlight across town.

The fresh breeze filled my lungs with crisp early autumn scents. How was it a single conversation could make the whole world seem brighter?

A few of the locals I passed shot me—and my bulging equipment bag—odd looks. I found myself remembering the middle-aged woman who'd badgered me at the grocery store a few days ago about what I was doing in their town.

But while that hadn't been a fun encounter, it wasn't the norm either. At least twice as many of the faces I passed offered friendly smiles.

One older man wiping down his store window even called out, "Good practice, I hope, Miss Lou?"

"Always is," I replied cheerfully.

I walked right down the main street because I'd already been planning on making a quick stop on my way home. The doctor's office was open for ten more minutes when I reached the front door.

I went past the now-empty chairs toward the reception desk. To my surprise, Dr. Ribeiro, the woman I'd seen at the café a few times now, was standing behind it. Her receptionist must have already gone home.

"Oh!" she said when she saw me, and motioned me the rest of the way over. "You're our new skater in town. I've already heard all about you. Small town gossip, you know."

She gave a soft laugh that had the same inflection as her mild accent. Portuguese, I was going to guess based on the little Brazilian flag tacked to her bulletin board alongside various informational papers.

"I guess you probably were the subject of a lot of that when you first moved in too, huh?" I had to say.

Dr. Ribeiro laughed again. "Some, I'm sure. Most are too polite to gossip about me to my own face. But the doctor who was just retiring when I showed up was a curmudgeon, from what they gossiped to me about *him*, so people were happy to have a new face around pretty quickly. What can I do for you?"

I could see how Hobb Creek's citizens would have warmed up to her in a flash with her easygoing, welcoming attitude.

I flicked my hand toward my body. "Because of all the bumps and tumbles I take in a typical day, I figured it'd be good to schedule regular checkups. And I haven't had a proper physical in ages."

Back home, I'd never seen a regular doctor. Mom had always had a guy with medical training in the crew, and he'd looked after any pressing health issues.

"I can write you in. I believe we have some openings next week. What time works for you?"

I ended up with a mid-morning appointment the following Thursday and headed out with a spring in my step with another mission accomplished.

Dr. Ribeiro's voice followed me out the door. "And if you ever need a hand getting your footing here in town, don't hesitate to get in touch."

This had to be small-town life at its best. Friendly neighbors, simple schedules—everything perfectly *normal.*

My satisfaction with how the day had turned out after all buoyed me the rest of the way back to the bungalow. I walked straight to my bedroom to set down my equipment bag—and stalled two steps inside.

The evening breeze was wafting in with even greater force than usual, through a neat rectangular hole that'd been cut into the window screen.

And on the floor beneath my bedroom window, like someone had pushed it in through that hole, lay the limp carcass of a dead, blood-smeared squirrel.

EIGHTEEN

Luciana

I WAS STARTING to get used to seeing Hobb Creek at three in the morning, but that didn't mean that I had to like it. All I wanted in life was a little peace, and I was *going* to get it.

If that meant I had to crouch on the roof of a building three stories high down the street from the gang's shitty hideout, then so be it.

I sighed and adjusted the binoculars I'd purchased specifically because they were supposed to be enhanced for dark conditions. Finally, when I'd gotten the settings just right, the shapes around the storage building came into focus.

A few lights were on in the building. I noticed that the gang members had taken to parking their cars close to the entrance, where they could be more easily monitored, rather than scattered across the lot.

I smirked. That showed that they were at least a little bit scared of me.

They thought torturing forest animals was going to make *me* run scared? They had no idea who they were dealing with. I could do worse, much worse, if I wanted to.

They were lucky I didn't.

Mass murder was still off the table, even if that was what Mom would have said they deserved. There had to be another way I could make life so difficult for them that they'd move somewhere else.

Somewhere with a competent police force, somewhere that would eat small, poorly run gangs like theirs alive. I wouldn't have to bloody my hands, and Hobb Creek would finally be free.

Headlights appeared from the far end of the road. I ducked beneath the low wall that ran around the edge of the flat-roofed building to keep out of sight and peeked cautiously over the edge.

The lights were attached to a delivery truck similar to the one I'd tampered with a few nights ago. That one was still sitting hood-up right where I left it, but this new vehicle seemed to be in fine working order.

At least, for now.

When the truck stopped in front of the building, the garage-style door to the shipping area whirred upward. A few scruffy young men emerged from inside and heaved open the back of the truck.

One of them hopped up inside and began to hand boxes down to the others, who hauled the cargo into the shadows inside. I couldn't make out any details on the sides that revealed what the boxes might contain.

I'd messed with the goons' vehicles. Maybe next time I'd need to target their merch.

If I could figure out a way to get to it without getting myself caught in the process.

I lowered the binoculars with a frown, debating my next steps. Then a hand dropped onto my shoulder so unexpectedly that a squeak burst from my lips as I jerked away.

As I spun around in a defensive stance, I found Rafael glowering at me, his arms crossed over his chest.

"What are you doing out here?" he demanded, pitching his voice low.

Shit. I could have sworn he'd been fast asleep when I'd snuck out. How had he found me?

I knew better than to ask. He wouldn't want to give away his secrets and make it easier for me to sneak off on him again.

Instead, I glowered right back at him, rubbing the rings I'd been tempted to drive into his face before I'd seen who he was. My voice came out hushed but harsh with irritation.

"What the fuck are *you* doing, other than trying to give me a heart attack? You're lucky I didn't brain you with the binoculars. If I'd wanted you to come along, I'd have invited you."

"You'd have to try awfully hard to get in a decent blow with those things," Rafael said without a hint of concern or amusement. "And in case you've forgotten, my *job* is being wherever you are, making sure you don't get yourself into even more trouble than necessary."

"And here I thought I got to make the decisions about what's necessary in my own life, not you."

Rafael's jaw tightened. "You know what I mean. Why the hell are you taking off on your own in the middle of the night—without even telling me?"

"Why should I have to tell you?" I retorted, my temper rising at his insistent tone. "I'm the most dangerous thing in this town other than you. If I want to go out for a late-night stroll *on my own*, you have nothing to worry about."

Rafael snorted. "You're obviously not out here just to stroll."

"How's it your business either way? Is it so horrible that I want to do one or two things without you hovering over me?"

His voice took on a growling note. "It is when those things involve messing with a gang of idiots you can't be sure won't shoot you by accident if not purposefully."

I rolled my eyes. "I've dealt with plenty of men with guns before."

"But you don't need to be dealing with these ones. Come on, let's go home. You need to get some sleep."

He turned toward the ladder that had given us access to the roof, like he assumed I'd just go along with him.

My pent-up frustration boiled over. I planted my feet firmly on the concrete surface. "Don't tell me what I need to be doing, Rafael."

My bodyguard's head jerked around, his eyes flaring for just an instant before settling into a darker smolder. "*Someone* needs to tell you, because you're not doing the best job of taking care of yourself."

My teeth set on edge. "You're not my mother, thank the Lord, so you sure as hell don't need to start acting like you are."

Rafael grimaced. "That's not—just tell me what you're up to. What's so important about these pricks that now you're spying on them at three in the morning?"

I balked automatically at admitting the full truth. Imagine how much more overprotective the man in front of me would get if he found out how the gangsters had started harassing me directly.

"All you need to know is that it's important to me," I said. "And I've been handling it just fine on my own, or it wouldn't have taken you this long to notice."

Rafael's eyes narrowed. "This long? What *else* have you been up to that you haven't told me about?"

Okay, I probably shouldn't have said that part.

I set my hands on my hips. "It doesn't matter. They're my problems, not yours, so I'm handling them—my way."

Something in Rafael's expression deflated. Worry replaced the frustration in his eyes.

"What problems? Lou, if something else has happened—you know why I came here with you. We can do things your way, but I've got to have some idea what's going on if I'm going to have your back."

"Is that really it?" I couldn't stop myself from asking. "You want to have my back—or you want to decide that where I go and what I do meet your standards?"

Rafael was silent for a long moment. He shifted his weight as if he'd considered stepping closer to me and then decided against it.

"I'm sorry," he said finally, his voice gone a little rough. "I've obviously made you feel like you can't trust me to not just protect you but respect you as well. I know you're not a kid anymore—I know how well you can look after yourself. I realize I was out of line with Jasper the other night, and if I've been crossing the line in other ways, I'm sorry for that too."

My own temper simmered down. "Are you sure you mean that and you're not just saying it because you think it's what I want to hear? Because it sounded like you didn't actually think you should have to apologize right after it happened."

Rafael ducked his head. "Maybe I was still kind of pissed at the time. But I can admit I was wrong. Lou… I just hope you can understand that even if I don't plan on changing our relationship, I do care about you. A lot. I want to see you reach for those dreams of yours—I want to help you get there."

All the rest of my rancor seeped out of me. My arms sagged at my sides.

This was the man who'd been by my side for almost a decade. The one who'd heard all my rants and excitements over the years.

The one who'd thrown away his career in an instant to make sure I had the chance to pursue my own.

"Okay," I said quietly. "I guess it's just hard to accept the whole protect-Lou attitude when everything else about my situation is different. But—I mean, I do appreciate everything you've done for me."

Rafael lifted his eyebrows. "Does that mean you're going to tell me about the problems that brought you out to a rooftop in the middle of the night?"

I blew out a breath, my stomach twisting. But the truth was, I wouldn't mind a little guidance, if Rafael was committed to letting me figure out my own path in the end.

"A few practices ago, I found a doll hanging from the door to the rink—done up to look like me, and tied like it'd been hung from a noose."

Rafael's eyes flashed. "And you didn't tell me?"

"It was right after you freaked out about Jasper! I had no idea how you'd react, and I didn't want to get into another argument about whether I was actually safe at the arena."

His mouth settled into a grim line. "What else?"

Now that I'd come this far, I might as well admit the rest. "This evening when I got home, I found a dead squirrel on the floor in my bedroom. Someone had cut open the screen and shoved it in."

"What?" Rafael sucked a breath through his teeth. All I could think looking at him was that it was a good thing for the culprit that Rafael hadn't caught them, or they'd have been lucky if their next of kin could identify their body when he was through.

"Stupid, gross pranks," I said. "It's obviously the guys from the gang harassing me."

"Have you done anything else to provoke them?"

I grimaced. "After the doll thing, I pulled that trick Frasco taught me with the steel wool in a few of their car engines. No one saw me, but they'd have been pretty pissed after the engines went up in flames. I was hoping it'd finally scare them off, but obviously not."

"Hard to scare pendejos who're too stupid to realize they're outmatched," Rafael muttered.

I glanced back toward the storage building, knitting my brow. "I don't totally get why they're sticking to little tricks instead of blustering right at me. That seems more their style. I have been careful—maybe they don't actually know it's me, and they're just intimidating a bunch of people in town to see how we react?"

"Could be." Rafael rubbed his chin in thought. "All it'd take is one really unhinged prick in the bunch. Or maybe it's got nothing to do with the stunts you've been pulling on their territory, and they're just hostile to any newcomer in town."

"Jasper and Niko didn't mention anything like that."

"They're famous. Bigger consequences. And you're a woman and, well, you stick out a little compared to the typical Hobb Creek inhabitant."

I tugged at a strand of my dark hair, knowing what he meant. Other than Dr. Ribeiro, I was the only Latina I'd seen in town.

All the wannabe gangsters were pale as anything, so that could totally be a factor.

I sucked my lower lip under my teeth. "Well, it doesn't really matter why they're doing it. I'm going to run them out of town either way, prove I'm no one they should have been messing with. And without stooping to the kind of brutality my mother would have expected me to."

Rafael gave me a long, pensive look before beckoning me toward the ladder. This time I came.

"I'm not sure if that'll be possible," he said. "Guys like this..."

"It *has* to be," I insisted. "Maybe we have to get more creative, maybe we've got to find the right pressure point—but I'm not going on a killing spree. I'm not a mafia princess anymore. I never wanted to be in the first place. I'm leaving all that *behind.*"

Rafael rested his hand on my shoulder, warmth washing through my body from his touch.

"Lo sé, Lou. I know you're not that kind of woman. We'll figure it out."

I clambered down the ladder after him, wishing I could believe he knew that for sure.

NINETEEN

Luciana

"FORGET THE DINNER," Jasper said with a satisfied groan that did funny things to my internal temperature. "I'd eat here every night just for dessert."

As he popped the last bite of his maple peach crumble into his mouth, Niko waggled his fork at the other guy from across the restaurant table. "You want maple on everything. I'm lucky you didn't pull out that bottle you carry around and cover the whole plate with extra."

Jasper shot him a baleful look. "Do you know how hard it was to track down anything with real maple syrup where my family was living in the US? I've got to make the most of it while I'm here."

Niko chuckled. "I suppose it's a good thing you're indulging at dinner rather than breakfast, or you'd be lumbering around the skating rink tomorrow with all that in your belly."

A different sort of twinge passed through my body, and the bite of apple pie I was chewing soured in my mouth.

We hadn't exactly been lumbering today, but Jasper and I still hadn't quite found our rhythm. How were we going to impress an audience and a bunch of judges if we couldn't even pull the routine off smoothly in practice?

I had the niggling worry that we were going to make total fools of ourselves. And whose fault was that more likely to be—the renowned professional skater's or mine?

Jasper hadn't commented on our difficulties, but he was clearly still in a prickly mood, even after I'd cleared the air about Rafael.

"I have amazing digestion," he informed Niko, continuing to glower at him, and then pushed back his chair. "Syrup does make a bit of a mess, though. I'd better wash my hands before I hand over my card."

"You do that," Niko said cheerfully. But the moment the other guy had disappeared into the restroom, he pulled out his own wallet. He set down enough money to cover all three of our bills and a generous tip.

I nudged my plate aside. "You don't need to cover me, Niko. I've got plenty of cash."

"It's my treat today. You can give me the gift of accepting it without arguing."

He winked at me and brushed his fingers back through his smooth hair, where the pink strip I could tell he'd freshly touched up seemed to wink too.

I grumbled under my breath but resisted protesting further as he motioned for me to get up. I did have a good nest egg squirreled away, but it wasn't infinite. And skating necessities added up quickly.

As we headed over to the door of the cozy restaurant to wait for Jasper there, Niko rested his hand on the small of my back in a familiar, warm gesture that made my heart skip a beat. I still wasn't used to having a guy act so sweet with me.

It hadn't ever occurred to me that I'd *want* sweet, but now that I had it, I could admit it was pretty addictive. At least in the gorgeous form of Niko Okabe.

By the door, he turned to me and lowered his voice. "I wanted to ask you about what you told us the other day—about your family. You don't need to give me any details, but are you sure you're safe now? Is there anything I can do that would help?"

My heart swelled with more emotion—gratitude and affection mixed with a little pang of pain that I couldn't be as open with him as he'd been with me. "Everything's good now. You don't need to worry. I just had to get away—there's no reason anyone would come looking for me here."

At least, I sure as hell hoped that was true.

"I'm glad to hear that. It was obviously the right thing for you, seeing how you've bloomed on the rink without anyone downplaying your talent." His dark eyes twinkled. "And maybe I'm a little selfish, to be thankful that leaving them behind meant you ended up where I am."

He teased his fingers along my jaw to tilt my head up and claimed a quick but tender kiss. A giddy shiver ran through my chest as I kissed him back.

Niko's arm tightened around me just for a moment, and I could feel him force himself to ease away. He laughed lightly and gave my temple a peck too.

"But as much as I enjoy your company, I don't want to distract you from what's most important." He glanced across the restaurant to where Jasper was just emerging from the restroom. "I feel that right now it's your skating partner you should be focused on."

"Yeah," I said with a lopsided smile. "I'm still working on that whole partner thing."

"You paid?" Jasper demanded, striding over to us with a frown at Niko.

Niko held up his hands. "What is it you say—guilty as charged?"

Jasper let out a huff but seemed to already realize he wasn't going to get very far trying to change Niko's mind.

After we'd stepped out onto the sidewalk, Niko offered us a cheerful wave, turning toward his apartment, which lay in the opposite direction from where both Jasper and I would be heading. "Well, I'm off. Good work, you two. We'll keep at it tomorrow."

I waved back and glanced at Jasper, catching a flicker of a deeper frown that crossed his face as he watched Niko vanish around the corner.

Was he beating himself up about how our training was going, just like I was? Fretting that we were disappointing our coach, who'd come so far specifically to drag him out of his slump?

Maybe Niko had made a good point just now. We could stand to focus more on each other—possibly without anyone at all looking on.

I wet my lips, a little nervous about Jasper's possible response. "Hey, do you want to head back to the arena for a bit right now? We could get in a little extra practice off the ice—see if we can at least nail the position for that one lift. Niko left the storage room set up with the foam padding."

Jasper looked at me, shoving his hands in his pockets. I got the impression he was evaluating me, and with a certain amount of wariness. "You want to go back?"

I offered a cautious grin. "What better things do I have to do? Maybe we'll surprise Niko tomorrow with our newly perfect form."

My partner wavered for a few seconds longer and then tipped his head, although I still got a reluctant vibe from him. "Fine. Couldn't hurt."

Gosh, what an enthusiastic endorsement. I restrained myself from rolling my eyes, which definitely wouldn't help smooth things over.

We walked back to the arena, the awkward silence making me twice as glad for Hobb Creek's small size. It was only five minutes before we reached the darkened doors—but Jasper had his own key.

No breaking and entering necessary!

I refrained from making that comment out loud and glanced behind me while he unlocked the door. Rafael would be shadowing me from somewhere nearby.

Slipping one hand behind my back, I made a quick gesture with a flick of my fingers, giving him the signal that I needed some privacy.

He'd do a quick sweep of the arena just to be sure no dangers were lurking, and then he'd hang back near the reception area rather than keeping me in view. That way I really could focus completely on Jasper without worrying another tumble—of whatever kind—might bring out Rafael's protective impulses again.

My partner and I tramped over to the storage room Niko had converted for our off-ice training. The foam rectangles still littered the floor.

I brushed my hands down my tartan pants and decided they and the long-sleeved band tee I had on would work just fine for a brief stint of training. I'd already dropped my sweaty athletic clothes back at the bungalow, if I'd even have wanted to get back into them.

"So," Jasper said with a hint of doubt in his expression as he looked around the room. "You wanted to practice that last lift."

I squared my shoulders. "Yeah. It seems like the one we're having the most trouble getting in sync for."

He nodded, not disputing my assessment, and motioned me over to him. His expression stayed grim, all business, but I thought I caught a flicker of heat in his gray-green eyes when he lowered one hand to settle on my hip.

An answering heat coursed through me, having his brawny frame so close. I could smell his woodsy, musky scent, even more delicious than the dinner I'd just eaten.

"Ready?" he asked, with the slightest husky note in his voice.

I lifted my hands into the best starting position. On cue, Jasper grasped my fingers and hefted me up and over his broad shoulders.

I arched in his hold, noting every place my weight needed to balance, tightening my muscles to make the position as easy as possible for him. Getting into the pose from standing rather than skating into each other wasn't the same—no momentum, no flow of movement. When he set me down again, without the benefit of a glide to carry us through the motion, his hand slipped against my leg and I teetered too far to the left.

"Whoa!" Jasper caught me around my back before I hit the pads and helped me straighten up. He grimaced. "Sorry."

I waved off his apology, hoping my cheeks hadn't flushed too much from the momentary embrace. "It's a little different from what we're used to. At least we were steady while I was up in the air."

"While I was standing still," Jasper muttered.

I managed to laugh. "We'll work on that too."

As we went through the motions of several more standing lifts, I felt the tension radiating off Jasper gradually loosen. When I suggested that we'd proven ourselves enough that he should try carrying me around the room in the pose, he even let out a laugh of his own, if a short one.

"Sure, Punk. If you trust me to swing you around on the ice, I guess this is actually safer."

I prodded him in the bicep. "You can carry me anywhere you like."

I'd spoken without thinking, tossing out the generic flirting remark, but the definite flash of interest in Jasper's gaze got me heated up all over again. As he stepped up to me, my pussy clenched.

Down, girl. This is work time, not play time.

Some part of me didn't see why it couldn't be both, though.

Jasper's solid hands gripped me firmly and hoisted me into the air with new confidence. I caught a wobble before it became a problem and lifted my arm and upper leg into the right configuration.

He stepped forward tentatively and then with a little more speed, rotating in a circuit of the room similar to the loop he'd skate on the rink. He'd almost made it all the way around when his body swayed a little to the right, and I started to slide in his hold.

"Shit!" he mumbled as he tried to steady both of us, but gravity took over. In his hasty attempt to catch me, he ended up tripping over one of the pads.

We both fell in their midst, me landing partly on top of Jasper with an *oomph* of breath from his lungs.

Jasper tipped his head back against the foam chunks. "Great. So we can handle lifts as long as we're staying perfectly still. That'll work out well."

I snorted. "It was only our first attempt. And walking is pretty different from skating."

I eased myself a little upward, and the feel of my body shifting against his muscular frame sent a spike of arousal shooting through me.

Jasper's gaze jerked to mine, his face flushing as if he'd felt it too, and suddenly I couldn't help saying, "Maybe we should take a little break to make sure we're at our best."

Jasper studied me with an inscrutable expression. "A break, huh? Trying to get out of the hard parts?"

But there was no animosity in his tone, and he didn't make the slightest move to nudge me off him.

Taking a gamble, I sat up over him and pressed my hands against his sculpted chest as if to pin him down. I gazed down at him through my eyelashes, tamping down the rush of need rising up from between my legs.

"We had fun the other night, didn't we? It seemed like we were getting in sync in other ways. You know the whole thing with Rafael was a misunderstanding. Is there some other reason you've been keeping your distance?"

Jasper's voice turned rough. "Lou, I— I figured maybe it would be better to keep things professional after all."

I cocked my head. "Because that's what you want or that's what you think you're supposed to do? We don't *have* to go there again. But I'm totally on board, and I don't think it'll be a problem professionally either."

His eyes smoldered as he took me in. I'd swear I could feel his skin growing hotter through his shirt.

But he still hesitated. "The thing is… it already has gotten kind of messy even though we decided we'd avoid that. I'm not really the type to go for a quick lay and then forget about it. I don't want to just screw around like it doesn't mean anything."

I blinked at him with a flutter in my chest. This wasn't where I'd expected this conversation to go.

"Is that your way of saying it *would* mean something to you?"

His gaze darted away from me for a second as if he were embarrassed. "Maybe I wasn't the friendliest ever when we met—"

I couldn't hold back a guffaw at that understatement.

Jasper made a face at me before continuing. "I wasn't sure what to make of you. But you're obviously… a lot of things that I really respect. And admire. Along with being one of the hottest women I've ever seen." His smile turned a bit sly despite his awkwardness.

My throat constricted for a moment before I managed to speak. "Oh. I didn't—I guess I've been around too many guys who only think with their dicks. I wasn't going to push for anything like a commitment, especially when I've been seeing Niko too. But that doesn't mean— It'd be more than just screwing around to me too. Even when you're being a jerk, you're really something, you know."

"Something?" he repeated, definitely teasing now.

I mock-glared at him. "Incredibly frustrating. But also passionate and determined and with that artistic mind I wish I could even halfway match."

Jasper raised his hand to trail his fingers down my arm, sparking giddy quivers even through the layer of thin cotton. "So what are *you* saying?"

I leaned forward until my face was just a few inches from his. "I'm saying somehow I've ended up caring quite a bit about both Niko and you, Mr. Not-the-Friendliest. And who knows? Maybe we'll be better partners on the ice if we embrace all the other ways we'd like to, ah, 'work together' instead of fighting our feelings."

"Well, when you put it like that…" Jasper pushed himself up those last few inches to press his mouth against mine.

Oh, he tasted delicious too—like the sweet maple and tart peaches from his dessert. I kissed him back hard, running my hands down his chest to the hem of his shirt and reveling in the groan that reverberated over his lips.

I didn't have any patience left in me after going unsatisfied the other night at my house, and the same sense of urgency seemed to have gripped Jasper. He claimed my mouth again and again with a swipe of his tongue between my lips. We devoured each other as if we'd been starving for this.

He sat all the way up, sliding his arms around me to pull me even closer, and I gasped when my pussy collided with the bulge behind his track pants. Jasper groaned at the contact. He ran his fingers up and down my thighs before massaging my ass in a way that just begged for me to grind against him.

As I whimpered with need, I edged my hands up under his shirt over the jackpot that was all his heated, muscled torso. I felt like I'd won another reward with his eager hitch of breath when I gently raked my nails over his washboard abs.

Jasper tangled his fingers in my hair, heedless of my loosening ponytail, and kissed me so deeply stars spun behind my eyes. Then he pulled back just enough to chart a scorching trail along my jaw to nip my earlobe.

"Fuck, I want you so bad," he growled. "I've wanted this since the first moment I saw you on the ice."

My own longing flared hotter at his declaration. Who would have thought—behind all the grumbling and glowering, Jasper St. Pierre had been hungry for me all along.

I rewarded him for the confession by swiveling my hips against his even more enthusiastically. The press of his groin had us both gasping in unison, pleasure flooding my core.

Jasper yanked my tee right off me, and I reached for the waistband of his pants. When my fingers grazed the bulge of his erection, he arched toward me with a hiss.

"God, Lou."

Our mouths collided again. I stroked his rigid cock through the fabric of his pants until he let out a desperate sound and practically tore them off with my help.

As he yanked off my bra, I tucked my hand right into his boxers. He groaned at the squeeze of my fingers and then bowed his head to suck the peak of my breast into his mouth.

Bliss raced through my chest. I groped at the waves of his auburn hair and rocked against him with my own growing desperation.

"Fuck, that's good."

Jasper hummed against my nipple, drawing it to an even sharper peak. One of his hands slipped between us.

When his thumb flicked across my clit, I bucked into his touch, seeking more. *Needing* more.

At my encouraging moan, Jasper stroked my entire pussy through my pants. Then he shoved his hand under to finger me skin to skin.

His breath came out shaky. "You're so fucking wet, Lou."

"Your fucking fault," I replied with a stuttered laugh, and tipped my head back with another moan.

Intent on paying him back in kind, I gripped his cock and ran my thumb over the head already slick with pre-cum. Jasper only allowed me a few pumps before he captured my attention by slipping one finger inside me.

My grasp wavered as my concentration did too. His movements were slow and deliberate, and he watched every reaction with growing satisfaction.

His cock twitched in my hand as I breathed out his name. With a ferocity that would have soaked my panties if I'd still had them on, he dragged the rest of my clothes off me and threw them aside.

"Condom," I mumbled, snatching at my purse. I dug out one of the few I kept in there for just in case—thank you, Past Lou!

Jasper kicked off his boxers and tore open the foil packet without a second's hesitation. As he rolled the contents over his shaft, which was as impressively built as the rest of him, I took a moment to admire the view.

All those chiseled muscles on display, honed by years of pushing himself to the limit on the ice. Broader and bulkier than Niko's lean form, but equally delectable.

A girl could appreciate a little variety.

He tipped me back on the pads with another kiss, both determined and lingering. I'd almost melted beneath him when he lined himself up.

I was so slick and ready that he plunged all the way in one go, the heady friction making my head spin. He pulled back and then thrust even deeper, propelling a moan from my lungs.

I closed my eyes, unable to process anything else other than the sensation of him taking me, filling me, stroking me from the inside out. He kissed my lips and my neck almost savagely while running his fingers over my hair with clashing tenderness. My heart swelled at the impression that I was being both claimed and cherished.

Every guy I'd been with back in Austin, every hasty hookup, had felt like something only about bodily urges. Scratching an itch, relieving tension, nothing all that personal beyond finding the guy hot enough and unobjectionable enough that I didn't mind the momentary physical vulnerability.

With both Niko and Jasper, the experience was totally different. The act reached beyond our physical collision and tugged at my heart.

I didn't think I could give this kind of intimacy up. I *had* to be the woman they saw me as; I had to keep all the darkness of my past as far away from them as possible.

With a surge of deeper desire, I lifted my legs to urge Jasper closer, and he followed me without breaking his rhythm. His cock hit the spot inside that made my whole torso pulse with pleasure, and I caught his mouth in another wild kiss.

My breath had broken into pants. I arched to meet him, welcoming him in every way I could, soaring on the pleasure rushing through my body.

He thrust harder, faster, our skin sliding together with the sheen of sweat that'd broken over it. He squeezed my ass, driving all the way to the hilt at just the right angle, and I blazed over the finish line with an explosion of sparks behind my eyes.

As I clenched around him, shuddering with my ecstatic release, Jasper's hands wrapped around my leg. He hoisted it up almost as if this were a new pairs lift, pounding into me.

I dug my fingernails into his bare back, and he slammed into me with a groan that told me he'd reached his own climax.

We stayed melded together like that for a long moment, coming down from the high. I smiled a little deliriously, my happiness only heightened by Jasper's returning grin and the playful kiss he pressed to the corner of my jaw.

"I don't know about you, but I think that's all the practice I can handle for today," he said lightly as he pulled back to clean up. "You've worn me out, Punk."

I laughed and tapped his side with my foot. "Maybe we should add this to our workout regimen."

The gleam in Jasper's eyes suggested he didn't totally object to the idea. He stole one more kiss, and we scrambled back into our clothes.

As Jasper turned toward the door, though, a pensive shadow crossed his face. His stance was so much more relaxed than when we'd come in, but I couldn't shake the sense that something was still bothering him.

I bumped my shoulder against his arm on the way out. "We got in some good work on the lift too. I bet we'll nail it tomorrow."

"We should definitely be closer," Jasper said easily enough, but his expression didn't totally lighten.

However much I'd gotten through to him, he was still keeping me at a distance. But I didn't know what to do about that other than wait and see if he'd eventually let me all the way in.

And maybe he was right not to, considering how many secrets I was keeping from *him*.

TWENTY

Luciana

I'D BECOME QUITE the regular at the Blueberry Café.

Not only did they have fantastically authentic pierogies, the coffee was ten times better than what I could make with the cheap machine that'd come with the bungalow. The place had become my comfort spot and a regular stop before practice. Sometimes after too.

And on Sundays, I could hang out at my leisure. I'd dropped in today earlier than usual to dig into a stack of the café's trademark blueberry pancakes, drenched in so much maple syrup that I probably should have invited Jasper along too.

Scratch that. He'd have tried to eat my pancakes.

It seemed that some of the locals had noticed my regular appearances there. As I polished off the last pancake, an elderly woman I'd seen in the place a few times before shuffled over to my table. She clutched her purse in her wrinkled hands like it weighed a hundred pounds.

When I looked up, she aimed a bright smile at me, her mouse-like eyes crinkling. "You're our newest resident, aren't you? How are you liking our town, hon?"

I had to smile back. "Loving it. It's a wonderful little place."

"Oh, that's lovely to hear." The old woman's expression got even sunnier. "We don't get many young folks moving into Hobb Creek—mostly they're off searching for their big adventures. Do you expect to stay very long?"

I caught a prying vibe in her comments but simply ignored it. I didn't mind small-town nosiness as long as people weren't pushy about it.

"I'll have to see, but right now I feel like I'd be happy staying here forever," I told her.

"Oh, perfect, perfect. You aren't at all concerned, a young lady living on your own?"

Rafael had done such a good job of keeping a low profile she obviously hadn't even noticed his presence.

My lips twitched with amusement at the thought of Hobb Creek being any kind of a danger to young ladies. "Yes, I like it that way."

"Well, that's good to hear. If you need anything, you ask around for Laurel, and I'll see what I can do."

"Thank you, Laurel," I said, restraining a laugh. She might have been both nosy and a little clueless, but she obviously meant well.

This was what a home was supposed to feel like: acceptance and support. Two things I'd never felt even within my own house back in Austin.

As my new friend ambled off, I paid my bill and headed out into the crisp but warm early autumn sunlight. I'd parked the Grand Marquis down the street so that I could swing by the grocery store and carry my haul back to the bungalow without straining my already sore arms.

My glow of happiness faded the second I set eyes on the car. It was parked exactly *where* I'd left it, but not *how* I'd left it.

Something was lying at the base of the windshield. Something that'd left ruddy smears on the glass.

With a hitch of my pulse, I hustled over and then stopped when I made out what the things were.

Three dead pigeons lay on the hood of the car, their feathered bodies limp. Well, *most* of them was lying there.

Their heads had been cut right off.

Nausea surged up from my stomach. I clamped my mouth shut against it and the string of curses I wanted to let out.

What the fuck did those assholes in the gang think they were playing at now?

With brisk steps, my heart thumping hard and fast, I yanked open the trunk, grabbed a plastic bag that'd been abandoned there, and used it to scoop the dead birds off the car. With a silent apology to the garbage man, I chucked the bag in the nearest public trash can.

The feathered corpses hadn't been lying there long. A few squirts of the wiper fluid were enough to rinse off the blood. But I sat there in the driver's seat for a few minutes after that, my thoughts and my stomach churning.

This latest threat wasn't aimed just at me. There'd been *three* birds.

They were telling me that they figured Jasper and Niko would be dead meat too.

My teeth set on edge. Those fuckers couldn't get away with menacing my men as well as me.

I didn't know what I was going to do, but I had to do something. Now.

They'd been bold enough to leave their sick little gift in broad daylight. Well, I could be plenty bold too.

I yanked the ski mask I'd used on past expeditions out of the glove compartment and shoved it into the back pocket of my jeans. Then I pushed myself out of the car.

Groceries could wait.

I stalked through the streets, my hands curled into fists, possible plans unfurling in my mind. I didn't have to worry about Rafael interrupting my retaliation, because for once he'd decided I would be safe enough simply going to the café and the grocery store and agreed to take a break from bodyguard duties, but that also meant I was on my own again.

When I reached the last few houses before the edge of town, I veered into the shadows. From there, I studied the parking lot and storage building across the street.

Two men were standing out front drinking beers near the garage-style door. In the several minutes I took stock, no one came in or out of the main door.

And there was another entrance around back. I'd seen it when scoping out the place in the past. I could make it over there without the goons seeing me, right?

All the things they wouldn't want fucked with the most lay inside.

I walked a short distance up the street, past the stretch of trees to the lot around the neighboring warehouse. Then I crossed the road at a jog and circled around through the trees.

When I'd come up on the back of the gang's hideout, I tugged the ski mask over my head. It might not help me hide, but it would at least stop them from getting a good look at my face if I ran into any of my enemies.

A span of scruffy field lay between the yard around the other warehouse I was now standing near and the back of the storage building that was my target. I watched for a couple more minutes, my pulse racing through my veins, and then darted across the uneven ground.

I slowed as I reached the asphalt around the building. Muscles tensed, I walked right up to the back door and pressed my ear to the gap.

Nothing. No music, no laughter, no loud conversations.

Something inside of me jumped for joy. A tug of the doorknob proved it was locked, but I knew just how to deal with that.

In a matter of seconds, I'd applied my pins to the minor security issue as quickly as I had the door to the arena my first day in town. Yanking on the knob again, I whisked myself inside the hideout in one fluid motion.

The douchebags were *so* going to regret messing with me.

My eyes darted around the dim hallway I'd come into, searching for an ideal objective.

Farther ahead, the hall split like the head of a T. Muffled voices carried from around the bend to my ears, but there didn't appear to be any activity in the rooms closest to me.

Setting my feet quietly, I tried the doors in my stretch of hall.

The first opened into what looked like a workout room with exercise mats, weights, a ratty punching bag, and a rowing machine. The second revealed stacks of boxes and plastic crates.

Bingo.

I slipped inside, letting the door shut behind me, and pried open one of the crates. A smirk stretched across my face.

Oh, this was just perfect.

I whipped out several of the bags of white powder tucked inside. When I dug into the plastic with my fingernail, the sharp scent confirmed what I'd suspected.

These guys were holding a whole bunch of cocaine. Too bad for them it soon wouldn't be in any condition to sell.

I ripped the hole wide and poured the powder all over the floor like a deluge of fine snow. Then another and another, until the dirty cement surface was coated with it.

As I tore apart another bag, I did a little dance across the room, the powder hissing under my sneakers. Grinding it into the cracks and grime for good measure. I had the urge to fit in a little jumps practice too, mashing the stuff with Axels and Lutzes, but there wasn't quite enough room.

How many tens of thousands of dollars was I losing for these guys in a few short minutes? I pictured the cash going up in flames as I continued my stomping dance.

Maybe that would piss off whoever they were supplying or storing the stuff for enough that *those* assholes would run these ones out of town for me. Extra bonus.

I was just grabbing another bag close to the bottom of the now nearly empty crate when a shout filtered through the wall.

"Hey, Delroy, that you messing with the merch?"

A jolt of panic raced through my nerves. I'd gotten so caught up in my revenge that I hadn't been cautious enough—someone must have heard me.

Without risking a second to think, I dashed out into the hall. Footsteps sounded around the corner as I hurtled past the back door.

I sprinted toward the patch of woodland—I could vanish in there like I had the other night. Running on into the woods, I winced at the yells I heard in the distance. But none of them sounded at all close to me.

The gangsters sounded pissed off, but also like they had no clue where the perpetrator of the vandalism had gone.

A tiny smile tugged at my lips. Keeping my head down, I wove between the trees, determined to put more distance between me and the storage building before I let down my guard.

I veered around a steep section of earth jutting up from the ground—and found myself face to face with the flabby guy named Barry who I'd watched berate the high school kid by the lake.

He jerked to a halt, one hand clutching the strap of the bag he had slung over his back. He must have been returning from some illicit business of his own. Shit.

"Who the fuck are you, and what are you—?" he spat out.

I didn't wait around to hear the rest of his question. I just flung myself in the opposite direction.

My feet pounded across the fallen autumn leaves and crackling twigs. I swerved left and then right, until I found myself coming up on the road on the edge of town.

I paused, my chest heaving for breath, my ears pricked. No sounds of pursuit reached my ears.

Was it possible he hadn't bothered to run after me? I was probably in better shape than most of those pricks anyway. Or maybe I'd simply lost him in the woods, and he'd given up.

With a sigh of relief, I tugged off my ski mask and looked down at myself. My stomach lurched.

My star-dappled Henley and distressed jeans were dusted with a fine layer of cocaine. There was no missing it against the black fabric of my shirt especially.

Hell, it was dappled all across the front of the mask too.

Barry might not have been able to identify me specifically with the mask covering my face, but with one glance at my figure in the fitted clothes, he wouldn't have had any doubt that I was a woman. Or that I was the one who'd created the mess he'd find when he returned to his base of operations.

I hadn't been sure whether the gang was targeting me because they knew I'd been making their lives harder or because I was new in town and different. Now they'd definitely be able to narrow down their list of suspects when it came to the assaults on their property.

I swiped the evidence of my crime off my clothes as well as I could with the help of some strips of moss and then trudged across the street, apprehension settling over me like a cloud.

Now that the goons would be that much surer who'd been targeting *them*, how would the assholes come down on me next after I'd screwed up their business so thoroughly?

And how the hell was I going to make sure that confrontation went in my favor—without ruining not just my life but those of the two men who'd lifted that life into something out of a dream?

TWENTY-ONE

Luciana

I KNEW BETTER by now than to assume any of my problems had been solved even when it felt like I'd made progress, off or on the rink. No matter how well things appeared to be going, it seemed like a monkey wrench would inevitably lodge itself directly into the turning gears of my good day.

Today, that monkey wrench was tall, broad, and Jasper-shaped.

My partner had been relatively chill with me—you know, as chill as Mr. Grouchy ever got. He actually smiled when I showed up at the rink and managed to laugh rather than grumble after our first collective stumble during a lift.

Maybe because the subsequent fall in which he'd cushioned me had reminded us both of how enjoyably we'd ended our last training session together.

But as we moved into the sections of the routine that were more about synchronization than directly working together, a different sort of tension seeped in. And not between him and me.

"I think if you just loosen up your stance a little more, you'll land that much better," Niko said to Jasper after his fourth shaky finish in a row. "Why don't you try this form again a little slower to see if you can feel where you're going wrong?"

Jasper scowled. "A little slower. Right. Like that's going to fix all my problems."

A new storm cloud seemed to have descended over him since Niko had started focusing on his most difficult individual spin, and it was only getting darker. I paused, my stomach knotting as I watched the two of them together.

I'd seen prickly moments between the two men before—well, prickly on Jasper's side—but I'd thought that was just Jasper being himself. It didn't make sense for him to get all snarky with our coach when he was in a good enough mood to brighten up with me.

Unless there'd been more than prickliness underlying their dynamic all along, and I hadn't noticed because our own tensions had overshadowed the trouble until now.

Niko shook his head with a twinkle in his eyes, but I thought I could make out a strain in his attempt at a typically lighthearted tone. "I'm not saying it'll fix *everything*. We've got to start somewhere, right? I know you can hit the mark perfectly if you just get your head in the right place."

"Oh, so now I'm only just starting?" Jasper rolled his eyes. "Aren't you supposed to be building off what I could already do, not sending me back to square one?"

Niko's mouth twisted. He was normally so relaxed, but there was no mistaking the tension in his stance now as he tried to talk Jasper down.

"You know that's not what I meant. Of course you're drawing on all your talent. But you've got to let people fully see it. You're so close to mastering this spin. Come on, from the top, let's keep at it."

Jasper's expression hardened, but he cast off to attempt the move on his own, not even waiting to see if I'd join him. He whirled himself around with a kick of his legs, but even I could see that his temper was getting the better of him.

This time, his whole torso swayed too close to the ice. He broke out of the spin a rotation early with a string of curses.

Niko held up his hands. "All right. Take a breather, skate a few laps around the rink to cool down, and then we'll come back to it. We're not giving up until—"

"Oh, come off it," Jasper interrupted in a snap as sharp as the blades of my skates. "You can quit coddling me. Maybe the problem is you're not half as good a coach as you thought you'd be, and you don't actually know how to solve any of this. You can stop treating me like a pity case and go skate your own fucking routine if you want to see it so badly."

He shot off toward the stands and was stomping up the aisle the second he'd wrenched his skates off.

Okay, then. I had no idea what that fit of anger was all about, but apparently we were finishing practice early today.

I glanced toward Niko, expecting the easygoing man to crack a joke to ease up the mood, but his shoulders had slumped. Defeat was written across his delicately chiseled features.

My stomach sank. I pushed off to glide right over to his side.

"Hey. Are you okay? I don't know what his deal is today, but you didn't do anything wrong."

Niko swiped his hand over his face. "I might not have this afternoon, but that isn't the real issue. I thought I could shake him out of his slump—I thought I could fix the problem… But maybe that was ridiculous when it's my fault in the end."

I frowned. "What do you mean it's your fault? You've been *helping* Jasper—it sounds like he'd still be holed up at his grandparents' house not even skating if you hadn't dragged him out here."

"He might not have ended up there in the first place if I wasn't so thoughtless."

Thoughtless? That didn't sound anything like the Niko I knew. I wasn't sure if he'd just picked the wrong English word for what he meant or something beyond my comprehension was going on here, but I wasn't leaving without getting to the bottom of this.

I nudged him toward the boards, and he meandered over with me. When he rested his arm against one, I set my hands on my hips.

"All right, I think you'd better tell me what's the matter. What do you think you did? How could you have had anything to do with Jasper dropping out of the competitive circuit?"

Niko sighed and seemed to shake himself. "I've probably already said more than I should. Jasper wasn't in the right headspace, and it seems I'm not either."

"Oh no, you don't. You're my coach too—he's my partner. If there's something more going on, you've already gotten me mixed up in the middle of it. I have a right to know."

His despondent expression wrenched at my heart, but he squared his shoulders as my comments got through to him. He raised his bright brown eyes to meet my gaze.

"It was just a quick moment. But sometimes something small can totally throw things off."

"Something small like what?"

Niko ran his hand back through his streaked hair. "After one of the international competitions early last year, a bunch of us headed out to get some drinks. A little friendly celebration after the rivalries had been settled. I was a little... tipsy, that's the word. And I think Jasper was too. We started chatting in a corner, and it seemed like there were... sparks. So I leaned in and kissed him."

My eyes widened. "You and Jasper hooked up?"

A blush colored Niko's cheeks.

"No," he said quickly. "It was just the one kiss. A *good* kiss, but—"

He cut himself off with even more obvious embarrassment. "That's not important. I don't know if Jasper had ever done even that much with another man before. He kissed me back as if he was happy to, but then he acted awkward and left. And the rest of the international circuit, he kept floundering with his performance..."

The pieces clicked together in my head. So much made sense that I'd never have figured out without this crucial detail.

All the odd looks I'd seen pass between the two men. Niko's determination to get Jasper back on his feet.

I stared at him. "Hold on. You think you kissing him sent him into his slump?"

Niko made a face. "He was doing so well before. And getting

confused about your personal life, attractions and all that, can really throw someone off. I didn't know where his head was—I shouldn't have assumed I could make an advance—"

I shook my head vehemently to interrupt him. "No way. That's the hugest of huge leaps, Niko. I'm sure he had other stuff going on."

"It still could have factored in." Niko hesitated. "It wouldn't be the first time I've messed things up, badly, that way."

I still wasn't buying this whole taking-full-responsibility stance. "So you came all the way around the world to coach him out of his slump because you felt guilty about it?"

"It seemed like the least I could do. And I did want to see him back on the ice. I believe everything I've told him. The world should see his talent."

I eased closer to Niko and looped my arms around his neck in a loose embrace. "Have you talked to him about all this stuff?"

Niko exhaled roughly. "I tried to bring up what happened between us before, but he was obvious about changing the subject when I even hinted at it. I thought it might be better to let him pretend it never happened—write over it as if it doesn't matter. The last thing I want to do is reopen old wounds. *He's* never mentioned it."

These incredible, hopeless men I'd found myself involved with. I blew out my breath with fond exasperation and peered up at him.

"You know how he is. So proud it might as well be bulletproof armor. He probably just needs a little more time to get over whatever's actually eating at him."

Which I suspected was not quite what Niko thought it was.

Niko lowered his head so his forehead rested against mine, his stance relaxing just a little. "I really hope so. I've been trying my best."

I shifted one of my hands to stroke his cheek, his closeness sparking heat all through my body. "I've been able to see that from the first moment I showed up."

My mind tripped back to the things Jasper had said about Niko when he'd dropped by my house—how impressed he was by the other man's coaching. It wasn't my place to share our private conversation, but I felt it was fair to add, "I'm one hundred percent sure that Jasper knows it too. It was just a bad day. The two of you will sort it out."

Niko hummed to himself. "Thank you for listening." He teased his fingers along my jaw. "You really are an angel, aren't you?"

I couldn't help grinning at him. "Only the most devilish kind."

I bobbed up on my skates to press a kiss to his mouth. My coach let out a rougher sound and kissed me back eagerly.

More heat flooded me as Niko's lean body pressed me against the boards. I breathed in, taking in the rush of adrenaline that came with his familiar cool scent.

When his tongue traced a sensual line across mine, I had to stop myself from stripping his clothes off him right there. He knew just how much to tease me and how to do it in all the right ways.

As our mouths collided again, I let him take the lead, following wherever he wanted to take me. But I couldn't resist stroking my hands over his chest and then his back.

I wanted to feel all of him. It'd been too long since our delicious encounter by the lake.

Niko's hands roamed down my body to my ass. He tugged me tighter against him with my back braced against the boards.

He was already rock hard behind his pants, and his rigid groin settled into just the right place between my legs. At the contact and the flare of hunger that came with it, a whimper seeped from my throat.

As I rocked against him, reveling in the friction, my head tipped back. Niko branded the side of my neck with his mouth, massaging my thighs at the same time.

Oh, God, he knew how to work me over just right. As if he'd been created just to get me off, and he was nothing but happy to do so.

A very large part of me wanted to urge him onward, to have him fucking me right against the boards. He slid his fingers along my waist, tracing the top of my leggings, and I knew he'd strip them off me and take me if I let him keep going.

But another part of me, maybe not quite as big but insistent, reminded me that off in the shadowed stands, Rafael was watching over me like some kind of guardian angel himself. He'd be seeing every kiss and every caress.

I had no idea how he'd feel about it. I had no idea how he really felt about me. But after seeing how he'd reacted to my make-out session with Jasper, I was pretty sure those feelings were conflicted.

I wasn't going to give up on a love life just to make sure my bodyguard never got unfairly jealous, but that didn't mean it was kind to rub it in his face.

Dipping my head, I sought out Niko's lips for one more kiss. Then I eased back regretfully. "This is *really* good, but can I ask for a rain check? I've just—I've got a lot on my mind."

Niko cupped my cheek. "Of course. You should never feel like there's any pressure from me."

I grinned at him. "Only to be the best figure skater the world has ever seen."

With another laugh, Niko winked at me. "You've already got that one down pat."

Ignoring the unfulfilled ache between my thighs, I sat down in the stands to pull off my skates. My mind spun with all the things I'd just learned.

There was another problem, one I could never have expected, forming cracks in my partnership with Jasper and our dynamic with our shared coach. I'd solidified the connection with my skating partner… Could I smooth over this lingering tension too?

It was so hard to figure out what was really going on behind Jasper's grouchy front, he wore it so adamantly. But then, I'd never have guessed at the guilt Niko was carrying either.

And obviously neither of them had any idea how far *I* actually was from being an angel.

Maybe all three of us were putting on a sort of performance, not just on the ice. Showing the world what we thought it should see even though that wasn't totally accurate.

Something about that last thought sent a bolt of inspiration through me that had nothing to do with my skating life at all. I sprang to my feet, grabbing my bag.

Yes—yes, that just might work.

And then I could solve the biggest threat looming over me and get back to focusing on the guys who really mattered.

TWENTY-TWO

Luciana

MY NERVES JUMPED ABOUT HALF a mile when Rafael strode into the motel room, only settling when I saw it was him. He shut the door behind him with a thump and a rasp of the heavy deadbolt.

After hearing about the pigeon incident and the gang's unfortunate sighting of me in the woods yesterday, my bodyguard had insisted that we temporarily relocate to a strip motel about a half hour down the highway from Hobb Creek. The rooms seemed to mostly be vacant, the walls scuffed and the carpet musty, but at least the security features appeared to be sturdy enough.

I'd spent the hour since I'd gotten back from practice pacing in front of the dated television set and stewing on the idea that had unfurled during my drive from the arena. I'd whittled away at it until it felt foolproof, but I was still nervous as hell.

If this didn't work, I had no idea what would. And the grim expression Rafael was wearing sent a fresh jitter through my nerves.

"What?" I asked. "Did something happen?"

He sighed. "It's pretty bad. Those trumped-up gangsters are barging all around town looking for you."

I tensed instinctively. "Looking for me how?"

"I saw them openly harassing regular people on the street—pushing them around, demanding to know where 'she' is and what they know about 'her.' Meaning you, obviously. No one over there has a clue what they're talking about. I can't even tell whether the buffoons know exactly who they're looking for or if they're trying to scare someone into tattling."

A shiver ran down my back. "Have they hurt anyone?"

Rafael grimaced. "Not yet, but with tempers running that high… I wouldn't be surprised if they get there soon."

Shit. I sat down hard on the stiff mattress. "It's my fault. If I'd been more careful…"

"They provoked you," Rafael said evenly, though I was pretty sure he wasn't happy about my stunt with the cocaine bags either. "I can't blame you for retaliating."

I dragged in a breath, my fingers curling into the blanket. When I'd first thought about interfering with the gang, I'd assumed I'd have to vanish if they caught on to anything I'd done against them.

But I couldn't leave now, not when they were wreaking havoc against the townspeople because of me.

Not when I'd come up with a plan that could truly end this once and for all.

Resolve wound around the guilt that'd clenched my gut. "We can't let this go on any longer. We have to hit back as hard as we possibly can before they do hurt someone innocent—or manage to track me down."

Rafael gave me a wary look. "Somehow I have the feeling you've already come up with a strategy you're just waiting to get me on board with."

I shot him a tight smile. "My plans haven't been bad so far. Our opponents are just too idiotic to take the hint and realize they're beat. But I think what we really need are some theatrics."

"Theatrics," Rafael repeated with undisguised skepticism.

"Yes." I straightened up, the energy of my brainstorm buoying me up. "We're going to do major damage to their business, *and* in a way that makes me seem way scarier than I actually am. Convince them once and for all that they can't win, that they're better off cutting their losses and leaving town—because the consequences of sticking around would be so awful. And in a way no one would ever associate with the Deadly Rose."

Rafael's tone turned dry. "For the record, I already think you're plenty scary. But what exactly did you have in mind?"

My smile turned fiendish. "I made a list of supplies. That might start to give you an idea."

I tapped my phone's screen to bring up my notes and held it up so he could read it.

Rafael's burgundy eyes scanned the list. He smirked when he came to the final item and shook his head, his tight black coils swaying slightly.

"You're crazy," he said. "But this… I can see how this could be good. Let's get going. We have some serious shopping to do."

One benefit of Jasper inadvertently ending our training session early was that the army surplus store in the next town over was still open when I parked around back.

Rafael headed down the street to pick up some supplies he'd have an easier time locating, and I sauntered into the unassuming building with my spirits high.

Those pricks weren't remotely prepared for the hell I was about to unleash on them.

The bell over the door jingled as I stepped inside. An old man with low jowls that gave him a bulldog-like look peered at me from behind the register.

"Hello there, miss," he said in a croaking voice that was more bullfrog. "Can I help you find anything?"

I glanced around the shop's cluttered interior, densely packed with shelves of equipment and racks of clothing, mostly in black, brown, and khaki-green. The stuffy air made my nose itch.

I'd rather not give him any more time to think about my planned purchases than necessary. "I'd like to browse for now and see what turns up, thanks."

"Well, let me know if you need a hand. I've got a ladder for the stuff that's high up."

Good to know, since some of those shelves were at least a foot higher than I could reach on tiptoe.

I moved through the aisles, my eyes on the merchandise. Ammunition boxes, canvas satchels, piles upon piles of camo. I shook my head, my mouth twisting to the side in a crooked frown.

No, no, and no. None of this would help me.

I turned the corner around a rack of cheaply made ghillie suits and ran an anxious hand over my ponytail. I'd realized I might not find what I wanted right away, but I'd been hoping I could get everything together quickly.

Who knew how quickly the gang might escalate their anger?

I'd just knelt down to check a stack of boxes along the far wall when the door chimed again. Had Rafael already finished and come looking for me?

I peeked past the ghillie coats and froze with a hitch of my pulse.

Jasper stood at the counter, his broad shoulders blocking my view of the clerk. I let go of the coats, my heart thudding hard in my chest.

If my skating partner saw me here, how was I going to explain my sudden interest in army gear? It didn't jive with my usual style. I definitely didn't lean toward military punk.

If I claimed I was broadening my horizons, would he buy that excuse or get suspicious? Especially if some strange events happened near Hobb Creek shortly afterward…

My mouth had gone dry. I shifted my position, my ears pricked to track his movements.

If he simply never realized I was here, problem solved.

Jasper's brusque voice carried from the front of the story. "Hey. Looking for a parka. Got any in at the moment?"

"Sure, right at the back. We were cleared out a few weeks ago but just got some more in. Preparing for a cold winter, huh?"

Jasper managed to chuckle, a little darkly. "Isn't that what they all are around here?"

His footsteps treaded through the store—right toward my hiding spot. I craned my neck and noticed the rack of heavily padded parkas just five feet away.

Stomach churning, I edged to the side around the other racks. Suddenly I was grateful for the tightly packed stock that made for easy hiding places.

As I sank deeper into my crouch, out of view of the parka rack, a flicker of embarrassment passed through me.

Was I being ridiculous? Maybe Jasper wouldn't think twice about noticing me in here. I could be making the situation so much worse by hiding rather than showing myself like a normal person who wasn't up to anything at all sketchy.

But the possibility that he'd realize my real purpose here gnawed at me deeply enough to keep my legs locked in place. Understanding crept up over me with chilly fingers.

I didn't just want to keep my old life separate from the new one I was building. I was *terrified* of Jasper and Niko finding out who I'd once been.

If they realized the things I'd done, the acts I'd carried out on Mom's orders… If they knew the world I'd moved in and the people I'd associated with…

How could men like them see me as anything other than some kind of monster?

Neither of them could have blood on their hands—not anything like what weighed on my conscience. They'd never be able to wrap their heads around what I'd been through, what I'd been forced to become.

That version of me had died the second that I'd crossed the Texas border. I was becoming something different now, as well as I could. I couldn't let anything jeopardize the happiness I'd found here.

I couldn't lose the first people who'd really welcomed me in and made me feel like I deserved something more.

Unexpected tears pricked my eyes. I closed them and took a slow, deep breath, praying that the clerk wouldn't call out to me and alert Jasper to my presence.

From the rustling of fabric to my left, I could tell that Jasper was picking up parkas and trying them on. I could even imagine them draping his muscular frame.

It made a pretty sweet visual. Would have been nice if I could have checked it out for real.

I forced my eyes open and pretended to be fascinated by the row of canteens in front of me.

Jasper muttered under his breath, followed by more rustling. "Have you got anything else in the back? The biggest size here is still a little snug."

"What we got is what we got, son."

Jasper let out a long sigh. "Right. Thanks again."

I only let myself relax after I heard the door chime again with my skating partner's retreating footsteps. That had been way too close for comfort.

I swiveled around—and found myself staring at one of the objects I'd most wanted to stumble on.

A grin stretched my lips, my worries falling away. Reaching out, I plucked the simple gas mask from the floor where it'd tumbled off a shelf. "Come to Mama."

But as I tramped over to the counter with my prize under my arm, my spirits deflated a little. How could I be triumphant when I was living a double life?

As long as I was making plans like this, taking on the criminals who lurked around this town, everything I did and said with Jasper and Niko was a sort of lie.

But as long as the gang kept terrorizing Hobb Creek, I didn't have much choice. So I'd just have to end their reign as fast as I possibly could, whatever it took.

TWENTY-THREE

Luciana

I FILLED my lungs with the chilled air of the rink, closing my eyes as I glided across the ice. Tomorrow was the qualifying round for the competition, and I wanted to be as one with the routine as I could possibly be.

They said if you told yourself something enough times, you'd actually start believing it. So I rehearsed what I wanted to believe in my head.

I was confident in myself and in my skills. I was cool and calm, knowing that I was going to skate well in front of the crowd.

I'd be able to put my troubles with the gang on hold, at least for a couple of days. Thankfully, Rafael hadn't observed anything more frightening since their initial round of harassment in town.

The final pieces of my plan were still coming together—with a delivery that should arrive tonight. I'd see it through when we got back from Dellville.

There was only one thing I had to worry about right now: my skating partner.

I glanced across the ice to where Niko was discussing leg positioning with Jasper. The vibe between them had relaxed again after Jasper's blow up a couple of days ago, but the younger guy still looked a little tense.

And now that Niko had filled me in on their history, I was noticing little signs I would have simply dismissed before. The way Jasper's gaze lingered on Niko's face when the other man's focus was elsewhere, just a little longer and more intensely than you'd expect from a guy simply paying attention to his coach. The faint hint of a flush that colored his cheeks when Niko patted his upraised leg in approval.

It was like a suppressed version of the markers of attraction that'd revealed his interest in me. Maybe he was even more hesitant to let his feelings show when it was another man, especially if Niko was the first guy he'd crushed on.

Or it could be he was hiding it as well as he could because he assumed our coach didn't return that interest. As far as I could tell, both from watching them and from his comments the other day, Niko was totally oblivious to the signals. Maybe he did see them and was afraid to read anything into them after what he saw as his epic blunder with that first kiss.

So they continued, Niko shooting Jasper a bright but professional smile and turning back to me with a beckoning gesture, Jasper drinking in the graceful planes of the other man's face with his eyes before jerking his gaze away with another trace of a blush. The tension in his shoulders wound tighter.

No wonder he'd been prickly with Niko—and with me intruding on his time with Niko. The guy had followed him all the way around the world after what sounded like a pretty fantastic kiss and now was acting like he didn't want anything from Jasper other than to coach him. That'd be enough to throw anyone for a loop.

And naturally Jasper wasn't going to simply open up his mouth and say something about it.

These men really were hopeless. Possibly it was just as lucky for them that I'd crashed into their lives as it was for me.

I might have brought an unexpected threat down on our heads, as hard as I was working to deflect it, but I could do at least one good thing for them too.

"Are you two ready to try that one again?" Niko asked, smiling at me too.

"Sounds good." I rubbed my hands and checked with Jasper, who nodded.

We set off together, cruising across the ice. At the right spot, we both kicked our legs up in a single flip jump flowing into a spiraling shotgun spin.

My thigh ached with the stretch of holding my leg as straight and high as possible. Jasper matched my movements in perfect synchronization. But as we dropped our skates to the ground with a whirl of motion, he jerked just a little to the side before catching his balance.

Jasper muttered a curse under his breath as we skated back to Niko.

"Remember to let out your breath while you're lowering your leg," Niko said. "That should help keep you steadier."

Jasper narrowed his eyes at our coach. "I think I know how to *breathe*. I'm not quite that inept."

Niko clicked his tongue playfully. "It's not about inadequacies. Anyone can forget the basics in the moment when they're focused on something more complicated."

"I'm not forgetting," Jasper grumbled. "I know what I'm doing. It's just not happening right. How about you figure out the cure for that?"

I caught Niko's wince before he schooled his expression to placid again, and my gut twisted. We *had* to get in sync before tomorrow—all three of us. If Jasper couldn't get his head on straight before the competition, my own nerves wouldn't be the deciding factor.

But I didn't think he'd be able to shake off his uncertainties until we addressed the elephant in the room that they'd both been so studiously ignoring.

I cleared my throat before Niko had to reply to Jasper's snarking and crossed my arms over my chest, looking from one of them to the other. "You know, when a hugely respected skater comes halfway around the world just to coach you, it seems like you could try to listen without biting his head off."

Jasper aimed his glower at me. "I listen. That doesn't mean I'm going to hear anything helpful."

"But you are still here training with him, even though you keep complaining about his coaching." I tapped my finger against my lips. "Did you ever think it's kind of odd that Niko Okabe would have come all this way to shake you out of a slump, like he's got nothing better to do?"

Jasper's posture stiffened a bit, and Niko's expression tightened. I could tell from the awkward smile he shot at me that he suspected where I was going with this, but he kept quiet, not interfering. So far.

"Maybe he was bored," Jasper muttered.

"I guess it could be that," I said, as if I really was thinking it over. "Or it could be the fact that you guys shared that amazing kiss last year right before you fell into your slump, and Niko has spent this whole time thinking he caused the whole problem."

Jasper's face outright flared, blazing nearly as red as his auburn hair. "How did—" His gaze jerked to Niko. "You—"

He couldn't seem to get out more than those few sputtered words.

Niko's throat bobbed with a thick swallow. "Lou," he started, his voice thin.

I shook my head at whatever he'd been about to say, letting the corner of my lips quirk upward in a teasing smile. "You came racing to the rescue like a knight in shining armor because you thought you broke Jasper with that kiss. But he's still been struggling even with your help, right?"

"Jasper's made a lot of progress," Niko said quickly.

"But there's still something off. And as far as I know, you haven't been kissing him anymore since last year, huh?"

"No," Jasper mumbled, looking like he wanted to vanish into a crack in the ice.

"Well, there you go." I held Niko's gaze firmly, aware of Jasper at the edge of my vision. "Obviously he's dealing with a lot of things that have nothing to do with kissing. So you're not to blame. No need to feel like you have to make up for any mistakes. You can go home with a clear conscience and get back to your own skating career."

If I'd thought Jasper had been tense before, it was nothing compared to how rigid his body went at my last comment. Oh, he didn't like that suggestion at all.

But Niko was already frowning, his bright eyes gone momentarily stormy. "No. That's not the only reason— I made a commitment to see Jasper make it back into the competitive circuit. The world's losing out by missing the performances I know he could give, and *he* misses it too."

He paused, flicking a tentative glance toward Jasper. "As much as he might try to pretend he doesn't. I can tell, and I want to watch him shine the way only he can."

"Grouchiness and all?" I prodded.

Niko's expression softened. "That's part of the package, so I'll take it with the rest."

Determination rang through his words… along with unmistakable affection. A triumphant grin tugged at my lips, but I held it in while the two men studied each other.

Jasper's shoulders had come down with Niko's declaration. How many of his spats of temper had spawned from insecurities not just about his interest in Niko but whether Niko would stick around at all? Wanting to push the other guy away first so he could say it was his decision, rather than watch Niko give up on him?

"I wouldn't hold you to that commitment," he said hesitantly.

"I know." Something had relaxed in Niko too, having the tensions between them out in the open. "I want to be here, Jasper."

From the warmth dancing in his eyes, I had the feeling he wanted a whole lot more than that too. But this didn't seem like the time to push my luck that far.

Jasper ran a hand through his hair with a duck of his head. "Well… should we get back to work, then? I'll try to keep the grouchiness to a minimum. And remember to breathe."

The last remark felt like a peace offering. Niko nodded. "Why don't we run through the whole routine from the top? It's easier to get into the zone when you're feeling how it all comes together."

As Jasper and I skated into the middle of the rink for our starting position, I could feel the loosening of Jasper's posture. He caught my eye and offered me a crooked smile.

"You really like to shake things up, don't you, Punk?"

I grinned back at him. "Seems like some things come out better after a little shaking."

"Well, here goes nothing."

His freer attitude seeped into his movements from the first glide across the ice. The sense of his higher spirits buoyed me up too.

We whirled from one move into the next, only getting a little wobbly on that one tricky lift. I salvaged it without outright falling, and we skated on toward the end, but I braced myself after the song shut off.

"That was wonderful," Niko said, back to his usual shiny self. "Just watch your right hand on that lift—you don't want to loosen your grip until she's most of the way down."

To my relief, Jasper tipped his head in acknowledgement without any grumbling or snark. "Right. I can do that." He swiveled toward me. "Let's give it another go."

The same energy carried us through three more run-throughs and some more focused work on specific jumps and lifts. My own chest felt lighter as we soared across the ice.

With our final attempt, I might as well have been flying. My limbs moved like they were one with the music—and with Jasper.

He hoisted me up and around like I weighed nothing at all, and we spun together with perfect balance. There was nothing but perfect control in his grasp as he lowered me, my body adjusting to follow his lead.

I touched down and spun out without missing a beat.

We'd done it. We'd pulled off every part of the routine without a hitch.

Only once, but that meant we could do it again.

When we came out of our ending position, Niko was applauding us enthusiastically from the stands. "Fantastic. You're going to blow them all away tomorrow!"

Jasper beamed back at him with a joy I didn't think I'd seen from him on the ice since he'd performed his old routine on my request. When I threw my arms around him in a hug, he squeezed me back and then tipped my head back so he could steal a quick kiss.

But even with plenty of joy thrumming through my chest, my nerves kept prickling away too. We'd pulled off the entire routine once —and now we had to perform it in front of my first set of judges tomorrow. We might not even make it all the way to the actual competition.

I'd better keep my own head in the game, or I could screw this up not just for myself but for the two men who were starting to mean more to me than I'd have ever imagined was possible.

TWENTY-FOUR

Niko

I COULDN'T HELP LEANING BACK against the boards as Jasper and Lou unlaced their skates, my gaze lingering on both of them in turn. My heart had been thumping a little faster than usual ever since Lou had staged her surprise intervention on the ice.

The two of them exchanged a few teasing remarks, looking more at ease with each other than I'd ever seen before. The brightening of Jasper's face sparked something inside me too.

I'd been afraid to insist on talking about that night in Munich in case the subject stirred up even more uncomfortable feelings that would bog Jasper down. But it seemed like the opposite had happened, as if he'd cast off a burden he'd been carrying.

And somehow, Lou had known or at least suspected that would be the case. I knew she'd wanted to help us today, not upset us.

I studied her for a moment as she smoothed a few loose strands back into her ponytail. Why had she decided we needed to clear the air today?

There was something more going on with *her* than she'd said. She smiled at Jasper, but a shadow crossed her face when she was concentrating on her own tasks. For the past few days, I'd increasingly had the sense of a dark cloud hanging over her, and it'd only gotten thicker.

Was she simply nervous about the upcoming competition, or was something more going on?

Jasper gave a spine-cracking stretch that made the muscles in his torso flex in all kinds of ways I could appreciate and aimed another relaxed grin at his partner. "Better not to get too wound up before a performance. You should take it easy tonight. I think a nap is on my agenda."

Lou laughed, but the good humor didn't quite reach her dark brown eyes. "If even *you're* telling me it's good to chill out, I guess I'd better listen."

"You should *always* listen to me, Punk," he said in a teasing tone, and lifted his gaze toward me. He hesitated for a moment, and then the corners of his mouth lifted with another small but genuine smile. "Thanks for everything today, Niko."

My heart just about flipped right over, but I kept my rush of exhilaration under wraps. "That's what I'm here for. Go get your rest. You two are going to stun them all tomorrow."

Jasper lifted his hand in a wave to both of us and loped up the aisle to the exit, his gym bag swaying against his back.

When Lou moved to grab her bag too, I stepped forward. "Hey, before you take off, I have a few more pointers. Since it's your first competition and all."

Lou perked up as if she lived for nothing more than for me to tell her how she could skate better. Which honestly, having seen her in action, maybe she did.

"Sure. What were you thinking? Have I been messing up that tuck position again?"

"No, no, nothing like that." I sat down on the edge of the bench across from her. "Jasper's right about relaxing before a competition. You also want to make sure you're well hydrated before you go on, and you're best off having a solid meal a couple of hours before our performance but nothing too heavy."

I could see Lou making mental notes to herself with each point. "Okay, got it."

"And…" The perfect way to get at the questions I wanted to ask popped into my head. "You should also keep in mind your facial expressions, especially performing in front of the judges."

She cocked her head. "There's something wrong with my face?"

I couldn't hold back a chuckle at her mock-offended tone. "You've just looked a little tense sometimes. Your face should give the impression that everything your body is doing is perfectly easy, no strain at all. It's an… illusion it's always good to convey."

"That makes sense."

I peered at her, watching for a clue about her mood. "Have you been feeling like you're under pressure lately? You know this competition in Dellville is very low-key. Even if something goes wrong, it won't affect your career at all."

Lou shrugged, but I caught a flicker of uneasiness in her eyes. "Oh, you know, it's hard not to be a little nervous when it's my first time performing for an audience."

"Of course. Is there anything else on your mind? You can talk to me about whatever you want, you know."

She gave me a gentle smile that lit me up just as much as Jasper's could. "I know, Niko. Really, I'm fine."

I didn't believe her, but I couldn't see how to push any further without becoming obnoxious. I wasn't her keeper—I wasn't even officially her coach.

She'd share her concerns with me when she felt ready to. I could respect her need for privacy, as much as I wanted to smooth out any strain she was feeling.

A hint of mischief tugged at her lips. "And you didn't figure Jasper needed this pep talk too?"

I raised my eyebrows. "He's been through dozens of competitions much more intense than tomorrow's. It'll be good for him to just get back out there again and remember how much he loves it, but I can't imagine there's anything I could tell him that he doesn't already know."

He did love it—being on the ice. I'd been able to see it in every performance during his high period. That was one of the things that'd drawn me to him to begin with.

"Maybe not about competition prep," Lou said, arching her eyebrows right back at me. "But about other things… You obviously care about him a lot if you came all the way here and put up with all his grumbling just to get him back into competitions. No way did you go to all that trouble just because you felt guilty about a kiss that couldn't have lasted more than a minute."

My throat constricted. "I wouldn't have kissed him if I hadn't already liked and respected him quite a bit."

"Like? Respect?" Lou shook her head in apparent exasperation. "Come on, Niko. He's more than that, right? You've got a thing for him, that for some reason you've been keeping ever so quiet about."

A flush of heat crept up my neck. "It didn't seem… relevant. Jasper's never acted as if he—"

"Jasper can barely seem to figure out what *he's* really feeling half of the time through all his hang-ups," Lou interrupted, the insult tempered by the obvious affection in her voice. "How the heck was he supposed to know that you're interested when he hadn't even seen you for more than a year after that one kiss? Did you really expect *him* to make the first move?"

I grimaced. "Well, I—I didn't want to impose on him."

"Has he ever said anything that made it seem like he's upset about what happened between you two? I didn't see any sign that he was bothered about the kiss today."

"No, we've never even talked about it until now."

She tossed her hands in the air. "Why not? Why don't you go for it to see what could happen?"

I grappled for an answer, my feelings in such a muddle it was hard to tell what was actually accurate. "It's complicated. I'm here to coach him—I didn't want to confuse things. Or upset him again."

"He's obviously not getting upset about it. And I think he was a hell of a lot more confused by you *not* saying how you felt."

Lou tapped me on the chest. "And you're not technically his coach any more than you are mine. There's nothing official tying you together that'd make it hard for him to walk away if he wanted to, right?"

I didn't know whether I should be pleased or frustrated that I couldn't brush off her arguments. "I guess there isn't."

"There you go. That's my pep talk for you. Get out of *your* head, take a deep breath, and tell him everything. I'm not making that part of the confession for you."

I shot her a baleful look, and Lou grinned back so sunnily that I couldn't take any offense. The sight of her gorgeous face sent a strange wobble through my pulse.

My feelings and Jasper's weren't the only ones that mattered.

"You wouldn't have any problem with it if—if something more happened between him and me?" I had to ask.

Lou's snort doused all my worries in an instant. "Of course not. You haven't minded sharing me with him—why should I mind sharing him with you?" Her smile turned coy. "I'd get to see my two new favorite guys find a little more happiness. Sounds good to me."

A swell of affection rose up through my chest and propelled me toward her. I touched her cheek and captured her lips with mine, hoping she could feel just how much I meant the tenderness of the kiss.

"Thank you," I said after, running my fingers over her soft hair. "Apparently I did need a pep talk too."

Lou beamed at me. "Glad to be of service."

She leaned in for one more quick peck and then hefted her bag. "See you tomorrow!"

I watched her go, emotions whirling inside me. They didn't feel as jumbled as they had before.

I hadn't wanted to risk the mostly friendly dynamic I'd established with Jasper… but getting closer with Lou hadn't thrown anything off in our working relationship. If anything, we understood and trusted each other more.

Our hookup and the moments we'd shared since hadn't interfered with her performance, so why would simply talking about the possibilities with Jasper ruin his?

Maybe we could have something special, a deeper bond than I'd dared to let myself hope for before.

I wanted that. I had to admit that fact at least to myself now. I'd traveled around the world to work with Jasper because something about him had caught hold of my heart, and my admiration had only intensified as we'd worked together.

I wasn't going to bring up the subject immediately. He had plenty on his mind already with tomorrow's qualifying round and the full competition I was sure they'd make it to the day after.

But once that milestone in his career return was over… Then I'd find out just how good things between the two of us could be.

And take the blow if he didn't reciprocate my feelings after all.

TWENTY-FIVE

Luciana

BREATHE IN. Breathe out. In again.

Jasper and Niko had told me to relax before the performance, but that was a hell of a lot easier said than done. My nerves had been buzzing since the moment I'd woken up in the dingy motel room this morning.

I'd kept up my deep breaths every time my heart started pounding a little too fast. Now I was hunkered down on the questionable motel-room carpet, stretching my muscles just for something to do.

I'd be heading out in just a couple of hours so we could make it to Dellville with plenty of time for our qualifying performance. And then… then it would all come down to whether I actually deserved the faith my coach and skating partner had put in me or not.

Imagine how it'll feel at the end if the judges say you're through to the full competition. Not how painful it'll be if you screw things up for everyone.

I was just pushing myself off the floor when the lock clicked on the door. I perked up, expecting the pastries Rafael had offered to grab us from town, but one look at his grim face when he hustled inside sent my spirits spiraling downward.

"What?" I said before he could speak. He hadn't even brought his intended loot—no paper bakery bag dangled from either hand.

Rafael's mouth pulled tighter. "That gang of bozos has stepped up their campaign to find you. When I got into Hobb Creek, there were store windows busted all down main street—including the bakery. They're smashing things up when people can't tell them what they want to know.

My stomach plummeted in the same direction my good mood had gone. "Shit."

"That's not even the worst of it." He rubbed his hand over his face. "One of the store owners tried to intervene, and they stabbed him in the shoulder, bad. The doctor rushed out to help him, but the assholes were shouting about how everyone would pay for it if the cops got called in. I don't know if anyone will dare."

I hugged myself, nausea unfurling from my gut. "*We* can't call the police either—who knows what the pricks will do to the other townspeople. It's not like the cops have managed to get the gang in line before now." I paused. "Why didn't they just come after me at practice yesterday if they're so worked up?"

Rafael shook his head. "It seemed like they're still not sure who exactly was giving them trouble. The bits I heard, they were carrying on about 'that woman who's been messing with us,' not using your name or anything more specific. Beats me how they haven't put the pieces together when they were already targeting you."

I grimaced. "You did say that they might have been harassing me as a newcomer, not because they had any suspicion I was connected to the sabotage at their hideout. It's not like they're the sharpest tacks in the box."

"Yeah, the idiots might assume it has to be someone who's a long-time resident. They wouldn't figure a new arrival would be invested enough to bother." Rafael sighed. "They don't know you."

His words sent a spike of determination through my veins alongside the thudding of my heart. "No, they don't."

Rafael eyed me. "What are you thinking? Don't we have to head out for your competition soon?"

I glanced toward our pile of supplies, the latest bits we'd received to go with what was already stashed in the trunk of the Grand Marquis. My pulse kept thrumming, images of broken glass and splatters of blood flashing behind my eyes.

How much more damage would the gang do if I let them keep rampaging while I spent the weekend skating?

What if they did finally figure out I was the one who'd messed with their property… and they tracked me down to Dellville? It wasn't just the town under threat but Jasper and Niko—and everyone else who'd be at the competition—too.

A chill swept across my body. No, I wouldn't let that happen.

"We can't put off the plan," I announced, moving to grab the bags in the corner. "It's *my* fault that any of this is happening. The locals shouldn't suffer any more because of what I did."

Rafael frowned. "Are you sure you want to do this? Right before you're supposed to perform—"

"We have to," I interrupted. "We have to end this stupid war once and for all and show them that *they're* the ones who are going to pay. We'll just do it fast."

It'd take a half hour simply to get back to Hobb Creek. We were going to be cutting it so close—and I couldn't rush through the plan without getting every piece in place, or it'd flop and we'd end up worse off than before.

But there simply wasn't any other option. The gang had decided their fate.

Better that I let down Niko and Jasper with a late arrival than bring the wrath of a bunch of rabid wannabe gangsters down on the entire local skating establishment.

Rafael didn't wait to be told again. He grabbed the rest of the bags and rushed after me out of the motel room to the waiting car.

I ducked back in to snatch up my equipment bag, which thankfully I'd already packed for the competition, and heaved that in the back of the car. Rafael dropped into the driver's seat, and I didn't bother arguing about who would take the wheel.

All that mattered was getting to the gang's hideout ASAP.

Rafael turned the key in the ignition, and the car rumbled to life. "We'll make it work. If those bastards aren't pissing their pants and running for the hills by the time you're done with them, they're certifiably braindead."

I glanced over at him as he hit the gas, with a flutter of warmth rising through the tension that gripped me. We might have had our conflicts since coming to Hobb Creek, but I knew without a doubt now that this man was my rock in the storm, the person I could count on no matter what hell we faced.

He gunned the engine all the way to Hobb Creek, veering around the few other cars on the country highway at a breakneck pace. I pulled on the one piece of equipment I could prepare this far in advance over my head and let the thick fabric of the sort-of poncho settle over my arms. Then I tapped my foot against the floor, my mind leaping ahead to every stage of the not-at-all-beautiful performance I intended to orchestrate just for our enemies.

Rafael only slowed the car slightly when we came around town to where the storage buildings sprawled. He parked behind a warehouse a short distance from the gang hideout where we wouldn't be seen making our final preparations.

I leapt out of the car the second it stopped moving and flung open the trunk. First things first—I tugged on my ski mask and tossed another to Rafael.

"Grab your stuff and get over there."

His mouth twisted. "I don't like the whole splitting up part of this plan."

"It's the only way this is going to work." I shoved the bag with the things he needed toward him. "There's no time to argue about it. Just get as many of them out of the building as you can."

As he slung the bag over his arm, my gaze dropped to the bulge of the concealed holster at his hip. "And remember that I don't want you to shoot any of them—not to kill, anyway. Not if you can help it."

"Yes, boss," Rafael said in a dry tone. "You are definitely not your mother."

I managed a breathless laugh. As he loped off, I stuffed my own supplies into my backpack, getting a whiff of a heady chemical scent that made my eyes water. I tossed the bag onto my back and clutched my fingers tight around the gas mask I'd left in my hand.

With frantic steps, I hustled around the side of the warehouse to where I could see the back of the storage building. A couple of men were standing guard by the rear door, slouched and scowling.

Rafael would have gone around front. I just needed to wait until he—

The first hiss and boom of a firework punctuated his arrival. From my current position, I couldn't make out the parking lot, but the crackle of breaking glass suggested he'd aimed well, right at one of the gang's cars.

We really were making them go through a whole lot of vehicles. This time we'd need to leave at least a few for them to flee in.

"Hey, assholes!" my bodyguard bellowed. "Come get a taste of this!"

More shrieks and bangs reverberated from the roman candles he was carrying. The thugs at the back door looked up with matching expressions of shock and then took off to see what the hell was going on.

The yells carrying from the front of the building suggested a fair number of other goons had stormed out from that doorway as well. Good. Now was the time to make my move.

I sprinted from the warehouse to the back of the storage building. The chaos from up front covered the pounding of my footsteps.

I snatched at the door, already reaching toward my sock for my pins—but the knob turned in my hand.

Ha. The dipshits had left it unlocked, presumably so the guards could easily go in and out. They'd made my job that much easier.

Tugging the gas mask over my mouth and nose, I slipped inside. The hallway was empty, but raised voices filtered to my ears from the front of the building.

No problem. Everything I wanted was back here.

I hauled the big container of gasoline out of my backpack and yanked the cap open. Then I shouldered into the room where I'd found the bags of cocaine last time.

The stacks of crates and boxes still filled the space. I didn't know how much of the stash they had on hand was drugs and how much other was illicit merchandise, but pretty soon it was all going to be ashes.

Breathing through the gas mask with faint wheezes, I splashed gasoline over every stack and then drizzled a train out the door. From the hall, I darted into a couple of other rooms and found another heaped with sacks and more boxes.

Hasta la vista to all of those supplies too.

I doused the second storage room with another trail into the hall and poured a thin line of gasoline all the way to the back door. The fumes would have been dizzying if not for the mask. I'd take the rubbery scent filling my nose instead any day.

Pushing open the door, I tossed the now-empty gas container down the hall and pulled out a lighter. Buh-bye, criminal livelihood!

With one flash of sparks, the liquid trail lit up. Flames shot along the stream of gasoline toward both of the rooms and licked straight under the doors.

In a matter of seconds, the warbling sound of a raging fire resonated down the hall along with clouds of smoke gushing from beneath the doors.

Grinning beneath my mask, I jogged backward a few steps and fumbled in my bag for a tube of special gel that'd been our last acquisition along with the poncho. With a forceful squeeze, I got a big blob of it and smeared it all across my neck, hands, and my face as far as I could reach, pressing beneath the gas and ski masks. I even slathered some onto the fabric of the ski mask itself for good measure.

The cool, slick sensation made me cringe, but I didn't dwell on it. I shoved the tube back into my bag and dashed for the front of the building to reunite with Rafael.

I charged into the parking lot to find him handling the situation there pretty well on his own. Three of the gang members were lying on the ground, moaning and holding various parts of their bodies. Another handful of guys were advancing towards him, but he didn't look worried.

I watched in admiration of his strength as he jabbed one jerk in the stomach and brought a huge fist crashing into another guy's nose, only to toss the loser into the dirt a few feet away.

The few remaining gangsters circled him warily. One glanced back at the building and let out a shout at the sight of the smoke now streaming up into the open air.

A flicker of relief passed through me. Maybe I wouldn't even have to take this last, crazy step. Maybe we'd done enough to have them running scared as it was.

But as that thought passed through my mind, a truck roared down the road with two cars flanking it. They tore into the parking lot and skidded to a stop with a screech of their tires.

A dozen more guys sprang out, all of them clutching pistols or knives. And all of them clearly furious.

TWENTY-SIX

Rafael

IF I'D HAD it my way, every one of the so-called gangsters who'd just torn into their parking lot would have charged toward me. Instead, most of them ran at Lou where she'd emerged from behind the smoking storage building, some twenty feet away from me.

She was both closer to the scene of our main crime, and she must have looked a hell of a lot more vulnerable than I did. The combination of ski mask and gas mask gave her an almost alien appearance, but she was more than a foot shorter than me and slimmer besides, and her feminine curves showed even beneath the black poncho draped over her.

They probably figured they could use her as leverage against me.

Gritting my teeth, I hurtled after them as fast as I could run. If they sent one bullet or blade into her body…

I couldn't let it get even that far. The thought of Lou injured, her petite frame swaying with pain, sent a pulse of fury through my veins.

My hands clenched into fists, and my fingers itched for the gun at my hip.

I'd promised her I'd only shoot if I needed to—but our current situation had to count as an emergency. Better if these pricks all ended up dead on the pavement than to let even one of them lay a hand on her.

Lou tensed in a fighting stance, her sharp-edged rings glinting in front of her knuckles. One of the assholes *laughed* at her.

He raised his gun, just a few steps away from her. My hand leapt to my holster. My fingers closed around the grip—

And Luciana Cordova flew into action.

She lunged forward before the guy in the lead could reach her and drove her ringed fist right into his face with a smack that rang across the pavement. As he reeled backward, clutching at the scratches dribbling blood from his forehead, she knocked the gun from his hand with the crack of broken fingers.

As that guy swore and sputtered, Lou was already whipping to the side to slam two other men's heads into each other with a thud that I knew would leave bruises if not concussions as well. They stumbled dizzily while she kneed the next approaching attacker in the groin.

That thug's knees had barely hit the pavement before she was kicking another goon's legs out from under him with a swift sweep of her foot.

Her poncho billowed out around her limbs like an all-encompassing cape, as if she were some strange superhero vigilante. She definitely was a sight to see.

Even as I rammed my fist into one of the guys at the rear of the pack and drove my elbow into another's ribs hard enough to provoke a *crack!*, I couldn't stop glancing at her. And not just to make sure she was okay.

I'd known her mother had trained her in all kinds of fighting techniques. I'd been around for some of those sessions, not to mention a few missions that'd devolved into gang warfare.

But I'd always stepped in to make sure I took the brunt of any attack. Mireya had never pushed her daughter to her limits, at least not in front of me.

It seemed the coldhearted bitch had taught her daughter to fight better than even I knew. Or maybe it was simply that now Lou had something to lose, something she truly cared about.

My heart twisted. She was thinking of those two guys. *Her* guys. Niko and Jasper.

Not me.

But no matter who'd inspired this show of force, she was incredible. A whirling dervish of lunges and blows, leaving her attackers scattering in her wake. Not just fierce and powerful but bringing the same grace to the battle that had always taken my breath away watching her on the ice.

"Jesus Christ," one of the slower guys muttered, easing back from the brawl. "She's fucking crazy!"

Oh, he didn't know the half of it. But she was my kind of crazy, all the way through.

I couldn't have been prouder to be standing here by her side than I was in this moment.

I kneed him in the gut and toppled him to the ground for good measure, but I wasn't sure Lou even needed me for that much. She already had half a dozen guys sprawled and groaning around her, and the remainder had slowed their roll, eyeing her from a careful distance with their weapons drawn.

One of the men still standing had a pistol. I grabbed my own, ready to intervene if he decided that outright killing her was a better option than taking her hostage, but then Lou launched into her final trick.

I didn't even see her reach into her pocket. There was a click and a flash of a lighter by the edge of her poncho—and then the entire specially-treated piece of fabric burst into flames.

My heart stuttered with the urge to dash in and save her from the terrifying scenario she'd just created. But we'd gone over this—she'd protected her skin and hair, she'd read all of the safety measures.

She needed to convince these idiots that they weren't going to win this war, not against her, and for that she needed to pull out all the stops.

The flames sizzled all around her torso as she strode toward the remaining men without a hint of hesitation. Her voice bellowed through the mask, the hollow effect it created making her words sound twice as threatening.

"If you assholes know what's good for you, you'll pack your shit and get the hell out of this town. If I ever — and I mean *ever* — catch you in Hobb Creek again, it'll be your stone-cold corpses I burn. *Do you understand me*?"

The men jerked back when she struck out with her flaming arms, their jaws gone slack, their weapon-arms faltering. I'd bet these imbeciles had never seen anything like this little but potent force of nature before.

"You're all dead men the next time I see you," she growled in calm ferocity. "I'll bury you right where I ice you."

She whipped a fiery blow straight at one of the men standing, and a flicker leapt from her poncho onto his shirt. He shrieked like a baby and swatted at it as he scrambled away from her.

That was the straw that broke the camel's back.

"Let's get the fuck out of here!" someone shouted.

A few of the injured men were heaving to their feet; their colleagues yanked others off the pavement. They fled for the working vehicles like the hounds of hell were snapping at their heels. I noted the damp spots on a couple of crotches where the goons had pissed themselves.

"Fuck, fuck, fuck," one of them mumbled under his breath. Several of the faces had gone sickly white.

One of the guys leaned out of the driver's seat of the truck as he started the engine. "This crappy town is all yours, you freak!"

I enjoyed a brief moment of triumph that was mostly Lou's watching the truck and cars speed out of the parking lot and then groped at my bag for the fire-retardant blanket. The longer Lou let the fire rage on, the more chance—

I didn't even have time to really worry. Lou dropped and rolled on the gritty pavement, pressing her body into the hard ground. The flames hissed as she smothered them, smoke wisping off the special poncho.

The second the worst of them were out, she yanked the poncho right off and stomped on the lingering flares of fire for good measure. Then she chucked her gas and ski masks into the smoldering heap.

She spun around, a grin stretched across her shining face, and swiped at the gel smeared across her jaw and cheeks with her sleeve. "We did it. We fucking did it!"

"You did it," I had to say. "That was fucking spectacular, Lou."

She pumped her fist in the air and bent down to snatch up her cast-offs. "Can't leave any evidence around. Let's get back to the car. I've got to skate! We're going to have to break a few speed limits to get to Dellville in time."

"We will." I silently resolved that I would get her there unharmed and on time, no matter what I had to do. "Don't even worry about it."

But of course Lou leapt into the driver's seat before I'd even loped all the way to the car. She shot me a sassy grin that lit up her dark eyes, and my heart skipped a beat.

As I dropped into the seat beside her and leaned back with her slam on the gas pedal, an undeniable realization sank deep into my gut.

I'd let the cheeky attitude she'd had since she was a teenager, her size, and our age difference lull me into thinking she was still the same girl I'd been protecting for years. But that couldn't have been further from the truth.

She was a woman now. I hadn't let myself see just how confident and capable she'd become. Sure, she was nineteen and technically an adult, and I'd told her I knew all that, but since we'd gotten into town, she'd shown an assurance and sense of strategy way beyond those years.

She was every bit the leader her mother had wanted to mold her into. She could hold her own against forces even I would have avoided tackling.

How could I have still seen her as a victim too vulnerable to take care of herself? How could I have treated her like one, even after she'd made this bold bid for independence?

I glanced over at Lou as she lifted a hand to wipe away a little more gel from her neck. Her eyes gleamed, but there was a distance in them now, as if her mind were miles ahead of us already.

She'd put the situation with the gang behind her. I could tell by her expression that she was entering that realm of grace and balance and beauty, the space in her mind where I could never join her.

It was a place reserved only for skating, for the art that had truly left its mark on her soul. Niko and Jasper might belong there, but I sure as hell didn't.

But God, did I wish that I did.

That was the worst part of the revelation that'd just struck me. In all my refusal to see what was right in front of me, I'd pushed her away, turned down her advances.

I'd known that she'd wanted me, and I'd felt the same desires humming through me every time I looked at her in the past year, but I'd decided I knew best. That I needed to protect her from myself.

As if *I* could possibly be too much for *her* to handle. So totally fucking absurd.

But it was too late to take back the decisions I'd made now. What the fuck could I even offer her? Reminders of the life she longed so badly to leave completely behind?

She'd found something good with two men who understood the most important part of her existence so much better than I did. All I could do now was watch while the knowledge of my mistakes tore my heart out.

TWENTY-SEVEN

Luciana

RAFAEL GLANCED over at me from behind the steering wheel. "That's the arena up ahead. Are you ready?"

I peered at myself in the mirror on the sun visor and smoothed down a few errant strands of my hair that were threatening to escape my ponytail. My pulse was outright thundering now, but I couldn't see anything to be nervous about in my appearance.

Rafael and I had switched off driving halfway to Dellville, when I'd briefly ducked into a service center restroom to scrub the last traces of gel off my skin. The high of my victory over the wannabe gangsters had carried me careening along the highway that far, reveling in the lingering adrenaline and the thrum of the engine, but it'd been a necessary transition.

Because all the rest of my prep I'd carried out while Rafael handled the Grand Marquis like a race car, weaving through the thickening traffic. In the less busy stretches, I'd squirmed out of my stealth gear and into the skating outfit that was only a temporary costume until

Jasper and I saw how this initial routine landed with an audience. While my bodyguard had been cruising swiftly but steadily, I'd tamed my hair into this sleek ponytail and applied some basic makeup.

All thoughts of the other performance I'd put on today had gradually faded to the back of my mind. My routine on the ice called for grace and elegance, nothing like the violent chaos I'd just created.

Some kind of celebration should be in store, but not until Jasper and I made it through the qualifying round and had that to celebrate too.

If we made it through the qualifying round.

The butterflies in my stomach flapped harder. But I said to Rafael, "Now or never."

As he pulled the car into the parking lot outside the big, pastel yellow arena building, I swallowed hard at the sight of the rows and rows of cars already stretched across the space. But the time on the dashboard clock said it was still ten minutes before our assigned performance time.

I'd made it, if only barely.

I grabbed my equipment bag out of the back and hauled ass to the arena doors. I was still several steps away when Niko and Jasper burst out to meet me, Niko's eyes shining with relief but Jasper in a furor.

"Where have you been?" he demanded before I could say anything, raking his hand through his tousled hair. "You missed our warm-up time. We're supposed to be going on to perform, like, *now*."

"Ten more minutes," I said with a gulp of breath. "Sorry, I didn't mean to cut it so close. I tried to take a shortcut and then we got delayed by an accident on the road."

It was a reasonable enough story, and Niko nodded. "We're just glad you made it."

But Jasper's eyes had narrowed as he looked at my ponytail. "Your hair…"

I frowned. "What?"

He reached over and fingered the strands, tugging a lock over where I could see it from the corner of my eye.

See the brittle, blackened tip where that bit had gotten singed.

Oh, shit.

I fumbled for a reasonable excuse and let out a laugh I hoped didn't sound nervous. "Just a little accident with the straightener. Come on, we've got to get inside and into our skates, or we really will be late."

That spurred my partner into action. A strange cosmetic detail was nothing compared to making it to the competition ahead.

As we all hustled inside, Niko waved to Rafael. "Come with me. You should sit up front for this performance—bring all that moral support."

A hint of a smile touched Rafael's lips. When the two of them split off from Jasper and me, a bloom of warmth filled my chest.

All three of the men who mattered most to me were here together, supporting me as a team. My two skaters had no idea about the trouble I'd gotten involved in, and now that was over. I could really put my past behind me and move forward.

I couldn't have asked for anything more.

The inside of the arena was only a smidgen nicer than the one in Hobb Creek. Along with the other skaters and the judges, there were several dozen onlookers in the stands, but not anywhere near enough to bring news crews. Just a small portion of Dellville's population curious to see the competition all the way through.

As we slipped into the rink area, the pair before us was gliding across the ice. Curiosity tugged at me to check out their routine, but I couldn't afford to give them even a few seconds of my time.

Jasper rushed me onward to the prep area at the base of the stands. I dropped onto the bench and yanked on my skates at record speed.

With each cross of the laces, I breathed in and out, willing my pulse to steady and my mind to clear of everything but my love for the ice.

Images from beautiful routines I'd watched in awe in the past floated through my mind—some of them spectacles put on by the very men who'd helped me reach this moment. Jasper and Niko had taken my breath away so many times.

I could make art like that too. Even if it wasn't a kind of art that could ever hang on a museum wall or be displayed at a gallery, it was art all the same.

But the fact that you had to be there in the moment to see it made it even more special. The beauty was so fleeting, so pure and so brief, that it had to be magic.

Determination wound through my limbs as I knotted the laces. I'd just defended the town I'd made my home and won, and now I was going to win this opportunity for myself and the men I was falling for too.

The song for the pair before us petered out. I looked up just in time to see them in their ending position before mild applause carried through the stands.

As they glided over to the boards, I quickly brushed my fingers over the pocket of my bag that held my childhood lace, for whatever luck it would offer me.

Jasper and I stood up in anticipation of our summons onto the ice. Jasper's shoulders looked stiff, his forehead furrowed.

When a woman with a clipboard motioned for us to take our starting positions, my partner's stance didn't loosen. The tension wound through his body while we skated into the center of the rink, storm clouds gathering in his eyes.

My own nerves had formed a twitching ball in my stomach, but they were as much excitement as anxiety. But then, maybe it made sense that he would be worrying more than I was.

This was my first chance to show the wider world what I could do. The possibilities were endless.

He'd already experienced the highs of success… and the lows of failure. He knew exactly how awful it would feel if he faltered out there.

It wasn't right. *I* knew what an amazing skater he was.

And maybe by working together, we'd find our way to a place where he could believe it again too.

Just before we settled into position, I tucked my hand around Jasper's neck and pushed up for a quick but tender kiss. When I drew back, he was staring at me with a hint of a flush in his cheeks but the storm clouds parted.

"Lou…"

I tapped him on the chest with a playful smile. "I just want you to know that I can't wait to be your partner—in this and in all kinds of other ways. We're going to make something really beautiful together."

His shoulders came down as an answering smile crossed his lips. "Yeah. Yeah, we will."

We arranged ourselves in our planned poses, my ears pricked for the first strains of our music. When the opening note reached my ears, my heart leapt.

Jasper and I took off at the third beat of the song, a dreamy nocturne that we had both agreed captured the emotion we wanted to evoke in our viewers. In that first moment, I realized he was just a tad ahead of me, not quite in sync. I pushed myself to catch up and wobbled, and my pulse stuttered.

We matched each other as we swept across the ice, every lift of our hands mirroring each other. When we whirled into our first set of spins, I caught a brief waver of Jasper's leg, but he straightened it in less than a second.

Keep breathing. Keep moving. We could do this.

We veered apart and circled back toward each other in preparation for the first—not quite as tricky—lift. Jasper's eyes met mine, and everyone off the ice seemed to dissolve from existence, as if we were the only two people in the universe.

When he hoisted me into the air, the cold air breezed by my face, stinging my cheeks. But I didn't care. This was what I was put on this planet to do.

I arched my back, letting my arms reach out wistfully, and hoped that my expression conveyed the gentle, heavenly emotions of the music.

Maybe I focused a little too hard on what my face was doing rather than the rest of me. As Jasper moved to lower me back down to the ice, my body shifted, and I sensed in an instant that I'd missed a moment when I needed to adjust my position more.

My weight wasn't even; my balance was off kilter. And Jasper had set his hand a little farther down my hip than was ideal, so I couldn't quite get it back on my own.

With a jolt of panic, I felt myself wobble. I hit the ice at an unsteady angle, already sensing gravity pulling my knee toward the ice.

But I pushed myself against its tug, and Jasper caught my elbow in a move that wasn't technically part of the routine but blended in well enough. I righted myself without outright hitting the ice.

The judges would have seen the awkward landing, even if it hadn't been as bad as it could have been. But as we set off to begin the next series of spins and jumps, I reminded myself that it was over.

We had so much more to show ahead of us, and we were going to knock their fucking socks off like no one else could.

I caught Jasper's eye and shot him a grin, hoping he hadn't been thrown by the error either. His expression relaxed, and he gave me a slight tip of his head just before we launched into our double Lutzes.

We hit the ice in perfect synchronization and whipped straight into the next sequence. With every breath, the pump of our legs felt even more aligned.

I experienced each breath Jasper took as though it were my own, our chests rising and falling together. We were even more united now than when we'd hooked up in the training room.

This was something different, something hovering on a soul-deep level I'd never felt before.

Our jump combo was effortless; our landing without fault. A smile lingered on Jasper's lips—not aimed at me but for the simple joy of the routine.

He was reveling in the art of skating itself, falling in love with the sport all over again. My heart soared at the sight.

This was what Niko had been working so hard for. I hoped he could see my skating partner's expression from his place in the stands.

Our toe loops descended to the ice at the exact same moment. My outstretched hand met Jasper's, and he pulled me close enough that I could feel his pulse hammering.

A twinge of anxiety rippled through me under the swell of the music. This was the lift that'd really given us trouble before. We'd failed in practice more often than we'd succeeded. If we hadn't even pulled off the easier one properly…

I shut out those doubts and gave myself over to the movements. We *had* done it before, just yesterday. We could do it again.

Jasper's fingers squeezed around my hand and against my thigh.

My body soared upward in his grasp to twirl three full times in quick succession.

I followed every shift of his body in time with the peak of the melody. We were still united, still in sync in every way that mattered.

Yeah. We could do this. Watch us now.

I came down at the perfect angle, the tips of my skates' blades connecting with the ice like they were magnets. A whoop of approval carried from the crowd.

We glided around into the last jump-spin combo and twined together in our ending pose. We were both panting for breath, but I could feel Jasper's triumphant grin against my cheek.

Applause thundered through the arena. My own grin stretched so wide my cheeks ached.

We'd done it. We'd recovered and proved just how good we could be.

Jasper took my hand, raising it high towards the rafters. The clapping only grew louder.

My gaze veered to the row of judges with a rush of relief at the smiles on their faces before they ducked their heads to consider their notes.

Jasper nudged me in the arm on our way back to the stands. "You were really something out there, Punk."

I beamed at him. "So were you. I'd say that was a pretty good start to our competitive partnership." I paused with a slight listing of my stomach. "Well, as long as the judges think so too."

Niko didn't appear to have any doubts on that score. Our coach welcomed us to the bench with his face lit up so bright he outshone the overhead lights.

"You two were amazing!" he crowed. "I knew you could do it!"

Even Rafael couldn't completely contain a smile. He studied the judges. "What about their scores?"

"Just a moment." Niko motioned to the judging table. "Look, they're handing them over to the announcer now."

My heart started pounding so hard it drowned out every other sound. The announcer raised his microphone to his lips, but all I heard was the frantic thudding and another round of cheers from the crowd.

Niko grabbed my arm and Jasper's and pulled us both into a joint hug. "You're in! Not that I had any doubts *before* watching you, let alone after."

I blinked at him, breathless. "But—aren't there still some more pairs who need to compete?"

"It doesn't matter," Niko announced gleefully. "Your score is the third highest out of everyone who's performed so far, and there are only five more pairs left. Even if they're all geniuses, you're guaranteed to be in the ten who'll compete properly tomorrow."

He wrapped his arms around us, happiness radiating through our little huddle. "I'm so proud of you two. This is just the start, and it was a fantastic one."

A giddy laugh burst out of me. I hugged him back and then pulled Jasper into an embrace just the two of us. Even after I finally sat down on the bench to swap my skates for my sneakers, the sensation of floating stayed with me.

Rafael leaned over from behind me, murmuring by my ear so that only I could hear him. "I'm going to take a walk around the perimeter. I just want to be sure everything is fine, if you know what I mean. But that performance was incredible, Lou."

I nodded, understanding completely. I couldn't blame him for wanting to be on the safe side after what we'd accomplished earlier today. And a big crowd celebration wasn't really my bodyguard's style.

As for me, I was riding the wave of adrenaline coursing through my veins with nothing on my mind but this first small but perfect victory.

I had arrived, and I was already making my mark.

TWENTY-EIGHT

Luciana

TAKEOUT HAD NEVER BEEN SO delicious in my life.

I dug into a mound of white rice and duck sauce, scooping faster than I could swallow. A veritable feast was laid out between Rafael and me on our little dining table in the bungalow, and all of it tasted like success.

"This was definitely the right choice for a celebratory dinner." I dipped a wonton in soy sauce as it wobbled between my chopsticks. "God, I was starving. Today really took it out of me, I guess."

Rafael only hummed in response, unusually subdued even for the deadpan bodyguard I was used to. I glanced up at him, taking in the distant cast to his eyes and the solemn shadow that'd come over his features.

He'd long since finished his helping of Mongolian beef. The container sat empty on the coffee table, judging me silently as I chowed down. He hadn't touched anything from the myriad of soups and appetizers I'd ordered.

Now he leaned back in his chair, his mouth setting in an even sterner line than before.

Was he still worrying about our hijinks before the skating competition this afternoon?

I wagged my chopsticks at him. "I don't think we need to worry about that pathetic excuse for a gang ever again. I mean, they wouldn't have cleared out the rest of their stuff from the storage building if they weren't taking off for whatever they figure greener pastures are, right?"

We'd stopped by the old hideout on our way back into town and found the building a burnt-out shell and the parking lot totally vacant other than one car Rafael's fireworks must have done too much of a number on. There'd been no sign of the wannabe gangsters anywhere.

"They're not going to come back," Rafael said brusquely.

His confirmation reassured me but left me even more confused about his mood. I prodded a morsel of duck. "I'm glad that's over with. Now we can live our lives in peace."

All I got in response was a grunt. Where had this new stick up his ass come from? He'd seemed upbeat enough, as much as he ever got, right after I'd skated.

But he'd become increasingly quiet and solemn the whole drive home. I'd thought it was concern about our previous problems, but that clearly wasn't the case.

My stomach ached with all the food I'd stuffed into it and a little apprehension as well.

I set down my chopsticks. "Well, if you're not eating anything else, we'd better pack the rest up. I don't want to gain twenty pounds right before the actual competition."

Rafael got up with a scrape of his chair legs, his attention finally focusing on me. "You're going to be fine tomorrow. Better than fine."

"Oh, yeah?" I said with a teasing lilt as I started closing up cartons. "Then why are you going around like you expect the apocalypse to begin any moment now?"

The corner of his mouth twitched. He gathered up a couple of cartons in a stack in front of him and then simply gazed down at them as if he'd forgotten what he was supposed to do with them.

He lifted his head and met my eyes again. "I'm sorry, Lou."

Say what now?

I cocked my head, trying to hide just how confused I was. "What've you got to be sorry for? I couldn't have gotten through today without you—you had my back every step of the way. You know how much I appreciate that, don't you?"

"It's not… It's not about that." He grimaced as if he was grappling with his words.

My stomach started to sink.

Rafael was normally taciturn, sure, but he spoke his mind bluntly when he did have something to say. What was he so uncomfortable about telling me?

Was he thinking about leaving—going back to Austin to rejoin Mom's operations? Maybe our battle with the small-time criminals here in Hobb Creek had left him missing the bigger thrills of his former career.

He squared his shoulders, and I braced myself for the pain I imagined was coming.

"As much as I said I wouldn't, I've been treating you like a kid," he said. "Like you're a victim—or like you can't make your own decisions. But today showed me just how wrong I was. I should have seen it so much sooner. I should have—"

He cut himself off with a growl, the sound containing so much frustrated emotion that my pulse kicked up a notch.

I shook my head. "It's okay. You don't have to apologize for that. You *have* been watching over me since I was a kid—it makes sense that it'd be hard to shift your frame of reference."

"Maybe. But it shouldn't have taken me so long. If it hadn't…" He let out his breath in a rough sigh. "I've noticed the woman you were becoming in *other* ways for years. You're strong and funny, talented and gorgeous—I can't say there wasn't a tiny part of me that was tempted even when you took your shot when you were sixteen."

My mouth went dry, my heart thumping even faster. "You turned me down."

"I did. I don't regret that—that's a line that should never be crossed. But you waited until you were old enough that no one back home would have batted an eye and gave me another chance, and I blew that one too. I wanted you so badly, but I convinced myself I shouldn't go there, that I'd somehow be taking advantage of you because you couldn't realize what you were really getting into."

As I stared at him in stunned silence, he hung his head. "That's what I'm sorry about. I rejected you even though you were everything I could possibly want because I was arrogant enough to think you couldn't know what *you* really wanted, and now—now I've obviously lost my chance. I probably shouldn't even be telling you this, but I wanted you to know that you weren't wrong. It was my screw-up."

I swallowed thickly, so much emotion welling up inside me that I could barely breathe.

Rafael had been my first crush and therefore my longest. I'd always wanted him more than any other man I'd met, even after he'd made it clear nothing was going to happen between us.

Well, until I'd blown into Hobb Creek and met Niko and Jasper.

I paused on that thought. Was that why he assumed he'd lost his chance?

But all those old feelings still thrummed through my body, propelling me toward the man I'd loved for so long. I walked around the table, hardly feeling the floor beneath my feet.

"Rafael, I fell for you all the way back when I was thirteen years old. Because you *are* everything I could imagine wanting. Just because I'm falling for other men too doesn't mean those feelings have vanished."

He lifted his hand only to leave it hovering in the air between us, not quite reaching all the way to me. I wrapped my own much smaller hands around it, his solid palm engulfing my fingers.

The warmth of his skin sparked a headier heat right up my arm. But I knew I had to make one other thing clear.

"I *am* falling for Niko and Jasper," I said, keeping my voice steady but soft. "There are other things I want in my life—need in my life—that I never realized before, that I've found with them. I'm not going to give them up."

Rafael's voice came out gruff, but I thought I saw a glint of hope in his burgundy eyes. "I wouldn't expect you to."

I smiled up at him. "And that's exactly why I still need you too, however you're willing to be a part of my life. That's what it comes down to, really. You haven't lost your shot. It's just a question of whether you can handle sharing me with them."

His jaw worked as he considered his answer. "I don't know. A lot of me wants to whisk you away from everything and claim you all for myself. But you're not a woman who can be claimed. I realize that. I'd like—I'd like to see what we could be even with them in the mix, if you want that too."

I grinned up at him with a rush of joy. "Oh, believe me, I do."

I bobbed up on my toes, and thankfully Rafael knew exactly what I was aiming for. He wrapped one brawny arm around me and leaned in to meet my kiss.

His searing heat washed over my body. I sighed into the kiss and tilted my head to angle it even deeper.

For all the hardness of his muscular frame, Rafael's lips were soft as velvet. His tongue slid like a flame against my own.

With each kiss that followed the first, my head spun faster. His fingers trailed over my hair, sparking jolts of pleasure through my scalp.

I matched his passion with my own blazing desire, wanting him more and more with each passing moment. Wanting to savor every bit of the connection I'd believed I was never going to get.

My hands teased up under his shirt to stroke his sculpted back skin to skin. Rafael groaned and kissed me even harder—

And a loud *thump* filtered through the wall from outside in the front yard.

I jumped with a flinch of my nerves, my head jerking toward the door. The passion that'd been flowing through my limbs ebbed with a pang of apprehension. "What was that?"

Rafael's eyes had turned even darker. He strode toward the door, and I dashed after him, my hands balling into fists.

We stormed down the front steps, scanning the yard for any sign of an intruder. In the thickening darkness of the evening, I didn't make out any movement.

Then my gaze caught on a furry form slumped on the hood of the Grand Marquis.

Rafael saw it in the same moment. He held out his hand to ward me off. "Maybe you should go inside."

I shot him a pointed look. "Didn't you just get done saying how I'm a strong woman who can handle myself?"

I marched over, my gut twisting as I made out the details of the tableau that'd been arranged on the hood.

It was a raccoon. Limp and lifeless, its beady eyes glazed, its severed neck leaking blood across the pale blue steel.

And next to its head lay a figure skate with a bloody blade. The blade that'd been used to cut the animal's throat.

My stomach was outright churning now. "Rafael," I murmured, wrenching my gaze back to him. "We ran the gang out of town. And they didn't even know it was me. They wouldn't come back just to pick on the new girl in town some more."

Rafael scowled at the carcass. "No, they wouldn't. I don't think this is about them after all."

A shiver ran through my body. "We assumed we were dealing with one set of enemies… but it could have been two all this time."

If my latest bloody gift wasn't from the idiotic gangsters, then the doll, the squirrel, and the pigeons hadn't been either. Those two pieces of the puzzle had never really fit together—because they weren't connected after all.

I peered into the deepening night with a deeper chill prickling under my skin.

Whoever was harassing me with unnerving "presents" was someone separate from the gang we'd just run off.

Someone deranged. Someone dangerous. Someone smart enough to play their disturbing tricks without getting caught.

Someone who intended to torment me in every sick way they could, and who wasn't remotely close to stopping.

PIVOT POINT

BLADES OF HAVOC #2

ONE

Luciana

THE BLADES of my skates clicked against the ice as I stepped onto it. With a soft hiss of steel against the frozen surface, I glided toward the center of the rink next to my partner.

I'd imagined what this moment would feel like my entire life.

I'd always thought—always been *told*—that entering any kind of competition was out of my reach. I'd been stifled, kept in the dark when it came to my true skill.

I'd been lied to, manipulated, and emotionally beaten down by the people I should have been able to trust most.

But today made all that anguish worth it.

Today, I would let out the truth of who I was—who I was meant to be. I would fly free in front of an audience, if only for a few minutes.

I wanted to cement this memory into my brain. After all, it was my first competition since I'd started skating fourteen years ago.

I'd only get this moment once.

And no creepy stalker was going to ruin it for me, no matter how hard they tried.

I couldn't stop my gaze from flicking toward the stands with a nervous twitch. Watching for a tell-tale flash of blood red, as if the psycho who'd been haunting me might have left one of his bloody presents here in Dellville's rink, two hours from the town where he'd been harassing me before.

He *could* be here among the decent-sized crowd that'd gathered to see the full competition after yesterday's qualifying round. I didn't really know anything about the creep who'd left dead animals in my bedroom and on my car, who'd taunted me with a doll hung by a noose.

My gut clenched at the memory. I couldn't imagine many *other* figure skaters had to worry about a psychopath while they got into position for their first ever official competitive performance.

Was he already planning his next moves? How far would he take his sick game next time?

I closed my eyes for a second, gathering myself. I couldn't think about that asshole right now.

I had to focus on the men who were standing with me rather than against me.

Jasper caught my gaze, and a small smile touched his lips. The arena lights shone off the pale planes of my partner's stunning face beneath his shaggy auburn hair.

He let out a shaky breath that maybe he thought I wouldn't notice.

A lot was riding on this moment for him too. Jasper St. Pierre, once known as Saint Jasper by his many avid fans, hadn't competed since he'd been sunk by a major slump more than a year ago.

This could be his comeback—or a nail in the coffin formed by his uncertainties.

Our not-entirely-official coach, Niko Okabe, gripped the top of the boards where he was standing by the edge of the rink. At my glance, he shot me a broad smile, but I suspected there was a little anxiety in his twinkling brown eyes too.

He'd come all the way from Japan to dedicate himself to pulling Jasper out of his slump. And I'd discovered that he was invested both professionally and personally, with feelings that were warmer than friendly.

As he swiped his slender hand through his smooth black hair with its stripe of neon pink, my attention slid higher in the stands just for an instant.

I couldn't see my bodyguard, but I knew with every fiber of my being that Rafael was standing up there, watching over me. Silent, unseen, but ready to leap to my defense at a moment's notice.

We'd get through this, the four of us, together. Even if my two fellow skaters had no idea just how much I had to worry about.

I was starting to live my dream, and in the end, that was the only thing that mattered. I had to keep my focus, not just for my men, but for myself.

For five-year-old Lou who'd fallen in love with skating at a random ice show that her mother had taken her to out of boredom.

For ten-year-old Lou who'd practiced for hours each day after school, determined to do better, to *be* better.

For fifteen-year-old Lou, who'd already seen and been forced to participate in so many horrors, who only found solace on the ice.

Skating had been my only source of peace for so long, the one place where I could experience something beautiful and graceful. I couldn't let this chance slip through my fingers.

"You ready, Punk?" Jasper murmured as we struck our poses, giving his nickname for me a teasing lilt.

"As I'll ever be."

I found that I was actually telling the truth. All anxiety had fled my heart. I was left with nothing but quiet resolve.

The moment the familiar melody began to play over the speakers, my heart started to pound. On the third beat, we pushed off across the ice in graceful synchronization.

Our measured breaths became one, our heartbeats thudding along in the same rhythm. Confidence wrapped around me like a warm blanket, more than I'd felt performing the same routine yesterday, even if there were more onlookers this time.

Jasper and I would do our best. I knew every move, every spin, lift, and jump, and I simply had to show it.

It seemed that Jasper felt the same way. I caught his expression: the gentle, expressive smile that curved his full lips up.

Even as we swept into our first sequence, I had to marvel at his grace. He was all broad shoulders and powerful limbs; it didn't seem like he would be able to glide across the ice with so much elegance, but he seemed more at home on the rink than off it.

We spun, jumped, and landed together to spiral around each other. I imagined a trail of color, sparkling silver and gold flowing behind me as I swayed in time to the music.

Jasper and I swiveled toward each other. At the music's highest trill, my hands found his. Our arms twined together, necks tilting, backs arching.

The melody swelled, the sweeping arrangement filling both my ears and my heart. I barely felt myself land the next jump.

There was nothing in me or around me but the resounding symphony and the beauty of our routine. My heart soared along with every note, every spin, every pose.

No matter what any psycho stalker did, no way could I ever give this feeling up.

We breezed through the first lift without even the slightest hint of a quake in my skating partner's arms or my own stance. I'd been so caught up in the joy of the routine itself that I'd had no time to worry about whether we would struggle.

I swung through the air, perched on Jasper's palm, without a care in the world. The routine felt as natural as breathing.

When he lowered me back down to the ice, I reveled in the power and strength contained in his brawny arms.

We shot into our synchronized double Lutz without hesitation, our bodies twisting midair simultaneously. This routine had followed me into my dreams, replaying over and over like a tape stuck on repeat, but one that I could watch for eternity without getting tired of it.

I backpedaled until I was flying in reverse, my dark ponytail whipping around my face. These were the moments I lived for.

My heartbeat quickened as I circled back around, facing my

skating partner. We were coming up on the lift that had always been hardest for us.

If we could just pull that off, then I could believe we'd really see this through to the end as the entire routine was meant to be.

Resolution shone in Jasper's eyes as he glided forward. His hands reached for me, and I leaned into his hold, giving over my trust to my partner.

He lifted me up, higher and higher until I was truly soaring now. His powerful arms supported the pose I struck with a surge of strength that made my body crave his touch even more.

One rotation.

Two.

A third time, each whirling motion perfectly in time with the music.

As he lowered me, my arms swept outward. I landed soft as a dove feather.

We'd done it. We'd *nailed* it.

A grin stretched across my face. My body careened through the last part of the routine as if floating on joy.

Jasper caught my hand and held it up in our final pose. Even if the power had gone out right then and there, my partner's bright smile would have been enough to light the room.

And he aimed it right at me.

A whoop I knew was Niko's carried from the boards. A pang ran through my heart at the connection I felt to both of these men who'd come together to build my dream with me.

With the last note of the song fading, a moment of silence gripped the arena. My pulse only had the chance to stutter with concern once before a thunder of applause broke out through the stands.

I looked up at them, watching rows of spectators stand as they brought their hands together. So many more smiles beamed down at me. One old man in the front hastily wiped away a tear with the back of his glove.

My grin stretched even wider, happiness surging up inside me as if it would carry me all the way to the ceiling.

Was the sicko who'd been harassing me watching up there too? Let him.

I was a force to be reckoned with. I hadn't let my mother destroy my life, and I sure as hell wasn't going to let any psycho stranger do it either.

And this was only the beginning.

TWO

Luciana

WAITING for our scores felt like the longest few minutes of my life. We'd gone last, so the number the judges were calculating would determine exactly where we placed in the rankings.

The thing was done. We could sit back and celebrate the fact that we'd made it through the routine so flawlessly, no matter how we did in the actual competition itself. Nerves or not, I wanted to savor this moment for all it was worth.

And it was worth the world to me.

My hands wound tightly together as I rested them in my lap, my butt freezing from the chilled metal bench. Beside me, Jasper's knee jiggled up and down in his anxiety.

Niko, though, was as still as a cat who had spotted a mouse, his bright brown eyes on the judges as they marked down our scores. My eyes flicked over to the announcer as another employee handed him a sheet of paper.

Oh, Lord. Here it comes.

My stomach lifted as though I were about to go hurtling down a roller coaster's steep first drop. The announcer adjusted his glasses and squinted down at whatever was written there.

"And the score for our final pair is… fifty-two point three-nine! That puts them in first place."

First place.

Those two words beat around in my skull, echoing like a shout into a cave. Jasper and Niko let out a joint cheer.

The crowd was whooping and clapping, but I could barely even hear them. I was frozen, stunned by what we'd just accomplished.

With this being our first routine as a pair and there not being much time to prepare for the small local competition, we hadn't included the most complex moves that could have made an even higher score possible. I'd already calculated the maximum we could possibly achieve with the jumps and lifts we were going to perform, and we'd come just a couple of points shy of total perfection.

A grin broke across my face, and I spun toward Jasper to wrap my arms around him. He laughed and hugged me back.

This was real. We'd not just competed but *won.*

As I let go of Jasper, Niko grabbed me in an embrace of his own. "I hope that puts all those doubts your old coach gave you out of your head."

A choked giggle sputtered out of me. "I guess it has to."

Had Coach Balakin ever imagined I'd be capable of this? Would he have been surprised or sad because he'd always known he was holding me back under my mother's orders?

Niko pulled back and beamed at the two of us. "I only wish you could have seen your routine from the stands. It was breathtaking. Just stunning. I got it on video, but that won't compare at all to the experience you just gave these people. Congratulations!"

"Congratulations to you, too," Jasper said, nudging Niko's shoe with his. His smile was sunnier than I'd ever seen it. "You're the one that got us here."

"We won." I breathed out in a giddy rush. "We… we really did it!"

"Yeah, we did." Jasper grinned. "We showed this competition what we're made of, huh?"

All of our hard work and all of that effort had actually paid off. My years of training under Coach Balakin had done a lot of good, even if he'd never admitted how much.

The man might have been forced to lie to me about my skill, he'd still done his best for me, had tried to give me everything he gave his other normal students whose parents didn't happen to be leaders of a vast criminal organization.

And he'd died for his efforts.

Tears blossomed in the corners of my eyes. I didn't wipe them away in time for Niko and Jasper not to notice.

"Lou, you alright?" Jasper asked, his voice low. "If you want to go somewhere quiet—"

"No, no." I brushed a hand across my face, reining in the swell of grief that had momentarily overwhelmed my hammering heart. "It's just that… I don't know, I thought this moment would never come. I didn't think I would ever get to feel this way—not once in my whole life. I just can't believe we pulled it off!"

My eyes traveled up to the stands; I knew that somewhere, Rafael was watching me with pride glowing in his burgundy eyes. I only wished that he could be down here with me now, and then my heart would truly be full and complete.

For now, though, it was enough to know that he was here, that he had seen my routine. That he had seen me finally win.

The announcer had just finished reading out the names of the winners—mine with the fake last name I'd had Niko register me under—calling us onto the ice. Jasper and I made our way down to the center of the rink again.

Our winnings weren't much: two fifty-dollar gift cards for local eateries, two more to the sporting goods store in between here and Hobb Creek, and a small metal trophy in the image of an ice skate. You couldn't expect much more than that from a competition this low-key.

But I didn't need grand prizes to revel in the moment. I gripped Jasper's hand as we grinned like fools in the center of the rink, clutching our gift cards and our cheap trophies.

Jasper grabbed my hand as we returned to the stands to a little more fanfare. "We should probably go get changed, huh? Meet you in the front hall after? We should go out to celebrate."

"You bet." I squeezed his hand hard before letting go.

We snatched our equipment bags and made our way to the locker rooms, Niko following at our heels. He nodded to us, still smiling as bright as the afternoon sun outside.

"I'll be right here."

Jasper pushed the door to the men's locker room open. "Let's go somewhere that's serving breakfast for dinner. I'm dying for some waffles."

"Of course you are," I called after him with a snicker, and headed into the women's locker room, my thoughts spinning in my head in a joyful daze.

This is so surreal.

The dream-like feel of the moment only increased with the various skaters who offered their congratulations as we changed side by side. I smiled and thanked them and complimented their performances even when I couldn't remember the routine, my hands whipping through the motions.

I just wanted to get back out there and see my men again. My lessons with Coach Balakin had always been solo, so I wasn't used to this community vibe, as nice as I imagined it could be once I got used to it.

These other women were my peers, not people who I had to gaze at from afar, wishing I could be one of them. Not anymore.

I wriggled out of my skating costume and pulled on my faded black skull tee and pinstriped leggings before slipping my clunky rings that could serve as weapons as well onto my fingers. I only took a moment to glance at myself in the mirror.

Okay, I had to admit I'd earned Jasper's nickname.

Despite my haste, my partner was already waiting for me in the hallway, Niko beside him. The sight of them together, happy and relaxed, was enough to make my heart sing.

Even in the artificial arena lights, I didn't think I'd ever found them more striking—or irresistible.

My heart thumped faster, and so did my steps as I closed the gap between us in urgent strides.

Jasper's eyes gleamed as he took me in. "Lou, we—"

I didn't give him the chance to finish his sentence. I snatched them both by one arm and dragged them around the nearest corner, away from the locker rooms and the distant murmurs of the exiting audience.

The only thing I wanted was to feel their bodies against mine, to taste victory on their lips.

The moment that I was sure we were alone, I thrust myself into Jasper's arms and kissed him. He hesitated for only a split-second before he pulled me closer, his lips parting against mine.

He tasted like fire and ice all at once, steaming hot in desire and chilled from the rink. I nibbled on his bottom lip briefly, then teased his tongue with my own.

His hands moved up into my hair, his fingers mussing my ponytail. He let out a tiny gasp that tickled me somewhere low in my belly, his eyes darkening when he pulled away to meet my gaze.

Now *that* was a victory kiss.

"You were really amazing out there," he said, his voice gone rough. "So fucking beautiful."

As my cheeks flushed at the emphatic compliment, he glanced over at our coach. I caught a flicker of uncertainty in his expression before he squared his shoulders and stepped closer to the other man.

"And you've been amazing too."

Jasper leaned in to quickly press his lips to Niko's. It was something softer and more cautious than the embrace we'd just shared, but the sweetness of the gesture was palpable.

A different sort of joy swept through me as he eased back with a cautious smile. My lovers were finally working through their own crap to find their way back to where they'd started.

Niko blinked at Jasper and then grinned, at least as pleased as he was startled. "I'll accept the compliment and the gift that came with it. But I can't leave my favorite girl out."

He flashed that impish grin at me before pulling me in for a kiss as well. I smiled against his lips, a giggle bubbling up in my throat.

I loved the playful part of him so much. His lively personality had become a source of comfort to me.

My two skaters contrasted with each other, but together they made something more special than I could have ever imagined being possible back in Austin.

And then there was Rafael now, too.

My good spirits dampened just slightly at the memory of my bodyguard's confession—and the brief makeout session we'd had last night. I was going to have to tell Niko and Jasper that my relationship with the other man was shifting in a new direction.

They'd known I wasn't exclusive, but I'd explicitly told them that he was just a friend. I didn't want them thinking I'd lied about that.

Although we shouldn't get into all the things I *had* lied about, or at least avoided telling the truth about. I hadn't even competed under my real name.

My gut knotted. My past had to stay in the past. It was safer for all of us that way.

But I was going to be honest with them about Rafael.

We'd need to go somewhere more private for that conversation. I wasn't going to get into my complicated love life when any of the other skaters could come around the corner in the middle of my explanation.

Maybe at dinner we could get a cozy booth in a not-too-busy restaurant that would give us the space we needed. Or I'd invite them over to the bungalow after. Niko hadn't even seen my house before.

I tugged at both men. "Come on, let's go get that dinner. I'm starving."

We made our way back out to the main hall, still grinning like shy middle schoolers who had just shared their first kiss. A few of the other skaters were still standing around chatting, adding to the community vibe I was just starting to appreciate.

Someday I'd really fit in with the rest of them.

We'd almost reached the lobby when a trill of a voice called out from behind us. "Jasper St. Pierre! Oh, and your lovely partner is with you too. What luck."

All three of us turned to see a middle-aged woman making her way down the hall toward us, waving for our attention with just the tips of her fingers. The thudding of her clunky high heels echoed through the hall. Her startlingly bright blue eyeshadow should have clashed with her sunflower-print dress, but somehow the contrast gave her a quirky poise.

"Oh, I'm so glad to have caught you." the woman said. "It was so wonderful to see you performing again, Jasper. That performance was absolutely moving."

Jasper peered at the woman with a hint of confusion before he pasted on a smile in an even more impressive performance than he'd given on the ice. I could tell that he didn't actually recognize her, and he probably wanted to tell her to buzz off, but he knew better than to let his usual grumpy self show in front of a fan.

"Thank you," he said, tucking his hands behind his back. "I'm glad that you thought so. Creating a visual that's emotionally compelling is always my main goal."

The woman laughed like a crow with something caught in its throat. "And you do it so well." She turned to me. "And I don't believe we've met, but you rose to Jasper's level quite spectacularly. I can't wait to see more from you."

Feeling a little out of my depth, I didn't know what to say other than a repeat of Jasper's "Thank you."

She arched her eyebrows at me. "And I do expect to see more of you. Will you be competing for Canada or coming down to join us at U.S. Figure Skating?"

I opened my mouth and closed it again, and latched on to an appropriate diversion. "You work for the association."

"Oh, yes, look at me not introducing myself. I'm Martha Maderline. I'm not high enough that it'll do you much good to butter me up, I warn you, but I can still tell you how much we'd love to have you on board."

Understanding dawned in Jasper's eyes as he must have remembered seeing her before.

I couldn't help asking, "What are you doing all the way up here in Dellville?"

Maderline gave her croaking laugh again. "I heard from a local friend that Jasper was performing again and I just had to take a quick jaunt up here to see it for myself. And imagine my surprise when I saw who was coaching you! Niko Okabe, what an unexpected delight."

"Yes," Niko said with obvious amusement. "It's a little far from my usual territory. But you don't get the chance to coach a talent like Jasper St. Pierre every day. And Lou, too. She's a big up-and-comer, you know."

"I could see that with my own eyes." The woman patted my arm so fondly that I found myself warming to her despite her overblown personality. "Congratulations on holding your own with big names like these two. You're really going somewhere, I'm sure of it."

This time my smile came with a little uncertainty. "That means a lot to me."

Maderline set her hands on her ample hips. "Well, I'll let you get on with the celebration I'm sure you're planning after that win. I just had to say hello, and also to *insist* that you come compete in the qualifying series if you're at all inclined to return to Jasper's home country. You still have a week to sign up before the cut-off. Don't miss it!"

Jasper rubbed the back of his neck. "We'll certainly think about it. Thank you again."

She waggled her fingers at us once more and sashayed out into the parking lot. A giggle bubbled in my chest, but a prickle of nerves held it in place.

Jasper glanced at Niko. "She really thinks I'm back at that level again?" There was no mistaking the hope in his voice.

Niko snorted. "Of course you're at that level. You'd breeze through the qualifying competitions, as long as you don't get in your own way." He prodded me with a teasing finger. "Both of you would."

A softer smile curved Jasper's lips, but one that looked totally genuine. "Maybe we *should* give it a go. The way I felt on the ice today… It was almost like it used to be. Or better, just a little different than I'm used to."

He aimed his smile at me, and my pulse fluttered. Getting such an eager vote of support from someone who worked for the national skating organization was huge—and it lit me up inside seeing Jasper acting more sure of himself.

"I guess it could be worth trying."

"Worth trying?" Jasper gave my ponytail a tug of mock-consternation as we stepped out into the warm late-afternoon sunlight washing over the parking lot. "You should be chomping at the bit for this, Punk. Place high enough in the early competitions, and we could be at Nationals in a few months."

It should have made my heart soar to see him talk about that possibility with nothing but happiness. Instead, a chill trickled through my veins.

If we started competing at larger competitions, especially south of the border, the chances that my mom would catch wind of my location would increase exponentially. I knew from my own figure-skating viewing that the qualifying competitions were mostly broadcast on specialized channels that people who moved in her circles weren't likely to be tuning in to.

But Nationals? That'd be shown on any station with significant sports coverage.

Coach Balakin's sallow, lifeless face flashed behind my eyes, and I had to restrain a shudder.

Every step further I took on this journey toward my dream, I put the two men with me in more danger. Danger they couldn't possibly anticipate.

But how could I tell them that we should stay here and stick to tiny local competitions? How could I drop out of my partnership with Jasper when he'd just started finding his way out of his slump?

Nausea congealed in my gut, but I knew there was only one answer.

I was going to have to come clean. Tell them the whole story of who I was and where I'd come from.

And then I'd find out whether they even still wanted me around, let alone competing with them.

THREE

Luciana

I WISHED I could have appreciated my introduction to Niko's apartment more. The four of us tramped up the stairs next to a cute thrift store and stepped into a bachelor pad lit by the last rays of the sinking sun through its broad front windows.

I could tell that during the day, the whole place would be as bright as Niko's attitude. His personal touch to the place was minimal, probably because he hadn't been able to bring a whole lot of possessions over from Japan with him, and the space had a tidy feel. But his presence showed in the postcards pinned to the fridge with magnets and the collection of weights and other training equipment next to the futon.

It even smelled like him, warm and tart. I should have been loving this moment.

Instead, my stomach had twisted into one big knot.

Rafael glanced at me with a questioning expression. On the drive over, he'd asked me if I was sure I really wanted to do this.

"You know I have to," I'd told him. "If I leave Niko and Jasper in the dark with the danger I'd be putting them in, I'd be *worse* than Mom."

Rafael had grimaced. "We don't know how they'll react. They could panic and do something… unwise."

I'd rolled my eyes at him. "I don't think they're going to call the cops on me. And if it looks like they might, we'll just have to disappear again."

Better that than I got the two men I'd started falling for killed by dragging them into the line of fire unaware.

Niko smiled as he swept his arm toward the cozy space, but his expression was curious too. At the end of the dinner which I hadn't been able to enjoy all that much either, I'd told him and Jasper that there was something important I needed to talk to them about and suggested we go back to one of their places.

I didn't trust the bungalow, not really. Not when my stalker had already targeted it more than once.

Jasper wasn't one to beat around the bush out of politeness. He turned to face me and folded his arms over his chest.

"So? What's the big important news?"

"It's not exactly *news*…" My throat constricted.

I dragged in a breath and sank down on Niko's couch. My heart hammered at my ribs.

I'd only just found real happiness here in Hobb Creek with these two men. Was I going to lose it already?

Would the admiration and affection I'd treasured in their eyes fade away into disgust and horror?

But I did have to tell them. Maybe I should never have hidden it this long to begin with.

I swallowed thickly and looked up at the three men. Rafael moved to stand by the arm of the futon beside me.

His brow furrowing, Jasper gripped the back of the boxy armchair. "Is everything okay?"

Niko settled onto the futon next to me and gave my knee a quick but reassuring squeeze. "Let's give our angel a moment to work through her thoughts. If you need anything, just say so, Lou."

He was being so sweet about it that I winced inwardly. I was even less of an angel than I'd ever claimed to be.

I set my hands on my lap, where they twisted together awkwardly. "The thing is, there's something you should know before we decide about competing on a larger scale. I—I haven't told you the whole truth about how I grew up."

Niko frowned with obvious concern. "You mentioned that you had a hard life at home. We didn't need the details."

"You do, though. Because… the *reason* it was a hard childhood is that my mother is the ruler of a major criminal organization. Like, think the mafia, but with even more influence and power."

Jasper's eyebrows shot up. "You ran away from the *mafia*?"

I shook my head. "Not even the mafia. Listen. It's—she's—even worse. She commands legions of underlings and has control over business all around the world, and she's not afraid to kill. And she expected me to become just like her."

Silence fell over the room. It pressed down on me as if a sack had been pulled over my head, but I forced myself to push on. I had to get it all out.

"That wasn't—that wasn't what I wanted to be. *Who* I wanted to be. I've always wanted to skate. I never lied about that. But she… I think she paid off my coach to tell me I wasn't good enough, to make sure I never thought I should be competing or going anywhere with it. And then, when she thought I was old enough that I should be taking more responsibilities as her heir…"

A shiver ran through me with the memory of Balakin's corpse, the blood-stained ice, the knowledge that he'd died because of me.

Just like these two men might if Mom ever found me.

"What happened, Lou?" Niko asked, quietly but gently.

I stared at my clenched hands. "She had my coach murdered. Left him for me to find. Acted as if it was a good thing because I could finally move on in the direction she wanted."

Jasper sucked in a ragged breath. "Holy shit."

"Yeah," I said, fighting down my nausea. "That was when I knew I couldn't stay any longer. I grabbed what I could and took off—and Rafael insisted on coming too. He's been my bodyguard for years. I needed to find someplace she'd never think to look for me and, well, we ended up in Hobb Creek. You basically know the rest of that story."

Rafael's gaze slid from one man to the other, his expression grim. "She's felt guilty about not telling you everything, even though she didn't owe it to you. Even now, she could have cut and run rather than getting into it. Remember that."

Jasper rubbed his hand over his face and blinked at me. "That just sounds crazy. Why *are* you telling us now?"

He wasn't recoiling in disgust, which I guessed was a win. But now I had to get into the hardest part.

"My mom will be searching for me. If she figures out where I am, I don't know what she'll do, but you could become targets. I'm already getting harassed by a stalker who could be connected to her somehow —we don't even know."

I lifted my gaze to meet Jasper's and then Niko's eyes. "She might kill you if she realizes I've been skating with you, like she did to my old coach. The more publicity we get, the bigger events we compete in, the higher the chance is that she'll catch on and you'll be in danger. I don't want that to happen. And I totally understand if you don't want anything at all to do with me now. I didn't mean to get your hopes up under false pretenses."

Niko leaned toward me, searching my face. "How much danger are *you* in, Lou? You said someone's already been bothering you?"

Really? After everything I'd just told him, he was worried about *me*?

"I don't know," I said. "Some sicko has left dead animals around my house and things like that, but I have no idea who's doing it. But it just proves that I'm a magnet for trouble."

Jasper snorted. "Well, we already knew that, Punk."

The joke came out a little strained, and his smile was stiff around the edges. But he looked at me steadily.

"There was always something that sounded a little strange about your story," he added. "This whole thing *is* crazy, but somehow I don't even feel that surprised. It's not okay that anyone's messing with you, doing psycho shit like that. If you need to crash somewhere else for a while—"

"You're welcome to stay here, as long as you need," Niko jumped in before Jasper could make the offer it'd seemed he was leading up to.

I gaped at both of them. "Are you listening to me? Your lives could be on the line. I'll do whatever I can to make sure she doesn't discover what I'm doing and to keep you safe if she does, but it's a huge risk, no matter how you slice it. A risk I can't ask you to take."

Jasper flexed his shoulders, a scowl crossing his face. "I'm not going to run away and let you take all the heat on your own."

Rafael cleared his throat and aimed a glower at the younger guy. "I can look after Lou just fine."

Oh, shit, if they weren't kicking me to the curb, I still had to explain about my evolving relationship with my no-longer-just-a-bodyguard too.

Were my skater men really taking my confession in stride? I studied both of them again, afraid to let myself get relieved just yet. Not sure I even should be relieved.

"You'd really want to stick with me? Both of you? I don't know how—Jasper needs to get out there and compete in bigger events—I don't want to hold him back."

"We'll figure something out," Jasper said without hesitation. "You deserve to be out there in the spotlight too."

He cut his gaze to Niko, who nodded emphatically. "We aren't going to abandon you, Lou. We're a team." He glanced up at Rafael. "All of us."

I swiped my hand across my mouth. "Um, if that's the case, then about the whole team thing… I should probably also tell you that while Rafael and I *weren't* anything more than friends when I introduced him to you, it seems like that may be changing."

As both of the other guys' attention zeroed in on the man standing next to me, Rafael drew himself even straighter, his expression as impenetrable as usual.

"That doesn't mean I don't want the two of you too," I added hastily. "The way I feel about all of you… Maybe it's selfish. But there's something there, something special even if it's different with each of you. Again, it's up to you what you do with that information. I just felt I should keep being honest with you about seeing other people."

To my shock, Niko broke into a laugh. "Well, when you have all that history with him, and he cared enough to stay with you even after you ran away—honestly, I was surprised when it sounded like there was nothing more going on."

He caught Jasper's gaze, and some wordless communication appeared to pass between them. I resisted the urge to fidget as another silence fell over us. Of course they needed a little time to process everything.

"I can go," I said. "If you want to talk about it just the two of you, or—"

Jasper shook his head and sat down in the armchair. "I don't think that'll be necessary. We *are* a team, we're in this together, and we're going to get out there on the ice again. No more-than-a-mafia mom is going to get in your way."

As Niko nodded, hope flooded my chest. I couldn't judge how well they understood what they were really getting into, but I'd told them everything I could. From the firmness of Jasper's tone, he was taking the situation seriously.

Niko rubbed his chin. "The qualifying series competitions aren't very widely publicized. I doubt they're the type of thing most gangsters would be watching."

"That's true," Jasper said. "I don't think it'd be all that much risk giving one of those a go. We could pick somewhere you don't think your mom has connections—there are a bunch of the qualifiers all over the country. And if we get farther than that, into events that are broadcast more widely, we could change up your appearance so you're less recognizable in general."

From his intense expression, he was already imagining disguises he could design like he did his skating costumes.

I stared at them, my words shocked out of me. They were willing to risk so much just to keep me in their lives.

I hadn't let myself give up, but deep down, I'd been sure they'd walk away. That the truth about my past would be too much for them.

Instead they were committing themselves even more than they had before.

Jasper took in my face and grimaced. "Don't look like that. Of course you shouldn't have to give up your dream—not for your mom or any crazy stalker. I just wish we could have done more to protect you sooner."

Niko raised his chin, any playfulness vanishing. "Well, now that we know, we can be better prepared. We won't let your stalker win, whatever they're after. Rafael, you're just going to have to get used to Jasper and I looking out for Lou as well."

I half expected my bodyguard to argue, but instead he let out a low chuckle. "I guess I can't complain about sharing the workload. But you have to take this seriously. These people mean business. It's like nothing you'll ever have dealt with before."

"Then we'll learn," Niko said. "That's always been a part of this job."

The rush of joy and affection overwhelmed me. I scooted over to pull him into a hug and then moved to the armchair to embrace Jasper as well.

He hugged me back tightly. "We've got you, Punk. No matter what they throw at you."

"Thank you," I mumbled.

My spirits were soaring… but a thread of doubt remained coiled around my gut.

If they didn't fully comprehend what they were signing up for by throwing their lot in with me, would I really be able to protect *them*?

FOUR

Niko

I STUFFED my last few shirts into my second suitcase, unable to stop myself from hearing my father's voice in the back of my head, chiding me for not being more careful to avoid wrinkles. As if a few creases in my clothes were worth worrying about right now.

Every time I slowed down in my packing, I saw Lou's face as she'd made her confession to us. The anguish in her expression and her voice replayed in my head.

I should have been rejoicing that the skater I'd come around the world to coach had regained his confidence enough to want to enter the next round of official competitions. And I was thrilled that Jasper had agreed. But I couldn't help worrying about the other pupil I'd ended up taking on.

Whatever exactly Lou had been through in her childhood, she hadn't deserved it. I'd seen how compassionate and generous she was.

She lived on beauty and grace. And her family had tried to drag her down into grime and violence.

I had no experience dealing with organized crime directly. We all heard stories, of course—of the yakuza back home, of the "mob" in America—but I could admit I wasn't sure how to protect her.

I only knew I was determined to do it one way or another.

Cursing my past self for insisting on bringing so much with me from Japan, I lugged the two suitcases and my equipment bag down to the car I'd leased. It'd seemed extravagent when I'd signed the contract, but I'd quickly realized that getting around Canada required a personal vehicle. You couldn't simply hop on a train from Hobb Creek to anywhere.

As I pushed the suitcases into the trunk, my ringtone pealed out from my back pocket. I pulled out my phone and hesitated for a second at the sight of the unknown caller.

But how would any criminal or stalker have gotten *my* phone number?

Shaking my head at myself, I tapped the answer button. "Hello?"

A woman's no-nonsense voice carried from the speaker. "Is this Niko Okabe?"

"Yes, it is. What's this about?"

"Oh, good, I'm glad I reached you. This is Sally Bakers from Whetstone Sporting Goods. You reached out about some talent looking for sponsorships—Jasper St. Pierre and a Luna Garcia?"

My spirits lifted even with my momentary jolt of confusion. Right, I'd registered Lou for the qualifying competitions and submitted her and Jasper for possible sponsorships using the fake name from one of the assortment of passports she'd turned out to own. We'd gone with the Luna one because it meant she could keep the nickname "Lou" without anyone finding it odd.

"Yes, I did. I hope you enjoyed the video of their most recent performance."

"We were *very* impressed with what we saw. I'm prepared to offer you a sponsorship for the two of them. Especially if they're going to be competing at larger scale events… That is the case, isn't it, Mr. Okabe?"

"Absolutely." I shut the trunk and pulled open the driver's-side door. "Actually, we're on our way to Boston now to prepare for a qualifying competition there before hopefully continuing on to Finals and Nationals."

If anyone pressed further about why we were moving to the United States weeks before the actual competition, I'd have told them that I wanted my skaters to get comfortable in the new setting well ahead of time, even if we couldn't train in the exact same rink where the main competition would be held.

The full truth was that I also wanted to get Lou away from her stalker here in Hobb Creek, and the Boston competition was the one farthest from Austin, where she'd said her mother's organization was based. It also happened to be the site of the Pairs Finals this year, so we'd already be in town if my two skaters accomplished everything I knew they were capable of.

"That's excellent to hear," the store representative said. "I can tell they'll go far. I'll be emailing you the contract and additional details. If you could look it over by the end of the week and get back to me with any questions or concerns, I'd appreciate it."

"Absolutely, Ms. Bakers!"

I'd be reading through that email the second it arrived in my inbox. I hung up with a smile tugging at my lips.

This was definitely good news. Skating was an expensive career at the best of times. With a solid sponsorship, Jasper and Lou wouldn't have to worry about how they'd cover their rink time, equipment, or the materials Jasper would need when he got down to making his fully custom costumes.

There. I might not know how to fight off career criminals, but I could support Lou in plenty of other ways that she needed too.

And if I needed to protect her by facing off against literal threats, I'd do that too. I could stand up for people other than myself.

I was going to do right by her, like the man I'd always intended to be. No slip-ups this time.

There was even more on the line now.

My smile tightening with determination, I dropped into the driver's seat and cruised the short distance to Jasper's apartment. We were going to drive down together while Lou and Rafael took their own car, meeting up for meals and a rest overnight at the halfway point.

As I parked outside the house with its large, detached garage that held Jasper's temporary home, my thoughts veered in a totally different direction. To the press of his firm lips against mine three days ago at the Dellville arena.

The memory sent a quiver through my veins. My heart thumped a little faster as I stepped out of the car, anticipating seeing his impressive form and handsome face appearing at the top of the stairs outside the apartment's entrance.

I'd known we needed to talk since Lou had insisted on bringing up the subject of our original kiss from almost two years ago. I hadn't wanted to distract Jasper before his first competition in ages, but I didn't have that excuse anymore.

We needed to clear the air. I needed to find out where we stood, what he wanted out of our relationship, even if it was possible I wouldn't like the answer.

Who knew if he was looking back on the kiss as happily as I was?

I bounded up the steps to see if he was finished packing and was just reaching to knock on the door when Jasper opened it. He peered out at me with his eyebrows raised.

"There you are. I thought you were going to make me wait around all day."

I couldn't help laughing. "Me? You're the one I usually have to drag out of this place. I thought you might need help getting organized."

"I can organize just fine. But you might as well come in, since I'm sure you'll want to confirm that."

He'd taken on a typical grouchy tone, but it was light enough that I knew he wasn't actually in a bad mood. He was just being Jasper.

Grinning, I followed him into the cramped space.

He did already have his own suitcase packed—just the one, as well as a backpack and his equipment bag. Of course, he hadn't come from anywhere near as far away as I had.

I cocked my head as I considered the space. "Do you want to stop at your grandparents' house before we head down south so you can pick up more things?"

Jasper shook his head. "Nah, I have everything I need." He shot me a sideways glance. "You just want to let my Grandma ply you with her butter tarts again."

I held up my hands. "I was only looking out for you. Although if there were certain delicious tarts involved in the visit, I wouldn't complain."

Jasper let out a rough chuckle that did something funny to my stomach. Of its own accord, my gaze lingered on the firm line of his jaw. Then it dropped to the sculpted brawn of his chest under his fitted T-shirt.

Those muscles flexed as he hefted his bags and stepped close to me where I was waiting by the doorway. "If you're satisfied, let's get going."

His scent filled my nose, warm and musky—perfect. It would have been easy to nod and put off the conversation again, but I knew once we were stuck in the confines of the car, I'd feel even more awkward.

I cleared my throat, and Jasper paused, probably sensing the shift in mood.

"I actually—there was something I wanted to talk to you about first."

Jasper knit his brow. He set down his suitcase and studied me. "Sure. What's up?"

I opened my mouth, closed it again, and forced out the words. "We kissed the other day at the arena—that is, of course you know that—and before, after the competition in Munich— Is that something you want? For our relationship to shift in that direction? If you'd rather keep it totally professional, I can. I never expected, just because I came out here…"

As I trailed off, Jasper smiled crookedly. "That's pretty obvious from the fact that you've never brought it up or made a move the entire time you've been here."

I grimaced. "I did try to lead up to the subject a couple of times, but you'd get tense. I didn't want to push."

Jasper ducked his head for a moment. "I don't know. I— You know my head hasn't been in the best place. Maybe I was a little scared if you kept talking about it you'd end up telling me it'd been a mistake. Because I do. Want something like that. With you. Um."

He glanced up at me, his face flushing adorably. I wanted to kiss him again right then.

"I never thought it was a mistake," I said quickly. "Unless it really had thrown off your skating career—but it never was for me."

"Yeah, I guess that should have been obvious from the fact that you traveled halfway around the world to help 'fix' my skating. And just to be clear, that first kiss had nothing to do with my slump. I promise." Jasper's smile grew, smoothing out my jangling nerves. "I don't want to rush into anything. I've never done anything with another guy before. I didn't even know I could be attracted to guys until that night in Munich. But I definitely am—to you. I'd like to see where that could go. If you would too."

I beamed back at him. "Yes. Absolutely. There's no rush."

Seeing his stance relax at those words sent a rush of pure joy through my body. He looked so pleased that I couldn't resist the urge that gripped me next.

I crossed the small space between us and touched his jaw to bring his mouth to mine. Jasper hummed low in his throat, the reverberation passing through the kiss.

So what could I do but kiss him a little harder? I held myself back from jumping into everything I'd imagined doing with this man but reveling in the feel of his lips as they parted against mine. Celebrated the flick of his tongue as he gained enough confidence to flick it briefly into my mouth.

Slow. I could do that. I could move at a snail's pace if it meant Jasper was right here with me like this, figuring things out as we went.

He drew back gently, shooting me an even brighter smile than before. "I guess we'd better swing by Lou's place before she starts thinking we must have gotten lost on the way."

I grabbed one of his bags to help him carry them out. "Can't leave our woman waiting."

The bubble of warmth that seemed to surround us as we tramped over to the car left my heart singing. But at the same time, a darker thread wound through my chest.

I needed to defend this relationship with all I had too. It was on me to make sure I didn't screw things up.

FIVE

Luciana

THE CHILLED air rushed through my ponytail, my skates gave a soft click as they met the ice, and a song swelled around me. Pure bliss.

The feeling was no different here in Boston than it'd been in Austin or Hobb Creek, even if the arena was a little bigger and fancier. And more crowded.

I veered neatly around a couple of other practicing skaters, timing my movements with the beat of the third song among the options Niko had offered for our free skate. We could use the same routine we'd performed in Dellville for our short program, just increasing the difficulty of a few of the moves to meet the official standards, but we needed a longer one with other specific criteria as well, and that meant we also needed more music.

I skipped up in a tiny bunny hop alongside the melody and laughed when I caught sight of my skating partner's and coach's faces.

"What?" I pumped my legs back towards them as Niko killed the music. "I thought the song was fun. Not sure it's exactly what we'd want to go for with the routine, though. What do you think, partner?"

Jasper tilted his head as he considered. "I usually go for something more emotional rather than upbeat. I did like the second one you put on, Niko. Play that one again?"

"Sure." Niko thumbed through the list on his phone.

The song started right where he'd cut it off before, a little under halfway through. The tune wasn't quite as poignant as the classical piece we'd used for our short program, but the dramatics of the mix of strings, guitar, and drums were definitely enthralling.

It would be a difficult song with its shifts in tempo, but if we could nail it, it would totally be worth it. The impression it would leave on the judges and on the crowd would be overwhelming. I could already picture us whirling across the rink, catching them up in the picture we made.

I pushed off against the ice and kicked my heels up in a waltz jump. My emotions lifted alongside my body.

Yeah, this melody was something I could really skate to.

I circled around another skater seconds before I veered too close, abruptly self-conscious. I wasn't used to sharing the rink with anyone other than Jasper, and even his presence was still new to me.

But Niko had said it'd be good for us to go out during the freestyle session. We'd get a chance to see some of the other skaters we'd be up against and what they were capable of, their styles and strengths.

Of course, that also meant they were getting a look at *us*.

Ignoring the prickling over my skin brought by other skaters' gazes—real or imagined—I glided back to Niko and Jasper as the song ended. They were standing closer together than I'd ever seen them, their shoulders nearly brushing. There was an ease to their closeness that lit me up from the inside.

They'd obviously started to figure out whatever was happening between them. Good for Jasper, going for that kiss in Dellville. I hoped Niko had finally opened up about his feelings too.

"This song is definitely the best," I announced when I reached them. "Let's be ambitious. You only live once, right?"

Jasper snorted, but he also reached out to tug my ponytail affectionately. "Spoken like a punk, Punk."

Niko grinned with a faraway expression. "You two could create something spectacular with this. And I know exactly where we'd want to include some of the jumps already."

He pulled out his notepad and started scrawling his thoughts out in kanji. His primary language helped ensure no one else would be able to steal his inspiration, although I wished I could read it myself.

I craned my neck to scan the music app on Niko's phone. "You've got a huge collection of playlists there. Are they all for skating?"

"Oh, they're for everything." Niko slid his phone back into his pocket. "Cleaning, shopping, eating..."

"You have a playlist for eating?" Jasper arched an eyebrow up at him.

"You don't?"

As the two of them fell into a light-hearted debate about the importance of background music, I watched the rest of the skaters do their thing. One of the other women landed a triple Axel before my eyes, sweeping across the ice like it was nothing.

I clamped my jaw to stop it from dropping. Jasper and I weren't casual skaters either—I'd pulled off triple Axels before—but this was my first real official foray into the professional scene. I wasn't used to being surrounded by this level of skill.

These were skaters who had likely competed over and over, who had already been able to show the world what they could do. They would have backers and fans and maybe were even a few favorites of the judges. And I was going to go up against them?

But when I looked at Niko and Jasper again, none of that mattered. I had the two of them and Rafael watching over me from somewhere in the shadows at the back of the stands, my safety always on the forefront of his mind.

This was a new start for all of us. If everything had gone according to plan, my stalker had been left to eat our dust back in Hobb Creek. We were moving on to bigger and better things.

There was an entire world here just waiting for us to crack it open like a golden egg.

A cocky voice with a hint of a rasp broke through my reverie. "Look who's here. Jasper St. Pierre finally shows his face again?"

I whirled on my skates to see a man who probably wasn't more than a year or two older than my nineteen propping his arms against the boards a few feet away. The arena lights glinted off his golden-blond hair, slicked back from his forehead without a strand out of place. He was dressed like a skater—long-sleeved thermal and gloves—and his wiry frame held plenty of lean muscle to support that assumption.

And really, what else would he be doing here? He definitely wasn't old enough to be coaching.

Jasper's shoulders tensed as he turned to meet the stranger's piercing blue eyes. This guy obviously wasn't a stranger to *him*.

"You're training here too?" he said with an unmistakable edge in his voice.

The new guy shrugged and straightened up, pulling at his gloves. "It's the best option in town. Or maybe you forgot after all that time away. How long has it been since you last showed your face at a rink? A decade or so?"

His arrogant tone had me bristling in an instant. If any of the guys back home had talked to me or someone I cared about like that, they'd have been getting a knuckle sandwich.

But this wasn't back home; this was a professional skating venue. I had to deal with the jerks here a little more politely.

Something about his looks struck a chord of recognition in me: hard-edged but handsome with his smooth, pale skin broken by a faint scar that ran up his chin to his lower lip. I probably *should* know this guy.

Jasper glowered at him. "I needed a break."

The other guy guffawed. "Sure. A break from knowing your time in the spotlight was limited with all the new talent coming up. The nerves could get to anyone."

I stepped forward, narrowing my eyes. "Funny, I'm not seeing a whole lot of talent from you so far—other than for shooting your mouth off. Maybe you're talking about yourself."

The blond guy's gaze darted from Jasper to me, startled and then sparking with vicious amusement. "Who the hell are you? Jasper's coach brought on some fresh meat so he'd look better in comparison?"

My teeth gritted, but Jasper touched my shoulder in a gesture that felt like a warning. He fixed the jerk with a glare.

"This is Lou, my *partner.* And you wouldn't be talking shit like that if you'd seen her." He turned to me. "Quentin Wolfe. Sorry you had to meet him."

His terse but dry tone got a laugh out of me.

Quentin Wolfe—I did recognize that name. He'd made his mark in the Juniors competitions that I'd sometimes watched when there wasn't enough new higher profile stuff to study. He'd gotten onto the national team last year, though he'd been one of the less prominent members.

Quentin let out a low chuckle of his own. "Your partner? You're skating *pairs*, St. Pierre? I guess you figured that way you wouldn't have to go head-to-head with me."

"Hard as it may be for you to believe, I haven't given you much thought at all," Jasper retorted, but his jaw was tight.

"You're going to find it hard to ignore me now. I look forward to watching you crash and burn all over again, old-timer."

Quentin tossed aside his skate guards and pushed off across the ice without giving either of us a chance to respond.

I rolled my eyes at his retreating back. "Old-timer? Who inflated his head so big?"

When I turned back to Jasper, my partner was scowling. "He's a fucking prick. Better to ignore him."

I took in the storm clouds that'd gathered in Jasper's gray-green eyes, and my stomach knotted. "Is he like that with everyone?"

"Probably. But he's worse with me." Jasper sighed. "When he first transitioned from Juniors, the media liked to pit us against each other in their coverage because we were close in age and our styles are so different. He took that as his cue to make my life hell. It figures he'd be training here."

"You have nothing to worry about," Niko piped up. "The last time you were competing against Quentin, you made it to the international circuit and he was stuck at home."

"Yeah, but last year he made it to Worlds. Which obviously inflated his ego even more." Jasper let out another breath and shook his head. "Whatever. It's true that I don't have to go up against him directly while we're competing in pairs. It's all just hot air anyway."

He didn't sound like he totally believed that, though.

Frowning, I glanced over to where Quentin was going through his initial on-ice warm-up.

It was easy to see the contrast between him and Jasper, even in the basic spins and jumps he was working through right now. My partner was all fluid motion, wrapping you up in the story of his movements.

Quentin angled every limb with perfect precision. His expression stayed locked in analytical intensity, as if he were calculating the exact degrees of every turn, every lift of a leg or arm.

Technically, he hit every mark. There was no denying the power that showed as he whipped through the air.

But even as I admired his overall form, the performance left me cold. It was almost mechanical in its deliberateness, no sign of the artistry I admired so much in Jasper.

I let out a humph. "Even if you were competing with him, he couldn't hold a candle to you."

That got a smile out of my partner, even if it was a strained one. He slung his arm around my shoulders. "Thanks for the vote of confidence."

As he spoke, one of the female skaters glided over to join Quentin where he'd stopped for a moment not far from us.

She tilted her head at a coy angle and batted her eyelashes, thick and dark with mascara. "Hey, Quentin. We ended up at the same arena again. Must be meant to be."

Quentin grinned at her, the expression as sharp as his moves. "I guess I can look forward to my off-ice time now too, Jess." He gave her ass a swift pinch.

Jess let out an exaggerated gasp and then giggled. "You betcha."

She swiveled around to flash a red-lipped sneer at me before soaring off across the rink again. Irritation prickled under my skin.

What the hell was the matter with these assholes?

To my further annoyance, Quentin glanced over right then and caught me watching. He aimed a broad smirk at me that felt like a challenge and shot off after Jess.

I turned my back on them and touched Jasper's cheek. "We'll just ignore him. Both of them."

"That's right," Niko said. "You've got to get used to the competitive atmosphere again."

Jasper let out an inarticulate grumble. "Quentin will definitely get me up to speed in that area fast."

Our coach squeezed his arm. "Focus on your own skills. No one will be mocking you after they see how far you've come. Let's stick to this corner of the rink. I'll play that song again, and we can work out how some potential moves could come together."

As I floated over the ice next to Jasper, I tried to envision an ideal free skate. This was a much bigger deal than the small, amateur competition in Dellville—this was serious.

People were watching.

And not just watching. In between spins and jumps and a few quick lifts that Niko had us run through, my gaze slid to the stands.

Even for this practice, several figures sat on the benches—friends and family members here to encourage the skaters. And a few of them had their phones out, filming the moves.

They'd inadvertently be recording *me* too, here and there.

A shiver ran down my spine that had nothing to do with the chilly air.

I was here under an assumed name. That should have granted me all the anonymity I needed at this level of competition.

But if people posted those videos online—if the wrong person happened to see them…

All it'd take was one bit of bad luck, and my mother would be racing up here to put me in my place. And do who knew what to my men as well.

My throat constricted. The hiss of my blades over the ice suddenly sounded more ominous than exhilarating.

I couldn't let that happen. My men had promised to protect me—and I had to protect them in turn.

I had to do everything in my power to make sure there wasn't the slightest chance the wrong person would see me and think of Luciana Cordova, the Deadly Rose's daughter.

SIX

Luciana

IT TURNED out that applying eyeliner was like riding a bike—once you learned, you didn't forget.

I hadn't bothered with flashy makeup since I'd left Austin—and even back in Austin, I'd stuck to a little mascara and lip balm when I was in mafia princess mode. I'd saved my fun, striking looks for my periodic club nights. Since I hadn't gotten the chance to compete on the ice back then, I'd never done a performance look for my skating sessions.

Even Mom had rarely seen me with cat-eye liner, vibrant shadow, and vivid lips. Her associates wouldn't connect the me I was creating in front of the mirror to the old Luciana Cordova at all.

What would Mom have thought of me now? I could hear her voice in the back of my head: *Women in our position don't need to paint our faces like clowns.*

She'd been all about keeping it simple and a little severe rather than artsy. But I didn't think I looked anything like a clown.

I turned my head from left to right, assessing myself. The bright green eyeshadow dusting my lids paired with the turquoise in the corners really popped in contrast with the red hue I'd dyed into my dark hair.

I hadn't been sure about the bangs the hair stylist had chopped across my forehead, but as I brushed my fingers through them, I decided they were definitely cute rather than dorky. And they were one more way my appearance was transformed.

Every day, I'd put on this face for our practices. Even if someone who'd known the old me caught a glimpse of a recording, it shouldn't trigger the slightest jolt of recognition.

I blotted the deep red lipstick to tone it down just slightly and gave my reflection a smile. "Right. I think that does it."

I set my new makeup bag in the cabinet alongside Niko's razor and Jasper's aftershave. It was a little weird suddenly living with not one but three men in the three-bedroom apartment we'd been able to find not too far from the arena, but I had to say I loved having easy access to my guys.

Like right now. I pushed open the door to find Niko and Jasper hanging out on the sofa in front of the TV, Jasper flipping channels restlessly. Time for the first trial run of the new look.

I didn't even have to clear my throat to get their attention. Both their heads turned my way at the squeak of the bathroom door.

I couldn't imagine anything much more gratifying than the way their faces lit up at the sight of me. The genuine sign of approval made my heart leap.

Jasper let out a low whistle. "You look amazing. But I hardly recognized you. I guess that's the point, right?"

Niko chuckled. "I almost thought we were being held up by some mysterious, red-headed robber. You're an expert makeup artist as well as skater."

My smile faded a little. "It kind of sucks that I'll be going out there not exactly looking like myself. But it's fun putting it on. And I'll be able to refine the look to go with our costumes once we get those sorted out."

Niko clicked his tongue and leapt up to give my bangs a light ruffling. "Your spirit still shines through. You'll never stop being Lou, no matter what we're giving as your full name."

I laughed, warmed by the affection in his tone. "Thanks for the vote of confidence."

"Speaking of costumes…" Jasper got up with a stretch of his arms and checked his phone. "We'd better get going if we're going to make it to the fabric store with plenty of time to look through the options before closing. Do you want to come along, Lou?"

I shook my head. "Nah. I trust your artistic eye a lot more than my own. I'm sure whatever you pick will look amazing."

And it might not be a bad thing if he got a little one-on-one time with Niko to foster whatever relationship they were growing between them.

Jasper bumped his shoulder against mine. "No pressure, huh?"

"Hey, I've seen what you can do. I have total faith in you."

I bobbed up to give him a quick peck, brushing my lips lightly so I didn't leave an imprint. Niko leaned in to kiss my temple, and the two men headed out together.

"Oh, hey," Jasper said a little awkwardly after he'd opened the door. A second later, Rafael stepped past him with a brusque nod. My bodyguard was just returning from one of his periodic sweeps of the neighborhood.

After the other men had left, Rafael checked the lock and then turned to me, his face showing no reaction to my mask of cosmetics. He'd already seen the new hairdo, watching over me at the salon.

"See anything concerning out on the streets?" I asked.

Rafael was still very much in bodyguard mode. Along with his patrols around the apartment building, he'd insisted that he'd take the sofa at night rather than sharing one of the bedrooms, so that he could be our "first line of defense" against intruders.

His dedication didn't surprise me, but part of me couldn't help hoping he'd warm up to the other men beyond simply tolerating their presence in our lives. Eventually.

He pulled off his jacket and hung it on one of the hooks by the door. "No sign of danger that I could pick up on. I'll do another circuit later tonight."

"So, it seems like we've left my psycho stalker back in Hobb Creek?"

"As far as I can tell." He aimed a faint smile at me, which from Rafael was practically a grin. "He hasn't left any calling cards yet, and I'm not sure how he could have figured out where we are. But I'm not letting down my guard until we're sure."

"Of course you aren't." I grinned back at him and then struck a modelesque pose. "So what do you think of my full disguise?"

His gaze swept over my face, leaving my skin tingling in its wake. There was analytical precision to it, but also a heat in his eyes that he didn't attempt to suppress.

I'd been longing to see that kind of desire in him for so long. It was hard to believe he was finally offering it.

"You know how to pull off an extreme look like that," he said. "You'll be drawing lots of eyes, but I don't see how anyone from the old life will recognize you. I think you look best as yourself, but this is a good shield."

I think you look best as yourself. Had he ever expressed any opinion about my appearance before?

The guys at the clubs had preferred flashy Lou. But Rafael had known me for all the most important parts of my life—and he'd finally decided that he wanted me. No pretenses, just as I was.

He finally recognized the woman I'd become instead of only seeing the girl I'd been.

A flutter passed through my chest, and for a second I lost my words. "Well, I'm glad to have your approval."

The corner of Rafael's mouth quirked upward into something more like a full smile. "Lou, you know I've never *not* thought you were gorgeous."

The flutter grew into full-out beating wings. I swallowed thickly and tipped my head toward the bathroom.

"I don't really need the disguise right now. Just wanted to try it out. Help me get all this crap off so I can go back to being myself?"

I could have washed up by myself, but I wanted to see if he'd agree. And, okay, I also appreciated the excuse to have him with me in the tighter space.

We stood next to the sink, and I poured out some of the remover onto a cloth. Then I offered it to him and tilted up my face with my eyes closed so he could ensure every trace of shadow and liner was wiped away.

Rafael brushed the damp fabric over my skin so gently my heart skipped a beat. My pulse kept thumping faster, every inch of my body aware of his closeness, the heat of his brawny body.

He set his other hand on the side of my neck, his thumb braced carefully against my jaw while he wiped off the other eye. My breath caught, and he paused.

His voice came out rough. "I'm sorry. Did I hurt you?"

"No," I said, hearing my own voice gone husky. "It's just… nice, having someone take care of me. You've always been good at that."

"Not that you need all that much taking care of anymore," he said dryly. "You're very capable of doing it yourself, as you like to prove on a daily basis."

I wrinkled my nose at his teasing. "Yes, I absolutely *can* look after myself. But that doesn't mean I can't enjoy having help."

"Well, you have it. As long as you want me. I can't think of a job I'd rather do than protecting you."

More heat unfurled under my skin. When he lowered the cloth, my eyes slid open.

Rafael met my gaze, both of us unspeaking. I took another cloth to wipe off my mouth and the foundation I'd laid over my forehead, cheeks, and chin. Then I lifted my face again.

"All done?"

"All done."

I set the cloth on the sink and wet my lips. Rafael's gaze tracked the movement. Every nerve in my body was screaming at me to throw myself into his arms.

Instead, I set my hand on his chest. Just testing, to see how he'd respond. The last time—the only time—we'd kissed before, my stalker had interrupted us. I wasn't really sure how to pick up where we'd left off.

His thumb stroked over my cheek, lighting flames in its wake. "Lou…"

"You like me best like this?" I asked, gazing up at him.

There was no mistaking the fire burning in his eyes. "Siempre." *Always.*

"Then why don't you show me just how much you do?"

The words had barely left my lips before he was claiming them with the crash of his mouth into mine.

SEVEN

Rafael

LOU WAS the sweetest thing my tongue had ever tasted. I could never have imagined how addictive her kiss would be, and now I couldn't imagine ever pulling away from her.

She nibbled on my lip with a gentle scrape of her teeth that struck me like a bolt of lightning. I swallowed a groan, not wanting to show how desperate for her I already was.

Instead, I let my fingers run rampant in her newly colored hair. The strands were so soft, so delicate, so fragile.

Something inside me tightened. More than anything in the world, I wanted to make her mine. Dominate her body and soul until every inch of her was quivering with need like I was.

Show her all the passion I'd kept under wraps for so long and how well I could bring it to bear.

As her arms wound around my back, her nails tracing fine lines through the fabric of my shirt down my back, I reined in the impulse.

This was still new, whatever we had together. I had to be careful with it.

She might be all woman, but she'd had a crush on me since she was practically a kid. I had to make sure she was totally on board with the change in our relationship every step of the way.

Her tongue darted between my lips again with a playful swipe. I closed my eyes, savoring the sensation for all it was worth.

My hands slid down to stroke over the sleekly muscular planes of her perfect shoulders. Lou hummed encouragingly, the sound setting me on fire.

I kissed her harder with a growl and pulled her tight against me. She *was* mine now. Maybe she had feelings for two other men as well, but in this moment it was just me and her.

I'd accepted her as a woman, and that meant I could enjoy all the benefits that came with it.

But not too forcefully. Not too demanding. Simmer down, Rafael.

She might have left the mafia princess life behind, but she'd always be royalty in my eyes.

As I loosened my hold, Lou dipped her head to plant a trail of kisses along my jaw. Her lips drew a scorching line all the way to my ear.

When she nipped the lobe, I couldn't suppress my groan. My cock twitched within my jeans, achingly hard.

Lou shot me an impish grin before continuing her torturous course down my neck. It was all I could do not to slam her against the wall and grind the proof of my arousal against her pussy until she was pleading for release.

I wasn't going to cede all control over the situation, though. I grabbed her wrists and backed her up until I had her caught against the door. She dragged in a tiny breath, her eyes on mine, but she didn't tug against my hold.

No, the heat in her gorgeous eyes was nothing but welcoming.

She wasn't the only one who could tease. I lowered my head to the crook of her neck and flicked my tongue over the smooth skin there. When I sucked on it, she rocked against me with a gasp.

Fuck, I needed more. I wanted to drown in this woman.

No other lover had ever consumed me like this. It was as if I'd been waiting my whole life to give in to Luciana Cordova.

Catching both her wrists in one hand and keeping them raised over her head, I slipped my other hand beneath the hem of her shirt. My fingers splayed across her toned stomach.

I couldn't resist the swell of her breasts. Without thinking, I jerked at her bra hard enough to snap the band.

As my palm closed over one breast, Lou squirmed against me with a whimper that both inflamed me and made me hesitate. What kind of animal was I going to be here, ripping up her clothes?

But as I forced my touch to gentle, my fingers to stroke tenderly rather than urgently over her curves, Lou peered up at me through her eyelashes.

"Don't hold back with me, Rafael. I've wanted this for so long. I'm not afraid of you."

I inhaled with a hiss and let my mouth crash down against hers again. As I tweaked her stiffening nipple between my thumb and forefingers, she moaned against my lips and wriggled her hips.

The friction sent a flood of heat through my groin. I hefted her up, balancing her against the door with her legs splayed around my thighs so we could lock together even more fully.

With a yank, her shirt was on the floor. I'd had to release her wrists to accomplish that, and she wound her arms around my neck again, reclaiming my lips.

After she'd ravished me so thoroughly my head was spinning, her fingers groped at my own shirt. She wrenched at the buttons and then heaved the whole thing off so we could press together skin to skin.

The feel of her breasts against my bare chest had my cock throbbing twice as hard. Lou kissed my shoulder and traced her hands down over the ridges of muscle, setting off sparks everywhere she touched.

"I don't think this is how you really want me, is it?" she said coyly, and let her fingers drift lower. She traced the waist of my jeans. "I can tell that a very important part of you is begging for attention."

"I don't beg," I muttered, even though I was the barest of threads away from it when she talked like that.

"No? Hmm, I wonder if I could change that."

She flicked her fingers right over the bulge of my cock, firmly enough to make me groan but so quickly the sensation passed before I had a chance to enjoy it.

Another growl slipped from my throat. I pushed her against the door with a thrust of my hips, and Lou's head tipped back with a hitch of breath.

A sly smile crossed her lips. "Am I being too much of a brat for you?"

My pulse stuttered. "What?"

"You're making that face—the one you always do when I get up to something you don't totally approve of. Don't lie. You *totally* think I'm a brat sometimes."

"That's not—" I started to argue, and then she skimmed her fingertips over my groin again. My sentence cut off with a growl.

Lou's grin widened, and suddenly my hesitation seemed ridiculous. The connotations of the term obviously didn't bother her. She thought it was funny.

We both knew she was my equal in every possible way. It didn't matter that I had twelve years on her or what labels we put on things.

"You are *definitely* being a brat right now," I said in a low voice, tipping my face close to hers. A twinge of discomfort ran through my chest as I said the word, but it faded at Lou's laugh.

"And what are you going to do about it, old man?" she murmured in a husky tone that went straight to my cock.

How were those words so hot? How did this suddenly feel so *right*?

Because she was owning it. And if she could lean into the parts of our dynamic that I'd once found so worrying, then I could too, couldn't I?

Bracing my hand against her thigh, I whipped her off the door and yanked it open. Another giggle spilled out of her as I strode across the apartment toward her bedroom.

"You're in for it now," I informed her.

"Oh, no." She squirmed in my arms, her pussy brushing my cock. "Whatever shall I do?"

I didn't know whether to snort with amusement or groan with unfulfilled desire.

I pushed into her bedroom, kicked the door shut behind us, and spread her out on the bed with me looming over her. Her dark red hair fanned out around her gorgeous face, a tempting combination of devilish and angelic.

"What are you going to do with me?" she asked, a little breathless.

"I'm going to return a little of the torture."

I ran my hand up her leg and hooked my fingers under the waist of her leggings. They had to go.

And go they did. I slid them down inch by inch, stroking my thumbs in teasing arcs across the skin I bared as I went. Holding Lou's eager gaze every step of the way.

Her eyes glazed with hunger. She wiggled her legs as if to urge me faster, but I held them down and pressed a kiss just above her knees on both sides.

"Rafael," she said, stretching my name out in a mock-whine.

I couldn't restrain my smirk. "Brats get what's coming to them."

"Fuck, yes."

When I reached her ankles, I whipped the leggings the rest of the way off her. Then I drank in her nearly naked form—the perfect curves, the smooth light brown skin marked here and there by paler scars.

Some of those wounds she'd taken in gang fights, others on the ice. Both were a testament to how strong and committed this woman was.

And she was mine.

Lou pushed her elbows behind her and arched her back to emphasize her breasts. "Like what you see?"

"You know I do."

She wet her lips. "I want to hear you say it."

Her tone was all seductress, but the longing in her eyes didn't look like only lust to me. Behind the confident woman, was she still a little scared that I'd shut her down before we took this encounter to its obvious end?

I'd turned her away so many times before. I had to show her that would never happen again.

"You're perfect." I reached for her last remaining piece of clothing, the thin panties clinging to her hips. "There's never been anyone I wanted more. And now I finally have you to myself."

I punctuated each word with a suggestive tug of her panties. In a matter of seconds, they joined her leggings on the floor.

I took Lou's entire body in, wanting to memorize the sight and keep it locked in my memory. Her breasts rose and fell with her giddy breaths. A gleam of arousal shone on her beautiful pussy.

She was ready for me, but I wanted to savor this moment. And I wanted her to as well.

I might not be the only man in her life, but I was damn well going to make sure she never forgot how good it was with me.

I leaned forward to press kiss after kiss down her stomach. She lay back, enjoying every brush of my lips, every trail of my tongue and nibble of my teeth.

When I came to her pussy, I let my heavy breath rush over her clit. She shivered, her legs shifting farther apart as if in offering.

I finally gave her what we both wanted. I swiped my tongue across her exposed pink nub.

A guttural sound reverberated from Lou's lungs. She pressed up against my mouth, not hesitating at all about encouraging me to keep going.

She tasted like everything I'd ever dreamed of. Her pussy pulsed against my tongue, her thighs grazing my cheeks.

When I inched lower to slide my tongue into her slick slit, I got a chorus of whimpers as my reward. She raised her knees, giving me more room to work.

"Good girl," I murmured, and her fingers stroked over my scalp with another moan.

I circled her clit with my thumb, pressing down on her while I still gave her everything I could with my tongue. I used every ounce of knowledge I'd gained with other women—all the women who'd never meant half as much to me as the one I was pleasing now.

Her hips rose with every delving thrust of my tongue. My thumb swiveled over her tender nub. When her fingers curled into the sheet on either side of us, I knew she was close to her peak.

And I was going to take her all the way there.

I threw myself into eating her pussy with wilder abandon, bringing my lips and the tips of my teeth to the task alongside my tongue. Lou bucked, a cry breaking from her throat.

Then her body stiffened, her pussy clenching around my extended tongue. I suckled her as she rode out the wave of her release with a string of noises that were close to sobs.

As her body went slack, I raised my head—and found myself being shoved back by those slim but powerful arms.

Flushed but grinning, Lou yanked at the fly of my jeans. Before I'd really recovered from the bliss of having her writhing under my mouth, she'd gotten the zipper down and delved her hand inside my boxers.

"Dios mio." At the careful graze of her fingernails around my shaft, my hips swayed toward her of their own accord. "Fuck, Lou."

She wrapped her fingers around me and stroked me from base to head. "I think we both want this in the same place as soon as possible. What are you waiting for, Rafael? Are you going to take me or what?"

I reared up and caught her face in my hands, kissing the satisfied smirk off her face. The brat was definitely asking for it now.

As I jerked off my jeans and boxers, Lou grabbed a foil packet out of her nightstand. I wasn't sure I'd ever seen a sexier sight than her tearing it open with her teeth.

I snatched the condom from her and unrolled it over my straining length. Then I pinned her back down on the mattress.

"Is this what you want?" I rumbled, rubbing the head of my cock over her folds.

She gasped and arched toward me. "Hell, yes. Give me all of it."

I'd meant to tease her longer as payback, but I couldn't resist when she made a request like that.

I pushed into her an inch at a time, knowing I was a big man in every respect. But Lou's pussy was so hot and slick it was like I was meant to fill it.

Before I was even halfway in, she started rocking to urge me onward, and then I was a goner.

I thrust into her, carefully at first and then with increasing speed.

Lou ran her fingernails down my back and squeezed my ass, and a groan tore from my lungs.

Any reservations I'd once held had melted completely away as if they'd never existed. Lou had made damn sure of that. All that was left was our desire, melding together and becoming one, just as we were now.

I grunted, giving her everything. My hands splayed against the sides of her head, my fingers digging into the pillow as I pounded into her.

She bucked to meet me just as eagerly, clutching my body to her. I snagged a fistful of her silky hair and pulled.

Her mouth dropped open, her breath coming in hot, heavy gasps as she panted for me. Her dark brown eyes reflected hints of gold as the sun fell across her from the window, her brows lifting high.

"Holy shit," she mumbled. "Rafael, harder… Yes, yes, just like that."

I lifted one of her legs to let me enter her even deeper, and a thrill of pleasure slipped from her lips. Her pussy gripped my cock with the perfect blend of friction and heat.

She jolted beneath me, her eyes closing as our hips slammed together. Her breaths shortened, and her nails dug into my ass with pinpricks of pain that only heightened my desperate pleasure.

My own breaths had become unsteady gasps as well. There was a gauge inside of me that was quickly filling, rising like a thermometer in Death Valley.

"Fuck, I'm close." As I spoke, I felt myself lose a little more of the control I did have. "You feel too goddamn good."

Her response was to wrap her free leg around me, forcing me further inside of her. She'd lost all words now, her lips parted only to pant.

She started to tremble beneath me. My name burst out of her in a gasp, and her pussy clamped tight around me.

I couldn't hold back any longer. A wave of pleasure washed over me with a blazing release of pressure in my balls. I came harder than I ever had before in my life.

I kept bucking into her as I spent myself. Lou clung on to me, her breaths gradually evening out.

Finally, my head drooped over hers. I couldn't quite bring myself to pull out of her yet.

Lou didn't appear to mind. She raised her head for a brief kiss and trailed her fingers over the tattoo on my arm with my brother's name. Her fingertips absently spelled out *Edmundo*.

"That was fucking fantastic," she informed me. "You see, we should have been doing this all along."

I couldn't stop the guffaw that sputtered out of me. "Not *all* along."

She gave me one of those cheeky smiles. "Okay, the last year, anyway."

It hit me then that she might even be right.

I nuzzled the side of her face. "I'll just have to make up for it by getting you off all over the place in all kinds of ways from now on."

Her eyes sparkled. "Is that a promise?"

As I gazed down at her, I realized it wasn't the promise I most wanted to make. I wanted to tell her it could be like this forever—because I'd make sure no asshole gangsters or crazy stalkers got close enough to so much as frighten her ever again.

I only hoped I was strong enough to truly stand beside this incredible woman I'd underestimated for so long.

EIGHT

Luciana

JASPER GLIDED to a stop next to me and rolled his shoulders with a sharp exhalation.

"I know we're technically not done with practice, but I'm going to head to the locker room a few minutes early. Can't quite shake the ache in my back, but the heat from the showers usually does the trick."

That sounded fair enough, especially considering Niko had taken off ten minutes ago for a meeting with another potential sponsor.

I gave Jasper's hand a quick squeeze. "Sure. I'm going to work on that spin a little more on my own, and then I'll be heading out too. I'll see you at the apartment."

Jasper shot me a smile and pushed off toward the stands. As I watched him go, my stomach knotted.

Were his sore muscles only because of the training we'd been putting in here over the past week, or was it more than that? I couldn't help wondering if his apprehension about tackling this competition with a total newbie coupled with the bomb I'd dropped on him and

Niko about my past were catching up with him, especially now that we were surrounded by skaters more at his level.

There was nothing I could do but give him whatever time and space he needed, though. And make sure my skills reflected the time I'd spent on the ice rather than my competitive experience.

I whirled through the spin we'd been working on a few more times, counting out the beats in my head, picturing my partner whipping around next to me. Another skater cruised by, but my focus didn't waver.

Niko had booked us some private rink time, but we often took part in the freestyle sessions as well. By now, I was used to skating on the same rink as my competition. It hadn't taken much for my anxiety to dissolve.

No one was looking at us. They were all too busy worrying about their own routines to pay all that much attention to ours.

And when they were evaluating us, I thought we'd put on a pretty good show so far as our free skate program came together.

Seeing the time slot was just about up, I pulled off my skates, gave the blades a quick wipe, and sat down on the bench to pull on my sneakers. My own muscles were twinging with exhaustion, but it was a welcome burn. The feeling of work well done. Of dreams I was chasing so much more closely than ever before.

I got up with a heft of my workout bag just as the skaters taking the next time slot spilled into the stands. Right at the front of the pack was Quentin Wolfe.

And just my luck, the cocky jerk strode straight down the aisle toward me.

His eyebrows arched as he looked me over. He stopped in front of me and tsked his tongue.

"I almost didn't realize it was you, Mrs. St. Pierre. What's with the new look? Figured you needed to play up that pretty face as much as possible to distract everyone from your partner?"

I rolled my eyes at him. If he'd had any idea what my disguise was actually protecting me from, the pompous asshole would probably have wet his pants.

"Some of us know that our looks are part of our performance too. And my name is Lou, by the way."

"Lou," he said with a mocking drawl, eyeing me with his piercing baby blues. "And where's the great Saint Jasper? Did he run for the hills when he heard I was coming?"

I didn't bother to hold back my guffaw. "Some of us also aren't paying that much attention to when everyone else comes and goes. Neither of us had any idea you were in the next time slot. I guess I'm just slow."

I shot him a sickeningly sweet smile that I knew would look obviously fake.

Quentin snorted. "I doubt that. From what I've seen, he's the one who'll be holding you back. Don't know why you decided to put your money on a fading star like him."

"You obviously haven't been looking very hard if you think he's fading," I retorted. "And after what I've seen of *your* version of skating, I'd rather be on the ice with him any day."

Quentin flashed his teeth at me, but the expression had the quality of a restrained snarl. "Considering who you call talented, my feelings aren't exactly hurt. You'd think him wimping out last year would give you enough of a clue, but I guess you'll find out who's willing to put the real work in."

I gave him a pointed look. "Says the guy who's standing around heckling a girl he's not even competing with rather than getting on with practice."

Quentin let out a cool laugh, but his eyes gleamed with what looked almost like appreciation. I'd seen how Jasper acted with him—doing his best to stonewall and ignore the other guy.

Maybe he liked having me sass right back at him.

I grimaced inwardly at the thought of this prick liking anything about me, but at the same time I couldn't deny that my heart had kicked up a notch too.

His antagonistic intensity made for a good target to let out some of the tension churning inside me, that was all. And as volunteer punching bags went, he was pretty easy on the eyes. The sharp angles of his handsome face matched his penetrating gaze.

It really was a shame those striking looks had been wasted on such a trash bag of a human being.

"*I* can recognize talent," he said with a hint of a sneer. "But it's not like I can stop you from wasting yours."

I flipped my ponytail over my shoulder and batted my brightly shadowed eyes at him with a confident smirk. "Come up with whatever excuses you want to justify this growing obsession with me. I think you're just glad you don't have to go head-to-head with Jasper again."

The light in his eyes sparked brighter with what might have been a flare of heat too, but before Quentin could shoot off another caustic remark, his phone buzzed in his pocket.

Muttering a curse under his breath, he pulled out the device. When he glanced at the screen, his stance tensed. His jaw flexed as he tapped out a response with his thumb.

He'd just sent it off when the woman who'd glommed onto him before sashayed down the steps and draped her arm around his shoulders. "Why are you bothering with this dope, babe?" She pursed her hot pink lips and narrowed her eyes at me. "Your time's up, isn't it, newbie? Let the professionals get to work."

She thought she was being professional? Jasper and Niko would never in a million years have stooped as low as these two did.

I tilted my head to the side with another stiff smile. "Oh, I've been trying to leave, but your boyfriend here just couldn't bear to let me go."

Quentin's lips curled. "Won't be the first time I'm in your way. Better get used to it."

He grasped Jess's hand and tugged her toward the ice, clearing the aisle. Swallowing my last snappy retort, I turned my back on them and hustled up to the doors.

Neither of them deserved any more of my energy. They were only on our case because they knew how good Jasper and I were.

Quentin should be thanking his lucky stars he didn't have to face off against Jasper this year. And Jess—I might not be totally confident in my competitive abilities yet, but I was sure I could wipe the ice with that catty bitch.

I even had a rival now. I really had arrived.

I laughed softly to myself and quickly changed, eager to get home and relax with the men who actually mattered. Should I tell Jasper about how antsy *his* rival obviously was around his return? Or would it just make him irritable hearing about Quentin at all?

Better to wipe the jerk and his stunning asshole face right out of my mind.

When I stepped out of the arena, I drank in the cool outside air, not caring about the tang of car exhaust. Boston was a hell of a lot bigger than Hobb Creek, but I loved that I still got to walk home from the arena when I wanted to. The guys had done an amazing job picking out our apartment.

I strolled down the street through the thickening twilight, peeking through store windows and perking my ears at strains of music that filtered through doorways. We'd be here for at least another month, and I couldn't wait to check out the clubs and music venues this city had to offer.

As much as I'd enjoyed Hobb Creek's peacefulness, I had missed a proper nightlife.

The cool air wound around me, but my jacket kept me cozy and warm. Knowing Rafael would be following along at a discreet distance warmed me even more.

Blending in with the big city bustle, I was ten times as anonymous as I'd been in Hobb Creek too. Anonymous and safe.

My bodyguard had never been one to actually hit the dance floor, even though he'd followed me into Austin's clubs often enough. Would I be able to convince the other men to take a different kind of spin with me?

Niko would probably jump at the chance to let out more of his buoyant energy. Jasper would grumble about the idea… but he might get into it if I could convince him to give the scene a shot. If he brought the same athletic grace to the club that he did to the rink, he'd have everyone watching in envy.

The daydream brought a real smile to my lips. Tonight might not be the best time to go for it since Jasper had been extra sore, but maybe this weekend we could take a little break and work our muscles in all kinds of other ways…

I rounded the corner to our apartment building, my eyes flicking up to instinctively look at the windows of our unit. My steps slowed.

The lights weren't on, but I hadn't caught up with Jasper yet either. I'd assumed he'd gone on ahead of me and would already be here.

Hopefully he wasn't waiting back at the arena someplace I'd missed him.

I hurried up the steps, wanting to check what was up before I sent any worried texts. When I burst into the third-floor hallway, my breath rushed out of me in relief.

Jasper was standing right there at the threshold of our apartment, the door open in front of him. For a second, I thought I'd caught him just as he was about to step inside.

But rather than walking on in, he glanced over at me. The sight of his sallow face made my heart lurch.

As I dashed over to see what was wrong, Rafael thundered up the stairs and charged into the hall after me. He must have noticed my sudden urgency and been afraid something was wrong.

Well, that wasn't incorrect, even if I hadn't known exactly how wrong at the time.

"Lou," Jasper croaked, stumbling backward. My eyes trailed from his unnerved face to his trembling hands and through the doorway.

Something lay on the floor in the beam of light that spilled from the hallway. Something white and red and feathery.

I blinked a few times before my mind fully processed the shape.

It was a dead dove.

Its body had been placed carefully in the apartment's front hall, its wings spread wide in a pool of dark blood that stained the tips of its pale feathers. And a rose lay next to it… No, *through* it.

The thorny stem had been shoved straight through the bird's neck.

My stomach lurched. I backed up too, colliding with Rafael who'd come up behind me.

"Shit." I ran my hands through my hair, brushing my bangs away from my face. "Shit, shit, *shit.*"

Rafael's voice came out in a growl. "Stay here. I need to make sure whoever left that isn't still in the apartment."

He strode into the apartment, radiating protective fury. If the intruder *had* stuck around, they'd regret it very soon.

As Rafael's feet creaked through the apartment, the facts of the situation sank in with icy clarity. By the time he'd returned to us with a grim shake of his head indicating the space was all clear, my stomach had balled into a twist of anxiety.

"He followed us all the way here," I said, hugging myself. "That fucking psycho figured out where we went—he found the exact apartment in all of Boston…"

"He isn't going to get away with this," Rafael insisted, but I could see the concern in his dark gaze too. He didn't like this development any more than I did.

Jasper sucked in a breath, bracing his hand against the wall to steady himself. "We'll figure this out, Lou. We'll find a way to make sure he doesn't come back."

I swallowed thickly, my arms tightening around my torso. "I don't know if getting rid of him would be enough to keep us safe."

My partner peered at me. "What do you mean?"

Rafael would have already figured it out, but I had to say it out loud for Jasper's benefit.

"The rose… My mother's name, as part of her empire, is the Deadly Rose. The only reason he'd have included that detail is if he knows who I am."

And if this unhinged lunatic knew I was my mother's daughter… how long would it be before he tipped *her* off about my new life, and everything I'd achieved came crashing down?

NINE

Luciana

BY THE TIME Niko arrived back home with a few bags full of groceries, most of our collective shock had faded into a foggy confusion and burning fury. Rafael had gone through the apartment several times, yanking open closet doors and checking underneath all of our beds, examining every fixture for recording bugs.

At the very least, the stalker wasn't in our home anymore. It was another question entirely whether or not he was still nearby, but the only clue he'd left us was the dove itself.

Rafael and I had cleaned up the mess, but the horror that crossed my coach's face when we filled him in was like he'd seen it himself. My stomach twisted, half expecting Niko to rush to his room and start packing his things.

I'd told him about the "gifts" my stalker had left me before, but that'd been well after the fact. And we'd hoped we'd left the sicko behind.

But after I'd explained everything, Niko sank into one of the armchairs, the horrified expression giving way to something more pensive. The rest of us sat down around him. I folded my hands over my belly as if I could hold back the ache that'd formed in my stomach.

After a minute of silence, the normally cheerful man glanced up at me with a somber expression that only deepened the ache. "What do we do now? Should we leave the apartment?"

I grimaced. "It'd be hard to find another one on such short notice, especially furnished, and it's not like we have the funds to set us all up in a hotel for days on end. If this asshole tracked me down here, I'm not sure moving would do us any good anyway."

"We wouldn't even need to think about that if he hadn't gotten this far," Jasper grumbled, and shot a dark look Rafael's way. "Isn't keeping psychos away from Lou supposed to be *your* job as bodyguard?"

Rafael's eyes narrowed. "I took every possible step to keep our location under wraps. I'm not the weak link here."

Jasper's shoulders stiffened. "What's that supposed to mean? I didn't tip anyone off. I don't know anything about all the criminal stuff."

"Exactly," Rafael growled. "So you'd better shut up about it instead of mouthing off as if you're in any position to point fingers."

"When Lou's safety is on the line, I think I—"

"Guys!" I pushed to my feet to stand between them, holding out my hands. "Arguing isn't going to get us anywhere. We need to work together if we're going to deal with this prick."

The aggression deflated from both of their stances, though Rafael's scowl lingered. I pressed onward before he could toss out any more cutting remarks.

"We need to figure out who the stalker is, exactly what he knows, and what he's planning on doing with that info. Apparently he's figured out my ties to the Deadly Rose, but if he'd informed my mom of my location, her people would already be here. So he's up to something else."

Jasper let out a ragged sigh. "Okay. Could we put up some kind of security cameras? If he comes back, catch him on video?"

Niko perked up. "There's a camera in the lobby."

Rafael shook his head. "I already checked the footage. There was a guy who came in during the right timeframe, who's probably the right one, but he obviously knew he was being recorded. He had a cap on so the brim would hide his face, baggy clothes so I couldn't even tell you what his build is like, nothing distinguishing."

"But if we had a camera right in the apartment, he wouldn't be expecting that," Jasper said.

"Technology isn't really my forte," Rafael admitted reluctantly. "I wouldn't know how to set up something that'd go unnoticed—especially since he's already cased the place. If we stick a stuffed animal or a lamp or something like the typical hidden cameras, he'll be suspicious."

I frowned. "Well, we can try. It's worth a shot. But if it doesn't catch anything visible that we can use to ID him, it doesn't help us much. We won't even know he's been in the apartment until afterward."

Niko snapped his fingers. "You know, my sister's good with technology like this. She helped out a friend of hers who had a persistent ex-boyfriend hanging around messing with her things. She might have some ideas."

I shot Rafael a glare at his automatic skeptical expression and nodded at Niko. "Sure. It can't hurt to check."

"We don't want people all around the world knowing our business," my bodyguard muttered as Niko pulled out his phone.

"I won't tell her why we're asking. Just a general hypothetical situation." Niko tapped on the screen. "Let's just hope she's not too annoyed at me for waking her up. It's only eight am in Japan, and she likes to sleep in."

His eyes brightened, and he spoke into the phone. "Ohayo, Emi! Warui warui."

He launched into more animated Japanese that the rest of us couldn't follow, gesturing with his free hand as if she'd see his body language as well. I could make out a female voice on the other end in his pauses, so faint I probably wouldn't have been able to decipher the words even if they'd been in English.

I got the sense that she was offering some suggestions when his tone turned a bit serious again. He asked a few questions, I suspected in clarification, and turned cheerier with what I could tell was an expression of gratitude.

"Fine, go back to sleep, lazy bones," he added in English in a teasing tone, and turned to the rest of us as he ended the call.

"Well?" Jasper said, on the edge of his seat.

Niko beamed at us. "She said we could set up a motion detector by the door. It can be programmed to send us all an alert on our phones if someone enters while it's active. Then we'll know as soon as an intruder arrives."

Rafael leaned forward, his expression becoming more intense. "And I can get back here and catch the motherfucker." His lips curled into a fierce smile.

Jasper cleared his throat. "Whoever's closest and available should head back. Even if it's Niko or me. We don't want to risk losing our chance to nab the jerk."

Rafael raised an eyebrow. "It should be the one who'd know how to take him down. Which would definitely be me."

"No, Jasper's right," Niko said. "If he or I are close and can get here faster, we're not going to ignore it and risk him getting away. I'm sure we can manage to tackle one man and keep him from leaving at least until you get here." He flexed his bicep with a grin. "We've got plenty of muscle too, you know."

"Yeah." Jasper smacked his fist into the opposite palm. "And I'd like to take a few shots at the asshole who's trying to terrorize Lou. He deserves that and more."

The vehemence in his voice and Niko's unshakable enthusiasm sent a rush of anxious affection through me. I hadn't expected my skater men to be so determined to protect me in *every* possible way.

But here they were, declaring their intention to do battle for me without hesitation. Even though they weren't remotely prepared.

"He'll probably be armed," I reminded them, sitting back down next to Jasper and grabbing his hand with a tight squeeze. "I don't want either of you getting hurt."

Jasper shot me a steely look. "And we don't want this prick doing anything else to mess with you. We can handle it."

"We won't do anything more than we need to in order to make sure he doesn't get away before Rafael arrives," Niko assured me with total confidence.

I didn't know how to argue with that, even though every particle of my body screamed to keep them out of this part of my life completely.

But I'd drawn them into it. I'd told them who I was and all the baggage that came with my old existence.

And they'd stuck with me willingly.

What were the chances that they would be more available to get here than Rafael would anyway? He'd be on patrol or guard duty, and they'd usually be at the arena with me.

"Fine," I said, with a firm glance at Rafael. "Whoever can come, will. Including me. But don't be afraid to fight dirty if you need to. A good swing of a skate or a heavy duffel bag could do as much for you as a knife."

And maybe we should get the guys some knives too. And make sure they knew how to use them well.

The thought made my head start to ache too. I pressed the heels of my hands against my forehead.

"We'll get it all sorted out quickly," Niko said, tapping on his phone again. "Emi knew a brand she's used before—she texted me a link to it at an American store where we can get it quickly. I'll place the order right now. There, done."

Jasper scanned the living room warily, his fingers twining with mine protectively. I didn't think I could stand to see all of my men so unsettled on my behalf any longer.

I got to my feet, tugging him with me. "Then we have a plan. I think we could all use something else to think about after all this stressing out, don't you? Why don't we check out that Cuban restaurant down the street? Rafael, you said you wanted to try it."

My bodyguard considered me, but maybe he could recognize my inner turmoil. Or at least that there wasn't much else any of them could do to protect me in this exact moment.

"I did," he said. "That sounds perfect, if these two gringos are up for it."

Niko laughed as he stood. "I'm always interested in trying out a new cuisine, especially with expert guidance."

As we tramped out the door together, a little of the tension inside me unwound. But the ache of anxiety lingered in my gut.

My men were as determined to defend me as I was to protect them… but what if this trick wasn't enough to stop the psycho who had me in his sights?

TEN

Luciana

AS OUR SERVER took away two empty plates that had once held heaping piles of masitas de puerco and empanadas, Niko leaned back in his chair with one hand on his stomach. "Now that's some food. I've never had anything like it."

Rafael raised an eyebrow at him. "Not many Cubans in Japan, huh?"

"Nope. I should encourage some to join us! The ones who already want to open restaurants."

Jasper laughed and licked a fleck of sauce off his thumb in a gesture that got me heated up just to watch. "I'm sure they'll really appreciate your enthusiasm. Those were only the appetizers, you know."

Niko straightened back up. "Oh, I'm ready for more. But maybe we could get another plate of those little pork things too?"

To my surprise, Rafael let out a chuckle. "I think I could manage to put away a few more. This place can't quite match my abuela's masitas de puerco, but they're pretty good."

A smile touched my lips as I watched the guys. Rafael hadn't really hung out with my skaters before, joining us briefly for meals in the apartment but otherwise keeping his distance. He'd still been his usual quietly stern self since we'd headed out to the restaurant, but the other men's enthusiasm for the food he loved had obviously warmed him up to them a bit.

"Well, now I feel a lot better about letting you do the ordering for all of us," Jasper said with a relaxed grin of his own and perked up at the arrival of our server. "And here come the main meals!"

Rafael nodded to my partner's heaping plate as the waitress set it down in front of him. "That ropa vieja should be full of flavor. If it doesn't kick you in the taste buds, I'll just have to make my own version for all of us one night."

Jasper dug his fork into the shredded steak and hummed happily as he chewed. My mouth watered as I took in the Cuban sandwich arriving in front of me.

When I raised it to my lips for a massive first bite, Rafael shook his head at me. "I can't believe you. Out of all the traditional things they have on this menu, you go for the sandwich."

"Hey, I like what I like." I shot him a teasing smile. "You should be glad I didn't insist on us going out for Polish instead."

Niko peered at me with curiosity. "You don't like Cuban food, Lou?"

"Not everyone's into the food of their background," Jasper pointed out. "And Lou isn't even Cuban—your family was from Mexico, right?"

"Yeah, four generations ago—pretty distant." I waggled my sandwich. "And I don't dislike it. I just like other stuff more."

Niko had turned to Jasper. "You aren't one to talk. You weren't even born in Canada but you pour maple syrup all over everything."

Jasper mock-glowered back at him. "I'm not that far removed. My parents only immigrated to the States a couple of years before they had me. Anyway, maple syrup objectively makes everything better." He glanced down at his ropa vieja. "Well, maybe it wouldn't work on this."

"Lou's nanny when she was a little kid was Polish," Rafael put in with a fond glance my way. "Got her hooked on pierogies and cabbage rolls. It's a goddamned tragedy."

"They're, like, the most comforting foods ever," I protested. "And pyzy—oh, man, if you've never tried those…"

Rafael pointed his fork at me. "You're not allowed to drool over Polish food while you have a Cuban sandwich right there in your hands."

I shrugged innocently and took another big bite. The savory pork was an awfully good treat too, but I wasn't going to admit that to him while he was heckling me.

"It makes sense that everyone has their own tastes," Niko said, between bites of his braised short ribs. "But I wouldn't trust a fellow citizen who doesn't love Calpis."

Jasper rolled his eyes. "I'm pretty sure not everyone in Japan loves milky soda, Niko."

"Everyone with good taste does." Niko smirked at him. "And one day I'll convert you too."

Jasper let out another laugh, and his free hand brushed across Niko's thigh. The other man's gaze darted to the gesture, and a soft flush colored his cheeks that I didn't think had anything to do with the spice in his food. He scooted his chair a little closer so their knees rested against each other.

I couldn't restrain a grin as I watched. The romantic side to their relationship was so new and fresh—it warmed me up knowing that I'd helped them finally figure out what they both wanted.

Maybe after Jasper got a little more comfortable with the physical side he'd never really explored before, the three of us could have a lot of fun, all together. Not that I'd mention anything along those lines just yet. Knowing Jasper, too much of a nudge would send him running in the wrong direction.

I squirmed a little in my seat with the pang of desire set off by the images that'd formed in my head and shelved them for another day.

Seeing the way their faces lit up when their eyes met and they exchanged smiles, I knew we'd get there.

Then Jasper turned to Rafael. "You've obviously known Lou for a long time. How did you get into the bodyguard business anyway? That doesn't sound like something you'd find a job posting for online."

Rafael snorted. "No, it's a pretty different side of job searching." He paused, looking down at his plate for a moment, with a hesitation I didn't totally understand.

Was he still uncomfortable about the fact that we were hooking up now after he'd known me as a kid?

I reached over and gave his hand a quick squeeze. "My mom's… operations were pretty prominent. Anyone in town who wanted to get into that kind of work would have known she was the person to impress."

Rafael's odd reaction appeared to have smoothed away with my interjection. He nodded. "It's not the kind of thing most kids dream about, but I ended up getting wrapped up in the life… I still wanted bigger things than the local gang I started out with, though. Working for the Cordovas offered more opportunities."

Niko cocked his head. "Even when you ended up mainly protecting one person."

"One very important person," Rafael said firmly. "And I did get to travel a lot with the family. It wasn't all kiddy stuff. Especially once this one got older and wilder." He narrowed his eyes at me.

"As you should very much appreciate," I retorted with a cheeky flash of my teeth, but the conversation had reminded me that I'd never gotten much of Rafael's history out of him before. I knew I'd asked him basic questions when I was younger, but from what I remembered, he'd always deflected them.

"Your parents weren't in the criminal life, were they?" I said. "You always wanted to keep them away from that stuff."

Rafael's expression darkened again. "They worry less not knowing. I made the choices I made—my parents shouldn't carry any burden from them."

He shoveled another bite of his dinner into his mouth with a firmness that suggested the topic was closed. I eyed him for a moment, wondering at his sudden clamming up after he'd gotten more talkative earlier.

Was there something about his early career that he didn't want *me* knowing? Or could it be that he was afraid of how the other guys with their much less questionable pasts would see things?

This wasn't the time to push him about it. Maybe when we no longer had the looming threats of both my stalker and my mom, plus the impending competition, hanging over our heads.

The waitress returned a few minutes later and beamed at us. "Look at all these clean plates. That's the perfect compliment to the chef. Is anyone ready for dessert?"

Niko elbowed Jasper lightly. "This one is always game for something sweet."

"Hey!" Jasper protested before his mouth slanted into a self-deprecating smile. "Okay, he's right. Rafael, should we put our trust in you again?"

My bodyguard appeared to relax a little more as he rubbed his jaw. "I think I can be worthy of that faith."

We ended the night with a coffee and a sweet each. Jasper and I both spooned rice pudding into our mouths while Rafael and Niko both powered through miniature caramel flan.

The taste of cinnamon filled my nose as I relished every bite. I set the spoon down and was about to comment on how obscenely full I was when a phone alert pealed out from Niko's side of the table.

All of us stiffened, my heart skipping a beat. Niko yanked his phone out of his pocket. Then he glanced around at the rest of us with a rough chuckle.

"It's just a text—from Emi, complaining that she couldn't get back to sleep. We haven't even set up the motion detector yet."

A giggle tickled up my throat. No, we hadn't, but that was exactly what I'd been thinking of.

As the giggle tumbled out of me, the tension broke with the guys joining my laughter. Jasper rubbed his temple. "I can't believe I nearly jumped out of my skin over that."

"I guess we're all a little on edge," I said, still smiling, but inside my stomach had knotted.

Tonight had been a good distraction, but we were going to have to face the psycho harassing me sooner or later. I just hoped that finally confronting this prick would be the end of it. I'd never asked for any of this.

All I wanted was a normal life, and it seemed like the universe was determined to block me at every turn.

ELEVEN

Jasper

THERE WAS nothing like having the rink to ourselves after the shared time slots we'd had for some of our practices. Lou and I swept across the ice in sync, my legs pumping at exactly the same beat as hers.

I glanced at her to check that she was still ready to try the adjusted lift that Niko had suggested we switch to for our short routine, switching to a one-handed hold to make it more impressive. She smiled at me with a barely perceptible nod and reached out her hand.

I swept her up, pushing her slender form into the air as I whipped us around. Her body balanced in my hands, stretched out as if she were literally flying.

My arms tensed slightly as I let go with one hand to stretch it out into the air as well. But I managed to stop myself from stiffening up too much, and Lou stayed poised above me like she was never meant to be anywhere else.

I swung backwards as I lowered her, watching her skates touch down without a single wobble. She grinned at me, her eyes alight with the exhilaration that took her from pretty to absolutely fucking gorgeous. My heart skipped a beat as I grinned back.

We went through the rest of the routine just to feel how it all came together, my spirits buoyed by the initial victory. When we locked into our final pose and then glided over to the boards to meet Niko, he clapped his hands in approval.

"That looked fantastic," he crowed. "Here, take a look."

He held out his phone to show us the recording he'd taken. Watching Lou and me soar across the rink was almost as amazing as experiencing it.

"I need to keep my elbow a little higher there," I noted with a momentary frown.

"And I need to keep that foot totally pointed," Lou put in. "But it's so close to perfect! We should be able to have it down by competition time."

She prodded my bicep. "When are you going to have those costumes finished, partner? I want to see the full visual, and we've only got a week left."

I narrowed my eyes at her even as her enthusiasm had another smile tickling at my lips. "Hey, good sewing takes time, Punk. I'm just finishing up the details."

"Having seen the fabrics you picked out and your past designs, I know it's going to bring the whole routine together," Niko said with the unshakable confidence he so often managed to exude.

Sometimes it irritated me that I couldn't totally buy into his confidence. Now… I couldn't help thinking it might be warranted.

I'd found myself partnered with two skaters who understood what was important to me on the ice—and were doing everything they could to help me get there. It'd been a long time since I'd felt this at home at the rink.

This might be the best I'd *ever* felt about my skating aspirations.

The thought hit me with a rush of affection. I couldn't help teasing my hand along Lou's jaw.

"It'll be incredible, because I've got two incredible people helping me make it happen," I said, and tugged her into a kiss.

The arena's air might have been chilly, but Lou's lips seared against mine with blazing heat. Just like that, I wanted to meld her whole body against mine, to indulge in the other sort of partnership we'd proven to be awfully good at too.

But even with the rink to ourselves, the open air felt way too, well, open. I let my tongue flick over hers in a teasing promise of more fun to come later and drew back.

My eyes met Niko's, my other partner on—and possibly off—the ice, and the urge gripped me to yank him to me too. To show him I was embracing every part of our collaboration.

The same hesitation that had held me back from outright grinding against Lou gripped me again. What if someone walked in at the wrong moment?

Getting romantically involved with one's pairs partner wasn't that unusual. Openly hooking up with your coach—especially when you were both men? That would definitely raise a lot more eyebrows.

The twinkle in Niko's eyes suggested that he'd picked up on my desire. I almost overrode my hesitations—but was relieved that I hadn't when the door banged open at the top of the stands.

Quentin Wolfe's coolly arrogant voice traveled down the aisle. "What are you misfits still doing here? It's our time now."

Just our luck, we had to cross paths with this asshole even when we'd booked a private timeslot. I let out my breath in a huff, but Niko spoke first in his usual friendly way.

"Don't worry, we're just wrapping up. I assume having two skaters packing up in the stands won't interfere with your practice."

Quentin strode down the aisle, that girl Jess who was always hanging off him and two junior skaters his coach was working with trailing behind him. "I get that you'd want to spy on our brilliance, but you'd better get out of here fast."

I snorted at both the ideas of us wanting to spy and of him being brilliant, and Quentin fixed his piercing gaze directly on me. Because of course he did.

"I'm sorry I missed any of your practice," he said. "I bet it'd have been a laugh riot. I'll have to show up a little early next time for some entertainment before the professionals get to work."

"Fuck off, Wolfe," I muttered, unable to stop the remark from dropping from my mouth.

"Let's hope your skills are a *little* better than your insults, or I'm not sure I'll be able to enjoy our inevitable win."

He slid on his skates and stepped onto the ice without a backward glance. I wiped down my blades, fighting a grimace.

He just liked jerking my chain. I knew that. I shouldn't let it get to me.

As much as his comment about spying had rankled me, I couldn't help glancing over at him and his fellow skaters as I swung my duffel over my shoulder. We hadn't crossed paths with Quentin here in a while. I had no idea what he'd been working on.

It wasn't as if it mattered what we saw when we were competing in different—

Wait a second. What the fuck?

Quentin and Jess were gliding across the rink side by side, glancing at each other to get into sync. As I watched, they leapt up and whipped around in matching double Axels.

Their landings were slightly off, and their coach beckoned them over to give a few tips. My stomach sinking, I strode up to the boards.

"What the hell are you two doing?"

Quentin cut his gaze toward me. His tone went from cool to outright cold. "You didn't think I would let you weasel out of a proper competition that easily, did you, St. Pierre? It wasn't a problem to get me switched over from singles to pairs."

"But—you haven't even been training—"

He scoffed. "It isn't as if working with a partner is that hard."

"Especially when he's got one like me," Jess put in, slinging her arm around his waist and cozying up to him.

Quentin offered her a smile that wasn't much more than a smirk and leaned in to nip her earlobe. Her breathy giggle set my jaw on edge.

I couldn't tell if he even actually *liked* her. This was just one more way to piss us off.

"You're such a fucking idiot," I snapped. "You can't possibly be properly prepared to make this work. Why would you rearrange your plans for that?"

Quentin ignored me long enough to flick his tongue across Jess's jaw and squeeze her ass. She giggled again and nuzzled his neck as he returned his gaze to me.

"We actually tried out a little pairs skating this year already, just to see how it'd go. So it won't be too hard to pick up where we left off. You bowed out before I had the chance to beat you last year. I'm not letting you run away again. It's going to be *so* much more satisfying to crush you head-to-head."

Lou let out a guffaw behind me. "Somehow I think we'll be the ones getting all the satisfaction. Including the satisfaction of not having to listen to your crap any longer." She grabbed my hand. "Come on, Jasper. We've got more important things to focus on."

Fuming silently, I let her drag me away, my free hand balled into a fist. That fucking prick and his oversized ego…

"I'll meet you two out front," Niko said as we ducked into our respective locker rooms.

I peeled off my sweaty clothing and rushed through a hasty shower, but even the cool water I set it to didn't cool my temper. When I stalked out into the hall, my jaw was still clenched, my nerves jittering with annoyance.

How was I supposed to relax and enjoy the strides we'd been making when I knew I'd have to face that jerk's stupid mug throughout the competition? Fuck, was he going to keep up the whole pairs thing all the way to Finals?

If *we* even made it that far.

My teeth gritted harder. Why was I letting him get to me? I was letting him screw me up when I should have just ignored him.

But I couldn't quite will the anger away, and that only made me more pissed off.

Lou emerged a minute later, took one look at my face, and tsked at me. "You're still stewing."

"He just—he did this *on purpose* to try to mess with me."

She stepped closer, setting her hands against my chest and peering up at me through her eyelashes in a pose I had to admit was totally delectable and at least a little distracting. "So don't be messed with. We're better than those two—we have to be when we have months more practice at skating together."

She had a point. Even through my frustration, I could admit that.

"I just wish I didn't have to think about him at all," I grumbled.

"You don't." She cocked her head. "Why do you care what he does anyway? He's just one more skater we'll be up against, right? There are lots of others."

I exhaled in a rush. "I know. But none of the others are set on taking me down a peg like he is. He just—he gets under my skin. All that talk about how there's no way I could be good enough…"

I trailed off at the ache that came into my gut with the admission. A familiar ache, but not one that'd originated with Quentin.

Lou's expression softened. "What? Did something bad happen between you two, more than just heckling?"

"No," I said quickly. "He's never done anything but mouth off."

I hesitated, wanting to shove the other memories that'd risen up back into the recesses of my mind where I preferred they stayed. But the concern in Lou's eyes loosened my tongue a little more than usual.

I owed her some honesty, didn't I?

She stayed silent, giving me the space to decide how much I wanted to tell her. Affection overwhelmed the painful pang inside me.

If anyone could understand my situation, it was her, considering that what she'd been through with her mother had been even worse.

"My dad," I said finally. "Whenever Quentin lays into me, it reminds me of the kinds of things my dad would say. He hated that I wanted to pursue this as a career so much—it practically broke up my parents."

Lou winced in sympathy. "I'm sorry."

"We're past that now." I hung my head. "I've just always had this doubt in the back of my head about whether it was really worth it. If I'm going to accomplish enough to justify the stress I put them through over my choices."

"Jasper."

Lou raised her hand to touch my cheek. When I met her gaze, her dark brown eyes shone perfectly clear.

"It's already been worth it. You inspired me—you must have inspired hundreds of other skaters, maybe thousands, with your past performances. And all the people who've been touched by seeing you skate… I know you've got tons of fans."

"People I let down by not showing up at all last year."

"You didn't owe them anything if you weren't in the right place to compete. And now you're back." She beamed up at me. "And we're going to be amazing."

More of the ache melted away, but the tension didn't disappear completely, even as she tugged me toward the entrance where Niko was waiting.

She hadn't been there for all the fights and the cold silences and the snapped remarks. She hadn't seen the one person who'd always been there to support me break down in tears because of where that had led.

Maybe I'd accomplished enough already, but I didn't feel like I had. And if I failed now, I'd let down not just myself and anyone out there who still believed in me, but the incredible woman beside me too.

TWELVE

Luciana

AS I HEFTED my equipment bag over my shoulder and stepped out into the fading late-afternoon sunlight, my stomach grumbled in anticipation of an extensive dinner that would make up for all the energy I'd burned on the ice. I'd hung back for an extra hour during one of the group practice times to work on some of my forms while Jasper and Niko headed out to search for a final embellishment Jasper wanted for our costumes.

He'd better show me what he'd come up with soon. I'd only caught glimpses and gotten a vague idea from the measurements he'd taken.

I set off toward the apartment, picturing the heaps of pierogies I could be shoveling down soon if I could convince the guys to go for Polish tonight. But I hadn't even reached the end of the block when a hand caught my shoulder.

I jumped half a foot in the air and spun around with my fists raised, only to see Rafael looking both tense and sheepish.

"Sorry," he said. "I thought you'd hear me coming."

I shook away my nerves and lowered my hands. "I was dreaming about dinner. What's going on?" The turmoil roiling in his burgundy eyes set my pulse thumping double speed.

His mouth pulled even tighter. "The motion detector went off."

My heart outright skipped a beat with a jolt of chilly exhilaration. "Perfect. Let's go catch that fucker and put him in his place."

Rafael gave me one of his patented long-suffering-bodyguard frowns. "*I'm* going to put the prick in his place. But first I'm going to put *you* in a room at the nearest hotel. I don't want you anywhere near him or on the streets where he could find you."

My eyebrows shot up. "Are you kidding me, Rafael? This asshole has been harassing me, so I'm damn well going to be there to take him down. Don't start treating me like a kid again."

Rafael let out a huff of breath. "It's not about seeing you as a kid. I'm still going to do whatever I can to keep you safe."

"Only as much as I'm going to let you. We're together in this. Now come on. If we stand around arguing any longer, we could miss the guy!"

Rafael glowered at me, but I stared right back at him with my chin raised. He knew I had a point.

With a growl of frustration, he turned on his heel. "Fine. But I'm going in first."

"No arguments here. I can play backup this once as long as I'm still in play."

"This isn't a game, Lou."

I set off next to him, matching his swift stride even with my shorter legs. "I know. And it's time my stalker found that out too."

We hustled back to the apartment building at a measured jog, Rafael scanning the street ahead as we went. I peered around us too, but I had no idea what I should be looking for. It wasn't as if the psychopath was going to show up draped with his bloody idea of presents.

Just as the building's brick face came into view up ahead, an unnervingly familiar figure ducked out from the entrance. I didn't get a glimpse of the guy's face amid his clothes, but he had on a cap with the brim tipped low and a baggy coat with the collar turned up, just like Rafael had mentioned when describing the man he'd seen in the security footage two nights ago.

Rafael obviously made the same connection. He swore under his breath and paused while the figure veered in the opposite direction from us.

He motioned toward the building. "Stick your duffel in the lobby so you're more mobile and let's keep on this motherfucker's trail."

I darted inside, shoved my bag into a corner, and rushed out, falling into step beside Rafael when he immediately started walking. He moved slower this time so we'd keep a safe distance from our target.

"Too many bystanders to tackle him out in the open like this," he muttered to me. All kinds of regular pedestrians were strolling along the sidewalks around us through the waning evening light. "We wait until he goes off the beaten path, and then we strike."

I nodded silently, my lungs constricting in anticipation. The man who'd been messing with me for weeks was finally right in front of me. I longed to sprint right after him and slam my fist into the back of his head, knocking off that stupid cap, but then we'd look like the aggressors to everyone watching.

We needed a little privacy to do this right.

Instead, I studied everything I could see of the guy from where we were trailing half a block behind. The tan coat fell to his thighs, the rest of him covered by dark baggy jeans and large tan boots. Like Rafael had said before, it was impossible to get a good read on his body type with that outfit.

I flexed my fingers with their heavy rings. What kind of fighter would he be? Was he carrying any weapons?

Well, if need be, I'd start by kicking him in the balls. That worked with just about anyone.

We'd only followed him for a few blocks when he swerved abruptly to the doorway of a large chain clothing store. As soon as he'd disappeared inside, Rafael motioned to me.

"We can't grab him in there either, but we might be able to get a look at his face and ID him. And we don't want to lose track of him if he tries to slip out the back."

We loped the rest of the way to the store and stepped in after our target. For a second, my gaze skimming over the other customers, my nerves jittered with the thought that we'd lost him.

Then I spotted his blue cap at the far end of the first floor, beyond several clusters of clothing racks. I snatched Rafael's hand. "Let's go!"

"Better idea." Rafael steered me in a roundabout route that took the guy out of our line of sight for a few seconds.

My heart pounded faster. "But—"

"Here."

My bodyguard had drawn up next to a shelving unit that rose from floor to ceiling, a checkerboard of open squares. Over the top of a stack of folded jeans, I realized we had a perfect line of sight to my stalker.

But he couldn't see us watching him. As I stared, he turned toward the front of the store, clearly checking for someone.

For us. He'd realized we were following him, and this was some kind of gambit.

But none of that mattered when I was now getting my first clear look at his face.

Tufts of blond hair showed beneath the cap, topping a pasty face with a hooked nose and a speckling of acne scars. His jawline was still hidden by his coat collar, but I made out a brutal-looking slash of a mouth that set off alarm bells in my head.

This was my psycho stalker. And I had no idea *who* he was.

"I've never seen this asshole before in my life," I whispered to Rafael, and then noticed my bodyguard's expression.

Rafael's gaze had hardened, his muscular shoulders tensed and his jaw taut. "Of all the bad fucking luck," he growled under his breath.

"What? You know him?"

Rafael didn't answer, only pushed forward. Was he going to confront the lunatic right here in the store after all?

But before he could corner the guy, the baggy-clothed figure strode straight past us like he'd just realized he was late for an important meeting. Rafael sucked his breath in with a hiss and marched after him, shooting a wary glance around the store in case anyone noticed our pursuit.

We burst past the doors only a few steps behind my stalker—just in time to see him jumping into the back of a car with a wave of his phone at the driver.

He must have called an Uber surreptitiously while he was in the store and waited until it arrived before he left. Fucking hell.

The car pulled into the street. There was nothing we could do but watch it go, unless we wanted to end up in a jail cell.

I gritted my teeth, resisting the urge to stomp my foot in annoyance, and spun toward Rafael. "Who the hell is he? How do you know him?"

Rafael sighed, his narrowed gaze still fixed on the back of the car as it cruised off down the road. He spun on his heel and motioned for me to walk with him.

"Let's get back to the apartment and see what he got up to there. I'll explain on the way."

I wrapped my arms around my chest as we set off. "I'm ready to hear it."

Rafael grimaced. "That prick's name is Martin Haggard. He ran with the gang in Austin for a few years back when you were a kid, but your mother got fed up with him pretty quick. He was too unhinged, too unpredictable—lashing out when it wasn't called for, making trouble in our own ranks. He crossed some line, and she told him to get his ass out of town. I heard he went north, but not specifically where."

My heart sank. "All the way to Canada, apparently."

"Seems like it. Maybe he ended up doing business with those amateur thugs near Hobb Creek and that's how he happened to see you." Rafael shook his head. "Maldita sea! The shittiest possible luck."

So, my stalker really was a literal psychopath. Wonderful.

I suppressed a shiver. "Why do you think he's harassing me? It doesn't seem like he's told my mom that he's seen me—she'd have tracked me down herself by now."

"No doubt. Who knows, with him? I always got the impression he didn't even care about the money—he just liked doing whatever he could to make people squirm… or scream. And I doubt he has fond feelings toward your family after your mother ran him off."

Fuck. And this freak had stumbled into my new life? Into Jasper and Niko's orbit?

It was even worse than I'd been afraid of.

"You don't need to worry," Rafael said firmly, as if reading my thoughts. "I'll track Haggard down, find out if he's mentioned anything about you to anyone else, and end this."

The cool certainty in his voice settled my nerves. Then he glanced down at me, and something shifted in his expression.

"Do you want to be a part of that? Of ending him? It'd be your right, after what he's put you through."

It probably didn't say anything good about me that a flutter of affection passed through my chest at the offer. Rafael was proving that he did recognize me as an equal force in our relationship—even the darker side of it.

I hesitated, turning the question over in my head as we reached the apartment building and clambered up the stairs. "I'm not sure. Scaring him off would have been one thing, but this… I don't know if I want to get my hands *that* dirty again."

Rafael clearly intended to kill the asshole. It sounded like doing so would benefit all society. And a part of me longed to at least watch the jerk suffer the way he'd tried to torment me.

But I'd hoped I could put the murderous side of my old existence behind me completely. I'd only killed a few people under my mother's orders, and each of those times had left me feeling sick both physically and emotionally.

"You don't have to do anything," Rafael said. "I can take care of it all on my own. I'm happy to. But I wanted to give you the option."

"Thank you." I exhaled in a rush. "Let me know when you figure out how to find him, and I'll make a final decision about how involved I want to get then."

It was clear as soon as Rafael unlocked the door that Jasper and Niko weren't back yet. Small mercies. Although they'd have gotten an alert too, so we'd have to tell them something.

Rafael flicked on the light and took in the space. "Motion detector is where it should be. Looks like he didn't notice it."

I couldn't see anything out of place at first glance around the living room. No dead animals or obscure messages.

I eased over to my bedroom and braced myself as I shoved open the door. But my crumpled bedspread and my half-unpacked suitcase looked completely undisturbed.

A noise of consternation reached me from the opposite direction. I dashed over to find Rafael making a disgusted face as he fished something out of the refrigerator into a plastic bag.

"I'm taking care of *this*," he said over his shoulder.

I wrinkled my nose and held my hand out. "At least let me bring the bag to the trash chute."

He passed it over. By the time I returned from down the hall, he was almost finished scrubbing the shelf where Haggard had left his latest "gift."

I glanced back toward the apartment door, my stomach knotting. "I'm surprised Jasper and Niko haven't gotten back yet. You'd think they'd have headed over as soon as the alert went off. I didn't think they were going too far."

Rafael shrugged and gave the shelf a few more swipes along with a squirt of cleaning spray. "They probably realized we'd be closer since we were at the rink and finished up whatever they were doing first."

After seeing how determined my skater men were to defend me, I wasn't so sure they'd have taken the development that lightly. Swallowing thickly, I pulled out my phone to try texting them.

Before I'd done more than tap out a few letters, a key clicked in the lock.

I spun around just as Niko and Jasper stepped inside, their gazes searching mine but their mouths set in matching sheepish smiles—and a new face bobbing up to peek over their shoulders.

"Oh em gee!" the slim Japanese woman cried out with a clap of her hands, her voice holding the same light accent Niko's did. She pushed between the two men with a swish of her sleek black bob. "You must be Lou! I'm so excited to meet you."

The next thing I knew, she was throwing her arms around me. I hugged her back automatically gaping at Niko.

He let out a rough chuckle. "Ah, we were a little delayed because of a surprise visitor. Emi decided it'd be fun to drop in from Japan."

"It's going to be *so* much fun," his sister declared with unshakeable enthusiasm, pulling back to grin at me.

I plastered a smile on my own face, wishing I could mean it more. But any happiness I might have felt at meeting part of Niko's family was drowned out by the roar of uneasiness reverberating through my head.

Just seconds ago, Rafael had been cleaning animal gore out of the fridge. Just how much more were my two way-too-different worlds going to collide now—and who else might get caught in the crossfire?

THIRTEEN

Luciana

I LOOKED DOWN at my plate of spaghetti as the waitress set it in front of me and suppressed the flash of memory provoked by the bright red sauce. My stomach clenched, but I made myself pick up my fork.

Jasper gave me a glance with a flicker of concern as he leaned over his own plate, but I'd had a chance to talk to him and Niko briefly away from Emi before we'd headed over to her hotel to dine in the lobby-adjacent restaurant. Not wanting them to worry too much, I'd told them that Rafael and I had followed up on the motion detector's alert and IDed my stalker.

My partner was clearly still in protective mode, but he also knew how well I could take care of myself. Jasper dragged his gaze away and brandished his own fork.

"This looks great. I'm starving, and I've got a bunch more work to finish tonight to get those costumes ready to go."

Emi clapped her hands together eagerly. "Niko said you make your own. I can't wait to see them!"

I couldn't suppress a genuine laugh. "Join the club. He's been keeping them secret even from me, and I've got to wear two of them."

Jasper aimed a teasing kick at me under the table. "Tomorrow we'll try them on. Promise."

"I'm sure they'll only make your performance more spectacular," Niko said with a grin.

"That's why I had to fly all the way out here," Emi declared. "It wouldn't be the same watching on TV. And it's been too long since I've been able to check up on my big brother."

Niko pressed his hand to his chest in mock-offense. "It's my job to check up on *you.*"

She giggled. "Well, you can do that better when I'm in the same city as you. But it looks like your friends have been taking good care of you."

She beamed around the table at us, and I felt a little of my uneasiness subside. It was hard to worry too much about psycho stalkers with a presence as warm and upbeat as Emi right in front of me.

Obviously friendliness and good cheer ran in Niko's family. And her vibrant chatter helped drown out the questions that'd been whirling in my head since I'd seen my stalker's face.

I was glad she'd suggested we get out of the apartment to eat, though. We had no idea whether Haggard might come back there… especially now that he'd noticed Rafael and me tailing him.

Emi paused her eager remarks to dig into her seafood fettucine, only to start swooning a moment later. "So good! It's been too much time since I had authentic American food."

Niko clicked his tongue at her. "It's Italian, not American."

"Well, we're *in* America, so almost the same thing. They don't make it the same back home."

A strange twinge passed through my chest, watching them together. You couldn't miss how much they cared about each other.

I'd never had a relationship like that. No siblings, and even my interactions with my mother had been far from warm. She'd warned me not to get too close to anyone at school, and it wasn't like I could have felt comfortable inviting any classmates over to our house anyway.

It must be nice, having family you could joke around with and count on like that.

"I bet they cook it differently in Italy too," Rafael put in, but he softened the remark with a chuckle. "But I do like the American version."

Niko pointed his fork toward Rafael. "This one will introduce you to all the Latin cuisine you could fill your stomach with. Can't get much of that in any way back in Japan."

A hint of a smile, enough to make my own stomach flutter, crossed Rafael's lips. "Always happy to expand my culinary horizons."

I had to appreciate how gracious he was being about the sudden visitor when he must have been dying to get out there and track down Haggard. He hadn't totally forsaken his bodyguard role—I saw his gaze sweep the restaurant every couple of minutes, watching for threats.

No doubt as soon as we left Emi at the hotel, he'd be off tracing leads.

I still had to decide how involved I wanted to get in his investigation… and the consequences that would follow.

The thought made my gut knot all over again. I managed to force down about half of my pasta, but the heaping plate was too much for my scattered nerves.

During a lull in the conversation, I dabbed at my mouth with my napkin and nudged back my chair. "I'm going to hit the ladies' room real quick before dessert."

Emi popped up from her chair. "Oh, I should freshen up too. I think I saw the restrooms on the way in. Here, I'll show you the way!"

She walked ahead with buoyant steps and pushed into the polished restroom with her purse swinging from her elbow. I ducked into one of the stalls and emerged to find her touching up her glossy pink lipstick.

As I moved to wash my hands, Emi gave the stalls a quick scan. We were alone in the room.

She lowered her voice to a conspiratorial tone anyway. "I hope my idea about the… what do you call it in English? Motion tracker? That it helped with your security problem."

She'd spent five years of her childhood living in the US and attending an English school just like Niko had, but it wasn't surprising her vocabulary had some limitations.

I hesitated, not sure exactly how much she'd figured out or what Niko had told her—on the phone or since she'd arrived. "Um…"

"It's crazy that fans get so obsessed," she went on. "He was telling me in the car that you've been coping really well, though, not letting it affect your focus."

Not too much. But I was grateful that Niko had been able to come up with a reasonable story on the fly that wasn't as unnerving as the real one.

"Yeah," I said. "The motion detector did help, actually. We know who's been coming around the apartment now, so we should be able to make sure he backs off."

"Oh, perfect. I'm so glad. It must be very stressful."

She aimed a softer smile at me, and I realized with a jolt that she really was concerned on my behalf. It seemed she shared not just Niko's upbeat attitude but his sense of compassion as well.

"It has been," I said. "But your brother—and the other guys—have been a lot of support."

"Hmm, yes." Emi's expression turned sly. "In all kinds of ways."

My face flushed. How much had she figured out about my relationship with the guys? "Well…"

She waved her hand as if dismissing my embarrassment. "They've obviously all fallen for you. And good for you juggling all of them and keeping them happy. Why wouldn't a woman want three men's attention if she can handle it?"

I coughed, still off-balance. "I guess that's one way of looking at it."

Emi shot me a sideways glance and patted my shoulder. "Every time I've talked to Niko since he started training you, he's been in a brighter mood. So it must be good for him too. I'm glad he has you, even if you're—how would you put it?—keeping him on his toes."

"Good," I said, grappling with my awkwardness. "It's important to me that he's happy. That we're all happy. I've tried to be upfront with all of them, because it has gotten kind of complicated. I just… like all of them too much to want to pick just one."

"And why should you if they're happy? I'm impressed." She flashed me another grin and tucked her lipstick into her purse. "We haven't known each other for very long, but from what my brother has told me and what I've seen, you're a very interesting woman. It makes sense that they would all be interested. And I hope we can be friends."

Friends. The word shouldn't have made me balk like it did. But what the hell did I know about having a real friend, someone who wasn't paid to look out for me? Another woman I could gossip about relationships and all that other stuff with?

On the other hand, if having a BFF was like this, chatting away with smiles and encouragement, why wouldn't I want *that*?

"I hope so too," I said honestly. It might take me a while to get used to the idea, but Emi seemed like she'd make a pretty awesome friend if I was going to have one.

I hesitated and added, "I'm really glad you decided to drop in and surprise us with this visit. It's been great to meet you."

Emi's eyes sparkled. "I'm glad too. I needed a break anyway, but always better to spend it with good company. Now let's go see about that dessert!"

She tugged my sleeve, and we ambled together back to the table, Emi exclaiming over the posh hotel décor the whole way. When we dropped into our seats, Niko raised an eyebrow at her.

"Don't worry," she told him cheekily. "I didn't tell her *too* many of your embarrassing secrets."

Niko snorted, and Jasper cocked his head. "When do I get to hear these secrets?"

Emi set her chin on her folded hands. "Maybe if you let me have a peek at those costumes…"

As we drifted back into light-hearted banter, a weight settled in my chest, dampening my temporary high spirits.

My new friend had no idea what she'd arrived in the middle of—and how could I explain the whole story to her?

I'd just have to make sure she never ended up in a dangerous position. Keep myself between her and any potential threat.

We shouldn't have her over at the apartment again. Stick to meeting out on the town and at the arena.

Unless my stalker had already found out about her and worked her into his plans.

My teeth gritted, and my fingers tightened around my fork.

Haggard had better not touch one hair on her head, or I'd lose any qualms I had about dealing out a brand of justice even my mother would be proud of.

FOURTEEN

Luciana

I GLIDED over to the boards with a relieved exhalation, reveling in the burn of well-worked muscles that was spreading through my body. My hands moved to smooth the ruffles of my training skirt automatically.

We weren't going to wear the gorgeous costumes Jasper had finally revealed to me until the actual competition, but we'd stuck to similar if much simpler outfits for our last few practices so we were used to the overall feel. The skating dress wasn't quite as comfortable as my usual leggings and thermal tees, but I was too excited about tomorrow's competition to care.

Especially when we'd whipped through our routine today several times without any slips.

I shot a grin at Jasper, who'd skated over to join me. "That was a perfect way to end the last practice before the official competition."

He beamed back at me. "I don't think it could have gone better."

"You're going to knock it out of the park over the next couple of days," Niko informed us, his eyes sparkling, and checked his watch. "You don't need me for the packing up part. I've got to go meet that representative from the winter clothing chain that's thinking of coming on as an additional sponsor."

"Give them a good pitch!" I said with an encouraging wave.

As we sat down on the benches to chuck off and wipe down our skates, a trickle of figures passed through the doors, ready for the next time slot, which appeared to be a larger group one. I tensed briefly in anticipation of Quentin's snark, but it appeared he hadn't managed to bookend our practice time today.

Instead, all of the kids hustling ahead of their two coaches were junior competitors in their early to mid-teens. A few of them shot us glances as they sat on other benches to lace up, but one kid who looked to be about thirteen paused and stared at Jasper, his eyes wide in his dark face.

I tapped my partner with my elbow, and he looked up. When he met the boy's intent eyes, his expression turned just as awkward. "Oh. Hi."

"I'm sorry," the kid said in a rush, swiping his hand back over his hair, which was twisted into short dreadlocks over a neat fade. "I just—it's so cool seeing you, Jas—I mean, Mr. St. Pierre. I've been watching you since you were in Juniors. Got a bunch of your performances recorded to study them and everything."

I'd swear Jasper's cheeks pinked a little. "That's—that's very flattering." He straightened up, gathering confidence in the face of the younger skater's admiration. "It's totally fine for you to call me Jasper. We're all colleagues here."

The kid hunched his shoulders as if in embarrassment. "I don't know if I'll ever get to the same level as you. I try."

Jasper hesitated and then pushed to his feet. "I bet you can. How would you like it if I gave you a few pointers? I don't need to rush right out."

The boy's mouth dropped open. "For real? That would be amazing!"

Jasper glanced back at me in question. I shot him a smile and a thumbs up. I couldn't think of any better way for him to end the day before the competition started than by basking in awed respect of a fan and up-and-comer.

"I'll see you later," I told him. "Have fun!"

Watching my partner step onto the ice with the younger guy set off a flutter of warmth through my chest. Jasper could still be a grouch, but getting back into the competitive circuit was helping him get his own bearings again. And when he wasn't all tangled up with insecurities, he was a sight to behold.

And not just for his looks, as incredible as they were too.

After a hasty change into street clothes, I headed out into the mid-afternoon sunlight with high spirits. My hand brushed my phone in my pocket, but the motion detector alert hadn't gone off since Haggard's intrusion the evening Emi had arrived.

He didn't seem inclined to take me on in public, and I'd have made him sorry for it if he had. Besides, Rafael would be trailing at a discreet but not immense distance behind me.

I was rarely completely alone.

I veered down a quiet side-street that offered a little peace on the walk to the apartment, daydreaming about how I'd spend the night before the competition. It was time to get out of my head and just relax. We'd done all the prep we could.

Maybe the four of us could meet up with Emi for dinner again. Then cuddle up on the couch with some popcorn and a movie, like a real date night. And afterward… who knew what we might get up to?

Just as my lips curled into a smile, engines roared down the street. I spun around to face two sleek black sedans that tore across the road and screeched to a halt by the curb right next to me.

Several burly men leapt out—and leapt *at* me. I dashed away, but another car pulled up just ahead with a few more thugs barging out in front of me.

Shit. I had no idea what this was about, but it obviously wasn't *good.*

Two of the closest men lunged at me as if figuring they'd grab my arms. In their dreams.

Thankfully, when I'd gotten changed I'd adorned my fingers with their usual chunky rings. Shrugging off my duffel bag so it thumped on the ground, I sent a fist slamming into one guy's nose. Another bashed the second guy's jaw, the metal edges scraping open his skin.

While the first prick stumbled, blood pouring down his face, the other snarled and snatched at me again. I ducked and punched him right in the balls.

He staggered, but his companions were closing in on me in a tighter ring. I blew at my bangs with a huff of exasperation, glancing around at them.

"I guess you guys don't want to talk this out like gentlemen? Well, okay then. Your funeral."

A couple more loomed over me, and I lashed out with both my fists and my feet. My heel rammed into one guy's shin hard enough to provoke an audible crack of bone, and my rings slashed open another thug's brow deep enough to send a stream of blood into his eyes.

But there were still more of them, and they were backing me toward the wall of the nearest building. I couldn't let them get me pinned.

A few of them were pulling out guns, another a knife. I swallowed thickly. My rings wouldn't be much match for those.

My gaze darted around. There was an alley opening just ten feet away. If I could take off down there—

I didn't even need to complete that thought before a massive body charged into the midst of my attackers with a roar.

"Get the fuck away from her, you pieces of shit!"

Rafael's fists whirled through the air. He pummeled two of the thugs' heads together before they could even shift the aim of their guns and kneed another in the gut so hard the jerk spewed vomit as he crumpled.

Another asshole jabbed a blade at Rafael, and my bodyguard snatched his wrist. He snapped the bones like they were toothpicks. The idiot swayed backward with a howl.

Another goon raised his gun from a safer distance, his arm swerving between me and Rafael. "Not another fucking move."

"That's my line," Rafael growled, drawing his own pistol. "Try to take a shot, and it's a bullet in *your* skull."

The sound of languidly clapping hands broke the tension. Yet another man was emerging from the sedans, this one in a collared shirt and wool jacket that gave him a greater air of professionalism than his colleagues' jeans and hoodies. A shock of white hair sprouted up over piercing green eyes.

"Enough of that," the newcomer said in a gravelly, authoritative voice. "Everybody, knock it off for a minute or two."

His gaze flicked over the thugs and the two of us with an expression of bemusement, as if he wasn't sure whether to be annoyed or amused. A few lines veered from the corners of his eyes and mouth, but overall his face was smoother than I'd have expected given his stark white hair. Based on everything else, I'd guess he was in his forties.

The goons backed up a few steps, a couple of them limping, the one whose nose I'd broken still clutching it. One guy remained on the ground, groaning.

"Who the fuck are you?" Rafael demanded, his gun still raised.

The white-haired man didn't appear at all concerned about it. His eyes narrowed as he focused on us for a longer beat.

"Not someone you want to mess with. My name's Sheeran, and I speak for the Harvester. I assume I don't have to tell the Deadly Rose's daughter who that is?"

A chill ran down my spine. The Harvester was another member of the Devil's Dozen, alongside my mother. One of the leaders of the thirteen biggest criminal syndicates that controlled all illegal activity around the globe.

He'd found me? How? Why?

"What do you want?" I asked, smoothing the nervous rasp from my voice as much as I could. I'd never actually met any of Mom's equals, but knowing how dangerous she was and how careful she was with the rest of them, they obviously weren't people you wanted to offend without knowing exactly what you were getting into.

The man smiled at me with all the warmth of a lion about to dig into an antelope. "My boss has heard that you've shown up in town to make claims on his territory on behalf of your mother. But you and she should both know that all of Boston belongs to the Harvester, and attempting to steal it out from under him is an act of war."

The bottom of my stomach dropped out, but I forced myself to simply scowl at him. "Where'd you get that load of bullshit from? I've got no interest in stealing your territory, and the Deadly Rose has no idea I'm even here."

Sheeran snorted disdainfully. "If you're going to lie, you could come up with a better story."

"She isn't lying," Rafael snapped. "It's the truth. It'd be a pretty shitty takeover, trying to orchestrate it with a single nineteen-year-old girl and one guy for backup, don't you think?"

My hackles rose at him calling me a girl, but I knew he was only downplaying my strength to help us get out of this. Unfortunately, Sheeran didn't appear to be swayed.

"The two of you tore through half of the force I brought out here," he said. "That's not convincing me you're here to make friends."

I scoffed. "We're not looking to make friends *or* enemies. I didn't even know this was the Harvester's territory! If you come and attack me, obviously I'm going to fight back, but I came to the city to skate." I motioned to the duffel bag I'd dropped by the wall behind me.

"Skate?" Sheeran let out a guffaw.

"Yes," I insisted. "I've cut all ties with my mother. I'm not interested in her empire or your boss's. I'm a figure skater."

"Now that's the most ridiculous story I've ever heard." Sheeran's gaze turned into a full-out glare. "You can quit with the crazy lies. The Harvester wants you *gone*, ASAP. If you ignore the warning, there'll be consequences you won't want to deal with. Next time we won't go easy on you, no matter whose daughter you are."

Without waiting for my response, he beckoned his men toward the cars. "Let's get out of here, boys. Leave the little princess alone… for now."

"You've got it totally wrong!" I shouted after him as he slid back into the front passenger seat, but Sheeran ignored me. The thugs helped their injured comrades into the cars, and the sedans drove off down the street, leaving us standing there stunned.

Rafael quickly jammed his gun back into its concealed holster. "Mierda. That motherfucker… Come on, let's get back to the apartment before any other armed idiots come at us."

I set off next to him, my pulse thumping fast and my nerves

jangling. "What the fuck was that? Who the hell would have told him I'm here to steal territory?"

"I have a pretty good idea," Rafael muttered. "Who's the only person we know of who has any idea who you are and that you're in town?"

My head jerked around so I could stare at him. "You think *Haggard* tipped off the Harvester?"

Rafael shrugged. "Who else could it be? It was bad enough luck that the one prick recognized you—it'd be insane if we'd somehow crossed paths with *two* of the Deadly Rose's former employees who had a bone to pick."

I rubbed my hand over my face. "This whole situation is fucked up. Now we've got the Harvester breathing down our necks because of that lunatic's stupid lies. And Sheeran wouldn't even listen to me!"

"Haggard does like tormenting you every way he can." Rafael grimaced. "If I can figure out where he's holing up in town… but that won't stop Sheeran from gunning for you."

I looked at the apartment building coming into view up ahead, but it didn't offer any comfort. Nowhere in the city felt safe now.

How was I going to compete tomorrow with this new threat hanging over me? With one of the Devil's Dozen expecting me to take off the second he'd snapped his fingers?

"I can't just run," I said even as the idea crossed my mind. "I came all this way—I'm so close—and I'd totally let down Jasper and Niko."

"Your life is more important," Rafael said.

"Skating *is* my life." My hands clenched. "I can't let myself down either. We'll figure it out. We managed to deal with that gang back in Hobb Creek."

Rafael hummed in his deep baritone. "I don't know, Lou. These guys are a pretty big leap above those idiots."

I lifted my chin. "I know they are. But so are we."

FIFTEEN

Luciana

JASPER GRIPPED the top of the boards as we watched the pair before our free skate whirl across the ice. "Those two are pretty good. Costumes aren't as nice as ours, though."

He shot me a wry grin that made me laugh. It was easier to be relaxed after yesterday's short program performance, which we'd swept through to receive high marks. Going into the free skate, we were practically tied with two other pairs for the top spot.

Even the fact that one of those pairs was Quentin and Jess hadn't gotten Jasper down. Hell, if there was one area we should be able to beat the two of them without breaking a sweat, it was in the artistry I knew our routine exuded.

I ran my hand down the sea-green fabric of the skating dress Jasper had custom made for this performance. It shimmered under the brilliance of the arena's fluorescent lights.

The rink where the qualifying competition was being held was even larger and grander than the one we'd been practicing in. Despite having spent yesterday here already, my breath still caught when I took the space in.

"They are pretty amazing," I said to Jasper, giving my hips a little shimmy so the short silky skirt rippled over them. "You captured the oceanic vibe that fits the flow of the music so well. We're going to look like mer-people soaring through waves."

Jasper outright beamed, a more open smile than I usually got from him. "That's exactly what I was going for." He looked me up and down, and his gaze turned sly. "And that color looks amazing on you."

I tapped him on the chest. "You look pretty damn stunning too, partner."

The color set off the gray-green in his eyes, and the fit showed off his brawny physique to impressive effect. He looked like the spitting image of Atlantean royalty, something melancholic yet hopeful all at the same time.

"I expect to hear at least one collective gasp while you're out there," Niko informed us, giving both of our shoulders a squeeze. "Probably two or three."

I glanced up to where his sister perched eagerly in the stands. "Or Emi will cheer loud enough to drown everyone else out anyway."

It'd taken her several minutes to calm down from her exclaiming over yesterday's performance. The memory brought another smile to my lips.

The pair before us struck their ending pose, and my pulse hiccupped. It was almost time.

But there was no room for insecurity. I was going to finish this, my first fully professional competition. The girl from Austin who'd been told over and over again that she wasn't good enough couldn't exist any longer. I had to leave her in the past and claim my future.

The judges conferred and passed over their score. Behind the glass of the press box, the announcer moved closer to his microphone. He announced the number—in the low nineties, good but not great—and then cleared his throat. "Our next pair will be Luna Garcia and Jasper St. Pierre."

I let out my nerves in one quavering breath and stepped onto the ice with Jasper. Niko gave us a confident smile and a thumbs up, assurance shining in his dark brown eyes.

Up in the stands, Emi whooped and cheered as we found our positions. I closed my eyes, imagining that I was here on the ice of our regular rink, that I was just about to skate for pleasure with my favorite people surrounding me.

When my eyes opened and found Jasper's steady gaze, I felt much better. All of Niko's confidence and Emi's enthusiasm found its way into my heart, and there was no doubt that my partner was just as dedicated to this moment as I was.

The music started. Jasper and I pushed off across the rink side by side with wide sweeps of our legs. From my peripheral vision, I caught the way my flowy sleeves billowed in the breeze my skating created—they fluttered and rippled with every lift and dip of my arms as if I were underwater, performing an aquatic dance for the visual pleasure of my viewers.

In this moment, I was a siren, a creature of music and art and desire. And I was going to make this audience fall in love with me—with both of us.

I knew I was succeeding the moment that we nailed our first lift. The applause rang out while I was still in the air. As Jasper carried me across the ice, my hands raised high and my head tilted back, I said a quick mental prayer. I could only hope the judges thought it as impressive as the audience did.

Four minutes of perfection, that was all we needed to make it into Finals. And from that point, there were only greater heights waiting for us to make it there.

We soared through our next sequence of jumps and spins without a hitch. I breathed through every motion, matching Jasper's rhythm.

My gaze slid across the audience, taking in their avid expressions in brief glances. Every pair of eyes wide with awe lifted my spirits even higher.

We swerved closer together in preparation for our next lift, and my gaze snagged on one particular audience member. A broad-shouldered man a few rows up, with a shock of hair so bright red it was really orange and a navy track jacket.

I only saw him for an instant before he blurred back into the crowd, but a chill washed over me. Hadn't one of the Harvester's men who'd confronted me and Rafael two days ago looked like that?

Had the Harvester sent his people to hassle me again since I hadn't left town?

My thoughts scattered. Jasper was here with me, and Niko, and Emi. I couldn't protect anyone from the ice, and Rafael might not see the threat in time.

If it even was a threat. I couldn't be sure that was the same guy in the fleeting glimpse I'd gotten.

In my distraction, I nearly missed my cue. I pushed toward Jasper a little harder than I should have needed to, and could tell from the second he hefted me into the air that my balance wasn't quite right.

Shit. My heart thudded against my ribs as I flexed my limbs, holding my position but also attempting to adjust my weight just a little.

It wasn't enough. My error threw off Jasper, but he managed to tense his arms before they wobbled too badly on the descend. Still, my blades hit the ice at not quite the right angle.

I stumbled, my fingers swiping just inches from the ice before I righted myself. Inches from a total fall.

A sense of sinking dread filled my stomach. I whipped around into the next sequence of the routine, but I'd lost the exhilaration that'd been buoying me up.

I launched into our synchronized triple Lutzes just a tad short on momentum and had to spiral out after just one and a half turns instead of the full two. Another jerky motion on the landing.

Shit, shit, shit. Everything was falling apart.

I focused on the music and the hiss of our blades over the ice, doing my best to tune out my worries. I'd probably just imagined the resemblance. I'd been on edge since the fight.

We could still pull this together. I couldn't let Jasper down.

We spun, crossed paths, and whirled around each other. Jasper gave my hand a quick squeeze before releasing it as if to reassure me he was still here with me, and affection flooded my chest.

It carried me through our triple Salchows—not as difficult a move as the Lutzes, but close enough to maybe make up for it. I still didn't feel the same grace and emotion I'd meant to convey with the whole routine, but at least we landed in perfect sync.

We had one more lift left too. At the swell of the melody, Jasper's hands found their way into mine, clasping my fingers firmly.

The moment that the violin began to trill, I pushed off and he whirled me high into the air. I let myself stretch out in his arms, one arm arcing over my head as if beckoning the judges and the audience to join us in the world we'd attempted to create for them.

I came back to earth in a rush, but only for a moment. The sequence ended with a series of jumps.

I pushed off, tossing myself into the air at the same moment as Jasper did. Twice around, down, and then flinging my body up again. For a few seconds, I flew like the angel Niko always said I was, spinning once, twice, the full three times.

If my foot didn't point quite as tightly as I'd like on the landing, I could forgive myself after that finale. I beamed at the crowd as Jasper and I raised our clasped hands up in our finishing pose.

Inside, my heart was still racing. Had I screwed up our chances?

Did we have bigger problems to worry about than our score—like a bunch of goons waiting to murder us all?

"Are you okay?" Jasper murmured to me under the applause as we skated to the stands. "It seemed like you got lost for a bit there."

I resisted the urge to hang my head while the audience was still looking on. "I'm sorry. I got distracted and didn't recover fast enough."

"You were amazing considering this is your first major competition." He slung his arm around my shoulders. "They were only minor slips. We should still do pretty well. Don't worry about it."

We both knew that he was just being nice, but I wasn't going to argue him out of his good mood. I swallowed down the lump of guilt that'd formed in my throat.

Beating myself up in front of him wouldn't change my performance. It'd just make both of us feel worse. As long as he was putting on a hopeful front, I could do the same for him.

Niko's bright smile shone at us from beyond the boards as if we'd been nothing but brilliant, and I could hear Emi letting out a few whoops as we reached the gap in the boards. But, just our luck, Quentin sauntered by right as we were easing off the ice.

"Is *that* what we were supposed to be worried about? All I saw was a couple of screw-ups and a lot of fumbling. And here I thought you might at least *try* to give us a real challenge."

"Go fuck yourself, Wolfe," Jasper muttered under his breath, and tugged me over to Niko.

Our coach grabbed both of us in a hug. "You were fantastic. Don't let the little things get you down. The judges will see through them. No one else has given them anything like that final sequence."

I tried to absorb his confidence, but it couldn't completely ease the tension in my gut. I found myself scanning the stands for the man with the orange hair and navy jacket. If I could spot him and confirm whether it was or wasn't one of the Harvester's thugs.

But I couldn't make out the guy in the crowd. I wasn't even sure which part of the stands I'd seen him in.

And he could already be moving—toward me, or toward Emi if the Harvester's people had spotted her with me and the guys.

I barely heard the judges announce our score. Jasper let out a sigh that was mostly relief, but I thought it had a slight tinge of disappointment. "One hundred and two point four eight. That's not bad at all."

My head jerked around. "Didn't the pair that went on second get a hundred and five? They were within a point of us after the short program. We're already down to second place."

Niko rubbed my back. "It's fine. Still a very good showing for a qualifying round. And there are only a couple more pairs left to perform."

"How high do we need to be to qualify for Finals?" I asked with a sinking stomach.

Jasper shrugged. "It's all relative. Depends on the top scores from the other qualifying competitions. Usually second at any of them would be enough."

He kept his tone casual, but his earlier good mood had vanished, his gray-green eyes turned solemn. I sank down on the bench, my shoulders slumping.

Niko pulled out his phone. "From what I recall, none of the other competitions elsewhere have shown stunning results. Let me look them up so we'll have an idea where you rank overall."

The couple on the ice right now weren't particularly inspiring me with their pedestrian song choice or their sluggish movements, but it was hard to tell how much that was an objective evaluation and how much my own low spirits coloring my impressions.

I dragged in a breath and scanned the crowd again, keeping a particular eye around the section of the stands where Emi was leaning forward.

No one had moved toward her or us since we'd sat down. Everyone I looked at appeared to be focused on the skaters on the rink.

If the Harvester or his lackey Sheeran had wanted to make a point, wouldn't they have gotten on with it by now? Really, it'd have made more sense for them to come at me before I'd had the chance to skate so they could ruin my chances.

I couldn't totally regret my paranoia, though. Not when dismissing the flash of possible recognition could have cost me or one of my companions their life if things had gone in the opposite direction.

Jasper nudged me with his knee, and my haze of thoughts evaporated. "Looks like there's only Quentin and what's-her-name left."

I made a face. "Not what I want to be looking at right now."

"Hey, we can heckle them quietly between the two of us. That could be fun."

I should have been relieved to hear Jasper talk about his rival so flippantly. But right then Quentin and Jess swaggered past us, Quentin shooting us a triumphant grin as if he'd already beat us and Jess pursing her lips in a mocking air kiss, and all I wanted to do was punch the both of them.

It was a hell of a lot easier to put on a good performance when you didn't have to worry about murderous criminals.

I'd have liked to surreptitiously mock them with Jasper, but the moment their music started up, my body tensed up.

They'd gone ambitious even though they'd come to the Pairs competition late. The accompaniment they'd chosen was much quicker and more intense than what Jasper and I had picked. But they must have believed they could match the pace.

I'd already known that Quentin could handle the technically difficult moves, but it seemed I'd underestimated Jess. My jaw went a little slack watching them whip across the ice.

It wasn't my preferred style of skating. Every movement was a bit stiff, a bit too calculated without the emotion and artistry that drew me in.

That didn't mean there was anything actually *wrong* with it, though. Beat after beat, they sped through each move without a single fault. Their music blared through the speakers, the notes pouring forth at their quick-paced tempo.

They missed nothing—every waltz jump and side swipe of their skates was rendered in just the right angles. I waited for them to falter, for them to fail at something, *anything*, but every move and position was flawless.

They weren't pouring their heart into this routine. That much was obvious to me. The only emotion I saw on Quentin's face was the moment that his eyes met mine as he skated by and he flashed me a cocky smirk.

My hands clenched at my sides. The dick did know how to push people's buttons.

Even so, I couldn't deny that he was something to watch. With the fiery red costumes they'd chosen that highlighted his lean frame and muscular thighs, he kept drawing my gaze back to him whether I liked it or not.

The two of them ended their routine in an abstract pose that gained a massive outpouring of applause from the crowd. My heart sank. It was undeniable that the two of them were incredibly skilled. The audience knew it, the judges knew it, and unfortunately, so did Quentin and Jess.

Niko tutted under his breath. "Impressive talent, yes, but they didn't have an ounce of the passion you two did. Artistry counts with the judges too."

My heart kicked around in my chest like a bad motor as we waited for the judges' verdict. It didn't take them long to settle on a score.

They handed it over to the announcer, whose voice boomed through the PA system.

"Quentin Wolfe and Jess Hendrix together have scored… One hundred and eleven point three seven points."

My hands dropped to my sides. They'd smashed us, a whole nine points ahead.

"We're in third," I said. The words came out flat. "I can't believe I fucked up this badly…"

Niko was quick to jump in. "Third is still going to get you into the Finals. I promise. This is the last of the qualifying competitions, and the average top scores are mostly in the ninety to a hundred and ten range. You're still going to be in the upper ranks overall, high enough."

"But at the bottom of the pack when it comes to Finals." I resisted the urge to hug myself, not wanting to show even that much weakness in front of my men.

I wanted to do better than scraping by. I wanted to earn the kind of cheers Emi had called out for us.

I wanted to rub Quentin Wolfe's face in our success. I wanted to make him and Jess eat their words.

Most of all, I wanted to show everyone who told me I couldn't that I *could*. Now Coach Balakin's admonishments were ringing in my head all over again.

No. This wasn't over, not by a long shot.

"We'll have a month to prepare," Niko went on. "And we know what we're up against now. The two of you will come back absolutely breathtaking."

Unless my nerves got the better of me again. Unless the other side of my life interfered at the worst possible time.

If I didn't get it together, I could ruin this chance for both myself and for Jasper and Niko. They'd both worked so hard.

If I screwed up again, we were out for the rest of the circuit. Rank low at Finals, and Jasper and I could kiss any hope of competing in the US Championships or the international competitions afterward goodbye.

SIXTEEN

Luciana

EVEN THOUGH WE'D only come in third, the Okabe siblings were not going to hear talk of defeat. The sound of Emi's high-pitched praise filled every room of the apartment as she fawned over me and Jasper.

"Anyone with eyes could see your performance was so much better than that blond guy," she insisted around a huge bite of her meatball sub. We'd picked up dinner from a local sandwich shop to celebrate our qualifying for Finals—which did deserve celebrating, even if we'd only made it by a hair.

I couldn't help smiling, even though the mouthful of Philly-style cheesesteak stuck in my throat before continuing down. "Pretty sure the judges had eyes."

She let out a huff and patted my arm. "They got too caught up in the specifics of the moves. But you had all the passion! The little mistakes don't matter when you both showed how much the routine meant to the two of you." She aimed a smile Jasper's way too.

Niko came back to the table with a beer and gave me a quick hug from behind. "That's what I keep saying. Once you get your nerves totally under control, your combination of skill and emotion will be unbeatable."

I inhaled deeply, fighting with my guilt and my irritation over having lost to Quentin, of all people. I hadn't been able to tell the guys exactly what had messed up my nerves yet, since Emi had been with us since we'd left the arena.

From Rafael's knowing gaze as he watched the rest of us in his typical solemnly quiet state, he suspected the truth.

"I sure hope so," I said to Niko, and gulped down another bite of my sub.

He tapped his pocket. "I've already gotten requests for a couple of interviews, reporters wanting to cover Jasper's comeback. They'd love to talk to you too, of course, Angel."

My heart gave a little lurch, both excitement that we'd gotten that kind of attention and panic at the idea of having more of a spotlight on me. I was supposed to be laying as low as I could for as long as possible.

I couldn't comment on that in front of Emi, but the carefulness of Niko's tone told me that he'd already guessed I'd want to decline.

I shot him a thankful smile. "I think I'll let Jasper handle the reporters for now."

Jasper shook his head in mock consternation. "Abandoning me now?" he teased.

I wrinkled my nose at him. "Not on the ice."

Emi bounced in her seat with her irrepressible energy. "Oh, I wish I could stay to watch your skills grow. But I can only take off so much time from work before they get upset. Maybe I'll be able to fly back in November to see you at Finals, though."

My spirits lifted in a way I hadn't expected. "Really? It's a long way to home."

She waved off my comment. "If I can make it work with my boss, I'll be here. I haven't had an excuse to travel in a long time. And it'd be amazing to see you skate in person again."

I offered her a smile that was totally genuine. I could definitely get used to this whole friend thing. "I'd really like that."

"Good." She clapped her hands together and then yanked out her phone. "We need to exchange numbers. You can let me know everything that's happening for when my brother gets too busy to update me."

"I always reply to your texts," Niko said in mock-offense, and Emi's laugh pealed through the room.

I was sorry to see her go, but when she glanced at the time after polishing off her sub, her eyebrows shot up. "Oh, kuso. I'd better get a ride. I need to be at the airport fast or I'll miss my flight."

Jasper stirred, a look of concern coming over his face. "Do you need a ride? We've got a car."

Emi had already been tapping on her phone again. "No, no. I've got a taxi coming now. You should stay and keep celebrating—you deserve it!"

She grabbed me in a quick hug and did the same with her brother. Niko picked up one of her suitcases to help her bring her luggage down to meet the cab. I found myself going to the window to give one last wave before she hopped into the car.

Rafael ambled up beside me. "You liked having her around."

My smile turned crooked. "There's something to be said for having a warm female presence in the room. Not something I have much experience with."

Jasper's brow furrowed as he joined us. "You didn't have many friends in Austin?"

I shook my head. "I didn't really have *any*. My mom didn't like me associating with people outside her circle, and most of the people working under her were men. And it's not like they were interested in making friends anyway, unless they were going to get something out of it." I rolled my eyes. "The few women who did work for Mom were always pretty standoffish, probably saw me as a risk. If they pissed me off, they'd have to deal with her."

Niko strode into the apartment a moment later, flicking back his smooth hair with its pink streak. "It is nice to have family around after so long. I'm glad you all got along with Emi."

"She's easy to get along with," I said, my full smile coming back. Then my stomach twisted. "But we need to do more than celebrate tonight. I've got to explain what happened that threw me off on the ice."

Jasper frowned and tucked his hand around my arm. "You don't owe us a justification. Nerves can get the better of anyone. We all get it."

"But it wasn't just nerves." I bit my lip and moved to the sofa to sit down, to help steady me for the conversation. "You know Rafael and I told you that some men working for one of my mother's colleagues, part of that Devil's Dozen group, threatened me?"

The guys joined me in the living room, Niko's cheerful expression darkening. "Did they bother you again?"

"No. It might have all been in my head. But it's because of them." I sighed. "I thought I saw one of the guys who attacked me in the stands. Afterward, I wasn't so sure anymore. It doesn't really make sense that Sheeran would have looked for me there when he didn't even believe I was interested in figure skating. But in the moment, without being able to really think it through, I freaked out a little. I was worried he'd try to hurt one of you… or Emi."

Jasper's frown deepened. He twined his fingers with mine where he'd sat next to me on the sofa. "Do you think they'll really try something like that because you haven't left town like they asked?"

"I don't know. They might stick to only harassing me. But with this on top of Haggard's tricks…" I rubbed my forehead. "We need to deal with Sheeran too, get him off my back before I have to find out what he'd do next. And before he says anything to my mom about the war I'm supposedly starting."

Niko glanced at Rafael, who'd stayed behind the sofa at my shoulder. "Didn't you say you were going to look into this criminal guy? And Lou's stalker too?"

Rafael nodded. "I've been working all of the connections I have access to. I don't know a lot of people in Boston, but I managed to get in touch with a few old contacts. They haven't been much help in tracking down Haggard yet, but they confirmed that Sheeran is the top dog in the city on the criminal side of things."

"Makes sense," I said. "The Harvester would squash anyone who tried to go against his people on his territory."

"And Sheeran's boss must be awfully happy with him, because he's got a huge mansion in the suburbs and a collection of flashy cars, from what I hear."

I grimaced. "If he's doing well under the Harvester, he's got every incentive to keep the guy happy. Which includes kicking me out of town."

Jasper knit his brow. "I guess we can't fight back in a literal sense. He must have tons of people working for him."

"Yeah. And a show of overt aggression against Sheeran and his men would only make the situation worse. Like I really am trying to go to war with him." I rubbed my mouth uneasily. "Plus the Harvester would almost definitely bring it up with my mom then."

Rafael inclined his head in agreement, though he looked unhappy about it. "There's nothing good that could come of going head-to-head with them. Even if we had the full backing of the Deadly Rose's power behind us, which we don't, it'd be a mess."

Jasper gave my hand a squeeze. "Your mom obviously had to deal with guys like this a lot. What would *she* have done if she wanted to force someone to back off but couldn't be direct about it?"

I leaned back on the sofa as I considered the question. My mind drifted to the memory of Coach Balakin's bloody corpse, and I winced.

"Well, she tried to force me to back off from skating by killing my coach. Manipulating me into thinking our enemies had done it because of his connection to me so I'd be afraid to keep at it."

I sucked my lower lip under my teeth to worry at it, thinking through everything Balakin had told me over the years. "I bet that's also how she kept him under her thumb the whole time, forcing him to always tell me I wasn't good enough. He loved his kids and his grandkids so much. All she'd have needed to do was suggest that they'd meet some horrible end if he didn't follow her orders…"

Niko shuddered. "I can see why you'd rather stay away from her."

"Yeah," I muttered, but the wheels in my head had started spinning. "But that doesn't mean her strategies couldn't apply here. What if we could figure out something that matters a lot to Sheeran and his most important lackeys and show that we could destroy *that* if he doesn't leave me alone?"

Rafael's eyes darkened. "You want to start hurting their families?"

My stomach lurched. "No, no, nothing like that. Nothing *real.* We'd be bluffing. I don't want to actually destroy anything they care about. But Sheeran believes that I'm dangerous—that I'm my mother's daughter. So he'd think I mean business. We'd have leverage that could level the playing field."

Niko's eyes brightened. "That all adds up. Where would we start?"

I turned to Rafael. "We'll need to find out everything we can about Sheeran and his right-hand men—which means mostly *you'll* need to find it out, since you have the contacts."

"Hold on," Jasper said, and indicated Niko. "We aren't going to stay on the sidelines for this. I'm sure we can manage to scope out a couple of these guys if you need it."

My chest tightened at Niko's emphatic nod of agreement. "These are criminals. They won't be happy with you if they figure out you're watching them."

Jasper drew himself up straighter. "The same goes for Rafael, doesn't it? And they've already seen him with you—they know he's part of your mom's crew. You said that Sheeran didn't take your comments about skating seriously, so chances are good that he never bothered to look into it. There's a decent chance he has no clue who Niko and I are."

Even as my stomach knotted, I couldn't deny he had a point. When I looked at Rafael, my bodyguard offered a grim smile.

"You might have an advantage over me, just this once. I'll still do most of the digging, but your lack of connection to the criminal world could work in our favor once we know who we're checking up on. If you're sure you want to go in this deep."

"No question about it," Niko said without hesitation. "It's to keep Lou safe and make sure they don't stop her from skating—I'll do whatever it takes."

Jasper's expression had hardened. "Same."

For a second, unexpected tears pricked at the backs of my eyes.

There was no denying their adamant devotion, even though I didn't feel as if I'd totally earned it after my screw-ups this afternoon.

But my men didn't see it that way. They were going to stick by me and support me no matter what.

I hated the thought of them putting themselves in danger, but how could I tell them no when I knew how far I'd be willing to go to help *them* if need be?

"We have to make sure you don't get into any situations that are too difficult," I said. "Nothing too far on the criminal side, just getting a sense of their everyday lives."

Niko took in my face and stepped closer to brush his fingers over my hair. "You know this world better than we do, Angel. We trust your judgment. But we aren't going to stand back while you and Rafael take on the problem by yourselves."

I raised my head. "All right then. Let's get started with Sheeran's closest associates—and we'll keep an eye out for the perfect opportunity to put the squeeze on the big dog himself."

And hopefully Haggard wouldn't throw any new wrenches into the works before we'd dealt with this one.

SEVENTEEN

Niko

AS I SIPPED my beer at the bar counter, the jumble of voices and raucous laughter around me had my nerves buzzing. I tugged at the hood of my new leather jacket, chosen specifically to help me blend into this crowd in a shadier neighborhood of Boston.

This was my third visit to The Hook and Tankard, a bar Rafael had determined was managed by one of Sheeran's main associates: Louis Elwort. The guy usually arrived in the mid-afternoon and left in the late evening.

If the skinny man with a receding hairline who looked more like a high school principal than a gangster could be a thug, then maybe my impersonating one wasn't such a stretch. I squared my shoulders, a little thrill passing through me at the sense that I was tapping into an inner tough side I hadn't been totally sure I had.

In any case, I'd managed to fit in with the regular clientele enough that no one had hassled me. My hood hid the telltale streak in my hair, although I doubted any of the patrons around me would have been familiar with my work on the ice.

They were all occupied with a different sort of skating: a hockey game broadcast on the widescreen TVs poised around the room. I studied the whirlwind of movement as the men around me let out a shout at a goal.

The hockey players surged across the ice, all sweat and muscular force. I'd bet they had the strength to pull off at least some of the moves I loved, but in their element, they showed none of the grace and precision I admired in a skater.

Imagining them spinning and leaping after the puck like one of my trainees made my lips twitch with amusement. No, they were simply doing what their job called for.

Still, there was something fascinating about the visceral aggression of the sport. Maybe sometime I could draw on it for inspiration for a particularly provocative routine.

At the edge of my vision, I noticed Elwort emerging from his office behind the bar. He'd left earlier than this the first night I'd come by but later the second night, so I couldn't read too much into his appearance.

Except that my instincts, honed by years of paying attention to the exact angles of a hand or a pointed toe, the tiny indications that a takeoff had come with enough momentum or a lift with the right height, caught a couple of telling gestures. Elwort tapped his hip pocket, where I'd determined he kept his keys. Then he shot a quick look in the mirror beneath the shelves of expensive liquor and flicked his fingers over his thinning hair.

He'd gone through those motions both times before, just as he was leaving. My pulse thumped faster.

I could take advantage of my observations. This time I might actually fulfill my mission here.

Leaving ahead of him would make me look much less suspicious. I drained the last of my beer and sauntered toward the doorway at what I felt was an appropriately macho gait.

The growl of Elwort's voice reached my ears as I passed him where he'd stepped close to the bartender. The chilling hostility in his tone dispelled the school-principal impression in an instant.

"If I catch you skimmin' tips, Larry, I'll have you more'n just fired. You won't be hard to replace."

The bell over the door jangled with my exit. In the cool evening air outside, I picked up my pace. The last two times, Elwort had headed east for a couple of blocks and then veered south.

The first time, I'd trailed a couple of blocks behind him all the way to a mundane apartment building that hadn't offered up any clues. The second time, he'd taken a turn and vanished from view by the time I'd reached the intersection.

I had to stay on his trail this time. Lou was counting on me.

And if I kept failing, Rafael was going to think he was right that Jasper and I couldn't hold our own when it came to protecting her.

Around the first bend, I ducked into an alley I'd noted before. The stink of the garbage cans farther down it had me wrinkling my nose, but the shadowed space made for an ideal hiding spot.

It was only a few minutes before the brisk thud of Elwort's footsteps approached. I pressed myself against the alley wall where the shadows were thickest and watched his slim form stride by.

After waiting for several seconds, I slipped out and started ambling down the street after him with an air I hoped looked reasonably casual. I kept my head low and my hands stuffed in my pockets as if I were lost in thought and paying no attention to anyone around me, least of all the man up ahead.

I'd never attempted anything like this before. My nerves jittered as I debated exactly how closely to follow the gangster.

Lou and Rafael had stressed how dangerous these people could be. I didn't think the knife Lou had ordered me to carry in my jacket pocket would do me all that much good if my target realized what I was up to.

But I was more than just her coach. I wanted to be a man she could turn to, a man she could count on for *everything* she needed. Lou deserved that from all of us, or how did I deserve to stand with her and call her mine?

I hadn't focused enough on other people's needs before, and that had led to the greatest mistake of my life.

Elwort glanced over his shoulder, and I pretended to be studying the windows of the buildings I was passing. Then he took an abrupt turn to the left that I hadn't expected.

Kuso!

I hesitated with my silent curse and then sped up to a jog so that I could reach the corner in time to be sure of seeing which way he'd gone next. When I peeked around it, I just caught the streetlamps' glow gleaming off his balding scalp as he veered down an alley.

It was as if he was worried about being followed and going out of his way to take a complicated route. My mouth went dry as I hurried after him, but the racing of my pulse came with a jolt of excitement as well as nerves.

If he was being careful, then that meant he was up to something important to him, didn't it? Exactly the kind of thing we wanted to discover.

I slowed before I reached the mouth of the alley and peered down it, the back of my neck prickling with the awareness of how easy I could be ambushed. But I made out Elwort's skinny form at the far end, swerving in a hasty right.

I loped after him, setting my feet as quietly as I could manage amid the bits of trash that lay on the uneven pavement. At the bend, I took a cautious glance around the worn brick wall.

It was a good thing I'd been cautious rather than hurrying right around it. Elwort had stopped at the far end of the alley where it met another street, his head turning as he scanned the sidewalk around him.

His shoulders hunched. I held myself perfectly still until he pushed himself forward, crossing the street.

Having seen his wariness, I let him get farther ahead before sauntering after him and stuck to the opposite side of the street. He was walking faster again, but he kept going straight for several blocks. Once, when he started to glance backward, I ducked behind a parked car before he could notice me.

Oh, Niko the spy was improving his skills for sure.

The shops we were passing, some closed for the night and others derelict, gave way to larger concrete warehouses. After we'd passed a few, Elwort stepped into a side entrance on the next looming building with a jangle of his keys.

I leapt behind a bus shelter poster just as he started to check his surroundings. There was a rasp and a click as he unlocked the door. When I peered around the shelter, he'd disappeared inside, the door swinging shut in his wake.

What the hell was he keeping inside there that he was so concerned about? Was it part of the gang's criminal activities, or something more personal?

I needed to find out.

Trying to sneak after him right inside the building didn't seem like a wise idea. Instead, I crept around the outer walls, peeking into each window I passed.

Around the back, I noticed a glow in one of the windows farther down. I stole over to it and found it mostly covered by a dingy curtain —but there was a gap that allowed me to see into the room.

Perfect. Between the narrow opening and the darkness cloaking me, it'd be nearly impossible for Elwort to notice me out here. The glass would be reflecting the light from inside.

I squinted into the starkly lit room, bracing myself for a scene of violence or drugged indulgence.

What I actually saw was… paintings.

Lots and lots of paintings.

Canvases stood against the walls in stacks, a few of them framed, but many not. A couple of them stood on easels—one a landscape lit with neon shades, another a portrait of a face with abstract styling.

As I watched, knitting my brow in confusion, Elwort walked into view with a palette. He dabbed his brush into a blob of paint and added a few small streaks to the landscape.

Wait. Had *he* painted all these pictures?

That possibility didn't fit with the principal image *or* the gangster image, which had already clashed in my head. Could these be part of his criminal activities after all? Forgeries he was passing off as originals?

None of the pictures I could see looked like any famous paintings or even styles I was familiar with, though. And the delicate care with which Elwort applied a few highlights to the sky of his landscape contrasted sharply with his harshly threatening words to his bartender.

What was this man up to?

He started talking, just loud enough that I could make out his crooning tone through the glass. "That's right. Just a little blaze of yellow here, and you'll be perfect."

Watching a man I knew to be a hardened killer cajole his artwork like it was a young child was one of the most bizarre sights of my life.

His head lifted. I understood why a moment later when a woman appeared in the doorway to the room, trim and professional-looking in low pumps and a dress suit. Her hair was coiled in a loose bun, but her spiky bangs showed a little edge.

I hadn't caught her footsteps from my vantage point outside. Her voice reached me as clearly as Elwort's had, though. "Are you still working on that one? I thought you were finished the last time I came by."

Elwort sighed and lowered the palette. "Sometimes you need to let the image sit for a while before you can see everything it needs."

"Yeah, yeah." The woman crossed her arms over her chest. "Do you at least have the others ready for me to photograph? You promised at least five new ones. I have clients asking about your work, you know."

Elwort waved toward a stack of canvases to his left with a distracted air, his gaze still fixed on the landscape on the easel.

The woman looked as if she'd let out a sigh. "All right, I guess I'll set them up myself. It wouldn't kill you to get a proper studio instead of this godforsaken warehouse."

The man stiffened, his gaze jerking to her. "You know I have to keep a low profile."

"But you could be making so much more of yourself! If you'd let me set up a single gallery show, you could bring in a hundred thousand in one night, easy."

"I've told you before," Elwort growled. "It's not about the money. All this… it isn't something that goes well with my other line of work."

The woman shook her head. "Yes, yes, your mysterious day job.

I'm just trying to do *my* job as your agent—as much as you let me act like one."

"If you don't want me as a client anymore, then drop me. But as far as I'm concerned, what you manage to do is enough. The pictures get homes. I don't have to worry about my stash getting too big."

"Whatever you say, Louie."

The woman dragged a few of the pictures over to where the light hit them better and took out her phone to snap a few photos. I stared, absorbing the conversation I'd overheard.

These paintings really were Elwort's. Work he cared about enough to keep doing it in secret even though he obviously felt his regular colleagues wouldn't react well to the pastime.

I guess art isn't really encouraged in criminal circles.

That shouldn't have surprised me after what I'd heard from Lou about her mother's insistence on squashing her passion for skating. It wasn't as if I hadn't gotten plenty of attitude for simply being a *man* and going into a career many saw as emasculating, let alone a man who was meant to present an image of toughness and danger.

But if Elwort cared about his artwork so much he'd risk discovery to keep doing it… then I'd found exactly the point of leverage Lou and Rafael had been hoping for.

A spark of triumph lit in my chest. All the furtive stalking had been worthwhile. And now I could return home victorious and be done with cheap beer and hockey games.

I pulled back from the window and rushed away from the building as fast as I could go while staying quiet. I didn't slow down until I'd put a few blocks between me and Elwort's warehouse.

As I pulled out my phone to summon an Uber, my high spirits wavered. The memory rose up of Elwort's eager intentness as he touched up his painting.

Were we really going to destroy *his* artistic passion?

Even knowing what he did with the rest of his life, my gut clenched at the thought. I set my jaw and shook off the momentary guilt.

Lou didn't want to actually destroy anything that mattered to these people, only to make them think she would. And she wouldn't have needed to go even that far if they hadn't attacked her in a far worse way already.

Whatever happened to Louis Elwort after I turned this information over was on him and his gangster colleagues, no one else.

EIGHTEEN

Luciana

I ONLY LET myself skate over to the boards when every inch of my body was aching and my breath coming in pants. Jasper trailed behind me.

"The adjustments are really looking nice." Niko offered us each a water bottle. "I think that with a little more work, the free skate will be even more stunning."

"It would have been absolutely stunning last time if I hadn't screwed us over," I grumbled. "I'll be more in the game next time, I swear. It's just —"

Jasper laid a hand on my shoulder. "You have a lot going on. We know. Don't worry about it, Punk."

I took a long sip of water, my body releasing its tension at his touch. They were both so confident in me, so sure of my abilities. If not for them, would I have ever realized the true depth of my abilities?

I wasn't sure, but I did know one thing: I would be forever grateful for their grand entrance into my life. The two of them had cemented themselves along with Rafael inside my heart for good. Those three men were all I needed.

Jasper chugged the rest of his water and crinkled the cheap plastic bottle. "We've got ten more minutes of ice time. You wanna squeeze in a little more practice or head out now?"

Niko cocked his head. "You two have been working really hard lately. Maybe loosening up on yourselves wouldn't be a bad thing."

Before I could answer, my ears picked up on a sound that now instinctively set me on edge—Quentin's laugh, ringing through the door at the top of the steps. Chock full of arrogance and spilling over with disdain. Something sharp twisted in my chest.

My jaw clenched. "Are you serious? What the hell is he doing here this early?"

Jasper sighed. "He probably found out we booked the time before his slot and figured he'd take the chance to mess with us. You know what he's like."

I grimaced. "Well, we can't stop even ten minutes early now. He'll say we're running away from him."

A second later, Quentin pushed past the door with Jess at his heels. Their coach and her other trainees were nowhere to be seen.

The two of them sauntered down the steps and lounged on a bench near the ice as if they were there only to watch. Which I guessed at this point they were.

Quentin's eyes glittered, hard with condescension and challenge. Jess simply wrinkled her nose at us.

I rolled my eyes as I turned back to Jasper. "No point in letting them see the little changes we've made. Let's go through the first lift a few more times."

He dragged his eyes away from the stands, his hands fisted at his sides. "Right."

"And here I thought you two were preparing to blow us away now that you've got a second chance," Quentin called. "Awfully boring performance so far. Oh, I'm sorry, am I distracting you?"

"Shut it, Wolfe," Jasper growled, his shoulders tensing more. He nodded to Niko to start the music.

As the opening notes pealed from the speakers, we glided through the first section of our routine. I tuned out all thought of the jackass watching us, focusing on the beats of the music and my connection with my partner.

But Quentin had always gotten to Jasper more than he did me. When Jasper raised me into the air, I could tell right away that his arms were a little too rigid. They wobbled slightly on my dismount, and my skate jittered against the ice before I fully caught my balance.

A snort followed us as we circled around to start over from the beginning. When I glanced at the stands, Quentin had slung his arm around Jess's shoulders, and she'd tossed her legs right over his lap. She nuzzled the side of his neck, and he tipped his head to the side encouragingly.

Excuse me while I barfed.

"I think I'm seeing your problem," Quentin said in a mockingly languid voice as Jess trailed her fingers down his chest. "No passion. Saint Jasper here doesn't know how to handle a woman—big surprise."

I had half a mind to stomp over there and see how well Quentin could "handle" me when I slammed my fist into his face. From Jasper's expression, he was gritting his teeth to hold back a hostile retort.

I set my hand on his bicep, ignoring the jerk. "Hey, don't worry about that prick. Nothing he says matters."

Jasper gave his broad frame a little shake. "I know," he muttered. But frustration still radiated off him.

If he tried again all wound up like that, he was bound to make a mistake, and then he'd only get even more upset.

My words weren't enough to distract my partner from his long-time rival, but as Quentin had just reminded us, that wasn't all I had to offer.

He wanted passion? I'd show him passion.

The idea set off a crackle of electricity down the center of me. I pushed myself forward, grabbing the front of Jasper's tee, and bobbed up on my skates.

Every thought featuring Quentin or Jess was erased from my mind as I curled my fingers into my partner's auburn hair, twisting the strands around my fingers.

"Lou —" Jasper started, but I cut him off with an eager kiss.

My mouth melded to his perfectly. His arm came around my waist, tugging me closer. At the flick of my tongue against his lips, he parted them so our breaths could mingle.

As I kissed him more deeply, reveling in the attraction and affection I felt with this grouchy but mesmerizing man, the stiffness released from his muscles. He stroked his fingers over my cheek and delved his tongue into my mouth in the start of a playful duel.

I gave his lower lip a graze of my teeth as I eased back, heat coursing through my veins. The same hunger shone back at me in Jasper's gray-green eyes.

His gaze didn't so much as twitch toward the stands. In that moment, he was all mine, his preoccupation with his rival wiped away.

I grinned up at him. "Feeling better now?"

Jasper smiled crookedly back at me. "Loads."

The silence emanating from the stands was telling. Neither of us gave Quentin and his partner a sideways glance.

Niko started up the music again, and the two of us soared across the ice. My heart lifted along with our movements. When Jasper hefted me up this time, I whirled through the air with him solid and steady beneath me.

The two of us felt like one person, connected where the palm of his hand met my center. I knew my expression was perfect, the angle of my arms spot-on, and his stance just as perfect. Pride rushed through my chest.

Jasper set me down at just the right speed and angle, and I glided a little ahead of him while grasping his hand. I knew I was beaming at him but didn't care.

"Once more?" I suggested.

"Sounds good to me."

We swept through the opening sequence with more confidence, and grace flowed through every movement. The exhilaration brought an awed giggle to my throat.

Jasper spun me around, poised in his arms—and my gaze caught on a reddish splotch on the door Quentin had stepped through several minutes ago.

Deep crimson red, like blood.

My heart lurched. Images flashed through my mind, each hitting me harder than the last.

Coach Balakin, his face sallow and twisted in pain.

The pool of scarlet staining his white polo shirt.

His body lying stiff and still.

An involuntary flinch ran through my body just as Jasper started to lower me. The jolt made me slip from his grasp. Before we could recover, I tumbled to the ice, landing hard on my thigh.

Pain bloomed through my leg. I was going to have a massive bruise there for sure. But I barely felt it over the blare of panic that'd set my heart thudding.

Jasper knelt next to me, his face taut with concern. Niko was hurrying across the ice to us too.

"Are you okay, Lou? What happened?" my partner asked.

My words came out in a breathless mumble. "The door—it looks like there's *blood* smeared on it. I—"

I clamped my mouth shut and shoved myself to my feet. Quentin shot out some stupid remark that I let fly right past my ears. All my attention was on the door.

I yanked on my skate guards in an instant and sprinted up the steps as fast as I could with my skates on. Jasper and Niko hurried behind me.

As we reached the door, Niko exhaled in a rush. "It's only paint."

This close, I could tell he was right. The splotch, about the size of a human head, looked as if it'd been smacked there by a swath of wet fabric with no clear texture. A few rivulets dribbled down from the main shape. The red was just a little too saturated, and a plasticky tang rose off it that was totally different from the meaty odor of actual gore.

The paint hadn't been there when Quentin and Jess had walked in. Someone had done this in the past few minutes. What the hell was going on?

I yanked open the door swiftly as if I might find the culprit standing on the other side.

Instead, I discovered that the paint didn't stop at the door. A longer smear ran along the wall in the hallway, fading out and then appearing again, all the way to the door to the women's locker room.

Just as I registered that, the locker room door burst open. A girl I recognized as one of Quentin's fellow trainees scrambled into the hallway with a shriek, her eyes wide with panic.

Shit. I hustled over to the locker room with the guys flanking me, wishing I'd had time to take off my skates. I shoved my head inside, called out, "Anyone in here?" and motioned for the men to follow me in when no one answered.

I took two confident steps before stopping dead in the center of the changing room. The streaky line of red paint continued all the way across the wall, cutting off at the widest, most blank part of the wall.

There, the smears thinned to form a picture—a sketchy body with its torn-off head lying across from a tattered neck. Crudely shaped letters arced across the wall above and below the gruesome drawing.

This will be you. That's what bitches get.

My stomach churned. I stared at the wall until the imagery was burned into my memory and then spun away, just as Rafael charged into the locker room after us.

He looked at the paint and then at me.

I held his gaze, holding back the urge to shiver. "It was Haggard. It has to be. He didn't figure he could get away with terrorizing me at the apartment anymore, so he's switched to the arena."

With every word, my shaky nerves hardened as anger flared inside me. How *dare* this fucking sicko bring his lunatic crusade all the way here, where he'd ended up terrifying girls who had nothing to do with me as well?

When was it going to end?

Rafael swore under his breath and gripped my shoulder with a reassuring squeeze that conveyed all of his own fury as well.

"That bastard keeps slipping through our fingers. When I finally catch him, I'm going to make him regret every fucking time."

"There's no way to set up a warning system here at the arena, is there?" I said. "It's not like motion detectors will do us any good when people are always coming and going."

Jasper frowned. “Do you figure he realized we had something monitoring the apartment, and that’s why he hasn’t been back?”

“Probably.” Rafael let out a sound halfway between a huff and a growl and spun on his heel. “Grab what you need and let’s get home, now. You can shower and whatever else there.”

I didn’t argue. There was nothing I wanted more than to get back to the apartment, slam the deadbolt into place, and curl up under a blanket with my men around me.

Of course, not even our current home was guaranteed to be safe.

We ducked back into the rink area to take off our skates and grab our equipment bags. Quentin and his fellow trainees were on the ice, except for the junior girl who’d dashed from the locker room. She was speaking to the coach while wringing her hands.

Good. Let Quentin’s coach figure out how to deal with the mess. I had enough to navigate already.

The four of us hurried out of the arena into the dimming late afternoon light. For the first time, I wished we lived far enough away that we usually drove. I’d have felt more secure with steel walls around me.

But Rafael stuck close by my side as we walked, Jasper taking up the opposite position and Niko striding ahead of us with his gaze scanning the streets. Their determination to protect me hummed off them, wrapping me in a small measure of comfort.

As our building came into view up ahead, Rafael grunted and raised his chin just slightly toward a car parked on the other side of the street. “Looks like Sheeran’s decided to keep a closer eye on you.”

Tensing, I followed his gaze. The sedan was exactly like the ones that’d pulled up in the ambush last week.

A couple of men were sitting behind the windshield, watching us as they passed. They definitely looked like the type Sheeran had on his payroll. “You recognize them?”

“One of them, definitely. I’ve followed him a couple of times. Just act normal.”

“No kidding.”

I strode on as if I hadn’t even noticed them, but inside, my emotions were roiling.

Why couldn't everyone just leave me the hell alone?

Niko glanced back at us. "The Harvester still thinks Lou is after his territory?"

I made a face. "Seems like it." I sighed and squared my shoulders. "But we've been building our leverage. Maybe it's time to start dealing with the people we *do* know how to tackle."

NINETEEN

Luciana

"YOU BETTER BEAT it if you know what's good for you, bitch!"

The man in front of me stared me down with an expression that wanted to be tough but just wasn't doing the job. No matter how firmly he set his jaw, I could see the fear in his eyes.

I had him by the balls—metaphorically, at least.

I cocked my head at a cheeky angle. "All I'm asking you to do is listen. You don't want to mess with me, I can promise you that. You definitely won't like me if you do." I craned my neck to look at the vintage car behind him. "And neither will your shiny little toy back there either."

The man let out a growl, his hands clenching, but he stayed where he was. I'd already told him that he and the rest of Sheeran's crew would be in *so* much trouble with the Deadly Rose if they kept harassing me.

The guy, Eddie Johnston, was another of Sheeran's top associates. It hadn't taken long to figure out what mattered the most to him: the gorgeous vehicle behind him, some foreign make that I didn't recognize but could tell was both classic and kept in tip-top shape.

I didn't really want to destroy a thing of beauty like that, but I'd reduce it to a pile of scrap if that was what it took to drive my message home and protect the people I cared about.

"I said get out of here," Johnston said in a not very convincing tone. "I don't want to have to hit a lady but —"

"But you will, is that right?" I gave him a mocking smile, hoping he saw the crazy in my eyes. "Don't make me laugh, asshole. Like I said, there's a very easy way out of this problem. I don't want any trouble. I'm not here in town to threaten your business. Convince your boss of that and leave me alone, and I'll happily steer clear of you too."

I raised a finger. "But if you mess with me, you can say adios to that sweet little ride. Hey, maybe Sheeran would let you borrow one of his. You think he likes you that much, Eddie?"

"Shut up," he mumbled. Any remaining fire was dwindling in his expression.

"I'd be ecstatic to stop talking and get out of your hair. I just want to make sure we understand each other. You're going to encourage your boss to stand down? It'll be even worse for all of you if the Deadly Rose finds out you came at me with no provocation."

Johnston bared his teeth at me. "I hear you, bitch. I got your message; I'll do what I need to. Just get the fuck outta here."

I slung my bag over my shoulder. "My pleasure. Hope I don't have to see you again, Eddie."

I strolled out of the garage feeling better than I had in ages. I wasn't going to let the Harvester's Boston crew push me around anymore; I wanted to do some pushing of my own.

Taking out some of my frustration on these pricks was more satisfying than I'd expected. They had it coming, and I had no qualms about making them squirm after the beatdown they'd tried to deliver the other day.

I slid into the driver's seat of my Grand Marquis, wiggling into the plush seat. "One stupid goon down. And one more to go."

The GPS directions told me that my second stop was in a

residential neighborhood across town. I passed through a swanky area that housed some of the city's rich elite—Sheeran's kind of place—and into a stretch of slightly rundown rowhouses that must have still commanded a decent price because of their history.

The looming brownstones with their artful styling caught my eye even in the darkness. But there wasn't much room for admiration in my gut when I thought about the asshole I'd be dealing with here.

Robert Cullen was a major player. We'd dug up connections to three different women he'd been stringing along for years, each of them believing they were his one and only. The second had given him a son he doted on when he came around, but having a kid hadn't been enough to make him clean up his act.

He didn't clean up much in general, it turned out. I passed his address, circled around the block to park, and made my way to the backyard with a series of furtive dashes and scrambles, only to find the yard full of overgrown grass, rusty patio furniture, and scattered, mud-streaked toys from when he must have brought his son around.

I wrinkled my nose as I crept up to the back of the house. Rafael had texted me to confirm that Cullen had headed out for some nighttime business, leaving his house unguarded. Perfect for me to set up the element of surprise—and show that I had the skills to deliver on any threat I made.

Like many criminals, Cullen was overconfident. The lock on the back door was a little too complicated for my picks, but he'd left one of the first-floor windows a couple of inches open. Just enough room for me to pop out the screen and shove the pane upward.

I rolled inside and onto my feet with a soft thump. Looking around, my mouth pulled into a grimace.

The inside of the house was worse than the yard. I'd entered into the dining room—at least, I assumed that was what the room was supposed to be based on the large table in the middle, which was heaped with newspapers and takeout boxes. More lay strewn across the floor.

If he hated cleaning so much, the guy could have at least hired a maid service, for fuck's sake.

I crept over to the living room and found more food wrappers there, as well as several pieces of clothing tossed over the sofa. An unpleasant odor, a mix of food going bad and stale sweat, hung in the air.

Could this guy get more gross? How the hell had he managed to pull not just one but *three* devoted girlfriends?

Somehow I was guessing he never invited *them* over to visit.

Thankfully there was one armchair that held nothing except for an empty chip bag and a few crumbs. I swept them off and planted my butt there, poised in wait.

Every few minutes, I checked my phone. We had no idea when Robert would return, other than our past observations suggested he rarely stayed away all night.

I hoped he'd get his ass over here soon, because the smell was starting to make me queasy.

I distracted myself with a puzzle game until the rumble of a car engine sounded outside. I shoved my phone in my pocket and sat up straighter.

Cullen whistled a jaunty tune as he climbed the steps to the front door. He shoved it open, swaggered inside—and jerked to a halt when I switched on the lamp next to me.

I aimed a sharp little smile at him without getting up. "Welcome home, Robert. Nothing all that sweet about it, though." I kicked at the trash. "I'm thinking your three girlfriends wouldn't keep screwing you if they got a look at this place."

Cullen gaped at me for a few seconds before he snapped into overconfident prick mode.

"What the fuck are you doing here?" he demanded, barging forward into the middle of the living room, ignoring the boxes crunching under his feet.

He didn't ask who I was, and the glimmer of apprehension mixed with the anger in his eyes suggested he already knew. He might have been present for Sheeran's attempted beatdown, or he'd heard about me from other discussions within the crew.

If he knew I was the Deadly Rose's daughter, then he should be well aware how deadly *I* could be… if I chose to live up to that name.

I folded my hands in my lap. "Relax, Robert. I'm only here to talk. I take it I don't have to introduce myself?"

More fury flashed across his face. "If you think you're going to weasel your way into our territory by—"

I held up my hand to stop him. "As I tried to tell Sheeran, I don't have any interest in your territory. I'm here on my own business that has nothing to do with your crew or claiming ground for my mother."

He scoffed. "Like we're stupid enough to fall for that."

I decided against telling him exactly how stupid I figured he was. "There's nothing to fall for. It's true. And you're going to go back to your boss and speak up in favor of staying *out* of my business."

"Why the fuck would I do that?" Cullen snarled.

I counted off the reasons on my fingers. "One, because it's true, and my mother isn't currently involved. But if you keep pushing, she will be, and I promise you that'll be awfully painful for everyone involved. Two, because I'm sure you have more important things to do with your time than spy on and harass me. And three, because if you *don't*, I know three lovely ladies I'll be having a chat with."

Cullen's eyes narrowed. "You can't even know—"

"What, about Bridget, Theresa, and Alison? I've got their numbers right here. I'm sure they'd be *very* interested in hearing about each other, don't you think so?"

For the first time since his initial shock, Cullen hesitated. A ruddy flush came over his face. "You wouldn't *dare*."

I shrugged. "I don't think I'm daring anything, Robbie. You're the one with something to lose. I know about Adam too. I wonder exactly how often Theresa would let you spend time with him if she knew you've been two—no, *three*—timing her since before he was even born."

Rafael had observed Cullen with his son, and so had one of his contacts. By all accounts, the jerk in front of me cared about the boy a hell of a lot more than he did any of his romantic conquests. He never missed a Sunday meet-up, went to the kid's school events and sports practices… The very picture of a devoted dad, if a fucked-up boyfriend.

We'd obviously planned our threat well. What I hadn't anticipated was just how upset Cullen would get about it.

"You fucking cunt!" He lunged forward, his face turning to purple, ready to snatch my wrists. Looking like he figured he'd snap my arms right out of their sockets.

I sprang to my feet, but I didn't even need to dodge. He hadn't made it past two steps before a deadly *click* sounded behind him.

Rafael stepped out of the shadows, his pistol aimed right at Cullen's head.

"I wouldn't," he snarled. "You listen to her, and your life goes on like it always has. You take one more step forward and I'll make sure the last thing you see is your brains all over the wall."

Cullen froze, but a lingering tremor of rage ran through his body. "Fuck. Who the hell are you?"

"You don't need to know that. You only need to know that you're going to regret it if you lay one finger on this woman."

Cullen wasn't stupid enough to imagine Rafael's warning was a bluff. He held in place, practically vibrating with frustration.

I brushed my hands together and fixed him with one last glare. "You've heard my terms. Talk to your boss. Tell him you've seen enough to believe I'm not actually threatening your territory. One more attack on me and my friends, and I'll make sure you never see your son or your girlfriends again."

Cullen sneered at me, but he also dipped his head in a slight nod of acknowledgment. That was enough.

I stepped around him and brushed my fingers across Rafael's arm. "Let's get out of here. I think Robert's finally got his head out of his ass."

We walked out the front door and strode around the block toward my car. Rafael stayed silent until we'd climbed inside and I'd started the engine.

"Nice work, there."

"Yeah." I swallowed thickly, realizing a lump had risen in my throat as the adrenaline rush of the confrontation waned. A knot of doubt echoed it in my stomach.

Would Sheeran's men actually act on my demands in the end? Or had I only succeeded in pissing them off more?

It'd felt good in the moment, but looking back, all I could remember was the fury that'd radiated off both men.

What did I really know about laying down the law? This was all part of my mom's legacy, the kind of life I'd meant to leave behind.

The life that kept nipping at my heels no matter what I did.

"Do you think this is actually going to work?" I couldn't help asking as I turned the car toward our apartment.

Rafael shot me a measured look. "I think it's a solid plan, better than anything I've been able to come up with. If I saw a better way, I'd let you know."

I blew out my breath in a huff, ruffling my bangs. "I just feel… weird. Most of the threats we've given I don't even *want* to act on. And this one… Cullen's girlfriends deserve to know he's been cheating on all of them, especially his baby momma. I just promised *not* to do that if he gets Sheeran to back off."

Rafael reached over and gave my shoulder a quick squeeze. "We all make deals we're not totally happy with to survive in this world, Lou. You've got her info. You can always find a way to tip her off after we're sure the Harvester doesn't have Sheeran gunning for you anymore."

"Yeah. I'll do that." If we ever got to that point.

But Rafael was right. When you were dealing with career criminals, there wasn't much you could do that would feel totally right.

This might not be how I wanted to live, but I had no idea how else I could defend the new life I was building for myself—or the lives of the men I'd inadvertently pulled into this mess.

TWENTY

Rafael

PATROLLING the neighborhood around the apartment always left me feeling a little more grounded than when I'd left it. Yeah, okay, maybe I was stalking the streets a little more often than was typical policy, but with all the stirring up of Sheeran's goons that we'd been doing, I wasn't leaving anything to chance.

If they tried to run Lou out of town again—or punish her for ignoring the Harvester's demand that she leave—I was going to be right here kicking their asses to kingdom come.

This afternoon, there was no sign of any trouble. Just regular people going about their regular lives with no clue about the darker underbelly their city held.

That was fine. They could keep their ignorance if I got to keep my peace.

As I rounded the corner to bring me back toward the apartment building, the phone in my back pocket buzzed. My hand leapt to it.

That was my newer burner—the one I'd been using only to reach out to my old contacts from my time working under the Deadly Rose. I'd wanted to keep the number those former acquaintances and colleagues got totally separate from everything else about my new situation.

You could never be too careful when it came to the Devil's Dozen.

This call could be more incoming information about the Harvester's Boston crew. Maybe even a warning about an impending attack—or the news that Sheeran had been ordered to move on to other things.

Hey, a guy could hope, even if I didn't put much stock in those hopes.

I hit the answer button and brought the phone to my ear. "Hey. What's up?"

The voice that carried from the other end didn't sound like any of the guys I'd been speaking to lately. "Rafael? That is you, right?"

My fingers tensed around the phone. I stopped in my tracks, every nerve going on the alert. "Who's *this*?"

"Hey, no need to pitch a fit." At the brief, hoarse cough of a longtime smoker, a picture started to form in my head—but it wasn't of anyone who should have had this number. "It's Gus. I'm sure you haven't forgotten me just yet."

Gus—Gustavo. One of my colleagues who'd worked out of Lou's family home. He'd generally been assigned to house guard duty, and I'd shot the shit with him maybe once a week, just to pass the time. We hadn't been close, but then, I hadn't gotten close to anyone in the Deadly Rose's outfit… other than Lou.

"How the hell did you get this number?" I demanded, alarm pealing through my veins even more sharply than before.

"No big deal. I heard from Manny that he'd talked to you and got him to cough up your number."

Next time I saw Manny, I was going to greet him with my fist. For fuck's sake.

"And?" I prompted in a voice stark with warning.

"And I just thought you ought to know what you left behind, you pendejo. Because it's a big fucking mess."

My teeth set on edge. "De qué hablas? Just get to the point, Gus, or I'm hanging up."

Gus sighed. "You took off with the daughter, right? Everyone knows you left town together. But Mireya is *pissed.* Like, I've never seen her like this before. She's crossing lines, launching beatdowns—she's a mad woman."

He was still talking in his typical don't-give-a-shit way, but a hint of a tremor crept into the last sentence. The Deadly Rose had gone so far she'd rattled even this asshole.

"I don't see what that has to do with me," I said tightly. "Luciana's a grown woman—she makes her own decisions. I didn't fucking kidnap her or anything."

"I don't think it matters, amigo. The boss is on a tear, like she needs the girl back *now.* I think there's some plan she was going to put in play that she needs Luciana there for, and she's raining down terror until she gets her way."

A chill coursed down my spine. "A plan for Lou? What kind of plan?"

"I don't fucking know. She doesn't fill me in on these kinds of things. But she's pulling out all the stops to find her, and when she does—it isn't going to be good for whoever she figures is even partly responsible."

"What exactly has she said about the thing she needs Lou for?" I asked, gripping the phone so tight the plastic casing started to crack.

There was a rustle as Gus must have shaken his head. "Nothing. She's just making it very fucking clear that we'd better cough up anything we know."

"So what are you calling me for, *amigo?*" I emphasized the last word with an edge of sarcasm. Gus definitely wasn't any friend of mine right now. "You figure you're going to trick me into giving up some intel that'll earn you a reward?"

"Fuck, no. And Manny didn't say anything about what he's talked to you about, so I haven't got a clue. I just wanted to tell you that if you know what's good for you, you'll make the girl come home or drag her back here yourself. There's going to be hell to pay for a lot more of us than just you the longer she's gone."

"Gus," I started, but there was a click and then dead air. The prick had hung up on me.

I glared at the phone, my lips curling into a silent snarl. Lou wasn't just *a* woman but her *own* woman, not her mother's tool. Who the hell was he to tell me to cart her home like she was a runaway kitten?

I debated smashing the phone but held on to it in the end. The burner couldn't be traced by its number, and if Gus passed the info on to anyone else in the Deadly Rose's crew, I wanted to find out right away.

A cloud of uneasiness descended over me as I stalked the rest of the way to the apartment building. My heart got heavier with every step up to the apartment.

What was I going to tell Lou?

I walked into the apartment to find Lou at the kitchen table, halfway through the plate of leftover roast pork and rice I'd made us for dinner last night. She glanced up at me with the fork halfway to her mouth and a mildly guilty expression.

"I hope you weren't saving this for yourself. I just had a craving, and it *is* lunchtime..."

The sight of her devouring my cooking should have filled me with warmth—and other kinds of heat—but I was still too chilled by my conversation with Gus. I managed to give her a crooked smile and kept my tone even. "That's all right. I'm never going to argue about you appreciating my work in the kitchen."

She grinned at me, all boldness and cheek, and a surge of affection and protectiveness swept through me in a tidal wave. Whatever Mireya had up her sleeve for her, I wouldn't let it happen.

Lou raised an eyebrow, and I realized I'd been staring at her too long. "What's with the face?" she asked. "Something wrong?"

She was already dressed in her training clothes, ready to jet off to the arena as soon as she'd finished eating. Her face was painted with the garish makeup she used as a sort of disguise out in public. I could see her leg swinging even as she waited for my answer, probably counting the beats to one of her songs as she replayed the routine in her head for extra practice.

I couldn't tell her everything I'd found out. I couldn't put all of it on her shoulders when she had to focus on her dream. She was already dealing with too much—so much it'd nearly cost her the last competition.

It wasn't as if she could help me fend off the Deadly Rose's plans when I had no idea what those plans even were.

"Just got an unexpected phone call," I said casually. "One of my old acquaintances from the Austin crew."

Lou's stance tensed just slightly—so slightly I wasn't sure anyone other than me would have caught it. "What did he have to say?"

I shrugged. "Nothing we couldn't already have guessed. Your mom's on a rampage, pretty pissed off that you disappeared. So it's a good thing we've been laying as low as we have. And obviously the Harvester hasn't addressed your supposed invasion with her directly yet."

Lou hummed to herself. "So expected news and good news. You should be smiling about it—or have you kept that grim expression so long you forgot how?"

She aimed a teasing smile of her own at me to show she wasn't serious and dug back into her lunch. I propped myself in the doorway, watching her as my conflicting desires and responsibilities churned in my chest.

She would want me to tell her the rest of Gus's story. But there was barely anything else to it. If I jumped the gun on this situation, assumed it meant more than it did… I could cause just as big a catastrophe as I almost had years before.

No. I wasn't rushing in all hotheaded again. I'd get the full picture, and then we'd figure out what needed to be done.

Lou glanced up at me again, with a fond gleam in her dark eyes that nearly undid me. "You really don't have to worry. I know how to keep a low profile. I've begged off any interviews—and no one cares that much about this level of competition outside of the skating crowd anyway."

She was trying to reassure *me*.

"You've been doing good," I said, hearing my voice go a bit gruff. "I just—you know what your mother is like. She's only going to widen her search."

Lou's gaze twitched. I caught a flicker of worry crossing her face before she squared her shoulders and got up out of her chair.

"She can search away. She's not going to find me. Especially when I've got you by my side, right?"

She sauntered over to me, her brightly painted lips curving up like a scarlet crescent moon. Her hands walked up the length of my arms to wind together behind the base of my neck. I breathed in a lungful of her sweet scent.

When she stood up on her tiptoes to kiss me, I met her halfway.

I was the luckiest goddamn man alive to experience this heaven with a woman so precious. I closed my eyes, sealing the moment behind glass, this tiny scrap of peace inside our whirlwind of a life together.

I wouldn't let myself mess up this opportunity for her. She deserved more than what she'd gotten in life up until now, and I'd go through hell and back to see her finally have everything she was owed.

TWENTY-ONE

Luciana

I COULD ALWAYS TELL when Niko had something up his sleeve. The sparkle in his eyes gave it away every time. But today he was being unusually closed-lipped.

"Can't you at least tell us what you're thinking?" I begged for the thousandth time that day. We'd stayed all the way through the group practice period at the end of the arena's schedule, and the last of the other skaters were just disappearing through the doors. Any second, one of the staff was going to come and tell us that we needed to get going too. "It's not like anyone's left to hear."

Niko smiled mysteriously. "I wanted to be sure there was *no* chance of anyone seeing what we're doing. The arena manager agreed to leave the building open for an extra two hours tonight, and I can lock up. There won't even be a janitor around." He patted his hip to a jingle of keys.

Jasper raised his eyebrows. "What's the big secret?"

Niko glanced around the stands, and Rafael emerged from the

shadows as if on cue. Had our coach even tipped off my bodyguard before telling us?

Rafael dipped his head to us with his usual stern expression. "I'll make sure no one comes back into the rink area from the locker rooms and then stand guard in the lobby once they've completely cleared out."

Curiosity itched at me as Rafael stepped out into the hall. "*What*, Niko?"

Niko rubbed his hands together, the gleam in his eyes only sparking brighter. "I was watching winning international routines from previous years, thinking I might get some inspiration. And I did. I want to change the second lift in your free skate to something even more challenging. We're going to add a throw at the end."

My heart skipped a beat. "A throw? It's already the trickiest lift in the routine." And it was the one I'd messed up in our qualifying competition.

But Niko was nodding avidly, bringing up a video on his phone. "That's exactly why it'll stand out—and impress the judges more than your competitors. This combination isn't seen very often because it's difficult, but I think you two are made for it. It works best when the woman is a lot smaller and lighter than the man, and most pairs are a little more evenly matched than you two."

Jasper and I gave each other an evaluating look. I couldn't deny that our size difference was particularly striking—that was something we'd played into more than once with our routines. Still, nerves gnawed at my stomach.

Niko held out his phone. I watched as a pair of skaters sped across the ice. The man—who was more than a foot taller than his partner and much broader—swept his petite partner up and over his head like it was nothing. She stretched out into a star position like our own while he gripped her with just one hand—and then in a near-blur of movement, she was spinning over his head again, descending to whirl across the ice in tandem, and immediately launching back into the air with a scoop of his arms to land a perfect triple Axel.

It was fluid and graceful and stunning—exactly the kind of vibe we'd been going for with the whole routine. I needed a moment to find my breath.

"It would be perfect."

Jasper nodded, his eyes alight now too. "I think we could pull it off with some practice. We have a few weeks left before Finals. Do you really think we can keep it a secret?"

Niko shrugged. "The longer we can, the less chance of anyone trying to top it. We'll only work on that aspect during our private ice time, and Rafael will keep a close guard. I wanted to be especially careful tonight when we try it out for the first time." He grinned at us. "If you're ready to try it out."

My pulse thumped quickly, but there was at least as much excitement as nerves in the swift beat. "Yeah. Let's do this! And smash the smirk right off Quentin's face."

Jasper laughed, the sound as sweet as maple syrup. "All right, Punk. We shouldn't rush it. Throws are where the most injuries happen. Even I know Quentin's not worth risking that."

I swatted him. "I just mean we should get started."

We watched the video a few more times and then a couple of other examples Niko had found. I studied every tiny movement from lift off to landing, watching exactly how the skaters adjusted their positioning and balance. Then we took to the ice ourselves.

"We'll start with a single rotation in the throw and work up to the triple," Niko said. "So you can get used to the overall feel of it before getting even more ambitious."

It quickly became clear that the skaters we'd been watching had made the move look easy when it was anything but. The transition from landing to Jasper propelling me back into the air left us wobbling, and once I slipped and bumped my knee, Jasper catching me just before I outright sprained it.

But we got up and went at it again and again. Sweat dampened my skin beneath my training clothes, but the assisted leap began to feel natural rather than awkward.

On my second complete single Axel, my blade hit the ice at a bad angle and I had to shove myself out of a fall with my hands. I brushed the frost from my gloves on my pants and straightened up with a surge of determination.

"Almost!"

Jasper smiled, his gray-green eyes fiery with matching resolve. "We'll get this. I'm ready when you are."

It must have been at least another half hour before we worked up to a double jump, but that change was easier than adapting to the initial throw. After a few shaky tries, I felt nothing but exhilaration as I whipped through the air.

When my skates touched down, one after the other, joy rushed through my chest.

This complex move would have stunned me watching it on television as a kid. Now I was actually performing it.

I raised my chin. "Let's go for the triple."

Jasper and I flew off into the lift one more time. The feel of his hands supporting me was nothing but familiar. My hair cascaded out in a crimson stream.

He shifted his arms, and I moved with them, tensing and flexing my muscles to match his movements. Then I soared out into the air, the momentum carrying me even higher and faster than before.

One—two—three!

I hit the ice already grinning. The impact radiated through my lowered leg, but I stuck the landing smoothly. I swung around in the finishing spin and then did a little happy dance on the ice with a whoop of victory.

Jasper was beaming too, his face flushed with exertion. Niko applauded avidly from his position by the boards.

"That was fantastic!" he crowed. "I knew you two could do it."

This would elevate our performance above all the others we'd seen in the qualifying round. It *had* to get us a top spot at Finals. And we'd already proven we were capable of nailing it.

The elation of that success coursed through my veins, and nothing could have felt more natural than grabbing Jasper by the front of his shirt and yanking him into a heated kiss.

As he kissed me back with total enthusiasm, an electric current zinged through my body. His hands were like lightning, the press of his mouth like rolling thunder. Our passion blended, mixing together to form an emotion so ravenous that I thought it would burst.

I wanted more than just a kiss—I wanted every part of him. And not just him.

I drew back from my skating partner to yank Niko over to us. An eager smile danced across his lips in the instant before they collided with my own.

His tongue delved in to tangle with mine while one hand trailed down my back to grip my ass. I arched into him, still clutching Jasper's shirt as well, my hungry growl reverberating between them. Jasper bent his head to kiss my shoulder.

The flashfire of our collision seared every other thought from my mind. We'd already been practicing far longer than a typical day—we'd accomplished more than we'd even imagined when we started.

There wasn't anything wrong with taking the opportunity to do a little celebrating as part of our cooldown, right? Rafael was standing guard in the lobby, making sure no one would interrupt our interlude.

We'd been so focused on training and dealing with my horrible problems lately that we hadn't taken any time to enjoy each other.

"Come here," I said in a demanding purr, dragging both men toward the stands. They came with an air of the same heady urgency that was racing through me.

We snatched up our equipment bags and hustled up the steps to the doors. In the hall, I shoved them toward the women's locker room, which would have emptied ages ago.

Pushing past the door, I tossed my bag aside, scanned the open space to confirm we were alone, and immediately tugged Jasper and Niko back to me.

Jasper's mouth collided with mine again, his breath scorching. Niko's deft fingers slipped beneath my shirt to stroke over the bare skin. The next thing I knew he was peeling both shirt and sports bra off me to drop them onto the floor.

"What a beautiful sight," he murmured before leaning in to suck the peak of one breast between his skillful lips.

I kissed Jasper hard, my whimper reverberating into his mouth, and raked my fingers into Niko's silky hair. My pussy clenched, and I could tell my panties were already soaked.

I wasn't quite far enough gone to forget about the sweat I'd worked up on the ice. There was a way to deal with that and make this encounter even more fun.

I hauled each of my men's shirts off in turn, drinking in their sculpted chests with appreciative eyes. Then I stepped toward the shower stalls and flicked one on with a swift motion.

As steam wafted into the air, the desire on Jasper's and Niko's faces flared hotter. Jasper reached for the waist of my leggings without missing a beat and dragged them to the floor, pressing a kiss to my hip as he went. "You're fucking spectacular, Lou."

I shivered with lust. "You're pretty amazing yourself. Both of you."

I made short work of Jasper's pants while Niko stripped off my panties. As I reached for Niko's pants, an even more delightful idea sparked in my head.

"Hey." I flicked my fingers toward Jasper. "Why don't you give me a hand?"

Jasper hesitated, his gaze jerking up to meet Niko's. His face flushed, but there was no mistaking the extra flare of hunger that lit in his eyes.

Niko smiled at him, sly but gentle. He reached out to Jasper, and the other man took his hand, awkward until the moment our coach eased him right over so their chests were almost touching.

With a sudden surge of boldness, Jasper touched Niko's jaw and brought their mouths together. A rough noise escaped his throat as they gave themselves over to the kiss.

Holy hell, that was one of the hottest things I'd ever seen. Two of the most attractive men I'd ever known locked together in their own passion. A different sort of joy glowed in my chest, knowing I'd helped them find their way back to each other and this shared desire.

Jasper's stance stayed a bit rigid, as if he wasn't totally sure what to do with the rest of his body. I stepped closer and stroked my hand across his back, dappling kisses along his arm and then Niko's. A little of that tension unwound.

Jasper turned back to me, cupping one of my breasts and branding the crook of my neck with his mouth. As I gasped, Niko joined in, claiming my lips.

Interlocked between the two of them, I couldn't suppress a pang of guilt that we were leaving Rafael out of the fun. But then, I wasn't sure he'd be up for sharing me in *quite* such an overt way just yet, when he'd only just gotten used to the idea of him and me hooking up at all.

We'd work up to that. Lord, imagine how amazing this would feel with all three of my men adoring me at once.

With a little help from Jasper, I finally got Niko's pants off. I pulled the two of them with me into the shower stall.

The water hissed down over us, the steam tingling over my skin. The stall was decently wide, but still a tight fit with the three of us. I couldn't say I minded being squeezed between my men's solid bodies, though.

They didn't appear to have any problems with it either. Niko leaned past me to capture Jasper's lips once more, and then they both focused their attention on me.

Jasper held me from behind, massaging my breasts with his thumbs swiveling over my hardened nipples, his tongue flicking over the shell of my ear to lap up a stream of water. "How do you like that, Punk?"

"Mmm, very good." My approval was punctuated by a gasp when Jasper positioned one of my breasts for Niko to devour it again.

As Niko offered up sweet torture with the flick of his tongue and the graze of his teeth, I squirmed between the two of them. My pussy was throbbing with need.

Jasper didn't leave me hanging. As my head tipped back against his shoulder, he dropped one hand to tuck in between my legs.

A full moan reverberated from my chest. I rocked with the rhythmic gestures of his fingers as they slid over my clit and the slickness of my opening.

"I think you could put that mouth to even better use, Okabe," he said in a low voice that practically made me come all by itself.

Niko released my breast to shoot a brilliant grin at both of us and sank to his knees. He made his way toward his destination with teasing care, pressing his lips to my belly, my hip bones, and my thighs. Then

Jasper made way for him, and Niko lapped his tongue right over my clit.

Between Jasper returning to fondling my tits, Niko eating out my pussy, and the hot water streaming down over all of us, bliss washed over me from every direction. I writhed between the two men, riding Niko's mouth and reveling in the bulge of Jasper's erection now pressing against my back.

I rubbed against him as I rocked with their attentions and then reached behind me to grip his shaft. As I pumped him up and down between my fingers, his breath spilled out across my neck with a ragged groan.

"Keep at it," he urged Niko. "Look at how she's loving it. I want to watch you make her come."

Oh, fuck. His heated words gave an extra jolt to the sensations building through my body. Pleasure spiked through me in giddy pulses with the movements of Niko's lips and tongue.

When I looked down, it was to see Niko caressing Jasper's thigh as he sucked on my clit even harder. The knowledge that he was getting us both off at once sent me right over the edge.

I bucked into his mouth, crying out and grinding against Jasper. Pleasure swept through my body, cresting higher with each stroke of their hands and mouths.

It wasn't enough. Even as the afterglow pulsed through my pussy, there was a void inside me that screamed to be filled.

As I recovered myself, I gripped Jasper's cock harder. "Fuck me."

He gave a rough, almost desperate laugh. "Hell, yes."

Niko had eased back with a satisfied smirk. I caught his gaze. "My purse—it's tucked in my equipment bag. There are condoms in it."

I didn't need to say anything more for him to dart across the room to retrieve a foil packet. As he dug one out, Jasper tipped me over on the tiled floor, my knees at the edge of the shower stall and my hands beyond it. He knelt behind me, the water drumming against his back and my ass.

Niko returned to us and passed Jasper the packet while stealing another kiss from the other man. I watched their mouths meld together with a growing ache between my thighs.

The second they drew apart, I pushed Niko down on the floor in front of me. "I'm not done with you yet either."

As foil ripped behind me, I bowed over Niko's sprawled form. His cock jutted from between his toned thighs, begging for attention.

I licked his length from base to weeping head, loving the hitch of his breath and the groan that spilled out after it. He tasted like salt and the sweetest of musks.

Niko stroked his fingers over my damp hair. "You have no idea what you do to me, Angel."

"Oh, I have a little," I murmured, and lapped my tongue right over the tip of his erection.

Then Jasper pushed into me from behind, filling my pussy with the delicious burn he offered so well, and all I could do was gasp.

My head arced backward for a second, the pleasure of that first thrust echoing through my limbs. My eyelids had drooped with the sensation, but even so, I caught the slight movement of the locker room door across the room.

Was that just a draft, or something more?

I started to tense, peering over without being too obvious about it in case we'd need to take an intruder by surprise. Then I made out the face in the narrow gap where the door was standing slightly ajar.

I could only see a sliver of it, but that was Quentin's cool blue eye staring at us, the slant of his blond hair above it, his sharp-edged features clearly recognizable even like that. The light streaming from the florescent panels overhead caught on the ruddy flush that'd come over his face.

Somehow he'd managed to evade Rafael's initial sweep of the arena. He'd figured he'd spy on us, huh?

He was sure getting an eyeful now.

The tension in me gave way to a fresh wave of giddiness, turned even more delicious by a competitive zap of energy.

Quentin had taunted us about our passion. Let him be shocked by just how much we could bring to each other. It wasn't as if we were doing anything wrong.

Let's see how much cocky arrogance he could produce the next time he saw us. I'd laugh in his face if he tried to convince us he and Jess were so in sync by letting her paw him.

I lowered my head and sucked Niko's cock right into my mouth. As I bobbed up and down over him, increasing the suction of my lips, Jasper eased in and out of me, matching my rhythm.

Niko's hips swayed to meet my mouth, his breath breaking into panting. When I swirled my tongue around his shaft, another groan thrummed out of him.

Jasper swore and thrust faster, deeper. I whimpered over Niko, letting the sound quiver through the movements of my lips and tongue.

"Keep going, Jasper," he whispered. "Fuck her just like that. Harder—she wants it."

He was right—I did want it. I rocked back and forth enthusiastically, willing Jasper to comply.

He didn't need more encouragement than that. To my delight, he pounded into me so forcefully stars started to sparkle behind my eyes.

My orgasm swelled inside me, overtaking me in a tsunami. I clamped my lips hard around Niko's cock, determined to take him with me. His tug on my hair sent me spiraling right over the edge.

My vision whited out with the final surge of ecstasy, the spurt of Niko's release in my mouth made it all the more satisfying. Jasper's thrusts turned almost frantic, chasing us to the tipping point, until he dug his fingers into my hips with the pulsing of his cock.

He bowed over me as he rasped for breath, his arm looping around my waist. As my own chest heaved, I spared a quick glance toward the door, but it had eased shut again. Our audience of one had vanished.

Let him stew on the spectacle we'd just given him. Ha.

Jasper eased me around so I was sitting between him and Niko. Niko scooted closer, encompassing us both in a joint embrace and gifting us both with playful kisses.

"Well," Jasper said with a chuckle. "That was definitely something."

Niko nuzzled my cheek. "Our angel is awfully special." He leaned over to nip Jasper's earlobe. "Not to mention our grouch."

"Hey!" Jasper grumbled, but a hint of a blush touched his cheeks as if pleased by the teasing affection.

I grinned at both of them, full of happiness. We still had a whole lot of problems waiting for us beyond this room, but for a moment they felt awfully distant in comparison to the passion and tenderness we'd just shared.

TWENTY-TWO

Luciana

EVEN AFTER SEVERAL DAYS, the memory of the locker room interlude still gave me a tingle, both of remembered pleasure and triumph.

Shockingly, Quentin Wolfe hadn't intruded on any of our practices since getting a look at just how much passion me and my partner—and our coach—shared. Maybe because he'd realized how pathetic any of his snarky comments about our connection actually sounded.

Rafael glanced over at me where we were waiting by the corner of the Chinese restaurant for our takeout to arrive. "What do you have that little grin on your face for?" His flat monotone didn't quite hide his amusement.

I drummed my fingers against my thigh. "I was just thinking about Quentin. And how good it's going to feel to absolutely destroy him in two weeks. I don't know if I can wait that long."

Rafael snorted. "Well, you're going to have to. And don't get too cocky. You should focus on your own routines, and then you'll be fine."

I knew he was right, but still, it felt good to know we'd thrown our rival for a loop. I allowed myself one more smirk of satisfaction and then put Quentin out of my mind.

The heavy scent of garlic, soy sauce, and five spice powder filled the room, making my mouth water. I did enjoy it when Rafael insisted on cooking dinner, but there was something to be said for variety. And not having to do dishes.

My stomach grumbled. Rafael met my eyes, the mirth clear in his expression now. "A little hungry, are you?"

"You know it. I'm starving after the workout we had today."

Rafael opened his mouth to speak, a half-smile lighting up his face. Before he could get a word out though, he froze, his gaze jerking to the restaurant's front window. His brows slanted down in a mask of fury, his burgundy gaze suddenly burning.

My pulse stuttered. "What?"

"I think I saw Haggard passing by outside. He had his head down low, but I'd swear— Wait here. If it's him, I've got to run him down."

He dashed to the door without waiting for my response. The jingle of the overhead bell melded with the thumping of his feet, and then he was gone.

I took a step after him with an instinctive urge to join the chase. The rustling of plastic bags being filled held me back.

Someone did need to stay for the food. And it wasn't as if Rafael couldn't handle one guy on his own. I didn't even know which direction he'd ended up heading in.

If he'd been sure it was my psycho stalker, I'd have followed him in an instant, no matter what he'd said. But maybe I should go along with his instructions just this once… to make up for all the times I undoubtedly wouldn't in the future when it mattered more.

When I turned back toward the counter, the older lady on the other side gave me a wary glance. Maybe wondering why my companion had taken off in such a furor. I offered her a smile I hoped was reassuring, and she dipped her head toward me.

"Just waiting on the pork belly," she said. "A few more minutes."

"That's fine." Hopefully Rafael would have finished his chase by then.

No, hopefully he'd actually caught Haggard and was ending that asshole's reign of terror right now by whatever means necessary. I still hadn't decided how much I wanted to be involved in delivering the well-deserved consequences, but if staying out of it right now meant I never had to worry about the psycho and his gory gifts again, I'd be okay with that.

My phone pinged in my hand. A text lit up the screen from Emi, packed with exclamation points and emojis in her usual way.

Hey! Can't wait for those Finals coming so soon! It looks like I can't get the time off, so you HAVE to send me all the vids!!!

I grinned. Emi, like her brother, seemed to know just when I needed a smile, even from all the way across the world. I hit the reply button and started typing out a response, but before I could, another text buzzed my way.

Especially some videos of that new lift and throw combo you told me about!! It's going be STUNNING!!

I promise I'll send you a video of our next attempt, I wrote back. *It's coming along really well.*

I had to admit that talking with Niko's sister was like a breath of fresh air after the wary and distant interactions I'd had with the women in my past life. Since we'd left, I'd found myself swapping stories about our interests and pasts with her.

I just wished I didn't have to deal with the twinge of guilt about how much of my past I was hiding from her. But I never wanted to be dragged into that world again. If I didn't have to worry Emi with all that garbage, then I wouldn't. I wanted her to see me as a normal person, not a former criminal or a charity case.

The woman behind the counter hooked a finger at me and set two bags down on the surface between us. "Your food is ready, miss."

"Thank you!" I pocketed my phone and grabbed both bags, one in each hand. The heat and the delicious scents wafting off them made my stomach gurgle again.

I considered the closed door that Rafael hadn't yet returned through and decided to wait outside. Maybe I'd see him already on his way back and I could meet him halfway.

As I stepped onto the sidewalk, the chilly fall breeze wrapped around me. The restaurant stood on a quiet side-street, just a few buildings down from a busy thoroughfare but with only the occasional passing pedestrian and car right in front of it at this time in the late evening.

No sign of Rafael in either direction yet. Frowning, I ambled a little farther down the street and decided to text him to see if he was finished checking up on his suspicion. If he didn't answer, I'd head back to the apartment on my own. It was only a couple of blocks.

I didn't even have time to reach for my phone before several figures burst from an alley across the street, charging straight toward me.

Sheeran's goons, I thought in the split-second it took to register the attack, and then I was whipping into action.

The thugs swarmed around me, throwing punches and ramming knees from all sides. I spun around, making use of everything I had in reach.

One takeout bag bashed into a prick's face, spurting hot sauce into his eyes. The other thumped a second attacker in the gut. I kicked it to send spicy noodles straight into a third jerk's mug, mourning the loss of our tasty dinner.

The second my hands were free, I lashed out with my ringed fists as well. The metal ridges carved lines through a goon's cheek, and I clocked another in the nose hard enough that he reeled backward.

It wasn't enough. There were too many of them, and they weren't holding back to deliver a warning this time. They wanted a total beatdown.

I whipped this way and that, stomping and jabbing, but there always seemed to be another fist to dodge. My breath turned ragged in my throat.

I fumbled in my pocket for the knife I kept on me, but the second I yanked it free, another thug caught my wrist. He twisted it so hard the bones creaked and the blade fell from my hand with a spasm of pain.

Shit, shit, shit.

"Get away, you fuckers!" I hollered. "Let me go!"

At this point, I'd welcome a police siren if it'd buy me an opening to flee. I knew when I was overpowered.

I managed to heel the guy who'd snatched my wrist in the shin and then kick him in the groin, but as he stumbled backward, two more goons leapt on me. One of them tackled me to the sidewalk, my skull glancing off the concrete. As my thoughts spun, they held me down.

"Sheeran sends his regards, Princess," one of them snarled. "You should have run when you had the chance."

I flailed with all my might, jerking my arms free, but it seemed like a dozen feet were slamming at my body now. Ducking my head, I raised my arms to shield it as best I could. More blows battered my chest and abdomen. Pain lanced through my torso.

The few grunts of discomfort I was able to provoke from the ground didn't come close to making up for my own growing agony. And then a sound reached my ears that turned my blood to ice.

The snicker of a switchblade flicking out.

This was definitely more than a warning. If I didn't get my act together, these pricks were going to slit my fucking throat.

Either the men we'd threatened hadn't been scared enough to act… or Sheeran hadn't given a shit what they had to say about it.

My eyes popped open. I spotted my own knife just a few feet away beyond the deluge of kicking legs. If I could just reach it—

"Get the fuck away from her!"

That voice was familiar. That voice was home.

Rafael barreled into my attackers' midst, colliding with the man who'd been going at my ribs like I was a soccer ball. My bodyguard clenched the asshole's throat hard enough to break the guy's windpipe, hurled him aside, and pummeled three other goons in quick succession.

The distraction gave me all the opening I needed. Gritting my teeth against the pain blazing through my body, I wrenched myself upright and lunged for my knife. With it held tightly in my hand, I jerked around so I was back-to-back with Rafael, glaring at Sheeran's men.

One of Rafael's victims lay on the ground, his head split open from the force of the impact against the corner of the sidewalk. My bodyguard let out a wordless roar, and most of the others took a step back, abruptly a whole lot less confident than when they'd been beating up on a lone woman.

"Two against all of you isn't good enough odds?" I taunted through breaths that felt like fire. "You're not going to try me now?"

Another of the thugs threw himself at me, but Rafael's fist got there first. The crack of a shattering jaw radiated through the night.

When one of his colleagues tried to hurtle past to get at me, I slashed out with my knife and dragged it through his shoulder. He swore, clapping his hand to the wound.

It still might not have been enough. The other goons were regrouping, massing together to form a solid offensive. I had no idea if Rafael and I could have dispatched all of them.

Then another bellow rang down the street with the thud of racing feet. "What the fuck do you think you're doing to her?"

Two of the men toppled as their heads were bashed together from behind. Jasper shoved into the fray, rage etched on his handsome face, his white teeth bared.

He might have been a figure skater, not a criminal, but he was built as tough as most of Sheeran's guys. And the odds had suddenly swung even more against them, lopsided as they still were.

Jasper got in one more swing before the bunch of them surged backward. "We're not finished with you!" one of them shouted in a dark voice.

They melded back into the shadows of the alley they'd emerged from.

Rafael probably would have given chase, but as he took a step forward, I wobbled and clutched at my side. The pain of my injuries was stabbing at me even more insistently now that my adrenaline rush was ebbing.

Rafael grabbed my arm. "Are you bleeding?" he demanded, his gaze searching my body for injuries.

I shook my head. "Nothing major. A few scrapes. But I think—" I took a strained breath. "I think I've at least bruised a few ribs. Maybe even cracked one." I restrained a wince and caught Jasper's eye. "Where did you come from?"

He stared at me, the anger now drained from his face and replaced with worry. "I finished up the mending that one costume needed and figured I'd walk over to help carry the food. Glad I did. Those were Sheeran's guys? I thought—"

"We obviously weren't convincing enough," Rafael snarled, and then shook himself. "Thank you for jumping in. You didn't need to do that. It helped."

"I wasn't going to just *stand* there." Jasper shifted his attention back to me. "You said they hurt your ribs?"

"Yeah. But I've dealt with that before. No big deal."

I put on a smile that might have been a bit sickly, but as soon as I started walking, the agony lanced through my chest again, making me sway.

Rafael caught my arm. "Take it easy. Come on, I'll carry you."

My dignity wanted me to argue with him, but I had enough brains to realize he was right. As he swept me off my feet into his bulging arms, my eyes caught Jasper's again, and the hint of panic I saw there reverberated into me with a sudden chill.

If I *had* broken a rib, how the hell was I going to perform in two weeks' time?

Sheeran's thugs hadn't succeeded in killing me, but they might have killed my career before it'd even really begun.

TWENTY-THREE

Luciana

THERE WAS nothing on the TV but daytime soaps and talk shows, both of which were full of drama so much more banal than my own life that it bored me to tears.

I groaned in annoyance and slouched on the sofa—and then winced at the flare of pain the movement sent through my ribs. We'd determined they were only bruised, not outright broken, but they still hurt like a mofo less than twenty-four hours after the attack by Sheeran's men.

The ache was a lot duller than it'd been last night, at least. More like a burn than knives being jabbed through my chest.

Niko walked by behind the sofa, stopping to tease his fingers over my hair and press a kiss to the top of my head. "I know you're not good at sitting still, but try to get a little more rest, Angel."

Jasper looked over from where he'd been prepping lunch in the kitchen. "Can I get you anything else? Glass of water, pillow, ice pack?"

The worry in his tone had a slightly frantic edge, which brought a totally different kind of ache to my gut. My guys had been hovering around me ever since I'd made it home, doing whatever they could to ease my pain and keep me comfortable, with no thought for their own needs.

"I'm good," I said. "And I'm coming over to the table to join you for lunch."

Rafael, who was already sitting at said table, stood up abruptly with a scrape of the chair legs. "You stay right there, Lou."

I made a face at him over the back of the sofa and pushed myself to my feet. The burn of the bruising coursed across my torso, but after a few steps I could mostly tune it out.

Not that my stoicism made any difference to the three men. By the time I'd taken those few steps, they'd all rushed to my side.

"You've got to know your limits," Rafael growled.

Niko nodded in emphatic agreement. "If you push yourself too hard, you could injure yourself worse."

I glared at the bunch of them. "I've had bruised ribs before. I know what I can handle. I'm just walking ten feet to the fucking table."

They took my grumbling in stride, helping me over to the nearest chair since they could probably tell it'd be more of a struggle trying to force me back to the sofa.

Jasper set a plate with the turkey sandwich he'd made for me on the table at my spot. "We wouldn't have minded joining you in the living room. I know you're tough, Punk, but you look like a truck slammed into you."

I grimaced, thinking of the vast purple-brown blotch I'd seen stretching across the side of my chest in the mirror this morning. "It doesn't matter what I look like. No one's going to see through my training clothes—or my costumes."

All three of the men froze in place. Rafael jolted back into action first.

He set one hand on the back of my chair and glowered down at me. "There's no way you should be skating when you're banged up this badly." He raised his head to glance at Niko. "Right? You're the professional—you tell her."

Niko's mouth had tightened. "With an injury like this, I'd never expect a skater to perform. Doctors would recommend a recovery period of at least a few weeks, and then—"

I sputtered a laugh. "Finals is in two weeks, so forget about that."

Jasper reached across the table and grasped my hand. "It's okay, Lou. I'm not going to blame you at all for what happened. Those shitheads fucked us over, and that's on them. You need your time to recover, and then we can take on the competition next year."

I shook my head with a jerk. "No fucking way. I didn't come this far to let some shitty gangsters ruin everything I've been working for. Everything *we've* been working for."

"It's not about 'letting,'" Niko said gently. "The body is only capable of so much."

Jasper let out a wordless growl. "If I'd just gotten there sooner, maybe they wouldn't have managed to hurt you so badly."

"No sense in beating ourselves up about it." I smiled at him. "Those goons already took care of that for us."

Silence. My joke had landed like a one-winged seagull. All three of them stared at me, incredulous looks on their faces.

"Nothing?" I asked. "Not a single laugh? Come on, we can't sit around moping. We've got work to do. My ribs are bruised, big whoop. I'll rest for another day or two so the worst of the pain has eased off, but then I'm back on the ice, no arguments."

Rafael considered me for a long moment with his best stern expression. "I can't stop you, Lou, but I wish you'd take your basic needs into account more. You know this is the only body you get. If you destroy it, then there's no way you can make skating a career in the long run."

I paused. He had a point.

"I can see a doctor if you guys really want me to," I said. "Just to make sure nothing's worse than it seems. And I'll pick up a cortisone shot to take away the pain so I can practice and perform no problem. Then I can get right back to skating as if none of this ever happened."

Jasper was still frowning. "A cortisone shot? Those things can be dangerous if you're not careful. If you mask your pain chemically and end up hurting yourself more, you could *really* damage your body."

I gritted my teeth. "It's my decision. It's only a couple of weeks before I can take a longer break, and I haven't had a real fall in ages. And, look—I'll be in a hell of a lot more pain if I let these bastards ruin my chances of getting my skating career off the ground."

I paused, glancing around at them, the twist of emotions in my gut rising to join the physical pain in my chest. "I hear what you're saying. I really do. But you don't understand. If I lose this chance… I don't know what's going to happen over the next year. How long I can stay off my mom's radar. Look at how quickly I ended up tangling with two different people who could report my whereabouts back to her. This could be my *last* chance to show what I can do."

Silence fell over the room. Niko and Jasper traded an agonized look.

They all knew I was right. My time with them was precarious. There was no guarantee I'd even make it to Finals without my old life coming crashing down on me, let alone all the way to next year's competitive circuit.

I picked up my sandwich, took a bite, and rallied against those awful thoughts while I chewed. "We do have to get the Harvester's Boston crew off my back before they ruin things even more. Right now, it seems like they're not going to stop coming at me until I give in and leave town. Which is not happening."

Niko's forehead had furrowed. "How are we going to do that? The threats we made didn't work. Are you going to go through with the threats?"

I sighed and swallowed thickly. I'd been hoping I wouldn't have to be part of more destruction. And— "I'm not sure that would actually do us any good. If anything, if we start launching attacks on Sheeran's people, he'll be even more convinced I'm working against him."

Rafael ran a hand over the wiry coils of his hair. "We went after Sheeran's main people before, but not the local boss himself. He calls the shots. We have to find *his* weak spot, something we can use against him."

I rubbed my mouth. "But none of your contacts knew any major dirt on him, right? And you haven't seen anything obvious."

"No. I'll keep at it."

Jasper tapped his fingers against the tabletop and then spoke up cautiously. "There is something… I don't know if it's enough, or anything at all for sure, but it might help."

All our gazes shot to him.

"What?" I demanded.

"From how you described him to us—I think I saw him last night, right before I rushed in to fight those pricks. There was an older guy, pretty slick looking, hanging back by the alley they all ran into when they took off. He was watching the others beat you down."

I perked up. "White hair, dressed in nice clothes?" When Jasper nodded, I did too. "Yep, that'd be him."

Jasper's eyes went momentarily distant in thought. "There was something that struck me, looking at him. The way he had his hands in his coat pockets, the angle of the seams…" He focused on Rafael. "You said that he seems to have an awful lot of money, right? More than you'd normally expect a local gang leader to have unless the main guy he works for was incredibly happy with him?"

Rafael gave the other man a contemplative look. "Yeah, it is pretty extreme. Not saying it isn't possible the Harvester just is that pleased, but it's a lot beyond what I'd normally see. Where are you going with this?"

A smile, nervous but determined, curved Jasper's lips. "I think if we can catch him at the end of one of the business deals he oversees here, we could get exactly what we need."

TWENTY-FOUR

Jasper

I PEERED at the old convenience store where Rafael had determined that Sheeran carried out a lot of his business dealings, just down the street from where we'd paused. The streetlamp overhead buzzed, casting a yellow glow into the darkness of the night. Niko's shoulders bumped against mine with a hint of nervous agitation.

Lou glanced at both of us from beneath the hood of her jacket. "You two don't have to go in with us, you know. I'd *rather* you stayed farther back, someplace safe."

I crossed my arms over my chest, gathering the resolve that'd brought me this far. "Nowhere's really safe until we deal with this asshole. And we're not letting you deal with him alone. Anyway, this was my idea. I should be there."

Niko nodded. "We said we'd stand by you through whatever danger you faced, and we're not going back on that promise."

Lou sighed but didn't argue. She shifted her weight from one foot to the other as she watched for Rafael's return, no sign of pain in her movements.

She'd gotten the cortisone shot she'd talked about a couple of days ago and today had been skating like she'd never taken a single hit. But I'd seen the thugs who'd come at her the other day. I'd seen how brutally they'd attacked her.

They'd wanted to hurt her way worse than we'd let them get away with. Maybe they'd even have killed her if they'd had the chance.

The idea of losing Lou—at all, but especially in such a vicious, painful way—made my gut clench up. How could I have ever thought *I* had it hard while she'd been dealing with shit like this every day since she was a little kid?

Rafael appeared across the street. He motioned us over to him and led us silently down an alley between the backs of the stores on either side of the block. I set my feet as carefully as I could, understanding that stealth was important.

Niko walked beside me, picking his way nimbly around the bits of trash that scattered the cracked pavement. He caught me looking at him and aimed a quiet smile my way, like a little stream of sunlight through the night.

This had to be done. If the four of us were ever going to live in peace together, we couldn't let Sheeran go any farther in his campaign against Lou.

Rafael held up his hand to stop us again. He moved forward, melding into the shadows with a skill I couldn't help admiring.

There was a muffled grunt and a rustle of clothes. Then a soft thump.

Rafael reappeared and beckoned us. "Come on, before they notice anything's wrong!"

We hustled past the slumped unconscious bodies of two men I assumed were guards Sheeran had posted, who obviously hadn't expected to encounter anyone like Rafael tonight. My skin tightened at the evidence of his violence, but I marched toward the shop's back door without hesitation.

Sheeran had made the rules here. If he'd left Lou alone, it wouldn't have come to this.

Rafael had taken out a gun that set my nerves even more on edge, though I knew it was for all of our protection. He took just a second to position himself and then threw himself at the door, bursting into the back room.

We barged into the thin artificial lighting to find the guy with the stark white hair I now knew was Sheeran and a few of his underlings standing around a metal table, which held a couple of baggies of a powder I assumed was some kind of drug and a pile of bundled bills set right in front of Sheeran.

He had one bundle in his hand as if counting it, but in the moment we hurtled inside, his other hand was dug deep into the pocket of his wool coat.

He jerked it out as he spun around at our intrusion, but I'd seen enough in the gesture and the angle he'd held his arm at.

I hadn't imagined anything the other evening. All my sewing work over the years had given me a strong sense of seams and clothing construction, and something was up with his pockets. And given everything else we'd discovered about him, I had a pretty clear idea what.

The three guys with him whipped out guns of their own and brandished them at us with threatening shouts. Rafael bared his teeth, positioning himself at the front of our group while Lou flanked him, her knife tight in her hand and her eyes fierce.

"What the fuck is this about?" Sheeran demanded, his jaw clenching as he took us in. He didn't look all that concerned, maybe because his side's guns outnumbered ours, but he definitely wasn't happy about the unexpected visit.

I cleared my throat. "We just wanted to check up on your operation. I was wondering how much money and product you've been skimming off your boss's profits and merchandise. Are your men on board with your disloyalty, or do they have no clue they're helping a backstabber?"

The three gunmen gaped at me, though their weapons hadn't wavered—yet. So, it was door number two, then.

Sheeran's face had hardened into a mask of horrified defiance, panic sparking in his gaze. "I don't know what the fuck you're—"

"Oh, it'll be pretty easy to prove it," I interrupted, stepping forward as if those guns didn't have my heart thumping double time. "Should we give these guys a show so they know who they're actually working under? Maybe it'd be a nice step up for them in the ranks, huh, if they could tip off the man at the top of the ladder about what his trusted lieutenant has been getting up to behind his back."

"They're making shit up," Sheeran snapped. "Shoot them already!"

Rafael fixed our enemies with a cool stare. "They know that's not a good idea. I can take down at least two of them before they could manage to stop me. Pretty poor odds, and for what? To support a traitor?"

"And we can prove we're not making anything up." I tipped my head toward his coat. "Your pockets will tell the whole story, won't they?"

The thugs glanced from us to Sheeran, looking increasingly uncertain. The fact that Sheeran had paled at my words couldn't have helped their confidence in their boss.

The older man appeared to make a hasty decision. He jerked his hand toward one of the thugs. "Give me that."

When the guy handed over his gun, Sheeran waved for them to go out the back door. "I can take care of this bunch. You make sure no other idiots are skulking around, looking to hassle us."

"But—" one of the gunmen started to say.

Sheeran glared at him. "Get the fuck out and follow your orders, or you'll be getting a bullet in the skull too."

Rafael waved at them with his pistol. "Go right ahead. I won't stop you."

Frowning, the three men filed out into the back alley. Lou positioned herself by the door so she'd hear their return.

She narrowed her eyes at Sheeran. "If you think you can cover up what you've been doing, *you're* the idiot. No matter what your men here know or believe, I can call up the Harvester directly and tell him the score."

Sheeran scoffed, though his knuckles had whitened where he gripped the gun. "You can't prove anything."

I raised my eyebrows. "Oh, no? You'll need to explain why you've got custom secret pockets stitched into this coat—and who knows how many other pieces of clothing. And why he'd find traces of the ink used on cash and maybe drugs as well in them. That stuff wouldn't wash out easily."

"We wouldn't give you a chance to try anyway." Lou smirked at him. "I could make the call while we have our little standoff, and I bet he could have someone checking your house in an hour or two, no sweat."

No sweat for the Harvester, anyway. A few beads of perspiration had formed on Sheeran's forehead. "You fucking bitch," he snarled.

She shrugged. "Look, I don't even care how you're screwing over your boss. Do whatever the hell you want… as long as you leave *me* out of it. I've told you before and I'll tell you again: I don't give a shit about your territory. I'm only here to skate. I've cut all ties with the Deadly Rose. I'm not a threat, and all I want is for you to leave me alone."

Sheeran snorted. "The Deadly Rose's heir wouldn't simply run off to take up figure skating. You might as well try to sell me on the story that you've joined the circus."

"How would you know?" Lou retorted. "You don't know a thing about me. Just because my mom pushed me out of her body doesn't mean I'm her carbon copy. I'm capable of wanting different things from this oh-so-fantastic life." She motioned around her at the dingy room.

"You have access to so much more than this. No one throws that away—not the power or the money."

"Speak for yourself, jackass."

Sheeran's lips curled into a sneer. We'd had him on the defensive, but now he was mocking Lou again. The possibility that she was telling the truth was so far outside the realm of what he could imagine that he hadn't even bothered to look into her story. Or maybe he figured she was spending all that time in the arena as a front for some criminal scheme.

My heart sank. Even this gambit wasn't going to work… because I didn't think Lou did have an immediate line to any members of the

Devil's Dozen. Not without her mother finding out and ruining everything anyway.

So how the hell could we—

A spark of an idea drew me up short. We could *make* him look.

I turned to Niko. "You have some recordings of our latest run-throughs of the routines on your phone, right?"

Niko blinked at me. "Of course."

I made an urgent gesture toward the bulge of the device at his hip. "Show this dickwad what she can actually do. What no one who hadn't dedicated themselves to years of skating practice could possibly pull off."

Without needing any further prompting, Niko whipped out his phone. As his thumb darted across the screen, Lou shuffled her feet, her stance tensing. "*No one's* seen the full routine except us."

I glanced at her. "We've got to convince him, right?"

Sheeran was rolling his eyes. "If you think a little video of her gliding around a rink is going to make a difference—I'm not an imbecile."

Niko ignored his comments, turning the phone's screen toward him. The familiar melody of our free skate music pealed from the speakers.

I knew the movements of the routine by heart, on or off the ice. With each beat, my muscles flexed instinctively, the motions playing out in my head. I didn't need to see the video to follow what it showed.

The wavering light played across Sheeran's grim features. He adjusted his grip on his gun, his sneer deepening. "Very nice. You set up this whole farce to pretend—"

His voice fell away with the swell of the music—the moment when we'd launched into our first synchronized jumps. The first lift would be next, Lou spinning over my head and stretching into a pose so graceful you'd think she was not just an angel but a goddess incarnate.

Watching her enemy take in her performance, Lou grimaced but didn't try to intervene. I couldn't imagine she liked him seeing this part of her life, the part she'd carved out through so much effort from the past he represented. But it'd been the only way I could think of to solidify our case.

Sheeran had tipped forward just slightly, his gaze now glued to the screen. The sneer was fading from his face. At the next set of jumps, a sequence hard for even pros to pull off, his eyes widened.

He was bull-headed but not stupid. He could tell there was no way Lou had simply picked up those moves in a few days' practice.

Niko watched the other man's face. His voice came out quiet but firm. "*This* is what Lou is in Boston for. It's the only reason she's here. She doesn't have time to worry about your criminal activities while she's training for the competitions."

I lifted my chin. "It's taken her years of practicing every day since she was a kid to reach that level. A lot of people *never* get there, no matter how hard they work at it. Are you so much of an imbecile that you think she did all that just to sell a cover story one day? A cover story no one in your line of work would believe anyway?"

Sheeran's lips parted at the lift-throw sequence we'd been working on so painstakingly. He shook his head, but not in denial, only as if trying to sort out his thoughts.

"I—" Sheeran yanked his eyes away from the screen with apparent effort. He looked at me and then Lou with a dazed expression before his shoulders came up slightly with a hint of shame.

"It *did* sound ludicrous," he said grouchily. "And I was specifically told otherwise—that you were here on a mission for the Deadly Rose."

Rafael hummed to himself. "Let me guess. Your tip came from a pale guy with a big nose and acne scars. Maybe you even dug enough to find out his last name is Haggard?"

Sheeran's attention snapped to him. "How did you know that?"

"That prick used to work for the Deadly Rose. *Used to* being the important part of that sentence. He's got a vendetta against her and everyone associated with her. He was only trying to stir up trouble for Lou for his own gain, and you bought into it hook, line, and sinker."

Sheeran grimaced. "What was I supposed to think? His version made a lot more sense than hers."

I glared at him. "Well, now you know. So, you'll pass on word to your boss that she isn't a threat and leave her alone from now on, right?"

Lou piped up before Sheeran had to answer. "We're going to take care of Haggard, so you don't need to worry about him. And if you back off on me, we'll leave all the Harvester's business and your own reputation alone. I'm sure you've got better things to do than keep track of what I'm up to anyway. Seems like a pretty sweet offer."

To my surprise, Sheeran looked back at the video still playing on Niko's phone before answering. He watched me and Lou whip through our final sequence with bewilderment in his eyes.

As Niko tucked the phone away, the gang boss inclined his head to Lou. "Fine. I can see I made a mistake, and I'll fix that as long as we're even. Consider it a done deal."

TWENTY-FIVE

Luciana

ONE PAIR of our competitors spun across the ice in their free skate routine, creating an image I could appreciate even as my stomach knotted with apprehension. I rested my hands against the boards, resisting the urge to fidget.

In some ways it was a good thing that Finals were being held in Boston this year, so we'd been able to stay in the same city and perform in an arena we were familiar with. But when I glanced around the vast space, I couldn't help flashing back to our qualifying competition performance.

The jolt of panic that'd raced through me. The wobbles and stumbles.

The shame of hearing our score and knowing it might not be good enough.

Jasper and I had performed our short routine yesterday without any significant errors, but the caliber of the competition was much higher at Finals. All the best pairs from across the country were here, and we'd only ranked fifth.

That was okay. We both knew that the free skate was where we really shone, and with the adjustments we'd made, it'd earn us all the points we needed to boost us up the ranks. It counted for twice as much of the total, after all.

As long as we didn't screw it up. As long as *I* didn't fuck it up.

We had to make it into at least the top three to be sure of getting accepted into the National Championships, the stepping stone to the international circuit. If we failed here, it'd be nothing but minor local competitions until the qualifying round started again next year.

I can do this. I just have to keep my cool, and I'll nail it.

The music wound down. The skaters struck their ending pose, bowed, and glided over to the stands.

There were still a couple more pairs to go before it was my and Jasper's turn, but my stomach clenched even tighter. This was going to be our first time showing off our new move in front of any audience. And a faint ache still radiated through my ribs despite the cortisone.

I'd rest some more, for at least a few days, after we got through today. That was a promise to myself.

But I still had to get through today.

A hand rested on my shoulder with a gentle squeeze I recognized before I'd even glanced up at Niko. My coach shot me his sunbeam of a smile, pride shining from his face as if we'd already proven ourselves.

"You're going to kill it, Angel," he said. "Both of you. Show them what you can do, and let them experience the beauty you have to offer the world."

I inhaled slowly, absorbing those words. He was right: my purpose was to add beauty to the world, not take from it. All I had to do was remember who I was—who I *truly* was, not who Mom had wanted me to be—and I would be golden.

I shot Niko a smile in return. "Thanks. I'm ready. It's just hard not to be a little nervous."

He gave a light laugh. "I don't think you'd be human if you weren't. But I've seen you face off against a lot more than a bunch of ice. I know you can do this."

The corners of my lips twitched higher. He wasn't wrong about that either.

My gaze drifted away—and caught on a set of bright blue eyes fixed on me from farther down the stands. My pulse skipped a beat, but I forced myself to continue my survey of the stands as if I hadn't even noticed Quentin's stare.

He'd been watching us—watching *me*—almost every time I'd glanced in his direction since we'd shown up for Finals yesterday. I couldn't tell whether the intensity of his attention was more unnerving or thrilling.

Was he trying to intimidate us? Hoping to rub his and Jess's third place spot after yesterday's routines in our faces?

Having trouble shaking the images from the night when he'd spied on us in the locker room?

I hoped it was the latter. Let him keep stewing on the passion he knew we shared, that he and his partner had no chance of matching.

Whatever the case, I wasn't going to let the jerk distract me.

As the pair on the ice launched into a jump that wasn't quite as impressive as our triple Lutzes, Jasper stepped up beside me. He stared out over the ice with a solemn expression that sent a pang through my chest.

He had to be nervous too. This was his grand return after his slump—and I'd already almost ruined it for him.

Had Niko and I really done the right thing, dragging him back into the spotlight? I didn't even know everything that was weighing on him.

I reached out and tucked my hand around his. "Jasper?"

His gray-green eyes slid to meet mine, warming as they did in a way that reassured me. "Yeah, Punk?"

I couldn't hold back a grin at the teasing nickname, even though it was still a little hard to get out the question I wanted to ask. "We never really talked about… about whatever it was that got you off track the last time you were competing. I know it wasn't because of Niko. Is there anything you're still worrying about?"

Jasper blinked, and then his gaze went momentarily distant. "Oh. That. I—I mean, it's mostly the same old thing, just it happened to hit me really hard at a time when I really needed my focus."

He rubbed the back of his neck in his awkward way, and I resigned myself to the fact that he might not say anything more. But then he caught my gaze again. "I've told you that my dad wasn't supportive about the whole figure skating thing."

I nodded. "Yeah. He sounds like a total jerk."

Jasper let out a rough chuckle. "That's one way of putting it. Well, a couple years ago, he and my mom took in the teenage son of friends of theirs—the parents had a great opportunity with work that was taking them overseas for a few months, and they didn't want to pull the kid out of school in the middle of the year. So he was living with my parents for the time being."

"That was nice of them," I said, wondering where this was going.

"It was." His jaw tightened, and he returned his attention to the ice. "The kid was on his high school football team, star quarterback, already getting interest from colleges even though he was only a sophomore. I went back home to visit for a few days around Easter, and my dad just wouldn't stop going on about how amazing this guy was, how impressive this game or that play had been, with little jabs implying *I* was a total letdown in comparison."

My hands balled at my sides. "Not just a jerk. A total fucking asshole."

Jasper shrugged. "I always knew he felt that way about skating. He just hadn't had such an easy point of comparison right there in front of him before to rub it in. That wasn't even the worst of it. My mom got upset with him, and the night before I left, they had a blow-up argument, yelling like they hardly ever did. And he stormed out of the house. He hadn't come back when I had to leave to catch my flight the next morning."

Good riddance, I wanted to say, but I suspected that comment wouldn't come across as all that helpful. "I'm glad you have someone who'd stand up for you."

"I guess there's that. But she still loves him even though he has that one hang-up. I could tell she was devastated. And then I went out and started practicing, and had a few bad stumbles, and all these doubts rose up about whether everything I'd been doing really was worth it. I got too much in my head, like Niko always says. Even worse when the pressure was on during the actual competitions."

Jasper paused and squeezed my hand. "I didn't know how to get back out of that spiral until the two of you showed up. I know *I* was an ass to you when we first met, but you have no idea how happy I am that you tolerated it enough to stick around while I got my head on straight."

A glow of affection lit in my chest. I bobbed up to give him a quick kiss. "I'm awfully happy I did too."

While we'd talked, the pair right before us had gone on. They were just wrapping up their routine, but as I watched them strike their ending pose, I found my own niggling doubts had waned.

Jasper and I really had created something special, and there was nothing I wanted more than to show it off in all its glory for the audience around us.

The announcer called out our names, and Jasper tugged me toward the ice. We skated into the middle of the rink.

Jasper aimed one more smile at me. "Okay, Punk. Let's show them how it's done."

As we assumed our opening position, I felt like I was made for this moment. The audience went silent, all their attention on Jasper and me.

Then, at the back of the arena among the logos for the event's various sponsors, a new banner unfurled before my eyes. A white sheet with red paint blazoned across it in the shape of a broken rose.

The picture was crude but unmistakable. My heart lurched.

It had to be Haggard's doing. He'd set up that banner here to taunt me—he was *here*, in the arena, probably right now to watch my reaction.

Through the flare of panic, my jaw set. Niko's words about how much I'd faced off against came back to me.

My men and I had overcome an entire crew of Devil's Dozen people. If this one psycho thought he was going to faze me, he was delusional as well.

The chill of fear melted in the wake of my anger—and a renewed surge of determination.

The music swept through the arena, and Jasper and I launched ourselves into motion.

The music carried us as if we were propelled by an ocean current. I caught Jasper's gaze as we whirled around each other and saw the same fierce certainty in his expression that'd steadied me.

He was in this to win just as much as I was. We had each other, and nothing was going to hold us back.

The melody flowed through me, and the routine became a blur. Jump, spin, lift. Every motion perfectly timed, the two of us in sync as if we had one body.

The poignant joy of the song wound through me and lifted my spirits. I let it play out in every tiny gesture of my hands while it shone in my face.

This was what skating was all about. We were spreading that joy to the hundreds of watching figures in the stands, transporting them to another place of our design.

Then it was time for the new combination.

Jasper's hands grasped mine. I whipped into the air over his head, finding my balance in his hold without a single wobble. The faces around us raced by with our rotation, and the music buoyed me even higher.

When Jasper propelled me up a second time, I whirled around with a sensation of perfect freedom. The air seemed to hold me up as my body spun, and my foot hit the ice at the perfect angle as if drawn by a magnet.

As my skates hissed across the rink with my landing, triumph swelled in my chest. Applause and cheers echoed from all around us. I had to hold back a victorious grin that wouldn't quite have matched the mood we were still trying to convey.

Take that, everyone who'd ever thought they could steal this moment away from me.

We swept through the rest of the routine hitting every mark and struck our ending pose with the last note of the song in one final dramatic touch. The roar of the crowd washed over us, and I finally released my grin.

Jasper beamed back at me, clasping my hand and thrusting it higher over our heads before we gave a quick bow.

As we skated back to the stands, my pulse thrummed in my veins. Niko grabbed us both in a hug, and shouts of congratulations carried from the seats around us. The energy coursing through the crowd after our performance exhilarated me.

But nothing mattered unless the judges had gotten caught up in our performance too. Had we done enough? Had they seen everything we'd meant to conjure with the routine?

The announcer took the scoresheet they handed over. He paused before leaning toward the mic, and my heart almost stopped.

"The score for Luna Garcia and Jasper St. Pierre is one hundred thirty-six point two seven."

Another thunderous cheer rose up through the stands. My jaw dropped.

We'd gotten over a hundred and thirty-five points? Even a hundred and thirty was rare. Holy shit.

My world spun. Jasper let out a startled crow of amazement and wrapped me in a hug. Niko flung his arms around both of us, and in that moment, there was nothing in my entire being but joy.

TWENTY-SIX

Luciana

BY THE TIME Jasper and I were called onto the ice for our second-place finish—our amazing free skate score tugged a bit low by our not-quite-as-spectacular short program—the giddy rush of excitement hadn't faded. I didn't stop grinning once as we stood side by side, basking in another round of applause.

Somewhere in the stands, Quentin and Jess would be watching. Their performance a couple of spots after ours had looked not just precise but rigid to my eyes, and Jess had lost her balance during one of the lifts, nearly kneeing Quentin in the face as she fell.

Despite their solid showing in the short program, they'd dropped down to seventh. I might have grinned even wider knowing that this was the last we'd have to see their smug faces around, since there was pretty much no chance they'd be welcomed at the National Championships with that placing.

Sure, I might miss the competitive thrill of facing off with our rivals a little, but it'd be more than worth it not to have to see Jasper's frustration when that jerk mouthed off at him.

It was hard to believe I'd made it this far when just months ago, I'd thought I'd never be able to compete at all. I resisted the urge to pinch myself.

I kept my arm looped around Jasper's waist as we skated back to the stands. When we reached Niko, I pulled him into yet another hug before aiming my grin at both of them.

"This is the best day ever. Obviously we need to celebrate. I'll run and get changed—then we can figure out where to go for dinner. I'm ready to pig out!"

Niko laughed and gave my cheek a quick kiss. We all tramped off toward the locker rooms.

The woman's room was crowded with my fellow skaters peeling off their costumes. As I eased out of mine, careful of Jasper's painstaking needlework, several of the other women came over to congratulate me on the performance.

"I can't wait to see what you and Jasper do at Nationals!" one of them, who I thought had placed toward the bottom of the pack, said with an eager smile.

I let out an awkward laugh, not used to having the attention focused on me. "Me too! Thank you."

I threw on my old Metallica shirt and a pair of faded jeans, restraining a wince at the slightly sharper ache of my ribs when I raised my arms. I had pushed myself pretty hard in the last couple of weeks—it was definitely time for some resting before we honed our skills for Nationals.

After I tucked my costume into my equipment bag, pausing to brush my fingers over my lucky skate lace from my earliest childhood lessons, I raised my head and noticed a door off beyond a row of lockers along the wall. It was narrower than the main entrance and scuffed. Probably for maintenance or something.

But what caught my eye was the smear of red paint just above the handle.

My pulse hitched. I froze for a second, my gaze darting around the room, but none of the other skaters appeared to have noticed it, let alone started worrying about it. Several were already taking off through the main door, eager to get home after a long, stressful day.

But I knew Haggard had been here. He'd left that broken rose banner for me to see.

What was he playing at now?

Simply ignoring the sign didn't feel like an option. I couldn't turn my back on an enemy without figuring out his new game.

I hefted my equipment bag and walked casually over to the side door. Setting the heavy bag down on the nearest bench, I gave the door a gentle tug.

It wasn't locked. When I peered out into the dim hall on the other side, a part of the arena that clearly wasn't generally open to the public, the streak of paint continued along the wall farther than I could see.

A shiver ran down my back, and my teeth set on edge. I was *not* letting Haggard fuck up the best day of my life.

I also wasn't going to throw caution to the wind. I pulled out my phone, tapped a hasty text to Rafael to let him know what I'd found and what I was doing, asking him to catch up with me as soon as he could.

I wasn't sure how he'd get into this hall while avoiding the woman's locker room, but this was Rafael. He'd find a way.

After putting my phone away, I reached for the knife in my other pocket. Holding it ready, I treaded slowly but steadily down the dim maintenance hall, following the trail of red paint. Splatters of it marked the floor as well, still gleaming wet.

A few other doors broke the sameness of the pale gray wall. I was just passing one when a hushed voice reached my ears, as if from someone standing right on the other side of it.

It was Quentin's voice.

I paused automatically, my ears pricking. As I leaned closer to the door, I made out the words of what sounded like one side of a phone conversation.

Quentin's tone stayed low and a little hoarse. "I'm sorry. I don't know what happened. It was fine when we practiced— Yes. Yes, I know that. Of course Jess and I tried our best. No, you can't blame it all on her. I was just— Mom, it wasn't like that. I still have another chance. I'll do better, I promise."

An uneasy twinge ran through my gut. This didn't sound like the arrogant prick I knew at all, but someone brow-beaten into submission.

I was way too familiar with having those kinds of conversations with my mother. Who'd have thought Quentin had a shitty one too?

Maybe that was where he'd gotten his shitty attitude from. I squared my shoulders and pushed myself onward.

I had bigger things to worry about. Our rival's family situation didn't even make the top ten.

I edged down the hall, stifling another shiver. The red blotches on the floor grew larger with every step I took. The smear on the wall continued on to a bend several feet ahead, where one more puddle of paint seeped around the corner.

I hesitated, inhaling the stale air and wishing Rafael had made it here already. My fingers tightened around my knife.

For all I knew, Haggard was already gone. Laughing to himself about how he'd freaked me out yet again. I'd just get to the end of the trail, see what was what, and then I could shut him out of my mind at least for tonight.

I pushed myself forward, my eyes peeled, alert for any hint of a threat. But I still wasn't totally prepared.

The second I edged past the bend in the hall, a gangly body in a denim jacket hurtled into me. As my attacker tackled me to the floor, a blade flashed in his hand.

The side of my skull slammed into the linoleum floor. I thrashed against the man's hold, my thoughts spinning with adrenaline and pain, and caught a glimpse of a hooked nose and a cruel mouth I recognized even in my daze as Haggard's.

He snatched at my wrists, brandishing his knife with his other hand. "I'm going to paint the place with your blood next, Cordova bitch!" he snarled, his spit flecking my cheek.

I shoved at him, squirming away from him with all my might, and the swipe of his blade only nicked a shallow line in my forearm. With a growl of frustration, he heaved me toward the floor again.

I'd gotten my torso briefly free, but he had my legs pinned beneath the weight of his body. Even as I flailed, I couldn't unseat him to aim a knee at his balls or any other vulnerable area that might have turned the tables.

So I did the best I could with my upper body. Ignoring the swipe of his blade, I jabbed at his chest with my own knife. When he smacked my arm to the side, he gave me the opening to punch him hard in the nose.

Haggard grunted and clamped his hand around my throat. "Fucking cunt. You deserve everything that's coming to you! You're a stuck-up, stupid whore, just like your mother."

Just like your mother. Those words echoed in my ears, sparking a blaze of denial that reverberated through me like a battle cry.

I was *nothing* like Mom, and I'd proved it out there just hours ago. I'd proved it despite this psycho's best attempts at shattering my confidence.

I hadn't let him win then, and I sure as hell wasn't about to roll over now.

Rage flared inside my chest. This prick had been hurling so much shit at me, messing up my life and dragging everyone I cared about into that mess, just to get back at someone I had no association with anymore.

I was nothing like Mireya Cordova, but I was still her daughter, with all the lessons that had come with the role. I would do whatever it took to end this sicko's campaign of terror.

With a renewed surge of strength, I wrenched to the side, just as Haggard stabbed at me again. His blade pricked my shoulder, but I rocked his balance. As he swayed, I rammed my elbow into his gut.

Haggard's breath spurted out of him in a pained huff. Anger twisted his features. He jerked around to pin me more solidly again, but I was already whipping up my hand at the perfect angle.

I grabbed his wrist with my other hand, yanking it down to clear the way, heedless of the scratch his knife drew along the side of my bicep. With all my strength, I jabbed my knife into the side of his neck.

It plunged in all the way to the hilt. Haggard's lips parted with a gurgle; blood splattered from the wound down over my chest.

As his body crumpled, I scrambled out from under it. My back banged into a pair of legs that had just jarred to a stop behind me.

I almost struck out before a big, brawny form dropped down to encircle me in his arms. Rafael held me tight and glowered over my shoulder at the slumped body spilling its life blood across the dingy floor.

I stayed frozen for a few more beats of my heart until Haggard's corpse sagged with total limpness. There wasn't a single sign of life left in him, not even a twitch of his fingers.

Rafael tucked his head over mine, his stance taut with tension.

"Are you okay?" he asked, his voice terse with strain. "That cabrón—"

I dragged in a long breath. "I dealt with him. I'm fine."

Only as I spoke did it sink in how true those words were. Not the slightest quiver of guilt or regret rose up at the sight of the man I'd murdered.

I raised my chin defiantly. "The world is better off without this prick. I did what I had to do to make sure it wasn't me lying there in a puddle of blood."

Rafael hugged me tighter for a moment and pressed a kiss to the top of my head. "You did fucking amazing, Lou. Both out there on the ice and right now. The bastard got everything he deserved. But maybe next time, wait until I'm there for backup."

I grimaced. "I didn't really expect to find him. He's never stuck around before."

A hint of wryness crept into my bodyguard's tone. "And he never will again. Let's get you cleaned up to go back to your celebrating. I can handle the mess back here. Somehow I don't think this asshole is going to be missed."

"You've got that right."

I pushed myself upright, standing next to Rafael as he checked over my minor wounds. My nose wrinkled at the metallic scent now lacing the air, but I didn't let myself look away from the man I'd killed.

He *had* deserved it. And now the world had one less psycho in it. My *life* had one less psycho in it.

I might not want to resort to my mother's bloody methods, but I'd done what was necessary. Come what may, no matter how far I tried to leave my past behind, I had to hold on to a little of what I'd learned.

I could never let myself get so afraid to turn to violence that I'd falter when it was truly the only answer.

TWENTY-SEVEN

Luciana

BY THE TIME Rafael and I emerged into the main hallway to meet Niko and Jasper, the full impact of what had just happened hit me.

I'd been ambushed by my lunatic stalker. He'd nearly *killed* me.

His blood was still clinging to my skin on the tee I'd covered up with a hoodie from the equipment bag Rafael had surreptitiously retrieved for me.

None of the blood or my minor wounds was showing, but Jasper took one look at me and frowned. "Are you okay, Lou? What happened?"

"I'm fine," I said, managing a smile that I could feel came out tight. "I just…"

As I trailed off, momentarily lost for words, Rafael stepped in. Ducking his head and lowering his voice, he must have conveyed the gist of what I'd just been through to the other two men.

Niko's eyes widened with a stiffening of his shoulders, and rage flashed in Jasper's eyes, but Rafael gripped the younger guy's shoulder.

"I'm going to take care of everything else. Lou will be okay—it was just a lot."

I shook myself out of my daze. "Yeah. And it's over now. So let's get on with the celebrating!" I aimed a steadier smile at my men. "I want to enjoy what we pulled off here today and forget about the assholes we've had to tackle. There's no one I want to think about other than the three of you."

A whiff of the bloody odor reached my nose, and I wrinkled it before adding, "And we should definitely go back to the apartment first, because I have some washing up to do."

Niko patted his phone in his pocket. "I've gotten a few calls, media enquiries and a possible new sponsor, but I already put them off until we had a chance to regroup. That can wait until at least tomorrow."

My bodyguard gave me a quick kiss and disappeared back into the maintenance hallway to take care of the body. Just this once, I was grateful for the connection Rafael and I shared with the criminal underground—it meant that he knew how to make problems like this disappear without a trace.

I let Niko drive and stretched out in the plush backseat. When we got home, I ditched the bloody shirt and dragged my sore and soiled body into the bathroom to start the shower running.

"You sure you don't need any help, Angel?" Niko asked, concern etched across his handsome features. "I don't mind if you need to lean on me."

"I'm good. I'll let you know if I'm feeling wonky. But I think I'm feeling more like ordering in than going out for dinner now. Why don't you two figure out something delicious for us to chow down on?"

When I stepped under the hot spray and inhaled a lungful of soothing steam, the last of the adrenaline rush faded away. I let out a relieved sigh.

Haggard was gone, and Sheeran was out of my hair. We'd skated to victory today, and we had every hope of reaching greater heights in the future. And now no one else was left to interfere.

I scrubbed my skin until it shone golden-brown, as though I could wash away the events of the day down the drain with the crimson-tinted water. By the time I left behind my steamy heaven, Rafael had returned. He passed me on his way into the bathroom to wash up himself, giving me a nod to signify that the deed was done.

I never had to even think about Haggard again.

The smell of fresh, cheese-laden pizza reached my nose from the dining area, setting my mouth watering. It might not be the most elegant of meals, but my men obviously knew me well. Next to pierogies, nothing said comfort like a big, greasy slice of pie.

As I headed over, something else reached me that was totally unexpected. A high feminine voice carried through the air. "Jasper, you both did so well. It was amazing to watch! I just wish I could have seen it live instead of just a video."

My eyebrows shot up. "Is that Emi?"

Niko beamed and motioned me over to where he was holding his phone so both he and Jasper could video-chat with his sister.

Emi waved from the small screen with both hands, grinning avidly at me. "There you are!" she cried. "Congratulations, a hundred times. I'm so proud of you, but then again, I just knew you two would come out on top."

Her eager words swept away any lingering tension from the day. My heart swelled with affection totally different from what I felt for my men but no less poignant.

I waved back with a grin of my own. "Thank you! I wish you could have been there too. We worked our butts off to give that performance."

She laughed. "And the judges must have noticed that! It was the best part of my day—no, my whole week. Now you get back to your dinner. I have to hurry to work."

As Jasper popped open the two pizza boxes so I could take my pick, Niko tucked away his phone and headed for his bedroom. "I have a little surprise to go with the celebration!"

He returned with a bottle of champagne—with a label that told me it'd been a pricy purchase. My lips parted in surprise as he dug out the cork with a satisfying *pop*.

"You must have bought that before the competition. We didn't stop anywhere on the way home."

Niko's eyes sparkled as he poured the bubbly liquid into the glasses that'd come with the apartment. "I had a suspicion that we'd find a good use for it sooner rather than later."

A rush of warmth flooded my chest all over again, and I only held myself back from jumping on him with another hug because that would have meant champagne splattering all over the place.

Rafael joined us, claiming a slice and a glass. I dug into my perfectly tangy meat-lover's and gazed around at the makeshift family that'd somehow formed around me.

My bodyguard offered a reserved but clearly amused response to one of Niko's enthusiastic remarks. Jasper had stepped closer to our coach, his shoulder brushing Niko's, with a comfortable companionableness that made me giddy. When he caught me watching, his smile was only a little sheepish, full of all the same fondness wound around my heart.

This was all the family I needed. It seemed like a miracle that we'd come together at all.

Rafael and I had figured out how to navigate the figure skating world, and Niko and Jasper were now holding their own against criminals. We'd met each other halfway and created something so much stronger out of our differences.

I polished off a second slice of pizza and washed it down with a healthy portion of champagne. The bubbles set off a headier exhilaration through my veins.

I was hungry for something better than food.

Setting down my glass with a forceful clink got all the guys' attention. My lips curled into a sly smirk.

"There are other ways I want to celebrate."

Without waiting for their response, I stepped toward Niko, who happened to be closest, and pulled him to me. He dipped his head to meet my lips, his mouth opening instinctively to allow my tongue entrance.

As he hummed his approval into my mouth, hands came to rest on my waist from behind. Jasper tipped his chin over my shoulder to kiss the crook of my jaw. "I think we've already proven we can collaborate on that kind of celebration *very* well."

I reached up to stroke my fingers down his face and then eased to the side so the two men could steal a kiss from each other. The growing confidence with which Jasper gripped the collar of Niko's shirt and angled his head to deepen the kiss sent a flush of heat through me that was both joy and desire.

But there was one other participant in our celebration—one whose reaction I was much less sure of. As Niko and Jasper drew apart, Jasper nuzzling my hair and Niko trailing his hand down my side, I glanced over at Rafael.

When I'd first met the skaters, he hadn't liked the idea of me hooking up with them at all. He'd admitted that he found it hard to accept sharing me. We'd gotten this far by keeping the most explicit parts of our relationship away from his watchful eyes.

But if there was a slight flicker of jealousy in his gaze as he stared at me now, it was barely visible amid the flare of lust.

"I'm not letting these two have all the fun," he rumbled in answer to my unspoken question, and stepped in to capture my mouth with his.

I tilted my head up to lean into the demand of his kiss, letting out a ragged sound when his fingers skimmed down my torso to squeeze my ass through my leggings. His free hand found its way into my hair and twined itself in the strands with a domineering grip.

He yanked my head back with just enough force to set my nerves singing, not the slightest prick of real pain. "You think you can handle three at once, huh, brat?"

I gave him my best bratty smile. "I know I can. The question is, can you handle me?"

He chuckled with a hint of promise that left me tingling from head to toe. "Oh, I'll make sure you're satisfied, all right."

Jasper raised an eyebrow. "I think we're all going to contribute to that."

Rafael's eyes smoldered. "Sure you will. Why don't you start by giving the side of her neck some attention? I hope you know how sensitive she is right at the crook of her shoulder."

The bossiness in his tone combined with his total confidence about what I'd like set me on fire. Even more so when Jasper followed his order, pressing scorching kisses down my neck and then nipping the crook with the edges of his teeth.

A gasp spilled out of me, and I ground my ass against him instinctively. Jasper let out a groan of his own at the friction I'd generated.

Niko smiled mischievously and curled his fingers around the hem of my shirt to lift it.

Rafael nodded approvingly. "Nice and slow. Tease her all the way up."

Oh, God. I didn't think I'd ever been so turned on in my life. My panties were soaking, and none of the men had even touched me below the waist other than Rafael's brief ass squeeze.

Niko eased my shirt up just as Rafael had directed, stroking his fingertips over my belly and then my breasts through my sports bra. My breath caught when he flicked them over my nipples, raising them to peaks simultaneously.

Jasper gave him room to peel the shirt right off me and grasped my bra in turn. He slid his hands under the fabric to cup my breasts, massaging them and swiveling his thumbs over the nipples. I swayed with the pleasure racing through my chest.

Niko turned to Jasper next. The other man went still for a second before raising his arms to let Niko strip his own tee off him. Our coach took the same teasing approach, drawing a flush across Jasper's chest that spread up his neck to his cheeks with Niko's playful caress.

Seeing their attraction to each other only fanned my own desire hotter. I wrenched at Rafael's shirt, determined to get as much delicious musculature on display as I had within reach.

Time slowed with a blur of stroking hands and hot mouths. More clothes tumbled onto the floor until we ended up kneeling together on the living room rug, stark naked.

I ran my fingers down Rafael's six pack to the jut of his impressive cock, and he growled. Without giving me a chance to do more than circle it with my fingers, he pushed me down on the rug.

"You," he said in the commanding voice that had me shivering with pleasure. "Get down there between her knees and give her what she deserves."

What I deserved?

His meaning became clear an instant later with Jasper's head bowing so it was sandwiched between my thighs. My partner's tongue darted out to lap over my clit and then lower to devour my entire pussy.

I keened and shuddered, rocking into his eager mouth. Jasper grasped my ass and tipped me up so he could work me over even more thoroughly. I melted against his lips and tongue.

Rafael's voice came out raw. "Good. Just like that. And you, take care of those tits."

Niko offered a light chuckle. "Nothing I'd rather do."

His slender hands palmed my breasts. As he pinched my pebbled nipples, sparking jolts of bliss, a full moan reverberated out of me.

Rafael wasn't leaving himself out. He eased toward me, tangling his fingers in my hair again, but all my attention was on the thick shaft between his legs. Carried on the waves of delight rushing through my body, I lifted my head and flicked my tongue over the tip of his cock.

Rafael gave a shudder of his own with a groan that made my pulse skip. I wanted to taste him, to take him all the way down my throat.

At first I thought he might pull back, but then he growled and slid forward. I took every inch, bit by bit, sliding my tongue along his shaft. My hand reached out to rake my nails against his bare thighs.

"A huevo!" he muttered, pumping toward my mouth. "So fucking good, Lou."

Niko lowered his head to suck one nipple between his lips, and my cry reverberated over Rafael's cock. He let out a ragged breath and pulled back, just as Jasper grazed his teeth over my clit.

I moaned again, but it wasn't enough for Rafael. Twin fires glowed in his dark eyes. "I say we fill her up properly. Are you ready to take a ride, brat?"

I licked my lips, but if he thought I'd turn right to him, it wasn't going to be that easy. As Jasper raised his head to take in the shift in the situation, I pushed Niko over on his back and straddled him. Then I shot a grin at Rafael. "Sure am."

Rafael didn't look at all put out—and Niko definitely wasn't. He slid his cock against my pussy with a worshipful sigh.

"You need—" Jasper scrambled away and returned moments later with a condom packet.

Niko's eyes shone as he watched the other man. "You want to prepare me for her?"

Jasper hesitated, but only for a split-second. His teeth grazed his lower lip in the most delicious way as he ripped open the packet and reached to roll the contents over Niko's cock. He delved his fingers into my wetness at the same time, taking my arousal as lubrication.

Holy hell. Lust gripped me, and I sank down onto Niko. He slid right into my slick channel, filling me all the way to the sweet spot deep within.

Niko groaned softly. "You always feel so good, Angel."

"You too," I murmured, bracing myself against the rug. I began to rock my hips against him, my tits bouncing with every thrust, welcoming him even deeper.

As we moaned in unison, his eyelids fluttered—and his gaze slid to Jasper, who'd planted himself beside me to return his attentions to my neck and breasts. Carefully, Niko lifted his hand and trailed it over Jasper's thigh. The top at first, and then easing inward in time with the rhythmic collision of our bodies.

Even through the pleasure hazing my mind, I couldn't help tracking the movement. Jasper paused, watching as if hypnotized.

Niko grazed Jasper's rigid shaft with the tips of his fingers, gazing up at the other man. Jasper closed his eyes, his throat working.

As far as I knew, they'd never gone quite this far with each other before, other than the brief help in "preparation" Jasper had offered a few minutes ago. Niko's caution seemed to confirm my suspicion.

The silent question hung in the air, and then Jasper nodded, opening his eyes with a blaze in his grey-green irises. Niko smiled.

His chest hitched as he plunged into me once more, and he wrapped his hand right around Jasper's cock. With a swipe of his thumb, he smeared the beading precum down Jasper's length and began pumping him as he pushed up to meet me.

Jasper's eyes rolled back. "Christ, keep doing that."

Niko did as he was told, his smile lingering on his lips. Jasper's breath stuttered, and he buried his face in the crook of my neck again, passing on some of the pleasure the other man was provoking in him.

Just when I thought the thrill inside me couldn't surge any higher, I felt a third touch at the small of my back. Rafael had positioned himself over Niko's legs behind me. He teased his fingers farther down, parting my ass cheeks and tracing the rim of my back entrance.

His voice spilled hot down my spine. "Would you like to be ridden at the same time, Lou?"

All I could manage to work from my throat was a strangled sound of encouragement. I felt Rafael's smirk in the press of his lips against my shoulder blade. Then there was a clicking sound.

When his fingers returned to my ass, they were slick with lubricant. I didn't know when he'd gotten it or how he'd anticipated this moment, but I sure as hell wasn't complaining.

Rafael worked one finger inside me and then another, provoking a different but equally heady burn of penetration. As he stretched me, readying me for his thick cock, I started panting.

The bliss rippling through me had already brought me to the brink. But I wasn't going to give myself over to it until I'd felt everything my men had to offer.

At the first nudge of his cock against my back entrance, I bit back a whimper. It turned into a giddy gasp as he slid in ever so slowly, swaying with Niko's motions beneath me. I slowed, allowing him to take me until he was balls deep and my whole body rang out with the pleasure of it.

Then we all started moving again, gradually gaining speed as we found our harmony with each other. The roar of pleasure drowned out every sensation other than the ecstasy roiling through me.

Jasper slipped his hand between me and Niko to massage my clit, and the extra jolt of delight made me determined to pay him back just as much. I arched over with a tug at his hips, urging him into a position where I could join Niko's efforts.

My tongue lapped over the head of his cock, and Jasper groaned. I let it slide between my lips with every vigorous stroke of Niko's hand.

A guttural sound resounded from Jasper's chest. "Fuck, that's amazing. Oh, fuck. I'm going to…"

The rasped words were enough of a warning, but I had no intention of pulling back. I reveled in the spurt of his cum into my mouth.

Rafael grunted behind me, driving into me with all the force I loved, while Niko pounded my pussy like it was his last day on earth. I tried to stretch out the bliss a little longer, but my self-control careened away from me.

I cried out my climax to the ceiling, quaking between my men, clutching on to them as I soared over the edge. Stars sparked behind my hazed eyes.

My orgasm caught Niko up in its impact. He groaned, and his cock pulsed wildly inside of me. He slowed his thrusting as he poured out his own release.

Rafael was not so easily won over. He looped an arm along my stomach and increased his pace. I worked my body against him, giving him everything he gave me. As he gripped my hips with both hands and let out a roar that set my skin quivering, I came again on the heels of my first climax.

We sagged together in a jumble of naked limbs. I hummed happily, totally sated. "Now all I need is a joint cuddle under the covers."

Rafael let out a peal of laughter. "You're going to need to get a bigger bed," he said. "Make room for all of us to fit."

Like he was already imagining the four of us tucked together on one mattress. Like he *wanted* that.

A grin stretched across my face with the almost unbearable happiness that we'd all come to accept our strange relationship. "I bet that could be arranged."

TWENTY-EIGHT

Luciana

I WOKE up early the next morning feeling parched but otherwise content. Despite my current bed only being a normal-sized queen, my three men had managed to squeeze onto it around me anyway. The heat of their bodies surrounded me, along with Rafael's soft snores and Jasper's and Niko's drowsy breaths.

For a moment, I just lay there, luxuriating in the sense of love and companionship unlike any I'd ever known before. But my throat kept panging with its demand for hydration, and my bladder twinged too.

Grimacing, I eased myself out from between the three sleeping men and managed to slip off the bed without waking any of them.

On my way out of the bedroom, I grabbed my phone, but Emi hadn't sent any new texts overnight. Sometimes she forgot that we were on totally opposite daylight schedules with her on the other side of the world.

I tucked the phone into the pocket of my pajama shorts, made a quick stop in the bathroom, and then ambled over to the kitchen to pour myself a glass of water from the faucet. Leaning against the counter in the faint dawn light, I took a few slow gulps until the itch of thirst retreated.

I was just setting the glass down, planning to clamber back into my manly nest on the bed, when my phone chimed after all.

My lips twitched into a smile, anticipating a barrage of emojis, but when I glanced at the screen, my body tensed.

The number wasn't anyone in my contacts, but the message made it clear enough who'd sent it.

Hey. It's Quentin. I need to talk to you.

I raised an eyebrow at the implicit demand. Maybe *I* needed to never see his stupid if admittedly striking face again. I debated ignoring him but then decided I might as well figure out what he wanted.

How did you even get my number? I wrote back.

Registration records are a thing, you know. And not exactly top secret. Can you come down? I'd rather talk in person. I'm outside your building.

Both of my eyebrows shot upward at that last sentence. *You tracked down my address? Stalker much?*

It was also in the registration records. No big deal. Are you going to come down or what?

Still an asshole, even to the end. I blew at my bangs in exasperation, but in spite of my snarky remark about stalkers, I didn't think I'd just picked up a new one. I'd never gotten a dangerous vibe from Quentin, only a jerky one. Over the years under my mother's rule, I'd gotten lots of practice at telling the difference.

That didn't mean I wanted to chat with the guy, though.

As I hesitated, the phone chimed with a follow-up text. One that said simply, *Please?*

Huh. Exactly how much pride had that single word cost Quentin's massive ego?

I shifted my weight from one foot to the other. What could he possibly want to say to me that was so important?

Whatever it was, if I didn't go along with his request right now, chances seemed good that he'd hassle me when Jasper was around—

and possibly hassle Jasper too. I'd rather spare my skating partner the frustration of dealing with his rival if I could.

And I couldn't deny that I was a tiny bit curious too.

Fine, I typed with jabs of my thumbs. *Give me a minute.*

I pulled on a hoodie over my tank top and shorts, both to cover me up and for the comfort of my knife in the hoodie's pocket. Just in case my instincts were wrong. After shoving my feet into my sneakers, I trotted down the stairs to the lobby.

Quentin was standing just outside the glass front door. His shoulders were slightly slouched, but he straightened up when he saw me coming with a glint of what might have been *relief* in his piercing blue eyes.

As I stepped out onto the sidewalk, he drew back to make room for me. No one else was around at this early hour, the sidewalks empty, only a single car puttering past while I frowned at the uninvited visitor with my hands shoved in my pockets.

Quentin swiped his hand over his hair, which was looking unusually rumpled, a few strands falling free from the slicked-back 'do. He glanced at the sidewalk and then back at me as if he didn't know what to say. As if he wasn't the one who'd called me out here.

"Well?" I said, raising my chin. "What's going on? What are you dragging me down here in the middle of the night for?"

Even now, he couldn't restrain that arrogant smirk. "Technically it's the early morning."

I glowered at him. "Who the fuck cares about the details? Everyone's asleep. What's so important it couldn't wait until after breakfast?"

His jaw worked. "I was hoping I could see you without St. Pierre as your shadow."

"Here I am. Are you going to get on with telling me what you want?"

Quentin cocked his head. "What if I just wanted to see you?"

"Seriously?" I let out a scoffing sound and spun on my heel toward the apartment entrance. "That's not even a real reason."

Before I could take a single step, Quentin's hand shot out. He caught me by the upper arm and whirled me around faster than I could have anticipated to push me against the wall next to the door. He leaned close, his arms caging me in.

He hadn't yanked me hard enough to hurt, but my temper flared anyway. In an instant, my knife was in my hand, the blade aimed at Quentin's chest.

My heart thumped away, an electric buzz passing through my nerves as Quentin glanced down at the knife and then back at me with a faintly amused expression. Not that I'd ever admit it, but something about his complete disregard for the obvious threat turned me on.

"I'm not done," he said, his voice low and taut with an intensity that quivered over my skin. "I was going to tell you that I'm going back to Singles. I can still compete at Nationals that way thanks to my placement last year."

My jaw clenched before I managed to speak through my annoyance. "And I should care because…?"

He smiled with a flash of his white teeth. "I'll admit that you and Jasper beat me, but I think it's mostly you. The way you skate…" He paused, the intensity in his eyes searing brighter as he held my gaze. "I haven't been able to stop thinking about you. You've gotten into my head, and I can't get you out."

The previous quiver turned into a full-out tingle, sweeping through my body against my will. I ignored the unwelcome reaction and scowled at Quentin. "That sounds like a you problem, not a me problem."

"Hmm, I wonder." He leaned even closer to me, his head bowing close enough that his breath grazed my cheek. "You knew I was there that night, didn't you? I could tell when you realized. Did you like knowing I was watching you take both of them in the locker room? Did it get you off?"

My face flushed, and I gritted my teeth, at least as pissed off because I *had* gotten off on the knowledge as because he'd brought it up.

I gave him an insistent shove, tapping the blade of my knife against his shirt. "Back the fuck off, Quentin."

"Not yet," he murmured, and then he slammed his mouth into mine.

The kiss hit me with a jolt of surprise, irritation… and a little thrill. Quentin claimed my lips with a determination that reverberated through my body in the fleeting second before he pulled himself away, just as I was about to shove him harder.

He stepped farther back, tucking his hands in his pockets. "We'll talk more later."

As the words rang in my ears like a promise, he turned and stalked off without waiting for an answer.

I wiped the back of my hand across my mouth, annoyed all over again at the shiver of heat that passed through me at the memory of the kiss. For fuck's sake, I didn't want anything like that with Quentin Wolfe, of all people. Hotness didn't trump assholery.

What the hell had gotten into him? I'd thought all he cared about was seeing Jasper—and therefore me—crash and burn. Now suddenly he wanted to strike up a relationship?

No, this was probably about Jasper too. Just a different way of trying to one-up his rival. He could forget about using me to accomplish that goal.

I peeled myself off the brick wall with a little shake. As I gathered my composure, a dark sedan cruised up to park on the other side of the street, directly opposite me.

A twang of alarm I couldn't explain resonated through my bones. I tensed, turning to dash into the lobby—

And the car door opened to reveal an all-too-familiar form, emerging from within to stand on the asphalt.

My legs locked. I stared, not quite able to believe what I was seeing. My heart pounded like a jackhammer.

My mother glided across the street with measured steps, raising her hand to hold it out to me.

"Almost as if you were waiting for me. How perfect. You've had your fun, Luciana. Now it's time to come home."

SKID SPIRAL

BLADES OF HAVOC #3

ONE

Luciana

THIS COULDN'T BE HAPPENING.

But it was, with sickening clarity. My mother was standing in front of me in the thin early morning light, just below the windows of the Boston apartment I'd called my own for the last several weeks.

Her eyebrows arched expectantly beneath the carefully sculpted waves of her dark brown hair—the same shade as my own, though mine was rumpled from sleep. I'd only given it a hasty finger-combing before I'd come down.

Her slender yet muscular body exuded the same aura of cool control it always had. She'd ordered me to come with her, and she expected me to obey without argument.

Knowing my mother, I was lucky she wasn't making the demand at gunpoint. No doubt she had a pistol concealed in her sleek pantsuit somewhere in case I forced the issue that far.

Her voice was equally cool. "Let's get going. The jet is waiting."

My legs stiffened with automatic resistance. "I don't want to go, Mom. I'm making a new life here."

Mom's eyebrows lifted higher. "What kind of life could you have running around this mundane city, living in a dreary building like this?" She flicked her hand toward the apartments behind me.

My heart lurched at the thought of her aiming her attention in that direction. I had no idea how much she knew about my exact living situation—or who I'd been living with. I had no idea how she'd found me in the first place, although I could make a few guesses.

Had Sheeran—the leader of the local gang that ran this territory for one of Mom's colleagues in the Devil's Dozen—complained to his boss after all, and the Harvester had brought my presence up with my mother? Or maybe Haggard, the lunatic who'd been stalking me for months, had tipped her off just in case our final confrontation hadn't gone his way?

I wasn't really the bloodlust-y type, but I wished I could drag that bastard out of whatever grave Rafael had dumped him in and kill him all over again.

As I searched for the right response to give Mom, apprehension prickled down my back. The three men I cared about more than anyone else in the world were sleeping two floors above us.

Rafael could hold his own in a fight, but Mom must have assumed he was with me. It'd have been too much of a coincidence for my bodyguard to have disappeared at the same time as I had unless we'd left together. She wouldn't have come unprepared to deal with him.

And if Niko and Jasper caught wind that something had gone wrong and raced in to try to help me… My skater men weren't remotely ready to face off against the Deadly Rose.

She could cut them down as easily as blinking.

I kept my voice low, afraid to make too much of a scene on the quiet street. This early in the morning, only the occasional car rumbled by.

"I can move up to better things than this. I'm just getting started. I'm making a real career for myself with my figure skating, and this is what I want to be doing. It's not like you need me back home."

Mom let out a light scoffing sound. "You're my heir. Of course I need you. I have significant plans in the works, and you're a key part of them. Be glad that I tracked you down before your absence became too noticeable, or I'd be *much* angrier than I am. The skating was always a silly dream."

I swallowed thickly. I hadn't really thought my argument would work, but I'd had to try. I still couldn't give up.

My hands dug into the pockets of my hoodie, one of them curling around the knife I'd recently held to Quentin Wolfe's chest. It was because of Jasper's rival that I was down here way too early in the morning at all—although maybe I should thank him for that. He might have saved us a confrontation right at the apartment, where I couldn't have kept my mother away from my men.

"It isn't a 'silly dream,'" I insisted. "I'm doing well enough that I've qualified for the biggest competition in the entire country. If I can score well there, I'll be brought onto the national team to compete overseas."

Mom tsked her tongue. "Whirling around on the ice like some kind of circus performer. You've even dyed your hair like a clown." She wrinkled her nose as she took in the reddish coloring I'd used in the hopes of disguising my identity. "You're meant for more than that ridiculousness, Luciana. Please don't keep me waiting any longer."

I stared at her, anger flaring up inside me. A dangerous emotion, but for the moment it held me steady.

"I told you, I don't want to go. Why should I? I know you had Coach Balakin murdered to try to get me to stop skating. He didn't deserve that, and it didn't stop me anyway. I'm an adult—it's my life."

My mother leveled her coldest glare at me, her eyes like fathomless pits. "It has never been only *your* life from the moment you were born. You belong to the legacy of the Deadly Rose, and you will return and take your proper place. And if you don't come along right now, your new skater friends will meet similar unfortunate fates to Balakin's."

Nausea unfurled in my gut. She wasn't denying what she'd done—hell, she was doubling down, threatening to do it again.

And I knew she wasn't bluffing.

Images flashed behind my eyes: the memories of my old coach's bloody body, slumped on the rink in Austin—then Jasper, then Niko, chests slashed open, gore spilling out of them…

A sweat broke out on the back of my neck. My gaze flicked toward the apartment above us, terrified that I might see one of their faces in the window right now, about to force my mother's hand.

The panes were empty, but Mom caught my glance. She shook her head. "That turncoat bodyguard of yours won't be able to keep you here either. Rafael had better stay out of my way if he wants to even keep his head attached to his neck."

She maintained the same even tone, but I knew her well enough to recognize the fury simmering beneath. Oh, she was pissed off with him, all right.

"Don't do this," I said, fighting to keep my voice from shaking. Every nerve in my body jangled with alarm. I couldn't protect my men from my mother and however many of her people she had on call here, not on my own, not even with Rafael backing me up. And then she'd kill him too. "None of this was their idea. It was all me."

"That's the only reason they aren't already in their graves." My mom swiveled toward her car, the sedan parked on the other side of the street, and snapped her fingers. "And they'll remain living as long as you come along without any more of a fight."

That was probably the only reason she hadn't immediately killed them as punishment. She realized they were more valuable to her as leverage than dead. If she tore the three men I'd fallen for away from me, she had no way to force my hand. I'd have nothing left to lose.

But I *really* didn't want things to get to that point. What was the point in winning my freedom if the people I cherished most in my new life were gone?

I didn't know what I wouldn't do just to keep even one of my men alive.

I hesitated just for an instant, and Mom moved as if to stride to the apartment lobby instead. My pulse stuttered, and I pushed myself toward the car. "Fine, fine, I'm coming."

What other choice did I have?

I had to go with her for now, figure out what she was planning, and hopefully put together a plan of my own that would let me find a way back to my guys while keeping them safe. I could play along if it stopped her from dealing out vengeance.

As I walked up to the car, my fingernails dug into my palms. The driver, an ugly brute with a crooked nose and heavy-knuckled hands, got out to open the back door for me.

I sat down and slid over on the smooth leather seat with a reluctant jerk of my body. The motion woke up the ache in my side where Sheeran's men had done a number on my ribs before I'd brokered a sort of peace with him.

I'd pushed my body awfully hard since then, relying on a cortisone shot to dampen the pain. I'd meant to spend the next few days resting and letting myself heal.

So much for that.

So much for any of my goals. The National Championships were happening in just two months. Was there *any* way I could sort this mess out in time?

I didn't just need to get out from under Mom's thumb before the championships—I'd need practice time too. We weren't going to impress anyone if I showed up two months out of shape.

And it wouldn't be only *my* skating debut ruined. Jasper's comeback would fall apart too.

A smothering weight filled my chest. I gritted my teeth against the prick of tears at the back of my eyes.

They were going to be so worried—all three of them. Rafael would go absolutely apeshit. They wouldn't even know I was still alive.

But telling them what had happened could draw them right into the danger I was trying to spare them.

Fuck, fuck, *fuck*.

Mom lowered herself into the seat next to me, all menacing grace. A shiver rippled over my skin as I watched her.

I hadn't seen her since the conversation when I'd realized that she'd had Coach Balakin murdered. Since it'd sunk in just how brutally ruthless she could be.

I hated her. Did she have the slightest clue how much acid ran through my veins when I looked at her?

Maybe, but she didn't give a shit as long as she got what she wanted.

She brushed her hands together and motioned to the driver. "Take us straight to the airfield. I want to get back to Austin as quickly as possible."

"Yes, ma'am."

Mom's gaze slid to me. I could feel her sizing me up, seething over the time I'd already cost her with this mission. But in front of her employee, she didn't harp on it.

I could probably look forward to plenty of harping later, when we were really alone.

I sagged into the seat and wet my lips, mentally scrambling for something to hold on to. I had to start strengthening my position as quickly as possible too. That was what Mom would have done in a situation like this.

To beat her, I'd have to think like her.

"You said you have plans that you need me for," I said with forced nonchalance. "Are you going to fill me in on what I'm getting into?"

Mom lifted her shoulders in an effortless shrug. "Oh, you don't have to worry about that yet."

"I'm not *worried*. I'd just like to start preparing myself. You want me to do a good job with whatever it is, don't you?"

I'd thought that appeal had a chance of hitting the mark, but Mom didn't look remotely swayed.

"Patience, mija," she said calmly. "I'll bring you up to speed step by step, as you need to know."

She added a firm note to the last few words—a hint of finality. She expected me to leave the subject alone now.

The ache of my ribs spread all through my torso, most of it not physical pain anymore. I tugged my gaze away, tuning out the growing sense of hopelessness as well as I could, and watched the last remnants of my new life drift by beyond the car window.

TWO

Niko

THE SUN WAS HITTING my eyelids from the wrong angle. Normally it didn't pierce right into them like this.

I knit my brow, trying to orient myself in my half-asleep daze, and rolled onto my side to put my back to the source of the light. My hand brushed a warm arm next to me.

My eyes popped open, and I found myself staring bleary-eyed at Jasper.

Oh. *Oh*. After last night…

After our very enjoyable time with Lou last night, sharing her between the three of us, we'd somehow all tucked ourselves around her on her bed and fallen asleep. That's why the window was in the wrong place. I was in the wrong room.

It was also why the man I found just as appealing as our shared lover was lying just a foot away from me.

It was only the two of us in the bed now. The covers were rumpled, pooled around our waists. Lou and Rafael must have used their criminal stealth skills to sneak out of bed without waking us and go get breakfast.

Which meant I alone got this fantastic view of Jasper St. Pierre's sculpted torso. Of his wild auburn waves tumbling across his pale forehead.

I resisted the urge to brush them away from his closed eyes. Asleep, he looked more at peace than I'd ever seen him.

Adorably so. Not that I thought Jasper would appreciate being called "adorable," so I'd keep that thought to myself.

Last night had really been something. I'd taken part in a couple of threesomes during my wilder days in my early twenties, but a foursome was a totally different level of passion. And acrobatics. Somehow we'd managed to all find our satisfaction while pleasing Lou together.

She was some woman, no doubt about it. I'd have to remind her of that the next time I saw her.

For now, I could enjoy watching my adorable grump of a boyfriend—if I was allowed to call him that. We'd never actually talked about labels.

Jasper stirred, and his eyes opened to reveal the gray-green irises. For once, they looked more curious than stormy. He gazed back at me, and his lips curved up to form the tender expression he'd been giving me more and more lately. An expression that made me giddy.

"Huh," he said. "Good morning."

I couldn't hold back a grin. "What if we make it an even better one?"

His smile grew. "I could possibly be persuaded. Give it your best shot."

How could I resist an invitation like that?

I scooted closer, tipping my head to seek out his lips, and he raised his chin to meet my kiss. The moment our mouths collided, heat rushed through my body.

This... This was fantastic too.

Jasper tucked one hand under my head, his thumb stroking over my cheek as he deepened the kiss. My pulse fluttered at the affection of the gesture.

Fondness and desire wound together in my chest. I trailed my fingers over the planes of muscle I'd been admiring moments ago, treasuring his hum of approval.

As I circled one of Jasper's pert nipples with my thumb, he flicked his tongue into my mouth. Then he withdrew it to test the edges of his teeth against my lower lip with an eager nip.

Pleasure jolted through my body. I teased my fingers down to his waist and back up again, and Jasper responded by grasping my hip through the sheets. In a gesture I suspected was more instinctive than conscious, he yanked our groins together.

The second our bodies aligned, it was obvious we were both already hard. My erection pressed into his with a spike of deeper arousal—and Jasper froze.

His lips lingered against mine, but the rest of his frame had gone still. His breath stuttered over my skin.

We'd never done more than kiss when Lou wasn't part of the equation. I was the first man Jasper had ever gotten intimate with. It wasn't surprising he'd have moments of hesitation and awkwardness.

His mouth moved against mine again, more cautiously than before. I could still feel the tension that had tightened his muscles.

Did he think he had to push himself farther than he was comfortable with to please me? Had I *made* him believe that, nudged him to experiment more than he was really comfortable with?

It wouldn't be the first time I'd overstepped with someone I cared about, too caught up in my own ideas of how our relationship should be to recognize their needs in time.

My stomach dropped. I returned Jasper's kiss carefully and then eased back with a smile so he wouldn't take my ending the make-out session as a rejection. I tugged my hips backward at the same time so I wasn't imposing so much down below either.

Apparently I hadn't been subtle enough in my withdrawal. Jasper blinked at me with obvious confusion. "Is something wrong?"

I could almost hear my sister calling me "Baka!" and making a rude gesture in my direction. Now I'd messed up in a totally different way.

I steadied my smile with all the genuine appreciation I could compel into it. “Of course not. I’m just starving. All that stomach grumbling can really ruin the mood.”

Jasper’s forehead furrowed, maybe because my stomach hadn’t actually grumbled. His gaze held me in place with its penetrating power. “You just want to get breakfast? Are you sure that—”

Before he could finish a question I’d have fumbled to answer, the bedroom door burst open. Rafael stood on the threshold, his massive form filling the doorway, his dark brown eyes unnervingly wild.

“Have either of you seen Lou?” he demanded. “Do you know where she went?”

As I took in his frantic state, my throat constricted. “No. She was already gone when I woke up. I thought she was with you.”

Jasper nodded, sitting upright. “Same. She isn’t in the apartment?”

Somehow Rafael’s expression managed to darken even more. I half-expected lightning to start crackling over his head.

“She was already gone when *I* woke up,” he said. “I thought she was getting takeout for breakfast to surprise us. But she’s been gone for a while—too long. I tried texting her five minutes ago, and it’s still showing as unread.”

My pulse stuttered. “It’s not like her to ignore you, is it?”

“No.” Rafael turned on his heel and stalked down the hall. “She wouldn’t have just *left*. There’s no sign of anyone breaking in. How could they have without me noticing? Fuck!”

His obvious agitation set my own nerves on edge. I scrambled out of the bed and hastily tugged on my track pants.

Jasper followed, his eyes gone wide with worry. “This is her room. She left all her stuff—her suitcase.” He opened the closet, where several outfits including her skating costumes hung. “The clothes she’s unpacked.”

Rafael’s voice carried down the hall. “Her equipment bag is over here by the door. Skates are still in there and everything.”

Jasper hustled to the living room, and I followed at his heels. Rafael was just picking up the purse Lou had tucked into her duffel bag.

He pulled out her wallet and clicked it open. “She didn’t even take her cash or her ID.”

My gut knotted. I had no idea just how bad this situation could be. I'd still been wrapping my head around the idea of Lou as a mafia heir who could be targeted by stalkers and gangs. How much worse could things get?

"What *is* gone?" I asked. "Did she take anything with her, or is it like she was grabbed out of the blue?"

Rafael spun toward me with a glower. "No one could have kidnapped her right from under my nose. She'd have put up a fight."

Jasper held up his hands. "We know. We're just trying to figure this out."

Rafael dragged in a deep breath. It was unsettling, seeing the man who was normally so intense and focused falling apart in a panic.

He seemed to gather himself and marched in another circuit of the apartment, taking stock. "I haven't been able to find her phone, and I didn't hear the alert when I texted her. So she went somewhere with that. I haven't found her keys either."

I forced my mind to think through the logic of the scenario. "Then she must have left the apartment on purpose. She stepped out but didn't expect to be gone for long enough to need anything else."

And then… someone had grabbed her beyond these walls? Had the Boston gang come after her again despite our truce with Sheeran—or was it some new enemy we hadn't been prepared for?

My hands opened and closed at my sides. I'd never felt so useless in my life.

Jasper picked up his own phone off the coffee table and flicked the screen on. He inhaled sharply. "She texted me."

"What?" Rafael was at his side in an instant. I hurried over to peer over Jasper's shoulder.

Jasper frowned. "It must have come in while I was still asleep. It was sent around six thirty. But—this doesn't make any sense."

I could read the message for myself. *I'm so sorry. I can't do this anymore.*

That was it. No explanation, no indication of what "this" even was.

Rafael rubbed his mouth. "No. She wouldn't have ended things this way. Even if she decided it was too dangerous for her to keep skating, which I can't picture happening in the first place, she wouldn't have left *me*."

I wanted to protest, but I knew he had a point. Lou had tried to protect Jasper and me from the darker side of her past again and again. There was a slight possibility that she might have decided she couldn't risk dragging us into more danger.

But Rafael had been with her for most of her past. She knew he could handle it. It didn't make sense for her to run off on him without a word.

Rafael raked his hand through the short black coils of his hair. "It isn't her. Not really. She wouldn't have left on purpose, and she wouldn't have sent you that text as the only sign of it. Someone has her—someone who made her write that message hoping it'd convince you that she's okay, just gone."

We stared at each other, a sense of doom descending over the room. I could barely breathe.

"Who?" I forced myself to ask. "Who would have taken her?"

Rafael let out a growl of frustration. "I don't have a fucking clue—and I have no idea how we're going to find out."

THREE

Luciana

WITH OTHER COMPANY, I might have enjoyed the flight. Mom's private jet boasted buttery leather seats with ample leg room and a wide variety of refreshments served by one of her employees. The small craft soared smoothly through the air with just a faint rumble of the engine.

All the turbulence was going on inside me.

Mom lounged in the seat across from me, sipping a Cosmo from the glass she periodically set on the burnished imitation-wood table between us. She gave every appearance of being relaxed, but I knew her too well to believe it.

Every time she gripped the glass's stem, her knuckles paled with unspoken tension. The perfect ovals of her maroon fingernails tapped an intermittent rhythm on the tabletop.

I yanked my gaze away from her, but the view outside the window didn't comfort me at all. With every passing minute, we left the gritty streets of Boston behind.

I'd liked living in Austin, even if I hadn't enjoyed the overall lifestyle I'd been forced into under my mother's roof. It was a vibrant city with a quirky atmosphere I'd have been able to enjoy even more if I hadn't needed to worry about keeping up appearances for Mom's crew.

But now it was the last place I wanted to be. Every mile closer we got was a mile farther from my dreams of the National Championships. From the men who'd helped me reach for that dream.

What would they have made of my disappearance? They must have noticed by now.

Would they believe the stupid text Mom had insisted I write before she'd confiscated my phone? I didn't know whether I should hope that they did so they'd stay out of the danger or that they'd have more faith in me… and be even more worried about my safety.

Mom set her glass down again with a firm clink. "That expression doesn't suit you. A good leader doesn't show her emotions on her face. Anything you give away, our enemies can use to exploit you."

That was rich, considering that my greatest enemy right now was the woman giving me advice. I bit my tongue against pointing that fact out to her and drew my posture up a little straighter before she could criticize it too, willing the tension out of my face.

Play along, figure out what she was up to, and then untangle myself from the mess ASAP. That was the plan. I could follow it.

Mom continued to appraise me for a moment that felt like an eternity, her attention making my skin prickle with discomfort. She let out a soft sigh. "I've dealt with our underlings who helped you in your little bid for adventure. You won't be counting on them again."

Despite her admonishment to hide my emotions, my forehead furrowed before I could stop it. Which was probably a good thing, because she should see my genuine confusion.

"What are you talking about? No one at the house helped me. Even—"

I snapped my mouth shut before I could mention that Rafael hadn't either—he'd simply followed me and insisted on coming along. I could have taken off all on my own if I'd wanted to.

Mom hummed to herself as if my answer had given something

away. I wasn't sure there was anything to be gained by arguing with her.

Instead, I gave her a little prodding of my own. "How did you know where to find me? I wouldn't think you'd listen to random tips."

She let out a chuckle, but there was acid in the sound. "Oh, I wouldn't call it 'random' when it came with video evidence attached. You should have known that with my connections, you couldn't expect to stay in hiding. But I suppose I should be glad you've gotten your restlessness out of your system."

Her tone carried a threat. I'd *better* have gotten it out of my system, she was saying, or I'd regret it.

I forced a slightly wider smile. "Yeah, I guess you could see it that way. Just, really—relying on a former employee you kicked out for being too much of a psycho... That had to sting."

I was taking a stab in the dark, but it landed. A muscle twitched in Mom's jaw before she shook her head without answering.

It had been Haggard, then. That fucking asshole, screwing me over from beyond the grave.

At least I knew my truce with the Harvester's people had theoretically held. I couldn't imagine Mom would have collected me this peacefully if I'd brought her empire to the brink of war.

She took another sip from her Cosmo and kept the glass in her hand as a faint vibration rippled through the plane. "Let's leave your mistakes behind us, Luciana. We have a lot of future to look forward to—and prepare for."

My heart thumped a little faster. "Are you going to tell me what those preparations involve?"

Mom glanced around, confirming that the small crew on the jet was tucked away at the front where the thrum of the engine would make it difficult for them to eavesdrop. "Now that we're on our way, we may as well go over our initial steps—and my expectations of you."

Oh, joy. I kept my obedient smile plastered to my face while I seethed. I did need to find out what she wanted me to do. "Go ahead."

She grazed her fingernails over the table with a soft but unnerving hiss. "You should join the physical training regimen all of our core employees participate in. No one knows the exact reasons for your absence, but it would be wise to remind them of your strength and combat skills to help you re-integrate as an authority figure among them."

"I can do that." It'd also hone my skills for getting those employees off my back if I was going to make a break for it. And keep my body in decent physical shape.

"Yes, you can," Mom said with a dry edge to her voice. "I'm also going to have you accompany me during some of my social engagements with our more powerful supporters. I want them to see that you're present and ready to step up. No one should be getting any ideas about our chain of inheritance weakening."

I hated that word on her lips — *our.* It tied me to her in a sticky web, one I hadn't managed to wriggle free of despite my best efforts.

I could handle being paraded around in front of her friends. Nothing she'd mentioned told me why it was ever so vital that I came home, though.

"None of this sounds very urgent," I remarked, studying her.

Mom flicked her fingers dismissively. "We'll get to the important parts once we've established the groundwork. But I wasn't finished. I'll also be setting up meetings for you with a few other members of the Devil's Dozen. I'd like you to feel out their respect for the Deadly Rose and confirm that none of them have seen your disappearance as an opening to test us."

A trickle of cold ran through my chest to pool in my stomach. "You want me to talk to your direct associates? Would they even have heard about me leaving?"

Mom's knuckles paled again with her silent tension. "It's likely some of them have found out. We all keep a fairly close eye on each other's activities. But they don't know the reason, and we're going to keep it that way."

I could agree with that. Meeting with the other Devil's Dozen members was like walking into a lion's den. I'd rather not give them additional ammunition against me.

At least with Mom, I knew she wanted me alive and well so I could support her. With the jockeying for power that went on within the Devil's Dozen, the thirteen most powerful criminal kingpins in the world, any of them might be happy to see me fall.

I'd never met with any of the others before. I only knew them by name. Even with the Harvester, he'd never confronted me directly.

But Mom was determined that I was going to fill her shoes one day. Apparently she'd decided it was time to fast-track me up the ladder to a full second-in-command.

I wanted that role even less than I'd wanted to be a foot soldier. The invisible shackles that chained me to this life seemed to tighten around my wrists.

The weight of those bonds dragged at me. I couldn't help making one last-ditch attempt at changing her mind.

"Mom… You know I've never been enthusiastic about the work we do. I'm not sure how good I can be at it when it's not something I want. Are you sure it wouldn't be better for you to mentor someone you trust from outside the family, someone who does have a passion for it, to eventually pass the reins on to—"

She held up one finger to silence me. Her voice came out chillingly cool.

"You were born for this, Luciana. Our family is a pillar, and if a key piece falls aside, everyone will be watching for the whole building to collapse. You know better than to even ask that."

I did, but I hadn't been able to help it anyway. I swallowed thickly, groping for the right words to convince her, but nothing came to me.

And then she went on, her voice dropping ominously low. "If I hear any further talk about returning to your silly hobby and the company you found there, you can be sure you'll run to those men of yours and find them ready for their graves."

Panic shot through my veins. I clamped my mouth shut and shoved my protests deep into the back of my mind.

"Understood," I said, managing to keep my voice steady. "I won't let you down."

Mom let out a faint huff and sank back in her seat again. "I certainly hope you won't. But we'll shape you into the woman you were meant to be, one way or another."

I peered out the window at the tufts of white cloud and kept as much of a mask over my expression as I could. My spirits had sunk lower than I could ever remember, a dark cloud rolling over me.

There really was no way she'd ever *let* me revisit my skating career. Not even as a hobby. For now… I had to give it up, even though the thought made me want to scream and bawl at the same time.

All I could do was accept her demands in silence and thank my lucky stars for what I did still have. The three men I'd fallen for were alive and reasonably well. Mom wasn't asking me to do any tasks that were especially dangerous and violent… yet.

The only way that I was going to win my freedom was by appeasing her until I had a chance to escape. I just wished I could see a clearer way through to the ending—one that wasn't drenched in blood.

FOUR

Jasper

I WALKED through the kitchen and back to the living room with no idea what I was trying to accomplish but desperate to do something. No clues about Lou's disappearance offered themselves up.

Niko was pawing through the trash bin in case she'd thrown something away that would tip us off, a similar air of desperation rising off him. Rafael had folded his arms over his chest as he surveyed the apartment's common areas, but I could see the panic behind his air of stern authority.

My teeth gritted of their own accord. The frustration I'd been trying to hold in burst out of me.

"How the fuck could this have happened? Isn't keeping Lou safe your literal *job*?"

Rafael's gaze jerked to me. "Shut the hell up. If I knew how to find her, I'd be doing it."

"What, like you managed to protect her so well when you were lying in the same fucking bed as her?" My hands clenched at my sides. "What kind of bodyguard are you?"

He narrowed his eyes. "You were sleeping in that bed too, asshole."

Niko stepped between us, holding up his hands. "Whoa, whoa. Let's calm down. We won't get anywhere if we're attacking each other."

I knew he was right, but the tremor that ran through his pacifying voice only pricked at the tension inside me. With an inarticulate growl, I spun away from both of them and marched back to her bedroom.

The worst thing was not knowing if she was in danger… or if she'd decided sticking with us was too risky and left of her own accord. She'd snuck away without disturbing any of us.

I swiveled on my heel inside the room, scanning the bed with its rumpled covers, the suitcase she'd only half unpacked even though we'd been living here for several weeks. My gaze caught on a flash of bright orange half-buried under a hoodie.

Frowning, I marched over and snatched the object up. For a second, I just stared at it.

It was one of the cheap plastic sports bottles the owners of Hobb Creek's arena gave out as a promotional item. Lou must have nabbed one during our training there, months ago.

The arena's mascot peered back at me. I had no idea what the artist who'd designed it had been going for—the thing looked like a mix between a walrus and a penguin. Somehow I suspected the arena owners hadn't broken the bank commissioning that illustration.

An ache spread through my torso as I took it in. Lou hadn't had any reason to hold on to this thing other than for the memories. Memories of the place where she'd first met Niko and me. Where she'd discovered that her dreams of making her mark on the ice could be more than just dreams.

I ran my fingers across the smooth plastic, my own memories playing like a film reel in my head: Lou, on the first day we'd met her, her eyes widening at the sight of us while she'd tried to play it cool. Lou, damp with sweat but still resolute during her training. Lou, grinning away, tears stinging her eyes during the announcement that we'd smashed the rest of the competition.

And now she was gone.

She'd cared enough to keep some tacky souvenir of our early training. She couldn't have cared *that* much and left anyway, without saying a word.

Right?

An impulse guided me to her equipment bag by the front door. I unzipped the side pocket she'd shown me once before, when we'd first been getting to know each other. The one that held the little scrap of fabric from her first childhood skates.

The fragile, grayed lace caught on my fingers. I lifted it up, rubbing the fabric gently between my fingers. My throat closed up.

"Guys!" I said, my voice coming out strained.

Whatever Rafael thought of my previous sniping, he hustled over in an instant, Niko beside him. My coach cocked his head. "What's that?"

"Her lucky lace." I tucked it back into the pocket for safe-keeping. When we got her back, it'd be right here waiting for her where she'd left it.

Straightening up, I turned toward the other two men. "There's no way she'd have left purposefully without taking that with her. She's held on to that thing since she was five years old. Something *must* have happened to her—something that forced her to leave."

Rafael sighed. "That's what I already thought. I don't suppose you've found anything that would give us some idea what or where."

My head drooped. "No. There's nothing in here." I paused. "We don't know why she left the apartment, but that might not have had anything to do with how she got taken anyway. What if she *did* simply go out to get breakfast or something, and got caught up in trouble along the way? There might be evidence out there."

"This isn't a crime show," Rafael muttered, but he reached for the door. "I already did a brief sweep of the area, but it couldn't hurt to look again."

Somehow Rafael ended up taking the lead, even though checking outside had been my idea. Niko and I trailed behind him like stray dogs.

There wasn't a whole lot to inspect on our way out of the building.

The lobby looked the same as always. So did the sidewalk beyond. I poked around in a hedge that lined a nearby parking lot and only spotted a few random pieces of litter.

Lou would have left a real message if she could have, wouldn't she?

What the hell were we going to do if she hadn't been able to? If all we had to go by was that final, vague text?

More irritation jittered through my veins. I couldn't help picturing how she'd looked after those assholes with Sheeran had pummeled her, how stormy black the bruises on her ribs had become.

Someone even worse might have her now. And we were doing shit-all about it. My hands curled into fists.

Then a figure stepped into view at the far end of the parking lot. A figure that was tall, blond, and guaranteed to piss me off even more in five seconds flat.

My stance tensed automatically. "What the hell are you doing here, Wolfe?"

Quentin had stiffened too. My rival studied me with the piercing blue eyes that always seemed to pick out the flaws I was most self-conscious of. But today his demeanor was unusually uncertain.

"I wasn't aware that you owned the city, St. Pierre," he retorted with only a trace of his usual snark. "A guy can go for a walk."

That might be true, but everything about his sudden appearance here—on this morning of all mornings—felt wrong.

I marched up to him. "Tell me why the fuck you're here or I'll give you a matching scar on the other side of that jaw."

Quentin's mouth tightened, making the pale line that cut through his lip stand out more starkly. "And of course you'd come at me like a goddamn caveman. It's amazing you can manage to stand up on the ice."

I restrained another growl. "You really don't want to fuck with me today."

"Because Lou's gone? Do you think you're going to find her in a hedge?"

If he hadn't caught me so off-guard, I might have grabbed him and slammed him into the concrete wall of the building behind him. Instead, I froze.

Rafael didn't have the same problem. He must have come up behind me while we'd talked—he definitely caught that last remark.

The bodyguard barreled past me and snatched Quentin by the front of his white tee, jerking him within reach of his balled fist. "Tell us what you know—now, before I have to start breaking bones you'd rather keep whole."

Quentin flinched but kept his chin up. To my annoyance, I had to respect his composure in the face of Rafael's threat, just a little.

"All right, all right," he said tersely. "I was going to tell you about it anyway. I just wasn't sure— I came by to see Lou this morning. I wanted the chance to talk to her without the three of you hovering around her like vultures."

I rolled my eyes at the description, my own hands balling. "Talk to her about what?"

"That's none of your fucking business." Quentin's shoulders hunched slightly, but I couldn't tell whether it was the subject of their conversation that he was uncomfortable with or what he had to say next. "After we had our chat, I made to leave, but I wanted to see what she'd do. So I stuck around over here where she wouldn't notice me."

Niko had come over to join us too. He knit his brow. "You know you sound like a stalker, don't you?"

Quentin glowered at him. "It wasn't anything like *that*. And you should be glad I did, because I saw what happened next."

Rafael gave his shirt another menacing tug. "And what was that?"

"A car showed up right after. A woman got out and walked over to Lou." Quentin's mouth twisted. "Lou obviously wasn't happy to see her. It looked like they were arguing, but quietly. I couldn't hear them from over here. Finally, Lou went over to the car with her and they drove away. But I don't think she wanted to go. She didn't even go back to the apartment to get any of her things."

Rafael swore under his breath and relaxed his hold on Quentin. "Describe the woman. What did she look like?"

Quentin tilted his head as he thought back. "Middle-aged, thin, long dark hair. Stylish clothes. Like she was on her way to some high-class business meeting. It was weird."

I could tell from Rafael's expression that this was not good. He raked his fingers back over his black coils and sucked a breath through his teeth with a hiss. "God fucking damn it."

Quentin focused on him. "You know her? Lou seemed to—not in a good way."

"No, it's incredibly fucking bad." Rafael turned away from him to face me and Niko. "That's got to be Mireya—Lou's mom. You know everything Lou told you about her. And that's only a bit of it. If she's got her claws into Lou again, there's no way she's letting her go. She figures Lou *belongs* to her."

My heart skipped a beat. "Doesn't she care at all what Lou wants?"

Rafael shook his head. "What Mireya wants, she sees that she gets. And she wants an heir, not a figure-skating sensation. She's already killed to try to ensure she's got Lou under her thumb."

A chill sank into my skin, sharper than the late autumn air. "What the hell are we going to do?"

Niko shifted his weight from one foot to the other. "She'll have taken her back to Austin, then?"

"Most likely," Rafael said. "That's her base of operations."

I grimaced. "No point in sending a text or making a call, I guess. We know her mom's gotten control over her phone."

Quentin cleared his throat. "I don't know anything about this woman, but we're going to go to Austin and get Lou back, aren't we?"

I swung toward him. "*We?* How the hell do you figure you're any part of this situation, Wolfe?"

He glared back at me. "I figure I'm the person who told you how to find Lou in the first place. If she's in trouble, I want to help get her out of it."

A harsh laugh tore from my throat. I could barely believe what I was hearing. "Are you for real? After everything you've put Lou and me through? I have no idea what you're playing at now, but you can fuck off."

"If I'd done that to begin with, you'd have no idea what happened to her."

"Great. Now you've gotten to lord that over us. If you imagine you have *any* right to weasel your way into some rescue mission when I know you'd rather spit on us than—"

"I wouldn't," he broke in. "I came to make peace."

I fell silent, blinking at him. Neither Rafael nor Niko seemed to have any idea what to say next either.

Quentin stuffed his hands in the pockets of his jeans, looking uncertain again and even a little deflated. He dropped his gaze to the asphalt before meeting my eyes.

"You're right. I've been a prick to you all through the competition. You're lucky to have her, and I—I'm not such an asshole that I'd want to see her get shit on just to spite you. Okay?"

I scowled at him. "Okay. Sure. And I should care why?"

Quentin appeared to weigh his words. "I don't know exactly what Lou is mixed up in. But I really might be able to help if it's anything like it sounds. I know the shady side of, well, life better than you or Okabe here possibly could. I grew up on the wrong side of the tracks."

Rafael snorted. "There's nothing you could tell us that I wouldn't already know."

Quentin gave him an evaluating look. "Are you completely sure of that? You'd really throw away the possibility that I might contribute something useful?" His gaze slid back to me. "What's more important—saving Lou or holding on to our stupid rivalry?"

It was always your *rivalry*, I wanted to snap at him. *I never asked for it in the first place.*

But maybe that was all the more reason to let that animosity go. As much as it burned me up imagining having this jerk around while we tried to extricate Lou from her mother, I had to admit I was totally out of my depth.

It couldn't have been easy for him to make this overture. To approach us at all. He could have run off and taken what he'd seen to his grave.

But for whatever reason, Lou mattered enough to him that he'd stuck around to tell us. That he was debating with me now, practically begging me to let him pitch in.

I would be the real ass if I refused him over my grievances, which I could admit were a hell of a lot pettier than what Lou would be facing at her mother's hands.

I glanced at Rafael. His mouth had set in a flat line, but he inclined his head to me slightly as if saying it was my call. Wonderful.

He wasn't arguing any more either. Apparently he was willing to accept Quentin's intrusion.

And Niko's mouth had formed a tentative smile, as if he was almost *happy* about the chance to make an alliance.

Oh, for fuck's sake. It wasn't really a choice, was it? If there was any chance Quentin could get us closer to Lou and to freeing her from her awful family, how could I not take it?

We might need all the help we could get.

"Fine," I said. "You can come along, whatever we end up doing. But I don't want to hear any more insults about any of us, or you can get packing."

Quentin's lips twitched with a smile of his own. "I think I can control myself for a little while," he said, with a gleam in his eyes that had me praying I hadn't just made the worst mistake of my life.

FIVE

Luciana

I STARED at Austin's downtown skyscrapers across the water, wishing I was anywhere but here. I had to admit, the scenery was at least nice. My present company, not so much.

In the late morning, the lakeside boardwalk only held a few locals strolling around—enough for us to easily blend in as if we were only out for a casual jaunt too, but not so many we couldn't steer clear of them for privacy's sake. This was business, after all.

The lean man ambling along at Mom's other side, flicking his hooded eyes toward her as he smiled at her latest comment, was the leader of the largest gang in the state. His long-time alliance with the Deadly Rose had benefitted both of them. She sent opportunities his way and ensured no larger forces infringed on his territory, and he filled her in on any news his contacts picked up while keeping the smaller gangs from making any trouble for her.

It was obvious from the deference in his tone and his posture that he recognized how much more power she held than he did, but you didn't become a gang boss without plenty of ruthless violence. If this man had been an enemy, he could have made a lot of trouble himself.

Which is precisely why Mom had him on a leash.

I'd zoned out of the conversation after it'd turned to exchanges of compliments over how well the two of them had handled past business deals. Now, Mom rested her hand on my shoulder.

"I'm particularly pleased to see my daughter coming into her own as I've always known she would. Luciana will be stepping up in all kinds of ways now that she's old enough to start taking the reins."

The boss eyed me with a mix of wariness and uncertainty. He saw me as just as dangerous as my mother—and just as important to impress. Too bad for him, nothing about his criminal inclinations was going to appeal to me.

Too bad for me, I had to pretend they did anyway.

His mouth formed a crooked smile. "You must be looking forward to getting to take charge and show what you can do."

Take charge, while my mom had me on a leash of my own? Show what I could do, when I couldn't pursue the one thing I was actually good at?

I stifled a dark laugh and forced my mouth to form a warmer smile than his. Time to give another Oscar-worthy performance, after I'd already contributed a few thoughts on territory lines and underling discipline earlier in the conversation.

"It's been a long time coming. I know my mother's made sure I'm fully prepared. I'm looking forward to standing more prominently by her side."

Mom's eyes burned into me, silently evaluating my response. I hoped my clown-smile was enough to satisfy her. I was here; I was doing what she wanted. Wasn't that enough?

It turned out that it was. She gave my shoulder a graceful pat as if any kind of physical affection was normal between us.

"Luciana has been doing exceptionally well at every task," she said. "She's going to be a great leader someday. I couldn't ask for more than that."

Other than me actually *wanting* to be that leader, sure. But this was the third time this week that Mom had trotted me out for one of her major local allies. She was putting on a show of how cohesive our family was, how stable the line of inheritance.

I had no idea why, though. Was she afraid someone would challenge her authority? Surely showing me off wasn't going to make much of a difference.

The wind picked up, blowing a lock of my hair across my face—dark brown strands that I swiped away. Mom had sent me to a salon within a day of my return to restore my dyed red waves to their natural color.

Even on that small scale, she controlled *me* completely.

We meandered on into the parking lot and parted ways with the gang boss with respectful nods on both sides. Mom rested her hand on my back, guiding me back to the sedan we'd arrived in. I slid into the backseat, thankful that the tinted windows meant I could drop my false smile for just a moment.

Until Mom eased in after me.

As her driver started the engine, she shot me a triumphant glance. "You handled yourself well, as you did before. But of course, as a Cordova, you're a natural at this."

A natural at faking my devotion to her life of crime? Wonderful.

"I learned everything from you," I said honestly. "What are all these meetings leading up to, anyway?"

Mom leaned back in her seat, but I knew her too well to believe she was actually relaxed. "Not every action needs to be building toward an immediate goal. It's important that you build your relations with the people we rely on. Speaking of which, I have a more important meeting scheduled for you tomorrow."

I restrained a groan. "Another gang boss?"

"Not exactly." She aimed a narrow smile at me. "You'll be having lunch with a representative from the March Wind—one of my colleagues in the Devil's Dozen. On your own. I want you to feel her out without me present, see what she might reveal if she lets her guard down a little."

My heart sank. I'd had my fill of dealing with Devil's Dozen people after getting harassed by the Harvester's associates in Boston. "I'm supposed to just show up and chat?"

"Well, the meeting is technically to set up the terms for a possible business trade that the March Wind and I are discussing. That's all the excuse we needed. What I really want you to do is figure out how friendly the March Wind is towards the Deadly Rose in general."

My brow knit. "That's all?"

Mom clicked her tongue. "That's all?" she echoed. "I think you'll find, Luciana, that determining who our friends are is critical—sometimes even more than discovering our foes."

Sitting on the sleek chair in the high-end Houston restaurant, I fought the urge to squirm. Fidgeting definitely wouldn't fit the white-tableclothed, sparkling-chandelier atmosphere of the place.

My brief reprieve alone at the table didn't last long. I could tell who the March Wind's representative was the moment that she appeared at the host stand. A twenty-something woman in a posh business dress, her sleek black ponytail trailed between her slender shoulders. The hostess smiled at her and pointed in my direction. My stomach flipped over.

I let out a slow breath, girding myself. Now was not the time to be uncertain. I definitely didn't want to piss my mom off by screwing this meeting up out of nerves. To top that off, the March Wind was just as dangerous as the Deadly Rose.

I had to keep my balance on this tightrope walk; I had to do this right. It wasn't just my happiness at stake but my guys' lives if I screwed up and Mom decided to punish me for it.

The woman sank into the chair opposite me and offered her hand over the table. "You must be the Deadly Rose's heir. My name's Mara Reilly. It's a pleasure to finally meet you."

Finally? I guessed there must be some speculation among the other Devil's Dozen inner circles about each family's heirs.

I smiled back at her, trying to mimic that same expression I'd seen

Mom use on the gang boss yesterday. "It's good to meet you too. Thank you so much for agreeing to this meeting so we can see what we can work out."

She bobbed her head. "My employer is very interested in what we might accomplish together."

Mom had gone over the initial negotiations for the deal with me in detail before I'd come here. She wanted to expand our weapons trade into one of the March Wind's territories in northern California. In exchange, he wanted to take over the distribution of certain drugs in the southern part of that state, which was currently under our rule.

We couldn't discuss any of that outright, of course. After placing our orders and a little more bland small talk, Mara got down to business using vague language to hide her real purpose.

She brought up a map on a tablet and slid it across the table to me. "These are the areas where we'd like to increase our reach. We feel it's an equitable balance with the access you're requesting."

I scanned the map, comparing it to the instructions Mom had given me, and tapped one county. "This one we'd like to keep full control over. There are some delicate relations that need to be maintained there. But we could offer this region or this one instead."

Mara cocked her head, considering. "I believe the second of those would suit our purposes as an alternative. We'd like to keep the transition as seamless and simple as possible."

I pushed my mouth into another forced smile. "So would we. I'm glad that our interests align so well."

It was my first attempt at feeling out her and her boss's attitude toward the Deadly Rose overall. Maybe a weak one, but I had no idea what exactly Mom wanted me to fish for. I couldn't exactly ask this woman if we could exchange friendship bracelets.

Mara returned my smile with the same blandly professional expression she'd kept up since she arrived. "It does appear that this arrangement will benefit both of us quite a bit. My employer appreciates your willingness to negotiate."

I didn't think I could read anything into that, warm or cold. The waitress saved me from having to figure out an immediate reply by arriving with our salads.

I couldn't have felt less hungry, but I jabbed my fork into the leafy green mix and chewed gingerly. Mara's gaze rested on me between bites of her own meal, and my skin prickled.

Was she studying me just as much as I was supposed to be evaluating her?

"Maybe there'll be other opportunities for us to collaborate with your employer in the future," I ventured in another tentative foray.

My probe was only met by a slight lift of Mara's thinly plucked eyebrows and a beat of hesitation. "If we see an opening for a satisfying exchange, we'll be sure to let you know," she said.

You couldn't get much more noncommittal than that. But then, I hadn't exactly poured on the enthusiasm either.

This whole conversation felt like an awkward dance—one where neither of us was willing to actually move close enough to touch the other person for fear of coming on too strong… or not being welcome at all.

I tried to earn a little more warmth from her by asking a few questions about her home territory in California—nothing at all sensitive, of course. Mara answered readily enough but with a cool air that gave nothing away.

By the time we were getting up from our seats, I couldn't shake the sense that whatever Mom had hoped for from this meeting, I'd failed miserably.

Mara dipped her head to me. "I'll have my employer pass on his confirmation of the agreement by the end of the day."

I let her stride out ahead of me and gathered my nerves as I walked out to the car I'd driven here on my own. I wasn't enough of a leader to warrant a driver yet, apparently, but then, I was grateful for the time to myself without any of Mom's lackeys peering at me.

I'd appreciate the freedom more if it hadn't also felt like a slap in the face. It was a silent statement that she would find me regardless—that there was no hope of escaping again, so she didn't need to bother monitoring me that closely.

Not letting myself zone out in the driver's seat like I wanted to, I turned on the ignition and pulled out onto the road. In a matter of minutes, I was on the highway heading to what I had to call home for now.

I was halfway back to Austin when my phone rang. I already had it set out so I could quickly hit the speaker phone button.

Mom's voice carried from the tiny speaker. She didn't bother with a hello. "How was the meeting? Did you learn anything interesting?"

I winced, glad she couldn't see me right now. "I'm not sure. It sounds like the deal is a go, according to the terms you were okay with."

"No further overtures of alliance?"

"No," I said cautiously. "I tried to put out feelers and suggest that we'd be open to more without being too blatant about it, and the representative stayed very detached about the whole thing."

Mom hummed to herself. "Well, that's a little disappointing, but not totally surprising. I wouldn't worry about it."

She wasn't upset with me? That would be a first.

In the face of her good will, I pushed my possible advantage. "So, what's up next? More meetings, or do you have something else in mind?" What big plans did she have in the works?

"For now, I do have one more meeting for you to attend. Tomorrow you'll be seeing the young man who's essentially the Storm now to have brunch and get to know each other better." Mom paused. "You should take some care with your clothes and hair. Make yourself look… appealing."

My stomach knotted. "Is this a business thing, or are you setting me up on a date?"

Mom laughed lightly. "You can make whatever you want of the opportunity. But it wouldn't be such a bad thing if that option was on the table, would it?"

Fuck. Not only was she holding my fear for my guys' safety over my head, she thought she could set up a replacement for them too.

My jaw clenched, but even as every particle of my body balked at the thought of so much as pretending I cared what another man thought of me, I knew I had to agree.

"Sure. I'll look every bit the mafia princess, Mom."

"I'm glad to hear that, mija."

A term of endearment she rarely used. I didn't know how to take it now.

We ended the call, and I stared blankly at the highway ahead of me. This was my life now.

And if I wanted the men I'd fallen for to have any lives of their own, I had to stick with it until I could find a real way out.

SIX

Luciana

EVEN IN THE LATE MORNING, tourists were bustling in and out of the colorful entertainment complex in downtown New Orleans. A couple of street musicians played a jazz riff as I walked past them to the restaurant where I was meant to meet the Storm. Or the guy who was practically the Storm now, from the way Mom told it.

I stepped inside to subdued air conditioning and tasteful beiges and whites accentuated with a pop of gold. Another fancy-schmancy place for another wary encounter with one of my mother's peers.

At least it smelled like the food would be worthwhile. Scents of seafood laced with citrus and herbs tickled my nose and set my mouth watering.

The tables were packed, but the Storm had gotten us a reservation—and showed up very promptly. When I told the hostess there was a reservation under Storm, she flashed a smile and led me over to a table tucked away in a quieter corner, where a blond guy who didn't look like he could be out of his twenties yet sat waiting.

He stood up at our approach, and I studied him as surreptitiously as I could, re-evaluating my initial assessment of him as being one of Mom's peers. He was more like *my* peer—definitely closer to my age than hers.

He swept back his sandy blond hair and shot me a warm smile that held none of the reserve the March Wind's representative had shown me. I might not be hoping for an actual date, but I could appreciate the way his tailored dress shirt and slacks fit his toned body. As much as his age might have been surprising for someone already taking the helm of one of the Devil's Dozen empires, his stance exuded a cool confidence that suggested he'd earned the responsibility.

I couldn't let his seeming friendliness disarm me. He could still be an enemy. With the constant jockeying for power Mom had told me about over the years, all of the Devil's Dozen members were potential foes.

As I reached the table, the Storm swept around it to pull out my chair before I could tell him I didn't need that kind of politeness. "You must be the heir to the Deadly Rose," he said, still smiling. "It's a pleasure to meet you."

To my chagrin, my mouth took a moment to start working. I definitely wasn't a natural at this politicking stuff.

"Same," I said, which sounded suitably neutral, and sank into the chair. I had the sense that the guy's gaze skimmed over me before he returned to his own seat.

He was sizing me up too. That was what all of these meetings boiled down to in the end, wasn't it?

I folded my hands on the table in front of me, wishing I had a menu to glance at and peek at him over. I still wasn't totally sure what Mom expected of me here. If she thought I was going to throw myself at this dude, she could forget it.

But this man, even if he was less than ten years older than me, held just as much power as my mother did. Controlled a criminal empire equally vast.

I had to tread even more carefully with him than I had with the March Wind's representative or with Sheeran back in Boston.

This was my first time meeting another Devil's Dozen member face to face. How had Mom even convinced him to go along with the meeting?

Maybe *he* was hoping he could score with me. A major notch in his bedpost, landing the heir to one of his colleagues.

The Storm signaled for a waiter, who appeared at his side in a blink. He had a couple of menus tucked under his arm, but my brunch partner didn't bother asking for them.

"We'll have the tasting menu," he said. "Water for me." He glanced across the table toward me. "What would you like to drink? The fresh-pressed juices here are excellent. But I won't be offended if you'd prefer something stronger."

Er, no, I thought I was much better off keeping as clear a head as possible for this conversation. "Orange juice sounds good," I said to the waiter.

As the man zipped off, I couldn't resist a dry remark. "I am capable of ordering for myself, you know, despite my feminine frailty."

The Storm chuckled. "I'm sorry—I wasn't trying to offend. I figured it was my duty to make sure you get the best possible impression of this place, considering my family owns the restaurant—and the rest of the complex as well. It's a matter of pride."

I picked up my fork and wagged it at him. "As long as you didn't steer me wrong."

"Oh, I think you'll be happy once the food starts arriving. And if you're not, you can smack me over the head with a menu and pick something else."

His gray eyes twinkled with amusement. I wondered if he would actually let me get away with dismissing his food choices—or with smacking him.

I wasn't going to let myself be charmed, but my posture had relaxed since I'd first sat down. This meeting was a far cry from yesterday's stilted conversation with Mara Reilly. It was hard not to admire the casual ease of this guy's banter.

Niko would have liked him. A pang shot through me as I thought of the men I'd left behind—the men I wished I was having brunch with instead, no matter how handsome or charming the Storm might be.

If he was planning on putting the moves on me, he'd be disappointed. My heart belonged to someone else. Three someones.

I just had to hope he'd take no for an answer without a fight.

Our drinks appeared in a flash, and I sipped my orange juice while I debated how to steer the conversation next. The burst of tangy sweetness over my tongue had my eyes widening.

Okay, this really was amazing stuff.

As I lowered the glass, the Storm aimed another smile at me, this one slyly knowing. Then his expression turned unexpectedly serious.

He cleared his throat. "You know, before we go any further, I should say—I'm not sure what your mother's told you, but I got the impression— Let's just put it as, if either of you were hoping that a more-than-friendly relationship would develop between us, you should know up front that I'm already taken."

A laugh of relief tumbled from my mouth. I found myself grinning back at him. "Oh, good. Thank you for clearing that up. Because I am too. But I'm not sure my mother cares about that."

I clamped my mouth shut, afraid I'd overshared with the honest remark, but the Storm's next smile was soft with understanding. "I bet she's putting a lot of pressure on you to meet her expectations, huh? Believe me, I know what that's like. I'm just glad we're on the same page."

I exhaled in a rush. "Yeah. Me too." I considered him more thoughtfully. Mom would still want to know where she stood with him—and for me to make a good impression. "I, ah, don't mean to make things with her sound bad. She's very good at what she does, and I know she mostly just wants me to follow in her footsteps just as well."

That much was true, even if I was leaving out how little I agreed with her about my calling.

"From what I know about the Deadly Rose, I don't have any trouble believing that," the Storm remarked cryptically. "But it's good to see she's also raised you to have a mind of your own."

Ha. That part wasn't so much Mom's doing as my one possible rebellion.

I shrugged, my smile going crooked. "I try."

The waiter reappeared with two small plates that contained a meticulously carved appetizer—some fruit I couldn't recognize in its current state, drizzled with spices. I dug my fork in and nearly swooned at the blend of flavors that laced my tongue.

My companion's mouth stretched into a full grin. "I can see we won't be needing the menu."

I mock-glowered at him. "Be grateful for your head."

Over the next few dishes, which were all equally delicious, it was easy to fall into a breezy back-and-forth as if we were acquaintances simply getting to know each other better. But I never completely let go of the tension coiled inside me, the constant awareness of how much influence the man across from me could wield.

It was still possible his charm was an act. That he was trying to lull me into complacency for some unpleasant goal.

Even if I wanted nothing to do with the criminal world, I had to keep up my role while I was here. And that meant I couldn't show any cracks, any weaknesses.

The Storm took a bite of cheddar grits that had proved to be as soft and fluffy as a cloud and swallowed. "I hope I've made a good impression. It's not often you get the heir to the Deadly Rose in your restaurant. What do you think?"

"It's wonderful, er, Storm. Really."

I could have face-palmed. *'Storm', Lou? Really?*

He brushed a lock of sandy hair away from his eyes. "These titles drive me nuts sometimes. They can be such a pain. You can just call me Beckett."

He was giving me his real name? I didn't think that was very common between the Devil's Dozen members, although I supposed it wouldn't be too hard for any of them to figure them out with a little digging.

But handing it over without a challenge felt like a peace offering.

I couldn't help relaxing a little more. I could offer him the same in return. "I'm Luciana, but everyone calls me Lou."

He tried it out. "Lou. Short and sweet, right to the point. I like it."

"Pretty fond of it myself."

He poked at a crawfish on his plate with seeming idleness, but his next question was anything but careless. "I have to admit, I'm curious why your mother wanted us to meet up right now. I'm assuming it wasn't just an attempt at playing Cupid, but she was vague in her request."

I hesitated. "And you agreed anyway?"

He shrugged with another glimmer of amusement in his eyes. "I was curious. I like to know what's going on with my counterparts."

"Well, I—I'm not totally sure myself." Maybe I could get more of an answer by acting ignorant than trying to play it cool like I had with Mara. "I haven't been very involved in the Devil's Dozen side of things before now. Have the Deadly Rose and the Storm families typically gotten along?"

How were relations between us now, in his perspective?

Beckett cocked his head, his gaze going pensive. "As far as I'm aware, we have. I don't think we've associated much at all outside of the monthly meetings and occasional communication around the places where our territories border each other."

I took a gamble. "I think maybe my mother would like to build more of an association. If you're open to it. I could tell her that, if you are."

The corners of Beckett's eyes crinkled with another smile. "I guess that would depend on what the association involved. I have been glad to see her at the table, giving us a little break from the monotony of old white guys who think they run everything."

I had to stifle a snort. "You're a white guy too."

Beckett laughed. "Sure, but hopefully you don't think I'm *old*. I'd like to think my ideas about good business practices are at least a little different from the others. My dad and I have argued about that subject often enough."

He was willing to challenge his father's views? Was that why he was seen as the Storm now, even though from what Mom had said, his dad was still alive?

I didn't know how to ask that without sounding way too nosy, but I filed the fact away for later and simply ventured, "It can be difficult getting the older generation to see things differently."

"No kidding. But I believe in following my conscience and carving my own path if I need to." His eyebrows lifted. "Just have to make sure I don't piss off anyone quite so much that they decide it's time to carve *me* up."

"Yeah." My heart beat a little faster, but it felt right to admit, "I don't always see eye to eye with my mother either. I'm… not sure I want to be in the whole business of running the Deadly Rose empire the way it is now."

That was much safer than saying I had no interest in anything to do with it no matter how you sliced it.

Beckett nodded without any sign of shock. "You'll get your chances to adjust course if you look for them. Once you start proving yourself, it's harder for anyone to squash you down."

"Right." Despite my best efforts, my answering smile felt stiff.

Beckett took a sip of water with a thoughtful air. Then he dug into his pocket. "Look, I don't know what your situation is exactly or how you're dealing with it. But I have been there. If you think there's anything I can do that might help, don't hesitate to reach out. I mean that."

He passed a business card over to me, a phone number and email address printed on it in bold lettering. I stared at it, my stomach flipping over, and quickly stuffed it into my purse.

"Thanks," I said, willing down a flush of embarrassment. Had I sounded like I *needed* help?

I did, didn't I? I was in over my head, and I had no idea how to swim to shore. Or where a safe shoreline even was.

But could I ever trust another member of the Devil's Dozen, even one who seemed as kind as Beckett did?

I tossed out a smart aleck remark I barely thought about and dug into my food again. All the while in the back of my head, my thoughts were spinning.

Even if things got really bad in Austin… would I be willing to take the help this guy had just offered me?

SEVEN

Rafael

A NEON SIGN in the shape of a beer bottle buzzed in the bar's front window, flickering for a second as it cast its red glow across my eyes. I scanned the sidewalk around me and the view through the glass before heading inside.

There was no sign of any of the Deadly Rose lackeys I could recognize. This place wasn't a typical hang-out of theirs, but I'd known a few people from my earlier life who'd frequented the place. Which was why I'd made it my first stop since arriving in Austin.

I stepped through the doorway into the reek of alcohol and surreptitious joints. The place was crowded with most of the seats around the table and the bar taken, raucous voices bouncing off the low ceiling. On the tiny stage at the far end of the main room, three dudes with scraggly beards were fiddling around with some instruments, squinting at their equipment as they tested the cords.

Maybe I could be done here before I needed to endure their musical stylings.

I didn't want to leave the loft for very long anyway. I *thought* the figure skaters had taken my warnings to heart about sticking to the quiet neighborhood on the fringes of the city where gang activity should be nearly nil. But the prick who'd insisted on joining the three of us in our search for Lou struck me as both restless and not in the habit of following orders.

Hopefully Jasper and Niko could keep him in line. I really didn't need another problem.

Lou would never forgive me if I got either of her other boyfriends too mixed up in the danger that waited for us here.

I moved over to the bar, ordered a beer since I didn't want anything that'd give me a real buzz while I needed to stay alert, and continued my survey of the bar-goers. My gaze caught on a slim middle-aged man in an untucked pin-striped dress shirt and jeans, sauntering from the restrooms over to the curve of the counter.

"'Nother Johnnie Walker on the rocks," he called to the bartender loud enough for me to make out his voice over the din, with a rap of his hand against the polished wooden surface.

The bartender fixed the drink without a word, and I moseyed around the counter to where I could lean against the empty seat next to my target.

"Hey, Albie. It's been a while."

The man swiveled toward me, and his eyebrows arched. "Rafael! It has been. Where've you been hiding yourself these days?"

I smiled grimly, knowing he wouldn't really expect an answer I wasn't going to give him. You had to be careful with Albert Thimbal. The small-time scam artist didn't pledge his loyalty to any particular gang, preferring to keep his ear to the ground and make use of any advantage he could get.

If anything major was going on within the criminal world of Austin, he'd know. And he wouldn't tattle on me to any of my former associates unless it seemed particularly worth his while—which was more guarantee than I'd get from most of my old contacts.

"Here and there," I said nonchalantly, and motioned to the bartender that I was covering Albert's drink. "Been out of the loop. Got a little time to shoot the breeze?"

He shot me a grin full of teeth that wished they'd seen braces in his teens. "If you're paying, I can talk."

He picked up his drink and we drifted over to a booth in the corner, as secluded as any seating in this venue got. Albert took a tentative sip and eyed me with obvious curiosity. "What's eating at you?"

I shrugged as if it was no big deal. "Oh, nothing urgent. I'm just trying to get the lay of the land now that I'm back. Any big news in the last couple of months?"

"I guess that depends on what you call big."

I narrowed my eyes at him and decided I'd better stop beating around the bush. "Have the Cordovas been up to anything interesting?"

Albert swirled his glass, the ice clinking against the sides. "Heard a lot of guys came out of the head lady's house worse for wear not that long ago. She was upset about something." His focus on me turned even more speculative.

I kept my expression vague. "I caught a few murmurs about that. Got the impression it had something to do with her daughter."

"Oh, yes, the heir. Whatever happened with her, Mireya Cordova is showing her off all over the place now."

I had to will the tension that gripped my body not to stiffen my stance. "Really? Showing her off how?"

Albert took another gulp. "Trotting her out in front of this boss and that one, lots of little meetings she's not being as secretive about it as you'd expect."

My stomach sank. "Any idea what all those meetings are leading up to?"

He shook his head and drained the rest of his glass. When he lifted an eyebrow at me in question, I nodded, and he made a grabby gesture toward a passing waiter to ask for another.

"Beats me," he said as I passed a couple of bills over to the waiter when he brought the drink. "She hasn't been *that* open about it. But I've got to say, there's something I don't like about the… the vibe in the city right now. It's got a feeling like there is something big on the horizon, and maybe not anything good."

An uneasy prickle ran down my back. I thought of the phone call I'd gotten from one of my former colleagues under the Deadly Rose not that long ago, warning me that Mireya wanted Lou back for some major plan. "You figure it's something the Cordovas are going to push forward?"

Albert sighed. "I don't know. It's just a feeling. But my hunches are usually pretty good." He pulled his drink closer and took on a tone that told me he was done with the conversation. "Thanks for your generosity, Rafael. Stop by for a chat anytime."

I stood up and made my way toward the door. I doubted anyone else I'd want to reveal myself to could tell me more, so there was nothing left for me here. At least I knew Lou *was* in town, and that her mother hadn't been so angry with her that she'd hurt her in any way that prevented public appearances.

I'd mostly been worrying about the slim chance of running into any of the Deadly Rose's goons. A moment later, I realized that could be the least of my problems.

I was five feet from the door when a burly man with distinctive patterns shaved in his close-cropped coils pushed through the doorway. My pulse stuttered. I would have turned and made for the back entrance if the guy's gaze hadn't already fixed on me.

He strode forward and clapped me on the shoulder. "Torres! Never thought I'd run into you around here. Seemed like you have better things to do now that you've moved on and up, huh?"

"I don't forget where I came from, Salvador," I said in a voice I forced to stay even. "I guess our paths just haven't crossed before." Too bad I hadn't kept up that streak.

Salvador looked me over with the air he always had as if he were an uncle sizing up his least favorite nephew. The asshole only had about five years on me, but he'd always enjoyed talking down to me as if he held so much more seniority.

He crossed his arms over his broad chest. "Oh, yeah? So you haven't forgotten Edmundo then, cabrón?"

My teeth set on edge. This was the last thing I needed while I was trying to run a stealthy rescue mission. "Never have, never will."

But getting into a fight in the middle of this bar wasn't going to help me or Lou.

Salvador shook his head chidingly. "That's funny, because I could have sworn we were supposed to hear about some big explosion, but it never came…"

A deeper chill rippled through me. I forced a mild smile onto my face. "Some things take time. Speaking of which, I've got a job to take care of."

"Oh, do you?" Salvador's voice carried after me as I sidestepped him on my way to the door. "Jumping to that rich bitch's tune now. Fucking sad."

I didn't bother responding, just pushed out into the evening hoping he wasn't invested enough to follow me.

I hurried down the street, wanting to get some distance from him before I hailed an Uber. My lungs were burning, and I realized I'd been holding my breath.

Fuck Salvador and whoever still stood with him. They had no fucking idea…

It'd been so much better when I'd been able to leave Austin behind. But I couldn't stay gone while Lou was trapped here.

I shoved my anger aside. When I'd left the bar well behind, I stopped by a dingy brick office building and pulled out my phone.

In the back of my mind, images were forming of Lou stuck in her old bedroom in the Cordova mansion, as trapped and alone as if her mom had shoved her into a prison cell. Without me, she'd have no one to count on there.

I had to get to her—soon. She needed to know she could turn to me. She'd have no idea I'd even tracked her this far.

I needed *her*. To see her sly smile, to hear her vibrant laugh, to wrap my arms around her. To know that I was protecting her every way I could, like that precious woman deserved.

I hadn't realized my heart could feel this empty until now.

As I ducked into the Uber, I kept my phone in my hand. We knew Mireya had gotten control over Lou's phone. But she and I had planned alternate means of communication back when I was still acting like a proper bodyguard, when she'd faced much more immediate dangers on a daily basis as her mother's heir.

Like she would be again now.

From what I'd seen and heard, those avenues were likely to be my best options of reaching out to her. I couldn't count on catching her at any of these meetings Mireya was setting up.

Lou had better have remembered those old schemes. Better be checking up on things just in case.

Que Dios me ayude if she'd given up because I hadn't gotten here faster.

In the phone's web browser, I brought up a forum for missed connections. Typed out a message that she'd recognize if she saw it, but no one else would understand.

For the skating angel I met at the crossroads, I heard that there's a lot of cheap equipment at the outlet store on Pine Street. Looking forward to shopping with you there if you're up for it — how's 6 o'clock Thursday night sound?

I hit the post button and sagged back in the seat. Now all I could do was wait and see.

"You sure she's coming?" Quentin asked for what had to be the twelfth time that night. He shifted on his feet, glancing around the abandoned outlet store at the few empty racks that'd been left behind when the last tenants had vacated it. A few lonely shirts hung dejectedly from their hangers. "You're sure she'd ever think we're going to meet her *here*?"

My voice came out in a growl. "She and I know each other well enough to understand this kind of thing."

The bastard had been getting on my nerves all day. The worst part was that his impatient skepticism was starting to infect the two men who should have trusted me more.

Jasper paced a few steps across the worn linoleum before returning to us, raking his hand through his shaggy hair. "What if she *doesn't* come? What would our next option be?"

"We'll figure that out if we need to," I said. "It's still a couple of minutes before six. She isn't even late."

Niko swiped his hand across his mouth and pushed his lips into a smile I could see was tense. "There've got to be other ways to get in contact with her, right?"

I restrained a glower. "If she doesn't come tonight, then we try again tomorrow, and the next night. She might not see the message right away, but she'll give it a shot when she does."

And if it went on for more than a few days without Lou turning up… Yeah, then we'd have a problem. One I'd rather not think about.

Niko glanced at his phone and typed out a message that was quickly answered with a cheery ping. I suspected he was talking with his little sister again.

Jasper sighed and shoved his hands in his pockets. And Quentin started prowling through the back of the store, wrinkling his nose at the discarded clothing. His mouth twisted into a sour expression.

If he made one more snarky remark, I was going to—

Thankfully for both of us, I never needed to complete that thought. Because just then the door I'd picked the lock on and left ajar eased open, and Lou darted inside.

Her new bangs, redyed to her previous dark brown, drooped across her face, and her shoulders were furtively hunched, but my heart leapt at the sight of her all the same. And when she raised her head and caught sight of the three of us in our cluster in the middle of the room, the smile that lit her face flooded me with the sweetest relief.

No, not just relief. Love. As I hurried to meet her, my chest swelled with the emotion I hadn't known I would ever feel. Hadn't known it was possible to feel this strongly.

But as I tucked my arms around her slender frame, a pang that was more bittersweet shot through my joy.

I loved this woman, sure—but even if she was with me now, I couldn't be there for her anywhere near as much as I wanted to. Not while she was still tangled in her mother's snare.

EIGHT

Luciana

I WASN'T NORMALLY the most emotionally expressive person in the world. Mom had taught me to hold my cards close and reveal my feelings cautiously.

But seeing my three men in front of me for the first time in over a week, I couldn't hold back the joyful tears that sprang into my eyes.

I threw myself at Rafael first, mainly because he was closest. As I wrapped him in the tightest hug I could offer, he chuckled, sounding just a tad choked up himself, and hugged me back with his chin tucking over my head.

"Glad you got the message."

"Glad you thought of using the forum," I replied. I'd cycled through our planned covert methods of communications a few times since Mom had dragged me back to Austin, but my hopes hadn't been high.

I forced myself to ease back from Rafael, but only so that I could grab the guy next to him in an equally emphatic embrace.

Jasper's brawny arms encircled me, and he planted a lingering kiss on my forehead. "It's good to see you've survived so far, Punk," he said, the gruffness of his voice not quite hiding the rasp of emotion.

His words brought a prickle of fear into my gut, but I ignored it for the moment. "It's so good to see you too. Even if you're still a grouch."

As he laughed, I turned from him to Niko, who was smiling bright as the sun. He gathered me up against his slimmer frame and nuzzled the side of my face. "We were awfully worried about you, Angel. All of us."

I would have assumed he meant all three, but as I pulled away to match his smile with a beaming one of my own, a fourth figure who I hadn't noticed at the edge of the room took a step toward us.

My gaze jerked toward the unexpected member of the group, and my stance went rigid.

Quentin stopped where he was, still several feet away between the sparse clothing racks, and ran his fingers over his blond hair, which was slicked back as neatly as always. His sharp blue eyes held some of the same wildness I'd seen when he'd called me down from my apartment right before Mom had grabbed me.

When he'd told me how he couldn't stop thinking about me and then kissed me.

In my shock, my voice came out cold. "What are *you* doing here?"

His mouth slanted at a crooked angle. Before he could speak, Niko jumped in. "Quentin helped us figure out why you'd disappeared. He saw your mother take you away."

Rafael nodded, his impassive expression giving away nothing of his feelings on the third skater guy he was now shepherding around. "He insisted on coming along, and I figured he'd make more trouble than it was worth if I couldn't keep an eye on him. Claims he knows the wrong side of the tracks and that he wants to help if he can."

His voice took on a slightly dry tone with the second sentence. Jasper simply scowled. I couldn't imagine he'd been happy about his rival coming along for the trip.

I was silent for a moment, taking in what they'd said and studying Quentin. The twist of his mouth had shaped it into a tentative if crooked smile. His gaze burned into me with its usual intensity.

When he'd come by the apartment, I'd figured he'd been looking for more ways to mess with me and Jasper. Or to get his rocks off and then move on. But he'd been willing to trek all the way across the country to try to get me out of this mess?

That didn't fit with the coolly competitive guy I'd thought he was.

I shifted closer to Jasper automatically, taking his hand to sling his arm around my waist. I was both starving for contact with the men I'd had to leave behind and determined that Jasper didn't imagine for one second that my interest in him had faded.

"How much does he know?" I had to ask.

Rafael shrugged. "The basics. Enough to realize he's stepping into a shitload of danger."

"We *tried* to scare him off," Jasper muttered, but he held me with a tenderness totally at odds with his tone. It wasn't me he was annoyed with, that was for sure.

"Well, thank you," I said to Quentin. "Never thought I'd see the day when you'd actually work *with* Jasper instead of trying to tear him down."

It was a purposeful jab—a test of his response.

Quentin simply bobbed his head in acknowledgement. "The least I could do if you're in trouble."

Which I was. The prickle that'd jabbed at me earlier spread into a larger ache.

And now my men were in trouble too.

I glanced up at Jasper, unable to resist rising on my toes to give him a quick kiss on the cheek. "*None* of you really should have come, though." I reached out to squeeze Niko's arm and then cast my gaze toward Rafael. "My mom… She might kill you if she finds out you're here. No hesitation, no questions asked."

Just saying it left me queasy.

Niko raised his chin. "We're not leaving you to deal with her on your own. There has to be a way to get you away from her."

"And we'll take whatever risks necessary to make it happen," Jasper added.

Rafael let out a light huff. "You know I'm not walking away from the danger."

I swallowed thickly and curled my fingers tighter around Jasper's hand. "But—there's Nationals too. You'll miss your chance—"

"Fuck that," my partner broke in emphatically. "I couldn't compete without you, and I sure as hell wouldn't want to anyway. If we get our way, you'll be right there beside me in time for us to skate together."

My heart sank. "It's not going to be easy. I can't just run away again. She'll know exactly where I went—and even if we laid low, now that she knows about you and Niko too, it'll be that much easier for her to track us down. And she's made it clear that if I go against her orders again, she's going to punish me by hurting all of you."

Rafael's lips formed a grim smile. "Then we have to make her believe that she's better off letting you leave."

"I wish." I exhaled in a ragged sigh.

"Is there anyone else in town you could join up with against her?" Quentin ventured. "Safety in numbers and all that. We could even put out feelers and—"

I shook my head with a jerk. "No. The four of you have to stay out of sight and not draw any attention—especially from the criminal underground. Anyone who's strong enough to even irritate my mom, she's got either under her thumb or too scared to even look at her funny. You have no idea how much power she can wield or how quick she is to use it."

Niko spread his hands. "We'll play it safe while we need to. But as soon as there's anything we can do to help, you've got to let us know."

"And fast," Rafael said with a hint of a growl.

I nodded, torn between reluctance to drag them any further into my problems and relief that I wasn't facing those problems alone after all. "I'll need more time to figure out a strategy that'll actually work. So far… I haven't seen any obvious way to get myself out of this. But I'm not giving up."

Rafael's subtle smile returned. "That's my girl." He cocked his head. "Do you have any idea why she was so determined to get you back right now? I've heard murmurs about big plans, but no one seems to know what they are."

I let out a rough chuckle. "Me neither. She isn't telling me any more than she has to—she knows I'm not committed to staying if I have any choice in the matter. But I am getting the impression that she's building up to something major."

I squeezed Jasper's arm one last time, leaned in to offer Niko a quick kiss, and then gave Rafael a final hug. An ache ran through my heart as I forced myself to pull away.

"Thank you for coming. Just don't make me wish you hadn't. I shouldn't stay any longer or she might get suspicious. We can pass messages back and forth through the forum to keep in touch."

"We'll be waiting for your call," Jasper said. "Whatever it takes."

I said my good-byes and hurried out before my eyes could overflow. My pulse thudded heavily through my veins as I walked back to my car, which I'd parked a couple of blocks away for caution.

But for all my fear and the sense of loss at leaving them again, my spirits felt lighter than they had in days. As I drove back to the Cordova mansion, my mind replayed those moments standing with my men, knowing they'd braved the wrath of the most dangerous woman in the country to come to my rescue. Even if they couldn't do any actual rescuing yet.

I strode through the deepening evening from the sprawling garage up to the broad front door. A few of Mom's lackeys were hanging around near the entrance, but all their smartass remarks had dried up since I'd gotten back.

Maybe seeing the furor Mom had gotten into when I was gone had given them a little more appreciation for my presence.

I headed past them up the sweeping staircase and along the hall to my bedroom. I wanted nothing more than to flop onto the bed and dream of running off with my men and leaving all this crap behind me.

But just as I reached for the door handle, a faint squeak of hinges sounded behind me.

"Luciana? I'd like a word."

Mom stood in her office doorway. Her expression was cool and impenetrable enough to set my nerves jangling.

Had she somehow figured out about my meeting with the guys? I hadn't seen her when I'd left the house, but I'd planted the idea that I was planning on going out for pierogies for dinner when I'd seen her earlier in the day.

If she'd seen through that lie, we were already screwed.

Avoiding her was hardly an option when she was staring right at me. I plastered an obedient smile on my face and ambled over at her beckoning. "Sure. What's up?"

Mom's nose wrinkled slightly at my casual tone, but she motioned me into the room without comment. "How was your Polish dinner?"

"Oh, you know," I said glibly, hoping she couldn't hear my heart about to thunder right out of my chest. "Not as fresh as when Zuzanna was here to make them, but it hit the spot well enough."

Mom hummed to herself and strolled over to her desk. She wasn't giving off an angry vibe, at least, so maybe I was safe after all.

I didn't think she'd asked me in here just to inquire about my meal, though.

She took her time getting to the point, a common tactic of hers designed to give her time to evaluate the other person's mood. As she straightened an already neat pile of papers on her desk, I held myself still and calm, waiting.

Brushing her hands together, she turned to face me again. "It's time to discuss our next steps. Across the meetings you've been a part of and my own outreach, it's becoming clearer who will side with the Deadly Rose, who's brushing us off, and who is inclined to stay neutral." She shook her head with a disproving click of her tongue. "I was hoping that boy who sees himself as the Storm would be a little more intrigued, but I haven't heard a murmur from him since your brunch."

She figured Beckett was brushing her off? "I don't think he knew what you were looking for," I pointed out. I sure as hell hadn't to be able to tell him. "Apparently he's already got a girlfriend, so framing it as a date wasn't a draw."

Mom flicked her hand dismissively. "An obvious overture of any sort warrants a particular response if there's any thought to a deeper alliance. That's fine. He can snub us all he likes… for now."

A chill ran down my back. "And what happens later?"

Her sharp smile chilled me even more. "We'll get to that. Before we make any significant moves, there are a few outliers I'd like you to approach. The most important of those is the new Blood Hunter."

"Another heir who's just stepped up?" I asked, still trying to untangle her insinuations about the future.

"No, a usurper." Mom's smile widened slightly as if she liked the idea. Maybe she did, as long as it wasn't her throne being stolen. "She has only a little experience within the Devil's Dozen. And she's not much older than you, so I'd imagine you'll have more common ground than there'd be between her and me."

"And we want to find that common ground because…?"

Mom shot me a look as if thinking I should keep up. "She's a wild card. But as a woman who's bringing new ideas to the table, I'm hopeful that she'll see the benefits that would come with adjusting the balance of power."

Adjusting the balance of power. And Mom was fussing over who wanted to ally with her and who wasn't taking the bait.

A horrible suspicion clawed its way up through my chest. "Are you… Are you trying to find allies so you can overthrow some of the other Devil's Dozen members?"

It wouldn't be a totally absurd move, would it? Banding together with a smaller group to shove out the others, dividing the losers' territory between the winners so there were fewer at the top, each with a bigger piece of the pie.

I could totally see Mom going for that. And becoming even more of a menace than she already was.

But if she failed… That kind of treason against her Devil's Dozen colleagues would warrant a death sentence.

Not a hint of agreement showed in Mom's expression—but she didn't look scandalized by my suggestion either. That convinced me I was right before she even gave her carefully bland response. "We're simply taking stock of where we stand—and what we might do from there. You should never leap into action until you're sure of your plan's success, Luciana."

Oh, yeah, that was as much of a yes as I could imagine Mom ever giving. Holy shit.

She intended to turn on some of those other top bosses—the kings and queens of the criminal underworld. How much territory was she hoping to gain? Did she figure she'd double her holdings? Triple them?

How many more people would be terrorized under her reign?

Did she really think it was worth risking everything we had on a crazy gamble like that? Or maybe she'd already found enough support that it didn't seem so crazy.

As those questions whirled in my head, a strange elation tickled up from my belly. I didn't like what I was hearing, but it also might be exactly the leverage I needed so much.

Mom was holding my men's lives over my head to get her way. If I could threaten something *she* cared about, it might balance out our own power struggle.

I tipped my head to the side as if I were thinking over Mom's words. "Then I guess we'd better make sure. When did you want me to talk to the Blood Hunter?"

NINE

Luciana

I RECOGNIZED the Blood Hunter the moment she stepped into the elegant coffee shop Mom had picked out for this meeting in downtown Atlanta, which apparently was neutral ground between their territories.

I'd never seen a picture of the woman before and only had Mom's brief description to go by. But I think even if I hadn't known to expect long black hair or dark eyes vivid against pale skin, I'd have identified her as a force to be reckoned with before she'd even crossed the room.

Despite her slim frame, the Blood Hunter's every movement emanated physical control and strength. Her steady gaze as she approached the table spoke of plenty of will power as well. I considered myself a skilled fighter when the situation called for it, but every inch of my skin prickled with the knowledge that this woman could have me pinned in a matter of seconds, no matter what I did.

Like Mom had said, she wasn't that much older than me, late

twenties at most, but when she stood over the small table I'd chosen, I felt like a kid. A kid who had no business trying to play the kinds of games my mother wanted to involve me in.

I had to anyway, though, so I'd better put on a good show.

I started to stand up as a sign of respect, but the Blood Hunter lowered herself into the chair across from me before I could get to my feet. She didn't show any sign of caring about those sorts of niceties.

It was far from standard protocol for her to be speaking with me at all. In Beckett's case, his agreeing to meet with someone who didn't even have the authority to sit at the Devil's Dozen table yet could be explained by the fact that there was still some uncertainty about whether he or his father truly held the title.

The Blood Hunter had no heirs. From what Mom had told me, she'd ruled for the past few years after killing the man who'd claimed that name before her.

Why had she done that? What had she been after?

Questions I definitely couldn't ask someone who could not just kill *me* in a snap but was a total stranger on top of that.

"It's good to meet you," I said with a quick smile. "Thank you for taking the time."

The woman studied me intently enough that my pulse stuttered. "What is this about? The Deadly Rose indicated that you had a time-sensitive issue to discuss with me."

Augh, why had Mom phrased it that way? Of course, maybe the Blood Hunter wouldn't have shown up at all otherwise.

She sure got straight to the point. There was none of Beckett's friendly warmth here.

Who would have thought I'd find myself wishing for another brunch with the Storm instead?

"It isn't really one specific issue," I said quickly, summoning the talking points Mom had coached me on. "But we're on the cusp of making some major changes with some of our dealings. It's an ideal time to build on our existing alliances and form new ones."

The Blood Hunter continued to eye me with a slightly skeptical expression. I had to fight the urge to shrink inside my blouse.

I was the Deadly Rose's daughter. I could be a force to be reckoned with too.

Never mind that I didn't actually want to be forcing a conversation like this on Mom's behalf. What unholy terror would Mom unleash on the world if she got her way and transformed the whole structure of the Devil's Dozen?

After a long enough silence that I was itching to fidget, the Blood Hunter rested her hands on the table. "And she wants an alliance with me? Why didn't she meet with me herself?"

Thankfully, Mom had covered her expected approach to that subject in depth. Admitting the truth wouldn't have gotten her what she wanted.

I lifted my chin. "I'll be taking over more and more authority within the Deadly Rose empire in the coming years." *If I can't get myself the fuck out of this hell.* "Since we're both relatively new to this kind of work, she figured you and I might have more common ground. If you'd prefer to speak to her directly—"

The Blood Hunter shook her head with a jerk. "This is fine. Is that your whole pitch? What would we be allying on?"

I motioned vaguely with my hands, hoping I didn't look as uneasy as I felt. "We could create more of a partnership between our empires. Combine some of our business interests. Work together against any threats. More people on your side can't be a bad thing, right?"

The woman across from me blinked slowly, pensively. "Depends on the friend. I've held the title of the Blood Hunter for years now, though. Is there something happening right now that's brought on this overture?"

"I've recently come of age to take on more responsibility," I said. "It's gotten my mother thinking about the ways our world could benefit from fresh ideas, a shift in the old habits and patterns. Reaching out to the colleagues she respects most is part of that."

I couldn't tell if the Blood Hunter appreciated or even believed that my mother might respect her. She flicked her thumb over her lips and then fixed me with an even more penetrating stare.

"Are any of the things you're saying *your* ideas, or are you just parroting what the Deadly Rose told you to say? She doesn't seem to have much respect for you if she's hanging around just a couple of blocks away, monitoring you."

A chill ran down my back. I'd known Mom was staked out in her car not far from the café, waiting for me to report back, but she'd been subtle about it. The Blood Hunter wasn't supposed to have noticed.

But she had, somehow or other. How could I explain that away when I was supposed to be claiming that Mom had put all this authority in my hands?

And if the Blood Hunter had picked up on that covert fact, what else did she know that we hadn't expected her to?

I hesitated with my lips parted, my throat aching with the honest answer I couldn't give. I didn't want to pretend I was wholeheartedly behind Mom's deeper treachery either, especially if this woman already suspected something was up.

Before I could fumble out a response, the Blood Hunter stood up with a rasp of her chair's legs against the floor. "That's enough of an answer. I'm not interested in all the complicated internal politics of the Devil's Dozen. You can tell your mother I'd prefer to simply be left alone."

With that, she strode out of the café, not even sparing me a backward glance.

A waitress breezed by, giving me a puzzled glance, and my face flushed with embarrassment. Who knew what she'd made of my oddly brief meet-up?

I gulped the last of the coffee I'd ordered while I was waiting, left a ten on the table that was more than twice my actual bill, and slipped out of the café a few minutes after the Blood Hunter had left. There was no sign of her outside, but it was impossible to know how she might be keeping an eye on us still.

Well, there was nothing to do but trudge back to Mom and make my disappointing report.

I took a couple of turns and crossed a crowded parking lot to where Mom had told me the sedan would be waiting. The Blood Hunter hadn't even been wrong, had she? Here I was, dutifully trotting back to my mother whose plans I wanted nothing to do with, like I was a puppy being brought to heel.

But the Blood Hunter had no idea what I had at stake. My nails dug into the meat of my palms hard enough to leave marks.

Mom had driven us this time, not wanting to talk with a driver who could overhear. I dropped into the passenger seat next to her. My heart thumped hard, but I dipped my hand into my purse as if I were making sure I hadn't forgotten anything back at the café.

I *wasn't* here just for her ends. Not that I could let her find out my private purpose.

Mom's gaze took me in assessingly. "That was a short meeting. What happened?"

I exhaled in a rush of frustration. "The Blood Hunter isn't interested. She seemed suspicious about the fact that we'd reached out at all, and after she heard my reasons, she told me she just wanted you to leave her alone and then walked out."

Her eyes narrowed. "That kind of a snub? I knew she was inexperienced, but…" She shook herself, but anger still simmered beneath her next words. "There are only three women in the Devil's Dozen. You'd think she could at least recognize the potential value in having each other's backs."

"According to her, she doesn't want anything to do with the politics in the Devil's Dozen." I knit my brow. Now I *really* wanted to know why that woman had claimed her spot at the table. She didn't seem to have any more interest in fulfilling her expected role than I did.

Mom scoffed. "She's taking that attitude, is she? No idea how much guidance she's losing out on that I could have offered." Her tone darkened. "Well, she'll regret throwing my generosity back in my face when she finds herself without any chair at the table at all."

A quiver ran through my veins. There. She'd just openly admitted that her end goal was to displace at least one of her colleagues.

My mouth had gone dry, but triumph sparked in my chest all the same. Because in my purse, my phone was recording this entire conversation. I now had a concrete record of Mom's illicit plans.

"We don't need her," Mom went on as she started the engine. "The fewer who join us, the less we have to share. Someone like her doesn't deserve her piece of the pie."

"I'm sure you'll find other people who'll stand with you," I said, careful not to indicate any personal support of her plans.

"Oh, I already have." A cruel smile curved Mom's lips. "And when it's time, *all* of the others will regret their choices."

TEN

Quentin

GO FIGURE. The muscle head had picked what must be the most rundown rink in the state of Texas for the three of us to practice.

My nose wrinkled reflexively as I took in the dingy arena. Several of the fluorescent bulbs fixed to the ceiling were flickering; a couple were burned out. The boards around the ice were smudged and in a couple of places outright cracked.

The stands hadn't fared much better. We tramped past a section of benches that were cordoned off with caution tape because the seats had slanted right off their bases with massive dents.

The smell of stale sweat and grease from fast food wrappers left in the stands made my stomach turn. As we reached the boards, I couldn't hold back a complaint.

"This is it—seriously? This is the best arena you could find in all of Austin?"

The massive man who was apparently Lou's gang bodyguard or

something like that swung around to fix me with his intimidating glower. My stance tensed, but I stared right back at him.

"The point isn't to skate in luxury," he said in his dark rumble of a voice. "The point is to keep a low enough profile that you all don't get *killed*."

Jasper let out a huff and hunkered down on a bench to pull on his skates. "I'm fine with those priorities."

My lips pulled into a grimace. "There wasn't anything even a *little* better maintained? Who knows if this ice is even—"

Rafael cut me off. "It's this or nothing. Up to you whether you skate."

He swiveled and marched back up to the door where he was going to keep watch.

I watched him go and let my gaze sweep over the dank space again. My stomach knotted.

The vibe of this place wasn't exactly unfamiliar. If anything, it reminded me way too much of the rink where I'd first trained as a kid. The crappy place near home that mostly got used for low-rent birthday parties and community center lessons.

My skin itched uncomfortably with the sense of having been sucked back into the past. I'd moved on to better digs than this in the years since then.

But I couldn't see that continuing to argue with Rafael was going to change my situation—other than it'd make him and the other two guys who'd grudgingly agreed to loop me in on this mission even less friendly.

I hadn't had the opportunity to do anything to actually prove my worth since I'd told them what I'd seen happen to Lou back in Boston. No doubt Jasper was chomping at the bit for any excuse good enough to send me packing.

Not that I really wanted to hang around him this much, but I knew there wasn't a hope in hell of me doing anything for Lou on my own. I wouldn't even know how to get in touch with her.

Squaring my shoulders, I dropped my bag on one of the benches and retrieved my skates. The ice looked decently smooth, at least. If there was anything that could make me feel better, it was honing my performance.

It'd be nice to get lost in the practice zone just for a little while. And I was going to need that practice to get up to speed with my routines.

By the time I'd laced up, Jasper and Niko had already moved onto the ice. Niko was saying something in a low voice and motioning to one end of the rink.

I wasn't sure how Jasper was going to get much done without Lou here, but I guessed he could work on his spins and jumps, if not the synchronization piece. It wasn't any of my business. They hadn't said a word directly to me since we'd come in—obviously they planned to have their own little practice session separate from me, like I wasn't even here.

Restraining a sigh, I pushed off across the ice. With each flex of my muscles, I felt how many days it'd been since I'd gotten a proper workout. Strength exercises and cardio routines in the apartment just didn't cut it.

I closed my eyes, playing the song from my short routine in my head from memory. Niko said something that I ignored until I caught my name.

I blinked and looked over at him. He shot me a wary smile. "How much practice do you expect to do without your partner?"

Jasper muttered something I couldn't totally make out but might have been along the lines of that I'd better not think I was stealing his. My teeth set on edge, but I answered with cool evenness.

"I didn't rank high enough to qualify for Nationals in pairs anyway. I'm going back to singles—I can compete based on last year's ranking."

Niko's narrow eyebrows arched slightly. "That could be tricky when you haven't been practicing your singles routines for most of the season."

I shrugged. "I'll manage."

He had no idea what I was capable of. I'd pulled off plenty of trickier tasks in my life—like getting to this point in my career at all.

The two of them wouldn't know anything about the kind of

struggles that'd taken. Especially Jasper born with that silver spoon up his ass.

I cast off into a brief series of warm-up moves, getting a feel for the ice. Niko went back to ignoring me while Jasper started his own warm-up.

I was just considering where to start my real practice when the door next to Rafael swung open.

A petite but curvy figure appeared with a swish of a familiar dark ponytail. Lou bobbed up to give Rafael a quick kiss and then hustled down the steps to the rink, where Jasper and Niko were already skating over to the boards to greet her.

The sight of her gorgeous face, lit up with the bright smile that stretched wider as she took them in, made my heart skip a beat. And the athletic slopes of her body in her tight long-sleeved tee and leggings… God, that woman was something.

Something that wanted nothing to do with me. She grabbed Jasper and then Niko in an embrace before yanking on her skates, the flush in her cheeks somehow making her even prettier. But as far as I could tell, she didn't so much as glance my way.

"I don't think Mom suspected anything," she told them in a breathless tone that made me want to capture even more of her breath from her lips. "But I can't stay more than an hour."

"I'm just glad you could make it at all," Jasper said in a tone I could have gagged at, especially because Lou responded by giving him an emphatic kiss.

It wasn't really disgust roiling inside me. Jealousy seared through my chest.

But what had I expected? I'd been a total prick to her and her partner for months, even if her partner at least partly deserved it.

It was going to take time before she realized I could offer something good too.

I turned away and narrowed my thoughts back to my routine. I knew the moves by heart. It shouldn't be that hard to trigger the muscle memory.

My mind drifted into the comfortable zone of calculation. I knew exactly how many inches I needed to lift my leg with this spin, or to get off the ice in that jump—and how many *more* inches would take me from acceptable to applause-worthy.

As much as I wanted to be at the latter stage immediately, it was better for my body to aim a little lower to start. A strained muscle or tendon could end the whole competition for me.

Piece by piece, I'd build what I could achieve back up.

I pushed off the ice, picturing the exact angle that my body would need to tilt to perfect the first move. My eyes narrowed as I sped forward.

Another powerful push, this time upward. I twisted my body in a perfect pre-rotation, and smiled when I came down under two thirds of a second later. A textbook triple Axel, from my airtime to the position of my body.

Maybe I'd even be able to push it to a quad before Nationals.

I probably should have stuck with my singles routines to begin with. But it'd been too infuriating that Jasper had found a loophole to avoid going head-to-head right when I was sure I could beat him.

Whatever. Competing one way or another was more important than showing him up. I could admit that much.

And he'd maybe even earned his victory over me and Jess at Finals. I could also admit that their epic free-skate performance hadn't relied only on Lou's skills.

At the other end of the rink, her laugh pealed out. I resisted the urge to glance over and try to guess what had provoked her amusement.

Going through the motions of the routine, I kept my attention on the precise angles and the amount of power I would need to make sure that each move was faultless. But every now and then, I couldn't stop my gaze from snagging on Lou. Her grace as she soared across the ice was close to hypnotizing.

When I was concentrating on my own run-throughs of both of my routines, I summoned a reasonable sense of satisfaction. I had them memorized—many of the spins and jumps were the same as I'd performed with Jess, just in a different order.

I didn't have that far to go before I could bring them up to scratch. And Niko had been worried about me.

I might have rolled my eyes, except right then I noticed Lou loping up the steps to the door, her skates slung over her shoulder.

Fuck! I'd gotten lost enough in my concentration that I hadn't noticed her hasty preparations to leave. Had it already been an hour?

Niko and Jasper were still on the ice, Jasper raising his hand in a farewell wave that Lou returned as she reached the door. My heart lurched.

I couldn't let her just leave—not when we hadn't exchanged a single word.

Ignoring whatever stares the other guys might be aiming my way, I flung myself toward the bench where I'd left my skate guards, tugged them on, and bolted up the stairs. Rafael didn't say a word as I barged past him, but I heard the rasp of his footsteps as he followed me into the hall.

Like he thought I might be a threat to Lou. For fuck's sake.

She was already halfway through the desolate reception area, just steps from the outer doors. My voice caught in my throat for a second before I forced it out.

"Lou, wait!"

Lou paused. I could see how she tensed in the instant before she turned to face me with wariness in her deep brown eyes. "Yeah?"

"Yeah?" I repeated. "Is that all you've got to say? I came all this way to help you—aren't you even a little glad to see me?"

Even as the words tumbled out, a flash of shame washed over me. Could I have sounded more pathetic?

But Lou's expression did soften a little, so maybe the sappiness was worth it.

She heaved a breath. "Look, I appreciate what you did—working with the other guys to find me. Thank you. But how much do you expect to change just like that?"

"Just like what?" I demanded.

She crossed her arms. "You *know* you acted like an asshole from the moment I met you—and even more so to Jasper, who you also know I care about a heck of a lot. Just because you admitted it the other day doesn't erase all those weeks. What, did you think all you had to do was lay on a little flattery, and suddenly I'd fall in love with you instead?"

My face heated, but I raised my chin. "I wasn't looking for 'I love you's. I just—I want to get to know you better. In all sorts of ways. You're not a one-guy kind of woman, and that's totally fine. I'd be willing to share you if it means you give me a chance to show you that I can be *more* than just an asshole."

Lou's gaze held me pinned in place. Her lips twisted in a wry smile. "It's not that easy, you know. I'm not sure if I want anything at all to do with you after the way you treated us. How long are you even going to be able to keep the peace with the three of them?"

"As long as it takes," I insisted. "You're more important than all that crap."

She let out a soft huff. "We'll see, I guess. It's going to take time before I can figure out how to feel about you, even if you mean that."

She spun on her heel, and this time I let her go without trying to call her back. How could I demand more from her right now when everything she'd said was true?

When she needed to get out of here to make sure her mom didn't come down even harder on her.

But as I watched her vanish beyond the double doors, my stomach sank. How the hell was I going to convince her to look beyond the past?

I strode back to the rink, gathering all my resolve. I'd just keep demonstrating my intentions until she believed me. That was all there was to it.

I'd never met a woman who awed me half as much as Lou did. I'd proven a lot of people wrong about me and what I could do, and I could prove to her that her first impressions had been wrong too.

When I returned to the rink, Niko was standing by the boards watching Jasper complete a jump, neither of them showing any sign of concern about my whereabouts. I didn't know whether I should be relieved or annoyed.

Well, they probably figured Lou could look after herself, which was fair enough.

I was just yanking my skate guards back off when my phone

buzzed in my bag. In my distraction, I picked it up on autopilot and raised it to my ear before I'd glanced at the call display. "Hello?"

My mother's voice crackled from the speaker. "Oh, good, you finally picked up. It's about time."

My shoulders stiffened. Shit. I'd been dodging her calls ever since we left Boston, just texting an excuse she obviously hadn't bought for a second.

My conversation with Lou had left my emotions frayed. I spoke more tersely than I meant to—more than I'd usually have let myself, knowing how easy it was to set the woman off. "What do you want? I'm trying to practice—which is what you *should* want me to be doing."

Mom sucked in a sharp breath. "Don't you take that tone with me, Quentin. Don't make it sound like I'm the bad guy here. When were you planning on having a real discussion with me? You up and disappear without a word, ignoring my calls, and all that after you fucked yourself over at Finals with your stupid idea to skate pairs."

My vision blurred with a toxic mix of emotion I couldn't afford to let out. "I've been busy."

"Busy? Busy ruining the career I worked so hard to make sure you could build. You can't even spare ten fucking minutes to talk to your mother? What did I do to deserve such a shitty excuse for a son? Where the hell are you?"

I'd gritted my teeth through the tirade, knowing there was little chance I'd get a word in even if she'd have cared about how I defended myself. At the final question, I rasped out, "You don't need to worry about that."

"Of course I'm fucking worried! My lord. Who knows what other braindead decisions you'll make without me watching over you? Now get your act together and start giving me the respect I'm owed—and I expect to see you skating your goddamn heart out at Nationals in singles, or you'd better believe—"

The tension inside me overflowed. "Don't worry," I interrupted. "I'm not going to throw a whole competition just to piss you off."

Then I tapped the button to end the call, bracing myself as if she could slap me across the head all the way from home. The way she no doubt would have if she'd been in front of me.

The way she had more times than I could count when I was growing up. Even left me with a pretty little scar on my face to remind me why I shouldn't cross her.

But I wasn't a kid anymore. I was twenty-one—in the eyes of everyone else in this fucking country, I was an adult by every possible measure.

So why the hell could she still make me feel like a cringing elementary schooler with a few well-placed insults?

I turned off my phone before Mom could launch into a barrage of texts or calls and slid it back into the pocket on my bag, only registering then how clammy my hand had gotten. My gut had tied itself in at least a dozen knots.

Fuck. How was I going to focus on practice like this?

I looked up, and my stomach sank all the way to my feet. Niko and Jasper had drifted closer while I was talking to Mom. They were both studying me now, Niko looking concerned, Jasper mostly just awkward.

He was the one who spoke first though, after a rough clearing of his throat. "What was that about? We couldn't help hearing—it sounded like a pretty intense conversation."

My face burned. Like I hadn't faced enough humiliation for one day. But telling Jasper off would only make it sound more like a big deal rather than less.

Instead, I shrugged, shoving all my uncomfortable emotions deeper inside. "It was nothing, really. My mom just doesn't know when to shut up. She has a lot of shitty opinions about my career, but I'm used to that."

A glimmer of startled recognition lit in my rival's eyes, one that horrified me even more as I realized what it meant. When I'd first gotten into the professional circuit as a junior competitor, there'd been a couple of public incidents after disappointing competitions… One where Mom had berated me outside an arena loud enough that a news crew had noticed and recorded some of it, and then the time when she'd smacked me hard enough that I'd banged my face against a railing and cut open my lip and chin.

No one had really tried to *help*, not that I could think of much anyone could have offered that would have been useful. They'd just reveled in the drama of it all until some other news story took over.

That'd been a long time ago. I'd gotten better at managing her moods and expectations over the years.

Jasper wasn't going to start pitying me now, was he? He'd probably assumed the tirades had stopped once I'd gotten older or forgotten about it entirely until now.

Something softened in the other guy's face, but instead of nauseating platitudes, his lips quirked into a wry smile. He rubbed the back of his neck before saying in an equally wry tone, "Well, I think I've had enough of the ice for today anyway. Anyone else up for waffles for dinner? That always puts me in a better mood."

I blinked at him. "Waffles?"

"Sure. Breakfast for dinner is totally a thing." He jerked his head toward his bag. "I even brought a bottle of maple syrup from where we were training in Ontario so we've got the proper Canadian stuff. I could spare you a dollop or two. If you ask nicely."

The glint in his eyes was more teasing than anything now, but in a way that felt almost… friendly rather than heckling. I didn't know how to respond.

Niko slung his arm casually around Jasper's waist and grinned at me too. "I know, the man is insane. But I have to admit the maple syrup is pretty nice."

I wasn't sure I'd ever had anything other than regular table syrup. I mentally flicked through my charts of calorie counts and protein quotas, and then shook myself.

The two of them weren't being weird about my whole mom situation. And they were volunteering to spend more time with me.

I wasn't going to get anywhere with Lou unless I was getting along with the guys she'd already chosen for herself too.

I aimed for the same dry but not hostile tone. "Jasper St. Pierre is trying to give me early diabetes—I guess it's my lucky day."

Niko laughed. "That sounds like a yes to me." He waved at my skates. "Get changed and let's head out. I'm sure we can manage to drag Rafael along too."

I sat down on the bench with a half-hearted grumble and snuck a sideways peek at Jasper as he wiped down his own skates. Watching for any sign that he was regretting his invitation.

Weirdly enough, he hadn't lost his smile.

Huh. I wasn't going to admit it out loud, but… maybe they weren't such bad guys after all. I might actually enjoy this dinner.

ELEVEN

Luciana

STANDING off to the side of my bedroom window, I watched as Mom got into the back of the waiting car. The sleek sedan pulled out of the mansion's driveway and headed down the main road beyond.

I'd overheard her telling one of her underlings that she had "errands to run." No telling exactly what those were, but I figured it'd give me at least an hour before she returned. And in the middle of the morning, barely anyone else in the house was roaming around.

Which made it the perfect opportunity to carry out a little "errand" of my own.

I slunk down the hall to her office door, twirling a lock pick between my fingers. When I caught no hint of anyone stirring in the rooms nearby, I knelt down, retrieved the second pick from my pocket, and went to work on the lock.

Mom had seen that I was well-trained. The lock was a good one as standard deadbolts went, but that only meant it took me ten seconds rather than five to disengage it.

Stuffing the picks back in my jeans, I turned the knob carefully. Not that anyone other than Mom hung out in this room, and I knew she was gone.

Voices traveled up the stairs from the foyer. I froze and then leapt the rest of the way into the office. Holding my breath, I eased the door shut as quickly as I could while keeping the click of its closing quiet.

No footsteps mounted the stairs. I stood there with ears pricked through several nervous thuds of my heart and then exhaled in relief.

I turned toward the rest of the room, my gaze skimming over the antique furnishings and their neatly arranged contents. Mom was a big believer in "everything in its place."

Her laptop sat in the middle of the elegant desk. She'd even left it open.

With a giddy skip of my pulse, I hurried over and rested my hands on the keyboard. My tap to wake up the screen brought with it a password window.

Shit.

I grimaced at the screen and made a couple of attempts—her birthdate, my name. But Mom was smarter than that. And also not particularly sentimental, as I was well aware.

The chances of me guessing her password before I got locked out and revealed my treachery were pretty much nil. With a sigh, I moved away from the computer.

The desk offered plenty of other opportunities to dig up some kind of evidence of Mom's plans that I might be able to use for additional leverage. I peeked through the few papers she'd left in a tidy stack at one corner and then tugged open each of the drawers in turn.

I found business receipts and contracts, financial statements and random notes, but nothing that looked like it related to her intended attack on some of her Devil's Dozen colleagues. But then, anything to do with that she'd presumably want to keep extra hidden.

I tapped on the back of the drawers in turn and couldn't suppress a grin when one wobbled a little. When I curled my fingertips over the edge, I was able to tug open a narrow hidden compartment that held a few more pieces of paper.

The first thing I pulled out was a piece of printer paper, folded once, with a list of names of what appeared to be companies: *East Marling Electronics. Fletcher and Co. Pawn Shop. Terry's Boutique.*

Next to each company name, Mom had added brief notes in red ink. *Weak security system. Manager gambles.* That sort of thing.

A list of vulnerabilities. She could be evaluating our own business ventures, but I didn't recognize any of the names.

I pulled out my phone and snapped a picture of the list so I could search for those companies later and see if I could figure out why they mattered to her.

As I fished behind the hidden compartment again, my fingers snagged on a more tightly folded paper. Easing it out, I discovered it was a map of the United States.

Sections of various states were circled in a few different colors. I wasn't sure what most of them represented, but I couldn't help noticing that a significant portion of Massachusetts including Boston had been marked off.

That territory belonged to the Harvester. Was she visualizing which pieces of the country she hoped to gain in her takeover, or was it just a coincidence?

I wasn't taking any chances. I snapped several photos of the map as well, a couple of the whole thing and then more closer up on different areas.

I was so intent on my documentation that the sound of footsteps didn't filter through my concentration until they were right outside the office door. My head jerked up with a jolt of panic.

My mother's voice carried to my ears, making my panic spike even higher. "You'd better tell Damien that I expect him to come to *me* next time, or he isn't going to have any fingers left to keep doing his work."

She must have been talking to one of her underlings. She'd come back early—someone she'd meant to meet had stood her up?

I didn't have time to wonder. As I shoved my findings back in the drawer as quickly as I could manage, keys clinked on the other side of the door. Fuck, fuck, fuck.

One of those keys rasped into the hole. I nudged the drawer closed and flung myself across the room toward the nearest viable shelter: a big potted fern spaced just far enough from the window that

I could crouch down and squeeze between the wide clay pot and the ledge.

I'd only just ducked into place when the door swung open.

"Stupid prick making me wait around for nothing," Mom muttered as she came in. "He won't be doing *that* again."

I could only imagine what horrible punishments she was devising in her head. My stomach knotted.

Please let her only be coming in to grab something before she took off again. If she stuck around and got down to work… Every passing second would mean another moment when she could unleash that anger on me.

Mom sank into her chair behind the desk. To my relief, I heard no sign that she'd noticed anything awry so far.

With a rustle, she withdrew her phone from her purse. She sighed and leaned back in her chair, making the wheels squeak faintly.

Whoever she'd called must have answered quickly. The tension smoothed from her voice, leaving it coolly nonchalant.

"Hello. I thought it was about time we touched base. I've narrowed down the list, and we shouldn't wait too long to get the ball rolling."

The list? Rolling the ball?

My pulse hitched. Was she talking to one of her co-conspirators? If she was going to say something incriminating, I needed proof.

Ever so carefully, I slid out my own phone and tapped the screen to start it recording.

Another squeak told me Mom had stood up. As she listened to the person on the other end, she paced behind her desk, her stilettos clicking on the polished hardwood.

Then, to my horror, she came around the desk and strolled across the rug toward the window.

"Oh, don't worry about that," she said languidly. "My people know how to keep their heads down when necessary. I'm sure yours can be circumspect as well."

Her scarlet fingernails dug into the curtain close enough to my hiding place that I spotted them through the fern's fronds. I held my body even more rigid as she yanked the fabric aside.

Starker sunlight streaked into the room. My mouth went dry. If she took even one more step and glanced down—

She stood, staring out the window, for a few seconds longer, and then turned on her heel to face the desk again.

"Oh, the others are smart, but they're not as sharp as they think they are. They've gotten complacent. It'll never occur to them to suspect anything like this until it's too late."

With every comment she added, I was increasingly sure this conversation was about her backstabbing scheme. I tipped my phone in her direction in the hopes that it would pick up her voice better, wishing I could hear the other side of the conversation too. Which of the other Devil's Dozen members was she talking to?

"Yes, I think that could be good to begin with, as we discussed before. The south end, around the square. What time do you think would give us the best balance of crowd cover and minimal witnesses?"

As she paused to take in the answer, I rubbed my free hand over the muscles in my thigh, which were starting to burn. I had plenty of muscle power and endurance, but this crouch wasn't a position I'd ever needed to hold in my figure skating practice.

The floorboards gave a soft creak under Mom's pacing feet. "Yes, and the water is a good option too. We'll put something in it—that'll do the trick. But not right in the Rosewood. We're better off going for a more discreet route."

Papers crinkled on her desk. Then she ambled back toward me. A cold sweat broke out down my back.

"That'll be fine. Let's get this done as quickly and quietly as possible. You know what your part is."

She whisked past me. If she'd glanced sideways, I'd have been a goner, but before I could do more than clench my jaw, she'd swung toward the door again.

Mom tucked away her phone and headed out of the office.

The second the door thumped shut in her wake, my shoulders sagged. I exhaled in a long but still cautiously quiet rush and stopped recording.

I wasn't home free yet. For all I knew, she'd just gone to grab a snack or convey a few orders and then she'd be back. I couldn't risk emerging until I was sure she wouldn't be close enough to see me.

I waited one minute, and another, straining my ears for her voice. When I heard it again, it was through the windowpane.

She was out front, giving orders to a couple of the sentries. Nowhere near the second-floor hallway. I had to get the fuck out of here before that changed again.

I had no idea what any of the things I'd overheard meant, but I could worry about that when my head wasn't on the line.

I squirmed out from behind the pot and dashed for the door. With my hand on the knob, I pressed my ear close and listened to make sure the coast was clear before yanking it open.

But, just my luck, as I eased it closed behind me, a voice traveled from the far end of the hall.

"What are you up to, señorita?"

I spun around to see one of Mom's higher-level lackeys leaning in a doorway several feet away. Shit.

Octavio pushed himself straighter and prowled closer, arching his pierced eyebrow at me. The twin gold spikes glinted against his darker brown skin. His dark hair fell raggedly to his chin, adding to his general air of menace. "You're not supposed to be in there."

I put on my best don't-fuck-with-me face, my eyes narrowing and my lips pursing. For the first time in my life, I hoped I resembled Mom.

"I think that's up to my mother, don't you?" I retorted. "I was grabbing something she asked me to get for a job she wants me to do, not that it's any of your business."

He made a scoffing sound. "Oh, yeah. And what is this thing you needed so badly, huh?"

I raised my chin at a haughty angle. "Did you miss the part where it's none of your business? If she wanted you in on it, I'm sure she'd have told you."

A spark of anger lit in Octavio's eyes. I was rubbing my higher position thanks to my familial ties in his face, and he didn't like that at all. The guy had been working for Mom for as long as I could remember, so I supposed I couldn't blame him for seeing me as a bit of an upstart.

But all he needed to believe was that he'd better not question his boss about how she handled her own daughter. Not when he couldn't be sure whether I was lying.

"She tells me plenty, pequeña rosa," he growled. "Pretty soon you're going to find out that you can't just bounce in and out of here whenever you want. It takes commitment to keep an operation like this running, and as far as I've seen, you've got nada."

I gave him a hard look in response. "As long as my mother's happy with my 'commitment,' somehow I don't care what you think. Unless you'd like me to mention your concerns to her?"

His mouth tightened, but he took a wary step back. "Just keep it in mind."

With one last glower, he stalked away.

I hurried back to my bedroom, my stomach twisted painfully tight. As long as he didn't call my bluff, I'd be fine.

He hated me because he wished he was in my place. Dios mío, I wished he was too. Let my mom pass on the torch to him instead of me, and we'd all be happier.

Somehow I didn't think he'd ever believe that. And that made him my enemy.

TWELVE

Niko

THERE WAS nothing I enjoyed more than seeing my two skaters whirl across the rink, hitting their marks with the same precision they had at Finals even though they'd been short on practice in the last few weeks. It was pretty amazing that I even *had* two skaters I could consider "mine."

But as I watched them from my spot near the boards, two worries nagged at me, dampening my spirits.

One was the unanswerable question of whether Jasper and Lou would be able to compete at the National Championships at all. We still had more than a month to go, but we hadn't made any definite progress in dragging Lou out from under her mother's thumb yet.

That didn't matter, of course. Whatever practice time she could make it out to this rundown rink for, we had to use as if we were sure we needed the preparation.

The other worry had to do with what I was seeing in front of me. Yes, my skaters were going through the motions, but something was missing. The soul-stirring emotion they'd provoked with this routine wasn't hitting me the same way, and I didn't think it was only because I was familiar with it. I'd seen it plenty of times before Finals too, and it'd brought tears to my eyes then.

No, Jasper and Lou weren't totally connecting with the material the way they had before. Which was probably understandable, given the tensions hanging over them as well.

It was my job to bring them back into harmony with the music and the movements.

After they'd struck the ending pose for the free skate program, I went over to join them. "Your rhythm and positioning is excellent, both of you. But I can tell you're a little distracted. Not your fault, obviously, but there's a little trick I'd like you to try out."

Jasper lifted his eyebrows in a typical skeptical expression, softened by his crooked smile. "A trick?"

I grinned back at him. "Just a little something that I've found helps me—how would you say it? Get into the groove?"

Lou rubbed her hands together in anticipation, always ready for a challenge. "Lay it on us!"

I tipped my head toward the speakers I'd set up on the boards. "When you go through the routine again, I'd like you to sing along with the lyrics, as much as you can."

Jasper's eyebrows shot even higher. "You want us to *sing*? We're figure skaters, not a band. Shouldn't we be saving our breath for the moves?"

I shrugged, still smiling. "I don't mind if you take it a little easy and adjust to fewer rotations. And you don't even need to use the right words, just make some kind of sound that matches the melody. The point is to get yourself fully in sync with the music and the emotion it's trying to convey."

Lou rolled her shoulders. "I've never been much of a singer, but I'll give it a shot." She elbowed Jasper. "Come on, it could be fun."

Jasper gave her a teasing glower. "You have strange ideas of fun, Punk."

Lou laughed and tugged him over to their starting position. I could tell from the loosening of his stance that he was going to give my suggestion a fair try too.

After I'd started their song playing again, my gaze wandered briefly to the other end of the rink. Quentin had claimed about a quarter of it for his own use. The last time I'd checked in on him, he'd been attempting a swift donut spin. It appeared he was still at it, his leg wobbling a bit before he managed to get it into its arcing position.

When he straightened up again, a dark scowl clouded his expression. I couldn't suppress a twinge of sympathy. It had to be hard for him, coming out here to Austin to help Lou while leaving his coach back in Boston, trying to train without professional guidance.

I'd have stepped in as well as I could, but he'd brushed off most of my overtures—and I had to admit that I wasn't sure I'd really do him more good than harm. I was new to this whole coaching thing, and I'd never really studied his skills on the ice before. I could advise Jasper and Lou from a position of familiarity. I didn't have anything close to that with Quentin, and he didn't have time for me to learn everything I'd need to in order to be really useful.

He shot a puzzled stare at Lou and Jasper when they took off across the ice, their voices wavering alongside the vocalist in the song. Their singing might not be the most in-tune I'd ever heard, but the eager gleam that was lighting in their eyes and the passion flowing through their limbs was all that mattered.

Partway through the routine, they ran out of breath and their voices fell away. But they swept into their final lift with the same vivid emotion that had captivated the audience at Finals. My cheeks ached with the stretch of my smile.

We weren't beaten yet, no matter what Lou's mother had to say about it.

Lou glided over to me, her whole face lit up. "That felt amazing!"

Jasper trailed behind her, rubbing the back of his neck, but I could tell from the pleased flush in his cheeks that he'd felt the difference too. "As long as we aren't doing that when we have an audience," he muttered.

Quentin took the opportunity to skate closer to the center of the rink where he could take a longer lead-up. He pushed himself into the spin again, whipping his leg up and around while curving his back.

It looked perfect to me this time, but clearly something about the attempt still failed to meet his exacting standards. With a curse, he jerked himself out of the pose. Without a word to us, he marched off the ice, yanked off his skates, and stomped off to the locker rooms.

Jasper frowned, watching him go. "Not so cool and cocky now."

His tone was wry but not really critical. I still felt the need to say, "He is kind of on his own here."

Lou let out a huff. "It's his own fault. I didn't ask him to make this big sacrifice in his career to follow me out here." She paused. "I mean, I'm not hoping he fails, but I wouldn't want him thinking that I owe him something when it was his decision."

I gave her shoulder a reassuring squeeze. "And he shouldn't think that. His past behavior hasn't exactly made it easy for you to, ah, appreciate his presence." My smile returned. "Speaking of appreciation, how about that singing technique? You two looked like you really got into it—it definitely showed in your performance."

Lou grinned. "Really? It did feel pretty good even if it was kind of embarrassing at the same time."

"You've still got the right spark," I said, directing the words at both her and Jasper. "I can see everything in you that made your performance at Finals amazing. Hold on to that, and you'll be golden at Nationals."

Jasper made a dismissive sound, but his eyes glinted playfully. "I guess eventually I'm going to have to learn to stop questioning your ridiculous advice, huh?"

I wagged a finger at him. "Because it's not ridiculous at all."

He laughed. "Only you could make stuff like this sound like a reasonable technique."

Shifting forward, he leaned in with his head lowering toward mine. I felt the kiss coming, and my pulse hiccupped—but not just in anticipation.

Before I had a chance to think about what I was doing, I pulled back a step. Jasper froze, his fond expression fading into uncertainty.

My stomach twisted, but I didn't know what to say. We'd just been talking about the sacrifices Quentin had made—what about all the opportunities Jasper had given up and was setting himself up to lose? Some of them were for Lou… but some were because of me.

I'd shoved myself into his life without really worrying about the consequences, hadn't I? And look where we'd ended up. The dreariness of the dim arena weighed down on me.

Jasper ducked his head and then looked up at me again, his forehead furrowed and his jaw tight. He looked so much like the frustrated guy he'd been during our first weeks of training that my gut twisted.

"What's going on?" he said, his voice gone rough. "You keep avoiding getting much into anything… physical. If you've decided you don't actually want that kind of relationship with me—"

My stomach lurched. "No, it's nothing like that. I do." More than I felt comfortable saying.

Jasper eyed me warily. "Then what is it? Because something's obviously wrong."

I fumbled for the words. "I just—I've been thinking about how we got started. I came all the way from Japan and badgered you into letting me coach you. But that—all of this—should be your choice."

Confusion still darkened Jasper's eyes. "It is. I thought I made that pretty clear. Why would you be worrying about it?"

Lou was watching me too. An ache expanded inside my chest at the thought of my deepest reasons. Reasons I'd rather not have admitted to with two people I'd come to care about so much.

But the feelings and trust we shared were exactly why I had to be honest with them.

My gaze darted away for a second before I wrenched it back to Jasper. "I've made… mistakes in the past. When it comes to my relationships."

Lou knit her brow. "What do you mean?" she asked softly.

Guilt soured my mouth. "A few years ago, I was dating a man I met in Japan. He wasn't a skater—not in the public eye at all. We'd gotten along really well, and I thought it could lead somewhere… But I've been out since I was a teenager, dealing with the judgments and the prejudice. I was so used to brushing it off like it didn't matter."

I paused, cringing inwardly at the memory, and forced myself to keep going. "*He* wasn't out, not even to his family. And during an interview on live TV, one of the hosts asked me about my romantic life, and I just said his name, automatically. Only good things, obviously, but there was no taking it back. His relatives, his friends, his employer and colleagues—I don't know how many of them ended up finding out, but they all could have, and he was horrified. And furious with me. To say the relationship ended badly is putting it mildly."

Thinking back to the flippant way I'd tossed out his name—with the arrogant assumption that if I could handle living this long in the spotlight with people knowing, it couldn't be that big a deal—left me queasy.

"Oh, shit," Jasper murmured.

My voice faltered. "His parents heard. They disowned him, shut him completely out of their lives. I screwed up his life with one stupid comment… He said I was selfish, that I only thought about myself, about looking progressive for my fans and making controversy—not caring how it affected anyone around me. And I can't say he was wrong."

Lou grasped my arm, her eyes wide. "It was an accident. Of course you wouldn't have done it on purpose."

I smiled wanly. "I didn't mean to hurt him, but I did it anyway because I wasn't thinking outside of my own perspective. I didn't consider the fact that he had a life beyond me with consequences I wasn't used to."

I shifted my gaze back to Jasper. "So it's really important to me that I don't get too caught up in my interests ahead of someone else's again. The last thing I'd want is for you to have felt pressured to go along with… any of this. The coaching, our relationship…"

For a moment, Jasper simply stared at me. Then a chuckle I wasn't expecting at all tumbled from his mouth.

"I get why you'd be worried after what happened before. But come on, Niko. Have I *ever* had a problem telling you when your approach was getting on my nerves?"

My lips twitched with the start of a warmer smile. "No, I guess you did let that inner grump out pretty often."

Jasper shook his head in amusement. "It was opening up about the fact that I did want to pursue something more with you that I had trouble with. I wouldn't have let myself admit it if I wasn't *one hundred percent* sure I want this, totally of my own accord, because it makes me happy."

I rolled that thought around in my mind. "I suppose you might have a point. But once the press finds out about our relationship—it's bound to happen eventually when we're together so much—"

He snorted and slung his arm around me, tugging me close. I couldn't help melting a little into the warmth of his solid frame.

"Fuck the press," he said with a hint of a growl that sent a shiver of electricity over my skin. "They can think what they want, and so can my family and anyone else who decides to have an opinion about it. The two of us—or, well, the four of us I should probably say—have something good, don't we? That's all that matters."

"Hear, hear," Lou put in, raising her hand as if offering a glass in a toast and beaming at us.

I found myself grinning back at the two of them, my spirits abruptly lightened. "That is what matters the most. And we do have something good—something *very* good. I'd imagine even Rafael would have to agree with that."

I hugged Jasper tight with one arm and drew Lou in with the other, tugging them together into a joint embrace. As Lou pecked my cheek and Jasper leaned his head against mine with a pleased hum, my heart swelled with joy.

This time, it seemed I'd done something right. Now if only I could free Lou from the shadows of her past, we could really get somewhere.

THIRTEEN

Luciana

THE PRACTICES I snuck away to were the only bright spots in my days. When I drove down the street toward the Cordova mansion after my latest skating session, my spirits still felt light from soaring across the ice with my men around me.

But as I pulled through the gate, all my remaining peace dissolved at the sight of a small army of Deadly Rose goons filing into a row of matte black SUVs.

Heart sinking, I parked in my usual spot in the garage and hustled back out to where Mom was standing by the front steps, overseeing the crowd. "What's going on?"

Mom motioned a few more men into one of the vehicles. In the wan light of the security lamps cutting through the dusk, her face looked tight. She smiled when she saw me, but there wasn't a particle of warmth in the expression.

"Oh, good, just who I was waiting for. You have work to do."

That was news to me. I searched my mind briefly for any memory of Mom telling me she had a task for me tonight and came up with nada. But telling her that wasn't a wise idea.

I crossed my arms over my chest in the sort of resolute pose she'd have encouraged me to take in front of our underlings. "What do you want me to do?"

It was an awful lot of underlings for the sort of jobs she'd sent me on before. I didn't think we needed two dozen guys to guard me at a meeting. Although I guessed that depended on who I was meeting.

Mom's smile only sharpened. "It's time I confirmed that you can handle yourself in action as well as in conversation. The Deadly Rose needs to crack down hard—one of our subordinate gangs tried to double-cross our people in a deal."

A chill flooded my chest. "And you want me to go with the guys?"

Mom's gaze pinned me in place. "I expect you to *lead* them. Take charge, direct the battle, make sure we come out on top. With an enemy this pathetic, it shouldn't be much trouble for you. A good starting place for building respect."

Without another word, she pushed a gun into my hand. I closed my fingers around it reluctantly, my throat constricting.

I knew nothing good could come from arguing with her, but charging off into a gang fight was the last thing I wanted to do. The violence and bloodshed was the part of the criminal life I'd always hated the most.

How could I say no? The second I defied her, especially in front of her underlings, she'd be sending a bunch of them to track *my* men down and deal out her sick brand of justice.

And they were even nearer at hand than she realized. It was a good thing my men had been holding on to my equipment bag and training clothes for me, so there was no hint of where I'd been to tip her off. God, if she found out that I'd been meeting up with them behind her back…

The fresh wave of icy fear propelled me into action. "Of course. I'll get the job done."

It was only criminals I'd be ordering our people to mow down, not innocents.

It could be worse.

Mom looked me up and down with penetrating eyes and then waved me toward the SUV at the head of the line. "Octavio will fill you in on the details and act as your second in command. I want to hear all about your victory when you get back."

Well, now it was definitely worse. I forced myself to stride over to the vehicle, where the man who'd hassled me after I'd searched Mom's office was watching me with a glower. He ducked into the back seat as I reached him and only let his lip curl into a hint of a sneer when he was out of my mom's sight.

"The pequeña rosa is in charge tonight, huh?" he said as I climbed in after him. "You got your brilliant plans all worked out?"

I narrowed my eyes at him. "I believe in hearing what we're up against *before* I start planning, if that's okay with you, hombrecito."

The dig did its duty. His full lips pinched together, the glint of his piercing flashing as his eyebrows dipped down. But he could say nothing. I was right, and he knew it.

The driver up front turned the key, and the engine roared to life. My heart thumped with a sickly erratic beat as the SUV headed onto the road.

Octavio swiped his hands together impatiently. "Listen up then. We're laying down the law with the Anacondas. They run things out of an old low-rise apartment building that was condemned a few years back but never torn down. The thing has four stories with a fire escape along the left side, leading to hall windows on each floor. There are three regular entrances on the ground: front, back, and right."

I nodded, picturing the layout as well as I could in my head. "Got it."

"Good. Most of those pendejos will probably be hanging out inside. The Anacondas don't do a whole lot of business, which I guess is why they got grabby and stupid. We can expect they'll have three or four people hanging around outside the building keeping watch, maybe a few more since they probably realize we're pissed. But we left it a couple of days so they'd start to get complacent. Now it's time to carve a message for the rest of the city in their blood."

I tuned out the churning of my stomach. "Got to make an example of them." My fingers tightened around the grip of the pistol.

Chances were I was going to have to fire the weapon tonight. I might very well need to kill someone myself. Why had these idiots decided to try and screw over Mom *now* of all times?

Octavio was studying me. "So you got a plan or what?"

If I faltered, he'd report it back to Mom. Hell, he'd probably give as scathing account as he could get away with no matter what I did. I couldn't leave any openings for him to criticize me.

This part of life under the Deadly Rose might make me nauseous, but Mom had roped me into enough discussions and past assaults for me to have a decent idea of how she'd have handled the assault. What I needed to consider. How to maximize their casualties while minimizing ours.

I could at least make sure as few of the men I was leading died as possible.

Not letting Octavio rush me into a careless decision, I spoke firmly and steadily. "We want to give the enemy as little time to prepare as possible. All the cars race in around the building at once—shoot the guards on sight. We enter through every available entrance including several guys going up the fire escape and smashing through the windows. All our force, all at once, before they even realize what's happening."

"The fire escape?" Octavio said with undisguised skepticism. "It's not like they'll have the ladder lowered for us."

I shot him a sideways glance. "I know. Park one of the vans right under it. Not that hard to hop from the hood to the roof and up, right?"

Octavio's silent scowl suggested he was pissed off that he couldn't find more to complain about in my suggestions. He shook his head with a sigh. "I hope you know what you're doing here."

"My mother seems to think I do," I retorted with an edge in my voice, reminding him of who had set this whole situation in motion. "Now are you going to relay the plan to the others or am I?"

He muttered something under his breath, but he got out his phone. In alternating English and Spanish, he conveyed my instructions to people in all of the cars.

I sank back in the leather seat, keeping my face composed in a mask of disinterest. Just another night, just another gang shootout.

Just another urge to vomit.

I wished I could close my eyes and completely shut out the horrible scenario I'd found myself in for a minute, but Octavio would take that as weakness. So I trained my gaze straight ahead and clamped down on my queasiness and flickers of panic as well as I could.

If this is what it took to protect those I loved, then I had to follow through. I wasn't letting down the men who'd done so much for me over a weak stomach.

I just hoped Mom would be happy with only one test and this wasn't the first of many.

Before that thought could fill me with even more horror, the driver jerked the wheel. "Coming up on the building," he said. "Just a few blocks away."

Octavio looked at me. "We hit them all at once?" Like he was giving me the chance to reconsider.

I stared right back at him. "The plan hasn't changed. Let's do this."

The driver pressed on the gas, and the SUV hurtled forward. The engines of the other vehicles roared behind us. Octavio pulled out his gun and rested it on his thigh before pressing the button to roll down the window.

The next several seconds passed in a frenetic blur. The driver whipped the SUV up onto the sidewalk and parked it with a jerk. Octavio was already firing through the window, other shots blaring as the rest of our army targeted the outside guards.

Through the open window, I watched two men near the brick building's front door jerk and crumple, bloody splotches dappling their shirts. The Deadly Rose force was already pouring out of the vehicles and charging toward the building.

Octavio heaved open the door, and all I could do was follow him. I wouldn't earn the respect Mom wanted by huddling in the backseat like a coward.

I was sending these men into the fight to their possible deaths. I'd damn well better have the guts to stand with them.

As I dashed across the sidewalk, a man ahead of me rammed his shoulder into the door. It burst open, and he headed inside, more shots ringing out. I lifted my pistol instinctively, grimacing at how familiar the gesture felt, how easy it was to fall in line with my mother's expectations. With the past I'd wanted so badly to shed.

I sprang through the doorway after the handful of men who'd taken that entrance. Shouts and footsteps were thundering from all around as the rest carried out my strategy to surround and overwhelm the building's inhabitants.

A man in a sweat-stained tee lunged out of a doorway with a knife. My hand jerked around; I blew a hole in his forehead before he could stab the blade at my chest.

As he toppled over, a shudder ran through me. I blanked my mind against the revulsion and pushed myself onward.

My ears rang with the booming of the gunshots. I moved from room to room, checking that any Anacondas in the place had been taken down.

Several other bodies lay sprawled across the floor. I didn't recognize any of them, and they were dressed shabbier than Mom would have tolerated. It looked like my army had cleared at least the first floor of opposition without any of our own falling.

I was just coming up on a kitchen at the back of the building when a skinny woman sprang at me, her fingers clawing at my face. My finger squeezed the trigger before I'd even processed that she wasn't holding a weapon.

Her head snapped backward with the close-range shot. Blood splattered the walls—and my face and shirt.

"Fuck. *Fuck.*" Bile rose up my throat, and I just barely swallowed it down.

Her body slumped lifeless on the floor. Had she been part of the gang or just a sort of groupie? Or even a customer partaking of whatever goods they sold?

Too late for that to matter now.

But Dios mío, this was not where I wanted to be. Not *who* I wanted to be. Who the fuck was I to decide who lived or died—to blast their lives away over petty squabbles?

I was supposed to be on the ice, conveying beauty and emotion for an audience, making them dream of things they hadn't imagined possible. Instead I'd been dragged into hell.

And now I was an instrument of that hell, this sick system that revolved around the most violent competition, all over again.

The kitchen beyond my latest attacker was empty. Nothing after it but the back door the Deadly Rose men had bashed down.

"First floor's clear!" I hollered out, my voice sounding distant to my ears.

A waft of cool night air washed over me from the open doorway. The shots were already slowing above me. They didn't need my leadership to finish this massacre, did they?

I drifted outside, taking a few steps into the shadows of the parking lot there. My head spun. I gulped a deep breath of the fresh air, wincing at the sticky patches of blood cooling on my skin—and two figures solidified on either side of me.

"What do we have here?" a hostile voice snarled.

They must have been Anaconda members who'd just arrived from someplace else. I whipped around, yanking my hand up, but I couldn't shoot both of them when they were in opposite directions.

I moved too slow in my uncertainty. One of my attackers hurled a fist at me. I dodged, but his knuckles caught my wrist, making me lose my grip on the gun.

I ducked and snatched after it—and a sudden thump sounded just a few feet away. Massive arms whipped forward to snatch one guy's head and shatter his spine with a wrench of his neck.

My fingers caught on the pistol. I jerked it up in time to put a bullet in the second guy's chest, just as the new arrival jabbed a knife into his throat.

I swung around to face off with this new figure, and the bottom of my stomach dropped out. The massive man's face was shadowed by the hood of his sweatshirt, but I'd have known him anywhere regardless.

"Rafael!" I hissed. "What the hell are you doing here?"

He frowned, pitching his own voice low. "I've been keeping an eye on you, like always. You think I'm going to let your mother just send you wherever? I couldn't let those pricks get the upper hand."

I wanted to protest that I could have handled myself, but I wasn't totally sure that was true, not when I felt so out of sorts. This slaughter was nothing like the operations I'd carried out of my own accord for my own purposes.

What would Niko and Jasper have thought if they'd seen this? Oh, God…

I yanked my mind back to the present and the one thing I did know. "You shouldn't have risked it! If any of Mom's people see you, if she finds out you followed me here and you're trying to help me, it's a death sentence."

Rafael's gaze seared into mine. Then, before I could react, he dragged me into a tight embrace.

"It's worth the risk," he murmured, insistent but strained. "It's always going to be fucking worth it to make sure you're safe. Lou… I love you. You know that, don't you?"

I shouldn't have been capable of the glow of happiness that lit in my chest. He'd never said that before, not in the actual words.

My throat choked up, and my legs wobbled beneath me. I'd never said it to him either.

I pushed myself back so I could meet his eyes. "Good. Because I love you too. And that's why you need to get out of here before anyone else sees you."

Rafael gave a curt nod with obvious reluctance. He hurried off into the darkness. With an ache in my heart, I let myself watch him go for just a second before I turned back to the site of the battle.

The guns had fallen completely silent. I'd only made it halfway down the first-floor hall when most of our men trooped down the stairs to join me.

A few of them held up bulging bags. "Got some loot to bring back too. Might as well take what we can, right?"

"Yeah," I said. "Waste not, want not." It wasn't as if stealing was worse than what we'd already done to these people. None of the corpses around us would have any use for their stash now.

Octavio appeared among the others, blood streaked across his cheek but otherwise the same as he'd looked in the car. "Every Anaconda in the place is down. I think we've made a clear statement about betraying the Deadly Rose."

I forced a stiff smile. "Then we're done here. Let's clear out before we have to deal with cops too."

The drive home felt like it took a million years. When the SUV parked outside the mansion, I peeled myself out of the back seat to find Mom waiting on the front walk, her eyes gleaming. Octavio had already called her to let her know how the raid had gone down.

She patted my shoulder with a smile that might have actually been genuine. "Good work, Luciana. I knew I could count on you. You really made a statement, both for our people and our enemies."

"I did my best," I managed to say, and motioned vaguely to my bloody shirt. "I think I'd better go get cleaned up."

"By all means. Then we'll have to enjoy a victory drink."

I trudged upstairs and swayed for a second before I managed to direct my body into my en-suite bathroom. The sight of myself in the mirror, hair mussed and face dappled crimson, brought back a surge of disgust and shame.

I looked like I'd orchestrated a bloodbath… because I had.

I couldn't squirm out of my clothes fast enough. After turning the shower as hot as I could stand, I stepped into the scalding spray and let it stream over me.

No matter how much I scrubbed my skin, I couldn't wash away the dirty sensation. I was soiled all the way down to my soul.

Mom was happy with my performance today. She said this was the *start* of proving myself.

What the hell was she going to ask me to do next?

I closed my eyes and leaned against the tiled wall, suppressing a sob. I couldn't keep doing this—I couldn't be what she wanted. Trying to meet her demands was killing *me*.

Finally, I shut off the water and pulled a towel around me. Back in my bedroom, I stared blankly at my closet without any ability to care about what clothes I put on.

My gaze fell on the purse I'd brought to my brunch with the Storm. The one I'd tucked Beckett's card into after he'd told me I should let him know if I could use his help.

Was there anything he *could* do for me? I couldn't be sure. But it was possible… and he might know how to reach out to the Blood Hunter too.

I knew that Mom saw them both as her opponents. The enemies of my greatest enemy should be my friends, right? At the very least, they might be able to help me gather more evidence so I'd have enough leverage to break out of her hold for good.

Even if it was a small chance, it was better than no chance at all.

I crossed the room to the chair where I'd left the purse and groped inside it for the card. Then I sat down on my bed with the burner phone I'd picked up to communicate with my men, staring at the number printed on the smooth cardstock.

Taking a deep breath, I punched in the digits and brought the phone to my ear.

FOURTEEN

Luciana

BY THE END OF PRACTICE, my muscles were burning in that familiar way I loved, but the sensation wasn't quite enough to wipe away the anxious tension that'd gripped me all day. I sat down on the bench and tugged my laces loose, unable to contain a sigh.

Jasper dropped down next to me, his forehead furrowed with obvious concern. "Are you doing okay? You've seemed a little out of it. I mean, your skating was great, but whenever we took a breather…"

I knew what he meant. It'd taken all my will power to stay focused when we launched into the moves of our routines. Any moment when I hadn't had that immediate goal in front of me, my thoughts had scattered.

I grimaced. "It's just getting to me, being back in that house. Being around my mom. I never know what she's going to ask of me next."

I couldn't tell him everything. I didn't want him to think of me blasting away desperate attackers in some rundown apartment building. As far as I could tell, Rafael hadn't mentioned anything to the other guys about the raid I'd led, and I'd rather they never knew.

I'd rather *I* never had to think about it again. In the back of my head, the memories of the jerking figures, the splatters of crimson, and the feel of the blood drying on my skin kept playing, flaring up behind my eyes at random moments.

Next time, Mom might ask me to do something even worse. And I had no idea what, when, or where.

My skin crawled just thinking about it.

Niko leaned against the boards across from us, his mouth slanting into a sympathetic smile. "It's understandable that you'd be distracted. I can't even imagine what it's like for you being trapped in this situation."

I squared my shoulders. "I'll get through it. It helps a lot that I can escape out here to the arena and see all of you. Gives me something to look forward to."

My gaze flicked toward the one guy I wasn't totally counting in my "all"—Quentin, still gliding around the far end of the rink as he perfected one of his step sequences. Since confronting me and demanding recognition for his efforts in tracking me down, he'd given me plenty of space. I hadn't heard him heckle Jasper once. In fact, this morning I'd come in to see them exchanging comments that had left Jasper *chuckling*.

Maybe Quentin really was doing his best to shape up not just his skills but his attitude too. And he was letting me decide how I felt about his efforts rather than getting pushy about it.

As I watched, he finished the final bit of footwork and paused to swipe a few strands of his pale hair back from his forehead. His gaze caught mine. His lips twitched with a hint of a smile, like he wasn't quite sure it'd be welcome but wanted to offer it anyway.

I wasn't going to be a total bitch. I shot him a quick smile in return and then looked away.

Why the hell had my love life needed to get even more complicated at a time like this?

Jasper slung his arm around my shoulders in a brief but emphatic hug. "You should just focus on what you need to get through this mess. We understand that you can't be one hundred percent on the ball with everything that's going on."

His supportiveness brought a lump into my throat. I yanked off my skates and reached for the rag to wipe off the blades.

A ping pealed out of my bag—the text alert sound for my burner phone, not my regular one. My pulse hiccupped, and I snatched at the pocket.

There was only one person who had that number who wasn't here in the arena with me. What did the acting Storm have to say to me today?

I tapped through to see the full text he'd sent. *It looks like one of the Deadly Rose's people tried to gain unauthorized access to a property of mine. I'll be dealing with the immediate response on my end, but I thought the surveillance footage might be useful to you.*

Then there was a link. I clicked on it and found myself staring at a list of image and video files.

Proof. Solid proof of my mom messing with one of her Devil's Dozen colleagues. The corners of my mouth lifted along with my spirits.

"What's up?" Niko asked, coming into the stands. "Good news?"

"I think so. A little more leverage to add to the stash I'm building."

I couldn't use it against Mom until I was sure I had enough to stop her in her tracks and shield me and the guys for the rest of our lives, but every little bit got me closer to that goal.

As I tapped hastily at the touch screen, transferring the files to a cloud server I'd set up to save all my recordings and other evidence, Rafael strode down the stairs from the rink's doorway.

"Everything's been quiet outside," he reported. "No sign of anyone having followed you or sniffing around."

I stuffed my phone back into my bag and let out my breath with a sensation of relief I knew wouldn't last—but that I'd treasure while I could. "Good. The one upside to Mom being busy planning a massive takeover is she doesn't have a huge amount of time to notice every time I leave the house."

Jasper glanced at the other two guys and then at me, a smile that looked a little sheepish crossing his face. "Speaking of that… Do you think you could get away with staying gone a little longer? I was thinking we could just go out and grab a coffee or something."

I blinked at him. "A coffee?"

His gray-green gaze held mine, so hopeful despite the careful way he was phrasing the question that it tugged at my heart. "I know you have to play it safe and there isn't much time for anything other than practice. But it'd be great to even have an almost-date, just the four of us hanging out like we used to..."

The lump that'd formed in my throat before expanded enough to momentarily choke off my words. I swallowed hard, wrenched by the recognition of how much I missed being surrounded by my men all the time. Sharing meals with them, watching TV with them, cuddling up on the sofa or in bed...

All the little pieces a relationship was made up of—the pieces we'd lost the moment my mom had dragged me back to Austin.

And she was ruining even this. Because I had to say, my voice gone rough, "I don't know if that would be a good idea. Risking being seen together anywhere at all public..."

But I needed him to know how much I missed him. How much I still wanted him.

Rather than trying to continue in words, I scooted closer on the bench and pulled Jasper into a kiss.

God, I'd missed all of this so much. I'd kissed him since we'd reunited in Austin—I had earlier today when I'd arrived for practice. But this time I threw myself whole-heartedly into the embrace as if there were no other demands weighing on me.

Jasper twined his fingers in my ponytail, tugging me even closer. As we both gave ourselves over to the kiss, his heat enveloped me. I wanted to melt right into him and never come up for air.

Except there were two other men I craved just as much. I let my lips linger against Jasper's for a few seconds longer, and then I pushed to my feet and grasped the front of Niko's shirt.

Niko beamed at me in the moment before our mouths collided. There was a sunny quality to his heat that was nothing like Jasper's but equally appealing. His deft fingers traced over my cheek while he tucked his other hand around to the small of my back.

I'd almost forgotten how well I fit against his slim but toned frame.

At a gruff clearing of a throat, I eased away from Niko to grin up at Rafael. "I'm not going to leave you out."

My bodyguard's eyes smoldered with a promise that left my skin tingling. "You'd better not, brat."

The low lilt he added to the teasing nickname had me drenching my panties. I hopped up on the bench above mine so we were practically the same height and threw my arms around his broad shoulders.

As he claimed my mouth, Rafael scooped me right off the bench. Enclosed in his brawny embrace, I felt invincible, untouchable. He couldn't really protect me from all of my mother's power, but I reveled in the impression anyway.

When he splayed his fingers across my ass, my pussy clenched. I kissed him with even more hunger, but every nerve in my body quivered with the knowledge that this wasn't enough.

I was going to take in everything my three men could give me. I'd had to deny myself too long as it was.

At the shift of my body, Rafael lowered me so I could stand. I teased my fingers down his solid chest and peeked at him through my eyelashes. "Secure the door and then come right back?"

His burgundy eyes outright blazed. He charged up the stairs two at a time, and I reached for the other two men.

Jasper and Niko watched me intently as I guided them back onto the rink rather than remain in the cramped stands. I tugged the down jacket Niko had been wearing off his shoulders, enjoying the quickening of his breath, and spread it out on the ice.

"Come here," I said, gripping their arms as I sank down on the makeshift cushion.

As he knelt next to me, Jasper drew me into another kiss. Niko settled at my other side and slipped his fingers up my back under my shirt. I hummed eagerly at their combined attentions, but the shape of another man drew my attention.

Quentin came to a stop several feet away from us, his posture rigid, his starkly blue eyes both scorching and uncertain. "I guess this is my cue to go?"

I paused, willing down the longing searing through my veins long enough to really consider the question.

I wasn't ready to invite Quentin *into* our little interlude. I didn't know if I'd even want to be kissing him again one-on-one, let alone adding him to the hard-won cooperative understanding that'd formed between the three men I'd already fallen for… one of whom he'd been a total asshole to up until a few weeks ago.

But a flicker of a memory rose up—seeing him at the locker room door while I took Niko and Jasper, all of us drenched by the shower. How hot it'd been knowing he was watching us.

He'd insisted that he could handle sharing me. Why not find out just how much he'd actually meant that?

I arched an eyebrow at him. "That's up to you. You got off on watching before. Maybe you could learn something about what sharing really means."

His pale face flushed. He drifted over to the boards, and I thought he was going to storm off. But he stayed there, his gaze burning into me, as Rafael strode onto the ice to join us.

I shifted my attention back to the three men I intended to fully enjoy this stolen time with. None of them looked remotely concerned about our spectator—if anything, I caught a competitive gleam in Jasper's gaze.

Oh, he'd like to show Quentin just how much the other guy was missing, no doubt.

As our mouths crashed together again, I slid my hands beneath my partner's shirt over his sculpted abs. At the same moment, Niko unclasped my bra with typical deftness. He reached around to fondle my breasts. The swipe of his thumbs over my stiffening nipples had me gasping into Jasper's mouth.

Rafael shed his own jacket to add to our padding against the icy chill. He stroked his hands up my legs to my thighs, chuckling when I arched into his touch, urging him farther.

"You've gotta practice that patience, brat."

I grunted dismissively and leaned forward to capture his mouth. Behind me, I caught a hitch of breath as Jasper turned to Niko for a kiss of their own. Despite the cool air, heat wafted around us, leaving me burning for more.

I yanked at Rafael's shirt and took a moment to run my hands and my eyes over the expanse of muscle I'd uncovered. As he smirked and gripped the waistband of my leggings, I twisted to free my other two men from their clothes as well, unwrapping them like they were Christmas presents.

Niko laughed as garments went flying, skimming his fingers over my bare skin and Jasper's at the same time. Jasper couldn't seem to decide whether he wanted to be branding Niko's lips or the side of my neck more, so he switched back and forth between the two.

I had no complaints.

As I wriggled fully out of my leggings, Rafael leaned in to press a kiss to my naked belly. At my encouraging murmur, he dipped his head lower to lap his tongue over my cunt.

I moaned, bucking toward him, and my gaze veered across the rink. Somewhere in the middle of our making out, Quentin had vanished.

I guessed it'd been a little too much for him after all. Or maybe the thrill hadn't been quite the same when he'd gotten permission, and he'd only felt awkward about gawking.

I wasn't sure if I should be disappointed, but the swipe of Rafael's tongue over my clit sent a rush of pleasure through me that washed any thoughts of the man *not* with us right out of my head.

A cry broke from my throat, but my hands felt too empty. I groped out and found the rigid length of Jasper's erection straining against his boxers.

When I dragged the fabric down and wrapped my fingers around his scorching skin, my partner groaned. He rocked into my grasp, pinching my breast and then tipping his head back to welcome another kiss from Niko.

Niko was still playing with my other breast. I swayed between the three of them, lost in the bliss they were conjuring in my body, wishing this moment could last forever.

Rafael sucked hard on my clit, and more pleasure spiked inside me. I could feel myself teetering on the verge of my climax, but this wasn't how I wanted to come, not just yet.

I dragged myself over onto my knees and nudged Rafael backward. "Payback time," I murmured, and lowered my head over his rigid cock.

It was hard to fit my lips around his thick girth, but I took him as far as I could go. Rafael cursed under his breath and wound his fingers into my hair, pulling it free from the ponytail.

As I slicked my tongue around him, my other men didn't neglect me. Jasper followed, leaving a trail of kisses down my back as he fondled my breast. His hand delved between my legs to mimic the motions Rafael had been performing moments before with his mouth.

Then I heard the tear of foil, and Niko's lithe hands grasped my hips. He positioned himself behind me and slid right between my slick folds until my pussy was perfectly full.

I moaned over Rafael's cock and began to rock more emphatically between the two men. The clench of Rafael's hand in my hair and the playful smack Niko gave my ass urged me onward.

Jasper was still working over my clit, his fingertips brushing the spot where Niko had joined me. Niko let out a ragged breath and turned partly toward the other man.

"Straighten up on your knees."

As Jasper adjusted his position beside me, I curled my fingers around Rafael's erection in place of my mouth so I could glance over and see what our mischievous coach was up to.

The gleam in Niko's brown eyes was all desire. He kept up his same eager rhythm inside me, pushing deeper at just the right angle to make me gasp, and lowered his head to suck Jasper's cock into his mouth.

"Oh, fuck," Jasper mumbled. He braced his hand against my back, stroking his fingers back and forth, and clutched Niko's hair with his other hand.

Seeing the two of them enjoying each other as well as me gave me the giddiest thrill I could have imagined. I bowed over Rafael again, determined to channel as much of the pleasure radiating through my body into him as I could.

Rafael's chest hitched, and his fingers tightened in my hair. He pulled on it with increasingly forceful tugs, spreading that blissful sort of pain through my scalp just the way he knew I liked it.

Niko thrust into me faster, hitting me at the perfect spot inside. I slammed back to meet him and drank in the panting of Jasper's breath beside us, the pleased sounds emanating from Niko's throat, the groan that reverberated from Rafael's chest.

Niko gave my ass another light slap that nearly tipped me over the edge. Then, still working over Jasper's cock with his mouth and pounding into my pussy with his cock, he delved one finger into the cleft between my ass cheeks. It circled my back opening and then eased inside.

Bliss flooded my body at the extra stimulation, and I moaned so hard Rafael jerked at the sensation from my mouth. With the movements of our bodies, the clothes beneath me shifted so one knee pressed into the frigid ice, but I didn't give a fuck. I was floating away on all this heady delight.

With one more press of Niko's finger, I came apart. My cry echoed off the high arena ceiling. Ecstasy swept through my nerves from every direction, casting me up and over like a tidal wave.

Even as I continued to shake with the pleasure of it, I clamped my mouth back around Rafael's cock. My hand slipped between his legs to cup his balls. Rafael shuddered.

"Lou," he growled in warning, but I didn't need it.

I sucked even harder, and his cum exploded into my mouth.

I drank it down greedily as if I'd been starving for it. Behind me, Niko bucked to his own release. His groan vibrated across Jasper's cock, and Jasper sputtered a curse as he followed us all over the edge.

With our limbs wobbly from the exertion and the impact of our orgasms, we collapsed together in a sweaty jumble on the pile of discarded clothes.

Niko stroked my hair and Jasper's simultaneously, his smile bright. "As much as I like working with both of you, I like playing even better."

Jasper let out a buoyant laugh. "And aren't we lucky that you're so good at both."

Rafael pressed a kiss to the top of my head. "*We're* lucky we had this stubborn woman to force us to get along."

I had to laugh too. "And here I was thinking I'm the lucky one."

Niko's hand drifted lower to trace the winged tattoo stretching across my shoulder blades. "We're here for you, Angel. Because of you. Because you're something special."

Jasper raised himself up on one elbow, catching my gaze. "Yeah. And don't you dare let your mom convince you of anything else."

My throat closed up again with a swell of emotion that was pure joy… and love.

This was where I wanted to be. Who I wanted to be with—always.

I'd told Rafael I loved him the other night without hesitation. It struck me now that I could have said it honestly to both of my skater men too.

The words itched in the base of my throat, but it didn't feel like the right time. I didn't want there to be any chance that they'd think I was babbling in the haze of fantastic sex rather than meaning it with all my heart.

I couldn't let anything stop me from returning to them again so I'd have the chance to tell them just how much they meant to me.

FIFTEEN

Luciana

I ARRIVED BACK at the mansion in a better mood than usual, the thrill of my interlude with all three of my men still humming through my nerves. The muted sound of music and voices filtered through the windows as I pulled through the gate. A bunch of Mom's underlings were taking a little recreational time in the backyard, their laughter carrying on the breeze.

The night, for once, felt welcoming.

I parked the car in my usual spot and got out. A quick glance over my street clothes confirmed that I'd brought no trace of my extracurricular activities with me. My skating stuff was safely stashed at the men's apartment. No reason for anyone to suspect I'd been doing more than grabbing dinner or taking in the city's sights.

Then I stepped past the front door and found Mom waiting at the base of the broad staircase.

She took me in with a cool expression, her arms crossed over her pale business suit that contrasted sharply with her tan skin and dark hair. My stomach plummeted with the immediate awareness that she was pissed.

"Luciana, come to my office, now," she said in a clipped tone, and spun with the expectation that I'd hurry after her.

Octavio's scornful expression flashed in my mind. Had he told her that he'd caught me slipping out of her office the other day? Shit. I'd been banking on his ego not wanting to risk mistakenly accusing me, but he had been acting pretty hostile toward me. He might have decided it was worth the potential consequences to try to screw me over.

That fucking prick. As if I even *wanted* any authority over him.

I had to play it cool regardless. My heart thudding, I strode up the stairs after Mom. "What's this about? Has something urgent come up?"

Mom didn't say a word as she stalked ahead of me. All I could do was trot along behind her like the little dog she'd trained me to be.

My teeth gritted, but I forced myself to keep walking. Defying her before I even knew what was up was a surefire route to disaster.

She stepped to the side of the office doorway to let me walk in and jerked the door shut in my wake. I stood awkwardly in the middle of the room while she marched over to her desk.

Then she whirled to face me. "How long did you think you could keep this up before I caught on? You don't really think I'm an idiot, do you?"

I bristled even as my nerves jolted with a deeper panic. What the hell was she talking about?

"Of course not," I said quickly, reining in the urge to babble. "I don't even know what you—"

Mom cut me off with a scoffing sound. "Don't give me that mierda. I know you're still skating."

I stared at her, my voice dying in my throat. She didn't know that I'd been gathering evidence against her, looking to undermine her schemes. That would have been good if she hadn't instead stumbled on the one secret that could destroy not just me but the men I loved too.

My mouth opened and closed a few times before I found my words. By then, it was probably too late to put on a believable show, but I gave it my best bewildered tone anyway. "Skating? I only went out to—"

"No," she said sharply. "Enough lies. I know how you look after you've been at practice, that head-in-the-clouds expression you get. Nothing else ever affected you the same way. I noticed it a couple of days ago, so I put a tracking device on your car. And where did that tracking device point to after you left today? It stopped just a few blocks away from a skating arena and stayed there for three hours."

Dread wrapped icy fingers around my gut. I couldn't deny her accusations when she had that much proof. It wasn't like I could convince her I'd been doing something else in the drab neighborhood around the rink.

Had she already sent someone to find out whether I'd been skating *with* anyone else? To hurt the guys as my punishment?

Oh, hell, no.

There was nothing I could do to fix this. Now that she'd caught on, she'd never let me leave the house without tracing my movements. I'd be lucky if I even got a chance to warn Rafael and the skaters.

There was nothing I could do… except play the hand I'd already been building.

A flicker of starker fear shot through my chest at the thought. I'd hoped that I'd have more leverage before I revealed my cards.

I'd gathered quite a bit of proof, though. It was probably enough.

It'd better be, because there'd be no coming back from this gamble.

I lifted my chin and drew on all the anger and frustration that'd burned inside me since I'd watched her step out of her car in Boston. "All right. I've been skating. So what?"

It was Mom's turn to stare. Her eyes narrowed. "So what? I told you that you're done with skating. You don't have time for that ridiculous hobby. Your attention needs to be here."

"It's my life," I said firmly. "I love skating, and I wouldn't *want* to live if I couldn't do it anymore. So I don't see why you should get to decide that for me. I've done everything you've asked of me even while fitting my practices in—you wouldn't even have realized if it wasn't for me being *happy*. What do you have to complain about?"

Mom's lips pursed so tightly it was a wonder they hadn't turned white. I'd talked back to her now and then in the past, but only brief throwaway remarks. Never such blatant, insistent defiance.

It was like I'd blown a fuse in her brain. There was no telling how viciously she'd retaliate when she got over the shock, but I couldn't back down now. I held her gaze unflinchingly.

When Mom spoke next, her voice was laced with venom. "I want you totally focused on the business. We're in the middle of something big, something that requires all your energy and attention. If you can't manage that in your current situation, then I'll simply have to rearrange your priorities *for* you."

There was no doubt what she meant by that. She hadn't tracked down my men yet, but she could be seconds away from doing so.

But then, she quite possibly would eliminate them no matter what I said next. So I'd better make this good.

I honed my own voice into a blade, even cooler than hers. "You're right, we are in the middle of something big. Huge, even. And wouldn't it be a horrible shame if the other Devil's Dozen members found out that one of their own is plotting against some of them?"

Mom's stance stiffened with twice as much shock as when I'd simply argued back. I didn't think it'd ever occurred to her that I might not just defy her but outright stab her in the back.

But I'd learned my methods directly from her. To get what you want from someone, hit them where it hurts.

Before she could snap out of her stunned silence, I snatched my phone from my purse and flicked through my recordings to one of the most recent ones. Then I slammed my thumb down on the track.

Mom's voice warbled through the speaker, distant but clearly audible. "My people know how to keep their heads down when necessary. I'm sure yours can be circumspect as well."

In the pause that followed, Mom lunged at me. Her arced fingernails snatched at the phone in my hands.

I yanked it out of reach, dodging backward at the same moment with years of trained combat instincts. My free hand came up in a fist, my feet falling into a defensive stance even as my pulse thundered in my ears.

Check. Mate.

"There's no point," I spat out before she could launch herself at me again. "Break this phone and nothing changes. Do you think *I'm* an idiot? Of course I've backed up the files—somewhere you could never reach them."

Mom's lips drew back in a snarl. "You little bitch—"

I glared right back at her. "I'm exactly the bitch you made me into, Mom. I learned from the best. And if anything happens to me, all the proof I've gathered will be sent out to the people you'd least want getting their hands on it. So don't think that taking me out will solve your problems either."

She didn't know how much I had. It could have been just that one conversation—but even that conversation had contained plenty of hints about her plans.

And for all she knew, I had a hundred times more.

Mom studied me for a minute, marinating in her rage. A shadow crossed her expression, and she drew herself back a step with a twist of her mouth.

"My own daughter, threatening everything I've worked for. Everything I've built *for* you. I can't believe it's come to this."

Beneath her obvious anger, she sounded almost sad.

I couldn't bring myself to feel sorry for her loss. I'd been telling her I wasn't the daughter she expected me to be for years. It wasn't my fault she'd never listened.

I squared my shoulders. "I don't want to destroy your empire. I simply don't want to be a part of it. You just won't accept that."

"Luciana—"

"I know, I know. It's my inheritance and all that. But skating is the most important thing to me in the world. I'm *good* at it."

Mom snorted. "Skating, *important*? Do you even hear yourself? Dancing around on the ice is a pastime for little kids. It should have stayed that way for you too. You're never going to be respected the way a Cordova woman should when you're prancing around in sparkly outfits begging for attention. What we do is in the real world, where the consequences actually matter."

I reined in my irritation at her dismissal. It wasn't as if I hadn't heard her talk that way about my dreams before. "Agree to disagree. It matters to me, and it's my life. It's about time I started fighting for what *I* want that life to be."

"Not a very good start," Mom said in an acid tone. "Throwing all your family loyalty out the window."

I shook my head. "I'm not, though. That part is up to you." I also wasn't such an idiot that I figured I could simply walk away with this threat hanging over us and trust that my men and I would be safe.

"I'll stick around and go along with your schemes," I went on. "I'll keep my mouth shut about the people *you're* betraying. On two conditions: You let me keep skating like I have been since I got to Austin, and you leave my men alone. You try to get in my way or hurt them, and you'll be the one ruining your plans. It's up to you."

Mom's gaze seared into me. "This is a dangerous game you're playing, mija."

I shrugged. "Like the work you have me doing isn't already incredibly dangerous?"

She exhaled in a rough sigh. "Fine. Have your ice time. Dally with these men you find appealing for some strange reason." Then she pointed a rigid forefinger at me. "But you'd better not slip up even slightly when it comes to carrying out my orders and fulfilling your side of the deal, or you'll be the one regretting it."

Even though I'd won this round, a chill prickled down my back, dulling my sense of victory. "I won't," I said.

But I had no doubt that from here on, Mom would be looking for any possible way to turn the tables on me and regain the power I'd stolen from her.

And if she managed to, there'd be no takebacks. My men and I were screwed.

SIXTEEN

Luciana

JASPER SWEPT me up into the air, and I glided along over him with my arms stretched wide. The chilly rink air washed over me, but I took nothing but enjoyment from it.

Especially since my recent confrontation with my mother had come with one upside. Now that she knew I was skating and grudgingly accepting the fact, we didn't have to hide anymore. Rafael had hooked us up with training times at a subdued but brighter and cleaner rink on the opposite side of town from our earlier digs.

Unfortunately, I couldn't take total enjoyment from the lift itself. A pang of strain ran through my legs and up my back, and my balance wobbled.

Jasper sensed my wavering and caught me in his arms before I could outright fall. As he lowered me to the ice, I grimaced.

When we eased to a halt, I swiped at the sweat on my brow. "Sorry. I should have had that."

Jasper waved off my apology. "Hey, none of us is perfect. You've been doing great."

Niko drifted over to join us. "It's understandable that you're getting tired. This is the longest you've been able to stay at practice since you got to Austin. You're going to need to rebuild your stamina now that you don't have to be quite as careful about your time."

I sighed, but I knew he was right. Even standing still, my legs still felt a bit shaky. The muscles in my calves ached. The physical workouts I'd done with the lackeys back at the mansion didn't compare to getting out on the ice properly.

I let out a growl of frustration. "I hate that I've lost so much time. How am I going to catch up for Nationals even with the longer practices now?"

Jasper squeezed my shoulder. "You'll get there, Punk. We've got a month to get totally into shape."

Niko flashed a smile at both of us. "I've seen you accomplish more amazing things than that already."

A hiss of skate blades announced Quentin's approach. He circled us with a teasing glint in his pale eyes. "You'd better not give up after you forced me back into singles and all."

I rolled my eyes at his gentle heckling. "You wouldn't have qualified for pairs even if we hadn't been in the running."

He laughed. "I don't know. Maybe seeing your skills scared the shit out of my partner and threw her off. I, of course, was totally unaffected."

"Of course," I repeated dryly. "Well, you don't have to worry about it. There's no way in hell I'm backing down."

Quentin's mouth stretched into a grin. "Just what I wanted to hear."

A twinge of affection rippled through the sense of defiant resolve he'd provoked in my chest. He hadn't actually been laying into me—he'd been trying to raise my spirits in his own way.

I was probably never going to receive gentle reassurance from Quentin Wolfe, no matter how badly he wanted to get into my pants.

I rolled my shoulders, revving myself up to take one last stab at the routine, but a text alert pinged out from my equipment bag. The sound I'd assigned only to my mom.

My pulse hiccupped. "I'd better see what that's about," I said, swallowing a lump of trepidation, and skated over to the stands. "It's my mother. Probably nothing important, just her finding whatever way she can to still mess with my skating time, but if I leave her waiting, she'll—"

My voice faltered as I took in the message that had popped up on the screen at the tap of my finger.

You're going to need to continue gaining the respect of our employees if you expect to retain any of my good will. I've set up a meeting Thursday night with the Hellborn for an exchange of our steel merchandise. I want you to lead the hand-off. Make sure you're properly prepared.

My stomach sank. Had she really not been able to wait to deliver her instructions in person, or was she so angry with me that she preferred to keep me at a distance for the moment? Or maybe she'd simply wanted to distract me from my practice like I'd initially figured.

But the real reason for my dismay was the job itself.

Jasper had joined me, peering at the screen over my shoulder. "The Hellborn? Somehow I'm guessing they're not a boy band."

I made a face. "They're a local gang in Dallas—a lot less powerful than my mom's organization but a significant ally in their territory. She said 'steel,' so it'll be a shipment of stolen cars we're handing off."

Niko studied my expression from where he was leaning on the boards. "Is this outside your usual responsibilities?"

"Not really." I shook off my nerves as much as I could. "It's just that the guy who usually handles the exchanges for the Hellborn hates me. I met him a few years ago on a job with my mom, and he kept taking jabs at me. So I had a few choice things to say in return… which a bunch of his colleagues overheard. He was obviously pissed off that I'd made him lose face, but he couldn't really retaliate against me with my mom right there."

The memories swam up through my mind of that prick Maverick and his sneering insinuations. Mocking me when I hadn't identified the exact make of a particular car, implying that I was just tagging along like a little kid, not contributing anything useful.

When he'd gotten a little bolder and suggested a few ways I could *make* myself useful, complete with crude gestures, I'd known I couldn't let it stand. So I'd informed him in vivid detail of just how pathetic I imagined his skills in that department were and how small a dick he had to work with.

The image of his glowering face, flushed with humiliation but also a crapload of anger, made every muscle in my body tense up.

Jasper scowled. "It sounds like he deserved the backlash."

I smoothed back my ponytail. "Oh, he absolutely did. And he's probably been waiting to pay me back ever since. This time I won't have my mom there to make him nervous about disrespecting her… She'll want me to prove I can handle him and the rest of those goons without relying on her."

Which meant this meeting was going to be a hell of a lot more dangerous for me than a simple exchange of merchandise. But I didn't want to spell that out for the men around me.

My fingers hovered over the screen. I had the momentary urge to tap out a message asking Mom if she was sure this was a good idea, but I reined the impulse in.

I was supposed to be showing how strong I was to keep *Mom's* desire for vengeance against me in check. This was the first big ask she'd made since I forced her into our own deal—I couldn't chicken out already.

No doubt she remembered that incident from three years back. I'd bet she was counting on Maverick giving me a hard time.

Well, if I could stand up to her, facing this asshole should be no problem at all.

Sounds good, I wrote back, as if there was nothing I'd rather do with my Thursday night. *I'll keep everyone in line.*

Then I stuffed my phone back into the duffel bag, pretending my gut hadn't turned into a ball of queasiness. My arrangement with Mom wasn't going anywhere near as smoothly as I'd hoped.

Even if I took care of the Hellborn no problem, what was she going to get me into next? Was she even still trying to groom me as her heir, or was she hoping someone else would take me out of commission to diffuse my threat against her?

No, she had no idea how I'd set up the evidence I'd stored. For all she knew, even me getting injured would prompt an email to her fellow Devil's Dozen members. She wouldn't take that chance.

But she'd tread as close to the line as she could if it meant making me regret crossing her.

Jasper gave me a tentative nudge of his elbow. "Do you want to go another round?"

I dragged in a breath, and all at once I felt more than ever how exhausted I was. I'd already gone two hours longer than I'd been able to any time since we'd reunited in Austin. My ribs, still a bit tender after getting badly bruised in Boston, were aching a little too.

Maybe I could use a break. If I pushed myself too hard all at once, I'd ruin my chances of competing that way instead.

"You know," I said reluctantly, "I think I'd better call it a day."

Niko's eyes twinkled. "Let's go grab some dinner, then. You two…" He paused and glanced toward Quentin. "You *three* could all use some fuel after all that exercise. And I'm sure Rafael would appreciate a change of pace from standing guard over the rink entrance."

I managed a genuine if tight smile. "Yeah. Dinner sounds good. Let's live a little."

And hope that I'd still be alive and well after Thursday night to live some more.

SEVENTEEN

Jasper

"PIZZA?" Quentin muttered from the passenger seat beside me. "Don't any of you count your carbs? Protein's what'll keep your muscle mass up."

My hands clenched around the steering wheel, but Lou swatted him from behind, saving me the need to respond. "Last time I checked, there's protein in cheese and pepperoni. And no one said you *had* to join us for dinner."

Quentin tensed up for a second before the playfulness of her tone must have sunk in. It was weird seeing him this on edge, eager to please someone other than himself.

Remembering how Lou had thrown my own emotions for a loop when I'd first met her, I could almost feel a little sympathetic.

Almost.

Quentin sighed, but his own tone lightened to match hers. "I suppose one slice won't hurt anything. I'll see what else they've got on the menu."

I restrained a groan of frustration and drew my focus back to the traffic around me. Quentin *had* been on better behavior since we'd come to Austin. I knew it was mostly for Lou's benefit even when she wasn't with us, but I could give him a little credit for self-control—and do my best to rein in my own irritation.

The right lane was packed with parked cars. I eyeballed them for my chance to veer over to make the turn I needed to. One started flashing its turn signal to pull out into traffic, so I switched to the brake to give it a chance to enter ahead of me.

Quentin let out a huff. "Jesus, St. Pierre, who taught you how to drive? We could have been halfway across town by now."

The jab raised my hackles in an instant. "Some of us learned to be courteous to other drivers on the road."

He snorted derisively. There was a familiar quality to the sound that cut right to the quick of my nerves. "There's polite and then there's being a total wimp about it. You know, if you want to get anywhere in life, you've got to—"

"Maybe I don't fucking care what you have to say about it," I burst out. "Let me drive however the hell I want to drive!"

The car jerked to a stop at a red light, and uncomfortable silence clogged the car. A burn of embarrassment spread up the back of my neck.

He'd only been casually hassling me. I hadn't needed to start yelling and swearing at him. So much for keeping my temper in check.

After a blip of shock, Quentin simply shook his head at me. His nonchalant reaction abruptly reminded me of what he'd said about his mother. How many times had he needed to deal with *her* snapping at him out of the blue like I'd just done?

Fucking hell.

As I sucked in a deep breath, trying to steady myself, Quentin clicked his tongue chidingly. "And there's another thing. You're going to keep getting distracted from your performances if you let people rile you up at the drop of a hat."

I managed to keep my voice at a normal volume, though it still came out sharper than I'd have liked. "Thanks for the tip. It'd be easier if you didn't have a knack for sounding just like my asshole dad."

Quentin let out a scoffing sound. "He couldn't have been that bad when he funded all your training with his posh job."

My anger flared back to the surface and crackled through my retort. "He didn't spend a goddamn penny on my skating. It was all my mom—until he made *her* stop when I was eleven and after that it was all on me and whatever sponsorships I could scrounge up. He *hated* me training."

Quentin's mouth opened and then closed again. I'd managed to stun him into silence. I guessed it wasn't totally surprising—given the kind of money my dad brought in from his job in corporate law and the trappings of privilege that I'd grown up with, people tended to assume that I'd never struggled to fund my pursuits.

Was that what Quentin had figured all this time? That I'd had everything I'd worked so hard for just handed to me?

The awkward silence lingered for a minute, and I cursed myself inwardly. It was the first night we'd been able to go out and do something with Lou, an actual date, and I'd ruined the evening before it'd even really begun with my stupid temper.

Then Niko's buoyant voice carried from behind me. "You know the only problem with a pizza place? They probably don't serve Calpis."

The remark was so out of the blue and yet so Niko that a laugh sputtered out of me. "I'm not sure *anywhere* in Austin serves Calpis. It's a good thing you seem to be able to survive without your fizzy milk."

"Just you wait until I get my hands on some and make you try it," Niko said. I could practically see the mischief dancing in his eyes. "You won't believe you ever doubted its deliciousness."

"I'd give it a try," Lou piped up.

I gave a brief grunt. "Now you're making me look bad."

Rafael backed me up with a low chuckle. "Don't worry—I'm with you. Milk and carbonation should not mix."

Niko gasped in mock-dismay. "Just for that, I'm force-feeding *you* the first bottle."

A smile tugged at the corners of my lips. "Shouldn't you save it all for yourself if you finally find some?"

"Hmm. You might have a point there. I'll have to reconsider my plans."

We all laughed, even Quentin, and the tension in the air seemed to fade. But as I parked outside the pizza place and stepped out into the cool early-winter air, apprehension still niggled at me. Niko reached over to give my arm a reassuring squeeze before we headed into the restaurant, and I couldn't miss the concerned glances Lou was shooting my way, as if she were evaluating whether I might be on the verge of melting down.

I grimaced inwardly. Why had I gone and said all that stuff about Dad? I'd mentioned my family issues to Lou before, but not quite how far he'd gone in his refusal to support my career. She'd probably assumed it'd been limited to criticizing *how* I was spending his money, not refusing to offer any cash whatsoever.

And it was humiliating to have lost my temper at all.

I placed my order half-heartedly and mostly listened as easygoing banter flowed around the table.

Rafael eyeballed the massive milkshake Lou had requested. "It's bigger than your head. You're really going to drink all of that?"

"I'm capable of incredible things," Lou informed him with a cheeky grin.

"I'm not sure you'll be capable of fitting any pizza in your stomach after that."

Quentin flashed a smirk. "I could always take it off your hands and save you from yourself."

Lou arched her eyebrows at him. "No rescuing necessary here."

Niko leaned toward Quentin with a sly glint in his eyes. "So you'll go for dessert, then? It's only pizza you object to?"

Quentin straightened up with an authoritative air. "The most important factor in an ideal athletic diet is balance. My body is the machinery I use to perform my routines. I'm screwing myself over if I load it up with too many useless calories."

Lou tapped the side of her glass. "Protein. Fat. Calcium. All necessary in a balanced diet."

He smiled at her. "That's why I'd take a milkshake off your hands but not a slab of chocolate cake."

Niko knit his brow in a show of bewilderment. "Your priorities seem very sad for your taste buds."

Quentin just shrugged with an amused expression, and it occurred to me that he was starting to feel like a normal part of our group rather than an unwelcome intruder. Somehow he was fitting in with us as if he actually… added something to the dynamic. Something not entirely horrible.

The thought sent a twinge of warmth through me at the same time as it made me want to throw the guy through the restaurant window. Okay, so my feelings about his presence definitely hadn't untangled themselves yet.

As I gulped down my last bite of my third slice of pizza, Niko got up and tugged on my shoulder. "I saw a dessert display case near the door. Come on, let's see what they've got. I know *you* have a sweet tooth."

I couldn't argue with that, especially when I took in the momentarily pensive light in his bright eyes. His request wasn't just about indulging in sweets.

Lou leapt to her feet and grabbed my hand. "You're not picking for all of us! I've got to have a say too."

I let myself be basically dragged over to the glass case just past the cash register. I couldn't really regret the trip once I took in the offerings. Choosing between tiramisu, cannoli, and sfogliatelle was not going to be easy.

As he studied the array next to me, Niko looped his arm around mine. "Is everything all right? The conversation in the car obviously brought up some bad memories, and you've been quiet since then."

Lou nudged her shoulder against mine companionably. "Yeah. If you want to talk about it, you know we're here."

In the face of their gentle support and the fact that they'd thought to pull me away from the two guys I wasn't as comfortable opening up in front of, my chest ached with affection. "You brought me over here to corner me, huh?" I said, but I didn't put any rancor into the words.

Lou pecked my cheek. "Just making sure you know we've got your back."

Yes, they did. I exhaled a little raggedly and forced a tight smile.

"I've already told you some of it, Lou. My dad was a jerk, criticizing everything I did, but especially the skating. He and my mom argued about it a lot."

Niko frowned. "I didn't realize they withdrew their financial support so early."

"It is what it is." I rubbed the back of my neck. "I guess I should be grateful he never brought out the insults when we were in public like Quentin's mom did. Although on the other hand, at least she *wanted* him to skate. My mom had some money of her own from an inheritance that she put toward my skating, but Dad got more and more pissed off about my 'sissy pursuit' as I got older, and finally he threatened divorce if she didn't stop."

Lou released a sound like a growl. "And she bowed to the pressure, huh?"

"It's hard to blame her. She was choosing between her entire marriage and something that was just one part of her kid's life. She couldn't have known back then that I'd manage to make a career out of it."

Niko slipped his arm right around my waist and gave me a sideways hug. "But you did, even without their money. You paid your own way."

I dipped my head. "Yep. It was a struggle sometimes, especially getting that first sponsorship—nothing big, just enough to keep me in ice time and basic equipment. It's hard to know what to say sometimes. Everyone always figured I had tons of support—financial and emotional—but I was teetering on the edge of having to quit more than once."

"He's a total prick to freeze you out like that," Lou said tartly, but with a vehemence that made me think it was a good thing she'd never encountered my father. Things would probably not go well for him, especially if she happened to be armed.

She flexed her hands before shaking off a little of the tension that had come over her. "You don't see him anymore, do you? You shouldn't let what he thought get to you. He was obviously wrong to dismiss your talent."

"Yeah." My head drooped. "I don't know. It's hard to set all of that history aside. My mom is great, really—she's always been there for me in every way she can without totally blowing up her marriage. I know how much it hurt her, fighting with him over me. Thinking she might lose him completely. When they weren't dealing with my skating interest, they were really happy together."

I paused and then admitted the doubt that'd weighed on me for so long. "Sometimes I wonder if it was really worth it. I was so set on pursuing skating that it messed up both of their lives, hers especially, and after all that, it's not as if I've accomplished anything so incredibly great so far."

Niko scoffed lightly and gave me a little shake. "What are you talking about? You're great already, and soon you'll be proving that to even more people than you already have. I wouldn't have chased you halfway around the world otherwise."

Lou poked me in the arm. "Yeah, you're a superstar who just needed a bit of a break for understandable reasons. Really, the two of us should start an Unsupportive Parents Club. It sucks, but we're not letting them win."

I couldn't help smiling at her enthusiasm. "I probably shouldn't complain when I know what *you're* dealing with. You're right. No one gets to win but us."

"That's the spirit!" Niko leaned closer to the display case. "Now about that dessert…"

In the end, we ordered five portions of tiramisu for the table, figuring that if Quentin turned his nose up at the treat, the rest of us could easily find a way to make his portion disappear. As we returned to the table, the waitress was already bringing the dessert plates over.

Quentin eyed his like he was scanning it for its calorie count, but he kept any snarky observations he might have had to himself. As I settled into my seat, he glanced at me, hesitated, and leaned closer so he could pitch his voice for just my ears.

"Hey, I—I'm sorry about before. About stirring up shitty memories. It's hard not to fall into the habit of getting on your case, but I really didn't mean to poke a sore spot like that."

I could tell from his awkward stance and the faint flush that'd come over his face that he meant it, as embarrassed as he was to be apologizing. Well, I guessed he would know what it was like having the baggage of harsh parents.

I offered a small, crooked smile in return. "I appreciate the apology."

Quentin paused again. Then he said in a halting tone, "It's actually pretty impressive that you got that far all on your own dime."

Somehow the acknowledgment did more to smooth over the animosity between us than his apology had. I had to answer, "Considering the challenges we've all had to deal with, it's pretty impressive any of us are here."

Quentin's eyes glittered with eager determination. "And not going anywhere."

He deigned to take a bite of his dessert and seemed to contemplate its flavors for several seconds while he chewed. When Lou tried to steal a chunk off his plate, he tugged it closer with a waggle of his fork.

Watching him, my urge to throw him out a window—or send him back to Boston on his own—faded away. He had been an ass, but I'd never have expected the old Quentin to admit he'd done anything wrong, let alone apologize for it.

If even Quentin Wolfe could adjust his attitude for the greater good, then there wasn't any reason I couldn't too.

EIGHTEEN

Luciana

THURSDAY NIGHT FOUND me in the last place I'd have wanted to be: the back seat of one of Mom's cars, being driven by a Deadly Rose lackey to a hand-off with a man who probably wanted to dance on my corpse.

And lucky me, I had *another* man shooting daggers at me with his dark eyes from the seat beside me.

"I hope you're ready for this, pequeña rosa," Octavio said in a disdainful tone, rubbing his forehead just above his spiky eyebrow piercing. "Maverick has been chafing in the Deadly Rose yoke lately, getting big ideas about who should really be in charge. I'd be surprised if he *doesn't* try to screw us over today to show off for the rest of his stupid outfit."

Oh, great. So not only did Maverick have personal reasons to want to stick it to me, he'd become even more of an aggressive asshole in general.

"Thanks for the heads up," I said, keeping my own voice even.

Octavio narrowed his eyes at me. "Your mom will expect you to put him in his place. Permanently." He drew his finger across his throat in a gesture that couldn't have been more unambiguous. "Make a clear statement to the rest of the gang."

My stomach twisted with a jab of queasiness. More blood on my hands to appease Mom? Not that I thought Maverick deserved to keep living his life of violence and assholery so very much, but every death I dealt out myself felt like another boulder weighing on my conscience.

Was that even what Mom would want? She hadn't given me any orders to that effect when we'd talked directly earlier this evening, only that she expected me to keep the Hellborn in line. If she had a specific opinion about how I did that, normally she'd have said it outright.

I kept my answer noncommittal. "We'll see how it goes."

Octavio shrugged and slouched back in his seat. "Your funeral if you disappoint her."

I studied him from the corner of my eye. He was laying it on pretty thick.

I already knew *this* asshole didn't have my best interests at heart. Was he promoting some agenda of his own under the guise of it being Mom's? Or simply hoping to trip me up by pointing me down a path Mom wouldn't have wanted at all?

No doubt he'd be oh so happy if I came out of this looking inept. Or dead.

Following his advice seemed like a surefire way to screw myself over. Whatever Maverick did, I'd just have to find some way of laying down the law that didn't involve murdering him. Then I'd be happier and Octavio would be unhappier, and at least it'd be a win in those two ways.

And if Mom didn't like it, she was welcome to hand over the role of second-in-command to this cabrón here and cut me loose.

Our car pulled into the chosen meetup spot first, a dusty stretch of hard-packed earth in the middle of nowhere, about halfway between Austin and Dallas. The transport truck carrying the high-end stolen cars collected by one of Mom's subsidiary gangs rumbled after us, followed by two more cars that contained my squad of backup lackeys.

Maverick wasn't the only one who needed to think about how he'd come across in front of his companions tonight. If I betrayed any weakness while Mom's underlings were watching, things could get *very* difficult back at the house.

I stepped out into the night. The fresh country air was a relief as it flooded my lungs, but I didn't dare step more than a few feet beyond the hood of the car. Even with supposed allies, you had to be cautious.

Our headlights caught on a few cars parked a couple hundred feet away. A cluster of figures peeled themselves out of the shadows around those vehicles and sauntered over to meet us.

I hadn't seen Maverick in three years, but it was easy to recognize the prick right there in the middle of the pack. He held himself like a tubby, redneck Napoleon surrounded by his shittily tattooed army. Arrogance radiated from his stance like a bad stench.

As they approached, I drew my frustratingly short frame up a little taller and held my ground.

He aimed a sneering grin at us with a glint of his crooked teeth. "Cordova sent her little girl, huh? Maybe I should take that as a gift."

I rolled my eyes. "The less time I have to spend anywhere near you, the better. You can see we brought the cars. Where's our money?"

He clucked his tongue at me. "Now, now. Don't get your panties in a twist. You shouldn't have come out here if you were on the rag."

His fellow goons snickered. Frustration prickled through my veins, but I kept my tone totally bored. "Do you have the cash or not?"

Maverick motioned at one of the guys behind him. The sunburned thug swung a duffel bag for Maverick to grab.

The asshole took a couple of steps toward me but then stopped rather than continuing forward to offer up the bag. Instead, he set it on the ground in front of him and unzipped it.

Normally it'd be my people doing the counting to make sure the Hellborn were giving us what we were owed. I would have said as much, except Maverick didn't just paw through the bag's contents. He immediately started pulling out wads of bills and tossing them in a growing heap beside him.

"What the hell are you doing?" I demanded.

He glanced up at me, a gleam lighting in his eyes that was both sadistic and a little crazy. "You're not the real woman in charge, now are you? I figure you're worth barely half my respect. So you get half the payment. Seems fairer that way, don't you think?"

Another chorus of guffaws, these ones both shocked and awed, carried from his crew.

My teeth set on edge. "Actually, I don't think so. I didn't drive all the way out here to be insulted, and I carry the full authority of the Cordova family. Deliver the agreed upon payment *now*, or you're going to regret it."

"Big words from a little pipsqueak of a girl." Maverick shook his head. "Nah, I like my way better." He took another handful of cash out of the bag.

Fury seared up through my chest. Fury that this idiot was mocking me. Fury that because of who he was and who I was, I was going to need to betray every shred of morality I had in me to set this right.

But his gang was watching, and so was mine. I couldn't let his blatant disrespect go unpunished, not if I wanted my deal with Mom —and the safety of the men I loved—to stay intact.

I had to act—and fast, while the element of surprise could offset the size difference between me and my opponent.

I could have gone for the gun tucked into the back of my ripped jeans. I could have blasted the prick away where he squatted. But that would be playing into Octavio's plans, not mine.

Instead, my hand dug into the pocket of my hoodie and closed around the handle of my knife. Without any warning, I launched myself at Maverick.

He might have had nearly a hundred pounds on me, but I'd trained against bigger guys my entire life. Helpfully, he was already crouched on the ground.

I slammed into him and knocked him onto his back before he'd even registered he had a fight on his hands. He grunted and swung a fist, which froze in midair as I pressed the blade of the knife to his exposed throat.

"That's right," I said in a tight, dark voice, my knee digging into his gut. "Stay right there, or this goes straight through your jugular."

I held out my free hand toward the Deadly Rose underlings.

"Another blade, please? I think Maverick here needs a more constant reminder of who has the real power."

One of the men darted forward and pressed a switchblade into my waiting fingers. I flicked it open and stared down at my victim.

I wasn't going to kill him, but I did need to make a statement. Well, I had always appreciated a nice visual.

Ignoring the queasiness winding through my gut, I brought the second knife to Maverick's forehead. At the first prick of the blade, he swore and thrashed in an attempt to buck me off him.

I pressed my weight down and dug the first blade into his throat deep enough that blood welled up along its edge. With a choked sputter, Maverick went still again.

"Better," I said. "You questioned the Cordovas' authority, so now I'm leaving our mark on you."

With several flicks of the switchblade, I carved an image into his forehead—the three-petaled rose with a spike of a stem that served as the symbol of both the Cordovas and the Deadly Rose, to those who knew enough to be aware of our empire's real name.

Blood seeped from the cuts over Maverick's forehead. He spat curse after curse at me that I ignored, my knife at his throat keeping him otherwise still.

He'd heal from that soon enough—but my etching would leave a lovely little scar for an awfully long time.

As I finished the last line of the pointed stem, a momentary hesitation gripped me. This was reasonable punishment for the insult to my family, but what about the personal humiliation he'd tried to subject me to?

I couldn't leave any doubt that Luciana Cordova, even on her own, was no one to be messed with.

An idea so perfect it made me a little sick swam up through my mind. Mom had taught me well in all sorts of ways I couldn't feel the least bit happy about.

But until I could get away from her, I had to play by the rules of this world.

I snapped my fingers toward my watching associates. "Two of you —pin down his arms."

"What?" Maverick sputtered. "You bitch! Get your hands off—"

I dug the knife into his neck again, and he cut himself off with a tremor that ran the length of his body. Maverick was a hotshot, all right, but he wanted to live.

Two of the Deadly Rose lackeys yanked at his arms and rammed their feet down to hold them in place. Keeping one hand at Maverick's throat, I adjusted my position to kneel beside him and yank up his sweat-stained tee.

"I feel like it's my duty to make sure *every* woman who considers getting up close and personal with you is aware of how you treat a lady," I said tartly, and tipped the switchblade into the flesh just below his belly button.

When Maverick squealed and thrashed, my knife drew another shallow line across his throat—and my lackeys stomped on his fingers hard enough to crack a few bones. As his protests dwindled into raging whimpers, I dragged my second blade through his skin to write out my brief but incisive message.

I AM A DIPSHIT.

When I'd finished the T, I shoved myself off the guy and took a couple of steps back, restraining a flinch at the sight of my gory artwork. I couldn't let any of Mom's people, especially Octavio, catch a hint that I had any regrets about how I'd handled the situation.

"Grab the money, and let's go." My words were hollow—I hardly recognized my voice as my own. "I don't want to have to look at this pig and the rest of his swine for another minute."

"You got it, *boss*." Octavio slid me a snake-like glance and strode forward to stuff the money Maverick had removed back into the bag. From the sharpness of his voice and his movements, he was pissed off at how the situation had turned out. Because I hadn't killed Maverick like he'd suggested?

But when I turned toward the rest of my crew, a few dipped their heads to me, unmistakably impressed. One guy even gave me a full salute.

I'd lived up to my mother's name. Hurray for me.

As Octavio hefted the bag, I marched back to the car without looking back. My men closed in around me to bar any thought of retribution from the rest of the Hellborn goons, although they hadn't risked making a move since I'd tackled Maverick.

My driver was still waiting at the wheel—I couldn't afford to so much as tremble as I slid into the back seat, even though I was shaking like Jell-O on the inside. It was all I could do to hold in the urge to vomit.

I'd done what I had to do. At least the blood on my hands wasn't an entire life I'd ended. My conscience was that clear.

It seemed to take forever before the trunk squeaked open and the duffel thumped inside. The driver gunned the engine, and Octavio sank onto the seat beside me.

As the car pulled onto the road, he glanced over at me, barely holding back a glower. "You good, chica? I told you to put that asshole *in* the ground, not just on it. Lost your nerve?"

I stared right back at him, letting my anger at being jerked around burn away my nausea. "Put him in the ground, and we leave the Hellborn rioting. Send him back to them with a message about what they get for defiance carved right into his skin, and no one fucking forgets. I think my mom will approve, whether you do or not."

His mouth twitched, but he didn't call out my implication that the order hadn't actually come from Mom. Even if he realized I thought he might have attempted to betray me, he was smart enough not to force my hand by pushing the issue.

As we settled into a tense silence, my burner phone buzzed in my back pocket. I yanked it out before another alert could go off.

Several texts came through in quick succession from a number I'd labeled as BH from my brief exchange of texts with the Blood Hunter after the Storm had filled her in on my concerns. Remembering the strength that the slim, dark-haired woman had emanated when I'd met her in the coffee shop, I couldn't help thinking she could be the key to holding Mom at bay, but she'd been noncommittal in our initial conversation.

She had a lot more to say tonight.

I think I might have some evidence for you to build your case. This was one of my front businesses.

That opening statement was followed by a link that took me to an article on a news website. The headline had my eyes widening. *Sports Club Littered With Bodies After 21 Die of Food Poisoning,* the title read.

My eyes widened. Twenty-one people all dead in one go—from food poisoning, of all things?

The article went on to report that the twenty-one people in question had all been employees or long-time regulars of the club. They'd stayed late into the evening for some kind of event, and the bodies had been found the next morning. Tests indicated they'd been the victims of severe food poisoning from a source that hadn't yet been definitively identified.

But one line in particular jumped out at me. *The Riverside Sports Club has been a long-time fixture in this suburban neighborhood, with sprawling grounds on the edge of the Rosewood River.*

A chill wrapped around my lungs. The Rosewood—Mom had said something about that in one of her calls. That they'd put "something in the water" but "not right in the Rosewood."

Something that would look like death by food poisoning? But why?

The Blood Hunter's following texts held the answer. *All of the dead were important employees of mine not far from my main base of operations. This feels like an attack, not an accident. And it can't be to simply take over territory. No one has made a move to claim the club or anything in the surrounding areas. I get the impression that for now they're just aiming to weaken my manpower.*

I'm increasing security and prodding the Deadly Rose in my own way to see if she'll reveal more, but I have no direct proof she was responsible. If you can do more with this information than I can, feel free. I'm not liking the direction this situation appears to be heading in.

My heart thumped for several halting beats before I typed out a hasty *Thank you* in response. After a moment, I added, *I'm sure my mom was involved, but I don't know if it was her people or a co-conspirator.*

The Blood Hunter deserved to know that much. There was no doubt in my mind that the "they" who'd set out to weaken the Blood Hunter was Mom and her allies.

Now I could prove that one part of a conversation I'd recorded was definitely Mom plotting to attack a fellow Devil's Dozen member. I hadn't gotten anything so concrete before. I couldn't say it was enough to upend her plans, but it felt like a major step forward.

A smile tugged at my lips. But as I tucked the phone away, I caught Octavio eyeing me suspiciously before he tugged his gaze away. His expression stayed dark as he stared out the window instead.

My smile faded. Had I really made the right call by ignoring his instructions? Now he knew that I definitely didn't trust him… which meant he'd be working even harder to displace me before I earned any more of Mom's trust.

I was balanced way too precariously already without throwing more problems into the mix.

I folded my arms over my chest, just shy of hugging myself, and held my posture straight. But my fears and misery in the life Mom had dragged me back into closed in around me with the whir of the car's engine, on the verge of suffocating me.

NINETEEN

Luciana

AS JASPER LOWERED me from the final lift, a twinge ran through my ribs. With our last few moves, it deepened into an ache. I hit our ending post with a hitch in my breath.

Jasper's gray-green eyes darkened with concern. "Are you okay?"

"Yeah." I rubbed my side instinctively, and his mouth tightened. He'd been there, rushing to my aid, when Sheeran's men back in Boston had battered my side with a flurry of kicks. "Maybe I just need a short break—and some water."

"Always good to stay hydrated," Niko piped up from where he was watching near the boards.

Jasper slid his arm around my shoulders in a quick but tender embrace and kissed my forehead. "We've been at this a while. Take all the break you need, Punk."

I had been pushing myself hard today, but getting to skate with my guys had helped me distance myself from the worst memories from a couple of nights ago. All yesterday, every time I'd glanced down at myself, I'd flashed back to the splatters of Maverick's blood dabbling my hands.

I'd still been a little shell-shocked when I'd shown up this morning, and my boyfriends had caught on immediately. But when Niko had asked if I wanted to talk about it, my throat had constricted until I felt like I was choking.

"It's all right," Jasper had told me. "You don't need to get into the details with us. We know whatever you needed to do, it's what you had to do to survive. It doesn't mean anything about who you really are."

Then I'd choked up for a completely different reason, tears of relief pricking at the backs of my eyes. But the burden of my unwanted duty had lifted as I'd skated, until I really did feel like myself again.

At some point, I might tell Rafael about what exactly had gone down with Maverick. He'd understand the violence I'd needed to turn to in a way the skater guys couldn't totally. But having permission not to lay out the gory details of my role as Mom's heir was the best gift anyone could have given me.

At least Mom had seemed satisfied enough. She'd even let out a sharp chuckle of amusement when I'd told her how I'd dealt with the asshole's mocking rebellion. Then she'd patted me on the shoulder and complimented my "creativity."

No mention of any expectation that I'd have killed the man. I was more sure than ever that Octavio's instructions had come only from himself.

When I skated over to the stands now, Niko had already grabbed our water bottles for us. I tipped mine to my mouth. As I took a few slow gulps, my gaze veered across the rink toward the other, lonely figure working on his routine alongside us.

Quentin whirled through a spin, the overhead lights flashing off his pale hair. His leg rose to the perfect angle with his body, his arms unfurling before he pulled in on himself again.

His form was incredible. I'd been able to see that even back when I'd wanted to punch him in the face every time he talked to us. But as he pushed off into a step sequence, I couldn't help thinking, like I had many times before, that there was something missing to all those strictly precise movements.

He came to a stop about ten feet away, and I set down my water bottle. We didn't normally talk a whole lot during our training periods, but the observation hit me hard enough that the words tumbled out.

"You know, you can pull off some really impressive moves. No one could ever say you're not a great skater. But there's something about your style that always looks too analytical to me. Kind of rigid."

Quentin raised an eyebrow and glided a little closer. "Did I just hear you call me a 'great skater'? And 'impressive' too? Go ahead and keep that praise coming."

He grinned, the faded slash of his scar lifting with the curve of his lips—a warmer expression than his usual smirk, but still a little wicked. And I couldn't deny that my heart skipped a beat watching his handsome face light up.

I arched my eyebrows right back at him. "I did also mention that you seem too stiff."

His grin widened. "And now you're offering tips. Trying to get into coaching too, Upstart?"

The nickname he'd apparently just come up with made me roll my eyes. "Just making an observation. If you don't want to hear—"

"No, no, it's fine." Quentin cocked his head. "It just sounds like you figure I need someone to teach me how to loosen up. Maybe you should take me on as a pet project, since you're so concerned."

There was no mistaking the teasing glint in his bright blue eyes—or the challenge in his voice. He *wanted* me to say yes, probably so he'd have an excuse to win me over however he imagined he was going to do that.

The truth was that he'd already been doing that, bit by bit, without trying directly. Possibly *because* he hadn't been laying it on thick.

He'd just been a more open, considerate version of the jerk he'd been before… and I'd been finding I kind of liked his presence in my life. The snark and the arrogance hadn't vanished, but balanced out like this, they'd become an acquired taste, like the bitterness in a good cup of coffee or the acidic tang of a grapefruit.

I wasn't sure I wanted him knowing how much progress he'd made toward his goal, though. And it wasn't just me he needed to prove himself to.

I tipped my head toward my partner, who'd leaned against the boards to watch the conversation. "You could learn a thing or two from me, sure, but Jasper's the expert at putting emotion into a performance."

Quentin folded his arms in front of him in a pose that initially looked defensive, but the raise of his chin was more determined than defiant. After a brief pause, his voice came out even. "Let's see what both of you could show me, then."

Jasper's stance tensed for a second, and I braced myself for an argument. But he eased over, giving Quentin a wary but not unwelcoming look. "You really want to do this?"

Quentin shrugged. "Why not? I won't be an idiot and say there's nothing I could learn from the great Saint Jasper."

There was a hint of wryness in his use of Jasper's fan-given title, but otherwise he sounded genuine. Enough that Jasper's mouth twitched with the start of a smile. "All right. Then let's get you moving."

Niko had headed to our portable speaker system. "It's easier to loosen up if you can relax into the music." He flicked through one of his many playlists and selected a lilting track that I knew would slowly swell with dramatic emotion.

I grasped Quentin's forearm and tugged him across the rink. Jasper skated next to us, his hand resting on the small of my back. He drew me away from the other guy and spun us around in a loose spiral before settling into a simple glide across the ice.

Quentin followed, his back straight, his arms by his sides. Jasper shook his head. "You look like a toy soldier, Wolfe. Can't you feel the melody? Let it work its way into your muscles and move with it."

Quentin frowned. "I've never skated to this song before."

"It shouldn't matter," I said lightly. "If you're *really* great, you can stop worrying about getting everything 'right' for a few minutes and let out what comes naturally."

The frown deepened into a grimace, but Quentin dragged in a deep breath. A mask of concentration came over his face.

He looked so stern I couldn't help laughing. "Stop thinking so hard. You're supposed to be *feeling*."

A hint of a slump came into Quentin's posture. He glanced away. "What if… I don't really know how that works?"

The hint of vulnerability brought a lump into my throat. A flicker of surprise passed through Jasper's eyes, and then he surprised *me* by nudging me toward the other guy. "Maybe you need the right inspiration."

I glided over to Quentin, and he lifted his hand automatically to catch mine. Even through our training gloves, the warmth of his skin seeped through. When our eyes met, a tingle raced up my arm.

"You think you can match my footwork?" I asked.

Something had softened in his expression. "I'll give it my best shot."

I shifted my feet into a series of basic steps, letting the rise and fall of the melody guide me. Quentin followed intently, but I caught a slight sway in his body and the motions of his free arm as he sank more fully into the music.

I swiveled toward him. "Want to try a sit spin?"

His gaze held mine, the smolder behind it heating me more than his touch. "I can manage that."

We pivoted together, his arms coming around my waist and mine lifting into the air. My knee brushed his thigh. He held me carefully, but I could already see his stance had loosened from when we'd started this impromptu joint coaching session.

His face, not so much.

"Come on, Wolfe," Jasper called from a few feet away, his tone playful in its heckling. "You've got a gorgeous girl in your arms. Try to look like you're happy about it."

Quentin let out a grunt, but then a smile crossed his lips—smaller but also gentler than any I'd seen from him before. Another tingle ran through my nerves as we gazed back at each other in the few seconds longer before we eased apart.

To my surprise, Quentin sent me gliding back toward Jasper. "You're already good with her. All that extra practice. Maybe I need you as a role model, old-timer."

Jasper only chuckled at the tongue-in-cheek insult and pulled me into his arms. "*Now* I get some respect. Let's see if I can get you to cough up a little more."

He picked up the pace a bit and lowered me into a dip as we swept across the ice with a crescendo in the song. Then Jasper handed me off to Quentin, watching expectantly. I gave myself over to the other guy's support, arcing back as he echoed Jasper's movements.

"Good," Jasper said. "Now a person would think you actually like her."

Quentin shot a glance over his shoulder at his rival. "Gotta learn from the best, huh?"

There was a new companionableness to their banter, as if they actually liked each other too. As if they might even be able to see each other as something like friends—if not right now, then in the not-so-distant future. Recognizing the shift warmed me as much as the feel of Quentin's arms around me.

"What've you got for me next?" Quentin asked, passing me over again.

I glided back and forth between them through several more simple moves, through one song and another. Niko shouted encouragement from his spot by the boards and after the first few exchanges hollered up through the stands. "You should come down and see this properly, Rafael. Cooperation in beautiful action."

My bodyguard emerged from his usual post by the main doors and came most of the way down the steps to take in our unusual training exercise. I sped from Jasper to Quentin and then back again with a breathless laugh. Both of the guys were grinning freely now, and there was a fluid grace to Quentin's strokes across the ice that I'd never seen before.

My heart swelled alongside the music. Somehow, we'd headed farther down the path of becoming a united group than I'd realized was possible with Quentin in the mix. Was there a chance he could fit in with the rest of us more permanently after all?

"You know," Quentin said as he caught me again. "This is almost… fun."

Jasper snorted. "You make that sound like a bad word. I think I see part of your problem."

"Hey, I'm working on it, aren't—"

The boom of the door slamming open cut off his retort.

As we jerked around with a hiss of our skates, a throng of men stormed into the room with a thunder of stomping feet and a few warning shots from their guns. I snapped into a defensive stance instinctively, groping at my hip, but of course I didn't have any weapons on me while we were training.

The torrent of attackers had already hit Rafael, a bunch of the men attempting to pin him to the ground while he thrashed against their hold. Niko scrambled backward, but a couple of the guys caught him too, one jamming a gun to his forehead. He froze.

The rest, a dozen or so of them, barged out into the rink. And right at the front of the pack stood Octavio, a wild light wavering in his eyes and his mouth twisted into a sneer.

"What the fuck are you doing?" I spat out, rage and terror colliding inside me. I wanted to bash open his ugly mug, but I didn't have anything to do it with—or any way to protect the men on either side of me who weren't armed or trained in fighting.

Octavio's lips drew back to bare his teeth. "You don't get to take off to play these stupid games and then prance home acting like you run the show. *I* put in the time, *I've* paid with sweat and blood, and I'm taking back the respect Mireya owes me, which you never deserved anyway."

Then he sprang at me, the rest of the men lunging forward at the same time.

"Get the fuck away from her!" Jasper bellowed, and Quentin let out a wordless snarl. They leapt to my defense as the onslaught of mutinous gangsters surged forward.

We had a slight advantage in that we were more at home on the ice. As a few of our attackers' feet skidded on the slippery terrain, Jasper managed to land a powerful punch on one jerk's skull. Quentin rammed his elbow into another goon's side while the guy was in mid-trip.

One of the other thugs grabbed at me, and I whipped him around in a ghoulish version of one of our spins before kneeing him hard enough to send blood spurting from his nose. As it smeared across the frozen surface beneath our feet, two more men closed in around me.

Inspiration struck. I didn't have any weapons I could hold in my hands… but I did have blades on my feet.

I swung around with a couple of swift kicks. The bottom of my skate slashed across one goon's cheek, slitting it open all the way to the bone. As he stumbled backward with a groan of agony, I jabbed right through the fabric of the other guy's shirt, sending blood spurting from a belly wound.

Grunts and thuds carried from either side of me, but I couldn't spare a moment to check on my skating partners. More thugs loomed on me.

I threw my fists and elbows, aimed another cutting kick, and yanked up a knee that caught one asshole in the gut. My feet rasped over the ice, veering this way and that.

The goons slipped and collided with each other almost as much as they did with us, but there were too many of them. Someone punched my shoulder just as I swung my skate again, and I wobbled for balance.

A hand snatched at my ponytail and wrenched me backward, pulling my hair at the roots viciously enough to leave my entire scalp throbbing. Octavio's face, ruddy with fury, appeared in my peripheral vision.

I lashed out at him with all I could, clocking him in the jaw and slashing at his calf with my skate blade. But then he slammed his fist into my side, right where my healing ribs were tender.

Pain exploded through my torso. I bent over, trying to shield myself, but he punched me again in the same spot, so hard that a spittle-filled gasp burst from my lips.

I doubled over, dizzy with agony, and Octavio kicked my legs out from under me. My ass hit the ice, sending another jolt of pain up my spine.

Octavio jerked on my hair to snap my head to the side. "I'm going to tell Mireya that the Hellborn tracked you down for revenge. She'll believe me, and then you won't matter at all."

He shoved me toward the ice with enough force that my temple glanced off the frigid surface. An ache splintered through my skull; my ribs were still on fire.

I manage to heave myself around in time to see Octavio raising his gun, aiming it at my head while his teeth flashed in an unnerving grin. "Good-bye for good, pequeña rosa."

His finger closed around the trigger. My sight swam as I screamed inwardly at my body to move.

A figure flung itself into view from the edge of my sight just as the bang of the gunshot tore through the air.

No new pain blazed through my existing aches. No bullet blasted through my skull.

Because Octavio was down. It was Quentin I'd seen charging at him—Quentin grappling with him on the ice before my hazy eyes.

Gritting my teeth, I shoved myself toward them, scrambling partway onto my feet. The two men twisted on the frozen turf, fists and knees jabbing at each other.

Just as I reached them, Quentin smacked Octavio's arm into the ice at an unnatural angle, and Octavio's fingers flinched open around the gun. I dove down to snatch at it, still fighting my dizziness.

My hand closed around the metal grip. I whipped it up, fit my finger around the trigger the way I'd practiced so many times, and rammed the muzzle against Octavio's forehead.

No final snarky remarks. I fired without giving him an instant to recover.

Octavio's head snapped backward. Blood gushed from the hole just above his brow. His body sagged onto the rink, his eyes rolling upward as if looking at the wound that had ended his life.

Dead. He was dead, and I was still alive.

I didn't have time to revel in the miracle that fact felt like. Instead, in defiance of the pain lancing through my side, I hefted myself as straight as I could and aimed the gun at his closest followers.

Most of the other men looked worse for wear by now, sporting scrapes and gashes, even more unsteady than before on the ice. They stared back at me—the daughter of their boss, the woman who'd just killed the man who'd convinced them to take up this rebellion.

"Listen up, assholes," I said, my voice crackling through the arena.

"You bet on the wrong guy. Get the hell out of here now before I decide to blast the rest of you away too, and maybe the next time I see you, I'll give you a second chance."

Whatever Octavio had said to them to get them on board, it clearly wasn't enough to outlive his demise. The men on the ice scrambled toward the boards without a backward glance.

Rafael was just tossing his last attacker off him. He drew his own gun and shot the prick in the face. That was plenty of motivation to get the last few goons hurtling for the doors as fast as their feet could carry them. The two who'd been restraining Niko fled for the stands after their departing colleagues.

My gun-hand dropped to my side. I found myself staring down at Octavio's corpse, at the blood pooling under his head, defiling the ice.

The image of Coach Balakin's murdered body flashed behind my eyes. A clammy sensation filled my lungs and crept over my skin. I hardly dared to lift my gaze and find out how my skater men were looking at me now—now that they'd seen just what violence *I* was capable of.

"Fucking bastards," Rafael said in a ragged voice. "I know someone who can get this cleaned up, Lou. Don't worry for one more second about that pinche cabrón."

Skates hissed closer to me. I raised my head, knowing I had to face the real music—and a jolt of shock raced through my veins.

"Quentin!"

He'd pushed himself away from Octavio and onto his feet while I'd threatened our other attackers, but I hadn't noticed—hadn't realized—

A blotch of red was spreading swiftly down his pale green thermal tee from a wound on his left shoulder.

I pushed toward him, my thoughts spinning, my pulse kicking up to a frantic pace. "You were shot! When—"

It hit me before I could even finish the question. My eyes darted up to meet Quentin's gaze. "You took the bullet he meant for me."

Quentin's face had gone sallow, his lips pinched with obvious pain, but he managed to lift his uninjured shoulder in a not particularly convincing shrug. "It's not that bad. Better my shoulder than your head, right?"

The rasp in his voice told me I couldn't believe his spoken assessment of the injury at all. I tore off my fleece and balled it against the wound in an attempt to stop the bleeding. "That was a fucking idiotic thing to do," I said, but my voice shook with panic rather than anger.

Quentin let out a thin chuckle. "Had to show those assholes that figure skaters can handle themselves in a fight too."

"Rafael!" I hollered toward the stands. "Get the first aid stuff—do you know a doctor we could go to?"

"On it!" he shouted back.

Jasper and Niko had come up around us, Jasper pressing his hand against a shallow cut on his jaw and Niko's forehead reddening where he'd have a bruise by morning, but neither of them showing any injuries beyond that.

Jasper's eyes were wide. His voice came out in a croak. "That... that was pretty goddamned amazing, Quentin. I couldn't have gotten there in time."

Niko set a careful hand on Quentin's shoulder, his face glowing with relief. "I was so scared for her. You were there for Lou when we couldn't be."

Quentin stared at both of them, apparently more shellshocked by their gratitude than by the injury he'd taken to earn it. It occurred to me that I should probably express a little more of my own.

I grabbed his hand in mine and squeezed it. "You saved my life, Quentin. Thank you. He could have killed *you.* I never would have asked—"

Quentin yanked his attention back to me. His eyes had gone a bit hazy with the pain, but their usual intensity returned as he held my gaze.

"No fucking way was I letting that prick hurt you if I could help it. I'm in this now—whenever you need me, however you need me. You never need to ask."

Rafael hurried over to us with a handful of sterile pads and a roll of gauze from my equipment bag. "I made a couple of calls. We'll get him fixed up."

Quentin dipped his head. "Thanks."

He said that, and he kept up his brave face, but he had to recognize that he hadn't totally won here. He'd been lucky enough to make it out of the fight alive, yes… but with a wound like that, he could forget about training properly for at least a few weeks.

One more in the long line of sacrifices he'd made to be here for me, and this one might have screwed up his own dreams completely.

TWENTY

Luciana

THE LIGHT from the broad but dingy windows of the guys' loft apartment streaked across Quentin's face where he was sprawled in a boxy armchair. His eyes were closed, his face still even paler than usual, but a little of the tightness from the pain had eased from his features.

The doctor Rafael had summoned had arrived just a few minutes after we'd gotten in, cleaned and stitched up the gunshot wound with brisk efficiency, and dispensed painkillers to both Quentin and me. She'd tested my ribs first and judged that they weren't broken.

From what I could tell, they weren't even fully bruised like they had been in Boston. Octavio's two punches had knocked me down in the moment, but they were nothing compared to the rampage of kicks I'd gotten during that previous fight.

That didn't mean they felt *good*, though.

The door clicked shut as she left the space as discreetly as she'd arrived. My gaze drifted over the rest of the apartment from my vantage point where I was propped up on the modern sofa's cushions.

Calling the place Rafael had found for himself and the guys an "apartment" was really a bit of a stretch. The sprawling open-concept room with its exposed concrete walls was obviously meant to be a commercial loft, not a living space.

It did have a sink and fridge setup at one end, and makeshift bedrooms had been cordoned off with office-style room dividers. The landlord had done his best to give it a homey feel with the furnishings despite the grungy industrial atmosphere, but it'd clearly been a losing battle.

Rafael prowled along the line of windows, peering over the street below into the stark mid-afternoon sunlight. He probably liked how open the layout was—easy to get the other men out if they needed to make a hasty escape, every part of the space accessible without real doors in the way.

Jasper leaned against the wall between two of the windows, and Niko sank onto the arm of the sofa near my feet. They'd both spent the last half hour bustling around, bringing water and rags as the doctor had asked for them, pitching in every way they could.

Jasper's mouth was drawn down in a worried scowl. His gaze caught mine. "Did you have any idea those guys would attack you like that?"

My stomach knotted. In our hurry to get back here and have Quentin looked after, we hadn't really talked about the fight… or what I'd needed to do during it.

I shook my head. "I had a feeling Octavio was trying to undermine me. He obviously wasn't happy about me being back or Mom priming me as her heir. But to come at me openly… He must have been totally sure he could win and cover up his involvement. Mom would have hunted him down to the ends of the earth if she knew."

Rafael had stopped his pacing. "You spared him the tortures she'd have dealt out," he said in his low voice. "Gave him a cleaner end than he deserved."

He knew how the guilt would be eating at me—how much I hated the violent side of this life. The other guys…

Niko simply cocked his head, moving on to the next concern.

"What'll happen to the rest of them—the ones who ran away? Do we need to worry about them coming after you again?"

"Nah." I pushed myself a little higher on the couch, relaxing as the painkillers took most of the edge off the lingering ache. "It was Octavio who had the big ideas. They were just following him—they won't want to show their faces anywhere near me or my mother after that mess. He must have told them he'd promote them once he was in charge. He figured he'd be next in line for leadership of the empire with me out of the way."

Jasper let out a light snort. "Jeez. And I thought Quentin had ambition."

In the armchair, Quentin's eyes popped open at that remark. He still looked more fragile than I liked, his normally neatly slicked-back hair rumpled across his forehead, but a healthy color was seeping back into his cheeks.

He flicked his gaze toward his rival with a flash of amused rancor. "Very funny, St. Pierre." As he shifted his attention to me, his tone softened. "How are you holding up?"

I blinked at him and half-sputtered my answer. "Me? You're the one who took a bullet."

Quentin lifted his good shoulder in one of his new partial shrugs. "Now I'm all patched up, good as new. Your ribs were already bothering you."

I touched my side, testing the sore spots. "I think he only set my healing back a little. They were almost back to normal."

Niko hummed and stood up. "I think you could both use some jasmine tea. It'll help you unwind and speed up the healing process."

As our coach headed for the kitchen area, Jasper raised his eyebrows. "Should we start calling you Dr. Okabe now?"

Niko shot a teasing glance over his shoulder. "Only if it turns you on."

Jasper flushed but laughed, and I couldn't suppress a giggle of my own. But my mind jarred against the weird sense of normalcy.

I'd just killed a man in front of these guys. Somehow, none of them seemed remotely bothered by it. The casual banter and the concerned affection in their gazes when they looked at me was all totally familiar.

They really had come a long way into understanding and accepting who I'd been before—who I was having to be again, while I was under Mom's thumb. They recognized as much as Rafael did that I'd only acted to save my life and protect them.

And miraculously, I'd managed to do both of those things. All four of them had made it out of the fight in one piece, if a little battered.

I just had to make sure they never faced anything worse.

Of course, I might have already lost that battle with one of them. The one who really couldn't have imagined anything worse than the fate his association with me had resulted in.

I studied Quentin's sharp-edged features. "It's going to be hard for you to compete with that injury." And Nationals were just weeks away now.

Quentin made a dismissive sound. "Getting anywhere at Nationals was already a long shot after switching to pairs and back again. No big deal. I'll be back in the game next year."

He didn't let any regret show in his tone, but I caught a flicker of disappointment crossing his face. He had the same fire inside of him for skating that Niko, Jasper, and I did. To have to call it quits on Nationals must be killing him, even if the bullet hadn't.

A lump rose in my throat. "I'm sorry I wasn't better prepared—that I didn't manage to finish the fight sooner."

"You said yourself that you had no idea that asshole would go that far. You don't have to apologize. I've got lots of time to skate. It's a hell of a lot more important to me that you're still in this world." His mouth formed a typical smirk. "Who else is going to kick my ass when I need it?"

Despite his nonchalant words, the intensity I was getting used to shone in his eyes as he held my gaze. He'd thrown himself in front of a bullet for me. He couldn't pretend it didn't mean a hell of a lot more than keeping up some friendly competition.

I opened my mouth, but the right response didn't come to me. While I was groping for it, Jasper pushed himself off the wall.

He peered down at Quentin and let out an impatient huff. "Why don't you just admit how much Lou matters to you without making it into a joke? It'll be easier for all of us if we're clear on where we stand—including you. The rest of us aren't going to run you off. It's not like you could make it any more obvious how committed you are."

Jasper lifted his gaze toward Rafael, who nodded, and then toward Niko by the kitchenette, who ambled back over, leaving the tea to steep.

"You risked your life for her," Niko said. "None of us could doubt how much you care about her."

Quentin stared at them for several seconds, looking lost for words. He wet his lips, and a hint of a smile touched his lips.

His gaze slid back to me. "I appreciate the vote of approval, but it's Lou's opinion that really matters. I don't— You said to give you time. I'm trying not to get pushy about—"

A rush of emotion swept over me, casting any hope of figuring out what to say out of reach. So much giddy warmth—for Quentin and the lengths he'd proven he'd go to for my safety and happiness, for my other men and the welcome they'd just offered him.

This one thing didn't have to be hard after all.

Since I had no words, I rose from the sofa instead. It was only a couple of steps to Quentin's chair. Only a thump of my pulse to lean over him, graze my knuckles across his cheek, and bring my lips to his.

Quentin must have seen my intent. He met my kiss without a second's hesitation, his mouth searing against mine. As the hunger of his enthusiasm reverberated into me, my hand rose to wind through his tussled hair.

This was so much better than our only kiss before, when he'd caught me by surprise and I'd still seen him as a total jerk. Quentin slipped his arm around me, his mouth coaxing mine open with a tenderness I'd never have expected from him back then—a little unexpected even now.

Then he eased back a few inches with a cocky smile that was much more typical of him. "Let's make sure you don't strain your ribs…"

With a heft of his good arm, he drew me onto his lap. As I straddled him, a laugh bubbled from my throat.

I gave his pale blond locks a teasing tug. "Always gotta try for more than you already have, huh?"

Quentin's eyes gleamed as he kept grinning up at me. "Hey, I didn't deny that I'm ambitious."

A snort from our audience brought both of our attention to the watching men. Rafael looked mildly amused, Niko was beaming, and even Jasper's mouth had pulled into a crooked smile, but I felt Quentin's body tense beneath mine.

I didn't mind them seeing this, but did he think they'd object? Or was he less comfortable with the idea of sharing me than he'd claimed back when we'd started down this road?

Niko cleared his throat, still looking delighted enough to burst. "Maybe the three of us should do a patrol around the building… for a nice long time. Just to be safe. I think these two need the chance to figure out how they're going to handle each other."

The corner of Rafael's mouth quirked upward. "You know I'll never say no to extra vigilance. Give me a call if you need us."

As I rolled my eyes at him, Jasper let out a rough chuckle. "I guess you do deserve a chance to sort things out without us breathing down your necks." He arched an eyebrow at Quentin that looked more friendly than his laugh had sounded. "Don't do anything I wouldn't do."

At Quentin's guffaw, the men I loved headed for the loft's door. A quiver of resistance ran down the middle of my chest, and my lips parted before I'd really thought the impulse through.

"You're not all going to leave without giving me a kiss goodbye, are you?"

If Quentin couldn't handle the fact that I was completely enmeshed with all three of these men too, then it was better we found out now rather than after I'd fallen for him more than I already had.

He didn't make a sound, just watching me with wary curiosity and running his thumb over my thigh. The other three guys made their way back over, understanding shining in their eyes.

Rafael reached me first. He tangled his strong fingers in my hair and pulled my head back to meet his demanding kiss as if I weren't currently perched on another man, as if I existed for him alone. And in the moment while our mouths melded together, that might as well have been true.

He eased back, leaving my lips tingling, and Jasper was there an instant later. My partner gave me one of his small but warm smiles as he leaned in to claim my mouth for himself.

Jasper kissed me deeply, thoroughly, as if to ensure I'd remember him after he walked out the door. Like there was any chance I'd forget his gruffly passionate presence. As he pulled back, Niko slid a hand up his arm to his shoulder in both a caress and a nudge out of the way.

Our coach tucked his fingers under my chin and offered a gentle kiss that was both short and sweet. He winked at me as he stepped away. "Have fun. The tea's there when you're ready for it. We'll make sure there are no unwanted interruptions."

My gaze dropped to Quentin's face. His eyes flicked from Niko back to me, and the heat I saw burning there set off an ache between my thighs. A faint flush had colored his cheeks, and when he wet his lips again, I saw nothing but desire in the gesture.

"Had to make a point, did you?" he murmured as the door clicked shut behind the other guys.

I gave him my version of his usual smirk. "I thought you liked it when I kicked your ass?"

He sputtered a laugh and reached for me, but his hand simply lingered against my face, his fingertips tracing my hairline down to my cheek. His bright blue eyes seemed to be drinking me in, like brilliant pools I could drown in.

I studied him in turn, grazing my fingers along the line of his jaw, stroking my thumb over the scar that notched his lower lip. There was no need to hurry. In a lot of ways, we were just getting to know each other.

But I already knew the most important things about him. That beneath the prickly, arrogant exterior lay a guy who craved affection and acceptance. That the man beneath me possessed a selfless streak deep enough that he'd put his life on the line for me without a second thought.

I hadn't been sure I could feel this way about him when I'd first seen him here in Austin. It'd taken time for those walls to come down, for him to show the vulnerabilities he'd been covering up and let the asshole front drop. Now, knowing I'd almost lost him, I couldn't imagine letting him go.

"I told you I'd convince you to give me a chance eventually," he said with a hint of a growl in his voice.

I laughed lightly and bowed my head over his so my breath would brush over his face. "And you only had to almost die to manage it."

Quentin made a soft scoffing sound. "Worth it."

Then he was pulling my mouth back to his.

Our early kisses were slow and lingering, tasting each other and testing what felt best while our hands explored each other's bodies, careful of our respective injuries. But with each meeting of our lips, the passion between us sparked hotter. Quentin's chest hitched, and he kissed me more fervently, dipping his hand right beneath my shirt.

I tilted my position to allow him easier access, and my pussy ground against the bulge at the crotch of his training pants. We both groaned, the sound reverberating between our lungs, and dove in for another kiss.

Quentin massaged my breasts through my bra and then slipped his hand behind me to unsnap the garment. As it drooped loose beneath my shirt, his slim fingers delved beneath the fabric to caress me skin to skin.

His thumb flicked over my pebbling nipple, sending a bolt of pleasure through my chest. I gasped and ground against him more insistently.

Quentin let out a full growl, devouring my mouth as he worked over my breasts. His hips rocked upward to press his erection against my throbbing cunt. I whimpered, a tremor of need passing through me, and he eased back with a shaky exhalation and a renewed smirk.

"I love how you tremble for me. Like you can't wait for me to touch you everywhere."

"So why are you taking so long to get on with it?" I grumbled playfully.

His answering laugh was lost in another kiss. But he answered my impatience by tugging my shirt off of me, and naturally I had to strip off his in turn, lifting it carefully around his bandaged shoulder. Then I raked my fingers down the compact but solid muscles of his slender chest and earned a tremble of my own.

Quentin ran his hands over every inch of me except the mottled patch where my skin was bruising over my ribs. Gripping my waist, he urged me forward. With a dip of his head, he closed his mouth around one of my sensitized nipples.

I moaned, rocking faster with the wave of bliss his lips and tongue sparked from my breast. The ache of need low in my belly expanded until I could barely think through the haze of lust.

He shifted his head to my other breast and tested my nipple between his teeth. My fingernails dug into his good shoulder as I arched into his hold. His pleased chuckle vibrated over my skin to delicious effect, but the straining of his cock against his pants told me he was at least as desperate for release as I was.

I wrenched at his pants, and he wriggled out of them with my help. Then his fingers hooked around the waist of my leggings. I lifted myself up so he could strip them and my panties off me, managing to wrap my hand around his erection and give it a few experimental strokes in the meantime.

"Fuck," he muttered through clenched teeth, jerking into my grasp.

"Working on it," I teased as if I wasn't equally breathless, and snatched at the purse I'd left on the floor by the sofa.

My fingers snagged on the condom packet I'd been searching for. Quentin snatched it from my hand and tore it open, his gaze never leaving my face. I felt him prep himself beneath me and swallowed a whimper as the head of his cock rubbed over my pussy, which was drenched with longing.

As he pushed upward, I sank down. Our moans entwined as our bodies joined, his shaft filling me at just the right angle. The heady burn I'd been craving raced through my nerves.

"God," Quentin mumbled. "I love seeing you on the ice, but this is my new favorite Lou."

I conveyed my own enthusiasm with the roll of my hips over his. He sucked in a breath and thrust up to meet me, penetrating me even more fully. With every little grunt and growl, he showed how much I turned him on—and fanned the flames of my own desire hotter.

He gripped my thigh and bucked up into me even harder. I threw my head back, my vision blurring as my pleasure started to sweep me away. Plenty of sounds were spilling from my own lips—gasps and a keening I couldn't hold in.

Quentin captured the tip of my breast in his mouth once more with a scrape of his teeth that had me whimpering. Then he lifted me high enough that he slid free from me.

His voice came out full of strained yearning. "Turn around. I want to take you as deep as I can go."

I couldn't resist the promise in his demand. I swiveled over him, and he yanked me back down, spearing me so abruptly and perfectly that stars swam in my vision.

Quentin raised his hand to cup my breast from behind. As I pushed back into his thrusts, he fondled it thoroughly, pinching and pulling at my nipple between his thumb and forefinger.

My body shuddered with the rush of bliss blazing through me. "Yes, fuck, just like that!"

He leaned forward to nip at my shoulder blade, pounding into me all the while. The jolts of pain transformed into something blissful in combination with the giddy friction he was creating from within.

He was taking me, making me his, leaving his mark on me. He hissed against my skin, the pace of his hips quickening.

"You like how I fuck you?"

"Yes—hell, yes."

He was panting now, but he managed to rasp out one more demand. "Say it. Let me hear how much you want this."

My mind was so scrambled with pleasure it took a moment to form a complete sentence. "I love how you're fucking me. Oh my God, keep going—"

My orgasm hit me like a tidal wave, crashing through me and leaving me washed out with ecstasy. My body shook over Quentin's, every nerve tingling with the force of my release, and he let out a choked sound as he followed me over the edge. His cock pulsed inside me.

We sagged together in a jumble of sweaty limbs. As our breaths started to even out, Quentin rested his head against my shoulder and then grasped my waist again. "I want to see you."

I turned in his arms and tipped my head so our foreheads met. Quentin touched my cheek, gazing up at me with so much emotion in those normally cool eyes that my pulse wobbled.

He didn't speak, only searched my expression for several thumps of my heart before gathering me against his lean chest. As his arms wrapped around me, I relaxed into his embrace, drinking in his tart, musky scent.

"I'm not sure I ever really believed I'd get this," he admitted after a few minutes in a voice so quiet it was almost a whisper. "The more I see you, the more I find out about what you've survived, the more incredible I realize you are."

I swallowed thickly and nuzzled the side of his neck. "You just talk a good game with all that cockiness, huh?"

"Fake it 'til you make it, right?" He gave a short laugh, and then a thread of tension wound through his muscles. "So… are we really doing this? Not just a 'thank you for saving my life' hookup—the whole relationship thing?"

He'd tried to keep his tone casual, but the fraught anticipation with which he waited for my answer told the real story. He wasn't sure even now.

I tilted my head to look at him. "If that's what *you* want, I'm up for it."

His voice thickened with emotion. "I don't think there's anything I've ever wanted more."

A pang of affection and compassion reverberated through me at those words. Quentin had survived an awful lot too, and I didn't know if he'd ever been able to admit it to anyone before now.

I adjusted myself against him so I could tuck my arm behind his back, returning his embrace. "Then we'll give it our best and see how it goes."

The gradual relaxing of his posture beneath me felt like a reward in itself. When he pressed a gentle kiss to the top of my head, my heart sang.

How lucky had I gotten to find not one, not three, but four extraordinary men who wanted to share their lives with me? I wouldn't have traded their devotion for any empire in the world.

So I'd damn well make sure I didn't lose them to the woman who believed I should.

TWENTY-ONE

Luciana

THE DEADLY ROSE mansion had rarely felt homey to me, even when I was a kid. But it'd never given me such ominous vibes as when I returned in the evening after Octavio's attack.

I pushed into the foyer, my gaze sweeping over the lackeys standing guard or simply hanging around near the grand staircase. I kept my stance straight and confident to hide my jangling nerves.

How many of these men had known what Octavio was planning? How many of them were going to be disappointed to see he'd failed? Could I hope that most would be glad that I'd come out on top?

Some of them nodded to me in the brisk gestures of respect that the daughter of their boss was owed. I thought I caught a flicker of surprise cross a couple of faces before they stiffened into emotionless masks. There might have been a twitch of a smirk here, a hint of a frown over there.

Nothing definitive. Nothing I could have pointed a finger at in accusation. Nevertheless, the certainty prickled over me that at least a few of these men knew what had gone down earlier today.

The goons who'd actually joined Octavio in his attack were unlikely to return, but he'd have picked low-level grunts without much direct connection to this household—the men most likely to be hungering for a step up in status. The men least likely to feel enough loyalty to Mom to warn her of an impending ambush on her daughter.

That didn't mean they had no connections at all to the men who worked out of the mansion, though. As they went into hiding, they'd have passed on news and warnings of possible retribution to come to whatever friends they had, even if those men hadn't known about the plot before.

Who could say exactly what they'd claimed about how it'd gone down? What kind of a picture they'd painted of me?

The one thing no one would have been able to deny was that I'd won. So I strode through the foyer and up the stairs with my head high and my expression stern, letting all of the watching lackeys see the cool, unshakeable mafia princess who'd stamped out a mutiny with blood and bullets.

It didn't matter that the memory of the fight still made me queasy. That my gut tangled up on itself even considering that I might face opposition like that from within my own empire again.

These men were never going to see the real Luciana Cordova. But they didn't deserve her. They couldn't understand me and my passion for skating or the love I'd found with four men, most of whom wouldn't have fit in here at all.

I was carved from totally different stuff than my mother and her horde. *That* was something to be proud of.

I'd meant to head straight to my bedroom, but another lackey moved to intercept me in the upstairs hall.

"Miss Luciana," he said, running a nervous hand through his greasy hair. "Your mother wanted you to meet her in her office as soon as you got back."

Of course Mom would send a human being to deliver her message instead of texting me like a normal person. She probably enjoyed reminding me of how much sway she held over her underlings—and reminding them of it too.

This goon's apparent uneasiness suggested she hadn't made the request in the friendliest way either. I judged his expression. "She was pretty impatient about it, huh?"

He managed an awkward grin. "I'd say you'd better get going."

At my signature knock, Mom whipped open her office door. She motioned me in with a sharp wave of her hand, the only outward indication of the tension I could tell she was holding in. She strode to the chair behind her desk and sank into it with her lips pursed.

When I'd settled into the chair across from her, willing down my own anxiety, she folded her hands on the top of the desk and narrowed her eyes.

"One of my top men is missing. Someone informed me that I should ask *you* what happened to him."

Oh, shit. I'd known Mom couldn't exactly fail to notice that a key underling had vanished, but I hadn't expected word to travel all the way up the ladder quite this quickly. I'd kind of been hoping no one would mention my involvement and she'd just assume Octavio had vanished.

At the bite in her voice, a chilling thought that hadn't occurred to me before prickled through my head. Had Mom known what Octavio was planning before he'd actually done it?

Was it possible she'd even nudged him down his traitorous path?

I could far too easily imagine her manipulating him into his attempted mutiny. She might have done it to test his loyalties, to see if he'd stay strong in the face of temptation. She might have wanted to evaluate how well I'd handle myself under attack from within her own forces.

She might even have seen it as due punishment for my own insurrection. I knew she didn't want me *dead*, but it wouldn't surprise me if she'd liked the idea of shaking me up, maybe seeing me injured beyond what that pendejo had managed.

Or she might have had no idea until an hour or two ago. The suspicions swimming through my mind were only speculation.

I gathered myself, watching her expression and pose closely. If she *was* at all disappointed that I'd returned relatively unharmed, I'd like to know just how wary I should be of her going forward.

At least I didn't have to worry that she'd be upset about what I'd done to Octavio. She expected her heir to handle insubordination with brutal efficiency.

If I hadn't killed him, she would have had to. It wouldn't have even been a question.

"I can tell you what happened to him," I said, keeping my voice cool and steady. "Because he and a bunch of goons he'd gotten to join him barged into the skating arena while I was training and tried to murder me."

Mom blinked. Her head tilted to the side as she took in my account, but I couldn't tell whether she was genuinely startled or only putting on a small show of shock.

Her mouth tightened. "Well, that is somewhat unexpected. Did he give any reason for his hostility?"

I grimaced at her. "He wasn't super talkative while he and his idiot friends were trying to bash me and my men around, but he's been grumbling about me coming back as heir from the start. He said he was going to tell you that the Hellborn had taken me out, and he obviously figured he'd be your clear choice as an alternate successor."

Mom exhaled in a rush, her eyes flashing. She was certainly putting on a good act if this was all news to her, but she was completely capable of faking it.

"I had noticed his ambitions seemed to be getting a little overblown," she said tightly. "You know what men are like—you give them a little authority, they think they're the next king of the roost." Her hands closed into fists. "But this—this is beyond the pale. If he thinks he'll get away with even attempting—"

"He didn't get away with it," I broke in. "I put a bullet in his skull. The rest of them scattered once he was finished. And now they know how deadly I can be if anyone thinks about messing with me again."

Mom's hands relaxed, a slight smile curving her lips. "You fit your role more with every new challenge, mija. I like seeing you blossom." Her gaze hardened again. "If you catch any of those traitors skulking around our territory again, you know how to deal with them. None of them should walk away from such a huge offense against the Deadly Rose."

I forced a grim smile in return. "My men and I delivered a decent beating in the moment. I'll do what I have to do if I see any of them again."

What I figured I had to do might not be what Mom assumed, but I didn't need to spell that out. I'd rather keep the corpses on my conscience to a minimum.

Mom exhaled slowly and seemed to gather herself. She'd definitely been angry—but because she was disappointed in how her gambit had played out or because anything had happened at all, I still couldn't tell.

She looked me over with an analytical air, and I drew myself a little taller instinctively.

"You're all right to continue with our usual business?" she asked.

My stomach sank, wondering what she had in store for me next, but I nodded anyway. "He didn't do any major damage."

"Good." She brushed her hands across the desk. "I have a few more meetings for you to participate in over the next week. Nothing too strenuous, but I expect you be ready to go and to represent me well."

At least I could be relieved that she wasn't sending me straight into another fight.

I stared right back at her. "I always do. I'm holding up my end of our deal."

Her smile turned a little sharp. "Yes, you are. So far. You may go."

So far. She might be proud of how I'd defended myself today, but we were still at odds, holding metaphorical knives to each other's throats.

I bobbed my head and headed out, a renewed sense of dread looming over me.

I hadn't conquered all the danger amid the Deadly Rose's ranks. The worst threat was sitting there right behind me.

TWENTY-TWO

Rafael

"IS your weapons dealer seriously named *Dolores*?" Lou asked with one eyebrow raised.

I glanced over at her as we headed down the alley to the back entrance of the building said weapons dealer worked out of. Her dark hair nearly blended into the evening's shadows, and I found myself feeling oddly nostalgic for the deep red shade she'd sported for a couple of months.

At least it'd meant I could always spot her in an instant.

I allowed myself a trace of a smile before I answered. "Old ladies have to make a living too, you know."

"Sure, I just wouldn't have expected that living to be in illicit arms." Lou kicked at a candy wrapper that'd drifted into our path, sending it crinkling away. "It's not like I really need another gun, you know. I've got the pistol Mom gave me, and now I'll keep it closer at hand. If I decide I want something else, there's plenty of selection at the mansion."

I gave a dismissive grunt. "Anything you do there is watched. I think you should own one piece your Mom and her lackeys couldn't know about. It's always better to have at least one advantage your enemies won't take into account."

"Lo sé, lo sé." Lou gave a brief shudder. "I know. I just hate lugging even *one* of those things around with me. I'm trying to avoid shooting people, not to give myself more chances to."

I glowered at her. "If it's that or someone shoots you, you'd better put all the bullets you can in them."

The memory of Octavio's attack at the skating rink flashed behind my eyes, and my gut twisted. *I* hadn't been close enough—I'd been too busy dealing with the thugs who'd jumped me to even try to defend Lou directly.

If it hadn't been for Quentin, I'd have lost her.

The thought sickened me, but I had to admit that gluing myself to Lou's side wasn't an option. She wanted to be free, not locked in a cage… or chained to a bodyguard.

So I was going to chase the chill of my fears away as well as I could by making sure she had every possible means to defend herself.

I spotted the right door with its faded blue paint and motioned to Lou. "Let me go first. I'll introduce you."

I rapped on the door to announce my arrival and then pushed into the room on the other side.

Dolores sat at a small table, looking for all the world as if she was engaged in an innocent game of solitaire with no other business on her mind. The amber glow of the dim fixture shone off the thick lenses of her glasses. She glanced up at me and grinned, bringing the smile lines on her worn face into sharper relief.

As I gestured for Lou to follow me in, Dolores swiped a few stray strands of stringy white hair under her vibrant pink shawl and reached for a case hidden away in one of the drawers on a nearby dresser.

Her voice was as crisp and crackly as autumn leaves. "Good to see you, Rafael. And this must be your 'friend.'"

The slight lilt she gave that last word indicated she didn't buy that Lou and I were only friends for an instant.

Lou took the wrinkled hand the old woman offered her and shook it, the picture of politeness if a little awkward. "Nice to meet you. I'm Lou. I, er, I'm here to buy a gun."

"Just the same as everyone else who comes to visit me," Dolores replied in a dryly amused tone. "You're a pretty one, aren't you? Rafael, if I were you, I'd hurry and put a ring on this one's finger!"

Heat rushed to Lou's cheeks. "I —"

Dolores laughed. "I'm just joking, darling. But not about how pretty you are. Goodness, you've got the face of an angel. And those legs! Appreciate them while you have them. One day you'll get to be just as old as me."

My stomach sunk at Dolores's words. I'd almost lost Lou so many times—there had been so many close calls. At this rate, we both would be lucky if we made it to forty.

She would if I had anything to say about it. As soon as we could get her out of her mother's control for good, she could live a normal life. Well, as normal as any other figure skating pro.

Dolores wasted no time popping open her case and laying a selection of guns out on the table. "I gather you want something discreet. Most of the young ladies prefer it that way. All of these will pack a punch without making you look like you're packing." She shot Lou a wink.

Lou picked up the compact pistols one by one, testing their weight and feel in her hand. A few of them she liked enough to pass over to me so I could confirm I approved with my greater experience when it came to firearms. But the decision would ultimately be up to her.

What mattered most was that she chose a weapon she'd feel comfortable enough with to use it when she needed to.

"These are all good," I told her after she handed a fourth option over. "Dolores is picky about what she carries. Which one feels best to you?"

Lou went through them again and settled on a sleek little Glock. "I like this one. Solid but small. I could fit it in the pocket of some of my jackets, even—definitely in even my smaller purses without being noticeable."

I nodded. "The closer you can keep it, the better."

I forked over the cash without thinking about the price. It was worth any amount of money to see Lou safe.

Lou slid the gun into the kangaroo pocket of her pullover hoodie, and her mouth twisted into a bittersweet smile. "I could even have it on me when I'm skating."

I didn't think either of us wanted to talk about why that might be a good idea.

We said our goodbyes to Dolores, who returned them cheerfully, and set out into the night. Lou rested her hand on the bulging purse she'd brought tonight, where I knew she was keeping her other pistol. She'd handled herself just fine, but I could sense the tension in her.

"You okay?" I had to ask.

Lou shrugged. "Sure. Hell, I might not ever need to use it. Really, you and the rest of the guys are the ones who should be concerned about protecting yourselves more than me. I've already taken down the biggest threat to my life."

My jaw clenched. "Your mom—"

Lou caught my gaze. "Is a stone-cold bitch, I know. But she doesn't want me dead. I can't say the same for you guys."

I couldn't help scoffing. "We can look after ourselves. Or I can, and I'll keep an eye on your skaters too. You worry about yourself."

I slung my arm around her shoulders at the same time to take the edge off my chiding. Lou immediately leaned into me, bringing the sweet scent of her hair to my nose. My heart stuttered at the same time as my cock twitched.

This woman had quite a hold on me, that was for sure. And if I had my way—

I jolted back into a deeper awareness of my surroundings with the thump of footsteps. In a matter of seconds, a crowd of aggressive figures had barged onto the narrow street we'd been walking along, their gazes fixed on us.

I jerked to a halt, my hand dipping to the pistol at my hip, and paused as recognition washed over me.

Salvador stood near the front of the group. A bunch of the others were men I'd known in my old neighborhood… members of the gang Edmundo and I had run with.

I'd hoped I'd make it through our time here in Austin without running into them again. It looked like they'd decided to force the issue.

Mierda!

A different guy stepped out in front of the others—no more than a couple of years older than me, with flinty eyes and an equally sharp jaw that jogged my memory. His attention was totally focused on me.

"I heard you were back in town, Rafe," he snarled. "Did you think you could skip a proper reunion?"

I swallowed hard and kept my voice calm. "I've been busy. It's good to see you, Anton. How's your cousin doing these days?"

Anton's lips curled back in a sneer. "Bruno está muerto. We lost him three years ago now. Not that you would care." His gaze flicked to Lou, who'd stiffened beside me. "Is this what you threw everything away for? Some Cordova puta?"

Lou glared back at him. "I'm no whore."

Anton ignored her, his eyes meeting mine again, smoldering with rage. "Your brother would be rolling over in his grave."

Even as I bristled at the insult he'd aimed at Lou, my innards turned to ice. Lou would have no idea what they were talking about—and I wanted to keep it that way. Forever, if I could.

These guys were clearly pissed, and there were a hell of a lot more of them than there were of us. What did they think they were going to do?

Were they just passing on a threat, or were they here to rain down judgment on me?

My voice tightened. "I've never betrayed anyone. Edmundo would be glad that—"

"Don't feed us that mierda," Salvador spat out. "You know what you were meant to do. You know who you owed."

"You have no idea what—"

Anton took another step forward. "Edmundo's not here to do it, so we're going to deliver the message he'd have wanted his traitor brother to get. And if you don't pay attention, next time we'll be sending you to your grave so you can make your excuses straight to his face in Hell."

The whole group surged toward us in a furious mass. I dove in front of Lou instinctively, my fists already flying.

My knuckles bashed in one guy's nose and clocked another in the jaw. I jabbed my knee into someone's gut before stomping an ankle hard enough that the bone cracked.

I had to take them all down—topple them all before they got close enough to hurt Lou.

I dared to reach for my gun, and maybe that was a miscalculation. In the small opening when one of my hands was out of commission, some prick hurtled into me from the side.

As I staggered backward, my fingers clenched around the pistol's grip—and the next thing I knew, something was slamming against the back of my head with a blast of pain.

A board, I registered as I grappled for balance. A few more assholes had come up behind us too—one of them had hit me with a fucking slab of *wood*.

More arms and feet lashed out at me. A bash to my forearm sent my pistol spinning away. I managed to grasp hold of two pricks' heads of hair and slam their foreheads together with a satisfying thud, but with each body that wobbled away, three more seemed to rush in to take its place.

As I swung in one direction, someone in the other rammed a kick against my shins. Multiple pairs of hands yanked and shoved.

I sprawled on my ass, sputtering curses, still hurling punches as well as I could. Then some cabrón drove his heel down on my knee with the full weight of his body behind the blow.

Agony exploded through my leg, like a thousand shards of glass digging into the joint. A groan burst from my lips.

They'd broken my goddamn knee cap. Fuck, fuck, fuck.

Anton loomed over me, clamping his hand around the short coils of my hair. He heaved my head into the pavement beneath me—once, twice, sending more white-hot pain fizzing behind my eyes. A throbbing sensation reverberated through my skull.

I blinked, but I couldn't clear the thickening haze from my eyes. The click of a safety sliding off brought my gaze jerking upward. Salvador stood over me by my broken knee, pointing his pistol at me.

I tried to thrash at him, but other goons jammed my limbs against the concrete. Salvador gave me a vicious grin, his fingers tensing—

And a shot rang out, but from beside me rather than in front of me.

Salvador crumpled, blood spurting from a wound on his chest. A short but fearsome figure shoved into view.

"Get the fuck away from him, or you're all dead!"

Lou fired another bullet into the thigh of one of the men pinning me down. He scrambled away with a string of expletives, clutching the gushing hole in his leg. She braced herself above me, the pistol she'd gotten from her mother clutched in one hand, the Glock I'd just bought for her in the other, murder in her eyes.

"If you don't get the hell out of here *now*, I'm just getting started," she snarled. In that moment, there was no doubting whose daughter she was, even if she'd only brought out the Cordova in her under duress.

Anton held up his hands, but his mouth had twisted with revulsion. "Está bien. We've already delivered our message. Oh, but one last present."

He stomped his foot down on my hand hard enough that a fresh explosion of pain radiated up my arm. I winced inwardly at the crack of bone.

I wasn't going to be holding a gun—or much else—for a good long while.

"Enjoy your goodbye present," Anton spat out, and waved to his men. Supporting the few we'd injured badly enough that they had trouble walking, the horde of them surged back into the side-street they'd emerged from.

Lou stayed poised over me, a tremor running through her body. Her arms quivered but held in place, keeping both guns aimed at the retreating men as they disappeared from view.

I groped at the gritty concrete beneath me with my uninjured hand, searching for leverage to heave myself upright. My head came up —and swam with a whirlpool of pain and dizziness.

Lou dropped down next to me, shoving one gun into her purse so she could wrap her arm around my shoulder. "Don't try to get up. You could make it worse. Dios mío, Rafael, your leg—there's blood all over the back of your head—"

I knew things were bad when she started slipping Spanish in there. The fact that when I opened my mouth, I nearly vomited was another major indication.

I swayed in her hold. My voice came out in a croak. "Sorry. I should have been… protecting you…"

"Fuck that," Lou snapped. "They practically buried you." She pawed through her purse and yanked out her phone. "I'm calling an ambulance."

"Lou," I protested raggedly. "No hospitals. No—"

"I don't want to hear it." The panicked note beneath her words startled me silent. "I don't care what the doctors think about how you ended up like this. I'm not losing you, and no back-alley doctor is going to be able to fix all of this."

I tried to find the wherewithal to keep arguing, but bright spots were forming in my vision, pulsing in time with the throbbing of my head.

"You saved my ass there," I mumbled instead. "Not supposed to be like that."

"Well, it is like that. So live with it. As long as you *live*, I don't fucking care what you think about it."

The desperation in her tone cut right through the center of me. Even as my sight blurred completely, guilt wrenched through the worst of the pain like a wound in itself.

I'd failed her yet again. And how the hell was I going to protect her after this, with my body broken and battered?

TWENTY-THREE

Luciana

RETURNING FROM THE HOSPITAL, Rafael scowled the whole way up to the loft. It was hard to tell whether he was more frustrated with his injuries or the help he was forced to accept.

"I can still *walk*," he muttered, thumping along on his crutches. "You don't need to coddle me."

I ignored his grumbling, shooting a grateful smile at Jasper when he opened the building's front door for us, and studied my bodyguard's face for signs of concussion. A large bandage swathed the back of his head where he'd been bleeding the evening of the attack, two days ago. When I'd come to pick him up this morning, the doctor had told me that the most dangerous period had passed, but that I should still keep a careful eye on him.

That bandage was far from his only lingering impediment from the ambush. He needed the crutches because of the cast encasing his left leg from calf to thigh to stabilize his broken knee cap. Another cast covered his right hand and wrist, where the one asshole had stomped on him right before he'd left.

I should have shot that prick too.

The broken fingers made maneuvering on the crutches significantly more difficult. Rafael swayed a little as we approached the elevator, and Niko extended a hand to steady him.

Rafael's scowl deepened, but he grunted a brief "Thanks."

Quentin jabbed the button to summon the elevator, and Rafael outright glowered at him. "What are you even doing down here trying to take care of me? *You've* got a bullet hole in you, remember?"

Quentin shot him a wry grin. "I've also got two working hands and legs, which is more than you can say, old man."

He kept his tone light enough that Rafael simply rolled his eyes. Their banter smoothed the edges of my distress. If they could joke around like normal, things couldn't have gone *too* horribly wrong, could they?

Every time I looked at Rafael, I had to reassure myself all over again.

I didn't even understand why that gang had attacked him in the first place. They'd said something about his brother and accused him of betraying them. How did that make sense?

I'd asked him about it in the hospital after he was bandaged up, and he'd brushed off the question, saying they were guys from his old neighborhood who'd taken it as a personal insult when he'd gone to work for the Cordovas rather than getting in deeper with them. That they'd gotten increasingly angry the longer he'd avoided them.

The explanation didn't sit totally right with me—but this didn't seem like a good time to badger him about it.

When he was healed up, I'd insist on getting the full story.

The elevator deposited us in the hall outside the loft. Jasper hurried ahead to open the loft's door, and Niko and I flanked Rafael on his lurching journey toward it with Quentin bringing up the rear.

Inside, Rafael thumped over to the sofa and sank onto it with a faint groan of relief. "Fuck hospitals."

Niko headed over to the kitchen. "I'll make us some lunch."

Rafael's mouth pulled even tighter, and I expected him to argue about being served. Instead, he simply said, "Hold off on that for a minute. There's something I need to say."

As the guys came up around the sofa, I sat down gingerly next to Rafael and rested a supportive hand on his abdomen. He slid his fingers around mine and squeezed.

"Lou, you were right," he said gruffly. "I was so caught up in protecting *you* that I wasn't thinking about the threats the rest of us might face, and look where that got me. Now I can't defend you at all."

A pang ran through my heart, and I twined my fingers with his. "It's not your fault. I don't know how anyone would have been prepared for—"

He shook his head to cut me off. "I know you're tough. I know you can look after yourself. But you'll still need help sometimes. And since I can't provide that until I've recovered, you shouldn't be afraid to let the other guys help you. So I'm going to make sure that *they're* as prepared as they can be—to protect both you and themselves. I already made the call."

I knit my brow. "Call? What are you talking about?"

Before he needed to answer, a knock sounded on the loft door. My gaze darted to it with a hitch of my pulse, but Rafael smiled. "Someone go get that. We don't want to leave her waiting."

Her?

My confusion mostly faded when Niko opened the door and I spotted a familiar bright pink shawl in the hallway beyond.

Dolores bustled past Niko and peered around the space, blowing a strand of her faded hair away from her eyes. She had a large case dangling from each aged hand.

"Nice to see you again," she said to me with a grin. "Wish it was under better circumstances. Not a bad place. Lots of pretty views." Her gaze flicked admiringly to Niko, who chuckled in amusement.

Rafael eased himself upright carefully enough that I didn't feel the need to jump in and admonish him. "Thank you for making the house call, Dolores. These guys need firearms of their own if they're going to take care of themselves and our woman properly."

Niko's eyebrows shot up, and a flash of surprise crossed Jasper's face. Only Quentin didn't look particularly startled, though he sucked in his lower lip for a second with a hint of concern.

I spun to meet Rafael's eyes. "Are you sure this is necessary? We've been trained to use guns. They—"

"I'll train them," Rafael said. "The basics, anyway. That'll be enough. We're up against experienced criminals, Lou. You can't let them go into this without the right equipment."

As Dolores laid out a selection of pistols on the coffee table, like the guns were pieces in a Tupperware party, I clamped my mouth shut. My gut stayed twisted.

I'd wanted to keep my skating life totally separate from my criminal past. But that past had become my present, and the guys had already been exposed to more violence than anyone should be. I couldn't pretend I could keep them totally innocent in this situation.

But arming them and preparing them to potentially murder people in my defense felt like a big step farther than they'd already come. A step that made me queasy just thinking about it.

How far would I end up dragging them into the horrible parts of my existence before I finally broke free?

But if I'd been right before, then Rafael was right now. I didn't know what threats we might face next. It wouldn't be fair for me to expect the other guys to turn down any possible tool they could use to keep themselves safe just to absolve my conscience.

I'd have a hell of a weight on my conscience if any of *them* got murdered when having a gun could have saved them.

Dolores stepped back so the men could gather around the table. Rafael studied the offerings and motioned to the other guys in turn.

"Niko, this Sig should suit you well. It's light and easy to carry, good for those slim hands of yours. Nothing too complicated. See how it feels."

Niko picked up the gun Rafael had indicated and eased his fingers around it. My stomach churned, watching him position it in his hand, the weapon looking completely incongruous with his cheerful demeanor.

"Most of my knowledge is from movies," my coach admitted with a nervous laugh. "But I'll do my best to learn. It doesn't feel *bad*."

I couldn't keep silent any longer. "You don't have to do this, you know. I mean, it's true that having a gun might come in handy. But if you're not comfortable carrying one, we're not going to force you."

Niko lifted his bright gaze to meet mine and offered his trademark sunny smile. "I can get used to it. If this is what it takes to keep all of us safe, especially you, then I'm in."

If he could smile like that while holding the pistol, then maybe this wasn't the end of the world. I dragged in a breath and nodded my acceptance.

Rafael had gestured to Jasper as he pointed out another of the guns. As he started to speak, I scanned the rest of the spread more closely.

"You might do best with this Smith & Wesson," he said. "It's a good beginner gun, not too heavy on the firepower."

I made a soft noise to cut in. "I don't know, Jasper has a pretty good grip. I should know from all those lifts. And didn't you tell me that your dad's taken you hunting before?"

Jasper paused, his shoulders stiffening. "I mean, he insisted. It's not as if I liked it. And those were rifles. But I guess I do have some experience with things like how the kick feels."

I nodded. "If we're doing this, we shouldn't skimp on power. I bet you could handle the Ruger." I pointed out the one I meant.

Jasper grasped it and held it up to get a feel for it. "Okay, that's a lot less cumbersome than a rifle. Just holding it, I think I'm okay with this one."

We both glanced at Rafael, who admittedly had a hell of a lot more firearms knowledge than I did. My bodyguard raised an eyebrow at me, but he tipped his head approvingly toward Jasper. "I'll never say a man should downplay what he can handle. I didn't realize you weren't a total newbie."

Quentin stepped closer with an impatient air. "What about me? I don't want anything wimpy."

Rafael contemplated his shoulder. "You're righthanded, aren't you? So the injury shouldn't mess with your aim."

I examined the remaining guns with a frown. "But better not to pick anything that's got too much of a kick. You've got to brace your whole body against that."

"I'll be fine," Quentin started to say.

I aimed a narrow look at him. "We're not making the injury worse."

Dolores, who'd been sitting patiently through our conversation, cleared her throat. "If I could make a suggestion… This model of Beretta has a good balance of power and subtlety."

Rafael took the pistol she'd indicated and looked it over, then passed it to me so I could check it out before Quentin finally got his hands on it.

He aimed it at the wall and then the window without putting his finger on the trigger. A smile crossed his lips. "I could get used to this."

"It feels all right?" I confirmed.

"Oh, yeah. I might not have fired a gun before, but I'm not squeamish about it. Just train me up."

The corner of Rafael's mouth ticked upward. "That's exactly what I've got on the schedule for tomorrow. I'm hauling the three of you out to a shooting range so you can get comfortable with firing those things."

After he'd handed over the cash for the three guns, Dolores cleared the others from the table and then opened her second case to reveal an assortment of knives. "Don't forget about these beauties. In close combat, a blade will often do you better than a bullet."

Niko immediately gravitated to a double-edged tactical knife. Just his initial swipe of it through the air made me think anyone stupid enough to try to take him on while he was holding that thing would quickly regret it.

Jasper went bigger, hefting a serrated hunting knife. He pricked his finger on the deadly tip and hissed before blotting beading blood from the scratch on his shirt. "Christ. This thing's pretty damn sharp."

"Of course it is. Dolores doesn't sell dull blades, young man." The old woman gave him a wink that looked suspiciously flirty.

I glanced over at Quentin, who was still eyeing the options. "Anything calling to you?"

"Maybe…" He turned a switchblade over in his hand, testing how responsive the blade was to the button. It snicked in and out. "I've always had a thing for these. You think it'd be a good choice?"

"Sure," Rafael said with a trace of amusement. "And it saves you worrying about chopping your own balls off while you're carrying it around."

Quentin guffawed. "Let's go with this one, then."

When Rafael had paid for those too, Dolores got up, beaming in her unnervingly grandmother-like way. "You're always a sweetheart, Rafael. And lately, my best customer. You send out a word if you ever need another house call."

"Will do."

As I deadbolted the door behind her, Rafael was already leaning forward to start instructing the other guys. "We'll deal with gunmanship tomorrow at the range, but I can go over the basics of knife combat right now. You might not get a whole lot of time to react, so you want to know the best places to strike to disable someone quickly and how to avoid a block."

He beckoned me over. "Lou, I'm going to need you to stand in for me here, since I can't play target very easily."

I wiggled my eyebrows. "Ooh, knife play. When did I get so lucky?"

Rafael just shook his head at me.

I did take the practice seriously once we got down to it—and the solemn expressions that had come over the skater men's faces might have been funny if I hadn't known their lives could be quite literally on the line. Rafael talked us through several scenarios, directing our positions and the tentative jabs and cuts the guys acted out, never actually doing more than grazing my clothes.

None of his three pupils made so much as a murmur of complaint. While I stepped back so that Rafael could demonstrate a grip and a twist with his good hand, my gaze traveled over all of my men, and a strange mix of trepidation and affection tangled in my chest.

I still didn't like seeing these three acting more like gang stooges than athletes… but there wasn't anything I could do about that. And when I let myself admit it, the fact that they were so committed to holding their own in the mess I'd dragged them into was something incredible.

I'd never have imagined they'd be devoted enough to get their hands this dirty for me.

A buzzing from my pocket broke through my thoughts. My burner phone.

The men looked up as I pulled the phone out and checked the screen. "It's Beckett," I told them with a leap of my pulse, and tapped through to see what the acting Storm had to say.

Would it be possible for us to meet in person in the next couple of days? There's something I'd like to discuss with you that I'd rather there wasn't any kind of concrete record of.

A quiver ran through my nerves. This could be something big if he was being so cautious about it.

I can manage that, I typed back and considered the demands Mom had made on my time this week. *Tomorrow afternoon?*

His reply was instant. *Perfect. Make sure you're not followed. I'll see you then—and fill you in on everything.*

TWENTY-FOUR

Luciana

I WOVE through the throng of shoppers that filled the thoroughfare of the huge mall complex. The constant shifting of bodies and the cacophony of voices had my unsettled nerves even more on edge, but I knew the setting was for both my and Beckett's protection.

As we blended into the mass of ordinary people that flooded the place in the late afternoon, no one was likely to notice our clandestine meeting. We wouldn't be visible from more than a few feet away.

And it meant neither of us could ambush the other with a larger force. You'd have to be insane to stage an attack with this many witnesses around, before even getting into the logistical problems of fighting amid a gazillion human obstacles.

No doubt Beckett had made the same calculations when he'd suggested this spot. Really, he had even less reason to trust me than I did him. I'd told him outright that my mother was scheming against him, and for all he knew, she might manipulate me into turning on him too.

You didn't survive long in our world without a healthy sense of caution.

Over the heads of the shoppers around me, I spotted the top of the marble fountain Beckett had mentioned. I made my way over to it and stopped by the tiled wall around the edge of the pool as if I were admiring the abstract sculpture. To my eyes, it looked like a gigantic flower an even more gigantic bird had chomped up and spit out.

Hey, there was no accounting for artistic taste.

The burbling of the water mingled with the voices carrying from all around me. I didn't hear Beckett's footsteps, only registered his lanky form and sandy hair ambling over at the edge of my vision.

He stopped a couple of feet away, gazing at the fountain like I was. Nothing about his stance indicated that he knew me or had any interest in talking to me.

"Thanks for meeting me," he said evenly, only just loud enough to be heard over the noise of the mall.

I matched both his tone and his volume. "I'm glad you reached out. What's up?"

"I'll keep this brief and to the point, because the less time we're together, the safer it is. I have reason to believe that the Deadly Rose has been trying to poach many of my top people."

I blinked, resisting the urge to peer over at him. "Poach?"

"Get them under her thumb rather than working for me. Thankfully, my employees are loyal, and several of them tipped me off that they'd gotten sudden, huge financial opportunities offered to them… on the condition that they cut ties with me first. Which naturally made them suspicious."

Mom hadn't mentioned anything about this to me—but then, she'd been cagey about her exact strategies from before she'd even realized I was collecting evidence against her.

"What kind of opportunities?" I asked.

"High level jobs with extensive benefits at a bunch of different companies, supposedly independent of each other. But obviously having them all come in short succession can't be a coincidence. I had my tech experts trace the businesses' operations, and ultimately they all led back to a couple of shell companies. We found significant but not undeniable proof that those shells are part of your mother's portfolio."

I made a face. "I don't need undeniable proof. What you said is enough—I'm sure it's her. Shit. I'm sorry. I had no idea she was planning anything like that, or I'd have warned you."

It was awfully similar to what she'd done to the Blood Hunter, only less fatal. Maybe there hadn't been a good setting to off a bunch of the Storm's key people all at once, so this had seemed like a reasonable alternative. Or maybe she figured the Storm would be a trickier opponent, and she'd been hoping his people would offer up inside intel once she had them under her sway.

Whatever the case, her ultimate motive was clear. She wanted to weaken the Devil's Dozen members she planned to move against so that it'd be easier to crush them later on. How many others of her colleagues was she messing with?

Beckett's lips curled in a slight smile. "You don't have to apologize. I wouldn't be here if I thought there was any chance you're on board with her plans. But you're in the best position out of anyone to do something about the overall situation."

"Aren't you going to take her to task when she went after your people like that?"

"Oh, I'll create some trouble for her to show the attempt didn't go unnoticed. But simply trying to win over someone else's top people would be seen more like reasonable strategy to my colleagues than a violation of our codes."

He darted the briefest of glances toward me. "You have the key pieces—and coming from one of her own, it'd be clear any accusations weren't a gambit of our own. If you get an opportunity to take her to task, I want you to have every bit of information available to make that as easy as possible."

I exhaled raggedly. "Right. Thank you." It all came down to me—I was the one living with the woman, seeing her every day.

I was the one she'd punish the harshest if I lost my grasp on the leverage I was using against her.

Beckett started to turn away. "I'll send you the proof we do have of the financial connections we dug up and a report of my employee's stories. Is the same phone number still good for that? I don't want to get you in trouble."

"Yeah, she doesn't know about that phone. I'll save the files to a separate server and delete the texts right away too."

"Good. You stay safe. I know it can't be fun finding yourself in the middle of this conflict. If there's any way I can help, let me know."

With those parting words, he vanished into the crowd.

I lingered by the fountain for a minute longer before drifting toward the exit. As I crossed the parking lot to my car, a heavy weight settled in my stomach.

More evidence meant more leverage. That was all great. But what would it take for me to be able to leave this life completely?

I had trouble even imagining having enough for that.

Just as I came up on the car, the sharp ringtone I'd assigned to Mom's number pealed from my purse. I groped for my regular phone and yanked it to my ear, knowing the conversation would be less uncomfortable if we didn't start it off with her complaining about a slow response.

"Hi, Mom," I said tentatively, bracing myself as I opened the driver's side door.

Her voice crackled through the line in an even more domineering tone than usual. "Luciana? Where are you? I need to go over a few things with you, in person. Immediately."

Oh, great. What plans did she have for *me* now?

My gaze slid to the nearby freeway. The mall was about an hour outside of Austin, but I'd rather give myself a little breathing room. "I'm not in the city. I can get there in a couple of hours."

I'd been checking my car over for tracking devices every time I took it out of the garage and hadn't found any since the first one Mom had admitted to. She shouldn't be able to tell exactly where I was.

"A couple of hours? What on earth are you doing? I need you to be ready when I have work for you."

I willed the irritation out of my tone. "The deal was that I get to have my own life too. If you want me for something important, you need to give me more than five minutes' notice. I'll get there as fast as I can."

"The deal was that you fulfill your duties as a Cordova. If you're not going to hold up your end—"

"I can't just magically teleport myself there in an instant," I snapped, and then reined in my temper before I could go too far. "I told you, I'm coming. We already had that meeting this morning. I had no idea there was anything else you'd urgently need me for."

"Well, now you know. If you expect me to believe you have any loyalty left at all, I expect to see you in my office by seven o'clock sharp."

She hung up without giving me a chance to respond. I gunned the engine, my blood boiling. After everything, she still saw me as a puppet whose strings she should be able to pull however she liked, whenever she liked.

As I merged onto the freeway, my heart pounded with a mix of anger and fear. Mom had no right to expect me to appear the second she beckoned, but that didn't mean she wouldn't punish me for failing to predict her demands. Part of me wanted to take my time driving back, to show up at seven and not a moment earlier so she'd know she hadn't frightened me. The part of me that *was* frightened wanted to flat-pedal it so I could diffuse her rage.

It took several minutes for the initial upheaval from the conversation to wear off… and a more subtle anxiety to creep in.

Why *was* Mom so desperate to get me back to the house? She didn't usually pull out the threats and show real anger unless it was absolutely necessary—she'd rather appear coolly in control.

She'd been awfully vague about what she wanted me there for. To go over a few things with me? If it was so urgent, why couldn't she have talked to me about it on the phone right away?

No, what she'd really been insistent about was getting me back to the mansion. Why? Because she had something bigger in store for me there?

Or maybe because she wanted to be sure I *wasn't* someplace else?

Once the idea had taken hold, I couldn't shake it. A chill prickled through my veins. Finally, I wiggled my burner phone out of my pocket and set it in the cupholder.

"Speakerphone on," I said in voice command. "Call Rafael."

Rafael picked up after two rings, his deep baritone a balm on my nerves. "Everything all right, Lou?"

"Yeah. I was just about to ask you that. Nothing strange has gone down at the loft?"

I could almost hear his frown in his pause. "Business as usual around here. We got back from the shooting range a couple of hours ago—your skaters didn't embarrass me too much. Why, what's going on?"

"Oh, maybe I'm just being paranoid. My mom—"

A sudden screech of a siren blared through the speaker, making me flinch. "What the hell is that?"

Rafael raised his voice to talk over the pulsing wail, sounding annoyed. "I think that's the building's fire alarm. They didn't warn us about a drill. Someone must have done something stupid in the halls."

A deeper chill pierced through my gut. I couldn't have said exactly what the problem was, but I had a bad feeling about all of this. "You should get out of the building just in case. And… be careful. I'm heading straight over—I'll get there soon."

The second the call ended, I pressed my foot to the gas pedal. Weaving through the other cars, I roared along the freeway as fast as I dared.

The loft was on the edge of the city, closer than the Deadly Rose mansion. I'd already covered a lot of the distance back to Austin. If all went well, I could cut the rest of the journey down to no more than fifteen minutes.

I just had to hope that didn't make me fifteen minutes too late.

I tore down the exit ramp and through the streets to the loft, only slowing when the building came into view up ahead. A small throng of residents milled on the sidewalk outside and across the road.

With a frantic flick of my eyes, I spotted all four of my men in a cluster near the parking lot. I pulled over to the curb, sprang out, and dashed over to them.

No smoke seeped from the building's windows. No flames danced behind the glass. My suspicions deepened with every thud of my heart.

Niko saw me first and welcomed me into their group with a sling of his arm around my waist.

Rafael swiveled on his crutches to face me. "What's going on, Lou? I didn't think you were coming over today."

I grimaced, my stomach churning with apprehension. "I don't think the fire alarm was a random coincidence. My mom's up to something. We need to check the loft."

He started to straighten up as much as he could with his leg in the cast, but I grasped his arm. "No. You've got to stay down here with the crowd. You know you won't be able to move fast—but you can keep an eye out and give us a heads up if anything changes down here."

And he'd be safer. I didn't want Rafael getting even more hurt than he already was. But if I said *that*, I'd wound his pride, and who knew what idiotic things he'd do.

My bodyguard's stance tensed, but he nodded in acceptance. I tugged the other guys around to the building's back entrance.

When I pushed open the door, the air inside smelled stale but not the slightest bit smoky. My certainty that this was some kind of a trick only grew.

"What do you think we're dealing with?" Quentin asked as we clambered up the stairs.

I let out my breath in a nervous rush. "I'm not sure. But be prepared for a fight."

They all accepted that order without hesitation or surprise. It'd have pained me more to see them adjusting to the craziness of my life so easily if it hadn't seemed so vital to their survival.

I slipped my hand into my jacket pocket and curled my fingers around the Glock that Rafael had insisted I buy from Dolores. If I had my way, I'd handle most of whatever fight we encountered.

We burst from the stairwell near the loft's door. The guys stuck close to me as we hurried down the hall.

Jasper hissed through his teeth. "The door's open."

It was—just an inch ajar. So slight we could almost have thought the guys must have simply failed to secure it properly in their rush to evacuate, but I knew Rafael would never have been that careless.

My whole body tensed. I took the lead, striding up to the door, girding myself, and then shoving inside with my gun held in front of me.

In the main room, three men in dark sweatsuits spun around. One held a knife that he'd been digging into the sofa cushions. Another looked like he'd been ransacking the kitchen cabinets, with cereal, dry pasta, and crackers strewn across the counters from their opened boxes. The third had been prying at a floorboard.

I recognized two of those faces. I'd seen them around the Deadly Rose mansion.

These were Mom's men. She'd sent them to search the loft… for evidence I might have stashed here, presumably, or a clue about how to get access to all the digital proof I'd stored in the cloud.

One of the men gave a shout. Another's hand twitched toward his hip where I could see the bulge of a pistol.

I jerked my gun toward him. "Don't even think about it unless you want to lose that hand."

Two more men came barging out from behind the dividers that separated the makeshift bedrooms. One of them lunged toward us with a growl, but then all three of my guys whipped out the guns they'd been practicing with earlier this afternoon.

"Just try me," Quentin gritted out, his pale eyes flashing with fury. He held his pistol perfectly steady. At my other side, Niko's and Jasper's stances were a little more awkward, but determination was etched in their expressions.

They'd blow these goons away before they gave them an opening to hurt me.

And the goons could obviously recognize that too. Four to five, with the four of us already prepared to shoot, it wasn't any contest.

The one who'd lunged and the one with the knife lifted their hands in a gesture of surrender. I motioned with my pistol at the one who'd reached for his gun, and he echoed the pose, scowling.

I glowered right back at them. "I can see what you were doing here. Get the fuck out of this building and tell my mother I won't be home until tomorrow. Maybe she'll be ready to treat me and my associates with all due respect by then."

Flickers of nervousness passed across a few of their faces. "The boss isn't going to be happy about that," one muttered.

"I don't give a shit what makes her happy. She should have thought about that before she went behind my back. Now get going!"

At the wave of my gun, the five thugs hustled over. We stepped to the side so they could file out the door, keeping our gazes and our weapons trained on them the entire time.

The thud of their feet resounded down the hall outside, and then they were gone.

My shoulders slumped as the tension released from them. Jasper's arm dropped, a strained chuckle tumbling from his lips. "Holy hell. I can't believe we just did that."

Niko set his gun down on a side table as if he didn't want to tuck it completely away just yet. He glanced at me. "Those were your mother's people—what were they looking for?"

I sighed. "They probably hoped they'd be able to get at and destroy the evidence I'm using as leverage against her. I should have realized she'd figure out where you're living and try to undermine me that way."

"It's not your fault that you don't think like that vicious bitch does," Quentin said firmly, scanning the loft. "Is there any chance they *did* get at your stuff?"

I shook my head. "Everything's online, and I know better than to write down passwords. It's totally secure." I paused, giving myself a moment to try to think like the Deadly Rose would. "But we need to search the place for surveillance bugs. They might have planted some during their search so she can listen in."

Niko rubbed his hands together as if the search sounded like a wonderful game. "What exactly do we look for?"

I pulled out my phone. "I'll show you some pictures… Can one of you go down to help Rafael get back up here? He'll be wondering what the hell's gone down."

Jasper reached for the door. "I'll fill him in."

I took in the mess Mom's men had left behind and restrained a shudder. We were going to be doing a lot of cleaning as well as bug-hunting.

But what would even be the point of relocating? Mom owned this city—I had no doubt that she'd figure out where the guys had holed up no matter where I set them up in town. And they'd made it amply clear that they had no intention of leaving Austin without me.

"All right," I said, putting on my best unfazable tone. "Let's start in the kitchen."

But as we crunched through the rummaged food that'd spilled onto the floor, my spirits were sinking.

Mom was getting awfully restless in our arrangement. How far would she go in her attempts to regain the upper hand?

TWENTY-FIVE

Luciana

THE ONLY UPSIDE that came with the shitty day was that it gave me an excuse to stay overnight with my guys. Once the confusion around the fire alarm had died down, we ordered in Thai—which had enough options that even Quentin was satisfied with the spread—and settled into the living room together, watching a cheesy old movie playing on one of the cable stations and shouting at the characters' wacky decisions.

It was so comfortable and cozy that I could almost forget the trauma we'd endured since arriving in this city.

Refusing the guys' emphatic offers to give up their beds, I took the sofa, pointing out that I was the smallest by far of the bunch of us and so fit it best. The loft had only come with twin beds, so it wasn't as if I could snuggle in next to any of them all that easily.

And so, in the middle of the night after the light beyond the thin curtains had dimmed and the only sound was the rasp of sleeping breaths from the makeshift bedrooms, I found myself sprawled on the sofa, staring at the ceiling.

The niggling thoughts I'd been managing to dismiss over the last few days crept in more insistently. Rafael was doing okay—but he still hadn't revealed anything further about the guys who'd jumped him. What had their warning even been about? What did they expect him to do now to avoid the threat of additional retaliation?

I understood where my mom was coming from, but what if they came after him again too?

And how did his brother fit into all this? I hadn't even known he *had* a brother. He'd never really talked about his family.

I should have pushed more. Asked more questions. Privacy was a precious thing in our line of work, but our lives were totally entangled now.

A soft grunt reached my ears from the direction of the farthest bedroom on the left, the one I knew belonged to my bodyguard. It was followed by the rustle of blankets as he must have turned over, and then a restrained sigh.

I hesitated for a second and then shrugged off my own blanket and pushed to my feet. If neither of us was sleeping, it couldn't hurt anything for me to go talk to him now. I didn't think he'd want to have this conversation in front of the other guys anyway.

I padded through the dimness to the dividers that framed Rafael's "room" and eased open the one that served as a door, just long enough for me to slip past it. As I pulled it closed again, Rafael was already raising his head to peer at me.

"What are you up to, brat?" he murmured with drowsy fondness.

Despite my worries, a smile tugged at my lips. I climbed onto the bed and tucked myself close against his brawny frame under the covers—both out of a craving for his warmth and out of necessity, given the size of the bed. Hooking one leg over his uninjured one, I rested my head on his shoulder and tipped my face toward his ear so I could speak quietly and not risk waking the others.

"I couldn't sleep. Too many thoughts spinning in my head. It sounded like maybe you were having a similar problem."

"And you figured misery loves company?"

I teased my fingers up his chest, rumpling the thin fabric of his undershirt. "Are you miserable that I'm here?"

Rafael let out a light chuckle. "Never, Lou."

I could have taken the moment in a very different, much more enjoyable direction right then, but the questions I'd been grappling with gripped me too tightly. "Rafael… the guys who attacked you talked about your brother. Would you tell me how he fits into all this?"

There was a long stretch of silence. Rafael's muscles had tensed against my body, but he reached over to stroke my hair with his good hand as if to show he was still with me, just figuring out what he wanted to say.

"It's a long story," he said finally.

"That's okay. I mean, you don't *have* to talk about him. But it'd make me feel better having a clearer understanding about what happened that night and why."

His fingers grazed over my hair in another gentle caress. When he spoke again, his voice was still low but rougher.

"Edmundo was my older brother—five years older. It's because of him that I got into this kind of life. My parents would never have expected it. They were totally law-abiding, just regular people. They ran a gardening and flower shop together, if you can believe that."

I pictured a tiny version of Rafael wandering between shelves of potted flowers and grinned. "You know, I think I can."

"It was their dream," he went on. "They worked their asses off getting the business off the ground, every bit of that a labor of love, and by the time I was in elementary school, it was just starting to take off. We weren't getting rich or anything, but they could buy take-out for dinner once a week, and we got a big TV to replace the old crappy one we'd bought at a garage sale. Stuff like that."

"That's great."

He nodded. "Yeah. But a successful business can attract the wrong kind of interest. There was a gang in the neighborhood that started hitting my parents up for protection money like they did other places in the area. Just a little at first, but then the demands grew. My dad got frustrated and made some snarky remark one time when they came around, and they took it as an insult to their authority."

My body stiffened. "Oh, no."

I felt more than saw Rafael's grimace. "Yeah. They broke into the shop one night and smashed up the place—the windows, the furniture, the merchandise. Most of it wasn't salvageable. It put my parents even deeper in the hole than when they'd first started out, and all they could do was struggle to get the store off the ground again. In most of my memories from after that, they were always stressed and overworked."

A lump rose in my throat. "I'm so sorry."

Rafael gave a brief shrug. "It is what it is. But Edmundo—he was twelve when it happened—it really got to him. Maybe because he'd been more aware of how hard they'd worked in the first place to build the business up, when I'd been too young to really pay attention."

"He must have been furious." I was plenty pissed off myself, even hearing about it decades later.

"Furious and determined. He decided he was going to get tougher than the gang—and make tougher friends—so they couldn't intimidate our family ever again. He ended up getting involved with another gang through some friends he met in high school. And when I was old enough that they could find some use for me, he brought me on board too."

The pieces clicked together in my head. "The guys who beat you up—they were part of that gang?"

Rafael exhaled raggedly. "Yeah. I don't know a lot of them anymore. It's been a long time since I ran with that bunch. But a few of them know me from back then."

I knit my brow. "But why were they so angry with you? Why did they think your brother would be?"

He paused, tipping his head back into the pillow. "They see me moving on to a bigger organization like your mom's as a betrayal. Like I was saying they weren't good enough. And—Edmundo was killed a while back, not that long before I came on board with the Deadly Rose, and they expected me to take his place. They were pissed that I jumped at a different opportunity."

Rafael turned his head toward me and kissed my forehead. "Not that I've ever once regretted the decision myself."

The affection in his voice sent a tingle of heat through me, but something about his story was still gnawing at me. "It seems like an awfully long time for them to hold a grudge. That all must have happened, like, ten years ago!"

"I guess they haven't had anything else offend them to take their minds off it," Rafael said dryly.

Before I could ask anything else, his tone dipped lower with a pained edge. "But I never meant to let it affect my ability to look after you. I was *useless* today because of the injuries those assholes gave me. I couldn't do anything to protect you or the other guys."

I bristled. "You've got nothing to apologize for. The assholes are the ones who screwed us over—they're the only ones I'm angry at. We all protect each other. It doesn't just go one way."

Rafael grunted. "I'm the one who knows this city. I'm the one who's seen what your mom is like. You need me to be at my best while we're here, and I—"

"Hey." I tipped closer to him and set my fingers on his lips to quiet him. His self-recriminations over his supposed weakness sent an ache through my gut.

Did he really think I saw him as less of a protector just because he'd been temporarily laid up? That I believed he'd let me down somehow?

Maybe it'd help if I proved to him just how much of a man I still saw him as—how much the strength I knew he still possessed turned me on.

"You're everything I've ever wanted you to be," I murmured, letting my hand trail down his neck and over his chest. "You always will be. And when you get knocked down for a bit, that just means I've got to work a little harder to show how true that is."

I rolled right onto him, careful of the cast around his leg, and leaned down to seek out his mouth. Rafael's lips parted beneath mine, his tongue sweeping in to claim my own, refusing to totally give up his usual role as the aggressor.

He tasted so damn good and felt even better under my body. His good hand rose to twine through my hair with the firm grip that could make me swoon. He might not have been all that mobile at the moment, but that didn't stop him from shifting his hips to press his erection against my pussy through our clothes.

I smothered a moan against his mouth. If we were doing what I hoped we were going to do, we'd have to stay quiet. No need to disturb the others' sleep while we got our rocks off.

Rafael wrenched my head back and branded my neck with another searing kiss. I swayed against him, grinding into his erection until both our breaths stuttered. When he briefly loosened his grip, I bowed my head over his again.

"You don't have to prove anything to me. I already know just how much of a man you are."

Rafael gave a muted growl. "Oh, I can show you that even more. I'm not too bashed up to satisfy you."

I swallowed a gasp as he rubbed his rigid cock against my pussy again. My panties were already soaked, and there was no ignoring how badly he wanted me too.

I'd always wanted him. Every single day from the moment I'd been old enough to know what this kind of wanting was.

With a slide of my hand, I palmed him through the boxers he'd worn to bed. He mumbled a curse as his cock twitched against my palm.

It only took a slight raise of my hips and some deft maneuvering to free him from the fabric without displacing myself. I pumped my hand up and down his thick shaft, humming in appreciation.

Rafael's eyes flashed in the darkness. He pulled me down over him, capturing my mouth as I claimed his cock.

"I hope you're not going to stop at just teasing me, brat," he muttered against my lips.

A breathy giggle tumbled out of me. If he'd had any idea how much I was aching for him, he couldn't have suggested that.

Deciding I could make a little show of it, I lifted myself up over him until I was standing and then shimmied slowly out of my plaid leggings. Rafael's gaze traced my curves, avid enough that I felt its heat coursing over my skin.

I wriggled out of my panties too and then hesitated. But he could guess my concern.

"Top drawer," he rasped, pointing at the crate-like nightstand. "I figured I should have a few on hand… just in case."

I snatched out a foil wrapper. Before I could open it, Rafael grabbed it from my fingers and tore it with his teeth. He managed to roll the condom over his cock at lightning speed even one-handed.

"Very impressive," I murmured, lowering myself over him. "I think you should get an immediate reward…"

I lined up and sank down, taking his entire cock into my slick cunt in one fluid movement.

Rafael muffled another groan and grasped my hair again. "I'll never get over how good you feel, Lou."

I rocked up and down over him, my vision already fizzing with the pleasure as he stretched me. "Right back at you."

We bucked against each other with as much furor as Rafael was capable of with his broken knee. His breath gushed hot against my neck and then my breasts as he shoved himself up to nip his way across my chest. His hand dropped as well, and I had to choke back a moan as he squeezed one nipple between his fingers.

"Shh," he said. "You don't want to wake everyone up, do you, brat?"

Instead of answering, I just rolled my hips faster, fucking him harder. He matched my pace, thrusting up into me with a power that took my breath away. His fingers moved to my ass and dug into the flesh there, sending jolts of pain and bliss through my nerves.

"Oh, fuck," I mumbled as the waves of pleasure rolled through me, sending me spiraling higher and higher. I bit my lip, squeezing my eyes shut as if closing my eyelids would help contain any sounds I'd make.

"Next time we'll let them hear you," Rafael said, his voice sizzling with dark promise. "Let them know how good I treat this pussy."

Oh, he was working me over good, all right. My breath came in short, hot bursts, my eyes unfocusing. I was dangerously close to losing hold of what little control I did have.

Rafael must have sensed my weakness. His voice took on a huskier note. "That's right. Come for me, Lou."

I did exactly as I was told.

My orgasm exploded through me in a whirlwind. I shuddered over

Rafael, my bliss spiking higher at the feel of his cock pulsing inside me. A cry I couldn't totally hold back burst from my throat.

Rafael yanked me back down to him and buried his face between my neck and shoulder. I muffled the rest of my ecstatic whimpers in the short twists of his hair while he groaned against my skin.

The world slowly fixed the tilt of its axis as I floated back down to Earth. My vision was still sparking bursts of color from the intensity of my release. Remembering the sound that'd escaped me, I listened carefully as I relaxed against Rafael's broad body. Maybe it hadn't been *too* loud.

At first I thought we'd succeeded in our attempt at discretion. No noise reached my ears from the rooms next to ours.

Then Quentin's voice, a little tired but with typical cockiness, carried from a couple of dividers over. "Next time you decide to have some fun in the middle of the night, I expect to be invited too."

A snicker followed that I was pretty sure was Niko's. Okay, so much for keeping our hook-up on the downlow.

Rafael chuckled under me. I let out a giggle of my own and offered up a rueful, "Sorry for disturbing your sleep!"

"You'd better get some now too, Punk," Jasper piped up from the nearest bed.

I couldn't deny that he was right. I considered slipping back to the sofa, but it was hard to peel myself away from Rafael's solid warmth.

He didn't show any signs of minding me simply sprawling over him like he was a human mattress. He tugged the blanket back up over the two of us and slung his arm over my waist. "You stay right here."

My eyelids slid shut. Sleep finally crept up on me, the pleasure having washed away the worst of my worries.

But in the last few moments before I drifted off completely, I couldn't stop one last question from prickling through my mind.

I'd told Rafael that I meant to protect him just as much as he protected me. Could I really defend the four men in this room from everything my mother had in store for us next?

TWENTY-SIX

Luciana

AS I PULLED through the gate outside the Cordova mansion, the music from my and Jasper's free skate kept playing on a loop in my head. I went through the motions of easing the car into the garage and parking, but behind my eyes I was playing out every move—every spin, jump, and lift.

Not even the ominous atmosphere that hung over my family home could dampen my spirits. It was less than a week before Nationals. Tomorrow we were all going to head up north to Portland, where the competition was being held, to get used to the rink ahead of time.

I'd warned Mom that I'd be gone for several days, and she'd accepted the news with cold silence. After her men had failed to destroy any of my leverage and I'd sent them running in an embarrassing fashion, there'd been a tense peace between the two of us. To try to ensure that she wouldn't sabotage the upcoming championships, I'd been as obedient as I could bear to be, following her orders efficiently and with forced enthusiasm.

I'd given her nothing to complain about. She'd survived without me for months before—she could give me a week now.

A bounce came into my step as I walked over to the front door, still hearing our song in my mind. If the few underlings hanging around keeping watch thought I looked dorky, I really didn't give a shit at this point.

I stepped into the foyer, switching to picturing the leftover Polish takeout I'd like to dive into to replenish some of the burned-off calories, but the clack of heels on the hardwood floor broke through my imaginings.

"I hope you're not thinking of heading off to your room."

My head jerked around. My mother emerged from the shadows at the top of the staircase like a grim reaper in Gucci. Her dark brown eyes narrowed dangerously. Both red-nailed hands were curled into fists on each hip.

She looked ready to deal out a wave of death. My stomach knotted. What had gotten her in a mood like that?

"I wasn't," I said carefully. "Not if you need me."

She smirked at me, and I hated myself. "Good answer. As a matter of fact, I do need you. Come down to the basement, and I'll fill you in."

My gaze flicked to the doorway off to the side of the foyer—the one that led to a narrow staircase and the maze of halls and rooms that stretched out below the mansion. Some of those rooms were just for storage, but I doubted Mom just wanted me to haul supplies.

The other rooms… Nothing good happened down there.

As Mom descended the stairs with brisk steps, I swallowed thickly. "The basement? You didn't mention anything about… work we'd need to do down there."

There was something oddly twitchy about Mom's movements as her head turned toward me. I got the impression that she was on edge, holding herself back from revealing even more coiled tension.

That didn't bode well for this afternoon's activities either.

Her gaze sharpened into a glare. "I'm mentioning it now. You'll come along if you know what's good for you—or do you need a reminder of who you're talking to?"

I held up my hands, even more uneasy than before. "All right. No problem. I was just asking."

With dread winding through my gut, I followed her down the stairs into the cooler air of the basement.

We passed several closed doors, making our way to the far end of the basement where most of the rooms were secured behind heavy locks. Where things went on that even most of the lackeys weren't privy to.

Mom stopped in front of a plain but solid door that I knew led to one of her "interrogation rooms." Heavily soundproofed so that no hint of what went on in there would seep through to the outside world.

She motioned to me. "Open it."

My throat constricted, but I didn't even know what was going on here to argue against it. Squaring my shoulders, I twisted the doorknob and pushed it ahead of me as I stepped into the room.

The second I'd moved past the door enough to see the far corner of the room, my feet stalled in their tracks.

A thin figure was standing in the corner, his hands raised over his head, restrained there by a chain that dangled from the ceiling. He'd been stripped to a wifebeater undershirt and his boxers, both soiled with sweat and in the case of the boxers, maybe worse. His skin looked sickly sallow, but he stared at me with a clenched jaw and a sullen expression.

Mom brushed past me and rested her hand against the prisoner's cheek. When he tried to move away from her touch, she slapped him with a rake of her fingernails.

Stark red lines formed across his face where she'd scratched the pale skin. He hissed and thrashed against the chain, but Mom stepped away, turning back to me.

"This young man works for one of my Devil's Dozen colleagues," she informed me in a cool voice. "We caught the snake trying to sniff around some of our operations. So now he gets to spill everything he knows about his boss's work. It seems he needs a little more incentive to start talking, though. Your job is to get all of it out of him."

My heart lurched. "*Me?*"

I wouldn't have dared let so much shock show if I hadn't been so very startled. Mom had forced me to watch a few of her interrogations in the past, but she'd never had me so much as pitch in with the actual torture, let alone direct it myself.

She was throwing me right into the deep end. And this was a pool I had zero interest in swimming in.

Her lips drew back, and a hint of a snarl came into her voice. "You. Everything's laid out. Get to work."

A metal stand stood next to the wall beyond the reach of the guy's feet. It held rows of vicious instruments, ranging from knives to clamps to a propane lighter and thumb tacks. Bile rose in my throat, but I willed it down, not wanting Mom to see my nausea.

I dragged my feet over to the stand and stared down at the tools. My fingers curled toward my palms, resisting the idea of so much as picking any of those objects up.

Mom tsked her tongue behind me. "Let's get on with it, Luciana. It's better that this pendejo gets a beat down than your beloved boyfriends, isn't it? Of course, if you'd rather see one of *them* tortured, I can certainly—"

"No," I snapped, fighting to keep my voice steady through the wave of horror her suggestion had provoked. I inhaled deeply, cringing inwardly at the dank smell of the room. "I'm just deciding on my approach."

I could do this. Prod him for answers, show that I meant business—maybe I wouldn't have to go too far to get him to open up.

If he was working for one of the other Devil's Dozen members and digging into Mom's business, he had to know the risks. He'd signed up for this. He wasn't some innocent.

Even more queasy at the thought of drawing blood, I settled on a steel baton. My palm started to sweat against the cool metal as I hefted it and turned to face the guy.

I tapped the weapon against my other hand. "We could cut straight to the chase. Tell us why your boss sent you to spy on the Deadly Rose."

A flicker of panic crossed the guy's face. "I have no idea what you're talking about. What's the deadly rose?"

So he was going to insist on making this difficult. I gritted my teeth and thought back to the lessons I'd learned from watching Mom in scenarios like this over the years and from my combat training.

I slammed the baton against the guy's side just below his rib cage, hard enough to send pain spiking through his organs but not to actually damage them. I'd rather I never had to get to that point.

The guy jerked and cried out. Tears started to leak from his eyes even as his body went rigid with resistance. "Please, I swear—I have no idea what any of this is about. Can't you—"

Another sharp whack on the opposite side of his torso. A jab right to his belly. A forceful smack across his knuckles, nearly cracking them.

With each spasm of his limbs and gasp that jolted from his lips, my nausea gripped me tighter. The only thing spilling from his mouth were frantic pleas of ignorance. It was all I could do to stop my own hand from shaking.

Lowering the baton, I clamped my free hand around his throat—not to strangle, just to warn and to lift his trembling face so his eyes would meet mine.

A sickly smell rose off of him—if he hadn't pissed himself before, he had just now. But the stink wasn't what made my stomach flip over as I stared him down.

He wasn't just a "young man." I hadn't seen it before with his head low, his hair hanging forward to partly obscure it, and the defiant act he'd initially been putting on, but this guy was a *kid.*

The face before me couldn't have belonged to a boy older than sixteen. That was grit smudging his jaw, not a five o'clock shadow. There was even a bit of baby fat still rounding his not-quite-mature features.

It took all my willpower not to blatantly recoil in horror. What the fuck was Mom playing at here? She really thought this *child* held some crucial secret?

What if he wasn't lying about having no clue what was going on? That possibility seemed increasingly likely with every second longer I gazed at his tear-streaked, agonized features.

My mind darted back to my conversation with Rafael the other night—to the young teen version of himself who'd been roped into a much smaller gang to appease his brother's hunger for vengeance—and my nerves rebelled even more than before.

"What kind of work does your boss have you doing?" I said, firm but quiet. "In general, I mean."

"I—I don't do all that much," the kid stammered. "Just hang around the house following whatever orders he gives me. Bring him coffee, clean his car, that kind of thing."

"Did he tell you to go someplace else and take notes about what you saw, or anything like that?"

The boy shook his head frantically. "No. I was just walking home and these guys grabbed me and brought me here. The boss doesn't let me in on anything interesting yet. He always closes the door if he's going to talk business, shuts me out so I won't overhear the important stuff. I don't even know his *name*—we just call him 'Boss.'"

Nothing about his demeanor or the tremors that were shivering through his body suggested he was lying. I *had* broken him already, and he simply didn't have anything else to say.

I'd tortured a teenager a few years younger even than me. A high school kid.

I had to clamp my lips tight against the urge to vomit. Stepping back, I dropped the baton with the other torture instruments and spun toward Mom.

"I'm done here. I'm not going to keep tormenting some kid, especially one who seems like he doesn't know anything and hasn't done anything to hurt us."

Fury flared in Mom's gaze. She caught my arm and yanked me toward the doorway.

Only once we were in the hall with the door shut behind us did she start speaking, her voice taut with a vicious edge. "You never undermine me in front of a prisoner. Aren't you already clear enough on the consequences of disobedience?"

I narrowed my eyes at her, my muscles rigid to stop myself from trembling but a surge of my own rage fueling my confidence. "You knew he wasn't anyone important to the Devil's Dozen, didn't you? You kidnapped some lackey from the lowest level specifically to prove that you could make me beat up a kid who didn't deserve it. Do you have any idea how sick that is?"

Mom's hand lashed out, too fast for me to dodge. Her palm connected with my cheek in a flash of pain.

I jerked backward, my face stinging, my hands drawing up into fists.

"I make the rules here, mija," Mom said, spittle flying with the words. "If you won't do as I say, I'm happy to bring all of the men you've been whoring around with here to offer them similar treatment."

With every word, my spine grew stiffer. I let my anger color my voice. "I wouldn't do that if I were you. You know how easily I can blow up all of your plans. Do you really want to push me that far?"

Mom scoffed and motioned to my hands. "You wouldn't want to blow up your own life either. You're complicit now—you've aided in the kidnapping of one of my rival's underlings. You're tangled up in my plans. Do you really think our enemies would spare your lives or your lovers'? Or that you'll get very far after you've flushed your inheritance down the drain?"

"I think *your* enemies will see that I've gone my own way, especially because I'm giving up that inheritance," I shot back. "And whatever they think, I'd rather take my chances with them than live under your roof if you're going to act like a total psychopath."

"I'm warning you, Luciana—"

"No, I'm warning you. When I say no, I mean no. And if I catch the slightest hint that you've sent anyone to mess with my men, all the evidence I've gathered is going to end up in the laps of the last people you'd want it to. And believe me, I've got even more than I did before."

Mom fell silent, her eyes blazing. We eyed each other for what felt like an eternity.

Finally, she broke the standoff. "I don't think you want to ruin your family that badly."

I raised my chin. "Feel free to call my bluff. I'm leaving town tomorrow for a week, like I already told you. If you can stick to your end of the deal, I'll stick to mine, and we'll see where we're at when I get back."

I swiveled away from the interrogation room and marched down the hall to the stairs. Mom didn't follow. My breaths shook as they spilled from my lungs. I couldn't believe I'd said all of that to her.

But I'd had to. There were some lines I wasn't going to cross.

More nausea unfurled through my stomach at the thought of the boy I was leaving behind. I wanted to barge in there and unlock his chains—but Mom had the key. And if Mom knew saving his life mattered that much to me, she'd gut him on the spot just to spite me.

His only chance of survival was if I didn't make a single gesture toward ensuring it.

I sent up a silent prayer as I hurried upstairs to my room. There, I grabbed my laptop and logged into the cloud server where I'd stashed all the evidence.

I'd set up the automated email with Beckett's help, CCing all of the Devil's Dozen members he had email addresses for. Every day, I scheduled it to send the following day if I didn't pop in to bump the time forward again.

If I ever disappeared for more than twenty-four hours, Mom would be totally exposed.

And I intended that exposure to be as total as I could manage. I dragged the latest files that Beckett and the Blood Hunter had sent me over to the folder that was linked in the email and then sat back on my bed with a ragged sigh.

I *didn't* want to have to burn down my entire family legacy, whether I wanted to claim that legacy or not. But if Mom pushed me any farther, she was going to find out that I hadn't been kidding around.

And after what I'd just seen, I couldn't deny that some part of me almost hoped that she forced my hand.

TWENTY-SEVEN

Quentin

AS I GAZED around the massive Portland arena under the brilliant overhead lights, I couldn't restrain a smile. Now *this* was what I'd been missing back in Austin. This was where skaters of our caliber ought to be performing.

Of course, I wouldn't be skating on that rink today. The gunshot wound had been healing well, but my shoulder still ached if I stretched the muscle there much. I hadn't been able to properly practice my routines since the injury.

Oh well. My chances of earning top marks after all my time off from singles would have been slim anyway.

This sophisticated setting would make a perfect backdrop for Jasper and Lou's routines, though. They were due up for their first chance to wow the judges, their short program performance, in just a half hour.

Seeing the glow that came into Lou's face when she glanced around her at the packed stands, it was hard for me to regret how the last couple of months had played out.

At least, she *had* been glowing a minute ago. When I glanced over at her now, tipping her head toward Rafael to make some comment to him, a shadow had darkened her expression. She clasped her hands together in her lap, her fingers twisting with tension. Not even the vibrant colors of the skating costume Jasper had sewn for her, which I had to admit was incredible, could disguise her uneasiness.

Rafael's frown suggested that he'd noticed the evidence of her nerves too, although on the other hand most of the expressions I'd seen the guy make involved frowning. I suspected he'd rather have been standing at the top of the aisle, watching over the whole arena for threats, but with his leg still locked in a cast, he couldn't have stood guard the usual way. He'd settled for taking a spot with us near the front of the stands.

Niko had vacated the spot at Lou's other side to go chat with a couple other skaters he knew. I sidled closer and nudged her with my elbow. "You okay there, Upstart?"

Lou's gaze twitched to me, the stiffness in her posture telling me the answer before she tried to cover it up. "Yeah, sure. You know, it's just a little nerve-wracking heading onto the national stage for the first time."

Her smile was unconvincingly tight, and her eyes darted away from me to flick over the stands in a wary circuit. My stomach sank.

She was worried about her mom—of course she was. It might actually be a surprise if that menace *didn't* try to interfere with Lou's big day somehow.

But she couldn't keep worrying about that. The rest of us were here to protect her. All I wanted her to be thinking about was taking her audience's breaths away.

I tucked my fingers around her arm and gave her a gentle tug. "You've still got some time. You know what always helps me shed the jitters? Getting moving rather than sitting like a statue. Let's take a walk up and down the hall."

Lou's gaze turned skeptical, but she stood without argument. I led her up the stairs, carefully avoiding a news team who looked like they were searching for people to interview, and ushered her down one of the quieter halls outside.

Lou gave her limbs a little shake as if trying to propel the tension right off her, but she kept scanning her surroundings at the same time. Always on the alert.

"Hey," I said, drawing her to a stop when I was sure we were out of anyone else's hearing. "You've got this. You know that, right? I can't wait to see you blow the rest of those idiots out of the water."

Lou arched an eyebrow. "I think it's a little early to assume we'll be that far ahead. We're up against the best of the best—and we only placed second at Finals."

I waved her protest off. "I've watched all of them before. And I've spent the last two months watching *you* as up close and personal as it gets. If anything, I feel a little sorry for them. They don't even know how badly they're about to get massacred."

That comment earned me a brief but genuine laugh. God, I could listen to that sound all day.

But then Lou's expression softened in the way that stole my heart even more. "Are you sure you're feeling okay—about not getting out there yourself?"

I shrugged, willing away the twinge of disappointment that was so small in comparison to all the things I was happy about today. "I've had a chance in the spotlight before, and I'll get it plenty of times again. This weekend is about you. You kicking a whole lot of figure-skating butt."

Lou lowered her eyelids to peer at me through her lashes. She touched the middle of my chest and walked her fingers slowly up to the collar of my fleece pullover, sending tingles racing through me with every brush of their tips.

"Who would have thought a few months ago that you'd be here with me at Nationals pumping up my spirits?" she said in a wry tone that was still sultry enough to make my cock rise to half-mast. "After all the insults you threw at me and Jasper—"

I held a playful finger to her lips, waggling it when she tried to give it a nip. "We don't have to talk about the distant past. Anyway, I might have been an asshole, but you have to admit it was great motivation to get you and St. Pierre pushing yourselves to do better."

Lou rolled her eyes. "Hmm. So suddenly your jerkishness is a heroic act. How convenient."

She offset the sarcastic remark by stepping close enough to offer up a kiss—brief but so sweet it had me wanting to drag her into the nearest room and see just how many times I could get her off before she was due on the ice.

I reined in my hormones. I hadn't brought her out here for a quickie.

I hooked one of her hands in mine and teased my thumb over the knuckles. The words stuck in my throat for a moment before I forced them out.

"It might not help all that much, but you know, I've been where you are, in a way. I know what it's like to have a mom who can make your heart plummet and your gut bottom out with a single word, where you never know how or when the next hit will come."

Lou's fingers tightened around mine. She hadn't been there when I'd opened up to Niko and Jasper, but I could recognize the dawning comprehension in her eyes. "I'm sorry. I've overheard you on the phone before—and I remember some of the news stories from a while back… I wish you hadn't had to go through all that."

"You shouldn't be feeling bad for me," I said firmly. "It isn't anywhere near the level of shit that you've experienced. But being with you, seeing how you stand up to your mom every way you can despite how dangerous she is—it's given me the strength to hold my ground with mine. I blocked her number the other day. Never have to hear her tearing me down again."

The smile that curved Lou's lips now was sadder than I liked. "That's good. You deserve to live a life where you're not being berated all the time."

I nodded. "And so do you. So I want to see you block your mom right out of your head so she doesn't get the chance to dim your shine out there, not by one tiny fraction. Do you think you can handle that?"

Lou inhaled deeply and drew her posture up straighter. Her eyes met mine with the determined glint I loved so much. "Yeah. We both got here by our own efforts, right? We're standing on our own two feet, and no one's going to hold us back."

I found myself grinning. "That's the spirit. Now let's get back to the rink before Jasper has a nervous breakdown thinking I've kidnapped you."

We made it back to the others just as the pair before Lou and Jasper took to the ice. Jasper caught Lou's hand, and they moved to the spot by the boards that they'd enter the rink from when called. I sank down onto the bench next to Niko, who was perched on the edge of his seat as if his skaters had already set off.

After the current couple finished up their short program, which I found boring as hell, the announcer summoned "Jasper St. Pierre and Luna Garcia." Lou was still competing under the assumed name she'd given to hide from her mother, since she'd been registered under that.

The two of them glided into the middle of the rink to assume their starting position. I found myself holding my breath as the music warbled through the arena.

And then they moved.

Synchronized spins leading into a triple axel, followed by some brisk footwork before they launched into their first lift. They hit every beat, their limbs flowing with the melody in a way I'd come to not just expect but admire.

Watching them without my pride getting in the way, I couldn't deny that Jasper was still better than I was. Maybe not by much, and maybe I could nail a few of the specific poses with slightly more accuracy… but he had a power and artistry that I couldn't quite match yet, no matter how much I'd heckled him before.

That was okay. It gave me a goal post to aim for. Someday, with enough practice and honing my skills, I'd get to the point where I could at least match the guy.

And the funny thing was, I could believe he'd now cheer me on when I did.

Beside me, Niko was beaming. "They're really something, aren't they?"

"Yeah," I said without a shred of resentment. "They really are."

I tore my attention away to steal a quick glance at the crowd. To my satisfaction, everyone's eyes were glued to Lou and Jasper with expressions of dazed amazement.

Well, everyone except for a few burly guys who looked unusually grim for an event like this. My gaze caught on them near the top of the aisle that led down to the opening where Lou and Jasper would come off the ice. One of them made a furtive gesture to the others, and they tramped down the steps toward that spot.

The hairs on the back of my neck stood on end. These guys definitely weren't typical figure-skating fans—they moved with an aggressive air that set off all my alarm bells. And the one with the heavy forehead and squinty eyes looked unnervingly familiar… Was he one of the thugs we'd caught searching our loft back in Austin?

Shit, shit, shit. Lou's mom really had decided to fuck this up for her daughter. What had she ordered those pricks to do?

My hands clenched at my sides. My first impulse was to dash over there and confront the assholes, getting right in their faces. Defend Lou like I'd promised her I would, like I had before.

But even as I tensed on the bench, an image played out in my head of how that confrontation would probably go—with just me, my injured shoulder, and a gun I'd never fired at a human being before against those three goons.

I'd already been more of a champion than she'd ever expected—and I had two guys beside me who were just as eager to protect her. It was a hell of a lot more important that we made sure Lou wasn't in any danger than that I got to take all the credit.

I cleared my throat. "Niko, Rafael, I think a few of the Deadly Rose's thugs have just joined the party."

When Rafael's gaze jerked to me, I tipped my head toward the men I'd noticed. His expression hardened with a flex of his jaw.

"Motherfuckers," he muttered.

Niko rested his hand against the side of his hooded sweatshirt. "I have my knife, if we need it."

Rafael inclined his head, fury blazing in his dark eyes. "We don't want to make a scene and distract from the performance. We go over there quietly and take care of things, fast and firmly."

It was kind of a relief letting the actual bodyguard among us take the lead. Gripping the one crutch he was making do with now, he eased past the two of us. We followed, hunching low so as not to block people's view on the higher rows.

We stepped out into the aisle as the thugs came to a stop just a few steps above us. Rafael moved toward them without hesitation, moving with his crutch as if it were an extra limb, so Niko and I flanked him.

When we reached them, he drew his gun in the space between us where no one else would be able to see it, keeping it low but clearly in view of the goons. He'd only gotten the cast on his dominant hand off days ago, but he held the weapon steadily enough. Taking my cue from him, I lifted the hem of my shirt to reveal the concealed holster at my hip.

"It's time for you three to take off," Rafael growled, low but forceful.

The guy in the lead eyed the weapons but adjusted his stance with a hint of a swagger. "Who the fuck do you think you are to order us around, you cripple?"

Rafael's lips drew back to bare his teeth. "I think I could outshoot you in my sleep with my hands tied behind my back. Last time I checked, I don't need my leg to pull a trigger."

One of the other guys snorted. "Are we supposed to be scared by that?"

Rafael did the most terrifying thing he could have—he pushed his mouth into the fiercest grin I'd ever seen. "Yes. Because I'd happily see you six feet under just for whatever you're *thinking* of doing to my woman. If you try to actually do it, the only thrilling news from the arena today will be about three strange goons who were gunned down because they didn't know what was good for them."

I was practically pissing myself, and I was on his side. The thugs exchanged a glance, and I hooked my fingers around the grip of my own gun.

With a sputter of frustration, they turned and marched back up the stairs. We watched them vanish through the doors. Rafael had tucked his gun away, but we didn't budge from our current position, guarding the woman we were crazy about while she flew on across the ice.

I turned to watch just as she and Jasper whirled through their final sequence. They struck their ending pose, and the crowd erupted into applause and cheers. A smile crossed my face, hard but genuine.

They were getting everything they deserved. And I'd put my life on the line as many times as it took to make sure that continued to be true.

TWENTY-EIGHT

Luciana

THE PAIR before us whipped into motion with the start of their free skate song, launching immediately into a sequence of swift and intricate footwork that took my breath away. And I didn't have a whole lot to spare.

Beside me by the boards, Jasper bumped his arm lightly against mine. "Those two know how to make a dramatic start, huh?"

"No kidding."

I swallowed thickly, willing down my nerves and trying to shoo the worries from my mind. We were third after yesterday's short program, a fact that should have overjoyed me, considering our free skate was where we normally shone the most.

It *had* made me rejoice yesterday. But after we'd arrived at the arena this morning, my stomach had gotten more and more twisted up with uncertainty.

My doubts hadn't been provoked only by the competition, although that was definitely tight. We were up against the best skaters in the country, some of whom had been competing for over a decade when this was only my first year. Only three pairs would be selected to compete for the United States on an international level, and while Nationals played a large part in that decision, it wasn't the only factor taken into consideration.

A bronze medal here wouldn't be a guarantee. If we could nab the silver or even the gold, then we'd be pretty much set. But that depended on us nailing every single move in the routine and nuance in our performance.

We'd done it before. I knew we could do it again. That definitely wasn't the only problem.

The pair on the ice pulled off a spectacular twist lift. Jasper gave my ponytail a light tug, careful not to shift the sparkly barrettes and carefully coiled ribbons that matched our costumes and kept all the strands neatly in place. "Are you ready to kill it, Punk?"

I shot him a grin, hoping he couldn't tell how tight it was. "You know it."

But with my head turned, my gaze slid past him over the massive audience around us. My eyes caught on trim blazers over collared shirts, elegant jackets over silky blouses.

These were the kinds of people who bought tickets to watch the National Championships. Sure, there were folks in sweats or chunky down vests in the crowd, but to afford the tickets, chances were they'd picked those outfits for comfort, not because it was all they owned.

I was surrounded by so many polished yuppies who could never have imagined the kind of life I'd led. Who had no concept that empires like my mother's even existed.

How had I convinced myself that I belonged here?

How would all those awed faces fall if they found out I'd killed people? How would they look at me if they'd known I had a gun in my equipment bag right now? That I'd shot a man right on a skating rink just weeks ago?

No matter what costume I wore or what makeup I painted my face with, I was tarnished underneath that mask. I wasn't the kind of skater they wanted to support. I'd just tricked them into thinking I was.

My ribs seemed to constrict around my lungs. When I tried to drink in a deep breath of the cool arena air, my chest ached.

The warble of the announcer's voice stirred me out of my uneasy reverie, but I didn't catch what he actually said.

Niko had come up next to us. He set his hand on my shoulder. "You two can beat that score—you have before."

Had we? I hadn't even heard what it was. But then, it wasn't how anyone else did that really mattered. It came down to our own performance.

The voice boomed from the speakers again, announcing our names. Jasper tipped his head toward the ice. "Let's show them what we can do."

What we could do. The thought spiraled out through my mind as I followed him to the center of the rink on autopilot.

I could shoot an attacker before they shot me. I could carve open a man's skin to leave my mark.

I could bruise up a literal kid trying to torture him into coughing up answers he didn't have.

The memory of the teen cringing and whimpering flashed through my mind, bringing a surge of queasiness with it. My lungs clenched even more—and my jaw tightened with a jolt of the same defiance I'd felt when faced with that scene in reality.

I hadn't wanted to hurt the kid. Mom had demanded it, threatening to do worse to the people I cared about most if I refused.

And when I'd realized just how innocent he was, I'd defied her anyway. I'd played the only card I had, been prepared to blow up my family's empire right then to avoid doing any more harm.

I was still prepared. I didn't stand with her or for the horrible acts she carried out. I might be the only person who could really stand against her—and I'd already taken huge steps toward interrupting her vilest plans.

My resolve broke through the vise of tension that'd been suffocating me. I raised my chin and looked up at Jasper, so striking in his sea-green and gold costume that coordinated perfectly with mine. As he looked back at me, his eyes gleamed, shining with affection and confidence.

He was nothing but eager to show the world what we were capable of.

I spared a quick glance toward the stands. It wasn't just my skating partner who believed in me and supported my dreams despite the hell that was my heritage. There was no missing Niko's buoyant enthusiasm where he stood by the boards. The quirk of Quentin's lips where he stood next to my coach brought back an echo of yesterday's pep talk when he'd reminded me of how much we could survive.

And right by the aisle, watching over me protectively as always, Rafael's stern gaze spoke of his own determined conviction.

My answering conviction steadied me. I could be more than a criminal heir apparent; I had to be, for both myself and the men I'd fallen for.

I *was* more than that already. Yes, I had blood on my hands, but I couldn't let that be all this audience saw. I could create sweetness and joy. I could make people feel things while watching my art, ease their pain, if only for a few moments. Even that—*just* that—was more light than my mom had ever tried to bring into the world in her entire life.

Maybe, just maybe, if Mom happened to watch this performance to see exactly what I was getting up to beyond her grasp, I could prove even to her just how much skating mattered to me. Why this was where I was meant to be.

I smiled at Jasper, and he smiled back, with all the faith he had in me. A rush of exhilaration propelled words I hadn't meant to say right now from my throat. "I love you."

His eyelids stuttered in surprise, but it took only an instant for his smile to widen, warming me from the inside out. "I love you too."

And then the opening notes of our song pealed out into the air.

My heart pounded in time with the melody. My body had never felt so light. It was as if I'd shed a hundred pounds of anguished weight that left me free to be no one but the woman I was underneath.

We swept through each move, leaping and twirling and soaring, every motion in sync with each other and the music flowing through me. I was the song and it was me, playing out through movements as small as the flick of my hand and as big as our most epic lift with its following throw. I landed the boosted triple Axel as if I'd been born on the ice and glided straight into the next sequence.

I *was* the routine—the ice and the art—and my body was just the instrument. Here there was no bloodshed, no fear or pain. There was only beauty and creation.

And love.

Jasper met my eyes as we landed our last jump. His fervor glinted within his gray-green irises. Our big finish was looming on the horizon —we either nailed it, or this was all for nothing.

I pushed off with my skates, gaining speed and momentum as I sailed across the ice like the angel Niko always referred to me as. Jasper's hands found their places against my limbs to boost me upward. We spun like one being, balanced precariously but melded together.

This was who I really was, and I was proving it to *every* person watching me, whether here in the arena with me or from a TV screen.

A collective gasp from the audience mingled with the music. Jasper lowered me to the ice, and we hit the last few beats before striking our ending pose.

The moment my body was still, a wave of exhaustion washed over me. I'd wrung every drop of emotion out of me into our routine—but wow, did it feel fantastic to have put it all out there.

Applause thundered through the arena. Jasper dropped our hands and grabbed me in a quick but emphatic kiss, and I'd swear the cheers got even louder. Grinning like a maniac, I skated with him to the stands.

When we reached the bench, Quentin was grinning too. "Hell, yeah! You two wiped the floor with the rest of these dopes. That was fucking amazing."

Niko laughed, his own face bright with joy. "He's not lying. Best performance yet, hands down. I didn't know you could top Finals, but I'd say you just did."

"Really?" My mind was reeling with giddiness and fatigue.

Before either of them could answer, the announcer's voice echoed through the arena. My spine stiffened as I waited for the judges' verdict.

"For Jasper St. Pierre and Luna Garcia, a score of one hundred and forty-five point five seven."

As a fresh wave of applause flooded the arena, my jaw dropped. That was a whole nine points higher than our previous high score. And—

Next to me, Jasper crowed with unexpected abandon. "Holy shit. Lou, that shoots us right to the top spot."

"And by a large margin," Niko said, beaming. "Knowing who's still to go, I've got no doubt those gold medals are yours."

A whoop spilled out of me. I caught Niko in a hug, and then Jasper and Quentin, and finally Rafael who'd come over to join the celebration. My bodyguard tucked his head over mine and squeezed me hard. "That was really something."

Niko clapped his hands, radiating excitement. "Ten weeks, and then World Championships, here we come!"

TWENTY-NINE

Luciana

I GOT no real welcome on my return to the Cordova mansion. A few of the underlings hanging around dipped their heads to me in acknowledgment, but it was hard to tell if they even realized I'd been gone for a week.

Better if they couldn't tell. Better if my absence had proven just how little my presence was needed in the running of the Deadly Rose empire.

I'd thought that Mom might be eager to drag me straight back into her schemes, but my phone had remained silent even though I'd texted her this morning to let her know I was on my way home. As I stepped into the foyer, I braced myself to meet her piercing gaze or hear her cutting voice carrying from the top of the staircase.

Nada. *Her* absence was so jarring that I hesitated for a moment at the foot of the stairs, feeling like I was an actress in a play who'd just realized she'd missed memorizing a few pages of the script. Now what?

I gathered the determination that'd carried me since our victory at the National Championships around me, as bright as the shine on my skating costume. I was wearing my gold medal, tucked under the collar of my long-sleeved band tee. The high of our performance still quivered through my veins.

I knew where I belonged, beyond any possible doubt. It was time to stop pretending and stride forward into that future.

And maybe, after all of this, Mom would finally understand that running the Deadly Rose empire wasn't the life I was meant for. She might be stubborn, but she wasn't stupid. It would be way better for her to have an heir who actually appreciated the role too.

Keeping my posture straight and confident, I motioned to a nearby lackey. "Let my mother know that I'm home—and that I'd like to talk to her as soon as possible."

He nodded and hustled off, pulling out his phone. That didn't tell me anything about where she was or when she'd get here. I tramped up the stairs and made my way to my childhood bedroom.

Sitting down on the edge of the bed, I glanced around the expansive space. Funny how this was the largest bedroom I'd had in all my jaunts around the continent, but it felt by far the most suffocating. It was barely even mine. Mom had picked out the décor, dictated what I was allowed to hang on the walls.

What here would I even want to bring with me when I left? I'd taken all the essentials when I'd first run away.

I hadn't been able to pack much in the way of clothes, though. There were some outfits I'd missed: my black cargo pants with the zippered pockets and buckles, my super-cozy hooded sweatshirt with the plaid sleeves, my black-and-neon-pink checkerboard leggings that I could just imagine Jasper's expression on taking them in. My studded leather jacket would have come in handy as the weather cooled off.

Well, I might as well pull everything together while I had the time. Go forward as if I expected to succeed—that was the best attitude, right?

I was just squishing a few pairs of stripy socks I'd always been fond of into a suitcase when my regular phone buzzed. A text from Mom appeared on the screen: *We can speak in my office now.*

My heart gave a little lurch, even though I'd asked for this meeting.

I took a deep breath, swiped my hands over my hips to make sure they weren't sweaty, and marched down the hall to face the music.

I rapped on the door in my usual pattern and waited for her terse reply: "Come in."

I entered the room to find Mom's back to me where she was standing by the window next to her desk. She waited until I'd come to a stop in the middle of the room before turning to face me.

Her face might as well have been carved from ice, and her voice was equally frigid. "You're back from your little vacation. It's time we get down to work."

Oh, no, I wasn't letting her direct the conversation this time.

I squared my shoulders and met her gaze steadily. "It wasn't just a vacation. My partner and I placed *first* at the National Championships —that makes us the best in the whole country." My hand rose to the disc of my medal under my shirt, but I didn't pull it out, gripped by the sudden fear that Mom would wrench it away from me.

Mom offered me nothing but a derisive snort in response. "The best at spinning around on the ice in a sparkly costume. What an honor." Sarcasm dripped from her tone. "You got what you wanted. Now that the distraction is dealt with—"

"Dealt with?" I broke in, frustration crackling through my veins. "I'm not finished. Placing that high means we've earned a spot at the World Championships, to compete with the best from every other country. Only a handful of people manage that every year. I worked my ass off to get good enough to make it."

"And I'd like to see you apply the same obsessive focus to our *real* work," Mom said. "You'll have plenty of opportunities to do so now that you've had your moment in the spotlight. I have you meeting with the head of one of our Houston affiliates tomorrow afternoon, and there's a deal I expect you to supervise the following night. I want to see you training with the troops every morning this week as well."

My jaw clenched. I shook my head. "No, Mom. You're not listening. I *can't.* Worlds is in just a couple of months—we have to keep training and—"

Mom cut me off with a flash of her dark eyes. "You *have to* get your head out of the clouds and be the Cordova you're meant to be.

I'm not going to tolerate any more talk of your ridiculous hobby. I think I've been more than lenient. It's time for you to give your full commitment."

My frustration erupted into full-out rage. She never listened—she never cared. She never even bothered to *see* the woman I was standing right here in front of her, too busy imagining the daughter she wanted me to be.

If anyone was obsessed around here, it was her. And it was time for that obsession to end. *I* knew who I was, and I couldn't squeeze myself into the box she wanted me to fit into any longer.

"No," I repeated, sharper this time. "If it's all or nothing now, then I'm done with everything to do with the Deadly Rose legacy. I never wanted the empire anyway. You can find someone else to inherit your throne."

Mom walked up to me, her expression still a frozen mask but so much fury seething beneath it that it wafted off her and sent goose bumps prickling up my arms. "You've entertained your stupid dream for long enough. You *will* get your act together now and play your part, or every one of the men you claim to care about will pay for it for *days* before I finally see them buried."

She meant that threat. She would torment all four of my men in every way she knew how, drive them to the limits of pain, just to shape me to her image. I recoiled inwardly, horror turning my stomach.

My hands clenched at my sides as I hardened myself against the instinctive panic. "You wouldn't dare. Not when I can expose your master plan to the only people who could make *you* pay."

Mom's eyes narrowed. "If you try to destroy me, you'll only be destroying yourself. I'll see that you and everyone you care about suffer until those men curse the day they met you and you wish you'd never been born, and then more after that. You won't get away with it."

With that last sentence, Mom sprang at me, swift as a cobra striking. She snatched at my ponytail and wrenched me against her into an embrace that was all venom. I struck out, thrashing in her hold, but Mom clamped me tight—and rammed a hard muzzle against my lips.

My mouth jolted open at the pain lancing through my face even as the rest of my body froze in recognition.

Still clutching my hair hard enough to send jabs of agony through my scalp, Mom shoved the barrel of her pistol between my teeth. I fought the urge to gag at the oily metallic flavor that seeped over my tongue.

"This is what your lovers will feel right before they eat their last bullet," she said, her voice so fraught it was almost a hiss. "Hold on to that memory. Remember it every time you think about defying one of my orders."

With that, she heaved me away from her. I stumbled and caught myself on a side table before I fell to my knees.

"Get out of my sight," Mom snapped. "The next time I send for you, you'd better be ready to play your role."

Blood trickled through my mouth from where the gun had scraped my tongue. My mind had gone blank. I groped for the doorknob and stepped into the hall on shaky legs.

She'd nearly killed me. She'd had her finger on the goddamn trigger.

She'd treated me like a minor underling—like a dog she'd put down if I didn't jump to fulfill her every command.

Like she didn't give a shit whether she had a daughter. She'd rather I was dead than happy on any path other than the one she'd chosen for me.

I made it back to my bedroom without much sense of how I'd arrived there. My head kept spinning. I wandered to the bed and gripped one of the posts for balance.

Something had broken inside me with that act of violence. After everything Mom had done over the years, somehow I'd never been prepared for her to go that far, to treat me so callously.

I could crumple like a rag doll and give in. The fear wavering inside me liked that idea. Pretend my heart out, protect my men, appease Mom's ego.

But even as the idea presented itself, the rest of me resisted.

I'd already tried playing along, and it hadn't worked. I couldn't live like that… Frankly, *I'd* rather be dead than become nothing more than a puppet carrying out Mom's bloody ambitions.

Nothing short of transforming into a person I could never be would be enough for her. No matter what I did, sooner or later I'd disappoint her. And then she'd go after my men as punishment.

I'd have proven that my threats really were a bluff. She'd want to get rid of the distraction they presented too, as soon as possible, with the slightest excuse she could use to justify it.

None of us would ever be safe as long as Mom was fixated on carving me into the heir she expected. Our lives were on the line either way.

At least if I gave her something bigger to worry about, it'd keep her busy while we made our escape. Maybe it'd even bring down her and her empire completely.

The second I made the decision, a lump of guilt formed in my gut. In spite of everything, she was still my mother. This empire had been built by my ancestors going back generations. I could be bringing that effort all crumbling down.

But the loss was on Mom's shoulders, not mine. I'd told her where I stood, and she'd refused to listen. All she'd needed to do to avoid disaster was appoint some trusted underling as her next-in-line and let me go.

Her refusal wasn't on my conscience.

I grabbed my burner phone and tapped out a message to Rafael with trembling fingers. *I'm on my way. Get ready to leave immediately—for good.*

Then I looked at the half-packed suitcase on my bed. It'd be a little more obvious than I liked if I walked out of here carrying that.

I pawed through my closet for a backpack, shoved my laptop and as many pieces of clothing into it as I could, and hurried through the house with it slung over my shoulder. My thumb darted over my phone's screen, summoning an Uber.

When I passed through the gate and walked down the block, the car was just pulling up at the corner I'd indicated as the pick-up spot. I slid into the back and peered down at my phone as the driver hit the gas.

I could log into the scheduled email I'd set up from this device too. I opened up the message with its explanation of all the evidence that the Deadly Rose was working to upend the very foundations of the Devil's Dozen and hesitated.

With one click, I could blow up the entire foundation of my life.

But I'd never really wanted that foundation anyway. Better to bulldoze over it and build fresh from the ground up.

I dismissed the scheduled send time and tapped the button to send the email now.

The phone chimed as the email flitted off to the inboxes of the Devil's Dozen's top dogs. A breath rushed out of me, shaky with a mix of terror and exhilaration.

I'd done it. I'd really done it.

As I sagged back in the seat, tears pricked at the corners of my eyes. I swiped at them, steeped in a strange mood that was more relief than anything else.

By the time the car reached the loft building, my head had started to clear like the first bright, refreshing sunlight after a thunderstorm. At the sight of all four of my men waiting out front, suitcases beside them, my spirits lifted.

I scrambled out to meet them, hauling my backpack with me.

"What's going on?" Rafael asked immediately, his words tangling with Niko's, "Are you all right?"

I found myself grinning at all of them like this was the best day of my life. Which maybe in some ways it was.

"I'm fine," I said. "I'm free. We're getting the hell out of here and never coming back."

THIRTY

Luciana

"AH," Niko said, taking a big sip of his Calpis as we walked through the doors into the rink area of the small arena. He waved to one of the men on the arena staff who was sweeping the stands at the far end of the room. "It's good to be home."

I couldn't help laughing at him. "Are you going to say that every time you drink one of those for the whole time we're in Japan?"

He grinned back at me with a familiar twinkle in his eyes. "If it's still true, why not? I can see you've started appreciating my country's many benefits too."

He nodded to the can I had clutched in my hand, what was technically hot chocolate except… cold. I never would have thought I'd get into drinking hot chocolate out of a can, let alone hot chocolate that wasn't even hot, but I had to admit I was finding the stuff strangely addictive now that I'd tried it.

Quentin took a chug from his bottle of iced green tea and stretched out his arms toward the rink below us. "I appreciate that even the out-of-the-way rinks look all clean and pristine. Maybe I'll have to move here."

Jasper elbowed the other guy lightly. "Who would have thought all Quentin Wolfe needed to put him in a good mood was tidy stands?"

"Hey," Quentin protested. "No one wants to skate in the middle of a mess."

I shook my head at the two of them and their mock-antagonistic banter before trotting down the steps to the benches nearest the ice. We'd been in Tokyo for two weeks now, training for Worlds, which would be held in nearby Nagano. With my family's empire in an uproar, it'd seemed safest to put plenty of ocean between us and my mother, and also not to train *too* close to the city she would first think to search for me if she had time to look.

No one had thought to look for us here at all. Niko fielded phone calls from reporters several times a day, giving them a vague story about our training progress after our win at Nationals and putting me or Jasper on to do brief interviews with the ones he felt would boost our profile the most, but we'd escaped all in-person media attention so far. He'd been able to keep the rest of the US team satisfied with the scraps of information he'd given them about our whereabouts too, other than a couple of video-chat meetings since we'd arrived.

Unfortunately, laying low had meant leaving Rafael back at the apartment Niko had found for us, because he stood out too much with the cast on his leg and his crutch. But we were hoping he'd be able to get the cast removed this weekend and be back to close to his old self.

From the bits and pieces of news he'd gathered from back home, the Deadly Rose's operations had been thrown into so much turmoil it wasn't likely she'd have had the manpower to search for me in the state of Texas, let alone all over Japan.

But still, it was best to be cautious. The Devil's Dozen had their fingers everywhere. I wasn't sure which of them owned territory in Tokyo, but no doubt someone had the local criminal elements under their sway. And we couldn't be sure whether that someone would be on Mom's side or against her.

I gulped the last of my chocolate drink and pulled on my skates, eager to get moving and stretch my muscles. By the time I'd stepped onto the ice to start warming up next to Jasper, anticipation was tingling through my nerves. "So, what's the latest word on our competition?"

Niko brightened up, always happy when he had new information to advise us with, and dug into his bag on the bench beside him. "I talked with another one of my friends from Team Japan last night. Like the others, he's being cagey about the specifics of their routines, but I did get him talking about the *other* countries' practices he's caught glimpses of."

Quentin rubbed his hands together. "Inside intel. Bring it on."

He wasn't going to be competing, of course, since he wasn't on the official US team. But we'd brought him with us to keep him out of my mom's sights, and he'd fallen into the role of unofficial assistant coach when he wasn't honing his singles routines for next year. His shoulder was almost back to full functioning now.

Niko tapped on his phone to bring up our songs. "One of the Russian pairs and maybe the Chinese too are trying out something a little new—adding some extra difficulty to their jumps. If we want to make sure we stand out equally well, I think we could adjust your routine to—"

The door at the top of the stairs slammed open, and a barrage of dark-clothed figures burst into the room. My heart stopped with a terrifying sense of déjà vu, hurtling me back to the moment in Austin when Octavio had come for me. Then my gaze caught on the semi-automatic rifles the strange men were jerking toward us.

"Get down!" I cried out, and snatched at Jasper's arm to haul him flat on the ice with me.

We hadn't ventured far from the stands in our warm-up. As bullets boomed through the air overhead, we cringed in the shelter of the boards. The tempered glass shattered, pelting us with a torrent of pebbles.

A hoarse cry rang out from the other side of the arena, where the staff person had been sweeping. I hoped he'd gotten out of the way fast enough.

The guns thundered for what felt like an eternity while I hugged the ice and clutched Jasper's arm. There was a brief pause. Just as I was sure our attackers would descend all the way to the rink and pick us off, sirens wailed loud enough to hear them through the arena walls.

Someone had called the police, and they were almost here. Thank God.

One of the shooters barked out an order I couldn't make out. Footsteps thudded as the men dashed off the way they'd come.

The second the door had banged shut behind them, I scrambled to my feet. My head jerked around as I scanned the stands. There—there was Quentin, the top of his blond head visible as he eased upright from where he'd hit the floor between the benches. And Niko—

I shoved myself closer to the stands and jarred to a halt. A cry broke from my throat.

Niko lay sprawled against the bench next to his bag, his head lolling and a scarlet blotch blooming on the front of his shirt.

DEATH DROP

BLADES OF HAVOC #4

ONE

Luciana

WHEN THE NURSE came into the hospital waiting room again, I felt as if I'd been sitting on the edge of my seat for hours. Jasper automatically grasped my hand as the woman motioned for us to get up. She only spoke broken English, but Niko's sister, Emi, had explained to her in Japanese that we'd want to visit after she and Niko's parents had seen the patient.

I scrambled to my feet and followed the nurse, my heart thudding against my ribs in a strange mix of relief and fear. Yesterday had been the worst day of my life: watching Niko's limp body loaded into an ambulance, failing to get anyone to tell me whether he had a chance of surviving. Pacing this waiting room until visiting hours were over, only getting sporadic updates from Emi, who'd looked equally horrified.

He'd been in surgery and knocked out on medication, but late this morning he'd finally come to. Naturally his family had wanted to spend time with him first. I couldn't resent them, as anxious as I was to see with my own eyes that he was okay.

Or at least as close to okay as you could get after taking a couple of bullets in the chest.

Jasper stuck close by my side as we strode down the hall, his gray-green eyes clouded with his own worries. His tall presence would have felt more reassuring if his broad shoulders hadn't been rigid with tension.

A police officer stood outside Niko's door, in consideration of the fact that his injuries had been due to an awful crime by assailants who hadn't been arrested yet. I knew that Rafael was monitoring the hospital on the outside, watching for anyone suspicious, but my stomach stayed knotted.

Would my mother's thugs make another attempt at Niko's life? Or at mine and my other lovers'?

Quentin had opted to help Rafael with his external surveillance, figuring Niko wouldn't want to see him all that urgently. But he'd given me a tight hug before I'd come inside this morning. "He'll come through. He might not look so tough, but that guy is made of strong stuff."

I couldn't have been more glad that he'd been proven right.

As we came up on the room, Emi emerged, ushering out a middle-aged couple while she chattered away in low but rapid Japanese. She shot me a glance over her shoulder with a swish of her sleek black bob and winked before guiding her parents in the opposite direction down the hall.

Emi and I had become fast friends when she'd come to visit Niko in Boston and eagerly cheered me and Jasper on in our qualifying competition. She'd realized I was dating not just her older brother but my skating partner and my bodyguard as well and accepted the unusual relationship without blinking.

But during our first get-together after we'd arrived in Tokyo to train for the World Championships, which were happening next month in Nagano, she'd told me that we were better off not trying to explain things to their parents. "The older generation," she said with a tsk of her tongue as if that explained everything. "They struggle enough with the idea that Niko likes girls *and* boys without him dating both at the same time."

Which he was doing. Jasper was as much Niko's lover as I was, even if they hadn't taken their physical relationship to quite the same level just yet. Considering that when I'd first met them, neither of them had been willing to even admit their feelings for each other, they'd come a long way.

The nurse motioned for us to stop just outside the room. As she slipped inside to confirm that Niko was ready to see us, the police officer gave us an inscrutable onceover. I hoped he was taking his job seriously.

Of course, *I* was the one who'd really failed here. It'd been my mother's goons who'd attacked us and shot Niko. Somewhere along the line, I hadn't been careful enough in covering my tracks.

Or maybe it went all the way back to my selfish desire to pursue my skating dreams. I'd known how angry Mom was about my decision to leave Austin. She'd threatened my men multiple times in the past.

I should have realized there was no way they'd be safe as long as they were with me.

The nurse returned and bobbed her head to us. "You may go now," she said in her halting English.

Jasper swiped his hand through his shaggy auburn locks and set his jaw before stepping inside. I hurried after him, my pulse thumping even faster.

At the sight that met me beyond the door, my heart just about leapt right out of my chest. Niko was sitting up in the hospital bed, propped against a couple of pillows. His warm smile somehow shone as bright as always, but I could see the strain in the rest of his face. And there was no ignoring the bandages bulging beneath his hospital gown or the IV hooked up to his wrist.

Jasper went straight to him and grasped his free hand. "How are you doing? No, that's a stupid question. I'm so glad you pulled through. Is there anything we can get for you?"

Niko let out a laugh that was only slightly raspy. "Who knew all it'd take to make you more talkative was me getting shot?"

I grimaced as I came up at our coach's other side, but my mouth sprang back into a joyful smile a second later. "It's just so good to see you awake and doing better. We were so worried. Jasper's right—if you need anything at all—"

Niko held up his hand, still clasped in Jasper's larger one, and his bright brown eyes twinkled with amusement. "I think the hospital staff has that covered. Not that I mind your kindness."

Jasper swallowed audibly. "Have the doctors said anything about your recovery? Or how long they'll need to monitor you for?"

Niko shook his head, the neon pink streak dyed into the smooth black strands swaying with movement. "They're running a few more tests. But it seems hopeful. Unless something unexpected appears, it sounds like I should be back on my feet in a day or two. Just... moving slowly for a little while after that."

"Of course." My throat closed up for a moment before I could force the words out. "I'm so sorry, Niko. It was all my fault. If I hadn't turned against my mom—"

Niko shook his head again, vehemently enough that my voice died. "Don't say that. I made my own choices—and I'm happy with them. I know the risks, and I still think they were worth it to see you and Jasper shine."

Jasper's mouth twisted. "Niko... You almost *died*."

Our coach shot him a firm look. "But I didn't die. We showed those gangsters we won't be stopped that easily. From now on, we'll just have to be even more careful."

My jaw dropped with a lurch of my gut. "From now on? You want us to keep training?"

Niko chuckled. "Of course I do. The world needs your talent. This was only a minor obstacle along the way to your glory."

"I'd hardly call this minor," I sputtered with a frantic wave toward his hospital bed.

"In a few weeks, it'll only be a memory," Niko insisted. "You have a... a gift. I'm not letting anyone scare you away from sharing it."

Jasper's voice went rough. "You shouldn't even be thinking about that right now. Not when we almost lost you completely."

Niko gazed up at him, his expression softening. "I'm still here."

My partner's Adam's apple bobbed. He blinked hard, a sheen of unshed tears coming into his stormy eyes. A flush crept up his neck to his cheeks, and he seemed to stumble over his next words. "And thank God for that. I—I'll get you something to drink."

He leaned in to give Niko a quick but tender kiss and then hustled for the door. As I glanced after him, I thought I saw him start to swipe at his eyes just before he disappeared from view.

I'd never seen Jasper get that emotional before. The poor guy didn't know how to cope.

But then, could I blame him? I hardly knew how to hold *myself* together after the trauma we'd just been through. Niko had gotten by far the worst of it—how could he still be so chipper?

When I turned back to our coach, his smile had deflated. His gaze lingered on the doorway after Jasper had left. I wished my partner could have seen how much our mutual boyfriend would rather have had him here, emotional or not.

Then Niko's attention shifted back to me. He reached across his chest to grasp my forearm. "Don't look so sad, Angel. It's over now."

I lowered my gaze. "But is it? We don't know when my mom might send more people. We don't even know for sure that you're totally okay now."

"We'll—how do you say it—cross that bridge when we get there? You've found ways to deal with her before." He paused and gave my arm a squeeze. "Enough about that. I need to tell you something."

I met his gaze, an ache spreading through my chest. "What?"

His smile returned, delicate but brilliant all the same. "I love you, Lou. I don't want to wait any longer to tell you that and risk losing the chance. And I'd get shot with a hundred more bullets just to watch you skate a few more times. So you're not allowed to stop because of this or to feel guilty about it."

My own tears blurred my vision. I set my hand over his, gripping his fingers tightly. "I don't think I can help the guilt. But I love you too, Niko. So much. That's why I'm so scared."

He lifted his hand higher to stroke his fingers over my cheek. "You're meant to be on the ice. And I think I'm meant to help you become everything you're capable of. It's simply destiny. You can't argue with that."

A laugh hitched out of me. I leaned in and gave him as much of a hug as I could without hurting him more. Niko tipped his head forward to brush his lips against my hair.

I eased up so I could claim a proper kiss, if a brief one. Then I met his eyes with all the conviction I had in me. "If it matters that much to you, I'll keep going. For me and for you. But I'm also going to do everything in my power to make sure my mom can't hurt anyone else."

Even saying that sent a chill down my spine. How much power did I have compared to Mom's empire?

But I had allies. I had the advantage none of her greater enemies had of knowing her well. If there was a way to stop her reign of terror for good, I'd find it.

Niko's face glowed with affection. "You wouldn't be my angel if you'd say anything else."

The door squeaked open again. I glanced over, expecting Jasper to have returned, but the nurse poked her head inside. She murmured something to Niko in Japanese.

He nodded to her and gave me a regretful look. "She says visiting time is over. They don't want me to push myself too hard when I've just woken up."

I choked up automatically and did my best to hide it. "I wouldn't want to wear you out when you need to be healing either. We'll be back as soon as we can."

He trailed his fingertips over my arm as I stepped away. "I'll be looking forward to it. And Lou, could you do one thing for me?"

I stopped. "Anything you want."

His smile turned crooked. "It's nothing big. I'm counting on them giving me a little more family time. Tell Emi that there's one more thing I need to talk to her about."

TWO

Luciana

I HAD no inkling what Niko might have been up to until Emi texted me the next morning to announce that she was picking up me and the guys—to bring us to our new rink.

"You'll like this place," she chirped as I got into the passenger seat of her compact Honda while Quentin and Jasper slid into the back. "They look after it really nice, and it's got some of the best security you'll find for an arena in Tokyo."

I glanced over my shoulder toward Rafael, newly cast-free, who was insisting on tailing us in the rental SUV Niko had arranged for us when we first arrived in the country. "How secure is that?"

Emi laughed and eased the car into the flow of traffic outside our apartment building. "Let's just say this is where a bunch of rich kids go to practice — and when I say rich, I'm talking about the kind of kids who think money will buy them a way into a fancy skating career. They're wrong, of course, but their parents don't want anything happening to them while they're pretending to be professionals."

"Rich, huh?" Jasper said doubtfully. "How much is the ice time going to set us back?"

"Nothing!" Emi shot him a grin in the rearview mirror. "I set things up through the owner's niece, who's a friend. I promised her uncle that if you two win a medal at the World Championships, he can tell everyone you practiced on his rink. It'll be the first time anyone who trained there even made it to a big competition. Might be a chance for him to get taken more seriously."

I guessed that was a reasonable trade-off. I didn't love the idea of hanging out some place funded by the city's elite, giving the trappings of quality even though apparently they weren't turning out any top skaters. But if no one prominent had ever come out of there, then the place wouldn't be on anyone's radar when looking for Worlds-level competitors.

And rich-people-level security sounded good to me. I'd do just about anything to avoid a repeat of our last practice's bloodshed.

As if he were thinking along similar lines, Quentin shook his head. "I can't believe Okabe was worrying about finding you a new practice space before he's even out of the hospital. That guy's a maniac."

"Only in the best way," Emi said cheerfully. "He's always been obsessed with skating. And now he has two other people to obsess over instead of just his own performance."

Jasper let out a rough guffaw.

I peered through the windows at the shiny skyscrapers we were gradually leaving behind. If I'd learned anything in the short time I'd been living in Tokyo, it was that any time I thought I understood how huge the city was, it got even bigger. It didn't have one downtown but something like a dozen of them.

Austin looked like some podunk town next to this metropolis.

Emi wove through the streets with total confidence, bringing us into a neighborhood of low-rise buildings in a hotchpotch of grays, beiges, and browns. She rounded the corner and drew into a small parking lot outside a silvery domed building. A red sign out front held thick Japanese characters next to smaller print in English that said SPORTS GARDEN.

Rafael parked next to us and got out, his dark eyes scanning the lot. I suspected the low but sturdy wall that surrounded the place garnered a little approval.

As we walked up to the front doors, Emi produced three key cards from her purse. "I got one for each of you skaters, and I have one for Niko too, after he's on his feet again. No regular keys, so no one can make copies. And there's always someone on watch at the security desk."

She gave the stern-looking man behind the desk in the lobby a friendly wave. He dipped his head slightly to us, his gaze sliding right back toward the parking lot.

Well, that was definitely a step up from rinks so low-key there was rarely anyone watching the reception area at all.

Emi led us through a couple of sparkling clean hallways and pointed out the locker rooms. "It looks like you're already in your practice clothing, though, so we can go right in to the rink. You've got the next three hours, but we can book longer sessions on the weekdays when most of the usual trainees are in school until the late afternoon."

She pushed past another set of double doors, and a waft of chilly air swept over me. My nerves settled a little at the familiar calm of the vast, quiet room. My hand dropped to my equipment bag, the urge gripping me to pull on my skates and vanish completely into the escape skating could bring as quickly as possible.

Emi gave me a knowing look. "You can get started. I have to meet with my parents. If you need anything, give me a call."

I nodded. "We'll see you at the hospital in the afternoon, if our paths cross."

She smiled back at me. "And not too long after that even if they don't. Have fun!"

As she slipped out, my men and I tramped past the stands to the rink itself. Rafael hunkered down on a bench about halfway between the door and the ice, turning so he could keep an eye on both at once.

I dropped onto another bench and groped in my bag for my skates and my gloves. The sooner I was on the ice, the better.

I tied the final knot, shucked off the skate guards, and stepped onto the rink. The first glide forward sent a wave of peace rushing through me.

Moments later, Jasper joined me. We automatically fell into the paces of our typical warm-up routine, stretching and getting our heartrate going, sweeping back and forth across the ice.

"Let's do some individual jumps and spins so we're totally used to the space before we get into anything more complicated," Jasper suggested when we'd finished.

Quentin appeared to be already doing that, whipping around at the far end of the rink, favoring his mostly-healed shoulder only a little now. I swiped my gloved hands together. "Sure, that sounds like a good idea. Double axels?"

My partner flashed me a smile. "You called it."

We took turns picking our next move, the hiss of our skates against the frozen surface providing the only soundtrack.

Too quiet a soundtrack. The sound was soothing, yes, but it wasn't enough. I couldn't stop myself from listening for Niko's voice calling out encouragement and advice.

None of this was the same without our coach here. How could we focus when the horror that'd taken him down was lingering in the back of all our minds?

If it hadn't been for Niko, Jasper and I would never have given this partnership a thought. He'd brought us together and bound us with his warm enthusiasm, which had proven to be unshakable even in the face of multiple gunshot wounds.

Maybe someday I'd be able to imagine doing this without him, but not any time soon.

Jasper paused when we eased apart after a joint spin, taking in my expression. "Are you okay?"

My mouth twisted. "Just… missing Niko."

A shadow crossed his face. "Yeah. Me too. I skated for all those years before I even met him, but now… it's like he's an essential part of this whole experience."

"He really is."

I dragged in a breath and was going to say that we should try with music, because that's what Niko would have suggested. A peal of a much more electronic-sounding tone than I'd had in mind cut me off.

"My phone." I pushed off toward the stands to check it. Maybe it was Emi with more news—or Niko himself, reaching out from the hospital.

What if something more had happened to him? Could Mom's goons have gotten past the police presence there?

My heart was thumping hard by the time I snatched up my phone. I stared at the text on the screen, my fear shifting from one source to another in an instant.

"Who is it?" Rafael asked, shoving himself to his feet.

"I… I don't know. Someone who knows who I am. But I have no idea how they got this number."

Hello, Miss Cordova, the text message read. *We've come to Tokyo to support you as the true heir to the Deadly Rose. I think we could have something to offer you. Will you meet up with us?*

Jasper had clomped over and checked the text over my shoulder. "What the hell? Is this some kind of joke?"

"I don't think so," I said slowly. "Why would anyone joke about that? No one who isn't part of my old life would know to mention 'Deadly Rose' or my real last name."

Rafael scanned the words with a deepening frown. "They want you to meet them? It sounds like a trap."

"It could be." Tension wrapped around my gut. "But I can't just ignore this, can I? If I don't answer, and they're out to hurt me, they'll force the issue. This way, we might be able to scope them out before we have to deal with them directly."

Quentin had joined us. When I held out the phone to show him the message too, he cocked his head. "We might as well find out what they want, right? You had other people from that Devil's Dozen group help you. Maybe they actually are on your side."

I rubbed my mouth. "Possible, but not super likely. But I'd rather find out what I'm up against than stay in the dark." It'd be better to confront them now than to wait and see if they burst into this rink with another hail of gunfire.

I typed out a hasty reply. *Who are you? And what are you offering?*

The answer came immediately. *I think that'd be easier to discuss in person. We'd rather not risk your phone being tapped and the conversation overheard. If Mireya hears about this, it'll go much worse for us than for you.*

Okay, I guessed that was a fair point, if they were planning to stand with me against her. I worried at my lower lip. *Fine. Where can I find you?*

Shinjuku Gyoen. We can get there in ten minutes. We'll wait near the bridge past the Rakuu-Tei tea house for an hour.

Rafael was already typing on his phone. "We can get to the park in half an hour. That'll give us a little time to study them before we decide whether to hear them out."

I lowered my phone to my side, my fingers clutching it tightly. "All right. Let's see who's come out to play."

Rafael found a parking space a few streets over from the park, which looked huge on my phone's map. The map did show the tea house the text had mentioned, with a pond and a couple of bridges nearby, so at least we had some idea where we were going.

The early February breeze had a nip to it but nothing outright biting. Niko had told us that it did snow in Tokyo, but only rarely. We headed into the park, where many of the trees had kept their greenery, although skeletal leafless branches showed in patches here and there.

Only a few visitors strolled beneath the trees. I hadn't visited this park before, and the serenity of it seeped into my skin despite my jangling nerves. I'd have liked to see it in the full bloom of springtime.

As we came up on the tea house, regularly consulting our phone maps, we slowed. Most of the bystanders were obviously Japanese locals, who paid us no attention. I saw two pairs I easily identified as tourists from the way they were holding up their phones and tapping away at the camera buttons. No one appeared to be looking for us yet.

Rafael peered at the map and motioned to the path ahead of us. "It looks like the trees thin up ahead and there's a pretty large clearing past the tea house, near the pond. If they're waiting there, we'll be able to get a good look at them without them seeing us yet. Keep your eyes peeled."

As we followed him off the path through one last dense stretch of trees, his hand rested on his hip. He had a pistol concealed there, under his leather jacket.

Just ahead of us, the trees gave way to a span of clear lawn. We slunk through the shadows to the edge of where we could stay concealed and peered out over the garden.

It was a pretty spectacular view. Maybe a hundred feet away lay a tranquil pond, rippling faintly with the breeze. An immense skyscraper and several other high rises showed over the tops of the trees that ringed the far side of the water, reminding us that this apparent wilderness lay in the middle of a vast modern city.

Then three figures ambled into view on the grass between our vantage point and the pond-side path.

I knew at once that they were the ones who'd sent that message. None of them were Japanese, but they didn't have the attitude of tourists either. They stuck close together, their eyes scanning the scenery as if they were as nervous of us as we were of them.

As I squinted at them, recognition crept over me. The big Latino guy with the lightning bolt shaved into his buzzcut—I'd seen him around the Deadly Rose mansion back in Austin. The woman too—her straggly bleached-blond waves and sharply arched eyebrows would have made her easy to pick out of a crowd even if female underlings hadn't been relatively rare.

The third guy, tall and scrawny with a thick scar that cut across his cheek just below his right eye, I'd never seen before. But if he was in with the other two, he'd definitely worked for my mom.

I glanced at Rafael, who was still contemplating them. "They were all part of the Austin outfit," he confirmed in a low voice. "In the middle of the ranks, not much authority but not newbies either. I never had much to do with any of them, though."

"They're *here*, like they said they'd be," Quentin pointed out. "It doesn't look like they brought any backup. We've already got them outnumbered."

I wet my lips. I could probably take at least one of them on my own, and Rafael definitely could. And we hadn't seen any sign of an ambush as we'd snuck over here.

If anything, the trio had put themselves in a weaker position, out there in the open with no shelter nearby. We could have shot them all down in a matter of seconds if we'd wanted to.

"You really want to do this?" Jasper asked me.

I shrugged. "We came all this way. They might have useful information."

Rafael sighed. "All right. But call them over here. I don't want *us* out in the open for this conversation either."

Bracing myself in case I needed to run or hit the ground, I stepped from between the trees at the edge of the lawn. "Hey! Waiting for me?"

The trio jerked around, the woman's face brightening in relief and the two men both looking vaguely grouchy but also awkward about it. I wheeled my arm, motioning for them to join us in the shelter of the trees.

As they stalked over, a tight smile curled the woman's lips. "You came. I'm glad to see I wasn't wrong that you've got plenty of guts."

Rafael flanked me, his gun in his hand now. "She's got more than that. You'd better start explaining what you're up to *now*, or we're out of here."

"Yeah," Quentin added. "You said you've got something to offer Lou. What is it?"

The big guy with the buzzcut gave Rafael a thoughtful look as if evaluating who would win in a fight—and seemed to deflate a bit when he must have decided it wouldn't be him.

His skinnier companion cleared his throat, spat on the ground, and gave us a crooked smile of his own. "Honestly, it's actually more about what we hope you can do for us."

"But we can help you too," the woman insisted.

I folded my arms over my chest. "What are you talking about? Let's get to the actual explanation faster, please."

The scrawny man narrowed his eyes, making the scar rise on his cheek. "You've seen how your mother has gotten. Going off the rails, lashing out at people—half the time when they haven't even done anything wrong. We figure we're better off not following her orders than trying to stay in line."

Mr. Lightning Buzzcut nodded. "She can't keep up like this for long, not with the mess she's gotten into. You'll be the new Deadly Rose soon. So we came to you."

The woman sketched a faux curtsy. "We're here to prove our loyalty. Take us under your protection, and we'll let you know anything we find out about your mother's plans. We'll stand with you if she sends anyone after you."

I had to hold back a laugh. These three figured *I* could protect them? I hadn't even been able to keep my coach and lover safe. They might be better off pretending they'd never heard of the Cordova family at all.

But they were here. They were making an appeal to me. There could be safety in numbers for both of us.

And if I wanted to keep my men out of the worst danger from here forward, having whatever intel these defectors could pass on could make all the difference.

"I can't make any promises," I said, unwilling to lie. "It's not like I have the kind of manpower my mother can wield. But if you're willing to work for me, I'll do what I can to take care of you."

As soon as I was sure I could actually trust them. I considered my options. "Do you have a secure place to stay?"

Scarface wrinkled his nose. "We've been hiding out in one of the local hostels. Not exactly prime digs."

I hummed to myself. "That'll have a lot of people coming and going. We'll have to fix that. Our apartment at the Izumi Tower is already pretty crowded, but I'll see about getting you a place nearby where you can lay low as soon as possible."

The woman let out her breath in a rush. "That would be an amazing start."

I took out my phone. "Let me get your names and numbers so I can get in touch."

It turned out the woman was Ursula, the big buzzcut dude was Dámaso, and the scarred guy went by Frankie. I saved their numbers in my phone and lifted my head to meet Ursula's gaze again, since she seemed the most eager of the bunch.

"How exactly did you get *my* number?" Only a few people in the

Deadly Rose ranks had gotten a direct line to the heir apparent, and the three lackeys in front of me weren't among that number.

The trio exchanged a glance. Ursula jabbed her thumb toward Frankie. "This guy managed to take a peek at Mireya's contacts and wrote it down. I told him he was insane, but I guess it worked out in our favor."

Frankie grinned. "Let's hope so."

We parted ways, the gangsters heading across one of the bridges and us backtracking the way we'd come. When we were well out of earshot, Jasper shot me a sideways glance. "What's the Izumi Tower? The place we're staying isn't called anything like that."

I smiled slyly in return. "I know. I noticed it during one of my grocery runs—it's a building a few blocks down the street." I turned to Rafael. "I'll need you to keep an eye on it for the next few days to see if my mother launches any attacks there. If she does, then we know our new friends were looking to double-cross us and passed the info back to her."

Rafael let out a low chuckle. "Smart thinking. I've made a couple of contacts on the wrong side of the tracks while you were off skating over the past couple of weeks… I can arrange to have the building watched."

I took a gulp of the crisp air and let it wash some of the tension from my lungs. "Well, our rink time would be over by now anyway. Let's head to the hospital. We can grab some lunch and eat with Niko if his parents are done visiting for the morning."

Quentin rubbed his hands together. "Sounds good to me."

It was a short trip from where Rafael had parked the car to the hospital where Niko had been admitted. I watched Rafael navigate the unfamiliar streets with a mix of affection and awe. He hadn't even been fully mobile for most of his time in this new country, still recovering from his own injuries after an attack by his brother's old gang back in Austin, but he'd managed to adapt in all kinds of ways already.

The hospital's underground lot was pretty full. We had to park a couple of rows over from the elevator. As we headed over through the artificial light, two men in well-fitted suits stepped into our path.

What now? I couldn't help thinking as I jerked to a halt, my body shifting into a defensive pose. Rafael's hand shot to his holster.

"You don't want to do that," one of the men said smoothly with a flick of his eyes toward the gun. "We're here on behalf of the Bright Dragon and the March Wind of the Devil's Dozen."

Oh, shit.

THREE

Luciana

FACING off against two representatives for the world's top criminal masterminds wasn't quite as scary as dealing with the head honchos themselves, but only by an increment. The thirteen crime bosses who made up the Devil's Dozen were the most powerful figures in existence, considering that between them they controlled all of the illegal activity around the globe except the pettiest of crimes that could escape their notice.

Mom was one of them. I'd met a couple who didn't seem all that bad. But the majority, to get where they were, had turned brutality into an artform. And the two men in front of us were no doubt sanctioned to act on their behalf.

I held myself still and steady, trying to keep a calm expression even as my pulse thundered through my veins. These weren't the kind of people I'd want to show any weakness in front of. "All right. We're listening. What exactly do you want?"

The man on the left, a burly dude who looked Asian but not like most of the Japanese locals I'd met—maybe Chinese?—flicked a discreet gun from a holster under his suit jacket and held it lowered but in view. He spoke with a polished British accent. "The Bright Dragon would like to know what your presence in Tokyo means in terms of your mother's intentions."

The other guy, his jowled head topped by tufts of bright red hair, palmed a pistol of his own. He aimed both it and a glare at me, spitting out his words with a mild Australian drawl. "And the March Wind would like to hear what the fuck you were angling for, sending around all those files about her operations."

His tone was sharper than his companions, and his posture undeniably aggressive. I fought the urge to take a step back from him, seeing Rafael's fingers close around the grip of his gun.

Mom hadn't just made enemies with her plotting against her fellow Devil's Dozen members. She'd had at least a few allies who were scheming right alongside her to take down some of their colleagues and divide territory they stole between them. From this guy's demeanor, I couldn't help wondering if my gambit had upended the March Wind's plans as well as my mother's.

Otherwise you'd think he'd have appreciated the warning rather than sounding pissed off about it.

"I think the answer to the second question should cover both," I said tartly, as if I were annoyed by the interruption, not terrified for the men standing with me. "I disagreed with my mother's tactics, and I figured the rest of you should know that she was hoping to tear apart the foundations of your organization. I also wanted to get her off my back. I'm not interested in inheriting her spot at the table."

The March Wind's man made a scoffing sound. "And we're just supposed to believe that?"

I glared right back at him. "Yes. Because if you did even a fraction of the research I'm sure your boss would have expected, you'll have seen that I'm here to compete in the World Figure Skating Championships. Which are taking place in Nagano, so of course I'm in Japan. We're training in Tokyo to try to avoid having my mom's people track us down, although that hasn't worked out so well after all."

The Bright Dragon's man studied me with a cooler gaze. "And what is your game plan after this skating competition? Are you aiming to wrestle your mother's empire away from her?"

I couldn't stop myself from rolling my eyes. "Did you listen to anything I just said? She can keep her empire. I just don't want her having *me*. She was using threats to keep me under her thumb, so I exposed her so that she'd have bigger problems to deal with. I'd be happiest if she forgets I even exist and I can focus on nothing but skating and regular life."

"As if the heir to the Deadly Rose would ever give up all ambition," the March Wind's man sneered. "We know where you came from. It sounds like this is all another game to me, one you won't win."

I folded my arms over my chest. "The only thing I care about winning is medals on the ice. I haven't had any contact with the criminal world since I left Austin, other than whatever my bodyguard has needed to do to keep us safe. But maybe you're more concerned because of what your boss thought *he* was going to win if my mother got to see through her plans."

I knew the second the accusation flew from my lips that it'd been a miscalculation. The stutter of the man's expression gave away that I was right, but his eyes flashed an instant later, his gun hand jerking forward. "I don't need to listen to a snake like you talk about my employer that way. Unless you want to know what the inside of your skull looks like."

None of us were slow draws around here. Not after all of my boyfriends had gotten weeks of practice with their own weapons that Rafael had managed to smuggle over the ocean.

A second after the threatening gesture, I'd tugged my tiny pistol from my purse into my hand, and Jasper and Quentin had retrieved their weapons from their concealed positions as well. The March Wind's rep flicked his gaze over all of us, a bit of the color fading from his ruddy cheeks.

He'd figured at least some of my men wouldn't be prepared. He'd bet wrong.

"Let's simmer down," the Bright Wind's man said in an even tone. "You have to understand that it's difficult for any of us to believe you gave up all of that power simply to skate."

Rafael stepped forward, gun ready but not aimed, his eyes glinting dangerously. "Is it really? Do *you* enjoy every part of this job? Lou's spent her whole life in a position where she has no more control over what she does and where she goes than you do. And she loves doing something her mother sees as silly. You've got to have enough imagination to see how all that supposed power could become a cage."

I'd rarely heard him speak at that much length, but his conviction rang through his words—and the March Wind's man lowered his gun just slightly at hearing it put that way. And maybe because it was coming from another man rather than a girl he probably saw as silly too.

My bodyguard had been part of criminal negotiations like this for nearly as long as I'd been alive. It made sense that he'd be comfortable talking at these men's level—and making the right points to start to diffuse their apprehension.

I raised my hand to rest it on the back of Rafael's elbow, surreptitiously encouraging him taking the initiative. "That's right. I don't feel powerful when I'm with my mother—I feel confined. And no amount of money holds a candle to the thrill of performing a routine that brings an audience to their feet with applause."

The March Wind's man scowled. "And with all those performances, you're risking bringing the Devil's Dozen into the public eye. There's already been too much talk on the news about the attack on your coach."

I sighed. "And who do you think orchestrated that attack? If you're upset about it, take it up with my mom. I'd rather it'd never happened in the first place."

Rafael nodded. "If anything, that should be more proof to you that Luciana is completely at odds with the Deadly Rose. She was almost killed in that ambush. The goons her mother sent didn't hold their fire."

"Yeah." I lifted my chin. "So if you have a problem with the spotlight that's being pointed on those crimes, you should be focusing on the Deadly Rose, not me. If there are no more attacks on me and my friends, then I won't even *think* about the Devil's Dozen again."

"And if there are?" the Bright Dragon's rep asked. "Are you threatening to expose us?"

Oh, for fuck's sake. I held myself back from gritting my teeth. "No, I'm just pointing out the natural consequences of my mother's insanity. She's the one sending people to shoot at me. Believe me, if I could make her stop, I would."

Rafael raised an eyebrow. "And your bosses should know how difficult it is to stop the Deadly Rose, considering the conflict with the entire Devil's Dozen hasn't managed to stop her campaign of vengeance against her daughter for even a couple of weeks. Are they coming down on their colleague as hard as you're coming down on Lou?"

The burly man's mouth twisted with a hint of a grimace. The March Wind's man raked his hand back through his fiery hair.

"I'm telling you," I said, just to drive the point home, "I'm not part of the Deadly Rose's empire or her family anymore in any way that matters. Everything you could possibly dig up about my activities here in Tokyo or the months last year when I left Austin should confirm that. My mother has all the control here. I'm just clinging to the little scrap of freedom I've been able to steal away."

There was a moment of tense silence. Then both of the men holstered their weapons.

"I'll pass on your remarks to my employer and see what he makes of them," the Bright Dragon's man said with a brief dip of his head.

The March Wind's rep let out a huff but nodded in a brusquer gesture than his companion's. "Yeah, yeah. We'll look into it. I don't think the boss will be happy about it though, so you'd better be ready to do some more explaining."

They split off from each other, moving quickly to their respective vehicles. I didn't take another full breath until the cars had rumbled, one after the other, out of the underground garage.

As the guys put away their own guns, my shoulders sagged. “Holy hell.”

I tipped my face toward the dark ceiling. “No more surprises, okay, universe? I can’t take another one.”

FOUR

Rafael

LOU HAD ALWAYS BEEN good at putting on a tough front. It would have been one of the very first lessons she learned living under her mother's roof. But I knew her well enough to see the slight stiffness to her movements as she reached for the plates to clear the table after our dinner, to notice the way her smile faded too quickly when Quentin made a teasing remark.

I could understand why she'd be stressed. Not only did she have Niko to worry about, even if he'd been looking even better during our visit this afternoon, but now she was facing more intrusions and threats from our old life.

If it'd been up to me, I'd have sheltered her from everything except the parts of her life she loved. But I hadn't managed to fully protect her even when she'd only wanted to train with Coach Balakin back in Austin. Who would I be kidding if I tried to convince myself I could shield her from everything coming at us now?

I kept an eye on her as she rinsed the dishes, but I didn't push.

When she was ready to talk through whatever was at the front of her mind, she would.

As I wiped off the compact apartment's small table, Quentin switched to hassling Jasper about some skating thing I couldn't give a shit about.

"I can't believe you'd put that Daimos routine in your top five. He didn't even manage to land the full triple Axel."

Jasper shot the younger guy a look that was more exasperated than outright angry. "Of course he did. I've watched that performance dozens of times."

Quentin shook his head. "No way. He pulled out a split-second too early. Anyone with eyes would have noticed that."

"The judges scored it like he completed the rotation."

"Right, and we all know that judges never make mistakes. Especially when they've got a world champion they're *supposed* to fawn over in front of them."

Jasper let out a huff and motioned for Quentin to follow him. "There's an easy way to settle this. I've got a video recording on my computer. We can even play it in slow motion if you insist."

"You'll be the one crying afterward."

Their voices dwindled as they stepped into Jasper's bedroom. Lou watched them go and rolled her eyes. "Boys."

I couldn't hold back a smirk. "Hey, you're the one who wanted them around."

"It's a good thing they have so many good points as well." She managed a wider grin and came over to grasp my hand. "But this means I can get a little one-on-one time with the only guy who won't argue about rotations or leg angles."

I laughed and let her guide me over to the sofa. Like the other furniture in the apartment Niko had arranged for us, it was smaller than I'd have preferred. I guessed there weren't a whole lot of Japanese men with quite my height and heft. But I could make do with the narrow cushions in exchange for a cuddle with my woman.

Lou tugged me down beside her and tucked her legs over my lap while resting her head on my chest. I slung my arm around her automatically. She sighed, relaxing into my embrace in a way that was as gratifying as making her moan between the sheets.

"Have you heard anything from the people who've been watching Izumi Tower?" she asked. "Any sign that my mother's people have poked around there?"

I stroked my thumb over the peak of her shoulder. "My main guy has only been in place for a few hours, but so far, nothing. I don't think we can draw any conclusions until we've given it at least a couple of days, though."

"Yeah." Her next sigh sounded tense again. "What do you think I should do about those three turncoats who came looking for me? Even if they don't tattle to my mom right away, that's no guarantee they won't later. And then there's the asshole reps from those two Devil's Dozen bigwigs... What if they're not satisfied with the answers I gave them?"

She was asking me? I hesitated, willing my muscles to stay loose beneath her body so she couldn't feel me tensing up.

I guessed it made sense for her to want my opinion. I was the only one she could count on here who had any significant experience with that part of her life. It wasn't as if the skater guys could offer much insight into the criminal mindset.

I traced more soothing patterns on her arm as I contemplated my answer. "I think you started off on the right foot. You didn't give the defectors any real information and found a way to test their loyalties. And you pushed the Devil's Dozen pendejos to focus on your mother rather than you. That's definitely the direction their attention should be pointed in."

"It just seems like hardly anything."

"Hey." I eased her closer and pressed a kiss to her forehead. "Listen to me. You showed them you're no one to be messed with but made your stance clear at the same time. No one could have handled it better."

"I think you might be a bit biased," Lou muttered, but she nestled against me as if she was meant to be nowhere but here.

For a few minutes, there was nothing but the soft whisper of her breath and the muffled voices as Jasper and Quentin continued their half-hearted bickering. I let my other hand come to rest on her thigh, relishing her warmth and the smooth skin I could trace through her thin leggings.

"So, I made a good start," she said. "Where do we go from here? It's obviously not the last time I'll have to deal with the rogue underlings, and it's fairly likely the reps are going to get on my case again."

My chest constricted again with an instinctive urge to avoid the question. Yes, I was her only remaining tie to her criminal life—but it wasn't as if I had all the answers. Hell, I'd come to the totally wrong conclusion about things in the past, to the point of nearly making a huge mistake that would have upended both our lives.

Who was I to give any kind of advice?

Lou lifted her head to glance up at me, her brow knitting at my silence. I cleared my throat as if I were getting ready to reply.

I had to offer her something—the best I could. We weren't going to rush into action.

If it looked like I'd led her astray, I'd just have to bust my ass course-correcting.

"Let's see," I said to buy myself more time as I mulled it over. "With the Deadly Rose turncoats, I would probably give them a few more tests—chances to see if they'll stick to the loyal path or backstab you. If they pass, then you can trust them a little, but I still wouldn't let them find out anything particularly important like where we're actually living or training."

Lou nodded. "Gradually let them in, but never too close. That makes sense."

"There might be a point when you can bring them on board completely," I felt the need to add. "If they do something that puts your safety ahead of their own—you'll be able to tell when you can really trust them."

"If that ever happens."

I shot her a wry smile. "It might. That's how your latest skater won us all over, isn't it?"

The image of Quentin's bloody shoulder after he'd leapt in front of a bullet for Lou would never leave my mind. Mostly because *I* should have been close enough to defend her.

But I hadn't been and he had, so he'd earned his place by her side. All the more reason I should help her this way if she could use some strategy suggestions, though.

"That's a little different," Lou said lightly. Then her expression darkened again. "And the Devil's Dozen reps? What if they don't let up on me?"

I let out my breath in a ragged huff. "That's the trickier situation, for sure. You just keep telling them the truth as emphatically as you can… and I guess if they refuse to listen to words, at some point you'll have to turn to force."

Lou made a face. "Attack them?"

I shrugged. "We'd have to figure it out when we got to that point. A little strategic destruction to show you're not an easy target. I know you've got it in you when you have to go that far. But the whole time, the message should still be that your mother is the real problem and you're just trying to keep yourself safe and away from all of them."

"If only they'd listen to that. If they'd stand up to her, maybe we could actually live our lives freely. Imagine that!"

Her tone was wry, but it didn't completely disguise the longing in the words.

I hugged her to me. "We'll get there. Look at how far you've come in half a year. We're all the way on the other side of the world."

Lou let out a soft snort, but she hugged me back with her arm wrapped around my chest. "I really hope you're right. It's just intimidating going up against people who have as much power as my mom."

"The reps don't," I pointed out. "They're more like tangling with Sheeran in Boston, which you did just fine. And not all of the Devil's Dozen pricks are total cabrónes. Those two who were passing on info to you back in Austin seemed halfway decent."

Lou's head perked up. "That's true. I was so focused on getting away from everything to do with Mom and the Devil's Dozen that I didn't think about where Beckett and the Blood Hunter fit in. I should give the two of them a heads up about the threats I'm getting from their colleagues. They could speak up on my behalf—they know I was working against her, not with her."

I smiled at her, even though I could feel her already pulling away from me. She had work to do, and I wasn't going to keep her from it. "Sounds like you've got a plan—and a good one."

Lou leaned in to give me a lingering kiss on the mouth that made me wish I could strip the clothes right off her. Well, there was always later tonight for that.

"Thank you," she said with a sly smile that suggested she knew how she'd affected me. "For reassuring me and helping me figure things out. It's not something I'd ever want to do alone."

I squeezed her hand before she stepped away. "You'll never be alone, mi amada."

Now I just had to hold on to hope that I'd guided her well—and not into total disaster.

FIVE

Luciana

THERE WAS nothing better than hearing our coach's voice ring out from the stands as Jasper and I came out of our short program's ending pose.

"That was a really good run-through," Niko called from his bench. He'd been cleared to leave the hospital a couple of days ago, but he was mostly staying off his feet to avoid straining himself—a precaution the rest of us were strictly enforcing. "You've managed to stay on track even without my help."

I laughed, relief flowing through my chest. "We're a lot better off with that help, though." I glided over to the boards to grab my water bottle, Jasper following behind me.

Emi, who'd insisted on coming along to her brother's first few practices after his release to watch over him, clapped her hands in excitement. "I can't believe I'm getting to watch future world champions perfect their routine right in front of me."

My next laugh was a little shakier. "We're not world champions yet."

"And it's not *quite* perfect," Niko said, with a playful twinkle in his eye that made the critique he was about to deliver go down easier. "I think you could hit the footwork in that first sequence even more precisely—really nail that beat. And you pulled off the second lift just fine, but I'd like to see Lou get a little more height. You'll always be good that way."

I ran through the routine in my mind, absorbing his suggestions. "We can work on that. We've still got five weeks to polish everything up."

Emi cocked her head. "Are you going to keep the routines the same as from Nationals, or add something new to spice them up?"

Niko nudged his sister. "I think we're better off sticking with what we already know works. They've gotten fantastic scores with the current routines."

The rasp of blades against the ice announced Quentin's arrival. He'd been working through his own routines with an eye to next year's competitions, but now he leaned against the boards next to us and held out his phone. "I don't know. After you see this, you might want to rethink getting complacent."

Jasper shot him a mild glower. "I wouldn't call our routines complacent."

"Maybe not," Quentin said, agreeably enough. "But there's great, and then there's holy fucking crap. One of the guys I know who made it to Nagano for singles is practicing at the same rink as a couple of the pairs. He sent me this. Check out what the main Russian contenders for the gold are up to."

He turned his phone's screen toward us. Niko leaned forward, and Jasper and I studied the handheld recording.

A lithe blond woman skated next to a tall, broad-shouldered man whose darker hair was slicked close to his skull. They swept across the ice with perfect synchronization, grace radiating from their movements. Both strength and artistry showed as they whirled around each other.

"Okay," Jasper said. "They're really good. But what's the big—"

His voice died as the two skaters launched into matching triple Axels, hitting the ice at the exact same time. They circled around and immediately came together in a stunning lift that ended with… a quadruple Salchow throw.

My jaw dropped as the woman touched down without any significant wobble, one foot still lifted, even her hands at exactly the right angle. Holy fucking crap indeed.

"Wow," I said when I got my breath back. "That's—hardly anyone's managed one of those."

Jasper was staring. "Their form is good, they've got the creative aspects, *and* the technical difficulty on top of that… Their scores are going to be through the roof if they keep up that standard in the actual competition."

Even Niko was momentarily speechless. "I had no idea anyone was attempting a quad throw this year. It's usually considered too much of a risk… but they do seem to be up to the challenge."

Emi blinked hard. "OMG. That looked amazing." She shook herself and glanced between the four of us. "But, I mean, Lou and Jasper are amazing too. Is that really going to top their routine?"

"If they do everything right, most likely," Niko admitted. "I think that was their free routine, from the pacing. Ours doesn't have quite the same level of difficulty."

Quentin grimaced. "That's why I thought you should see it. If you *are* going to make any changes, you should get on with that ASAP."

I bit my lip, dread pooling in my stomach. I'd never assumed that we'd win at Worlds, but it was hard not to despair at the idea that we didn't even have a chance. "What can we do? I've got the throw triple Axel, but I can't land a quad Axel even in regular circumstances. I guess we could try to switch it out for our own quad Salchow…"

"Then it'd look like we're just copying them," Jasper said grimly. "No one's ever properly landed *any* other throw quad jump, so I'm not sure there's anything else we could switch to either."

Niko pursed his lips. "It is a different form too—you haven't done a throw Salchow at all before now. Have you ever done a regular quad?"

"No," I admitted.

"I'm not sure we could get there in just five weeks, then. And it wouldn't do you any good trying for something you won't achieve and ruining your routine over it. That's why quad throws are rarely done by anyone."

My hands balled at my sides. "We can't just give up. Those two could pull the throw off at the actual competition just as well as they did in that training video, and then we'd be screwed. What about the rest of our routine? There's got to be something. We've found other areas to ramp up the difficulty and the spectacle before."

Silence fell over our group. My stomach started to sink, but then Niko raised his head with an unusual firmness that spoke of total determination.

"There is one addition we could try that will make you stand out. You're solid with your death spiral and your lifts. You'd get more points if you went straight from one to the other. We'd need to rearrange the existing choreography a little, but only shifting a few moves around."

My pulse hiccupped. "Right from the spiral into a lift?" I *was* confident at both, but I was also fully aware that the death spiral got its name for a reason. It was one of the most dangerous moves we performed. As were the lifts.

They awarded big points for linking the two—but only because it was so freaking difficult.

Niko nodded in acknowledgment, but his eyes gleamed brighter as he gained enthusiasm for the idea. "It isn't often done either, but it's absolutely possible. It's also a better balance of points to difficulty than any other option I can think of. And you already have both pieces. With the time we have, I'm sure you could get there."

My mouth had gone dry. There was getting there in practice and then nailing it perfectly in front of the judges. The former was a lot easier than the latter. If we failed during a performance, it could ruin the whole thing, just like Niko had said about the quad. Even attempting it could cost us any decent placement at all.

And that was assuming we didn't end up with a major injury on our hands before we even got to the competition.

But hadn't I just said that we had to give this our all? What was I here for if I wasn't willing to take that risk?

It wasn't any more dangerous than facing off with my mother's gunmen, that was for sure.

Jasper was watching me. "What do you think, Lou? You're the one in the most precarious position for both moves."

I squared my shoulders. "Let's give it a shot. What do we have to lose?"

Dios mío, let us not have to find out the answer to that question.

Emi let out a whoop and bobbed on her feet in excitement.

Niko waved us onto the ice. "Do some practice of the original spiral to make sure you're feeling totally confident in it. Think about how you'd need to adjust the exit to switch from it into a lift. I'm going to talk with one of my coach friends to see if she has any tips before we get right into it.

We ran through the spiral we were used to several times until I was dizzy. My brain kept cycling through the motion even when we were standing still. Niko motioned us over and gave us some suggestions about how to angle our bodies in the exit and quickly hit the right position for the lift.

Then we moved back into the middle of the rink. Quentin paused his practice to prop himself against the boards and watch.

I drew myself up straight and pretended my heart wasn't racing at a million miles an hour. We could do this. It was two things we'd already done, just pushed closer together. Piece of cake.

Maybe there weren't tons of pairs who'd pulled it off before, but a decent number had. I saw no reason we couldn't make ourselves one more.

We launched into the death spiral, my head whipping over the ice. Jasper's hand gripped mine as firmly as ever.

I counted out the beats, felt the shift as we transitioned into the exit, turned my body a little differently—

And stumbled before Jasper even had time to reach for me, let alone propel me into the air.

"Shit," I muttered as I caught my balance with my hand on the ice.

Niko applauded from the stands. "That was great for your first try. I can already see how it'll come together. Keep at it!"

The next two attempts had my temper fraying. No matter how

much I focused on the new position, some part of my body wouldn't quite adapt.

On our fourth try, a spurt of anger honed my attention even more. I whirled around, landed in Jasper's grasp, and launched myself upward with his added propulsion.

Unfortunately, while I'd been busy getting the angle right for coming out of the spiral, I'd ended up off-balance for the lift itself. Jasper's hand slipped before he'd quite hefted me above his head.

I fell to the ice, his grasp only slowing my momentum. My hip still jarred against the ice hard enough to make me wince.

"Fuck, I'm so sorry," Jasper said, kneeling beside me. "Are you okay?"

I patted my thigh. "Yep. Just a few more bruises to add to my extensive collection."

I pushed myself to my feet, my breath coming ragged. Niko stood up, making my attention snap to him.

"You're supposed to relax," I chided him.

"And you shouldn't push yourself too hard either," he said gently. "That's enough for today. We can go for this change, but we have to be smart about it. It won't help either of you if you end up hurt."

"You were *so* close!" Emi exclaimed. "I know after a few more practices, you'll have it."

Jasper squeezed my shoulder. "I am pretty exhausted, Punk. We've got lots of time. I'll put together some new costumes too—something even more striking so our artistry is at another level too."

I swallowed thickly and forced myself to nod. Inside, my stomach had knotted.

New costumes weren't going to elevate us enough to make us gold contenders—not if we couldn't elevate the rest of our routine too.

Just how far over my head had I gotten myself, facing off against the greatest skaters in the entire world?

SIX

Luciana

I FLOPPED down on my bed and stared at the ceiling, but I just didn't have it in me to relax today. Our ice time didn't start for another couple of hours, and my thigh still ached from yesterday's fall, but I wasn't going to feel okay until we'd conquered that combined move.

With a muffled groan, I pushed myself upright and stalked into the apartment's living room. Niko was puttering around in the kitchen making tea, and Rafael sat on the sofa, scrolling through his phone. Jasper had gone off to find fabric for the amazing new costumes he had planned, with Emi volunteering as translator and guide. Quentin had asked to tag along, saying he wanted to learn from Jasper's expertise in that area.

The sight of Rafael on his phone sent a different prickle of apprehension through me. I stalked over and leaned against the back of the sofa next to his broad shoulders. "Has there been any news from the other apartment building?"

He shook his head without looking up. "Your mother hasn't

launched any attacks there. And her rogue lackeys didn't take the other bait you gave them with that restaurant you mentioned you visited a lot, since she hasn't been terrorizing that place either. It doesn't look like the turncoats are passing on any information."

Somehow that didn't make me feel any better. I pushed away from the sofa to pace through the room. "So what am I supposed to do now? Even if they're not outright betraying me, that doesn't mean I can trust them."

Rafael set down his phone and raised his eyebrows at me. "Don't you have enough on your mind without worrying about that too? Forget about it until they do something that gives you an answer one way or another."

"Who says they're ever going to make a move that clear?"

"I do," he said with a hint of a growl. "Now sit down and relax for once in your life."

Oh, he thought he could boss me around just like that, did he? I set my hands on my hips. "If I wasn't the kind of person who takes charge and gets things done, we wouldn't be here at all."

Niko wandered over with a teacup nestled in his hands and a mischievous glint in his eyes. "I've heard of this concept called 'moderation' before..."

I made a face at him. "Oh, don't you start too."

He chuckled. "As your coach, I think I have even more right to give you a few orders. And in my opinion, you need to stay focused on your routine and unwind between practices rather than overworking yourself."

I sighed. "We both know I can't totally forget all my other problems. They're pushing themselves into my life way too insistently."

Niko cocked his head. "I don't see any of them dancing around the room right now. It seems safe to stop thinking about them for a few minutes at least."

I glowered at him, but at the same time, I couldn't deny he had a point. "Why do you have to make sense?"

His grin widened. "That's my job as your coach, isn't it? To guide you effectively?"

Something about the amusement lighting his face sent a flicker of heat through my veins. I couldn't stop myself from licking my lips. "Were there any other ways you were thinking of guiding me while I'm supposedly 'relaxing'?"

"Hmm. I might be able to find a few techniques to help you loosen up…"

He set his tea down on the side table and slipped his arms around me. My head tilted to meet his kiss. Our mouths melded together with the same perfect sweetness they always had.

He was back here with me again. I wanted to revel in that fact. I wanted to melt right into him, but I kept my hands careful as I stroked them over his cheek and down his side, avoiding the stitched up wounds on his chest.

The floor creaked as Rafael stood. My bodyguard circled the sofa to join us, making my pulse thump even faster in anticipation.

"Don't think you get to be greedy just because you caught a bullet for her," he rumbled, keeping his tone teasing. "This woman needs more than one man can deliver."

Niko eased back from me and grinned at Rafael. "If you think you can do better, then go right ahead."

Rafael loomed over me and dipped his head—to nip my earlobe rather than claiming my mouth. A squeak of surprise escaped me at the pinch of pain that brought a jolt of pleasure with it, and Rafael answered with an eager growl. He flicked his tongue along the crook of my jaw and finally planted his mouth on mine just as he slid his hand down to the elastic waist of the pajama pants I was still wearing.

A tiny moan slid between my lips. Rafael could always get me wet in record time. When he delved his fingers right beneath the thin fabric, my hips rocked to meet him, urging him onward.

"What do you think, brat?" Rafael murmured, loud enough for Niko to hear. "You want even more of this, don't you? You want both of us to carry you into your bedroom and give you the fuck of your life. Let's hear you say please."

His words sent a wash of heat through me. I couldn't deny they were true. "Please. Fuck me just right." I shot a glance over my shoulder at Niko. "Both of you. Ravish me."

Niko chuckled and stepped closer again. "Ravish, hmm? I think we could probably handle that..."

As Rafael captured my mouth again, Niko grazed his deft fingers over my chest to fondle my breasts. He pinched one nipple at the same moment Rafael circled his thumb over my clit, and I bucked in their joint embrace. A whimper tumbled out of me.

I couldn't forget that both of my men were still in recovery, even if Rafael was almost entirely healed. With a determined nudge, I directed us toward the bedroom. "This would be even more fun lying down."

Rafael clucked his tongue at me. "So impatient. But I do like a woman who knows what she wants."

As we passed over the threshold, he tugged off my pajama top. Niko didn't waste a second leaning in and lapping the peak of one breast into his hot mouth. I moaned and writhed with the pumping of Rafael's hand between my legs. My cunt throbbed with need.

For several seconds, we held there at the edge of the bed, too caught up in our shared desire to take the last couple of steps. Then Rafael slid his hand around to my hip and swept me right up to lay me in the middle of the mattress.

The two men clambered after me, and I clasped both of their shirts. "Off with these." I hesitated, my gaze lingering on Niko. "Or you can leave yours on if you'd rather keep the wounds covered up."

His smile turned only slightly crooked. "I'm not sure they'd be great for the mood. But I can strip down in other ways."

He reached for his pants. I openly ogled his leanly muscled legs as he exposed them, then switched to admiring the chiseled six pack Rafael had revealed.

My bodyguard smirked at me. "You look like you're enjoying the view. I certainly am."

I peeked at him coyly through my eyelashes. "I'd like you both to do a lot more than look."

Niko sank down next to me and trailed his hand down my belly. "You don't need to worry about that, Angel."

He tucked his fingers around my pussy to continue Rafael's work. Rafael chuckled and cupped my breasts. As he massaged sparks of bliss through my chest, he stole another demanding kiss.

My skin felt lit up with flames, heat flaring through my body from head to toe. When Niko curled his fingers right into my slit, I couldn't stop myself from crying out—or arching back against him. A second later, I froze, caught between my smoldering hunger and my concern for him. "I don't want to hurt you."

"I'm not that fragile," my coach reassured me, pressing an encouraging kiss to my shoulder. "Just don't flail around wildly, and we should be okay."

Rafael hummed to himself. "That sounds like a challenge."

A breathless giggle spilled out of me. "You can make me flail some other time!"

"Oh, I'm looking forward to it. Over and over again."

I shivered giddily and then let out another moan as he sucked one nipple into his mouth. Niko took the opportunity to lean over me and catch my lips with a kiss, still conjuring waves of pleasure between my thighs.

It was time I got a little payback around here. I groped for Rafael's sweatpants and slid my hand beneath them to grip his already rigid dick. His breath stuttered against my breast as he jerked into my grasp.

I stroked him up and down, and he sucked harder on the nub he'd already turned achingly stiff. At my determined tug, he helped me yank the pants right off him, his boxers following quickly.

Niko took advantage of my distraction to peel my own pants and panties off me. Rafael eased down the bed as if the other man had unwrapped a present just for him.

He gazed up at me for just a second, taking in every inch of my naked body. His attention seared over my skin. Then he buried his face where his hand had been teasing me minutes ago.

He knew just where to nibble and where to slide his tongue over the most sensitive parts of my cunt. I gasped and squirmed against his mouth, but his hand held me firmly. All I could do was shake with the bliss building at my core, alternating between clutching at the short coils of Rafael's head and twisting my own head to meet more of Niko's kisses.

Niko took over up top, rolling my nipples between his fingers to thrilling effect. My head spun, but with the most fantastic of sensations. Mumbles slipped from my throat—I was pretty sure I was begging them to never stop, but I didn't care.

Rafael swiped his tongue from my clit all the way to my slit one last time and then rose up, leaving me panting for more. "Not enough," he muttered as he snatched at my bedside table, knowing I kept a box of condoms in the drawer. "I can never get enough of you."

He tore open the foil and rolled the contents over him at lightning speed. As he parted my legs, he simply rubbed the massive head of his cock over my pussy, glancing past me to Niko.

"I think you'd like to satisfy both of us, wouldn't you, brat? Do you think you can take Niko and me at the same time?"

A heady rush flooded my veins. I grinned. "I know I can."

Rafael grabbed the lube I'd also stashed in the drawer and tossed it to Niko. My coach groaned in anticipation as he squeezed a dollop onto his fingers. While Rafael pulled my hips closer to him, gradually guiding his cock into me with us both on our sides, Niko worked my back entrance over with practiced fingers.

It was easier adapting now that I'd done this a few times before. In less than a minute, I was swaying between the two men, whimpering for more stimulation.

Niko nipped my shoulder and lined up our bodies so he could stay lying on his side as well. Rafael raised my leg higher so my knee came right past his waist, and Niko pressed into me from behind.

My breath caught at the indescribable sensation of total fullness that I'd never get tired of. Rafael bucked into me, and Niko started up a rhythm of his own—a little more careful, but still forceful enough to have me crying out.

The combined thrusts sent my pleasure spiraling even higher. My vision hazed. The sound of my men's ragged panting and the sweat forming between our bodies only turned me on more.

"You feel so good, Lou," Niko murmured. "So right for me. You always do."

"So right for both of us," Rafael grumbled without any rancor.

All I could manage was a needy whine in response. My head tipped back, and my climax tore through me like a lightning bolt.

Niko's chest hitched, and I felt him follow me. With a grunt,

Rafael pounded into me even harder. He cast me up, up, into the stars sparking behind my eyes and then groaned as he came.

We slumped together, our bodies sagging into the bed in the afterglow. I caressed Rafael's chest and rolled to nuzzle Niko's cheek, my heart full of endless affection for both of them.

"There," Niko said cheekily. "I kept up even with the bullet wounds."

Rafael gave a low guffaw. "And I'm sure you'll never let us forget it. You proved yourself well before this, Niko."

I made a light huffing sound. "What either of you deserve is based on a lot more than how good you are in bed."

Niko pecked a kiss to my forehead with a sly smile. "But it doesn't hurt our cases either."

Before we could fall into more playful banter, my phone chimed where I'd left my purse near the closet. My pulse hiccupped.

"That's the tone I programmed in for the Deadly Rose defectors."

Rafael shoved himself upright. "You'd better see what they want. It could be urgent."

As I scrambled off the bed, visions of a squad of gunmen swarming this apartment building swam through my head. I snatched up the phone, tapped on the message to open it up… and simply stared for several beats of my heart.

"Míerda! I can't believe— No. No, I totally can." My teeth set on edge.

Niko lifted his head, concern casting a shadow over his previously cheerful expression. "What's the matter?"

My mouth had gone drier than Death Valley. "None of us checked the news this morning, huh? It turns out someone defaced the arena in Nagano where Worlds is going to be held—just trashed the place."

"What?" Niko's eyes widened. "Who would do that?"

I raised my head with a grim smile, my stomach churning queasily. "Our new friends say they know it was people sent by my mom. A warning, or just a temper tantrum because she knows how important skating is to me. Either way, she's obviously not willing to let this vendetta go."

SEVEN

Niko

LOU STARED AT THE TELEVISION, raking her hands through the loose waves of her hair. The reporter on the news cast was speaking in Japanese, but the footage playing behind him made it clear what he was talking about. Imagery of Nagano's main skating arena, the doors bashed in, the light fixtures smashed and bent, and the walls streaked with crude spraypainted images slid by.

Lou let out a groan, one of many she'd voiced over the last several hours, and not the kind I liked to hear from her. "I can't believe this is happening. Threatening me directly is one thing. Now she's trying to fuck up the entire competition for everyone!"

Jasper came over and tucked his arm around her waist. "It sucks, but you know your mother plays dirty. No matter what she does, it isn't your fault."

Lou threw her hands in the air. "I still have to deal with it. Obviously the March Wind and the Bright Dragon did shit-all to keep her in line."

As if on cue, her phone vibrated where she'd left it on the coffee table after several past calls. I leaned over to check the number and made an apologetic face at her. "That's another one of the TV stations. Looking to get a quote from you, probably."

Lou rubbed her arms and tensed up all over again when a clip from her and Jasper's performance at the US National Championships played across the screen. "Oh, crap. Have they connected the vandalism to me after all?"

I stepped closer to the TV to listen to the commentary. After a few sentences, I shook my head. "No, it's the same as before. They're talking about the shooting incident here in Tokyo as another example of recent crime in the skating world—saying how they haven't seen anything like this before and how it appears figure skaters have become a target for criminal activity for unknown reasons."

"If they figure out it was all the same person behind those crimes —and that she's my mother…"

I came up at Lou's other side and squeezed her shoulder. "There's no way they could find that out. You're not even using your birth name, and your mother doesn't advertise her real business anyway."

My phone chimed in my pocket. It'd been even noisier than Lou's and Jasper's since the story had broken nation-wide.

Quentin raised his eyebrows at me from across the living room. "You're awfully popular too."

I grimaced and ignored the text that'd come in. "I was the main victim in the first attack, and I live here. It makes sense that they're even more eager to talk to me."

But I had nothing useful to tell the reporters. I'd responded to the first several inquiries with brief remarks about how I was saddened by the incident but recovering well from my own assault. Normally I enjoyed talking with the media, but I was getting tired of it. These new texts I could wait to respond to.

Lou sighed and flopped down on the sofa. "I'm going to have to reply to someone eventually, right? What can I possibly tell them?"

Rafael came up to the back of the sofa and rested his broad hands there in a protective pose. "You don't have to talk to anyone you don't want to."

I sat down next to her. "He's right. But it might be good to pick one or two places to give a statement to. Why don't we wait a little longer and then sort through the requests? I'll help you pick the best venues."

Lou's shoulders slumped. "I still don't know what to say."

"You don't have to say very much," I reassured her. "Remember, they don't know that you're personally involved in the new situation. We'll decide together, but you can say something along the lines of how you want to stay focused on your skating and you trust the local police to find the culprits."

"Right." Lou exhaled in a slow stream. "It doesn't need to be anything more than that. I *shouldn't* say anything else. If I get flustered, I might give something away."

Jasper crossed his arms over his chest. "Don't forget that you've got nothing to feel guilty about. You didn't do anything; you didn't know it was going to happen."

I couldn't tell if she'd really relaxed. Seeing her so distressed made my own gut twist into an uncomfortable ball.

Before I could think of anything else to offer, my phone trilled with an incoming call. Restraining a groan of my own, I checked the call display, drew up a chipper attitude, and answered in Japanese. "This is Niko Okabe."

"Mr. Okabe," the reporter on the other end said in our native language. "I'm glad I could reach you. I assume you heard about the incident at the World Championship arena in Nagano earlier today."

"Yes," I said, repeating the words that were rote by now. "I was horrified to see it. Who would have thought skating could draw so much hostility! All we can do is keep training and hope that the beauty of our art softens the hearts of those who want to attack us."

"Well said, sir."

"Thank you. I should get back to my trainees…"

"Yes, yes, of course."

And then yet another exchange was over.

My phone let out another ring before I'd even lowered it, but this one was a different tone. I let out a soft chuckle. "That's Emi. I'll let her know we're all surviving the chaos."

I stepped into my bedroom where it'd be quieter and answered the phone. "Hello, little sister."

"Hello, big brother," Emi shot back in a typical playful tone. Then she got abruptly serious. "I just wanted to make sure you're holding up all right. I can't believe they're dredging up all that stuff that's ancient history."

My stomach sank. "What are you talking about?"

"Oh, no—you haven't seen—never mind—"

I sat down on the edge of the bed. "*What*, Emi?"

She let out a disgruntled sound. "It's on TXN now."

I grabbed the remote and turned on the smaller TV in the bedroom. The second I flipped to the right channel, my skin went cold.

My face filled the screen. A reporter's voice droned on in commentary, with far less emotion than I'd have said the story warranted.

"Though dramatic on the ice, earning gold and silver medals at multiple competitions, Niko Okabe has seen plenty of drama and scandal off the ice as well. One of the best-known incidents of his past involved a former partner of Okabe's, Kenzo Kiyama, whom the skater outed on live television as his boyfriend, followed by a hasty break-up and Kiyama's firing from his prestigious job."

Oh, kuso. Why in the world had they needed to unearth that old drama? Shame flooded my chest, nearly as sharp as it'd dug into me five years ago when my most epic screw-up had just occurred.

"That has nothing to do with the skating arena," I managed to say through my daze.

Emi huffed. "I know! And you were the victim in last week's attack—it's not like you were creating 'drama.' Are they trying to say that you deserved to get shot or something? It's ridiculous. I'm going to call the station and tell them so. But first—do you need anything? You or Lou or the other guys?"

"No," I said quickly. "Don't call—let the subject drop as quickly as possible. And we're all right, just a little frazzled."

"I bet. Try not to let any of it go too much to your head. You made a mistake once—it's not *that* big a deal. And if you do need anything, you know how to reach me."

"I do," I said dryly.

After Emi hung up, I sank back on the bed and stared at the ceiling. Lou's mother had managed to bring not just her past back to haunt her but mine as well. I liked the woman even less than I had before, which was a pretty incredible feat.

My phone rang with another unknown number. I brought it to my ear automatically, preparing my standard reporter response.

"This is Niko Okabe."

"What the fuck is wrong with you, Okabe?" a far-too-familiar voice snapped in caustic Japanese.

My stomach lurched. I jerked upright again, my palm turning clammy against the phone. "Kenzo?"

"Don't talk to me like we're still close. I'm remembering all too well why we're not."

I could easily guess what had gotten my ex-boyfriend so upset. The more unexpected part of this call was that he'd still had my phone number saved someplace. "I have no idea why the news stations are bringing up our history again, Kiyama. If I could do anything about it—"

Kenzo broke in with a scoffing sound. "You'll just fan the flames even more. You can never get enough attention, can you? Five years later, and you have to drag my name onto the TV all over again."

Despite the weight of guilt in my gut, I couldn't help bristling a little at the accusation. "I told you how sorry I was when it happened, and I meant that. I definitely didn't *choose* to get shot or for the media to make a big deal out of the story."

"Sure. I know you, Okabe. You'll have played it up and encouraged them at every turn. Well, now you've gotten what you wanted. I just wanted to remind you that your selfishness affects people other than you. I hope you're happy with yourself."

"Kiyama—"

With a click, he hung up on me.

My voice died. My hand dropped to my lap, clutching the phone, and I simply stared at it for several heartbeats.

My insides felt as though they'd all tangled together. Shame still burned through my belly, but a spark of frustration had lit too.

I was sorry, and I hated that Kenzo was being put through the trauma of my previous actions all over again—and I had also been completely honest when I'd told him that I'd never wanted any of this attention.

His opinion of me had soured so much—and stayed sour even over the years. We'd had a joyful relationship before I'd screwed everything up. That one slip of my tongue had turned all the love we'd shared into total, unrelenting hatred.

As superpowers went, I could do without that one.

I swallowed thickly and tried to convince myself to get up. I couldn't quite find the will to propel myself off the bed.

A knock sounded on the bedroom door, followed by Jasper's voice. "Everything all right in there, Niko?"

I opened my mouth to give another rote answer. *Yes. Of course. I'm fine.*

I wasn't fine, though. And I didn't want to lie to this man. I wanted to be better with both Lou and Jasper than I'd been with anyone before. Be open with him, let him in, make sure we were always on the same page.

How else could I make sure I never made such a huge misstep again?

"Not… not exactly," I admitted.

Jasper nudged open the door. When he caught sight of me, he kicked the door shut behind him and crossed the room in a couple of quick strides to sit down next to me. He leaned his broad shoulder against mine. "What's going on? It looks like there's more bothering you than just pushy reporters."

I pinched the bridge of my nose. "No pushy reporters. Well, none of them who're talking directly to me." I motioned to the TV I'd turned off. "At least one of the news stations has started bringing up other dramatic incidents I've been a part of in the past—particularly, the time when I outed my ex."

"Oh, shit." Jasper slid his arm around me as easily as I'd seen him offer the same affection to Lou earlier. Despite the turmoil inside me, something brighter lit up in my chest, melting a little of the anguish. "I'm sorry. I guess reporters can be sharks all over the world."

I gave a rough laugh. "That's not the worst part. My ex saw and called to yell at me. He figures I encouraged the stories for more media coverage."

"What?" Jasper sputtered. "That's ridiculous. *I* know how awful you feel about that mistake, and I wasn't even there when it happened. How could he think that?"

"I did ruin his life in more than one way." I hung my head. "I can see how that would also have ruined his opinion of me. I tried to tell him that I never wanted it brought up again, but he didn't believe me. And then he hung up. I'm not going to chase after him trying to convince him."

Jasper let out a disgruntled sound and hugged me tighter. "He sounds like an asshole to me. It's one thing to be angry at someone in the moment, but to hold on to that much of a grudge years later—and take it out on the other person who's already shown how sorry they are…"

He scowled, which only made the fondness around my heart swell larger. "He has a right to his anger," I said. "And maybe I deserve to hear it. But it wasn't fun."

"No kidding. There's got to be a limitation on how long you can feel guilty over an honest mistake. He chose to live a double-life, with all the risks that came with it."

I didn't think Jasper fully understood the consequences Kenzo had faced. Both because things were somewhat different in Japan compared to the States, and also, maybe he'd never thought about himself being in the same position.

The moment that possibility occurred to me, I couldn't shake the idea. My mouth went dry, but I forced myself to look over at Jasper.

"Would you be all right if *our* relationship became public knowledge? If a reporter found out and spread it all over the news?"

Jasper paused, but not as if he was bothered by the question, only as if he was thinking it over. He cocked his head. "I guess it might make our situation a little more complicated—raising questions about you as my coach and the fact that we're with Lou as well. But it's not totally unheard of for skaters and their coaches to get involved, and our professional arrangement is a lot more informal than most anyway. I think it'd be fine."

I blinked at him. "And you wouldn't mind people knowing?"

He shrugged and offered me a sheepish smile. "I'm not saying there wouldn't be any awkwardness. It's hard to know for sure when I've never been in that position before. But I don't feel any need to *hide* our relationship. I'm not ashamed of who I'm with—not Lou and not you either. We're really good together. That's something to be proud of."

Gazing back at him, at his beautifully crooked smile and the warmth gleaming in his gray-green eyes, I was lost in a momentary rush of affection. The same poignant emotion that had nearly spilled from my mouth that first afternoon in the hospital—that would have if he hadn't taken off in the middle of our conversation.

But I could say it now. He obviously wasn't going anywhere.

I beamed back at him. "I love you. More and more the longer we're together. I'm so glad that we managed to find our way back into each other's lives."

A blush spread up Jasper's neck to his cheeks. He let out a rough chuckle. "I don't know if it was so much *finding* each other as you tracking me down halfway across the world."

Then his voice softened. He reached over to cup my jaw. "I love you too, Niko. Everything about you. *I* know you're one of the most selfless people I've ever met, putting other people's needs ahead of your own all the time. Cheering them up when they're down, putting in the work so that they can shine. You're something incredible."

With those last words, he guided my mouth to his. I gave myself over to his kiss, reveling in the eager firmness of his mouth, the contrasting gentleness with which his hand stroked down my side to my hip.

As he tipped me over on the bed, his fingers teasing up under my shirt now, the last knot of guilt released.

I'd fucked up in the past—massively. But I knew how to do better now. And I couldn't imagine anything as spectacular as the relationship I'd built with the woman on the other side of that door and the man who was right here with me when I'd needed him most.

EIGHT

Luciana

WHEN I EMERGED from my bedroom the next morning, my head felt stuffed full of wool, and I couldn't work the sour taste from my mouth. I found all four of my men gathered around the dining table, staring at an open laptop. Their gazes jerked to me, and their expressions made my stomach sink.

Bracing myself, I headed over to join them. "What now?"

They exchanged a glance, the skaters' gazes lingering on Rafael. He grimaced but shrugged as if to say there wasn't any point in trying to hide it.

Jasper turned back to me, his mouth tight with an unspoken apology. "The two incidents here in Japan have caught the interest of the international skating community. And they've been searching for new material to report on once they've covered the basics."

I raised my eyebrows. "So…?"

Quentin jerked his hand toward the laptop screen, which I could now see was open to a US news site. "They must have dug into the history of everyone who was at the rink when the shooting happened—which includes you. But all they had was your fake name."

"Right. That was the whole point—so they couldn't dig up anything incriminating." I hesitated. "What's the problem then?"

Niko reached over to give my forearm a gentle squeeze. "They haven't been able to find any information on you at all. No records of any competitions or even training and ice time under the name Luna Garcia before the past several months."

Jasper nodded. "Which means a bunch of reporters are now speculating about how it could be a pseudonym and why you'd have used one. Making up their own crazy stories about what your background might be."

My stomach plummeted. It was hard to imagine random reporters coming up with a past that was *worse* than my actual life, but that didn't mean I wanted them spreading their own stories around. "Shit. That's the last thing I need."

Rafael frowned. "For more reasons than your personal privacy. The Devil's Dozen pendejos didn't like that you were getting any media coverage at all. Reporters speculating about your dark secrets is *really* going to piss them off."

My heart stuttered. "Míerda. I hadn't even thought about that. It's a fucking awful situation all around."

Quentin braced his hands against the table. "I say we tell those assholes off. It's no one's business what Lou's been through."

Jasper rolled his eyes at his former rival. "Right. Because that'll totally get the news vultures to back off and apologize, not make them even more curious to find out what's up with her."

"I'd offer to take them all out for you," Rafael muttered, "but somehow I don't think that'll help put the rumors to rest."

I glowered at him. "I wouldn't want you to anyway." Queasiness wound through my gut, dispelling any interest I might have had in breakfast. "Maybe it was stupid to think I could get away with the fake name forever."

Niko rubbed my arm. "There was nothing wrong with wanting to keep a low profile and have people focus on what you're doing right now."

"That might be true, but trying to hide is what got us into this mess." I sighed and bit my lip. My stomach kept roiling, but from beneath the nausea, an undeniable truth rose up.

"I can't stay out of the spotlight anymore, can I?" I said. "They're going to be after me about my past no matter what I do from now on."

Rafael's muscles flexed as he crossed his arms. "You can ignore them. They can't force you to talk."

"They can't, but keeping quiet might look even more suspicious." I squared my shoulders. "I need to get used to this kind of attention. I wanted to compete on an international level, and this is what comes with the territory. I'm not giving up on skating, so I have to face the rumors head on."

Quentin cocked his head. "Which means doing what?"

I turned to Niko. "You helped me pick a couple of news outlets to give a quick statement to last night. Could you recommend a good show for me to do an interview on? Something that'd get enough coverage to reach everyone who's speculating?"

Niko wet his lips. "I could pick out a good option or two. Ones where they'd have someone with a good grasp of English on staff so it could be direct, too. But are you sure, Angel? You don't *have* to do this."

"No one should make you bow to the pressure," Jasper put in.

"I'm not bowing," I retorted. "I'm making the smartest career decision I can think of."

Rafael hummed to himself. "You voluntarily speaking to the press about your past could make the Devil's Dozen even more angry."

I smiled tightly. "That depends on the story I give them. I think I can spin a good one that gets everyone off my backs."

A glint of approval came into his eyes. "There's nothing wrong with showing the world you mean business."

I tipped my head to Niko. "I'm doing it. Set something up for me, as soon as you can get me in there."

❄

Stage lights glowed from all directions. Sweat had already broken out down my back, even though I was only standing off to the side of the main studio area. I swiped my clammy palms against my trim and professional-looking slacks.

I'd thought gliding onto the ice in front of high-level judges was nerve-wracking, but my skating competitions had nothing on this.

One of the program's staff caught my attention and motioned toward the small cluster of armchairs where the show's interviewer was waiting. That was my cue. I aimed a tight smile at her and strode out into the full glare of those lights on the set.

The interviewer stood by his chair until I'd sat down and beamed at me as he took his own seat. I could tell from the gleam in his eyes that he was hoping to get a juicy story tonight.

"Thank you so much for agreeing to speak with me and our viewers, Miss Garcia," he said, his Japanese accent only a little thicker than Niko's very mild one. "It's an honor to speak with such an impressive skater."

I forced my smile to relax as much as I could manage. "I'm glad to be here. I know there's been a lot of talk about me in the past couple of days, and I'm hoping I can clear things up."

"Of course. Why don't we start with the basics? I'd love to hear how you first became interested in figure skating."

This was comfortable enough territory. My smile softened even more of its own accord. "I fell in love with the beauty of the sport when I saw my first performance when I was five years old. Ever since then, I've spent every moment I can on the ice."

"Clearly all that hard work has paid off. I understand that this was your first year entering the major US competitions, and you and your partner, Jasper St. Pierre, placed first at the National Championships there."

I nodded. "That's right. It's been a thrill, finally getting to see my dreams through."

The interviewer folded his hands together on his lap. "And you're here in Japan now for the World Championships being held next month in Nagano. What are your hopes going into that competition?"

I couldn't restrain a laugh. "Obviously it'd be amazing if Jasper and

I could win a medal there too, especially the gold. But what's most important is giving the best performance we can on the ice—giving it our all, no matter how we end up placing."

"An admirable attitude." The man paused and leaned forward in his chair with a slightly conspiratorial air. "Now, Miss Garcia, I believe the current concern is that you've presented yourself under a false name."

Here we go.

I swallowed thickly, doing my best not to let my expression stiffen. I wanted everyone watching to see a woman who was making the most of the hand she was dealt, who preferred to be honest and trusted her community to accept her.

It was a precarious balance. I needed to sound genuine, but I also couldn't risk getting *too* truthful.

My pulse thudded in my veins. I drew in a breath and inclined my head. "Yes, that's right. I've been using an assumed name. But only for my protection."

The interviewer's eyebrows shot up. "Your protection? What have you needed protection from?"

My fingers twined together where I'd clasped my hands in front of me. I willed them not to clench so tight my knuckles would whiten.

The vague version of my story that I'd rehearsed spilled out of me easier than I'd expected. Like a valve opened to let the toxins flow out.

"It's my mother," I said. "I grew up in an abusive home. She was violent and mixed up with local criminals… I never felt safe there. It's been hard really feeling safe even after I ran off months ago."

The man's lips had parted in shock. Whatever answer he'd thought I might give him, it mustn't have been that.

Then he tutted disapprovingly. "Your own mother. That's very sad."

"Yes. I wish it hadn't been that way, but…" I shrugged in a "what can you do?" gesture. "The only thing I could control was how I handled it. I was scared that if I used my real name in the skating world, she'd realize where I'd gone and track me down. The last thing I wanted was to be found."

The interviewer's eyes widened. "I'm sorry that the recent news coverage may have made you feel as if you had to reveal all this now."

I shook my head. "It was bound to come out now that I'm competing on this level. I realized that I can't keep pursuing my dreams if I'm letting my fear of my mother hold me back. I just hope that whatever fans I have will support me in carving out my own, new life for myself."

"I'm sure they will," he said softly. "You mentioned criminal connections. Do you believe the recent incidents here in Tokyo have had something to do with your mother?"

"I can't say for sure." Which didn't mean I didn't know, only that I wasn't willing to admit it, but most people would assume I meant the former. "If either of them has been, I'm so sorry for any trouble that's been caused because of my family's associations. That's actually—there was a statement I'd like to make, if that's okay."

The interviewer swept his hand toward the main camera. "Go ahead, Miss Garcia."

I lifted my chin and gazed straight at the lens. My pulse kicked up another notch, but I focused on the idea of the people watching, the people I meant to speak to—every person in and involved with the Devil's Dozen, including Mom.

"I have no stake in anything my mother is doing these days," I said, firm and clear but allowing a trace of a quaver to come into my voice. I needed a hint of vulnerability for the benefit of the regular audience I wanted on my side. "I have no interest in any of her activities. All I want to do is skate—that's all I've ever wanted. Everything in my life is focused on my sport now."

I gulped another breath and continued. "So if anyone is trying to target me or other parts of the skating world because of who she is or things she's done, it won't get you what you want. You're coming after the wrong people. Please, whatever you're looking for, leave us out of it. It's got nothing to do with me and my colleagues."

I finished with a bob of my head that I'd learned from watching graceful Japanese interviewees on similar programs. My mouth felt like it was coated in ashes.

Please, let those words be enough. Please, let everyone believe them.

"That was a very impassioned plea, Miss Garcia," the interviewer said. "Thank you again for opening up with us today."

I aimed my smile at him again. "It was my pleasure. I hope it does some good."

When the cameras cut for a break, the interviewer stood again to see me off, with a brief bow of his own. I managed to walk off the set steadily, but my legs felt like jelly.

The same woman who'd motioned me on led me to the room reserved for guests and their entourage. My men hustled over as soon as I stepped inside.

"We saw the whole thing," Jasper said, pointing to the TV mounted on the wall. "You were fantastic."

Quentin had his phone out, his finger swiping across the screen as he scrolled down a webpage. "People are already posting about the interview all over the internet. Lots of sympathetic comments. Seems like you won the regular folk over, at least, Upstart."

A laugh of relief slipped out of me. "Let's just hope it makes the right impact on the less regular viewers I'm hoping will see it."

Niko waved his own phone. "I've already been talking with the Tokyo police force. They're going to assign officers to keep us under protection—for the next couple of days while the story breaks, and possibly longer if it seems necessary."

My next laugh was rougher. "I guess that buys us a little security if the wrong people *do* take it the wrong way."

I'd played the hand I'd been given as well as I could. Would it be enough to get the Devil's Dozen off our backs?

NINE

Luciana

AS WE WALKED through the new arena to the edge of the rink, my skin itched with the impression of stares. This was the place in Tokyo where several of the other World Championship skaters had been training, a more prominent spot we'd felt we needed to accept now that we had so much more media attention aimed at us.

Mostly at me. I sat down on a bench to dig out my skates, trying not to think about the fact that the handful of skaters already on the ice no doubt were aware of all my dirty laundry now. Who knew what they thought of the newcomer who'd admitted to bringing chaos into their midst?

Or about the police escort my confession had earned me. Two officers had followed us in and stationed themselves in the low area of stands to keep watch.

I tightened my laces with hasty tugs. "Did we have to come during a freestyle session?"

Niko grimaced apologetically. "I couldn't get us in for any private slots until next week—and only a couple that week as it is. We'll have to mostly keep training at the other arena. But showing our faces here will mean fewer questions overall."

It made me more visible, but if anyone wanted to attack me, maybe showing up here would make them less inclined to go searching for my other training location. I could hope, at least.

Either way, along with the cops, Rafael was doing his usual patrol around the perimeter, watching for anyone with ill intentions.

As I straightened up, I caught one of the female skaters on the ice giving me a wary glance just before she jerked her gaze away. My stomach sank.

Then a jovial voice rang out, clipped by a British accent. "Hey, St. Pierre! I thought that was you."

A blond guy nearly as burly as Jasper came loping over. He grabbed Jasper's hand and gave it a hearty shake—I guessed they knew each other from past competitions.

"Good to see you, Andrews," Jasper said, shifting his weight awkwardly. "You always know how to find the best places to train, huh?"

"What's the point in skating around the world if you're not doing it in style?" The big man laughed at his own joke and nodded to Niko and me in acknowledgment, his attention lingering on me with obvious curiosity.

To my relief, Niko interrupted any further conversation by waving over an older woman with silvery hair. "Patricia! It's been a long time. Look, I've joined you on the coaching side."

The woman skated over on the other side of the boards with a light chuckle. "I heard. And from what I've seen, you've been doing great things with your first trainees."

Niko beamed. "They've given me excellent skills to work with. I learn as much from them as they do from me."

I swallowed hard, trying to clear the lump from my throat. The other coach didn't comment on the other things his skaters had brought to the table—like gunfire and vandalism—but I could guess what she was thinking.

I'd already felt a little out of place among the experienced competitors before. Now I couldn't help suspecting I stuck out like a sore thumb as someone who didn't belong. My voice stayed locked at the back of my mouth.

Jasper gave me a knowing look and grasped my hand. "We'd better get on with our practicing so we don't put Niko to shame," he said, and tugged me with him onto the ice.

When we found a section where no one was currently skating, I exhaled in a rush and eased closer to Jasper so I could speak under my breath. "I don't think we should try the new part of the routine here. I don't want anyone knowing about it earlier than they have to… and it's not like we have enough room to really stretch ourselves anyway while other people are practicing."

My partner nodded. "We'll have lots of chances to work on it at the other arena without worrying about anyone seeing us take a tumble—or knowing what we're up to. We'll only be here for a couple of hours anyway. Let's warm up and practice that footwork we need to speed up a bit."

We glided around in our normal exercises and then got Niko to put on our music so we could work through the footwork sequence. As I matched the movements of my skates to Jasper's, every beat echoing through the music, my awareness of potential stares faded away.

That didn't mean no one was shooting any more skeptical looks my way. But as I gave myself over to the sport I loved, I found I didn't really give a shit.

I'd already proven that I deserved to be here. Jasper and I had earned our gold medals at the US Nationals. This news story could be only a blip, and then people would be staring at us for much better reasons. The skating was all that mattered, and I still had that.

Jasper and I ran through the footwork until I barely felt my feet touch the ice and the music lived in my veins. Then we ran through several iterations of each of our lifts, every bit of practice helping ensure that we knew exactly how to stick the raised pose and the landing when it was time for the competition.

We were good at what we were doing. I could feel it. But what if it wasn't enough?

By the time the other skaters around us started packing up, the freestyle session almost over, hunger overtook my doubts. My stomach let out a forceful gurgle as Jasper lowered me to the ice, and he paused to catch my eyes, chuckling.

"Should we go get an early lunch? It sounds like you're going to go feral if you don't eat something soon."

I grinned crookedly in return. "I can make no guarantees about my temper when I'm hangry. I saw one of those conveyor-belt sushi places down the street when we arrived—want to check if it's open yet?"

Jasper rubbed his hands together. "Conveyor belt sushi it is." As we skated over to our bench, he cocked his head. "I guess we should pick up some takeout for Quentin too."

The other guy had opted to stay back at the apartment and sleep in, complaining that freestyle sessions weren't worth getting up for when he wasn't even competing.

A softer smile tugged at my lips. "Are you actually starting to get *friendly* with him?"

Jasper elbowed me. "Friendly? Kindly tolerating, maybe." But he was smiling too.

It warmed me inside to see the guys treating each other like family, especially the one guy who'd initially made their welcome particularly difficult. My good mood buoyed me as we filled Niko in on the plan and rounded up Rafael on our way out of the building.

We stepped out into the parking lot, my gaze swept over the city streets around us—and my feet stalled in their tracks.

On the other side of the parking lot, a man was just setting off toward us, his hands deep in the pockets of his wool coat. There was no mistaking the bright red hair sprouting from his jowly face.

It was the March Wind's man.

"Shit," I muttered, my gaze darting from side to side. "What does that prick want now?"

Rafael moved a little in front of me, his hand resting on his concealed weapon. I carried out a brief internal debate and nudged him forward. "Let's go meet him. If this goes south, I'd rather it happened as far from the actual arena as possible."

I'd almost forgotten my new escort. The two cops had emerged from the building behind me. As I started forward, one of them made a brisk remark to Niko.

My coach turned to me. "He wants to know if this man is a threat."

My jaw clenched. The guy undoubtedly was, but not one I wanted the police interfering with if I could help it. That would make things ten times worse.

But that didn't mean I'd definitely be fine.

"Tell him I know him, and I think it should be fine. But they should keep an eye out just in case I'm wrong."

Niko passed on the message, and I hustled over to intercept the March Wind's man with Jasper and Rafael by my side. When I came to a stop by one of the parking lot's lamp posts, a few feet from the representative, I angled myself to the side so the cops would have a view of the unexpected arrival.

The March Wind's rep looked me over with a sneer curling his thick lips. I held my posture stiffly, my heart skipping a beat.

This was way too close to the parts of my life I wanted to keep separate from my past. Why the fuck had he needed to approach me here?

Well, I already knew the answer to that question. This was where he'd known he could find me. Maybe that was a good thing. They were finally figuring out I was actually serious about this skating thing.

"We need to have a little chat," the man spat out, his Australian drawl more pronounced in his apparent irritation.

I crossed my arms and answered his glare with a steely look of my own. "About what? I told you before that I've got nothing to do with any of your boss's business or my mother's."

The rep scowled at me. "The March Wind doesn't appreciate the public comments you've been making. The Devil's Dozen operates behind the scenes only. Any attention brought to it is a betrayal."

I narrowed my eyes even more. "It'd only be a 'betrayal' if I was still one of you. And I didn't say a thing about the Devil's Dozen. Or secret organizations or criminal masterminds. All anyone knows is that my mother is friends with some crooks. Sorry if that's not vague enough for you."

He bared his teeth. "It's not up to me what's good enough. If this is how you're going to handle your problems, we might just have to eliminate you from the picture once and for all."

Rafael let out a low growl. "That sounds like a threat. And I know exactly how to deal with threats to my woman. Are *you* looking to get eliminated?"

The man's stance went rigid, but he stood firm. "I'm just reporting the possible consequences."

Ignoring the clamminess of my skin, I wagged my finger at the guy. "How about the consequences of your boss's actions—or lack of action, more like it? I wouldn't have had to say anything about my mother if he and the rest of the Devil's Dozen had gotten her under control already. *She's* the one making public attacks that are obviously going to prompt the media to comment. I can't get away with saying nothing when she's forced my hand."

The March Wind's man let out a scoffing sound. "The thing is, between you and the Deadly Rose, it's a hell of a lot easier to deal with you."

He raised his hand from his pocket, a glint of dark metal showing, and my breath stopped in my chest. I jerked to the side instinctively—giving the watching cops an even better view of the goon.

Right—I had official backup here too. I tilted my head subtly toward the officers, holding the rep's gaze. "Really? Do you think the March Wind will be happy if you get arrested in broad daylight for pulling a weapon on a woman under police protection? Even if you manage to take me out in time before me and my men make you regret trying, you'll be going down too."

"But you're welcome to try," Jasper snapped, drawing his brawny frame up even taller.

The man's gaze darted from me to my men to the cops beyond us. He sighed sharply and slid his hands all the way back into his pockets. "I delivered the message requested. You'd better remember it. That smart mouth is going to screw you over someday, bitch."

Rafael shifted forward with a menacing loom, but the rep was already striding off toward his car. My shoulders sank as the tension rushed out of me with my next breath.

"Good riddance," I muttered. "What's next?"

Niko gave a laugh from behind us that only sounded a little strained. "I think now that you've dealt with him, next is sushi."

I managed to recover my smile. "Right. Let's get on with Mission: Fill My Stomach."

But despite my casual words, my gut stayed knotted as we headed off toward the restaurant, the cops trailing along behind us.

I was grateful for their presence and how it'd helped diffuse that situation. Things could have gone a hell of a lot worse with that asshole. But the problem he'd presented wasn't exactly finished.

Just how bad could this situation get before we could say goodbye to the Devil's Dozen forever?

TEN

Quentin

I COULDN'T RESTRAIN a low whistle as I followed Lou and Jasper into the fancy-pants new arena where they'd scored a private slot for the first time today. "And I thought the other place was nice. This is a top-level rink."

Jasper shouldered me teasingly. "Hope you're not too intimidated."

I guffawed. "Oh, I'll rise to the challenge, no problem." I cracked my knuckles and put on my best confident face even though my heart wasn't totally in it.

It was important to keep practicing. I wanted to be ready to blow everyone away when the next competition cycle started. But it was hard to throw myself onto the ice with full enthusiasm when I was surrounded by skaters who were getting to show off their skills on a stage I hadn't earned the right to.

Next year. Next year I'd make it to Worlds again. Anyway, I still didn't have total flexibility in my arm after the bullet wound that'd mostly healed. It was better to take things a little easy while I had the chance.

I'd just have to keep reminding myself of that.

The coach and skaters who'd had the slot before ours were just wrapping up on the ice. Lou and Jasper fell into a conversation about their twist lift, but when one of the guys stepped off the ice, Jasper waved to him. "Good practice, Andrews?"

The skater, who I vaguely recognized from the British team, shot him a jaunty grin in return. "Hopefully better than yours will be."

Lou tsked her tongue at him, her eyes gleaming. "Those sound like fighting words."

"It'll be a battle on the ice!" Andrews declared, chucking off his skates. As he wiped the blades, he glanced over at me and offered a more reserved dip of his head. "Wolfe, right? Quentin Wolfe?"

"Yeah," I said, and then just sat there awkwardly. We'd never really talked before—I wasn't sure we'd ever had much chance to. And Jasper had already asked the most obvious small-talk question.

The other guy loped by to the locker rooms before I needed to polish up my conversational skills. I guessed it wasn't really surprising that he hadn't tried to chum up with me. It wasn't as if I'd been particularly friendly with most of my competition over the past several years.

With *any* of my competition, really. Even the guy I knew who was training in Nagano and had helpfully sent me that video of the Russian pair I could only really call an acquaintance. I was pretty sure he was more sucking up to me as a guy he saw as having good connections rather than wanting to show his appreciation for me as a person.

That was fine. There was nothing wrong with being practical—the skating world could be a cutthroat place.

But not as cutthroat as the world Lou had come from. As she and Jasper eased onto the ice, I looked down at the skates I'd only finished loosening the laces on and then across the stands.

Rafael was prowling around somewhere nearby. The current police escort of two cops were stationed in the stands. Neither of those facts stopped a prickle of apprehension from creeping down my back.

My practicing didn't matter that much. If anything interfered with Lou's… I hadn't taken this fucking gunshot for her harpy of a mother to ruin her chances now.

"I'm going to grab a drink from the vending machine," I called to Niko, who was standing near the boards. He gave me a salute, and I used the excuse to justify heading out into the hall for a brief prowl of my own. Call it a very basic warm-up to stretch my legs.

I didn't see anyone lurking in the arena's halls—or walking normally, either, other than when the last slot's skaters pushed out the doors right before I returned to the rink area. Their upbeat chatter trailed after me until the door thumped shut in their wake.

On the ice, Lou and Jasper were running through that twist lift, Lou spiraling in the air over Jasper's arms. I paused for a second, catching my breath at the spectacle.

Her mother was an idiot as well as a harpy. Even a total imbecile should be able to see this woman was meant to skate.

And I should be skating too. Trying to skate off the restlessness that was still gnawing at me, I sat down to pull on my skates, only for my phone to buzz with an insistent vibration.

Maybe it was my not-quite-friend in Nagano with more inside info. I dug the phone out of my pocket and checked the number, but I didn't recognize it. But then, I couldn't remember if I'd bothered to save him in my Contacts.

With Lou and Jasper's music bouncing off the high ceiling, carrying on a conversation in here would be a pain. I jogged back to the doors and slipped out into the hall before answering.

"Hello?"

A sharp, all-too-familiar voice penetrated my eardrum even though it sounded a little tinny with distance. "There you are, Quentin. Don't you dare get off the phone."

My heart lurched. Shit. After all the turmoil it'd taken to finally block Mom's number, it'd never occurred to me to worry that she might borrow a phone or pick up a new one to hassle me from.

I'd never had to worry about that before, but I should have been prepared. No one knew better than I did how relentless my mother could be.

"I'm here," I said tightly. "What do you want?"

"What do I want? How about an explanation for why it looks like I'm blocked from my usual phone? No rings, no text delivered, for *weeks*—this is how you treat your own mother?"

I gritted my teeth, my stomach twisting queasily. But I'd dealt with gangsters pointing guns straight at me—I'd taken a bullet that could have killed me. Mom didn't have anything on the hell I'd faced in the last few months.

"Maybe I blocked you because of the way you're talking to me right now," I retorted. "I'm a grown man—I make my own decisions about my career and everything else in my life now. Including who I want to talk to."

"Oh, and look what happens when you throw away my advice and motivation. You go off the rails with this crazy pairs stunt, disappear, get yourself injured and totally screw up your chances of competing on any level at all. You honestly think—"

I broke in before she could try to tell me how wrong I was. "I'll be competing just fine next cycle. It's only one year. No big deal."

She sputtered a laugh. "The boy I raised would never have given up like that. What the fuck has happened to my tough competitor, huh? You've gone all soft without me to keep you in shape."

"That's not the problem," I snapped. "If anything, you were dragging me down."

"Oh, that's rich. I'm the only reason you got anyplace at all. I kept at you and hauled you to all those practices and competitions, kept on your ass about performing right, and you were really getting somewhere. Now you're going and throwing away everything we built."

Anger seethed inside me, so potent I wouldn't have been surprised to find smoke pouring from my ears like some kiddy cartoon. "Everything *I* built. And the only thing I'm throwing away is you and your shitty attitude."

"Don't be so sure about that. I've got half a mind to fly out there to Tokyo and see if I can't get you back on track. You won't be hiding from me when I'm right there whipping you into shape."

An instinctive flinch ran through my frame, but no real panic followed it. The chances that Mom could pull together the cash for a last-minute flight to Japan were next to none. She was bluffing, stewing in her own venom like she so often did.

"Feel free to test that theory," I said. "I can ignore you just fine no matter where the fuck you are. It'll be easier for you if you take a hint and leave me alone."

I jabbed the End Call button before she had time to reply. With another few swipes and jabs, I'd blocked the new number too.

As I shoved my phone back into my jacket pocket, my stomach sank. *Would* she catch a plane all the way out here, just to complicate my already hectic life even more? It didn't seem possible, but I'd just underestimated her once.

God fucking damn it.

I stood there in the hall for several minutes, breathing deeply as if I could flush my mother's toxic influence from my head alongside the air from my lungs. It didn't totally work, but I started to get worried that the others would wonder what had happened to me.

Putting on my best disaffected expression, I walked back into the rink area and made my way to my equipment bag. When I looked over at the rink, Jasper and Lou were just launching into one of my favorite sequences in the routine—the newest lift that flowed right into a triple Axel throw jump.

Jasper spun Lou around with ease, not showing the slightest strain in the bulging muscles that I had to admit were more impressive than my own, and launched her into the air. She whirled in flight like the angel Niko always said she was and landed with perfect grace.

The talent that emanated off them sent a flutter through my chest —followed by a painful pang. They'd get to show that talent off in front of the whole world next month. And me… I'd be stuck on the sidelines.

What if Mom wasn't totally wrong? How much of what I'd worked so hard for *had* I thrown away to be here with this woman?

The hours upon hours of practice, all of the sacrifices I'd made from every other part of my life—would it turn out to have all been for nothing in the end?

How could I honestly say to anyone that I knew that it wouldn't?

ELEVEN

Luciana

"I CAN'T BELIEVE I'm saying this," Jasper said, around a mouthful of linguine, "but I think Japanese Italian food is better than the regular version."

Niko chuckled triumphantly, the sound pealing through the bright restaurant we'd stopped in for dinner. "I will eventually win you over to all things Japanese."

Jasper arched an eyebrow at our coach and poked toward him with his fork. "Don't say it."

"Even Calpis!" Niko declared.

I snorted with laughter, and even Rafael cracked a smile.

Quentin shook his head, unable to suppress a grin of his own. "You're just never going to give up on that quest, are you?"

Niko dug back into his spaghetti. "It's the most honorable quest there is. But I guess I'll just be pleased that Jasper isn't feeling the need to pour maple syrup all over my country's cuisine."

I muffled another laugh. "This isn't even *your* country's cuisine."

Although I had to admit there was something about the Japanese take on the seafood fettuccine I'd ordered that really hit the spot. For some reason I can't figure out, Italian seemed to be the most popular foreign food offered around Tokyo. Every mall had a floor of restaurants up at the top, and every one of those sort-of food courts included at least one Italian place.

Rafael grunted. "If you can find someplace in this city that makes authentic ropa vieja, then I'll be impressed."

Niko beamed at him. "I'll see what I can do."

I chewed my mouthful of prawn and tomato sauce happily, letting the cozy atmosphere wrap around me. There hadn't been many moments in the past few weeks when we'd been able to simply relax and enjoy ourselves. It was nice to forget all our troubles for an hour or two.

Of course, Rafael never stopped his periodic scans of the restaurant. We'd shed our police protective detail the last time we'd been at the big arena—I didn't want the cops knowing where we were living or our non-professional activities, and Niko had managed to convince them to stick to guarding me at that rink. For all I knew, Mom or one of her Devil's Dozen allies had hacked into the Tokyo Police computer system and would find out anything they committed to record.

Those crime bosses could insert themselves into almost any organization. I wouldn't be surprised if at least a couple of the officers themselves were on one or another Devil's Dozen member's payroll. The criminal element in Tokyo would be under someone's domain, and they'd need ways of keeping the cops out of their business.

Quentin gulped down his last bite of chicken and cocked his head. "I could see spending more time here. If the rest of you were sticking around to keep some distance from the States."

Niko's eyes gleamed. "I'll have to get going with teaching you all how to speak the language."

Rafael guffawed. "Good luck with Lou. From what I heard, it was like pulling teeth getting her to even learn Spanish, and that's her family's heritage."

I wrinkled my nose at him. "My great-grandparents' heritage. Even Mom had to learn from tutors."

His voice fell into that teasing tone that never failed to get me all kinds of heated up. "I still think you could have a little more cultural appreciation."

I opened my mouth to give him a smart-ass reply, but a sharp trill from my phone cut me off. It was the ringtone I'd assigned to the trio of Deadly Rose lackeys who'd gone rogue.

The delicious flavors in my mouth turned to ash. I fished the phone out of my purse and yanked it to my ear. "Hello?"

Dámaso's thick voice carried through the line. "Luciana? Are you at the Sky Castle Mall?"

A chill washed over my skin. "How do you know that?" I hadn't talked to the defectors all day.

He swore under his breath. "We got a tip from one of our friends who's still working under Mireya—he's not ready to jump ship to your side yet, but he's hedging his bets. It sounds like someone working for your mom spotted you going into the mall, and she's sent a bunch of her people over to ambush you."

"Fuck." I pushed to my feet, my dinner forgotten.

"Yeah, exactly. Get out of there if you can. We're on our way over to see if we can help."

With that, he hung up.

My head spun for a second, but I squared my shoulders and willed down the worst of my panic. My men were all staring at me, Rafael braced like he could already guess what I was going to say. Which knowing him, maybe he could.

"My mom's people are heading to the mall to attack us," I said, snatching up my wallet to toss a handful of yen onto the table that should more than cover our meal. "We've got to leave—*now.*"

I didn't need to say anything else. The guys surged into motion like one being, as coordinated as any skating routine the three of them might have performed. They leapt up, and we hustled across the tiled floor to the glass doors, tugging on our jackets as we went.

I made a beeline for the elevator, my heart thudding. If the defectors had warned us in time, maybe we could make our escape before Mom's allies even got here.

Otherwise… things were about to get really messy.

The elevator car seemed to take years to arrive. We bolted inside, Rafael jabbing the button for the main floor. As the car whirred downward, he retrieved one of his pistols from its concealed holster and tucked it into his jacket pocket where he could keep it in his hand.

With a chime, the door opened. We hustled through the wide hallway past the main-level stores, most of which had already closed for the night. The darkened displays gave the mall an eerie quality, but I had to be grateful for the lack of bystanders.

The broad front entrance came into view up ahead. I picked up my pace, my spirits rising but my hand dipping into my purse for my own small pistol, just in case. "Looks like we made it in—"

The words died on my tongue as about a dozen men shoved past the doors and marched into the building. In my first glance, I registered that a few looked like locals, but the rest were a mix of ethnicities. Maybe the criminal organizations here had gotten more diverse, or maybe Mom had sent over a bunch of thugs from her other territories.

It didn't really matter. Either way, these goons wanted us dead. The second they set eyes on us, all of them whipped out guns.

"Take cover!" I cried out, and threw myself behind the shelter of a vacant information booth.

The guys hurtled after me, Rafael firing off a few shots as he sprang. A grunt and a thump told me at least one of his bullets had hit its mark.

Other bullets thundered in our direction, slamming into nearby pillars and shattering display windows. I winced and peeked around the booth, my pistol ready.

The thugs were advancing on us. I wasn't okay with that.

I took a couple of shots, nicking one guy in the shoulder and sending another toppling to the ground, clutching his belly. Our other attackers jerked to the side of the hall where they could use the pillars as shields.

Quentin swore and pivoted on his feet, his own gun clutched uneasily in his hand. "Is there another exit we can make a run for?"

I followed his gaze and grimaced. "Not without giving those assholes a clear shot at us." The booth would only hide us from view until we got a little ways away, and then we'd have a sprint of at least a hundred feet before the nearest side hall.

"Then we'll just have to go through the pricks," Rafael muttered, and eased to the side to take aim at our attackers.

I followed his lead, but my next two shots only clipped the pillars. The gunmen launched another spray of gunfire our way, and I ducked back into safety.

"They won't just hang out there forever," I said through my constricted throat. "When they try to get closer, we'll have a chance to pick them off."

Rafael nodded, but his expression was grim. We'd have to take down an awful lot of them. And out of the five of us, he was the only one completely confident with his weapon. I knew how to handle mine from lots of practice, but it'd mostly been against unmoving targets.

Our lives were on the line. If the thugs closed in on us, we'd just have to do our best to mow them all down.

Niko wet his lips, his knuckles pale where he was gripping his pistol. He raised his phone to his ear with his other hand. "I'll call emergency services. If we can hold the stand-off for long enough, the police will deal with them."

My pulse stuttered. We didn't know how many of the cops we could trust—and I hated the thought of having yet another violent incident associated with me.

"Make it an anonymous call," I pleaded. "They don't need to know it's *us* getting attacked."

His mouth tightened, but he nodded.

As he spoke into the phone in soft Japanese, I peeked around the booth again. None of our attackers offered a clear shot. Shit, shit, shit.

Then three more figures burst through the front doors behind Mom's goons. My jaw dropped as I took in the three Deadly Rose defectors, all of them whipping up semi-automatics.

Dámaso's eyes glittered with a fierce gleam as he opened fire on the thugs, the mall lights gleaming off the lightning bolt shaved into his dark buzzcut. Frankie cackled and swung his scrawny frame around, pelting out more bullets. And as she squeezed her trigger, Ursula's straggly, bleached hair flew out behind her like she'd leapt into this reality from an action movie.

It only took an instant for our attackers to realize they were now under assault from both sides. Even as a few bodies crumpled, streaking the floor with blood, some of the other men spun, firing their weapons in turn.

The defectors hadn't given any thought to shelter. One of the first bullets tore across Ursula's elbow, making her arm jerk and the gun fall from her hand. Another slammed into Dámaso's chest, sending him reeling backward.

"No!" The cry tore from my throat, and I launched myself from behind the booth. As my finger squeezed the trigger over and over, my men followed me, adding their own bullets to the fray.

The arrival of the defectors had driven our enemies from cover. In a matter of seconds, with the sound of the shots booming off the high ceiling, the rest of Mom's men slumped to join their colleagues on the floor. My mouth tasted sour with adrenaline and revulsion; I couldn't tell how many were outright dead, or how many of the bullets that'd landed had been mine or Rafael's or even from the skaters.

There wasn't time to worry about that. I dashed towards the trio of defectors, shoving my gun back into my swinging purse. Ursula and Frankie had drawn close around Dámaso, Frankie pressing his hand to the wound on his friend's chest and Ursula clutching her bleeding elbow while she spat out hasty orders.

"Let's go!" Rafael bellowed, catching up with me as we reached them. "We'll get him bandaged up once we're out of here. If the cops catch us, we're all in deep shit."

Sirens were just starting to peal into hearing beyond the doors. We dashed through the entrance and across the courtyard outside, Rafael supporting some of Dámaso's weight.

We'd come by the subway, but racing down there amid all the regular civilians didn't strike me as a wise idea. Rafael appeared to feel the same way, leading us past darkened office buildings into a narrow driveway well out of view of the mall.

There, he paused for a second to whip off his jacket and tear off a strip of fabric to use as a bandage. I pawed through my purse. "I've got a roll of gauze and some pads."

As the other guys and I took over bandaging up Dámaso and Ursula as well as we could, Rafael took out his phone. "I think one of the contacts I've made here can get us medical care without drawing any attention. And hopefully a vehicle too—fast."

Dámaso forced his voice through clenched teeth. "I can keep walking—put more distance between us and the cops."

Ursula hissed a breath through her teeth. "Mireya's going to know we had something to do with getting you out. We should probably switch to a new building just in case she's already been tracking us down."

Looking at the two of them bleeding on my behalf, a lump rose in my throat. Rafael had said I'd know when I could trust the turncoats because they'd do something to prove themselves. If this wasn't that moment, then what else could they possibly do?

The words tumbled out before I could second-guess them. "You should come back to our building. We'll make sure you're all patched up and okay, and then we'll figure out a safe place for you to stay nearby. From here on, I think we should all stick closer together."

TWELVE

Luciana

TEN MORE PRACTICES, and we still didn't have the new transition down.

I spiraled and straightened up, collided with Jasper's arms and let him launch me into the air, but I could feel before I was even halfway up that both our positions were off. In our haste, he hadn't gotten totally centered behind me; I hadn't tilted my body at quite the right angle to achieve the height of the lift.

I swayed and Jasper's elbow wobbled, and he jerked me back down toward the ice before it turned into a total collapse.

"Shit," I spat out, swiping my damp bangs from my forehead. I'd stripped my long-sleeved thermal off an hour ago, but even my cotton band tee was clinging to my sweaty skin. The tremor that ran through my legs as I fought to steady my breath told me I wasn't up to a whole lot more practicing today.

Niko skated over, not a hint of disappointment in his sunny smile. "That was so close! Every time we come here, you get better."

Jasper sighed, rubbing his arms, which had to be at least as sore as, well, pretty much every muscle in my body at this point. "Close isn't going to get us any golds—or even bronze. At this rate, even if we do master it, we'll barely have any time to get comfortable with the full routine before we have to compete with it."

Even though similar depressing thoughts had been passing through my head, my stomach listed uneasily. "What are you saying?"

My partner grimaced but didn't hesitate. "I wanted this to work, but it's fucking *hard*, and you're already under so much stress. Do you really want to keep at this? The old routine got us this far. We could trust that it's solid enough as it is."

I swallowed thickly. "But we know it won't give us enough points to beat at least one pair if they don't screw up. For all we know, there are other teams with higher difficulty levels too."

"It's unlikely that many do," Niko put in. "Your current routine is already close to the maximum anyone would be capable of. And the more difficult moves anyone else is attempting, the higher the chances that they *will* screw up."

Jasper sighed. "Just like we're making it more likely that we will too."

He was right. I knew that. But a pang of resistance shot through my gut even considering giving up.

"If we go back to the regular routine, then we're already good with the whole thing," I said. "We don't need a ton of time to work on it. So let's keep trying the death spiral to lift transition for a few more practices and then make a final decision."

Jasper offered me a tight smile, sympathy shining in his gray-green eyes. "That sounds like a reasonable compromise. You never like to back down from a challenge, do you, Punk?"

There was nothing but affection in his words—and in his embrace when he tugged me to his broad chest. Niko eased closer to brush a kiss to the top of my head, and just for a moment, their love washed away all the frustration I was feeling.

"If anyone can do it, it's the two of you," Niko said with total confidence.

Jasper nodded and lowered his head to plant a kiss of his own on my lips. As he drew back, his smile softened. "I know that's true. No one should get between Lou and her dream."

I exhaled in a rush and flexed my arms in front of me. "I think *I'm* getting between myself and my dream today. I'm not sure I can skate another inch."

Niko clapped his hands. "Come do some stretches to make sure those muscles stay limber."

I glanced over to where Quentin was just coming out of a jump at the other end of the rink and then let my gaze slide across the stands of the private arena where we'd been spending most of our practices thanks to Emi's connections. A little more of the tension in my chest unraveled when I took in the empty benches. "I've got to say, it is nice to have the sessions here without reporters watching our every move."

As soon as they'd gotten wind about my new sessions at the bigger arena, news crews had started hanging around in the parking lot hoping to get a quote, occasionally even barging right into the rink area.

"I'll second that sentiment," Quentin called out as he glided past. "No news is good news."

In more ways than one. Obviously reports on the shootout at the mall had been splashed across every news source, but so far no one had connected what Niko said the Japanese media was calling "an organized crime incident" to me. No one had even known I'd been in the building… other than my mom, who obviously wasn't giving interviews.

Several outlets had still tried to connect the violence to the recent incidents in the figure skating world, though. A couple of reporters at the other arena yesterday had shoved microphones toward my face and asked with the aid of translators whether I had any thoughts on the new bout of violence in the city.

Wouldn't it be sweet if someday I really could skate without anyone focusing on the shitty parts of my past life? Hopefully that wasn't too grand a dream.

I shed those worries as well as I could while I stretched out my limbs. Quentin joined us for the last several minutes, and then Rafael fell into step with us as we headed out to the car. There was something comforting about having all four of my men around me, knowing I had every bit of their support, even if the rest of the world looked at me with skeptical eyes.

When we reached our building, I spotted Ursula casually standing guard on the sidewalk outside. She had her hood pulled low and a scarf tucked over her mouth to make her difficult to identify, but I'd expected to see one of the turncoats out here.

She dipped her head to me in a subtle nod as we drove by into the underground lot. Her coat hid all sign of the bandage on her arm.

We'd managed to score the three Deadly Rose defectors a small apartment on a lower floor of the building, a furnished space normally used by short-term business visitors. Which I guessed they technically were.

Rafael had managed to get a doctor to Dámaso before he'd lost a dangerous amount of blood, and the bullet hadn't punctured anything vital, so at least he was getting to recover in relative comfort. When I'd stopped by to check on them this morning, he'd been walking around the apartment, if with occasional winces. When I'd thanked him for helping save our lives, he'd only chuckled and waved me off.

"I don't know what *we'd* do if we were stuck with just Mireya to answer to. It was for my benefit as much as yours."

I wasn't going to complain about that attitude as long as it worked in my favor.

We were just stepping into the plain but cozy living room of our own apartment when my burner phone pinged with an incoming text. My pulse skipped a beat.

There were only two people other than the guys with me who had this number. Neither of those two would be reaching out unless it was important.

My men all turned to study me as I pulled out the phone, their expressions darkening. We hadn't gotten a whole lot of good news by phone recently.

A text had popped up on the screen. My gaze skimmed over it. "It's Beckett—the Storm. He's asking to video-chat."

Quentin hustled over to the laptop we'd left on the kitchen

counter after Jasper had been consulting it for recipes. "I can set that up. On the coffee table so we can all join in?"

From the other guys' stances, they definitely wanted to be included in the conversation. I nodded and hurried over to the sofa.

I ended up sitting in the middle with Rafael at my left, Niko at my right, and Jasper and Quentin perched on the sofa's arms. With a couple of quick texts, I passed on the necessary info to Beckett. Seconds later, an alert appeared on the laptop's screen.

When I tapped to answer the incoming request, a window expanded to show Beckett's boyishly handsome face, his ash-blond hair slicked back from his face like usual and a wry smile curving his lips. The guy didn't look old enough or harsh enough to have a place at the Devil's Dozen's table alongside people like my mother, but so far he'd seemed capable of holding his own.

"Hey, Lou," he said in a typically smooth tone. "How are you hanging in there?"

I nearly choked on my laugh. "I've been better. What's up?"

"I thought you'd want to know about some recent developments that affect you… Good ones, I think."

Most of my panic dissipated. "I'm all ears."

His smile turned a bit crooked. "You know the Blood Hunter and I appreciated that you exposed your mother's treachery rather than holding on to it for longer as leverage. You saved us a lot of time, money, and unnecessary bloodshed, and we don't like what we've been hearing about how the Deadly Rose has repaid you for that favor."

I made a face. "Yeah. My mom definitely didn't see it in a positive light. But it was the best move I felt I could make for myself too."

"Still, we were hoping we could balance things out and see that you get the recognition you deserve. Or at least the peace. The two of us and a couple of other members of the Devil's Dozen who your mother was gunning for have been pushing hard on the rest of the group to enforce sanctions against the Deadly Rose. Including penalties if she continues attacking you, since you acted in the best interests of the entire organization."

My heart leapt in eager surprise. "Seriously? Is there any chance the other members will listen?"

Beckett's smile stretched into a full-out grin. "Based on this morning's conversation with the full Devil's Dozen, opinion has swayed in our favor. We've gotten a few more members speaking up in favor of our motion, which gives us a majority. Your mother finally agreed to a ceasefire while we sort out appropriate restitutions and so on."

Quentin let out an approving whistle, and Jasper squeezed my hand.

My jaw had gone slack. "She's said she'll back off—completely."

"In theory." Beckett's eyebrows twitched upward. "Whether she'll stick to it remains to be seen. But if you have any more trouble in Japan that you think she's responsible for, let me know, and the Blood Hunter and I can send people over to assist. Now that we have an official agreement within the organization, we can act against her without it being a betrayal."

A startled laugh rushed out of me. "That's amazing. Thank you so much. I've been doing everything I can to keep her at bay, but obviously I don't have a whole lot of resources on that side of things."

Before I could gush any more gratitude, Rafael leaned forward to draw Beckett's attention. "Hold on a second. What about the rest of the Devil's Dozen? We've gotten threats from representatives of the Bright Dragon and the March Wind."

"They've mentioned their concerns about Lou's presence in Tokyo," Beckett said. "But the Deadly Rose ended up confirming that you really are there simply to skate, and they've said they'll withdraw any hostilities. Although again, if they go back on their word, the Blood Hunter and I will back you up against them too."

He spoke with total confidence, the assured air that made it easier to believe he was one of the most powerful criminals on the planet, but Rafael didn't look the slightest bit intimidated, let alone cowed. "What good is your help going to do us if you're on the other side of the world? If more goons start shooting at us, we're going to need backup immediately."

My bodyguard kept his voice firm too, without straying into outright aggressive. I couldn't help admiring his cool-headed response.

Beckett definitely didn't look offended. If anything, he was a bit chagrinned. "That's a fair point. I can arrange for some forces to be immediately on hand on neutral ground near Tokyo, and I'll send their contact information along as soon as they're in place."

"That would be a huge help," I said. "Maybe you could make sure my mom finds out that you're prepared to intervene directly, to encourage her to keep her end of the deal?"

Beckett chuckled. "I can definitely pass word along through appropriate channels."

"All right. Thank you again. If this works out, it's a huge weight off my shoulders."

"That's what I'm hoping for too. Thank *you*, Lou."

As I ended the video call, Rafael rubbed his hands together. "He thinks a lot of himself, but I get the impression he can back that confidence up. And that he means what he said. Not a bad ally to have."

I elbowed him. "Thanks for your vote of approval." I paused. "But really, it was good that you stepped in there. I was kind of overwhelmed by the news—I didn't even think it all through."

A ghost of a smile brushed across Rafael's lips. "I don't mind helping where I can."

I kicked out my feet, thinking the moment called for some kind of celebration, but before I could even get up, my other phone blared its ringtone. A groan spilled from my lips as I reached for it, followed by another when I saw the caller ID. "It's another news station. Probably another reporter digging for info."

Niko glanced over my shoulder and clicked his tongue. "You should probably talk to them. They're with one of the biggest stations. Put it on speaker, and we'll handle them together."

Restraining a sigh, I slid my thumb to the answer button. I'd just have to do what I had to do to get through all this drama.

No matter how people like Beckett stepped in, even if the commotion around the violence faded without further incidents… would I ever really be able to put my past completely behind me?

If I was going to stop this new life I'd built from crumbling, I couldn't hide in the shadows anymore, no matter how much I wanted to.

THIRTEEN

Jasper

HOLDING MY BREATH, I eased the fabric shears through the shimmering ice-blue cloth I'd spread across the dining table. It wasn't an ideal workspace, but it was the largest flat surface we had in the cozy but sometimes cramped apartment, though Niko assured us this place was spacious by Tokyo standards.

The cloth hissed as it parted in the wake of the blades. I didn't exhale until I'd reached the end of the line in the pattern I'd pinned to it.

I didn't know if we were going to pull off that new transition to elevate our routine, but I was going to make sure our updated costumes took even more breaths away. That much I could guarantee.

Lou was going to look like starlight shimmering off a swath of frost. I could picture it perfectly in my head. Now I just had to stitch it all together.

Niko clicked his tongue against the roof of his mouth as he ambled over. "The fabric looks amazing."

I grimaced. "It's also a pain in the ass to work with. But it'll be worth it when I'm done."

He laughed lightly and leaned over to press a quick kiss to the top of my head, his slender fingers brushing over my neck in a caress. "I have no doubt about that. I'll leave you to it. Rafael wants to arrange a little more firepower for our new allies, and I think it'll go over better if he's got someone who can speak the local language along."

The bigger guy let out a huff from where he'd gone to the door to grab his jacket. "I'd let you go on your own if I trusted you to get a good deal for us. I don't like leaving Lou by herself."

Quentin aimed a narrow glance over the top of the sofa. "By herself? Hello, I'm right here."

"And so am I," I said, throwing a look of my own over my shoulder. "And aren't the Deadly Rose defectors taking turns guarding the front of the building and the hall outside our apartment?"

Lou raised her head from where she'd been stretched out on the floor, running through a workout routine. "They are. Not to mention that *I* can protect myself just fine all on my own even if I was by myself. Go do your negotiating. What did you train these guys in weapons for if you aren't going to trust them to use them when they need to?"

Rafael glowered at her before letting his gaze sweep across the apartment in one more wary evaluation. "We'll be back as soon as we can. Call me if you need anything—*anything*."

"Of course."

Rafael hesitated for just a second longer and then strode out into the hall. I caught Niko's friendly chatter starting up just before the door thumped shut, and my mouth twitched with a smirk.

I trusted Rafael to keep my boyfriend safe, but I wasn't sure how well the bodyguard would survive Niko's irrepressible good cheer.

Lou got up, shaking out her limbs, and let out a satisfied sigh. "I think I'm about ready for a nice, hot shower."

Quentin hooked his arm over the top of the sofa and raised his eyebrows at me. "I don't know about you, but I think that sounded like an invitation. We could heat things up plenty."

He grinned, his eyes gleaming slyly, and I found myself momentarily lost for words.

Part of me balked instinctively at the idea of going to Lou with this guy by my side. He'd been a *thorn* in that side for so long.

But he wasn't anymore. He'd shown how much Lou meant to him over and over. He followed her halfway around the world just to look out for her, for fuck's sake.

And there was no missing the fact that he was making the comment as a peace offering of sorts. He could have followed her without saying a word to me and made it a private interlude, just the two of them. Instead, he was holding out his hand and inviting me to come along. Showing that he was both willing to share and willing to see me as an equal partner in the relationship.

I rolled the idea over in my head, my initial reluctance gradually fading. I'd gotten it on with Lou while Niko and Rafael were involved before. Why not Quentin? It wasn't as if I still felt any animosity toward him anyway.

Hell, there were brief instants now and then when I almost liked having the guy around.

I folded the draped cloth over the table and stood up, meeting Lou's gaze where she was waiting for my reaction. "I wouldn't mind offering a little… assistance."

Lou shook her head in amusement. "Well, come on then. If you're going to make yourselves useful, you'd better get on with it."

We'd given her the one bedroom that had an en-suite bathroom attached, us guys sharing the one off the hall—other than at times like this. Lou sauntered into her room with a sway of her hips I couldn't help tracking with my gaze, and Quentin and I trailed right behind her.

She stripped as she rounded her bed and made her way into the bathroom, tossing her shirt and bra aside and then wriggling out of her leggings without a hint of self-consciousness. Quentin followed her lead and tugged his own shirt off. I yanked at mine, not wanting to be left out.

By the time I'd chucked off my boxers, Lou had the water running, steam already billowing into the air. She glanced back at us, her gaze sliding over both of us with an appreciative gleam, but when her attention fell to her own body, her smile slanted on one side.

"That new transition has really been giving me a beating," she said, grazing her fingers over the purple-and-brown blotches that dappled the tan planes of her arms and legs. "I'm more bruise than regular skin."

When I caught the hint of uncertainty in her tone, the last of my self-consciousness fled. I stepped right up to her and skimmed my fingers down her sides, careful of the bruises that spread up over her hips.

"I think they're gorgeous," I told her honestly. "They're a beautiful map of the art you're working on creating."

Quentin let out a low laugh and approached Lou from behind. He set his hands on her waist just above where mine had stilled. "And they make you look like a total badass. Of course St. Pierre would leave out that part."

The trace of doubt had been slight—maybe she hadn't been insecure at all—but I saw her light up at the compliments regardless. With a mischievous smile, she grasped our hands and yanked us with her under the spray.

I had to say that despite the tight quarters, the Tokyo apartment made for easier shower-sharing than the locker room back at our old arena in Boston. Instead of a single stall, the movable shower head pointed its deluge over the entire—if smallish—bathtub. Which meant there was plenty of room for me to start soaping up Lou's shoulders and chest while Quentin got to work on her back.

As I cupped my hands around her breasts, she hummed happily, swaying between us. She trailed her hands down my chest, and my cock sprang to immediate attention.

I couldn't resist leaning in to kiss her. Her lips melded with mine, damp and warm from the water.

I wanted to sink right into her, but Lou had other ideas. She tilted her head to nip my earlobe, and shivered as Quentin nibbled a path along her shoulder. Apparently he'd found just the right spot to spark her desire.

Carried by a competitive impulse, I massaged her breasts and stroked my thumbs over the soap-slick nipples. Lou arched toward me with a needy sound, and I claimed her mouth again with a sense of victory.

Quentin tsked his tongue behind her. "I'm going to need some of that sweetness too, Upstart." He grasped her thighs and tugged her back against him. From the pleased hitch of Lou's breath, he was hard enough to get her juices flowing too.

As she turned to face him so she could offer him a kiss, something twisted in my chest. But Quentin only let the embrace linger for a few seconds before cutting his gaze to me over Lou's shoulder.

"I've only got two hands here. I hope you're keeping yours busy—this woman deserves everything we can give her."

Not a competition—a collaboration. As I watched him tangle his fingers in Lou's hair with a brief jerk that brought an eager gasp to her throat, the twisted sensation smoothed itself out.

He had his own ways of pleasing her, of turning her on. Just like I did.

When we both worked together toward that end, it could only make a more spectacular experience for her, right? No one trying to do better than the other, but the two of us making the best possible moment we could for the woman we loved.

I palmed her breasts from behind and then slid one hand down Lou's belly to her pussy. When my fingers teased over her mound, she growled impatiently and ground her ass against my rigid cock. My breath caught—and then stopped completely when she reached behind her to grasp my erection.

I muffled my groan by pressing my mouth against her shoulder just above the feathers of her angel wings tattoo. Lou smirked as she stroked me up and down and then moaned when I delved one finger right inside her. With a chuckle, Quentin captured her mouth again, winding his hand tighter into her hair and fondling her breast with the other.

He let out a hiss, and I realized Lou was working over his dick now too. His voice came out low and rough. "Fuck, you know how to pump me just right. Keep that up, and I'm going to explode."

Dirty talk had never been a particular talent of mine, but Lou appeared to enjoy it. She licked her lips. "That's the idea."

Her grip on my cock tightened, and I couldn't hold back my next groan. "God, I want to be inside you."

"You are." Her hips rocked with the motions of my fingers where a second had joined the first inside her. Her cunt was so hot and drenched with arousal beyond anything I could blame on the shower. The feel of her made my dick throb.

Quentin ducked his head to suck one of her nipples into his mouth, and Lou released a full-throated moan that practically had me coming in her hand. I clenched my jaw, struggling for control, and rubbed the heel of my hand against her clit in time with the pulsing of my fingers.

Lou writhed between us, her breath breaking into panting. "Fuck. *Fuck.* Enough playing around. I need you—both of you—on the bed. Now."

Neither of us was going to wait for a second invitation. I slammed the shower faucet off, and the three of us stumbled out of the bathroom in a tangle of limbs.

Our feet tracked wet footsteps across the floor, but I don't think any of us gave a damn. We tumbled onto the bed like one being, Lou grasping my cock again, my fingers teasing between her ass now, Quentin dipping lower to flick his tongue over her clit.

Lou gasped and bucked to meet him. I grazed my teeth along the crook of her neck, and she rolled toward me to yank my mouth to hers. The sheets bunched beneath us, already damp from our untoweled bodies.

We grappled with each other and our shared desire. Lou shifted position between us again and again, and all we could do was follow her lead. I dove in to suckle her breast and then to nip my way down her spine when she rolled toward Quentin again.

For a brief moment, Lou jerked away from us to fumble in her bedside drawer. She tossed a condom packet toward me and then lowered her head over Quentin's jutting cock where she'd gotten him sprawled beneath her.

My fingers closed around the packet, but my gaze stayed on them.

I was getting a front-row seat to my woman delivering an obviously epic blowjob to the one guy I'd have expected to be most infuriated by.

Quentin's head sagged back against the pillows, his wet hair fanning around his head. A flush had reddened his normally pale cheeks.

"You know just how I like it," he muttered. "Take it all, Lou, like only you can."

Should I have been horrified by the sight? Somehow after the intimacy we'd already gotten wrapped up in, not the slightest quaver of discomfort traveled through my nerves. The scene before me simply looked *right*.

Especially when Quentin opened his eyes a slit and aimed a pointed look at me. "Are you going to get on with getting her all the way off, or what?"

I could only grin at the playful challenge in his voice. "Hell yes, I am."

I'd never rolled on a condom faster. I lined myself up and plunged straight into my lover's slick pussy in one smooth thrust.

Lou cried out against Quentin's dick, the sound electrifying me. It thinned out into a low moan as I began to thrust. She was so wet, so tight as her inner muscles clenched around me—my mind blanked out, and my primal instincts took over.

I gave her my all, just as I would on the ice. My muscles drove my cock into her with every bit of their coiled strength, and the avid noises escaping her throat only urged me onward. I pounded into her, deeper with each stroke.

Quentin was swaying up to meet her mouth with his own rhythm. His eyes had rolled back.

He was close. I was right on the edge, careening closer with every second her pussy squeezed my dick. But we couldn't come without her joining us.

I slipped my hand beneath Lou to rub her clit. The sounds leaking from her mouth turned more urgent, and her pussy clamped tighter around me. Then she shuddered with the first ripples of her release.

The sensation propelled me with her. I came hard, my balls

tingling, my vision whiting out with brilliant spots. The crash of ecstasy swept through me and left my breath ragged.

Quentin groaned as he joined us. Lou sucked his release down even through her own orgasm, moaning in approval.

I collapsed onto the soaked sheets next to her, glancing from her to Quentin and back again. "I think we might need another shower now."

All three of us burst into delighted, sated laughter. And just like that, it seemed ridiculous that I'd ever hesitated to join Quentin in this incredible encounter.

FOURTEEN

Luciana

SOMETHING about the morning light in Tokyo just hit a little differently. I sprawled under the covers, my eyelids at half-mast, watching the tiny dust particles float through the hazy glow of the rising sun like pixie dust.

It was nice to take a few moments to chill out amid the craziness of my life. For once, I could wake up slowly, and—

Just as I sat up with a luxurious stretch, my phone chimed with an incoming text. My regular phone, not the burner that Beckett or the Blood Hunter would have reached out to. And it was the tone I'd assigned to unknown numbers, my established contacts getting a different one, so it couldn't be any of my guys or the Deadly Rose defectors either.

My pulse hiccupped before I reached for the device I'd left charging on the bedside table. Probably it was Mom trying to reach out again. She'd tried a few different numbers after I'd blocked the ones I already knew, and I deleted every enraged and unhelpful message without engaging.

As my fingers closed around the phone, I thought about calling Rafael in to check the message and delete it for me. Seeing her words wouldn't stress him out the way it did for me. But my gaze had already grazed the screen, and I paused.

No, I didn't think this was from Mom at all. The message was short enough for the whole thing to show on the screen: *Am I talking to Luciana Cordova?*

I stared at the text for a few halting breaths, debating my next move. Who the hell *was* it? Who would know my name and have my number, but not be sure it was mine?

Maybe it *was* Mom, and this was some weird trick?

I wavered in indecision for a minute longer before kicking off the sheets and pulling a hoodie on over my pajama set for warmth. "Rafael?" I called through the door. "You there?"

He answered in an instant, sounding as if he'd bolted to my room as soon as I'd asked. "Of course, Lou. What's up?"

"I need your help with something."

He eased open the door and strode in, worry clouding his dark eyes.

I hadn't meant to involve the other guys, but Quentin caught the door and peered in after my bodyguard. "Is everything okay?"

I waved him off. "Yeah. I mean, nothing's terribly wrong. I've just got to figure something out."

Quentin propped himself in the doorway, and Jasper wandered over too. I resigned myself to having an audience. I guessed the skaters had a right to know what was going on too… even if *I* didn't know yet myself.

I offered my phone to Rafael. "I got a text from an unknown number—but they seem to know who I am. I'm not sure if I should answer it."

Rafael scanned the screen. "You have no idea who this could be?"

I shook my head. "It's kind of like when the turncoats reached out to me, but at least they were more specific about how they knew my name and that they were on my side. This is so… vague, it could be anything from a friendly overture to a threat."

Rafael hummed to himself and pulled out his own phone. He checked the number against his own contacts, his frown deepening. "It's no one I've had contact with either."

Niko had joined the other two skater men by the doorway and obviously picked up on what was going on. "Could it have nothing to do with your criminal ties at all? Someone you knew at your school or another ordinary place?"

I rubbed my mouth. "That is possible too. Although I don't know why they'd be reaching out now either."

Jasper gave me a crooked grin. "Maybe they recognized you on TV from the competition broadcasts and want to reconnect now that you're famous."

I rolled my eyes at him, but the thought of possible innocuous explanations settled my nerves a little. I exhaled roughly and glanced at Rafael again. "Do you think I should answer?"

He shrugged. "I don't see how it could hurt. Them knowing that they've got the right number doesn't give them any real advantage. And they might have something useful to say like the defectors did."

"Yeah." I hadn't really wanted to chicken out, and having him agree with my impulse to find out what was going on gave me the rest of the conviction I needed. "Here goes nothing!"

I took the phone back and typed out a quick response. *I used to go by that name. Who is this?*

I shifted my weight restlessly as I waited for their response. It only took a matter of seconds.

My name doesn't matter. I've got important information you should know about your close colleagues. Someone's looking to screw you over.

My heart lurched. "What the hell?" I looked over at the skaters while I showed Rafael the response. "They say someone I'm working with is going to betray me."

Rafael's lips drew back from his teeth in a silent snarl. "It's got to be one of that trio who came over from your mother's ranks. Shit."

I swallowed thickly. "I thought they'd done enough to show we could trust them."

"So did I." Rafael squeezed my shoulder. "This isn't your fault, Lou. They really pulled the wool over our eyes." He let go of me to pace toward the door and back, fury radiating off his stance. "But whoever it is, they're not going to live to see another sunrise."

His ominous words raised the hairs on the back of my neck. "We need to make sure we deal with the right one," I said, and tapped out another message.

Are you going to tell me who? It's not very helpful when you stay this vague.

Don't worry. I'll send you all the info you need.

I stood frozen as a series of images and videos popped up in the messages app. After a moment's hesitation, I tapped on the first image.

It was a screenshot of text messages between two people.

The bitch deserves everything that's coming to her, the first said.

No kidding, Rafe, the other replied. *There's no one better to get in there and do what needs doing.*

I'm going to make MC pay for what she did to my brother and every other fucked up thing she's pulled in this city. She'll have no idea what hit her.

The bottom of my stomach dropped out. I didn't know exactly what this was about, but it wasn't that long ago that I'd heard a gangster back in Austin call Rafael "Rafe." Was this something to do with him?

I swiped through a few more text messages that were more of the same: aggressive declarations from this "Rafe," encouragement from whoever he was talking to, and another reference to a "MC" who he was planning to savagely destroy.

Rafael loomed in front of me. "What is it? What're they saying?"

"I—I'm still trying to figure that out," I said, fighting to keep my voice from shaking, and tapped on the first of the videos.

A young black man with familiar coiled hair and broad shoulders was stalking back and forth in a dingy basement room. His muscles rippled through his arms as he appeared to pump himself up. "I'm going to smash that harpy into pieces. Tear the whole Cordova family down and stomp all over them until no one gives a shit about that name. They're never getting away with what they did to Edmundo."

Several other men were gathered around him at the edges of the frame. They let out whoops of approval. "That's right!" one of them shouted. "You get 'em, Rafe."

"She won't see it coming," announced the guy I could tell beyond a doubt was a much younger version of the Rafael I knew. "I'm going to get the bitch's trust and fuck her over before she has a clue she made a mistake. Take them down from the inside out."

"They fucking deserve it!" another guy hollered, and flung a knife toward a wall out of view. The camera swung to show a picture of a rose tacked to the wall, already pierced by a couple of other blades.

Rafael had gone still at the tinny voices when they'd first said his nickname. Now he lunged forward, snatching at the phone. "Don't— You can't watch that. It's not what you think. It's—"

I jerked backward so fast I bumped into the bedside table, making the lamp there rock. Hitting pause, I clutched the phone close to my chest, out of reach, and stared at the man I'd thought I'd known better than anyone in the world.

"It's a video recording," I rasped. "How could it be anything other than what it looks like? You obviously recognized it just from hearing what you were saying. I think I'd better watch the whole thing."

Rafael's hands opened and closed at his sides. He took a step toward me, his eyes wild. "It's only going to mess with your head. You should listen to me *now*, not that shit from years ago."

I stared back at him. "I'll listen to you after I find out what all of that shit was. Or are you going to beat *me* down to take it from me like you apparently wanted to do to all the Cordovas?"

The color leached from Rafael's face, graying his rich brown skin. He didn't reach for the phone again, even as his eyes burned a plea into me. "It's only going to fuck things up."

"I've already seen some of it," I said. "I'd say things are plenty fucked up already."

When I was sure he wasn't going to tackle me for the phone, I sank down near the head of the bed and played the rest of the clip. And the next. And the next.

It looked like the recordings had all been taken pretty close together. Rafael's clothing changed, but his looks stayed pretty much the same, and his attitude kept the same vicious swagger. Whoever had filmed him had caught him ranting and raving about his brutal plans in continued detail.

By the time I let my hands drop with the phone to my lap, I'd heard him explain exactly what order he'd want to cut off various parts of my mother's body and which animals he'd like to feed those pieces to. I'd listened to him laugh about how easily he was going to insinuate himself within her ranks.

For several seconds, I didn't speak because I was afraid if I opened my mouth, I'd vomit. I forced myself to raise my head and meet Rafael's gaze. Behind him, the other three men were braced in shock in the doorway.

"It's true, isn't it?" I said. I didn't see how it couldn't be. "You started working for my mother so you could destroy her and her empire."

Every muscle in his massive body was tensed, and his face was etched with agony. His voice came out strained. "It wasn't like that. It *isn't* like that. I was young and stupid back then—I hadn't really thought through what it meant—"

I shot to my feet. "Don't give me bullshit excuses! You obviously knew exactly how you wanted to tear my family apart. You were planning that while you were watching over me, acting like you wanted to protect me when really…"

My throat closed up. A shudder ran through my body. I'd trusted him so much for so long without the slightest clue about how much rage he was hiding.

"I never hated you," Rafael said urgently into my silence. "I would never have taken it out on you, even at first. Lou, you have to—"

"I don't have to do anything!" I interrupted. All the anguish that'd welled up inside me threatened to spill out of me in a flood. Could I really have been so wrong—could I have put so much of my trust in a man who'd wanted to destroy everything I was…?

Fuck, fuck, fuck.

I didn't know how to wrap my head around it. I couldn't think past the thunder of my pulse while Rafael was right there in front of me, an echo of the vicious figure I'd seen in the videos.

I swung my hand toward the doorway, fighting to keep my voice steady. "I need you to leave. Get out of the apartment. I've got to have some space to figure this out. I can't decide what to think or what I'm going to do when you're here."

Somehow, Rafael went even more rigid than he'd already been. "Please, Lou. I swear, I'll explain—"

"Not now. It's too much. Just give me some room to breathe!"

Rafael stared at me and swore under his breath, but he turned and stormed toward the front door. The other men parted in his wake. He shouldered his way out of the apartment, and the door thumped shut behind him.

He was gone.

I'd drifted into my bedroom doorway to confirm it. When the front door stayed closed in his wake, I sagged against the doorframe. My thoughts swam through the haze in my head.

How could this have happened? How could any of this be possible?

But it was. I had more than enough evidence right here in my hand.

Unshed tears burned in my eyes. As I sucked in a ragged breath, my skater men eased in around me.

Quentin's jaw was tight, his eyes flashing with vehemence that matched his voice. "We don't need that lying prick. The four of us will do just fine without him."

I suppressed a slightly hysterical laugh. I didn't know if that was true. Rafael had done so much to protect me from the moment I'd fled Austin—both times.

Nothing about this situation made sense.

Niko slipped his arm around me. "We'll figure everything out, Angel. No matter what happens, we're here with you."

"That's right." Jasper touched my cheek at my other side. "You do whatever you need to do to feel safe. We've got your back."

I pressed my hand to my forehead. "I can't focus—it's all such a mess. I can't believe he'd have hidden something that *huge*..."

"Here." Niko guided me over to the sofa. "You catch your breath and give yourself time to sort through things. We'll make some breakfast. Everything is easier to take with a good meal in your belly."

The gentleness to his usual cheer only made me choke up more. He'd only known Rafael for a few months, but he could tell how much this revelation had rocked me.

As the guys hustled over to the kitchen to try to whip up some kind of culinary masterpiece that would fix my broken heart, I slumped over on the sofa. When I closed my eyes, fragments of the video footage replayed behind my eyelids, no matter how tightly I squeezed them.

My stomach kept churning. Maybe it was ridiculous. I knew my mother was a horrible person. I knew she'd hurt tons of people. I'd been willing to hurt her myself to get away from her.

But for Rafael to have kept this huge a secret from me for so long… For him to have been capable of putting on a false front like that to begin with… How much else had I misjudged?

How could I know whether any of the choices I'd made had been the right ones?

I'd thought I loved him. I'd thought he loved me. Could I trust even that much?

How could I say I loved him when I hadn't known such a vital part of why he'd come into my life at all?

My bleary gaze roamed around the room. Finally it landed on my skates where they leaned against my equipment bag near the door Rafael had just left through.

Other images rose up in the back of my mind, ones I didn't need a video of to remember them. All those years when Rafael had motioned me out the door with him and driven uncomplaining to the arena in Austin. The hundreds of times he'd stood guard in the stands while I skated for hours on end.

The quiet smile I'd sometimes spot after I completed a particularly difficult move.

All the attempts I'd made at flirting with him, starting back when I was no more than thirteen. The times I'd outright propositioned him —at sixteen, then eighteen—putting my heart out there on the line.

He could have had me. He could have taken my hopes, used me, and ripped me to shreds. Wouldn't that have made a perfect revenge?

But he hadn't. He'd resisted my advances every time.

And despite that, he'd never left my side when I needed him. He'd volunteered to trek across the continent with me without hesitation, even knowing my mother would be out for my blood and his. He'd come back to Austin with me with the same threat hanging over him and done nothing that wasn't for my protection that entire time.

When I took everything I knew into account, I couldn't deny the facts. Even if Rafael had started working for my mother intending to betray her and tear down her empire, in the end he'd decided that supporting me was more important. He'd passed up all kinds of opportunities to undermine her so that he could look after me instead.

He was irreversibly interwoven into the journey that had brought me here—and I knew with a growing resolve that I'd come way too far to give up now.

But even with that certainty spreading through my chest, taking the edge off the pain, confusion clouded my mind. We couldn't go forward like this.

I needed to know exactly what had happened and why he'd wanted to hurt my family. Only then could I decide if and how I wanted to put the pieces back together.

I pushed myself upright on the sofa and glanced over at the guys in the kitchen. Savory smells drifted from the frying pan, but my mouth didn't even water.

"I think I'm ready to talk to Rafael some more," I said. "Get the whole story."

Niko nodded. "Whatever you think is right. You know him much better than any of us."

Jasper smiled tightly. "Yeah. We trust your judgment."

Quentin just scowled, but he didn't argue.

Inhaling deeply, I looked down at my phone and typed out a text to the man who'd been my rock for more than half of my life.

Come back? I'm ready to hear what you have to say.

FIFTEEN

Rafael

WHEN I REACHED the apartment door, I stopped. For a second, the burden of my omissions weighed on me so heavily I couldn't move.

All the secrets I'd kept from Lou.

All the casual deceptions I'd let myself pretend didn't matter.

All the horrible history that had brought us together, that hadn't gone away no matter how much I'd wanted to believe it had.

How the fuck was the woman I loved ever going to trust me again?

I wasn't going to find out unless I walked in there and talked to her. Even if she *never* forgave me, she deserved as much of an explanation as she'd let me give.

Girding myself, I raised my hand and turned the knob.

The door swung open to reveal an equally tense scene on the other side. Lou sat at the end of the sofa, one foot lifted to rest on the opposite knee, her back perfectly straight against the cushions. The other three men held themselves in a row behind her as if standing guard.

Niko and Jasper simply looked grim. Quentin outright glared at me. I could tell they were strung tight, probably ready to snatch at their weapons if I made a wrong move.

I couldn't blame any of them for their reaction.

Lou glanced at me with a cool expression. When she spoke, it was to the other guys. "I want to talk to Rafael alone."

Quentin let out a noise of protest, but before he could get any further into an argument, Lou held up her hand to stop him. "I'll be fine. Whatever he's got to say is about stuff from way before I knew any of you. I don't want any interruptions."

Jasper dipped his head, shooting me with a warning look. "We'll hang out in one of the bedrooms. Shout, and we'll be right here."

They headed off through one of the nearby doorways. As the door clicked shut behind them, Lou bent over and picked up the skate I hadn't noticed resting against the base of the sofa. She adjusted another object in her hand and brought the skate's blade to it.

Shrrrk!

I'd heard that sound dozens of times before. The sharp hiss of metal being sharpened against a hand stone. It raised the hairs on the back of my neck the same way nails on chalkboard might have, but I wasn't in a position to complain.

Lou didn't say anything to me, didn't even meet my gaze again as she angled her skate in rhythmic swipes across the stone. Honing the blade into just as much of a weapon as any knife she could have carried. I had no doubt that thing could slice through my skin if she wanted to cut me.

As she no doubt wanted me to be aware of while we had this conversation. A subtle yet unmistakable statement of her strength. I had to admire the gesture, even as it made my stomach churn.

She *had* said she wanted to talk. I took careful steps over to the sofa and eased down at the opposite end from her. She dragged the skate blade over the stone with another shrill scraping sound.

I let my eyebrows arch just slightly. "Should I be worried about whether this is a conversation or actually an execution?"

Lou's gaze flicked to me for just a second. "What are you talking about?" she said in a voice as smooth and cool as her expression. "I need to keep my skates in good shape. You know that."

"I do." I also knew that in this moment, she was every inch her mother's daughter. Not the awful parts that made the woman a vicious monster—the collected, professional aura of power that had made her a leader.

Lou could be a great leader too. Seeing her like this, I could imagine her keeping the Deadly Rose empire in line so easily.

If she'd actually had any interest in doing that.

What we were about to talk about now mattered to her. Keeping her self-control in the face of the potential threat I now might be mattered to her.

She didn't give a shit about world domination or racking up business earnings, and that was why she'd never be able to maintain the kind of authority her mother's heir would need long term. But she shouldn't have to.

She should be able to have whatever she goddamn wanted.

Not that long ago, that'd been skating, and the men she'd found on that journey… and me. More than anything, I wanted to pull her to me, wrap her up in all the protection I'd always offered, and show her she still had me.

That wasn't going to work. Not after what she'd seen. I had to use my words first.

Apparently it was up to me to start the discussion. That seemed fair too.

I swallowed my apprehension. "Lou, I'm sorry. More sorry than I can even say. I didn't tell you about any of that because none of it was true anymore. All the things you saw—they were from more than a decade ago. I haven't thought any of the things I said back then for a long time."

Shrrrk.

Lou kept her eyes on her skate. "But you did before. When you said it. You really did come to work for my mother planning to take her down, didn't you?"

"Yes," I admitted. "I thought I had a good reason to. The other guys you saw me with in the videos—they were part of my brother's old gang."

"The guys who confronted you in Austin? The ones who beat you up?"

"Yeah." I grimaced at the memory. "A few years after Edmundo brought me into the gang, Mireya lashed out at us what seemed like out of the blue. She killed my brother and a couple of other guys. I could barely wrap my head around living without him—I wanted to destroy the person responsible for taking him from me. The rest of the gang saw it as a flex of her power, just to show that she could and remind everyone to stay in line. Totally undeserved. I couldn't just accept it and shrug it off."

The pain of that long-ago loss prickled through me, dulled by time but not completely vanished. What would Edmundo have become if he'd lived? Who would he have been now?

The sad thing was, I wasn't sure it'd have been anything good.

I could have thrown away the best thing to have ever come into my life over someone who'd never truly earned that loyalty.

Lou had lowered her hand with the stone while I talked. She met my eyes with a pensive expression. "My mom did a lot of shitty things, but she didn't usually go around killing random people just for the hell of it."

"I know." I cleared my throat, trying to work the roughness from my voice. "At the time, I hadn't interacted with her at all, and I was reeling with grief and anger… I just wanted revenge."

Lou set down the first skate and picked up the other. She ran the blade over the stone, starting up the rhythm again. "And then?"

My heart sank with the memory. "After I'd been working with Mireya for a few years, working my way up through the ranks, I found out that it hadn't been random. Edmundo and the other two guys had tried to screw over a smaller gang in the city that we didn't know the Cordovas had a stake in. They'd killed a few people and stolen a bunch of merchandise."

Shrrrk. "And my mother retaliated with matching brutality. *That* sounds like her."

"Yeah. Reasonable retaliation." I shook my head, not knowing how to convey the full depth of my anguish to her—that I'd been so wrong, that Edmundo had made a move both so brainless and so heartless that it had nearly turned me into this spectacular woman's enemy. "I hate that I lost my brother, but as soon as I got the full story, I understood that it was his fault. He essentially attacked her first."

"But you stayed on," Lou said. "Why did you stick around if you weren't still planning some kind of revenge? I know you didn't *like* working for her."

"I didn't," I agreed. "I didn't like how she treated you or parts of how she ruled over her people... I had a bad feeling about the ambitions I caught glimpses of. I'd already been watching over you for more than a year then, and I could see you were better than her. I thought I'd stay, protect you and help you, and when you took over it could all be different."

"I guess you couldn't have gone back to your old gang empty-handed anyway."

My voice turned fiercer than I meant it to. "I didn't want to. I could see that I was doing something better by looking out for you. Even when you were a kid, there was something about you that shone through... It reminded me a little of my parents when they still had hopes for a better life. I couldn't abandon you and let her destroy that spark."

Lou let out a dry laugh. "So you stayed to wait for a preteen to ascend to her mafia throne."

I shrugged, affection clogging my throat as I thought of the girl I'd stayed for and the incredible woman she'd grown into. "It seemed like the best choice I had at the time. Although frankly, I'm happier here waiting for you to become a figure-skating superstar free of all that madness."

Her hand stopped, still clutching the stone. Her next words come out so low I barely hear them. "I'm happier like that too. Or I was."

That hint of the pain I'd caused her gutted me. I rubbed my hand over my face. "I should have told you sooner. After we got close. Given you the whole story so you'd know. But I—I didn't want you to think badly of me. I never thought I'd run into those cabrónes again, so it wouldn't matter. It could just stay in the past."

Lou put the second skate down next to the first and set the stone on the coffee table. Her hands clasped together on her lap. She looked down at them and then at me with so much hurt and determination smoldering together in her eyes I couldn't have torn my gaze away if I'd wanted to.

"I want to believe you," she said. "But it's so hard when you let me get blindsided like this… I need to know I can depend on you—now more than I ever have before. Everything I've worked for—everything *we've* worked for—falls apart if I can't trust you."

The faintest quaver ran through her voice with the last sentence. She couldn't completely suppress the blow I'd dealt to her faith and her confidence. I closed my eyes against the urge to bash my own head in for fucking things up so badly.

But taking my guilt out on myself wouldn't help her. She'd just said it—she needed me. I just have to prove to her that her faith had been justified after all.

Violence came easy to me. That didn't confirm anything. I had to give her something that hurt me in a different way, that went against all my instincts… except when it came to the woman I'd have died to save.

My heart gave me the answer. I pushed myself off the sofa onto my knees and bowed my head before her, resting my forehead on her knee. Lou sucked in a softly startled breath. Her stance went rigid.

"You're the only one in the entire world I'd give my whole self over to, Lou," I said, putting all my devotion into every ragged word. "My strength, my pride, my life. There's nothing I wouldn't do if you asked. You could tell me to jump into a volcano right now, and I'd do it, because you asked."

A sputter of a laugh burst out of her. "I don't think it's going to come to that."

"Maybe it should. Because if you can't trust me again, if you can't bear to have me with you, then I have no purpose left. Every decision I've made, every step I've taken, for years, has been to serve you as well as I can. I made a mistake, but it *was* a mistake. I've got no secrets left. Please, don't make me give you up now."

Lou inhaled shakily, and then she was grasping my shoulders. As I rose at her tug, she wrapped her arms around me, leaning into the embrace I returned automatically with a rush of relief.

"I don't want to lose you either," she choked out, muffled by my shirt. "I was so afraid I already had."

I buried my face in her hair. "Never. You'd have to *throw* me into a fucking volcano to get rid of me now."

Another laugh hitched out of her. Then she pulled back, her dark gaze searching my face. "If you haven't had anything to do with your brother's gang in all that time, why are they attacking you? It must have been one of them who found my number and sent all that proof, right? Do they expect you to still get revenge on me and my mother—they think they can force your hand?"

I grimaced. "Probably. I did try to tell them the real story after I found out how Edmundo had screwed over Mireya's people, but they refused to even hear it. It was obvious they'd never accept the truth after they'd spent so long blaming her for it. Seeing me back in town set them off again."

Lou glanced at her purse, which no doubt held her phone. "Well, I can delete all that crap, and then it's gone."

"From your life. Not from theirs." Uneasiness prickled through my gut. "They exposed me to you—I don't know what they'll try next. They might manage to cause even more problems for you with your mother because of me. If they go to her with those videos, and she gets it into her head that we're scheming together against her…"

Dios mío, I couldn't even picture how much more of a terror Mireya would become with that idea fanning the flames of her rage.

Lou grasped my hand and squeezed it. "We won't let it get that far. We'll take them on together—like we have so many problems before."

SIXTEEN

Luciana

"UGH." I tried to restrain a yawn as I rubbed at my eyes, rocking with the bump of the rental car's wheels over a pothole.

Rafael glanced over at me from the driver's seat. "You never were good at sleeping on planes."

"Unlike you," I muttered. He'd drifted off in the seat beside me before we'd even left Japanese air space. I'd done my best to doze during the long flight back to the US, but I wasn't sure I'd gotten more than a couple of hours of very restless sleep.

I had to push through my fatigue and the jetlag, though. We had bigger problems in front of us—namely, the members of Rafael's former gang and the peace we needed to broker with them to ensure they didn't stir up even more trouble now that it seemed like my problems with my mother might finally be under control.

Fly in, have a quick chat, fly right back to Tokyo. Simple as that.

Ha.

Anton, the guy who ran the gang these days, had grudgingly

agreed to our request to meet, as long as he could pick the location. We were heading into one of the roughest sections of Austin, no doubt smack in the middle of their territory.

My skin prickled with uneasiness, but the show of good faith had been necessary. They wouldn't have agreed to talk with us anywhere they thought we might be able to pull one over on them.

The one other time I'd met these assholes, they'd insulted me, accused Rafael of betraying them, and delivered a beatdown that'd left him in a cast and stitches. To say I wasn't looking forward to making any kind of deal with them was the understatement of the century.

But a girl had to do what a girl had to do.

Rafael eased off the gas as the grimy parking garage where the meetup was arranged came into view up ahead. "He's probably come with a whole horde of his goons."

I raised my chin. "That's fine. Whatever he needs to stay safe." I touched my gun in my purse and then the other in my jacket pocket. Rafael was armed too.

"You could let me handle it."

I shot him a narrow look. "It's my family they have the real problem with. Any way we hash this out, I've got to be involved. They need to know any agreement we come to is definitely from me as well."

My bodyguard sighed, but he didn't argue. We'd already had similar debates over the course of the past day while we arranged this impromptu trip.

He pulled into the shadowy cement fortress and parked not far from the entrance. Several figures shifted into view in the dimmer area toward the back of the structure.

I swallowed thickly and hardened my resolve. I couldn't afford to let any one of these pricks see that I was nervous. If they couldn't bring themselves to treat me as an equal, we were screwed.

About a dozen guys lumbered up to us, testosterone wafting off their flexed muscles and cocky smirks. Anton pushed to the front of the group with the broadest smirk of all, cracking his knuckles and studying us with his dark eyes.

"So, Rafe, you had the balls to come to us for once instead of making us track you down." He flicked his gaze toward me. "I'm surprised this one bothered to stick with you after she found out who you really are. I guess you really did win over some Cordova pussy."

A couple of his colleagues made crude gestures with their hips, and a laugh spread through the group. Rafael clenched his fists, but I touched his arm to hold him back.

Holding my stance firm, I rolled my eyes as if I didn't give a shit what he said about me. "I know who Rafael is now, unlike the bunch of you who seem stuck ten years in the past. After a decade, I think it's time we put this feud to rest."

Anton snorted. "Who are you to decide that, little puta? We still haven't gotten any payback for the shit your mother did. She thinks she rules this city, but we aren't going to bow down to any queen of míerda."

"No one's asking you to," I said evenly. "I don't work with her—I'm on my side, not hers."

Rafael tipped his head toward me. "It's true. Lou has completely separated herself from anything to do with Mireya."

With a sneer, Anton spat on the ground. "And we're supposed to believe that just because you said so? We've seen what backstabbing bitches you Cordovas can be."

A darker murmur rippled through the crowd behind him. He was getting his men riled up with thoughts of the supposedly unwarranted killings Mom had carried out.

But I didn't see any point in trying to convince them they were wrong about her. She'd done plenty of other awful things even if she'd been justified in taking out Rafael's brother. If these guys hadn't believed Rafael himself when he'd tried to tell them, they sure as hell weren't going to take my word for it.

We had to come at this from a different angle.

I clicked my tongue against the back of my teeth in a chiding sound. "Really? You do remember that I was only *eight years old* when your people were murdered, right? Are you seriously so pathetic that you'd hold a literal kid responsible for what her parents did?"

Anton's eyebrows shot up, but even as his eyes flashed, he couldn't restrain a grimace. The aggressive posturing of the crowd simmered down. Even these pendejos knew I had a point.

"You're not a kid anymore," one of the older guys snarled from where he stood by Anton's side.

Anton nodded with a jerk of his head. "Damn straight. And Mireya Cordova is even more of a tyrant and a terror than she was back then. You can't brush off your whole family history when shit is going down right now."

"I know she's gone off the rails," I said tightly. "She's been gunning for *me* too, as I'm sure you've noticed if you've been paying any attention at all."

Another gangster let out a scoffing sound. "You're still a Cordova. You've still got those ties."

Anton scowled at me. "You can't throw away all the responsibility for the family business when those riches will be going to you the second she kicks the bucket."

An edge I couldn't restrain crept into my voice. "I'd rather they didn't. I never wanted anything to do with the family business, and I'd be perfectly happy to see the whole fucking empire fall."

The man in front of me shook his head. His thugs rumbled discontentedly, skepticism stark on all their hardened faces.

We weren't getting anywhere just talking. I'd known making peace with just words was a longshot, but I'd wanted to give it a try anyway. Because the next step I was taking could come back to bite me if it didn't play out in my favor.

I glanced at Rafael. His jaw tightened, but he inclined his head slightly. We'd discussed what I'd do if I couldn't convince the guys to back down by verbally cutting ties with Mom.

So, I'd just have to offer concrete evidence of how little I gave a shit what happened to her.

I dug my hand into my purse, holding up the other hand when the men stiffened. "No weapons. I've got something that'll actually help you."

I pulled out a wad of folded papers. Opening up one, I held it out so Anton and his men could see the lines sketched across it.

"I can give you the layout of the Cordova mansion. Every room, every hallway, every entrance, with notes about how they're typically guarded. I've got two more floor plans here, of a couple of my family's main business locations in the city."

Anton licked his lips. He gazed avidly at the amateurish blueprint and then back at me. "Why the fuck are you showing me that?"

"I'm making a gift out of it." I refolded the paper and shoved the bunch of them toward him. "You can do what you want with them. Consider it a gesture of trust. Now it's up to you whether you trust Rafael and me to stop my mother our own way and save you the trouble, or if you want to go at her head on if it's that important to you. You've got the option. It all comes down to how much you want to put your heads on the line."

"There's got to be a catch," someone muttered.

I shook my head. "No catch. I wanted you to see that I'm willing to let my mom get even more pissed off at me, if that's what it takes to prove which side I'm on and get *you* off our backs. We aren't part of your fight with the Cordovas. We're fighting our own battle. If you want, you can sit back and let us do all the work, but I'm not asking you to wait if you'd rather stick your own necks out."

The gangsters jostled against each other restlessly, their expressions flickering between eager and uncertain.

Anton rubbed his mouth and frowned down at the papers he'd taken before lifting his eyes to meet mine. "How exactly are *you* planning to finish her?"

Rafael grunted. "You can't expect us to give away information like that. You worry about what you're going to do, and we'll worry about our own tactics."

It would have been stupid to give them that kind of information anyway, when for all I knew they could turn around and sell it to my mom regardless of their past anger. But there was also the fact that I didn't have the faintest clue how the hell we were going to end her reign of terror just yet, which Rafael knew as well as I did.

A different voice rose up from the crowd. "How much time is it going to take you to deal with her, huh? How much longer are we putting up with this bitch lording it over us?"

With great effort, I avoided gritting my teeth. "We're doing as much as we can as quickly as we can. If I could get this all over with tomorrow, I'd go for it. But upending an entire empire takes time."

Anton shoved the papers under his arm and cast one more grim look at me. "We'll do what's best for us, then. Maybe we'll wait and see how your way pans out; maybe we'll just get on with things ourselves. But we can cut you and Rafael here a little slack."

I shrugged as if it didn't matter to me either way. "I appreciate that. The rest is up to you."

He spun on his heel, and his goons turned with him. They stalked off into the shadows they'd emerged from.

As Rafael and I hustled back to the rental car, I didn't dare let my shoulders slump, even though I wanted to crumple in a mix of relief and trepidation.

We'd done it. I'd convinced the gang not to see me or Rafael as the enemy.

But I'd wanted more than anything to leave this part of my life behind forever. Now I'd made a commitment to staying with it until my mother was toppled from her throne.

And I had no idea how I was going to make that happen.

SEVENTEEN

Luciana

I MIGHT HAVE BEEN short on sleep, but we'd spent so little time in the US that stepping out of the Tokyo subway system into the crisp mid-afternoon air made me feel like I'd come home. My inner clock was back on the right schedule again, never having had a chance to switch over to across-the-ocean time.

I stretched my arms over my head with a yawn and glanced at Rafael. "The guys are probably training right now, but I think I need to sleep until tomorrow before—"

The trill of my phone cut me off—the ringtone I'd assigned to my guys. They'd have realized I should be in town by now. With a smile touching my lips at the thought of hearing their voices again, I dug out my phone. Jasper's name showed on the caller ID.

I brought the phone to my ear as I hit the answer button. "Hey! We just—"

"Lou! I don't know how long I'll be able to talk. We need help."

My partner's hushed but frantic voice crackled through the phone line. My pulse skittered.

"What?" I demanded, my fingers tightening around the phone. "What's going on?"

"We're at the rink," he rasped. "The smaller one. Your mother's people must have figured out we were training here. A bunch of men with guns stormed in—they've got us trapped in the stands."

My heart nearly lurched right up my throat. "What? She was supposed to—*fuck*."

A couple of distant gunshots rattled through the line. My pulse thudded even faster. "Have they hurt any of you?"

"No. Luckily the turncoats came along with us to practice, and they've helped hold the other guys off. But we haven't figured out how to reach an exit."

"Shit. We'll get there as fast as we can. Hang in there."

I shoved my phone in my purse and spun around, my thoughts whirling. Panic swept through my veins with its icy chill.

We were miles from the arena. I had no idea if we could get to them in time.

If I hadn't gone back to Austin—if I'd been there with them training, would I have seen a way out?

It might not have happened at all. Mom had probably picked this moment because she'd realized I'd left town.

No matter how hard I fought, the men I loved were being attacked from so many sides that I couldn't watch out for all of them at once. When was this going to end?

Rafael gripped my shoulder, his solid presence steadying me. "What's wrong, Lou?"

I blinked back the tears pricking at my eyes and strode forward, scanning the busy street next to us for a taxi. "My mom's people have attacked the guys at the arena. They've got them and the Deadly Rose defectors trapped by the rink. We have to get over there and give them backup."

Fury flashed in Rafael's eyes. "That maldita perra," he muttered, and sprang past me toward a cab that'd just pulled up to the curb to let out a passenger.

The second the passenger had walked away, Rafael dove into the front passenger seat. As I scrambled after him, he pointed his gun at the driver—low and careful with the safety still on, but that didn't make any difference to the guy, who stared at him with his jaw going slack.

Rafael spoke slowly and firmly. "I'm sorry. I'll leave the car for you to collect later. Right now we really need it. It's an emergency."

I had no idea how much the cabbie understood, but he didn't want to argue with a man with a gun. Leaving the key in the ignition, he bolted from the driver's seat, and I dashed around to take his place while Rafael re-holstered his gun.

"Was that totally necessary?" I couldn't help asking as I yanked the wheel to send the car back into traffic.

"No one's going to drive us there as fast as we need to go," Rafael retorted. "You put those daredevil skills to good use. I'm going to see what I can work out with Dámaso and the others."

He'd already swapped his pistol for his phone. As I wove between the other cars and hit the gas to fly through an intersection just before the light changed, his voice took on an even more authoritative tone than it had with the displaced cabbie.

"It's me. What's the exact situation there?"

He paused while Dámaso or one of the other defectors must have answered, and a couple of horns bleated their disapproval at my incredible driving maneuvers. My jaw clenched as I tore through another intersection.

Rafael nodded at whatever he'd been told, something about his unyielding posture beside me taking a little of the edge off my nerves. "That's not *too* many. Do you think there are more in the building? Okay. You know there's a back entrance, locked on the outside but useable as an emergency exit."

He fell silent for another longer stretch and then grimaced. "Fair enough. Listen, we'll burst in through the main entrance right behind these cabrónes. I want you six to move as close as you can to the upper hallway. Watch for the shooters to get distracted—run for it when you have the chance. Keep firing the whole time so they have to keep cover and can't take too good an aim at you."

He made it sound almost easy. Like he'd been giving orders in death-defying situations his whole life.

Well, he probably had. He might have been my main bodyguard, but he'd had to work with other members of my mom's security force on a regular basis. When it came to my safety, he'd had the ultimate authority over the rest.

"Stay on the line with me until then," he added. "I'll let you know when we get there. We're close now."

I tore around a corner and roared down the quieter streets of the wealthier neighborhood that held the arena. Somehow I didn't think *this* kind of attention was what Emi's friend had been hoping for when she'd made the deal to let us train there.

Could we possibly get out of this not only without any major injuries, but without making the front-page news yet again too?

The arena building came into view up ahead. I sped into the parking lot, wincing at the sight of a fallen security guard Mom's people must have picked off. So much for no major injuries. Míerda, this situation got worse by the minute.

I jerked up the parking brake, leapt out of the cab—and my breath froze in my lungs.

I could see through the broad glass doors that led into the fancy arena. And on the other side of the glass, cringing together with slim hands held over their heads while two gunmen pointed their semi-automatics at them, were three teenaged girls.

They had equipment bags at their feet—one had skates slung over her shoulder. School must have just gotten out, and these were the local trainees who used the rink, arriving for their own practice.

The men holding them hostage hadn't glanced over at us yet. Rafael shot me a determined look. "I'll go around through the back door. I can handle the lock. You keep them distracted, and then we go at them from both sides at once."

I nodded, my pulse now thundering in my ears. As he took off toward the back of the building, I headed toward the front doors, my fingers closing around the grip of the pistol in my pocket.

One of the men's heads jerked toward me. He pivoted, raising his gun, and I ducked into the shelter of a car parked just ten feet from the door.

"What the fuck do you think you're doing?" I hollered over the hood. "Those are *kids*. They don't have anything to do with me or this fight."

The guy shoved the door open to glower in my direction. "They're here. That means they're targets."

"You've already got plenty of other targets inside. Let the three girls go. There's no reason to keep them."

He let out a dark chuckle that raised the hairs on the back of my neck. "Your mother doesn't think so. She figures anyone who gets in our way is acceptable collateral damage. So maybe next time you'll think twice before you defy the Deadly Rose."

My stomach plummeted. I wanted to deny it, but I could imagine my mom giving the order all too easily. Even laughing at the thought of my distress at seeing innocent people dragged into our war.

She really had gone off the rails. She didn't care about the deal she'd made with her Devil's Dozen colleagues or the impact this rampage could have on her local connections. She'd gone fucking insane in her obsession with taking revenge on me.

And that made a woman who'd already been one of the deadliest in the world ten times more dangerous.

"I don't know why you're siding with her," I said past the dryness of my mouth. Keep him talking—keep him from thinking about anyone else who might be approaching. "She'll turn on you as easily as she turned on me."

"Oh, I don't think so. Because I know when I've got it good, and I'm not going to bite the—"

His words cut off with two swift bangs. I lifted my head to see Rafael framed by the lobby's archway, his gun raised and the two men crumpling to the ground.

A couple of the girls shrieked. I ran over, holding my own gun low in the hopes I wouldn't traumatize them even more.

The guy who'd been threatening me had fallen between the one door and the frame, holding it open. I yanked open the other door, closer to the girls, and motioned them out. "There's no one out here. You can go home. Get somewhere safe! We'll handle the rest."

My urgency must have conveyed enough of my meaning even if they didn't understand my words. Their eyes wide with fear, they hefted their equipment bags and darted across the parking lot.

I met Rafael's gaze. He tipped his head toward the interior of the arena, where to my anguish I saw the security guard at the desk slumped forward in a pool of blood. But no one came running our way at Rafael's shots.

"I took down a couple of guys who were patrolling the halls—quietly enough that I don't think the goons in the rink area noticed," he said. "How about we take a similar strategy going at the last of them?"

I smiled grimly. "I distract them while you sneak up on them?"

"I was thinking more the coming at them from different directions. You can come out into the base of the stands through the women's locker room, right? I'll go through the men's. From what Dámaso told me, that'll put us on either side of them. They'll be nearly surrounded."

I exhaled in a whoosh. "All right. Let's do this before they realize something's gone really wrong for their friends."

I slipped through the locker room as quickly and quietly as I could. By the exit that led to the rink, I paused and listened at the door. No shots, only a couple of annoyed voices.

"We've got to get closer. The Deadly Rose wants them kaput."

"How d'you figure we're doing that without getting shot, you idiot? Let them waste their bullets taking potshots, then we go in for the kill."

Oh, he thought so, did he?

Scowling, I eased the door open just a couple of inches. Across the way, I spotted Rafael at his own door. He gave me a brisk nod from the narrow gap.

We shoved all the way past the doors in unison, each shooting at the men standing closest to us. The cluster of seven scattered—two, then three crumpling before they'd taken more than a couple of steps.

The other four bolted toward the ice. Rafael raised his voice in a bellow. "Now!"

More shots rang out from the other end of the rink. The gunmen jerked and collapsed. One flung himself toward the shelter of the boards, but Rafael strode to an opening and put a bullet in his head too.

My arm sagged to my side. I stared at the carnage we'd left behind, my gut churning.

"Fuck. This is a mess."

"I'll deal with it," Rafael said in his impervious tone. "I'll get the turncoats to help me take care of this and the taxi. You just worry about getting these guys home."

I found myself nodding automatically. He sounded like he knew what he was talking about—which, of course, he did.

He sounded like a leader.

A spark of an idea tickled up in the back of my head, but I couldn't pay attention to it when the men I'd left behind were hustling over to join us.

"Lou!" Niko exclaimed. "You're okay."

I caught him in a tight hug. "I should be saying the same to you." I turned to grip Jasper's and Quentin's arms tightly, my throat abruptly choked up. "I was so worried about you."

My gaze slid past them to the three defectors. Frankie was frowning, but Ursula held her head high, and Dámaso looked almost smug despite the bulge of his remaining bandages under his shirt.

"Thank you," I said. "You were amazing. Now we'd better get the fuck out of here."

As Rafael motioned the defectors over with brusque orders, my skater men and I hustled out to the rental SUV they'd arrived in. Quentin pushed behind the wheel, and I found myself tucked between Jasper and Niko, clutching them like I was afraid they'd disappear on me.

"She's not going to get away with this," I muttered. "She won't. I won't let her."

Jasper stroked my hair soothingly. "Hey, it's over now, Punk. I'm just glad we made it out in one piece."

Quentin glanced over his shoulder at a red light. "I'm looking forward to a time when I'm never getting shot at again, but it's not your fucking fault. Did things work out in Austin?"

My stomach knotted all over again. "About as well as we really could have hoped. I don't think Rafael's old gang will hassle us anymore, at least."

My mother, well… Who knew what hell she'd rain down on us next?

As the adrenaline seeped away, the idea I'd had before swam up through my scattered thoughts. I studied it, turning it over in my head as my confidence grew.

That… That wouldn't solve all our problems. Not even our most immediate problems. But it was one piece of the puzzle that I'd like to put to rest if I could.

When we got back to the apartment, all my body wanted to do was drop dead on my mattress. I forced myself to stay up, cuddling with my men and sipping tea, until Rafael walked through the door.

He dipped his head to me. "It's all handled. We'll need to do a little damage control with the arena management because of the security guard and the girls they scared, but we might be able to keep our names out of the situation."

Niko's head came up. "I'll start talking to them right away. Get ahead of the situation."

As he grabbed his phone and headed into his bedroom for quiet, I got up and grasped Rafael's arm. He let me pull him into my own room. When I turned to face him, his expression was solemn but curious.

"What's the matter, Lou? You don't look like you're hauling me in here to jump my bones."

An exhausted laugh tumbled out of me. "I think I'm too wiped to do that even if I was in the mood. Nothing's the matter. I've just—I've been thinking."

Rafael furrowed his brow. "About stopping training? You know that—"

I held up my hand. "No. I think that ship has sailed. We're on this course, no matter what comes. But I'm looking ahead to after things are more settled, and where that course might end up taking *you* too."

The furrows deepened. "What are you talking about?"

I drew myself as tall and straight as I could. "You know I've never wanted my mother's throne, Rafael. But someone needs to be the Deadly Rose. And I think you would make a much better heir than I ever have."

Rafael blinked at me, shock blanking his expression. "*Qué?* Lou, you can't really mean—"

The fact that the possibility had never even occurred to him only strengthened my resolve. "Of course I can," I interrupted. "It makes way more sense than me taking over. You've seen the problems with my mom's approach—and how it's gotten even worse. You want to make things better. You're a good leader. You know how to take command but also be fair, and you haven't lost your compassion, even if you know how to hide it."

He still looked bewildered. "I don't know. I never would have asked for anything like this."

I gave him a soft smile. "I know you wouldn't have. But honestly, if I get control over the Deadly Rose empire, I'd hand it over to you in a heartbeat. If you're willing to take it. You should think about it."

I knew I would be thinking about it a lot… while I tried to see a way to wrench that power away from my mother before she destroyed us all.

EIGHTEEN

Niko

"PLEASE CONSIDER GIVING us a call back, Mr. Okabe," the reporter said as she wrapped up the voicemail she'd left me. "There's already a lot of speculation about how the recent shooting at the Sports Garden arena might be related to your attack and Ms. Garcia's family connections."

Beep!

Wincing, I set my phone down. In the past two days, the calls had been pouring in from both news stations and skating officials, and I hadn't had anything useful to tell any of them. The memory of cringing behind a bench, my heart racing faster than a bullet train at the thought of the actual bullets being fired, left my stomach knotted. And I wasn't going to admit to any of them that the incident was not only related to Lou but directly targeting her.

The worst wasn't even the nosy reporters. I could fend them off without any trouble—I'd been doing that ever since I stepped into the spotlight in my teens. But I'd generally kept on the good side of the professionals in our sport, even if they might have muttered about me behind my back from time to time.

The president of the Japan Skating Federation himself had left me a message this morning. His stern words lingered in my memory. *You still represent Japan even if you're coaching Americans. You should take more care in who you associate with. Think of what all these rumors are doing to our sport's reputation!*

That was the message I'd been getting over and over again from the skating world: my trainees were damaging the public's view of figure skating. The growing scandal was giving the wrong impression about what we stood for. Soon reporters would be eyeing all participants with more suspicious eyes.

And so on and so on.

What could I tell them? Yes, Lou had brought a lot of commotion with her, but it wasn't her fault. She was doing her best to put the horrors she'd experienced behind her and separate herself from that part of her life. Should she have been cut off from the sport she loved because of how other people were targeting her?

My phone pinged again, this time with a familiar custom alert. Emi. I snatched it up to see what she had to say after her talks with the arena owner.

As I scanned her message, my stomach sank.

Hey, big brother! I got everything sorted out with my friend's uncle. He doesn't blame you guys for what happened… but he said he's not sure he wants Lou and Jasper to mention that they trained there after all, even if they win a medal. I guess I'll keep you up to date on that part.

With a sigh, I sagged back in the sofa. Now even the people who'd been most excited about our potential success saw us as bad luck.

Rafael's voice carried from the kitchen. "What's the matter? Are the reporters still hassling you?"

I lifted my head. The big man was leaning against the counter with a steaming mug of coffee in his hands.

I'd almost forgotten Lou's bodyguard was here. He had such a quiet presence despite his bulky frame. Jasper and Quentin had gone out after dinner to see about some finishing details for the new costumes, and Lou had crashed in her bedroom, still recovering from all her recent air travel.

I didn't like to set a gloomy tone, but I couldn't think of a single way to spin the situation into something worth celebrating. "It's reporters and officials and everyone else who has an opinion or questions. They all seem to want to paint Lou as the bad guy. I don't know what to tell them to get them off her back. But I can't have them getting into *her* head. She needs to focus on her skating."

Rafael ambled over to the living room and sank into the armchair. His mouth curved into a tight but wry smile. "I guess she's been building up her team of representatives so she can do just that. She's got you as her skating boss, and now she wants me to be her crime boss."

I'd caught a few remarks between the two of them over the past couple of days that had given me the gist, but we hadn't discussed the subject as a group. "She's suggesting that you take over her mother's empire rather than her?"

He nodded, his mouth staying tight, his eyes going distant. "That's about the size of it."

As usual, it was difficult to read his reaction. "Would you *want* to do that?" I ventured.

His gaze came back to me, and he let out a dry chuckle. "That's a pretty important question, isn't it? Honestly, I don't even know. Obviously there's some appeal to having that kind of power, and knowing I could run things my way rather than her mom's… But am I really up to the full job? Just a few days ago, I almost lost Lou thanks to my past stupidity. My judgment is *better* now, but that doesn't mean it's perfect."

I'd rarely heard the man say so much at once. The decision must have been weighing on him a lot.

I'd also never expected to realize I had so much in common with the former gangster, even if we'd arrived at where we were from very different angles. Maybe it'd help him to hear that he wasn't alone in his doubts.

I glanced down at my hands and then back at him. "I think I know how you feel. I've had my share of epic mistakes. I once inadvertently outed my closeted ex on national TV and ruined his life." I waved toward my phone. "What if I end up saying the wrong thing again and damage the situation for Lou even more? That's the last thing she needs!"

Rafael took a long sip from his coffee, his expression turning contemplative. "I don't think you being too open about your past relationship has anything to do with how you'd handle Lou's career. It's not as if you know all that much about her past anyway, or that you'd ever think it's an important factor in her skating."

I paused, thinking that over. "They are pretty different situations. I mentioned my ex because I was happy being with him and wanted to share that happiness. There's definitely nothing to be happy about anything to do with Lou's mother."

Rafael gave a low guffaw. "Not at all. You've got to convince the officials that Lou is a great skater and not a liability, and that's what you already believe. Seems pretty straightforward to me, not much room for slipping up. Unless you were thinking you'd start pitching gunfire as a fun addition to the routine."

I couldn't restrain a snort. "No, there's no chance of that."

"There you go. You say what you mean, and that's what they need to hear, so there's nothing to worry about."

He sounded so confident that my nerves settled a little. He was right, after all. I wasn't hiding anything about Lou that I'd have wanted to say anyway. Everything I'd like the world to know about her was exactly the kind of things they *should* know to appreciate what an amazing athlete—and person—she was.

I smiled at Rafael, hoping I could return the favor. "You know, I could make a similar point when it comes to you. You made a big mistake years ago. But when you found out new information, you adjusted your mindset and took steps to fix things rather than sticking to the same course like the rest of your gang wanted to."

"I did what anyone should," Rafael muttered.

"But lots of people wouldn't," I said triumphantly. "Learning from your mistakes and being able to adapt and grow are things that don't come easily to a lot of people. But they are marks of a great leader."

Rafael opened his mouth as if he were going to argue and then paused. He frowned pensively before shaking his head in apparent bemusement. "Okay, you turned the tables on me. Maybe we're both being too hard on ourselves."

I grinned with the lift in my spirits. For a little while, faced with the barrage of accusations and requests, I'd felt alone and adrift. But we were a team—all of us, including Rafael.

We worked together in harmony, supporting each other, like any good relationship should work. The fact that we'd managed it even in one as complicated as ours was nothing short of incredible.

That's what we had here. Something totally incredible.

I picked up my phone. "I'm glad I could help—and thank you for your pep talk. Now I've got a couple of calls to make."

In the privacy of my room, I pulled up the number of the skating federation president. No time like the present to start setting everything else around us into harmony too.

To my relief, the secretary passed my call straight through. The president made a disapproving sound with his greeting. "It's good that you've finally returned my call."

"I appreciate you expressing your concerns," I said with all the cheerfulness I could summon. "I think there's a lot to say about Luna Garcia. Yes, she's come from a difficult past, but that means she brings a fresh perspective to the sport that we rarely see. Even in the short time I've been working with her, I can already tell she's going to transform figure skating in the best possible way…"

NINETEEN

Luciana

I SHIFTED my weight in the arena's bright yellow hallway, feeling like an elementary-school kid waiting to talk to the principal. Niko had gone into the manager's office alone to ask about booking rink time.

Beside me, Jasper glanced around the place. "I don't know if this is really our… vibe."

I grimaced. "We can't afford to worry about vibes. We can't go back to the Sports Garden arena now that my mom knows we've been training there, and there aren't enough slots at the big one to squeeze all our training in there. Even if we wanted everyone to catch on to the changes we've made to our routine."

"They're going to find out eventually," Quentin pointed out.

I shook my head. "It's bad enough us failing on our own without having a gazillion potential witnesses."

I still wasn't sure whether we should even keep trying the death spiral to lift transition. Our time before the competition was dwindling, and there'd been so many distractions. But I wasn't quite ready to let go of the hope that we could pull it off.

Neither was Jasper, apparently. He nudged my arm. "We'll find a place. If anyone can charm our way into some good ice time, it's Niko."

Quentin chuckled. "And if anyone can tackle one of the most difficult moves in skating, it's Lou Cordova."

Their affectionate encouragement lifted my spirits—which promptly sank again at Niko's expression as he left the office.

Our coach offered us an apologetic shrug. "He's booked solid for the next two weeks, which is the time we need it most."

Rafael and our newest allies were just sauntering over from a survey of the arena. The Deadly Rose defectors must have caught Niko's words, because Frankie propelled his tall but skinny frame forward with a scowl that pulled his cheek scar taut. "They don't have time, or they don't want to give it to Lou?"

A jolt of guilt jabbed my stomach, but Niko gave the gangster a mild look. "I didn't see any reason to think he was making false excuses."

Dámaso gave the hall a once-over. "The place doesn't seem secure enough anyway. Too many ways in and out."

"It'd be better than nothing." Frankie started to swagger over to the manager's office. "Maybe if I give him a piece of my mind—"

Rafael pushed in front of the younger guy with a glower. "We're not here to intimidate anyone. We're doing this by skating rules, not street rules."

Frankie let out a scoffing sound, but he stood down, eyeing my bodyguard warily.

Niko waved to us. "Come on. There's another place we can try in the next ward over."

We piled into our two cars and drove over with Niko directing, but when we came into the next arena's reception area, the guy monitoring the front desk gave Niko a series of deferential but obviously discouraging gestures while he talked.

Ursula frowned. "What's going on?"

I hugged myself. "I don't know. It doesn't look good."

Niko turned back to us. "He says the manager is busy and can't see us this afternoon."

"Fuck that!" Frankie strode up to the desk. "Listen up. My man here needs to talk to the people in charge, and—"

As the receptionist backed up with a panicked expression, Rafael grabbed Frankie by the shoulder. "Tell him we're sorry about our 'friend' here," he said to Niko, and yanked the skinny guy over to the opposite wall.

His voice lowered to a growl. "We're trying to make Lou look *good* here, not like a terrorist. We don't want people associating her with criminal low-lifes, so pull yourself together and stop acting like one, or you can sit this mission out."

My face burned with embarrassment as I dipped it in apology to the receptionist. But after Rafael's admonishment, Frankie did shut up, not even grumbling as he got into the defectors' car. Although he didn't exactly look happy.

After I'd slid into the back seat of our SUV, I raised my eyebrows at Rafael. "Look at you, stepping into the leadership role."

He met my teasing tone with a narrow look. "It doesn't mean anything. I haven't made up my mind about your offer."

"I'd vote for you as mafia king," Quentin piped up from the driver's seat.

Rafael sighed. "I'm still thinking about it." He brushed a strand of my hair back from my cheek with a stroke of his fingertips. "Let's say I'm giving it a try and testing out how I feel taking on a little more authority. We'll see how it goes."

I beamed at him and bobbed up to give him a quick kiss. "I can't ask for more than that." Then I gave the front passenger seat where Niko was perched a gentle kick. "Where to next, coach?"

Niko studied the list he'd made on his phone. "We haven't run out of options yet. And Emi is putting in some calls too. If I can just find someone who's impressed by my extensive star power…" He glanced over his shoulder to wink at me and froze as his gaze slid to the window.

My pulse hiccupped. "What?"

His throat bobbed with his swallow. "I think someone's here to talk to you."

I twisted around and found myself staring at the burly Asian man who'd spoken to us on behalf of the Bright Dragon not long after Niko's attack. He'd obviously just gotten out of the sleek sedan parked behind him, and now he was sauntering over with perfect poise, his gaze intent.

"Shit." I didn't want to have a conversation with any of the Devil's Dozen people in the parking lot of some random arena… but then, I didn't want to have any conversations with them at all. I guessed this was as good a place as any. No reporters around snapping pictures. No fans or pro skating colleagues looking on.

Actually, that was probably exactly why the guy had tracked me down here.

Gritting my teeth, I motioned for Rafael to open the door so we could both get out. The other guys followed. Seeing us emerge, the turncoats clambered out of their own car to see what was going on.

As my men and my new allies gathered around me, the Bright Dragon's rep came to a stop a few steps away. His expression stayed cool but mild.

He hadn't been as much of a jerk as the March Wind's lackey. I didn't think the Bright Dragon had been on Mom's side. But that didn't mean he was on my side either.

When I'd reported to Beckett that Mom had struck again despite the deal she'd made with her colleagues, he'd been pissed—and promised he was going to take it up with his colleagues immediately. He'd also informed me that his men who he'd given me contact info for had moved their forces right into Tokyo in case I needed help quickly in the future. I had no idea if the Bright Dragon knew about any of that yet or how he'd feel about it.

My fingers itched to call in some of Beckett's people right now for backup, but that might sour things faster when they weren't really necessary.

Instead, I propped myself against the SUV's trunk. "Fancy running into you here. Did you have something to say to me, or do you just hang out in random parking lots for fun?"

The rep held up his hands in a subtle gesture of peace. "Considering recent events, my employer felt we should have a talk."

"All right. About what?"

He cut his gaze toward the small crowd around me. "There are some things I'd rather not discuss in front of people who aren't part of our inner circle."

Before I could answer, Frankie stepped forward with a snort. "Oh, yeah? Well, we're her inner circle now, aren't we? After the way you dickwads have been treating her, you'd better give her and the rest of us some respect."

I whirled around. "Frankie, back off. I'm handling this."

He jabbed his hand toward the Bright Dragon's rep. "He's the one who should back off. These pricks are all the same, thinking they can bulldoze over everyone and call all the shots."

The other man's back had gone rigid, his eyes flashing with anger he didn't let seep into his flattened tone. "I can see my input is unwelcome here. I'll leave you to the counsel of your *wise* advisors then."

"Wait!" I shot a glare at Frankie and walked after the rep as he started to retreat. "He doesn't speak for me. I'm willing to talk. We're just all a little on edge after the constant attacks."

"Which *you* people have done shit-all to stop!" Frankie hollered before his voice cut off with a muffled grunt.

The Bright Dragon's man flicked one last dismissive glance my way. "You are who you associate with, Miss Cordova. You should remember that. We will. I've got better things to do than stand around being insulted."

He got into the sedan and jerked the door shut with a forceful thud.

Fuming, I spun around to see that Rafael had caught Frankie by the arm and clamped his other hand over the guy's mouth. As the sedan pulled out of the parking lot, Rafael let go.

"What the fuck were you thinking?" I snapped, marching up to Frankie. "He could have had something useful to say. He could have been offering an alliance to help keep my mom off my back."

Frankie scowled at me. "What do we need him and his stuffy boss or whoever for? It's not like they've done anything for us so far."

"That could have changed. You didn't give me the chance to find out."

"I told you to shut up," Rafael added, looming over the other guy. "If you're going to serve Lou, you've got to be able to follow orders—and recognize when she can handle a situation herself."

"Handle it herself?" Frankie sputtered. "These pricks keep coming at you. You can't make deals with them. At this rate—"

Rafael stepped closer, his gaze narrowed to a glare. "Now would be a good time to practice the shutting up."

"You've been going off half-cocked all day," I said, setting my hands on my hips. "That's not how I do things. The whole point is that I'm *not* constantly on the attack like my mother."

Frankie shoved away from Rafael, throwing his hands in the air. "Fine. Fine! You think you'll get far playing things like that, talking down to the people trying to tell you the truth? Handle it your way, then. I've got better things to do."

Dámaso extended an arm toward him. "Frankie, come on, man—"

The thinner guy shrugged him off and stormed away. I stared at his retreating back, wondering if he even knew how to handle the public transportation in the city to get back to the apartment building. I guessed he could always hail a cab.

I restrained a groan. "Well, that went horribly." How much damage had he done with the Bright Dragon? Had he just made me one more enemy when I was having enough trouble fending off the ones I'd already had?

Rafael's expression had clouded over with different concerns. "We're going to need to find another apartment. We can't trust him if he's getting into moods like that—and we can't have someone we don't trust knowing where we're living."

My heart lurched. I hadn't even thought that far ahead. "You're right. Let's get back and move our stuff out right now. We can always stay in a hotel until we get something more permanent sorted out."

Niko brandished his phone, smiling tightly. "I'll get on that right now."

As we turned to our cars, Ursula touched my arm. "I'm sorry," she said awkwardly. "He's been a hothead before, but I wouldn't have thought he'd go that overboard. He's just gotten real tense since the shootout at the mall."

Dámaso let out a derisive sound. "He didn't even get injured."

I heaved a breath. "We'll sort everything out. You two should pack up your things too. I'll let you know as soon as I figure out where we're going. And don't say anything to Frankie if he catches up with you there."

"Not a word," Dámaso promised solemnly. "He dug his own grave. He can deal with the fallout."

We scrambled back into our vehicles. Niko spent the whole drive making one call after another in animated Japanese, and announced just as we reached the apartment building that he'd found a couple of available short-term apartments in a place on the fringes of Tokyo. "Not as nice as this spot, but decent."

"The less flashy, the better," I said. "Okay, everyone—grab your stuff, and let's haul ass."

I don't think any of us had fully unpacked. I crammed my belongings into my suitcase, did a cursory sweep of the rooms, and hauled my luggage and my equipment bag down to the parking garage with my men at my heels.

My stomach stayed balled tight as we drove across the city to our new digs. We rode up in a plain but clean elevator to a three-bedroom apartment even more compact and spartan in décor than the last one.

But it was clean, and none of our enemies had any idea it existed.

We sorted out our rooms, and Niko, Jasper, and I ducked out for a quick grocery run. Niko handed off the defectors' keys to Ursula on our way down. When we made it back to the apartment, Rafael looked over our acquisitions and decided he could whip up some kind of dinner with them.

As the smells of boiling rice and sizzling garlic laced the air, I sagged onto the hard sofa and released some of my tension with a sharp exhalation. "Let's not do that ever again."

Quentin grabbed one of my feet and started massaging the arch.

"Hey, at least it's over now. We got out before that idiot could screw us over any more than he already had."

Niko let out a crow of excitement from across the room. "I found us a rink! One of the places I reached out to this morning says they had a cancellation and can fit us in now."

A startled but pleased laugh tumbled from my mouth. "Okay, I guess things are looking up a little."

Jasper stretched his arms over his head. "Some good food, a little relaxation, and tomorrow we can—"

The peal of a phone alert cut him off. Followed by a chime and a buzzing sound. And then a beep from a different direction.

All of our phones were going off.

"What the hell?" I muttered, groping for my purse.

Jasper pulled his from his pocket and stared at the screen. "Someone's asking me, 'Is this for real?' Is *what* for real?"

Quentin flicked his thumb across his screen and tapped on something. He flipped his phone sideways, squinted, and then went totally rigid in his seat. "Oh, fuck."

My gut lurched. "What is it?"

He opened his mouth and closed it again, looking too horrified to form words. All he could manage to do was beckon us over to see what had freaked him out so much.

TWENTY

Luciana

THE PHONE TREMBLED in Quentin's hand. I couldn't tell whether it was from anger, shock, or horror, because all three emotions were currently crashing through my body while I stared at the screen. I was dimly aware of Niko's phone pealing with another alert, but I couldn't tear my gaze away from the video footage playing within the frame of a public site.

Three figures moved together on a mass of rumpled bedcovers. There was Quentin, sprawled out with his head pressed into the pillow, his hips rocking. Me, bent over his thighs, my face blurred out to censor the most provocative areas while I sucked him off but identifiable in profile when I lifted my head briefly to grin at him. And Jasper, his entire hips area blurred as he pounded into me from behind.

Most of the time as we fucked each other, the average viewer probably couldn't have recognized us. The footage had been filmed from an angle that was off to the side beyond the foot of the bed. But every now and then we shifted position just enough that all of our features showed clearly.

Míerda. A shiver ran through my body, my skin chilling as if every drop of warming blood had left my veins. My legs wobbled under me, and Rafael grasped my arm to steady my balance. I barely registered the stream of curses mingling English and Spanish that flowed from his lips.

"It's already gotten more than ten thousand views," Quentin said in a hollow voice. "They're shooting up by the second."

Niko paced behind us with unusual urgency. When I managed to glance over at him, his expression was rigid. "A few major news outlets are already covering the story. They're calling it a scandal." His phone went off again, and he flinched. "Someone from the US Figure Skating organization is calling me. I've already gotten a message from the Japan Skating Federation. And several news stations."

"How the hell—how could anyone have recorded this?" I blurted out. "We were in the apartment. It was just the three of us."

Rafael's expression turned even more ominous. "Those fucking turncoats! They were taking turns guarding the apartment, remember? What day was it?"

I strained to think back through the whirl of my panicked thoughts. "The day you and Niko went to see about getting more weapons. That's why you weren't there."

Rafael balled his hands into fists. "Frankie was out there on guard duty when we left. That little prick."

Jasper blinked, looking totally dazed and a little queasy. "He snuck in and recorded us? Why the hell would he do that?"

Rafael grimaced. "The others said he's been acting off since the mall. He must have been starting to doubt whether he'd picked the right side."

The pieces clicked together in my head with sickening logic. "He was hedging his bets. Figuring if he should see if he could get anything to buy his way back into my mother's good graces if he decided to defect right back to her."

Quentin turned off his phone and then set it face down on the coffee table as if he couldn't stand to look at even the blank screen anymore. "And after you two told him off today, he did exactly that. It didn't take long for your mother to find a totally new way to attack us, huh?"

"It didn't." I swallowed hard and forced myself to check my own phone.

I had a bunch of messages popping up on my phone from unfamiliar numbers. When I opened up a couple of the social media sites and did a quick search for my skating name, a deluge of commentary on our threesome appeared. And most of it was caustic.

Slut.

Whore.

Must have slept her way into the World Championships.

I wonder how many judges she's done?

Can you imagine being that desperate?

Puking emojis. Vulgar gifs.

My blood was definitely pumping through my veins again, because my cheeks were burning with it. My stomach lurched, and I dismissed the app with a jab of my finger.

I was about to turn my phone right off when it vibrated with a notification of an incoming video chat request. An icon with Emi's picture popped up.

I hesitated, my hand tensing around the phone. Niko's sister had guessed at our joint relationship, but to have seen the proof of it in such explicit detail… I wasn't sure I wanted to face her right now.

On the other hand, she might be the only friend I had left outside this room.

Bracing myself, I hit the answer button.

Emi's face filled the whole screen, her eyes round with sympathy. "Lou, I just heard. This is crazy. Are you okay?"

How could I even answer that?

I made a vague motion with my free hand. "Not really. That video isn't something I'd ever have wanted anyone seeing. And it means one of the people we thought was an ally has betrayed us. We had no idea he even filmed us."

"I hope his ancestors rain down bad luck while they're watching over him," Emi declared with an angry huff. "I didn't watch it, of course—but people will be able to tell you didn't know you were being recorded, won't they? They'll know it's not your fault."

My mouth twisted with the misery tangling tighter inside me. "I don't know how much that'll matter. No one had any clue that I was dating Jasper *or* Quentin. For it to come out that I'm with both of them—and to come out like *this*… There are already a ton of judgmental comments all over the internet."

Emi gave me a firm look. "You're a good person, Lou. And an amazing skater. That should matter more than anything. The important people will see that."

I wished I could believe her reassurance, but it barely touched my jangling nerves. Still, I appreciated it.

"Thank you," I said. "I know you'll always see it that way. I don't suppose you have any idea how we get people focused on something else?"

Emi bit her lip. "I'm not sure. Usually it takes another big story, but you can't force that to happen." Then she brightened a bit. "But I'll think about it and let you know as soon as anything comes to me."

I had to smile at her enthusiasm, despite the nausea still churning in my gut. "That'd be great. And thank you for checking in on us too."

"Of course. Tell my brother he'd better update me as soon as he isn't so busy."

As I ended the call, I glanced over at Niko. He was still pacing while talking into his phone in brisk Japanese, sounding curter than I'd ever heard him. I'd been picking up the most useful basic phrases and bits of vocabulary here and there over the past several weeks, but I couldn't make out a single word in his rapid-fire delivery.

He ended the call and lowered his hand with a jerk. When he turned to face us, his expression was so grim it made my heart ache.

"One of our sponsors just pulled their support. I wouldn't be surprised if others do too. There are clauses in the contracts around professional conduct… I don't know how to fix this."

I rubbed my face, struggling to sort through the clash of emotions inside me. "Is there any way we could convince people that it isn't us? You can't see our faces *that* well."

Quentin frowned. "Everyone's already sure it is. Now that our names have been attached to it, I don't know how we'd change that. And it isn't like people haven't noticed the three of us skating together. If we didn't already have some connection, maybe, but…"

"Yeah." Guilt swelled up over everything else. This was my fault. "If I hadn't trusted Frankie—if my mom wasn't such a fucking *cunt*—"

Rafael slid his arm around me. "This isn't on you, Lou. You made the best decisions you could with the information you had. You three are the victims of a crime. There's nothing wrong with what you were doing."

"A whole lot of people seem to think there is." I looked desperately at Niko. "What are the skating officials saying?"

His anguished expression didn't shift. "I've only listened to a couple of the messages so far, but they're even more concerned than before about the publicity. Talking about lack of professionalism and things like that."

"Shit." Jasper raked his hand through his hair. "And the judges will hear about it—maybe even watch the recording. Even if they say it won't make them biased against us, you know it'll skew their opinions."

My agonized thoughts had already traveled even farther than that. "Will they even allow us to compete after this kind of scandal?"

Quentin's gaze darkened. "I don't know. I don't think there's ever been a scandal quite like this in the sport."

Niko looked haunted. "I'll talk to all of them. I'll impress on them that you were the ones violated—that it was totally consensual—that it has nothing to do with your careers. And I should be able to have the video taken down… from the more legitimate sites, anyway."

His attention shot back to his phone as he got to work on a task I doubted he could have ever imagined he'd need to take on as our coach. I dropped into the nearest chair, my head spinning so fast I was dizzy and my stomach clenched tight.

Was this it? The end of everything I'd worked to achieve—destroyed because of my sex life, of all things?

Was Mom going to win after all? I could just imagine her grinning at the thought of stealing my freedom out from under me.

You might keep living, Luciana, I could hear her say, *but it won't be happily.*

I didn't want to accept that. I wanted to fight her like I had in so many ways already.

But how the hell could I turn this catastrophe around?

TWENTY-ONE

Quentin

WITH EACH SECOND THAT ticked by leading up to my cue to walk on stage, my heart thudded harder. I stared out at the set hastily assembled for this US news station's time covering the World Championships, watching the polished blond woman chatting with one of the French skaters and barely processing a single word that reached my ears.

I didn't want to be here. I wanted to give every reporter in Japan, local or otherwise, the middle finger for making such a big deal out of the leaked video.

But the controversy wasn't going away. All three of us—Lou, Jasper, and me—had gotten requests for interviews, and strangely they'd focused on me the most. Maybe they saw me as the weakest link because I wasn't actually competing. Maybe they were curious about the potential drama of my once having been Jasper's rival.

In any case, we'd decided that someone should make a public appearance to set a few things straight, and I'd rather it was me than

Lou or Jasper having their focus shaken. A lot of the questions that'd started coming up were things only I could fully address anyway.

I'd taken a bullet for Lou. Handling a TV audience should be child's play.

But that didn't mean I was going to enjoy it.

There was a cut to go to commercials. One of the staff tapped my elbow. "You'll be on in a minute, Mr. Wolfe."

I nodded. The French skater had just vacated the seat next to the host's desk, where I'd be sitting in mere moments. The host sat stiffly as the makeup crew gave her face a quick touch-up.

Must be nice getting to ask all the questions and never having to be under scrutiny for anything other than your lipstick and eyeliner.

My hands twitched at my sides. I'd come alone, not wanting to expose the others to further speculation, but damn if I didn't wish I had Lou here beside me right now, smiling her fearless smile, squeezing her fingers around mine. She'd given me an emphatic kiss right before I left, and if I concentrated I could still taste her on my lips, but it wasn't the same.

I mentally smacked myself across the head. I'd survived just fine without any woman supporting me for years. I didn't *need* Lou holding my hand through this.

It just… would have been nice.

Before I could grapple with my longings any further, the man who'd warned me motioned me out onto the stage. I plastered a tight smile on my face and strode to the waiting chair.

The glow of the studio lights glared down on me. Blinking, I settled into my seat and clasped my hands on my lap. With each passing moment, my smile felt more rigid.

"Quentin Wolfe, gold medalist in the US Junior Championships a few years back, silvers and bronzes under your belt from recent years," the host said by way of introduction. "It's an honor to have you on the show."

Somehow I didn't believe it was my medals that had her salivating to talk to me. I bobbed my head and kept that thought to myself. "I'm glad to be here, Ms. Anderson," I said, lying through my teeth.

"Oh, call me Nancy," the host said with a flash of her brilliant teeth. "You've been in the competitive figure skating circuit for quite some time, haven't you?"

They were starting with the easy questions, of course. "That's right. I registered as soon as I was old enough—made it to Nationals in my second year."

I was allowed to still be proud of the victories I'd had, wasn't I?

"Indeed you did." Nancy Anderson flashed her teeth again. "You were considered quite a promising up-and-comer with the way you burst onto the scene. How did you cope with that kind of pressure?"

I already had a standard answer to that. "Honestly, it was nothing compared to the pressure I'd always put on myself. I just saw it as extra incentive to perform my best, which I always wanted to do anyway."

Nancy tilted her head to the side with a coy expression. "It is notable that in the past year, you switched from competing in singles, as you always have in the past, to pairs during the qualifying rounds. Was there any particular reason for that?"

I shrugged as casually as I could. "I had done a little pairs skating in the past and connected with my previous partner under our coach. It seemed like a good challenge."

"And it was around that time that you met Luna Garcia."

"Yes," I said, even though it wasn't a question. After years facing my mother's demands and barrages of criticism, I knew how to keep all emotion from my face and my voice. "We were training at the same arena in Boston."

I didn't know whether to be relieved or concerned that Nancy didn't continue prodding that particular subject just yet. She leaned her chin onto her hand. "Unfortunately, it seems the switch to pairs didn't work out all that well for you. You ultimately placed too low in the Finals competition to earn a spot at the National Championships. Did you consider returning to singles?"

I kept my tone even. "It crossed my mind, but in the end that didn't work out."

Nancy raised her eyebrows. "I'm surprised by that, especially considering the intense competitive spirit you just remarked on yourself. At what point during that period did you strike up a closer relationship with Miss Garcia?"

My stomach sank with the recognition of where she was heading with the convergence of questions, but I kept my annoyance under wraps. "It wasn't until after the Finals competition. Seeing her performances made me want to get to know her better."

"Would you say your early interest in her might have been somewhat… distracting when it came to your own performance at Finals?"

There it was. She was trying to insinuate that my failures were *Lou's* fault.

How fucking dare anyone blame the woman I adored for my screw-ups.

"Not at all," I forced myself to say smoothly. "If anything, she motivated me to do my best. But it was a gamble switching to pairs so late in training, and that gamble didn't pay off. I can only blame myself for the loss."

As the words fell from my mouth and my frustration with the interview simmered inside me, it struck me for the first time how true that was. I didn't hold the slightest bit of resentment toward Jasper or any of the other skaters who'd advanced ahead of me, not anymore.

I *had* made my own choices about how to handle my career—and my personal life too. Maybe I'd started with less than other people, but I'd probably had more than some. Could I really say that my overbearing mom had been a bigger burden than Jasper's frigid asshole of a dad?

I'd carved out a spot for myself in the professional figure skating world, and I'd arrived ages ago. At this point, it really didn't matter where I'd started, did it? I had to own the decisions I'd made and the paths I'd taken rather than finding excuses for the ones that hadn't worked out.

Nancy wasn't finished speculating yet. She tapped her chin with her finger. "You could have staged a comeback at Nationals with your solo routines. Is it fair to say that your budding relationship with Ms. Garcia diverted some of your attention then?"

I couldn't completely rein in my temper, a little heat creeping into my voice. "No, I wouldn't say that's fair at all. The fact of the matter is, I wasn't able to compete in Nationals mainly because of an injury that had nothing at all to do with Lou." Okay, that was a lie, but I'd *wanted* to save her life, so fuck anyone who'd claim it was somehow her fault. "Lou has always supported my skating and encouraged me to be even better than I already am."

"Even when you were competing against each other?" Nancy asked with a light laugh that made me want to punch her carefully painted face.

I drew myself up straighter in my chair. "Yes. Even then. If anything, *I* tried to distract *her*, but she was too professional to let me get under her skin. And since I've come around to realizing that I'm better off beside her than against her, she's pushed me to up my game and encouraged me to focus on areas of my performance I'd neglected before. I'm absolutely a stronger skater because of our time together."

Nancy hesitated, as if she wasn't sure what to make of the vehemence in my voice. Then she wet her lips as if she had a particularly juicy question to come. I braced myself.

"That's wonderful to hear," she said. "But it's recently come out that your relationship with Miss Garcia is rather… unconventional. It seems she's wanted more than what you two had together."

I barely held back a snort. "If anyone had a right to be bothered by that situation, it was Jasper, not me. He and Lou were together before I even met her, and I always knew that. But something sparked between me and Lou too, and Jasper's man enough to want her to be as happy as possible more than he wants to keep her all to himself. Like they've already said in their public statements, both he and I are totally comfortable with the arrangement we have."

I wasn't going to mention there were two other men in the mix. If the media was going to find out about Niko's or Rafael's more intimate roles in Lou's life, it wouldn't be from me. They were making enough fuss over just a threesome.

Nancy nodded in a way that felt condescending. "Yes, I've heard that. It's just a little hard to believe—as I'm sure many of our viewers will agree—that such an unusual twist to your personal life wouldn't have some impact on your career."

I flexed my hands to keep them from balling into fists. This woman really didn't know how to lay a subject to rest, did she?

Well, if she needed a target other than plain old me, I could give her one.

The idea that'd just struck me sent a jolt that was both exhilaration and apprehension through my chest. For a second, my tongue turned to lead in my mouth. If I said something, if I burned that bridge so publicly—

Then what? It'd simply make it that much harder for me to go back to what I knew was an unhealthy dynamic anyway.

Lou had found the courage to speak up about what she'd endured in front of the world. And the world already had a pretty big inkling what I'd gone through. Why shouldn't I confirm it?

I fixed the host with my firmest stare. "Look, I get that the video that got out startled a lot of people. But what you all really should be worried about is catching the prick who broke into our apartment to record it. As far as my ability to skate goes, there's only one person who's ever interfered with that, and it's not Luna Garcia."

Nancy's eyes lit up with eagerness. "Care to say a little more about that, Mr. Wolfe?"

"I do." I jerked my gaze toward the cameras. "The only person who's made it harder for me to give my all on the ice is my mother. But I got tired of her beating me down and trying to control my career, and I recently cut off all ties with her. So you can expect bigger and better things from me when the next competitive circuit kicks off."

With the last announcement, a rush of relief flooded my veins. It was out in the open—I couldn't have made the separation between me and Mom more definitive.

Nancy obviously hadn't expected that declaration. Her mouth hung open for a moment before she gathered herself. "Well. That definitely sounds like it'll be exciting to see. It sounds like you're really embracing your freedom as an adult skater and this… unique relationship you've found yourself in."

"Yes," I said automatically. "I absolutely am."

My mind tripped back to my time on the rink with both Lou and Jasper. Watching them train and getting their encouragement while I worked on my own routines.

But the best had been that day when the three of us had really skated together, both of them offering me tips and demonstrating, Jasper and I passing Lou back and forth between us. More than anything that happened with us outside of our sport, right then I'd felt like I was part of something bigger than just myself. Bigger than anything I'd ever imagined was possible.

A flicker of inspiration lit in my head. I hesitated, letting it weave through my thoughts, and a smile I actually meant stretched across my face.

"You know, Nancy," I said, "I think the world should keep an eye on us. Because we might have something to show off that's a lot more worth watching than that stupid video."

Curiosity sharpened the host's eyes. "And what might that be?"

I let my smile widen. The answer would depend on how Lou and Jasper reacted to my pitch, but I was sure I could convince them one way or another. "You'll just have to wait and see."

TWENTY-TWO

Luciana

NIKO LOWERED his phone with a sigh that he quickly did his best to compensate for with a smile. I sat up on the sofa where I'd been slumped, my chest tight with trepidation. "What did they say?"

His smile tightened. "The skating officials are going to have a meeting tomorrow to make an official decision. I've reminded them as clearly as I can that the current situation isn't your fault and has nothing to do with your skating careers. If they make the right choice, they should allow you to go forward with the competition."

Jasper let out a rough sound from the chair where he was slouching and rubbed his face. "*Should* being the operative word. They're really not happy with us."

Rafael grunted from his post by the door. "You'd think they'd appreciate the publicity you're bringing to the sport."

I grimaced. "Not this kind of publicity."

Niko wagged his finger at us. "Don't make any assumptions. We can't know what the verdict will be until they've discussed it. The facts are on your side."

The good humor in his tone didn't reach his eyes. I was sure he knew as well as I did that facts didn't mean shit in a case like this.

What mattered was that the most private details of my sex life were being shared all across the internet, and there was fuck-all I could do about it. For the rest of my life, I'd run into strangers who knew how I moved and what I sounded like in a threesome.

That wasn't the kind of fame I'd ever have wanted.

I wrapped my arm around my stomach, willing down the queasiness, and a new worry rose up. "Shouldn't Quentin be back from his interview by now?"

Jasper frowned. "It was only a half hour ago that he texted to say he was on his way back. I wouldn't call that late yet."

"I'm sure he'll be in a great mood too," I muttered sarcastically, not that I could complain when my spirits were at least as low as everyone else's in the room.

We'd come all this way. I'd worked so fucking hard. Surely all that passion and effort weren't going down the drain because of an illegal sex tape, of all things?

But I couldn't see any way out of the fate that felt more certain with every passing minute.

The lock in the apartment door clicked. I pushed to my feet just as Quentin stepped inside, his head high and his lips curved with a… grin?

As I stared at the newest of my boyfriends, blinking in my confusion, he kicked the door shut behind him and aimed his grin at all of us while he rubbed his hands together. "I've got an idea. It might be crazy, but it could actually be perfect."

His eagerness tickled into me with a jolt of hope. "What are you talking about?"

Quentin turned to Niko rather than me. "Okabe, do you figure you're up to the challenge of throwing together a very unique routine, incredibly quickly?"

Niko took a swig from the Calpis he'd brought from the kitchen and eyed the younger man with an air of growing amusement. "I'll never refuse a challenge. But what would this routine be for?"

Quentin gestured vaguely in the air, his gaze seeking out mine and Jasper's. "I want to show the world just how well the three of us can collaborate—and that our relationship isn't something they should see as dirty. It can be art too. It's something amazing when we decide what part of it they should get to watch."

The understanding of what he was getting at seeped through my thoughts. My breath caught in my throat. "That… that could really be something." Then I paused. "You're thinking we should try to get this publicized—covered on TV and all that. Are you sure you want to make a public performance focused on the three of us?"

"Why the hell not?" Quentin demanded. "They're already making all kinds of assumptions about us based on something we wouldn't have let them see. I love you, and I love this crazy relationship we've all built together. They might as well know that on our terms rather than your mother's."

"I'm in," Jasper said, quiet but determined. "It could be a total flop—or it could blow people away. I'm willing to take that chance."

A brighter smile had crossed Niko's face. "I can already picture the routine. It'll be an honor to choreograph something like that."

My mouth opened and closed again. They were all taking a much bigger risk than I was. They were the ones with the established names that'd be tarnished if this plan only made us look ridiculous.

I wanted to try, but I didn't want to screw up their lives any more than their connection to me already had.

Before I could decide on an answer, Quentin stepped up to me and caught my hand in his. "What we've got is something special. If the world can't tell that, then they're all idiots."

His eyes gleamed with passion, and he tugged me into a kiss. The emphatic claiming of my lips melted my reservations, leaving only the glow of hope behind.

Hope and another emotion to answer the confession he'd made. When he drew back, seeking out my gaze again, I beamed up at him. "I love you too. Let's do it. Let's show them what that love really looks like."

My attention slid away from him to the other men standing around me.

Rafael with his stoic confidence and unyielding support.

Niko and his boundless serenity and warmth.

Jasper, his soulful gray-green eyes coupled with his fire-hot touch.

And Quentin in front of me, stubborn and difficult but oh-so-brilliant in ways I obviously hadn't fully appreciated yet.

My heart swelled in my chest. "I love all of you. So, so much. I think what we've built together is pretty fantastic, don't you?"

Jasper reached out to twist a strand of my hair between his fingers. A familiar light was glinting in his eyes.

He cleared his throat as a flush crept up his neck. "You know, we haven't actually *all* collaborated together. Not at the same time. That could be the perfect way to get our creativity flowing. A little inspiration?"

His tone sent a flare of heat over my skin. Looking around at the other men, I saw the same desire mirrored in all of their expressions.

I loved them, and I wanted them. I wanted to remember how wonderful this collaboration between us really was instead of getting bogged down in other people's judgments.

A little passionate fun might be just what we needed to clear our minds of all that crap and then get down to work.

I wet my lips. "I'm up for it if you all are?"

Niko's lips curved into a sly smile that left no doubt about his interest. Quentin stepped toward me, his normally cool gaze searing my skin. "Hell, yes."

Rafael's mouth twitched with what might have been a hint of a smirk. "I'll make sure the door is fully secure."

"Good thinking," I muttered.

Then Jasper tipped my chin up so he could claim a kiss, and every concern left my head except how I could enjoy even more of this delicious man.

There was a click as Rafael checked the door, and then he was behind me, his large hands sliding down my body. He eased them beneath the fabric of my leggings and tucked his fingers against the divots of my hips. With a tug to bring my ass against his groin, he showed just how much he wanted me without saying a word.

My pussy throbbed for him. But when I lifted my head, it was Quentin I saw first. He yanked off his shirt as he approached me, revealing the leanly sculpted planes of his chest. I couldn't resist tracing my fingers over the taut ridges before he grasped my tee to give me the same treatment.

As soon as he'd tossed my shirt on the ground, he gripped my ponytail and tilted my head to the side so he could nip the crook of my neck. When he flicked his tongue right up to my earlobe, trailing sparks in its wake, I couldn't restrain a gasp.

Niko tucked his head over Jasper's shoulder, his smile turning momentarily a bit shy. But after Jasper leaned into the kiss the other man offered, our coach made short work of his shirt before wrapping his arms around Jasper's waist. Watching them fall back into another kiss, long and lingering, made my pussy clench even tighter while Quentin and Rafael worked me over.

Niko turned toward me and captured my lips with his. I hummed happily against his mouth, with a sharper whimper when Quentin tweaked one nipple between his fingers.

Rafael chuckled softly. "Let me get this out of the way for you."

With a brush of his knuckles against my back, he unclasped my bra. The second the cups fell away, Quentin ducked his head to suck the peak of my breast into his mouth.

Niko drew me into another kiss and then eased back while Rafael fondled the other side of my chest from behind. As I writhed between my men, Niko tipped his head toward the bedrooms. "Should we take this to a bed? I don't know if we'll all fit on any of the ones in this apartment."

A light laugh spilled from Jasper's lips. "I think we've finally found a flaw in your country's traditions: the beds are too small."

Niko let out a playful huff. "I'm sure if we end up making a more permanent home here, we could have something custom made."

I managed to speak around another whimper. "There's plenty of room right here on the rug. I think we're good."

As if to make sure of that, Rafael stepped away from me just long enough to shove the coffee table aside. Then he spun me around and pulled me down onto the sofa, straddling his lap.

I couldn't stop myself from grinding against his rigid cock. My panties were absolutely drenched—and the situation was made even worse when Quentin came up beside us and helped Rafael strip them and my leggings right off me.

I grasped both of their flies to make sure the nakedness was kept up on all sides and glanced over my shoulder at Jasper. "I trust you to take care of Niko. He's got *way* too many clothes on."

My partner blushed adorably but got right to work, stealing kisses from our shared boyfriend between each article he tossed aside. Then he bent over me and swept my hair to the side to nibble the corner of my jaw. "I'm not done with you yet either," he murmured in my ear.

"I'm not done with any of you, not by a long shot," I retorted, and delved my fingers inside Quentin's boxers.

His cock felt amazing, pulsing against my palm. I urged him toward me, and he knelt on the sofa, right where I could lower my head to lap my tongue over the bulging head.

As Rafael swiveled his hands against my breasts, I took Quentin all the way into my mouth. Quentin inhaled shakily and bucked to meet me, clutching at my hair again.

I felt ravenous for him, sucking harder and whirling my tongue around his length, but Quentin's grip on my hair tightened. "Slower," he rasped. "I want to enjoy every second of this."

I did as requested, my eyes finding his bright blue ones as I got back to work. His jaw clenched, his gaze burning with passion. I trailed one hand down his bare thigh where I massaged the taut muscle I found there.

When I felt his body tighten further, I pulled away. I wasn't ready for him to finish yet.

Instead, I turned back towards Rafael, moving my body in soft undulating motions against his. My hands slid across the broad expanse of his shoulders as I took in the twin burning flames that were his eyes. His kiss offered just as much fire.

I curled against him further as he bit down on my lip. With a gasp, I squirmed on his lap, desperate for release.

"You're such a brat," my bodyguard crooned. "You know how to make me want you so fucking badly. God, I want to take you right here, right now."

I dipped my head toward his. "So what's stopping you?" I whispered.

Something primal clicked inside of him. He picked me up while I giggled breathlessly in his arms and laid me flat on the rug. The head of his cock pressed between my folds. My lips parted in a gasp, but it was smothered by another kiss.

Somewhere in there, a foil packet ripped. Before I could register what was happening, Rafael pressed forward inside of me. I groaned, my eyelids fluttering closed. The sensation of him filling me up felt so right.

He thrust forward slowly, teasing me with his length, and then, all of a sudden, he pulled out. I whimpered in disappointment, but that only put a smile on his face.

"If you want more, you're going to have to work for it. Let's see what you can do. Get Jasper and Niko off at the same time, and then I'll let you have what you want."

Challenge accepted.

I shot him a teasing grin, and then eased off him to scoot towards my next two targets. They were willing victims; both Jasper and Niko were rock hard before I even got my hands on them.

They eased to the floor on either side of me. I kissed Jasper hard and then claimed Niko's mouth, tasting their flavors mingled together on each other's lips to thrilling effect. My hands raked thin red lines down their bodies as they swayed toward me.

Their warmth was enough to melt away all my previous worries. Every ounce of anxiety that had previously taken up space inside my head and heart evaporated into the atmosphere, leaving me with nothing but their protective, hungry love.

Still passing kisses back and forth, I reached out with both hands and grasped their untended erections. Their matching groans made a perfect symphony. Simultaneously, I ran my thumbs over the head of their cocks. Niko's teeth nicked my lower lip in the middle of our kiss, and Jasper thrust into my grasp.

"God, Lou," he groaned, "you can't just tease me like this."

Niko's hips jerked upward. "Right. That's my job."

I smirked at the sight. They were fully under my control—but that didn't mean that I would keep it for long. Jasper was gasping, but he was quickly gaining a handle on himself. As he rocked into my hand, he tilted my chin up to look at him.

The firestorm in his eyes sparked up a river of desire within my core. My legs shifted together, my pussy clenching in my center. I was desperate for satisfaction. Teasing Niko and Jasper was getting me hotter than I could stand.

As if sensing my need, Niko reached between my legs. He fingered my clit with the same eager energy he brought to so much else, setting of a flood of starker pleasure through my nerves. My knees wobbled. When he hooked one finger right inside me, I outright moaned.

Apparently Rafael needed satisfaction too. The next thing I knew, he was crouching on the floor behind me, his breath spilling hot down my spine.

"You did a good enough job," he growled. "I guess you deserve a little bit of a reward."

"I do," I gasped, writhing between the three of them. "I really do."

He wasn't stingy with rewarding me. His hands traveled around my body, leaving a scorching trail of bliss wherever they touched. My lips parted with a feverish panting. I allowed the pleasure to take over, to become my sole focus.

Quentin's cocky voice broke through my reverie. "Don't forget to share."

He'd hunkered down on the floor too. Before I could figure out exactly how to attend to him too, Rafael took over for me.

"Suit yourself up and get over here," he growled at the younger man.

As Quentin grabbed another condom, Niko and Jasper eased a little apart. I let go of them for just long enough for Rafael to lift me off the floor—to make room for Quentin to slide beneath me. He slid one hand down to adjust his pulsing member, inviting me to sheath myself on it.

I didn't deny him. The feeling of him sliding into me felt like fireworks in my core. I rocked my hips against him, keeping Rafael in my peripheral vision as he positioned himself behind me. When the bigger man nudged his erection against my back opening, I nodded in eager anticipation and leaned forward to allow him easier entrance.

His thick cock felt like fire at first, but after his first few strokes, nothing but ecstasy raced through my veins. The two of them filling me together felt like heaven. With every joint thrust, I was soaring higher.

"God, don't stop," I moaned, not even knowing which of them I was referring to. Both, really. "Please don't."

But I couldn't neglect my other two men, even if Rafael had decided I'd completed my duty. Through the haze of pleasure, I swayed to the side and hovered my mouth over Niko's straining cock.

"You're amazing, Angel," he murmured as he adjusted his position to allow me better access.

I caught Jasper's gaze and jerked my head toward our coach. "Let's make sure Niko has *all* the inspiration he needs."

Lust flared in Jasper's eyes. As I sucked Niko down, he positioned himself behind the other man. Careful of the still healing injury on Niko's chest, he tucked his arm around Niko's slim waist. The giddy shudder of Niko's body against mine told me when Jasper had slid inside him.

I took that as a cue to up my pace. I took all of him, as much as I was able to. It was all I could do to keep my mouth bobbing up and down over his musky skin while Quentin and Rafael send more bliss spiraling through me with their increasingly frantic rhythm. Every part of me was filled, but it wasn't just my pussy that felt close to bursting. Love and awe resonated through my chest.

As I careened toward the edge, Quentin gave a sharper jerk upward. He let out a ragged sound as he came. With him still inside me, I pressed back into Rafael's thrusts—and he flung me even higher with one final plunge of his cock. His strangled breath told me he'd joined me.

I moaned my climax around Niko's cock. As Rafael spilled himself, I stroked Niko's balls. He rocked between me and Jasper for a few more seconds before spurting his release into my mouth.

"Fuck," Jasper groaned from behind him. He bit down on Niko's shoulder as he joined our mass coming. Then, as I lifted my head, he leaned across the other man to claim one last kiss from me.

I rolled off Quentin to collapse between my men, my chest heaving, every part of me alight with the afterglow. The four of them cuddled closer, each finding some part of my naked, sweat-damp body to caress.

"Wow," Jasper said with a hoarse laugh. "We really pulled that off. What would you call it—a five-some?"

A giggle spilled out of me. Every shred of anxiety had left my body with that epic collision of passion. "That sounds about right."

Niko's eyes twinkled. "Don't doubt what we can accomplish when we work together."

A grin stretched my lips. Yes. We were capable of just about anything.

I tapped him on the chest. "Which means we can pull off Quentin's crazy plan too. So you'd better get started choreographing."

TWENTY-THREE

Luciana

A HANDFUL of the media channels we'd invited out to the arena were already there before we'd even arrived. More trickled in as we put on our skates and went through our warm-up. By the time we were ready for the actual performance, we had a whole row of reporters waiting for whatever we had to show them, the cameras in their midst blinking little red lights.

As I took my position between Jasper and Quentin, my chest tightened. I had to make a conscious effort to loosen my lungs with deep breaths. It was way too late to turn back now. We'd either pull this thing off or make total fools of ourselves, only compounding the disgrace we were in with the skating community.

Dios mío, let it be the first option.

I stared down at the ice for a moment as if I could see right through it. We'd only had a matter of hours to practice the hastily choreographed routine, not weeks or even months like we normally would have.

But Niko had made it as easy as possible on us by using moves from our existing routines in similar arrangements, just figuring out simple ways to expand and combine those elements—ways that were more about artistry than complex physical stunts. I *knew* we could handle every part of it.

We had to show the world the real beauty of our collaboration.

Jasper glanced over at me. His sea-green costume both contrasted with and complimented the flame-red one Quentin had on and my own pearly pale get-up. Since we didn't have matching costumes for all three of us, we'd gone with an array instead, and Niko had taken that visual aspect into account with the choreography.

"Are you all right?" my partner asked.

I shot him a quick smile. "Yeah. Nervous, but we've got this, right?"

The corner of Jasper's mouth curled upward. "You bet we do. This'll be a heck of a lot easier than some of the moves we've pulled off in the past."

I couldn't help laughing at the truth of his statement. "No kidding."

Quentin rolled his shoulders. "We'll go out there and skate and then head home. Let the reporters and the skating officials make whatever they want of it. After we do our bit, it's not up to us anymore."

I exhaled in a rush. "Sounds good to me."

If Jasper could smile through this—grumpy Jasper who had once scowled through a week's worth of practices—then couldn't I? If Quentin, the cocky asshole of the year, could come up with an idea that could bring us all together, how could I do anything other than believe in it?

I squared my shoulders. For them, I would fly to the moon just to snatch them a handful of stars.

Niko motioned to us from the stands, where he had the music ready to play. He was beaming as cheerfully as ever, but I could tell the crowd of reporters was getting antsy.

I nodded, and the three of us shifted into our opening poses. My blood pounded through my veins, but I let the rhythm lift my spirits rather than rattling them.

Just make it through this, and then we can go home. Just believe in the plan. Believe in the men who've stood by me through so much.

The song started to drift through the PA system. With the opening notes, the crowd of onlookers melted from my mind. All that was left was Quentin and Jasper, and the knowledge that Niko and Rafael were watching from the benches, full of love and support.

I allowed myself to be taken in by the gentle melody as I drifted gracefully across the ice. Between my two lovers, I could imagine that I floated in a soft bubble of protection that was much more tender than the world outside.

It was a short routine, about the length of a typical short program, but we were making the most of it—and of our trio. I spun from Quentin to Jasper and back again. Their hands lingered on my sides, my shoulders, love glowing in their eyes.

We pulled off a triple Salchow in perfect sync, three blades clacking against the ice with our landing in time with the music. My men whipped around me and grasped me on either side.

This was one of the trickier parts of the routine, but we'd kept the lift itself simple, knowing that having two men as the base would be a spectacle in itself. Quentin and Jasper hoisted me into the air by my calves and then my feet, holding me above their shoulders as we glided forward. I arced my arms gracefully through the air.

As they lowered me, I risked a glance at the audience. Everyone's eyes were glued to us, still and silent as they took in our performance.

Was that awe on their faces or doubt? Quentin swirled me around and sent me careening toward Jasper, and for a second, I lost track of my feet. I reached Jasper at a slightly wrong angle, off-balance for the spin we were meant to complete.

I wobbled—and Jasper's strong arms managed to right me. He swung me around, and my body loosened again as I felt it lock into the right position.

It didn't matter what the spectators thought. *We* knew that what we could make together was beautiful. If they couldn't see it, it was their loss.

We pranced across the ice in a swift sequence of footwork. I caught a brief sway from Quentin, who'd stretched himself the most to learn this specific section of the routine, but he caught himself so quickly I wasn't sure the audience would even have noticed.

We were moving in harmony, totally aware of each other's presence, totally united in our love and our passion for our art.

The music swelled and so did my pride. Quentin glided up at my left side, Jasper on my right. We were in the home stretch—just a few epic moves to end things with a smash. Well, hopefully not a literal one.

I gave myself over to the second lift, letting Quentin grip my shoulder while Jasper swept my hips into the air. We spiraled around as one being, my arm and leg lifting to add elegance to the pose.

Then, with the cue in the music, the two men pushed themselves faster. They launched me into the air so I could spin with a graceful double toe-loop jump. I could have tried for a triple, but we'd felt that would be too risky with the unusual launch.

Almost there. I wove between Jasper and Quentin, forming an infinity symbol with my path as we skated forward, and then fell back into synchronization with them. As much as I wanted to look into their faces and draw confidence from them, I had to focus on my own portion of this next move.

At the trill in the song, we all pushed off into our triple Axels. My legs whipped off the ice, my hands outstretched towards the stands. I was defying gravity, flying high, and connecting with the ice in a stable landing that reverberated through my lowered leg.

Next to me, Jasper's leg dipped to catch his balance. Not an absolutely perfect landing, but it was impressive that we'd pulled off the synchronized jump at all with so little practice. He regained his form in an instant.

We whirled together in a three-part spin that Niko had invented specifically for this routine. My heart soared as I leaned back with one hand extended. Watching this moment from the videos Niko had recorded had taken my breath away. I could only hope it was doing the same for our audience now.

But if it didn't, I still knew the three of us were creating something marvelous, something bigger than we were as individuals. If the rest of the world couldn't see that, there was nothing else left that we could show them.

The whirlwind that kept me in motion slowed, and we twined our arms in an ending pose that spoke of solidarity and devotion, our heads dipped together. My breath was coming hard, and I could hear the guys panting, but there was elation in the sound.

We'd completed the whole routine with no major mistakes. We'd offered up a performance like nothing the professional skating world had accepted before.

Now all that was left was the audience's reaction.

In the first few seconds after the music faded out, there was total silence. My pulse gave a nervous hiccup.

Then applause rang out from the stands, along with a couple of eager whoops.

A smile sprang to my face. We turned and bowed together with clasped hands while the clapping continued. A sense of resolve glowed in my chest.

Even if this performance wasn't enough to prove that we were more than a salacious news story and that our joint relationship was nothing to be ashamed of, it should have been. We knew what we stood for.

Now everything depended on just how closed-minded the skating officials decided to be.

TWENTY-FOUR

Luciana

VOICES RESONATED all around me beneath the rink's high ceiling. Jasper, Quentin, and I had been ambushed by reporters the second we'd stepped off the ice. They seemed to be running some kind of rotation, talking to each of us.

Thankfully, so far everyone had sounded upbeat and even excited about the performance. The man aiming his microphone at my face right now was grinning. "Finally, I have to ask: what prompted the three of you to pull together this unexpected routine?"

I had to laugh. "I think that should be pretty obvious. There's been a lot of talk about us in the news lately, and we wanted to show another side to the story."

As the man nodded and made a few concluding remarks to the camera, Niko leaned his head over from behind me. "The comments on the live broadcasts are blowing up," he said under his breath. "It's all been really positive. The fans are loving the performance—and all three of you."

A smile sprang to my lips, just in time for another reporter to dart into the gap in front of me. She pointed her mic toward me, her eyes shining.

"Luna Garcia, it's great to speak with you today. What were you hoping to get across with this routine?"

The answer came easily. "All three of us wanted to show the skating world that there's nothing wrong with us being together—in whatever way we'd like to be—and that we can create something amazing in collaboration."

She rattled off a couple more questions. After I'd answered, she lowered the mic, her voice dropping to a hush.

"You know, I've always wondered if it wouldn't be good to allow pairs skating with two women or two men and see how *that* would work out. It was thrilling to watch what you put together here—it makes me think there could be so many other possibilities."

My smile widened. "I'd love to see more variety in pairs too. Everything doesn't have to be so… so cookie-cutter standard to be beautiful."

"I agree." She lifted the mic back to her lips and glanced at the camera held behind her. "Well, there you have it, everyone—a statement from the woman herself. We can't ask for anything more than that…"

As she turned away, a deep sigh escaped me. Slowly, we were making the world see what we could do. It might take a lot of time and a metric fuck-ton of work, but they *would* accept us.

I was glad for the enthusiastic response, but we weren't in the clear yet. If the skating officials weren't convinced, we might still be banned from Worlds.

I glanced around at the crowd, bracing myself for another round of questioning, but instead my gaze caught on a figure bursting past the door at the back of the stands. Ursula hurtled down the steps with her straggly blond hair flying behind her, only slowing when she noticed the milling group of reporters around us.

At the sight of the tension gripping her face, my stomach flipped over. I ducked behind Quentin and hustled over to the steps. Ursula dashed down to meet me a little apart from the crowd.

"What are you doing here?" I murmured urgently.

She made a face. "I tried to text and call you, but you weren't replying. I didn't think this was news that could wait."

I winced. I'd left my phone in my purse—and on vibrate—while we warmed up and hadn't checked it since. It wasn't as if I had a pocket to keep it on me when I was in my skating costume.

"Sorry. What's going on?"

Ursula flicked her gaze toward the reporters and dropped her voice even lower. "Your mom just arrived in Tokyo with a bunch of her people. What I'm hearing is that she's determined to take you out of the equation once and for all, and to do it herself—she's pissed about the 'spectacle' you've made of the family or something like that. It sounds like she's gone even more off the rails than before."

My heart plummeted with a sudden desperate chill. Mom was right here in this city—and out for my blood? We'd just publicized our location all over the news.

We had to get out of here.

Niko sidled over to join us, his expression darkening as he took in my own. "What's the matter, Angel?"

I swallowed thickly. "We've got to leave—fast. My mom could be on her way to start a bloodbath right now. Can you give the reporters some kind of excuse to explain why we need to head out?"

Niko's eyes widened. "Not a problem. Leave it to me."

He strode back to the crowd and said a couple of brisk sentences in Japanese, followed by an English translation: "We appreciate that you've spent this time with us today, but my skaters have an important appointment to get to. We look forward to talking to you more after their next performance!"

As the reporters started to file out, I hurried over to take off my skates and grab my bag. Jasper took in my face and clenched his jaw. "That bad, huh?"

I nodded. "We have to head out as quickly as possible. And find someplace to strategize that we're absolutely sure my mom couldn't know about."

Niko hefted his own bag. "I can think of a spot where no one is likely to be looking for a group of skaters. Are we taking Ursula and Dámaso with us?"

"Yeah. Text the directions to Ursula so they can follow us."

We marched up the steps and out to our SUV. Rafael fell into step with me halfway across the parking lot. I shot him a look and simply said, "My mom's here."

From the twitch of his expression, I could tell he understood just how dire our situation was.

I scanned the parking lot before leaping inside, relieved to see no sign of Mom's presence yet. For all I knew, she was still at the airport going through customs.

But she wouldn't stay there for long.

As Niko hit the gas, Quentin gazed at the streets beyond the SUV's windows, his face paler than usual. "Do you really think she'll be able to figure out where our new apartment is? We just moved there."

I shook my head. "I doubt it. But I think we should take every precaution just in case. We don't know all the resources she might have in this country."

Niko drove through the city with focused intensity and pulled the car into a parking garage. We followed him out onto the sidewalk, where Ursula and Dámaso caught up with us, and up to a building with neon signs glowing in the windows and vibrant paint splashed across the building's face.

"This is a love hotel," Niko said as he motioned us to the front door. "We don't need ID, and we can pay by the hour. No way for anyone to know we're here unless they spot us going in."

I couldn't restrain a hitch of a laugh. "Imagine how much trouble we'll be in with the figure skating organizations if they get wind of this hang-out."

His logic made sense, though. We let Niko handle the room selection and payment, and within a matter of minutes, we were filing into a large hotel room with an obvious rose theme. There were fake roses smothering the walls, rose-print sheets and duvet, roses in a vase on the side table, and a thick rose scent clogging the air.

Dámaso sneezed. "This is… This is really something."

"It is," Niko said, chipper as ever, but his eyes had darkened. "I suppose we need to decide what we're doing next?"

I turned to the turncoats. "Have you heard anything else from your contacts who are still working with my mom?"

Dámaso waggled his phone. "It sounds like she got to the arena just a few minutes ago. We left right in time."

Ursula shuddered. "She's going to be hunting the city for us—me and Dámaso as well as the five of you."

"Has there been any word from Frankie?" I asked, holding on to the tiniest shred of hope that maybe he could change sides again and give us an inside advantage.

Ursula grimaced. "Nothing at all from that jackass."

"Okay." I clasped my hands in front of me and paced from the bed to the wall and back again. "We can't keep practicing while my mom is looking for us. It'll be too easy for her to find us that way."

Jasper frowned. "If you're going to suggest we give up on Worlds after everything—"

I held up my hand. "No. I'm just talking through our options." I heaved a ragged breath. "We could notify the police and hope they round her up—or at least her people—but she probably wouldn't risk coming here unless she or an ally in the Devil's Dozen has at least a few officers on their payroll, so that tactic might not work out in our favor after all. And even if not, it wouldn't be that hard for her to avoid them while she searches for me."

Rafael tipped his head to the side. "Didn't the Storm say he'd send people to help if we needed it?"

"Yeah. But I don't know how they'll find Mom and her people to take them out either. She'll know he's on my side by now—she's probably going to avoid any of the Devil's Dozen's usual haunts." My stomach knotted. "Her whole focus is destroying me."

"So far none of these options sound very good," Niko said gently.

"I know." I rubbed my forehead. The truth of the situation was creeping up on me; I just didn't want to accept it.

But there was no getting around it. Mom had forced my hand. I couldn't simply lay low and dodge her attacks.

It wasn't just my life on the line but my men's and my loyal allies' too.

I dragged in a breath. "I can't keep running away from her and pretending my family legacy doesn't exist. Worlds is coming up fast. Even if there was a way to practice in secret, we couldn't risk showing up at the competition if she might come and open fire on all those people. She's already shown she doesn't care about killing innocent kids to punish me."

Rafael was watching me, his mouth set at an even grimmer angle than usual. "Where are you going with this, Lou?"

I raised my head and met his eyes. "We have to end this conflict completely. I have to face her head on and make sure she'll never be a problem again."

A momentary silence fell over the room. Ursula cleared her throat. "You mean kill her."

Nausea swept through my gut, but I couldn't deny it. "I wanted to be done with the violence, but she keeps flinging more at me. The longer I've avoided that one step, the worse things she's done. It's time—and then maybe I really can leave the rest behind for good."

Quentin grasped my arm and gave it a reassuring squeeze. "If you decide you'd rather just take off and forget about Worlds, I don't think any of us will argue with you. We're sticking with you no matter what."

A lump rose in my throat. "Thank you. You have no idea how much that means to me. But no matter where I go, she's going to keep tracking me down. I can't live like that."

Jasper inclined his head. "Then you've got to do what you've got to do. None of us will judge you for taking that step either. I know this isn't how you'd have wanted to handle the problem."

"That's right," Niko said firmly. "Whatever you decide, we'll stand with you and do whatever we can to help. It won't change—"

The peal of his phone's ringtone cut him off. He fished his phone out of his pocket and glanced at the screen. His eyebrows leapt up.

"It's one of the skating officials I've been talking with. I'd better take this."

He took a few steps away and launched into a conversation in brisk but cheery Japanese. I couldn't understand a word of it, but that didn't stop me from trying to read his body language.

Of course, Niko was always so animated it was hard to guess how the discussion was going. I watched as his shoulders sank and then perked up again. His hand waved in the air even though the person on the other end couldn't see his gestures. I couldn't tell whether he was putting a good face on horrible news or happily accepting welcome news.

My heart drummed in a heavy rhythm. By the time Niko finished the call and turned back to us, my mouth had gone completely dry. Even with the threat of wholesale slaughter hanging over me and the people I cared about most, I needed to know the verdict.

Niko's broad grin soothed my nerves in the instant before he spoke. "We did it! The consensus is that you should be allowed to compete—and that's their formal position going forward. They are considering you to be on probation, but as long as no new sex tapes start circulating, I think we'll be okay."

Jasper's eyes lit up. "That's fantastic!"

The rush of joyful relief washed through me and seemed to leave me feeling hollowed out. We'd succeeded, we'd proved our point—but I couldn't fully enjoy that fact while my head remained on my mother's chopping block.

"It is great," I said. "Now we need to make sure we can actually show up at Worlds without it turning into a mass murder scene."

Rafael stepped closer to me, but even his looming presence wasn't as comforting as usual. "I can handle your mother if you want. You just say the word, and you won't have to be involved at all. I don't want you to get your hands dirty if it's going to weigh on your conscience."

I smiled up at him, my heart swelling with love. It didn't surprise me that he'd make the offer, but it meant a lot that he had all the same.

"Thank you," I said. "But I don't think sending you to take her out would make me feel better. You'd still be acting on my orders. I'd feel even more guilty sending you into the danger alone."

He let out a scoffing sound. "I can deal with that."

I grasped his hand. "I know you can. But it still doesn't feel right." I shook myself, trying to work the tension out of my nerves. "Anyway,

I have an even bigger problem than that. Once Mom is gone, the Devil's Dozen members are going to expect me to step up and take her place. Even if you're willing to take *that* role, I'm not sure they'll just take my word that you're qualified for the job."

Quentin rubbed his mouth. "So we don't only need to figure out how to off your mom but also how to handle what'll happen right after. Rafael killing her wouldn't be enough?"

"Not if he kills her as my bodyguard, protecting me." I let out a groan. "Why did I have to be born a Cordova?"

But I had been, and there'd been privileges to my life as well as downsides. Who knew how I'd have turned out in some other family? Maybe I'd never have found skating at all or never had the means to pursue it.

Speculating didn't get me anywhere. The fact was, as long as my mom was living, I could never be free. And as long as there was no one else to inherit the Deadly Rose throne, I could never live how I wanted to, even though I couldn't be less interested in the job. If only—

An idea struck me like a bolt of lightning. I had to pause and catch my breath as it unfurled through my mind. A giddy shiver ran through my chest.

I looked up into Rafael's dark eyes again. "I might know how to pull this off. But I'm going to need your help."

He didn't hesitate for even an instant with his response. "Whatever you need, it's already yours."

"Good. I'm going to arrange a meeting with my mom tomorrow."

TWENTY-FIVE

Luciana

I BREATHED in the dusty air with its scent of old, varnished wood and willed my nerves to settle. Not that I could actually feel calm, but I'd rather not be totally jittery if I could help it.

The theater that'd been out of use for a few years seemed like the perfect setting for this confrontation. I stood with Quentin, Jasper, and a few dozen figures that Beckett and the Blood Hunter had sent to support me off in the wings on one side of the stage, the curtains rippling around me. No one else was around—no unwitting citizens who could get caught in the crossfire.

Mom wasn't going to distract me that way. This one thing, we were doing on my terms.

I hadn't spoken to her directly. Ursula had ensured the message trickled through her contacts to my mother, and we'd gotten confirmation that the Deadly Rose had agreed to a parlay here just this morning. But I could easily imagine Mom's face hardening as she heard the request.

I could imagine her spitting her agreement into my face. *We can do this wherever you want, Luciana. Pick where you want to die, because that's all you'll get from me now.*

My heart thudding, I waited for her to arrive. My fingers curled around my pistol. I touched my knife in its sheath at my hip just to reassure myself of its presence.

Jasper and Quentin adjusted their own grips on their guns, scanning the rows of seats beyond the stage. We'd left Niko tucked away in the rosy love hotel room, because I'd insisted I wasn't putting him through physical combat while he was still recovering from the last time my mother's people had shot him. But he'd helped in his own ways.

All of the Devil's Dozen lackeys who'd joined us were armed and ready as well. Ursula and Dámaso crouched near the back of the stage, their gazes flicking over the theater. Beckett's and the Blood Hunter's people were clearly disciplined and focused. Not a murmur escaped them or a restless stirring passed through their cluster—a few in front of me as a shield and the others gathered behind me—as the seconds ticked down to my mother's entrance.

The door we'd left unlocked creaked open at the far end of the building. I made out the faint scuffing of various footsteps. My shoulders tensed, and my gun-hand bobbed up a few inches.

The curtains at the other end of the stage swayed. My mother stepped forward, surrounded by a mass of lackeys. She had to have brought at least as many people as I had around me. But that wouldn't matter in the end.

She peered between the two men standing guard in front of her with an expression as icy as I'd pictured. Her voice came out equally cold. "So you're willing to look me in the face after you stabbed me in the back. I'm surprised you didn't flee the country the instant you heard I was on my way."

My heart thumped so hard I'd swear I felt my ribs rattle, but I raised my chin, refusing to let my anxiety show. "I'm not backing down. I'm claiming my life to live it the way I want. And I didn't stab you in the back. You attacked me first, more than once. All I did was defend myself and the people I care about the only way I could."

Her lips curled with disdain. Spittle flecked the air as she hurled her next words at me. "So caught up in your silly little competitions. My daughter, prancing around on the ice. But you're not my daughter anymore. No daughter of mine would have made a mockery of our name and dragged me through the mud!"

A prickle of rage sparked inside me along with a tremor of confusion. "How did I drag you through the mud or anything else? I'm not even competing using my actual last name! No one has any idea that you have anything to do with Luna Garcia—or, at least, they'd never have known anything about my mother if you hadn't kept lashing out. You should have let me go quietly."

Mom jabbed her finger at me. "No. You belong to me. You're mine, Luciana, and you don't get to just wander off. After all the time I spent preparing you—everything I invested in you—this is how it's supposed to be. You're not allowed to walk away."

She was really raving now. Did her underlings hear how unhinged she sounded?

"I didn't ask for any of that," I retorted. "And I've invested *my* time in the things I care about—skating and people who support me in my dream. You could have chosen anyone else out of all the people who actually want the job to be your heir."

"That's not how this works! You're a Cordova—you're the heir to the Deadly Rose. I shouldn't have to settle for some pendejo off the street. But you're too stupid to see that. I never should have let you get wrapped up in skating in the first place. It's warped your brain."

I couldn't restrain a snort even as my hackles rose at her insults. "The only warped brain around here is yours. You sound like a lunatic. Why would I have wanted to stay with you, to keep learning the things you wanted me to learn? I chose my path, and you've turned it into a shitshow, not me."

She bared her teeth at me. "I won't take the blame for this. You and everyone you roped into your pointless dream are going to pay for it *today*. Or did you think you could beg for mercy?"

There was my perfect opening. I squared my shoulders, ignoring the chalkiness of my mouth and the thunder of my pulse, and took a step forward.

Quentin and Jasper stirred uneasily as I moved away from them, but they didn't stop me. They knew this part of the plan, as much as they'd hated it.

The men who'd shielded me parted to let me through. I took another steady step forward onto the stage, holding my mother's gaze. Then another, and another.

A nervous quiver ran down my spine. With every additional distance I put between myself and my supporters, I felt increasingly naked. But we weren't going to get anywhere I needed to go unless I put myself on the line like this.

Mom stared at me, her eyes narrowing as if expecting this move to be some kind of trick. Which maybe it was, but it didn't have to be. I was giving her one more chance to do right by me, to let it simply be over.

Not that I had any real hope she'd take that chance.

When I reached the middle of the stage, where a pool of starker spotlight fell across the polished boards, I stopped. As I held Mom's gaze, I lifted my voice to carry through the large room.

"Mom, this is your last chance to listen to me. The Deadly Rose was always a role you were trying to force me into, not something I wanted. I'd have been pretending the whole time, not really living, because it isn't what I'm meant to do. Ruling through terror, dealing out violence—it makes me sick to my stomach. It always did. That's just who I am; I can't help it."

I tossed my gun off the side of the stage, letting it land amid the empty seats, well beyond reach. Then I unsheathed my knife and chucked it in the same direction, leaving me totally unarmed. If I'd felt naked before, now I might as well have been bared to the bone.

Mom's lips parted with the slightest hint of shock.

I didn't let my gaze waver. "I'm making my stand. I don't want any more blood on my hands. You can accept who I am and let go of this idea that you have to use me as a puppet, or you can do whatever else you want to with me. How we end this stand-off is up to you."

I held my arms out, offering myself up as I was.

Mom's eyes burned into mine, those two dark brown orbs that

were so like my own. Her jaw worked. She might even have considered going with the first option I'd given her.

But if she did, it was only for a second before the sneer crossed her lips again. She lifted her head at a haughty angle and let out a bitter laugh.

Then she twitched her gun where she held it by her thigh. "A disappointment right until the end. At least you've made this final moment as easy for me as it could possibly be. I'll take care of the problem I raised myself."

She jerked her hand toward her men. "Make sure we're not interrupted."

At her gesture, the men around her surged forward—past me, to stand between us and my allies so no one could rush to my aid. Mom stalked forward in their wake, her fingers tightening around her gun. My body shook with the drumming of my heartbeat, but I held myself still and firm, while every nerve screamed at me to run.

Mom halted just a couple of steps away. She started to raise her pistol to point it at me, probably planning to shoot the bullet right through the middle of my forehead.

But she didn't get that far.

With a swift hiss, a figure plunged down from above. Rafael plummeted toward my mother, fixed to a cable like the kind I'd used when practicing the hardest figure skating jumps and lifts for the first time.

It worked just as Niko and the two men who'd helped him set it up had promised. My bodyguard soared through the air, dropping straight to the stage in the space of a blink.

Mom didn't even have time to glance up before he'd rammed the heavy knife he was holding right into the top of her skull.

A croaking sound escaped Mom's throat as her eyes fogged over. She crumpled to the floor of the stage. Her limbs shuddered and sagged. Blood pooled through the scattered strands of her dark hair.

Rafael stepped between me and her as if to protect me from the sight. As if I didn't need with every fiber of my being to be sure she was truly gone.

My stomach churned, but I held steady. With the image of Mom's death burned behind my eyes, I swiveled around to face the not-quite-empty rows of seats.

"My mother is dead," I declared, heaving my voice out into the room. Then I spun to face the gaping underlings poised between me and my supporters. "The old Deadly Rose is gone, which means you answer to me now. I won't have you hurting me or my people."

The goons hesitated in their bewilderment, not knowing what orders to follow when the woman who'd given their previous ones was dead. As they wavered, my allies charged into their midst, knocking guns from hands and slamming anyone who resisted against the floorboards.

In the time it took me to heave a few breaths, Mom's entire force was subdued—and now looking both confused and disgruntled. They stared at me as if waiting for further direction.

They were looking at the wrong person.

I swept my hand toward Rafael, who still had the bloody knife clutched in his large hand. "As the new Deadly Rose, my first act is to hand over the title and leadership over the Cordova empire to Rafael Torres. From now on, you answer to him. He's clearly proven he's up to the task."

The thugs' gazes darted between me and my former bodyguard, and I thought I saw respect starting to light in a few pairs of eyes. But they weren't the only ones I was speaking to.

I swung back toward the seemingly absent audience and projected my voice even louder. "Can everyone accept that, or do we have any questions?"

Along the railing of the balcony that jutted out over half of the lower seats, twelve figures stepped from the shadows into view. I immediately made out Beckett's confident stance and the Blood Hunter's watchful face. The reps I'd met for the March Wind and the Bright Dragon held up phones streaming video chats so that their bosses could take in the confrontation and its result from afar.

Most of the other eight spectators were reps as well, holding their own phones to send these events back to the Devil's Dozen bigwigs they stood for. A couple of the others, older men with stern faces, looked over the stage with their hands resting on the railing. Members who'd come to see these events in person, I guessed, though I didn't know what names they went by.

One way or another, every existing member of the Devil's Dozen had witnessed the death of the Deadly Rose. Everyone had seen Rafael take her life in spectacular fashion.

I'd needed them to not just see her gone, but also have it burned into their minds just how powerful the man beside me could be.

Beckett raised his voice first, with a subtle nod toward me. "I accept Rafael Torres as the new Deadly Rose. I welcome him into the Devil's Dozen as an equal and a colleague."

"I accept him too," the Blood Hunter announced, more bluntly. "Good to have you with us, Rafael."

Their voices started a cascade. One and then another face on the phone's screens spoke, and their reps confirmed their acknowledgment of Rafael's new position. The two other members who'd come in person hesitated the longest, but finally bowed their heads and added their agreement.

Even as relief washed over me, my stomach didn't completely unknot. The rest of the Devil's Dozen would be keeping a close eye on Rafael, no doubt, watching for any sign of weakness. Maybe even hoping for a chance to get the better of him.

I suspected their quick acceptance of my choice was partly because they hadn't wanted *me* to take my mother's place anyway. It had to be obvious to everyone other than her how bad I'd be at that job.

But I was okay with that. And I knew Rafael *was* up to the task.

Anyone who tried to take him down would quickly regret it.

Rafael's new band of underlings had crowded around him, professing their loyalty. This political segment of his life was novel to him, but I had all the faith in the world in him, just like he'd had in me for these past ten years.

My gaze dropped to my mother's discarded body, still lying center stage in a widening puddle of blood. Taking in her contorted features and the sharp angles of her strewn limbs, a pang of sadness hit me.

I wouldn't miss her. Every day from now on, I'd feel nothing but gratitude for the fact that she was no longer in my life. But I couldn't help wishing I could have had a different mother—a kinder one, a loving one who'd at least tried to understand me.

But it said everything anyone needed to know about what kind of woman Mireya Cordova was, that when faced with her daughter helpless and asking for peace, she'd instead come at me with a weapon and every intention of murdering me.

Now the monster she'd proved herself to be was gone. A new legacy could begin, one I wouldn't really be a part of.

Which was just fine with me. I had a different legacy to carve out for myself, one I could now pursue unhindered.

TWENTY-SIX

Jasper

IF YOU ASKED me what was worse, the war with Lou's mom and her goons or the challenge of facing the skating officials, judges, and immense audience at the World Championships today, I'd have had a little trouble answering. Okay, having guns pointed at me and fearing for Lou's life—and my own—was a nightmare. But I'd had plenty of nightmares about competitions like the one we were about to complete too.

Lou nudged me as our paths crossed during the group warm-up before the free skate routines started. "Don't look so grim. We've got this."

Her bright smile lifted my spirits, along with the memory of our last few practices, when we'd finally pulled off our new transition perfectly. Only a couple of times, and we'd still been shaky during the last practice, so we'd decided to wait and see how the competition went before confirming if we'd incorporate it here. But I couldn't help wondering if our heightened synchronization was because of the weight lifted off both of our shoulders.

There were no more gunmen stalking us. No more worries about the Devil's Dozen hassling Lou. Rafael was dealing with all that crap, and we could focus every bit of our energy on what mattered most to us: the skating.

Yesterday's short routine had gone as well as we could have hoped. For now, we were in fourth place, below two pairs whose greatest strength was their short program and the Russians who might be our greatest competition, just a single point ahead of us.

We both knew that our best time to shine was the free skate. Everything depended on what we did today.

I whirled around at one end of the rink and caught one of the other skaters staring at me for a second before he jerked his gaze away. The back of my neck prickled with the uneasy sensation of being watched.

He wasn't the first of our colleagues I'd spotted giving us skeptical looks, ranging from disapproving to unsettlingly curious. Of course our fellow skaters wouldn't have missed the scandal that'd nearly blown up our chances at Worlds before we'd set foot in Nagano's huge arena.

That was fine. I had nothing to be embarrassed about when it came to my personal relationships. With Lou, with the other men in her life, and with the other man in mine. My gaze darted across the rink, and I shared a quick smile with Niko.

My professional life, well… I did my best to ignore the niggling voice in the back of my head that pointed out every hint of a wobble or twinge in my muscles. But it was impossible to forget that the last time I'd competed at Worlds, I'd totally fucked it up.

People watching me would be remembering that incident too. They'd be wondering whether I could actually pull off something decent this time without crashing and burning.

I was wondering that too. Every jump of my nerves was as much anxiety as excitement. I had a lot to prove here today.

But then, I also had way more support than I'd been able to count on back then. I had my gorgeous and incredibly talented partner skating alongside me. I had the fantastic coach who'd tracked me down halfway across the world ready to cheer me on. I even had my former rival sitting in the stands after giving us a quick pep talk this morning.

Things were definitely looking up. I'd built success on top of success in the past several months. That was all *I* needed to remember.

As I ran through the rest of my warm-up, I reminded myself of those facts over and over. When Lou glided over to me as the group warm-up time came to an end, I tugged her to me for a quick kiss.

She beamed back at me and sank down next to me on our bench. We leaned forward in matching stretches to finish warming up off the ice.

I was just raising my arms over my head when my phone's text alert tone pealed out. My pulse stuttered for a second before it sank in that none of our calls warning of danger had ever come to *my* phone. Maybe Quentin had decided to give a snarky tip or two before we went on.

I pulled my phone out of my equipment bag and tapped the screen to see the message.

In the first second, I just stared at the name at the top of the text. *Mom*. I hadn't talked to her in ages—hadn't wanted to exacerbate her already shaky relationship with Dad by reminding him of the career she'd supported and he'd never approved of. We'd exchanged occasional texts while I was staying at my grandparents' place, but not since I'd started training again with Niko.

She might be following the competitive circuit on the down low. I glanced to the actual message, expecting it to be words of encouragement and good luck that would feel bittersweet no matter how much I knew she meant them.

Hey, honey. I know it's been a while, but that's my fault. And it's been too long. I realize I can't make up for all that lost time, but I still wanted to be here for you and show how much I believe in you!

I blinked, struggling to process what she meant. "Be here for me"? It almost sounded like—

With another ping, a new text appeared. *I can see you right now. Look across the arena, about ten rows up.*

My jaw dropped. She was literally *here*? In Japan? She'd come all the way from the US to watch me compete?

How had she explained that trip to Dad?

My head jerked up. I scanned the stands on the opposite side of the arena—and spotted a familiar slim figure with auburn hair like mine, waving eagerly several rows above rink-level.

As I raised my hand to return the gesture in a daze, my attention slid to the figure sitting next to her, and my arm froze in mid-air.

Dad was here too. Sitting beside her, looking a little stiff from what I could judge at that distance, his expression tight. But he lifted his hand in a brief wave as well, giving me a particle of acknowledgment.

Holy hell. How in the world had this happened?

I lowered my phone to my lap and realized Lou was peering at me. "What's wrong? What were the messages about?"

"Nothing—nothing you need to worry about," I said quickly, knowing she must be even more sensitive to unexpected news than I was. "My parents are here. They came to watch."

Lou's eyebrows leapt up. "Parents, plural? Your mom *and* dad? I thought your dad hated skating."

I swallowed hard. "He does. At least, he has my entire life, up until the last time I spoke to him a couple of years ago."

If my nerves had been jittering before, now they were doing jumping jacks all through my gut. As much as I appreciated Mom's gesture, even if I didn't totally understand what it meant, I kind of wished she hadn't told me until after our routine.

What if I screwed up in front of them? In front of Dad? That'd just be proving him right, wouldn't it? He'd feel justified in assuming my skating had always been a waste of time.

Lou squeezed my forearm. "Hey. Don't let it get to you. We'll still go out there and skate our best. What he thinks didn't matter before and it doesn't matter now."

I dragged in a breath, trying to absorb her certainty. Fighting against the sensation of Dad's judgment pressing down on me.

He was probably sneering mentally right now as he took in my shimmery costume and—

A hand clapped firmly against my shoulder from behind. I flinched and jerked around to see a middle-aged man I didn't recognize.

He made a gesture of apology. "Didn't mean to startle you, Jasper. I'm Jim Gunner with Skate Canada. Mostly I push paper, so we haven't gotten a chance to talk before."

Skate Canada was the official figure skating organization in my family's home country. I scrambled to set my thoughts in order. "Oh. Hi! Good to meet you."

Gunner laughed in a deep rumble that reminded me of dynamite. "No need to worry. I'm here to give my compliments. I wanted to tell you and your partner how much I enjoyed your trio skate with Quentin Wolf. It was beautiful work, especially considering that, from what I understand, you pulled it together very quickly."

His smile shone on both me and Lou. Lou grinned in response, and I found myself doing the same. "Thank you. I'm so glad it made an impact."

"Oh, it did that. I expect there'll be talk about this year's Worlds and your part in it for years to come. You've already left your mark no matter how you do today. If either of you ever decide you'd like to switch over to the Great White North, give us a call, you hear? That goes for Mr. Wolfe too!"

His praise washed over me, the warmth of his comments sweeping away the panic that'd gripped me moments before. "Thank you," I said again, more emphatically. "That means a lot to me."

"We'll give it some thought," Lou piped up, her grin widening. "And I hope you enjoy our routine today just as much."

Gunner caught Niko's eyes. "As much as I appreciate what you're doing with your coaching, I hope I see you on the competitive circuit again someday soon too, Mr. Okabe. Now I'd better get to my seat!"

With that, he shuffled off. Lou watched him go and shook her head with a light chuckle. "He's quite the character."

"Yeah," I said, my mind still reeling—but in a good way this time.

Maybe my career hadn't gone quite the way I'd imagined, but I'd still come so far from my early days learning the basic jumps and spins. I'd won medals; I'd gained enough fans to earn a playful nickname. There was no world in which that made me a failure.

I got to decide what success meant to me. My dad didn't get any say in it. Even if today was an epic flop, I'd still know I'd made it. I had so many chances to do even more ahead of me.

I'd climbed dozens of mountains to get this far. I'd struggled and fought and pushed with all my might to claw my way to this spot. Was I really going to let my asshole father pull me down now?

No way in hell.

With a renewed surge of confidence, I nudged Lou's shoulder. "You know what? Who cares what the other pairs do? I say we go for the new transition either way."

Lou's eyes widened. "Are you sure? We're not exactly solid with it yet. You seemed pretty iffy about incorporating it at the last practice."

"I know, I know. But listen. If we can pull it off, then that's it—we're almost guaranteed a medal, if not the gold. And if we fumble it… Isn't it better to fail at something incredible than to have our routine be flawless but uninspiring? If it doesn't happen this time, then we have another whole year to practice." My lips pulled into another grin. "So what do you say? You want to give it a shot, Punk?"

Lou laughed and took my hand, squeezing it hard. "More than anything in the world."

And just like that, it was all okay. No matter what happened now, I knew we were going to survive it. Whether Dad watched me fly or watched me fall, I wouldn't be shaken by him.

Not now, and not ever again.

TWENTY-SEVEN

Luciana

I THOUGHT I'd put on a good face with Jasper, but I'd be lying if I said I wasn't nervous.

As I watched the many pairs before us take to the ice, my heart pounded a million miles a minute. Why had we ended up toward the end of the line-up? All this waiting was killing me.

Of course, it might have been even worse skating early and then waiting over and over to see if our current rank would be displaced by someone else.

My foot tapped against the floor with clicks of my skate guard until I noticed and held it still. The pair who'd just launched into their routine were right before us—we were up next. I needed to find my inner calm and stay focused.

The truth was that despite my anxiety, my childhood self was doing somersaults in my chest. No matter what score we earned, just being here at Worlds was a longtime dream I'd barely allowed myself to consider might be possible.

I just had to keep reaching for the gold with each competition season, and someday I might be known among the greats. Skating here in Nagano was just one step along a much larger—and incredibly thrilling—journey.

My gaze followed the pair on the ice. They launched into an impressive lift that had me holding my breath, but the woman had to drop her raised foot too quickly on the dismount to recover her balance.

I couldn't criticize her. It was totally possible we'd have a much more epic wipeout when we attempted our spin to lift transition.

No, don't think about that. We had nailed it a couple of times. I knew it was possible.

All we had to do was repeat what we'd already done. When I thought about it that way, it only sounded slightly terrifying.

I glanced toward the stands. Niko, standing behind me and Jasper, caught my gaze with a typical sunny smile. He exuded nothing but warm confidence.

I found myself grinning back at him. Then my attention slid farther, to where Rafael and Quentin were sitting next to each other in seats a few rows up. They both nodded to me when they saw me looking their way, Rafael offering one of his subdued smiles that meant as much as a broad grin and Quentin offering a thumbs up.

A couple rows higher, Emi waved eagerly at me. She was beaming so bright you'd have thought she'd already won a gold medal.

As I drew my gaze away, it snagged on a face I hadn't expected to see. Beckett was sitting in the crowd, watching the current skaters intently with his hand at his chin.

My heart skipped a beat in surprise, and I scanned the rest of the seats more carefully. In a matter of seconds, I picked out not just the Blood Hunter but also the two older men who'd arrived for my confrontation with Mom—the ones who'd hesitated the longest before accepting Rafael as my replacement.

When they caught me staring, one gave a brief nod. The other kept up an impenetrably stern expression.

A fresh jitter ran through my nerves. Beckett and the Blood

Hunter had been my allies for a while—I could believe they were only here out of personal interest. But the other two…

Had they come to evaluate how serious I really was about my skating? To find proof that I really was giving up the Devil's Dozen life with this other career?

I took a deep breath. Let them watch. I knew how committed I was. They couldn't help but see that I was on the same level as the other skaters here—a level I couldn't have reached if I wasn't practicing like my life depended on it.

At least they'd believed in me enough to think it was possible I had a valid alternative. Mom had never bothered to do that much.

I was so far in my head that I barely noticed the end of the previous pair's routine. Seeing them heading toward the boards, I pushed to my feet with a rush of giddy exhilaration. Jasper and I stepped out onto the ice, knowing exactly what words we'd hear next.

"Our next skaters are representing the United States: Luna Garcia and Jasper St. Pierre."

Jasper and I pushed off across the ice. We glided in a loop around the edge of the arena, giving our muscles a slight additional warm-up and the audience a chance to take in our costumes.

My gaze sought out my other men again. Emi let out a whoop from her seat. A smile touched my lips as the sensation swept through me that they were all here with me on the ice almost as solidly as my partner, who was squeezing my hand.

We struck our opening pose. The rink had gone quiet, so still I'd swear the judges would hear my heart thudding away. But there was nothing left in it but joy and determination now. I was going to show everyone what I was put on this earth to do.

The first notes of our song resonated through the air, and I felt the music right down to my bones. I'd skated to this melody so often it might as well have been a part of me, like the rhythm of my breath and my pulse.

The two of us became parallel shooting stars as we shot across the rink. I kept my face relaxed, my expression languid. My brows flicked up only slightly as my partner lifted me up into our complex opening lift. One beat, two beats, a third—whirling across the ice with the lilting notes.

After Jasper lowered me, we took off again in a darting game of cat and mouse that went along perfectly with the swelling cadence that pumped through the PA speakers. We jumped high, spun fast, flowing from one move into the next like our bodies had been made for nothing else.

The entire time, the exhilaration that'd filled me buoyed me up. I'd won my way to freedom. I'd faced the world I'd come from, conquered it, and set off into new territory I was making my own. Now I was going to conquer this challenge too—and have a lot more fun doing it.

And I'd made it here with four amazing men who were still supporting me through every leap across the ice.

We whipped around, and Jasper grasped my hand to propel me into the spin that would lead into our next lift. My pulse hiccupped just once, and then I latched on to the peace in his gray-green eyes. The storm clouds so often there had faded away.

He was as immersed in the emotions of the routine as I was.

I leaned into his hold, letting him swing me across the ice. A chilly wind whipped up as I sped around just inches above the frozen surface.

A touch of cold slipped right into my chest. What if we screwed this up? What if it all came crashing down in the next few seconds?

Wait—why was I even thinking that?

Jasper's hand was perfectly solid and steady in mine. Jasper had always been there to lift me and catch me when I needed him to.

Maybe I'd still been holding back just a tiny bit, afraid of letting go completely and trusting him to hold my very life in his hands. But when I considered that thought, I could see how ridiculous it was.

I loved him, and I believed in him too. We could pull this off together. I wasn't alone, and there was no one left in my life who wanted to tie me down.

That last shred of doubt fled my body. Jasper yanked me up, and I soared into his arms like the angel Niko had dubbed me. A shared gasp warbled over the music as Jasper flung me up over his head straight out of the spin.

I could really fly without my mother's threats bearing down on me. I could launch myself far beyond the cruel world she'd tried to trap me in.

As my foot touched down again, I tensed my calf just before a wobble could creep through it. Then we were gliding across the ice again in perfect synchronization.

We'd done it. Maybe a hair away from a fault, but we'd fulfilled every requirement for full marks.

A laugh of pure delight tumbled from Jasper's lips, and I couldn't help echoing it. We swept through the rest of the routine on a rush of pure elation.

Then, hands clasped together, we lifted them high in our ending pose, my body arced against his. The song finished. Silence reigned.

And applause exploded through the arena.

As we skated over to the stands while the next pair took to the ice, I caught Emi chanting our names. More whoops carried out from across the audience. I sank down onto the bench where we'd receive our scores, trembling from the exertion of the routine and my own awed satisfaction.

Jasper slung his arm around my shoulders. "We really fucking did that, Punk."

I let out another laugh. "We sure did. You know, I feel like I've won something whether we get a medal or not."

"We'd better get *something*," Jasper muttered under his breath, but he hadn't stopped smiling.

The English announcer lifted his voice to declare our scores. "Luna Garcia and Jasper St. Pierre have earned in the free skate one hundred and fifty-three point two five."

My jaw dropped. I couldn't find the will to reel it back in. We'd gotten more than a hundred and fifty points—that had to be close to the record.

Niko cheered and grabbed us in a joint hug. "That's your best score yet. They saw just how fantastic you were—and how much you risked with the difficulty of those moves."

I gripped his arm, my mind whirling. "That—that puts us in first place, doesn't it?"

"You bet!"

"The Russians still have to go," Jasper reminded me as we moved to our spot in the stands. "They're up last."

I took in the grin that stretched from ear to ear across his face and elbowed him. "And you look so worried about it."

"Hey, I'll take a silver. I'm still having trouble wrapping my head around that score—and that we pulled the whole thing off so well here at Worlds. Holy crap—my *dad* saw that."

I hugged him close. Hopefully his dad would start to realize that Jasper's talent wasn't something that should be suppressed, but even if he didn't, it wouldn't mean a thing about the man beside me.

We watched the last few pairs compete, but the whole time I felt weirdly detached. I could appreciate the artistry of the movements, but the adrenaline rush had left me in a giddy state that gave the whole experience an unreal quality. Maybe I was actually dreaming?

Then the Russian pair glided onto the rink, and reality came back into sharper focus. I took in the woman's immaculate bun and their complimentary costumes, not a seam out of place. A lump rose in my throat.

Music drifted down from the speakers, and the pair became a pair of twin bullets, shooting across the length of the arena. The song they chose to accompany their routine was full of energy, a rock song that felt charged with electricity. The drumbeat matched their quick footwork; not once did the pair fall out of rhythm.

"Their quad throw should be coming up," Niko murmured at my side. "Any second now…"

And then there it was. The man lifted his partner high into the air, and she was airborne. She spun in four tight rotations. Her form was excellent, her landing beyond beautiful.

I could admit it was impressive to see. I stayed braced in my seat through the rest of the routine, admiring their poise and athleticism. I didn't see a single stumble.

When they hit their final pose, I sagged backward with a whoosh of a sigh. "Wow. They *are* good."

Niko clicked his tongue. "You two were very good too."

"I guess it comes down to what the judges think of it. The overall difficulty across all the moves is about the same, right?"

Our coach nodded. "No surprises."

"I have no idea how this will go," Jasper said. "They were stunning."

Niko raised his eyebrows at us. "I think yours had more heart."

I resisted the urge to squirm as we waited for the scores to be announced.

The announcer's voice crackled through the speakers. "Oleg Baranov and Yana Andreyeva have earned in the free skate a score of one hundred and fifty-one point five three."

My brain stumbled in its attempt to do math with the pressure of anticipation clouding my thoughts. All around us, people were clapping and leaning over to pat my and Jasper's shoulders. Shouts of congratulations rained down on us.

"You won!" Niko crowed. "You two got the gold. I knew you could!"

A choked laugh broke from my lips, and tears that were all happiness sprang to my eyes. I clutched Jasper and then Niko in the tightest of hugs. "Díos mio. Oh my God. We really did it."

Niko's phone started buzzing. He let out a laugh of his own. "There are all the reporters wanting interviews. And maybe some new sponsors too."

"Oh my God," I said again. My mind was spinning too fast for me to form any other words.

I blinked away my tears and smiled toward the stands where my other two men and my first real friend were watching. This victory was for all of us.

And maybe not just the people I knew of. I had to hope that everyone in the Devil's Dozen had been watching this competition, whether in person or on the TV. That they'd seen just how far my other interests had taken me.

If there were other heirs out there who weren't sure that the path most directly in front of them was the one that was actually right, then I'd just shown them there was another way. They could be who they wanted and still triumph.

TWENTY-EIGHT

Six months later

Luciana

I LEANED against the boards around the rink next to Jasper while our new coach rubbed his hands together, like he always did when he had something important to say. Niko had recommended Jerry Valdez to us, having worked with him for several months when Jerry was on an extended visit to Japan.

"Let me know what you two really think," he said in his gruff but warm tone that reminded me in a bittersweet way of Coach Balakin. "But I figure that since you two can pull off that tricky transition smooth as butter now, it's time to up the ante a little more. What if we added a throw at the end of the lift?"

My heart beat a little faster, considering how that would work. "It could be pretty fantastic. But we've only been really solid with the transition for the last few weeks."

Jasper cocked his head at me. "Could be worth a try, though, don't you think?"

I wet my lips and grinned. "Let's give the new routine one more run-through, and I'll imagine it to see how it feels in the moment."

Jerry swept his arm toward the ice. "Have at it."

We waved to Quentin, who'd also come under Jerry's wing and was practicing his singles routines alternating with Jasper and me. He gave us a thumbs up and a cocky smile before gliding out of the way.

It'd taken a while to hone our new routine for the next competitive circuit. We could skip the qualifying rounds because of our success last year, but we still needed to compete at Nationals in a few months. That should be plenty of time to make one more adjustment, though.

Jerry started the song, a bass heavy but still melodic pop song that had appealed to both me and Jasper, and my partner and I launched into the opening moves. We soared across the ice, every movement in harmony.

I'd done this hundreds of times now, but my heart still lifted when we jumped and spun together.

My nerves no longer jittered when we swept from the death spiral into our now-trademark lift. As Jasper whirled me around, I pictured what it would feel like for him to fling me into the air rather than lowering me like he usually did.

When we reached the end of the routine, my tee was damp with sweat. We'd been at this for hours already.

As we skated back to Jerry, I clapped my hands. "I think we could pull it off. Let's give it a shot!"

Jasper squeezed my shoulder. "I'm on board."

Jerry set his hands on his hips. "Perfect. I'll tinker with the moves afterward to smooth everything out, and we can get started tomorrow. Now, Lou, you could still lift your skates a little higher in that one footwork sequence. And Jasper, I think you could get more air with your triple Axel."

"Don't forget to remind them about their hand positioning in the first lift!"

At the cheerful voice, I glanced around Jerry and realized Niko had come back from his water break. He beamed at us while he shucked off his skate guards.

As Niko stepped onto the ice, Jasper wagged a finger at him teasingly. "You need to take off the coaching cap and focus on your own routine."

"That's right, old man," Quentin called out from the other end of the rink. "You've got a lot of work to do if you want to beat me once we get to Worlds."

Niko had decided to take a step back from coaching for a while and return to competing himself, joining us under Jerry's guidance. But he couldn't stop himself from weighing in here and there.

Thankfully, he also didn't take it hard when we chided him about it. He chuckled and tugged Jasper to him for a quick kiss.

"I can do that," he said, and blew a kiss to me as well before skating off.

Jerry simply shook his head in amusement. "All right, let's see you each go through your current routine one more time, and I'll give you a few more notes to run through in your dreams tonight."

By the time we were heading out the door, a pleasant burn had spread through all my muscles. I stretched my arms over my head and let out a glorious sigh. "This is the life."

"It is a pretty awesome one," Jasper agreed, and caught my hand to hold it.

Quentin came up by my side and took my other hand, not to be outdone. "I've got no complaints."

"As long as Emi keeps sending me those cases of Calpis, I'm right at home," Niko put in, making us all laugh.

We ambled down the Boston street that *was* feeling more and more like home with every passing week. I loved the noise and activity of a big city, and despite the Harvester's intervention, this had been my favorite of the places we'd stayed during our travels for training and competitions.

The guys had easily agreed to settling down here for the time being. Quentin had no interest in returning to his hometown where his mother would be more than happy to harass him, and we were close enough to Ontario that it wasn't difficult for Jasper to head up north to visit his family from time to time.

Right after Worlds, his mom had asked his dad for a divorce and moved back to Canada. Apparently bringing him to the championships had been her last-ditch effort to fix their relationship after she'd realized she couldn't tolerate his awful treatment of their son any longer. Mr. St. Pierre hadn't reformed enough, so she'd kicked him to the curb—like I happened to think she really should have done at least a decade ago.

But it was good to see how happy Jasper looked when I joined him on one of his trips across the border.

The loft we'd scored was just a few blocks from the arena where we were training. About halfway there, my phone chimed with an incoming text. I hefted my equipment back farther over my shoulder and pulled out the phone.

Emi had sent one of her emoji-filled messages. *Just booked my plane tickets for next month! Can't wait to see all of you!! You'd better be ready to go out on the town and have fun!*

My lips jumped into a smile as I typed my response. *I'm always ready. Just a few more weeks!*

A chance to hang out with my best friend was just what I needed. And Niko always brightened up even more than his usual cheery self when his sister was around.

As I slid my phone back into my pocket, Jasper gave me a subtle nudge. "There's another pair of them."

His tone was wry. I glanced up and noted the two brawny men in sports jackets sitting in a car across the street from our loft building. It took all my effort not to roll my eyes as a mix of irritation and amusement swept through me.

"Always keeping an eye on us," I said, matching Jasper's tone. "I wonder how long it'll take before Rafael's sure we're okay."

Quentin raised an eyebrow at me. "*You're* okay, you mean. We don't kid ourselves that it's the rest of us he's so concerned about protecting."

I elbowed him playfully. "Aw, he likes all of you too."

Niko looked as if he was suppressing the urge to wave at our supposedly low-key guards. "How's his alliance with the Harvester working out?"

I grabbed my keys to unlock the building's door. "Pretty well, from what he's told me. I guess that the business they went in on together has been really profitable. I'm sure he'll have lots to tell us about that tonight."

My heart lifted at the thought of Rafael's visit. In his role as the new Deadly Rose, he needed to spend a fair bit of time in Austin in the old Cordova mansion, keeping the main underlings in line. But after he'd gotten everything under control to begin with, he'd picked out some key people who could run things well when he wasn't there. Now he usually stayed with us for at least a couple of days every week.

But I always looked forward to those visits. As much as I understood why he couldn't be here every day like my other men, I treasured every minute I could get.

Once things were more settled for all of us, we'd find a way to be together all the time.

Rafael had made an alliance with the Harvester shortly after he'd taken over the Deadly Rose title, and part of their deal was that the Harvester's people in Boston kept a lookout to make sure no one threatened us. But so far the rest of the Devil's Dozen had left me completely alone since the World Championships, thank God.

The elevator let us out right outside the door to our two-story unit. With as many as five of us sharing the space at any given time, and some of them men with very strong opinions, we'd figured it was best to leave lots of room for people to spread out. We all had our own small bedrooms on the second floor, and the first floor was divided by the furnishings into several distinct areas with a different focus.

I was just raising the key to the lock when the door swung open on its own. A massive figure grinned down at me.

I dropped my bag and flung my arms around my former bodyguard. "Rafael! You got in early. I didn't think you'd be here until later tonight."

Rafael hugged me back tightly and then eased back to enjoy a lingering kiss. "I've been here for about an hour—and I made Cuban sandwiches for everyone. I figured all that work on the ice has probably left you awfully hungry."

Quentin's eyes gleamed eagerly. "You know it. Where's the grub?"

Rafael laughed and motioned us all into the loft. I made a beeline for the table, which he'd already set out with a sandwich at five of the six chairs. "Is everything okay in Austin?" I asked over my shoulder. "How's *your* work going?"

Rafael sank down next to me. "I've sorted out some things that needed sorting—faster than I thought I'd be able to. But you handed the job over to me because you didn't want to be bothered with all the details, right?"

I wrinkled my nose at him, but he had a point. "Fine. But if there's ever anything you *want* to talk about, you know you can. We all have a lot more experience with that part of my old life than I wish we did."

Rafael offered me a softer smile and gave my ponytail an affectionate hug. "And I'd like to make sure you never have to experience any more of it. Don't worry—I'm enjoying the challenge. And I'm happy with how the changes I've made are panning out. What about all of you? Anything new on the skating side?"

An answering smile sprang to my face. "We've really hit our stride with our new free skate routine. So much that Coach Valdez wants us to increase the difficulty."

His eyebrows rose. "Again? I thought you were already pulling off some kind of miracle."

Quentin smirked. "They do call this guy Saint Jasper for a reason, I guess…"

I got the impression that Jasper kicked his one-time rival—lightly—under the table. He turned to Rafael. "In the skating world, you always have to be looking for ways to stretch your abilities even farther. Because everyone else always is too, so otherwise you get left behind."

The corners of Rafael's mouth curled with amusement. "Sounds a lot like the criminal world, actually."

"Their routine is going to be jaw-dropping with the new addition," Niko declared around a big bite of his Cuban sandwich. "It'll be fantastic if we can all make it to Prague next year."

I glanced at him, knitting my brow. "Prague?"

Niko grinned at me. "That's where the Winter Olympics are being held, remember?"

Electricity zinged through my veins. I hadn't let myself think that far ahead. The idea of competing at the actual Olympics felt like a dream within a dream.

But it really was within our grasp, wasn't it? We'd won gold at Worlds. The Olympics would be a similar level of competition, even if it got a lot more fanfare.

Díos mio, the number of people who'd be watching if we performed there…

My heart fluttered with excitement, and I caught a matching gleam in both Jasper's and Quentin's eyes.

"Yeah, that'd be amazing, all right," Jasper said.

I thumped my fist on the table. "Then we'll just have to make it happen."

Rafael hummed to himself. "It sounds like I'm going to have to check out my new empire's European holdings so I can find plenty of excuses to be over on that side of the ocean by then."

I nudged him under the table. "You're the boss. You can make up excuses."

He laughed. "Good point. Now, come on, everyone. Dig into those sandwiches, or I'm going to think you don't like my cooking."

Quentin immediately stuffed the end of the sandwich into his mouth, carby bread and all. "You are never allowed to stop cooking for us," he insisted after he swallowed. "You can have all my cheat days."

Jasper shot the other guy an amused glance. "What does that mean—you won't eat any carbs at all the rest of the week?"

"Hey, I make it work."

"It's fine," Niko said serenely. "Anything he doesn't eat, I definitely will."

I leaned back in my chair amid the companionable warmth of their banter and couldn't hold back the smile that stretched across my lips.

This was a real home. This was exactly where I wanted to be. As hard as it still was to believe, everything in my life had clicked into place.

After all my clawing toward freedom to escape Mom and her influence, I'd been able to stop fighting and pursue the life I'd wanted. I could fill my days with different kinds of power—the kinds that came from agility and beauty rather than brutality.

I was in charge of my own destiny now. And with the four men I loved by my side, I knew I was finally on the right path, heading toward a future full of joy.

ABOUT THE AUTHORS

Eva Chance is a pen name for contemporary romance written by Amazon top 100 bestselling author Eva Chase. If you love gritty romance, dominant men, and fierce women who never have to choose, look no further.

Eva lives in Canada with her family. She loves stories both swoony and supernatural, and strong women and the men who appreciate them.

Connect with Eva online:
www.evachase.com
eva@evachase.com

Harlow King is a long-time fan of all things dark, edgy, and steamy. She can't wait to share her contemporary reverse harem stories.

www.ingramcontent.com/pod-product-compliance
Lightning Source LLC
Chambersburg PA
CBHW020324030826
48979CB00022B/1002

* 9 7 8 1 9 9 8 7 5 2 7 6 8 *